Ruined City

CHINESE LITERATURE TODAY BOOK SERIES

Chinese Literature Today Book Series

Ruined City

A Novel

Jia Pingwa

Translated by Howard Goldblatt

UNIVERSITY OF OKLAHOMA PRESS : NORMAN

This book is published with the generous assistance of
China's National Office for Teaching Chinese as a Foreign Language,
Beijing Normal University's College of Chinese Language and Literature,
the University of Oklahoma's College of Arts and Sciences,
and *World Literature Today* magazine.

Library of Congress Cataloging-in-Publication Data
Jia, Pingwa.
[Fei du. English]
Ruined city : a novel / Jia Pingwa ; translated by Howard Goldblatt. —
First edition.
pages cm. — (Chinese literature today ; volume 5)
Published in Chinese as Fei du (Xianggang : Tian di tu shu you xian gong si ;
Jiulong : Fa xing Li tong tu shu you xian gong si, 1993).
ISBN 978-0-8061-5173-1 (pbk. : alk. paper)
1. Authors—Fiction. 2. China—Fiction. I. Goldblatt, Howard, 1939– II. Title.
PL2843.P5F4513 2015
895.13'52—dc23

2015027958

Ruined City: A Novel is Volume 5 in the Chinese Literature Today Book Series.

The paper in this book meets the guidelines for permanence and durability of the Committee on Production Guidelines for Book Longevity of the Council on Library Resources, Inc. ∞

1 2 3 4 5 6 7 8 9 10

This is a work of fiction; any resemblance to real people is coincidental and unintentional. Truth, however, is at the heart of the work.
I await the laughter and condemnation that will follow.

—Jia Pingwa, 1993

Translator's Note

Some works of fiction excel at capturing the defining spirit or mood of their time, informing contemporaries as well as later generations of what it was like to live then, transcending aesthetic qualities to erect a mirror for society to view itself. Jia Pingwa's *Ruined City* (*Feidu*, 1993) ought to have been one of those, a literary snapshot of urban life in the early years following the culturally sterile and politically savage Cultural Revolution (1966–1976). But it wasn't—it was banned by government censors almost immediately after it came out, a ban that remained in effect for seventeen years. The reported offense was lurid sexual content. The bleak tone, the skewed relationships among characters, and a negative image of public officials and of society in general probably played a role in the decision to keep the book out of readers' hands, but it was mainly about the sex. It would be naïve to assume that, as a result, the novel went unread in China over all those years, for copies were smuggled into the country, usually from Hong Kong; more to the point, dozens of pirated versions made it, however briefly, into bookstores and private homes. Nonetheless, *Ruined City* could not be openly sold and read in China for nearly two decades.

In 1997, however, four years after its aborted domestic appearance, a French translation, *La capital dechué*, was published and was awarded the Prix Femina. Six years later, Jia was honored in France by becoming a Chevalier in the Ordre des Artes et des Lettres. The Chinese censors, we must assume, were both shocked and appalled. That did not, however, change their minds. In the early twenty-first century, rumors circulated that, given the evolving state of morality and a popular acceptance of sexual content in literature, the ban would be lifted. A government official squelched that idea: "*Feidu* has not been unbanned," he wrote. "Outside claims that *Feidu* will be republished in 2004 are pure hype."[1]

❋

Jia Pingwa was born in 1952 in the city of Xi'an, the site of perhaps the most significant archaeological discovery in China: the Terracotta Warriors. For many centuries, this Shaanxi city was the imperial capital of several dynasties, and it prides itself on being home to many of the country's most prized cultural relics and sites, including the famed Bell and

Drum Towers and the Giant Wild Goose Pagoda. Jia began writing in 1973, beginning with short stories, both for adults and for children, and essays. In the decades since, he has published a vast number of stories and novellas, plus more than a dozen novels, of which only a few have been translated into foreign languages. He is among China's most popular, and most controversial, novelists, a man of diverse interests and talents. A calligrapher, a fortuneteller, and a musicologist, in literary terms he is first and foremost a storyteller, one who finds much of his inspiration in the countryside, a writer who is culturally tied to the ancient traditions of China and does not shy away from dark descriptions when they seem warranted.

Yiyan Wang, Jia's literary biographer, has characterized his early writing as literary nativism, fiction that emerges from the soil and from the people who tend it. Set mainly in the impoverished mountain villages of northern Shaanxi province, these novels from the late 1980s and early 1990s were widely popular among readers, to whom Jia offered, in Wang's words, "an enticing story told in a lucid narrative language that is rich in local flavor."[2] They were less popular among critics, who either sought more sophistication in contemporary writing or were uncomfortable with literature that cast the heart of China in a dark and unforgiving light.

Much has changed in the two decades since the first appearance of *Ruined City*. Its author is now celebrated as one of the country's best-known and best-loved cultural figures, heralded by readers and critics alike; there is even an exhibition hall and museum in Xi'an devoted to Jia's art and archival material. The ban on *Ruined City* was officially lifted in 2009, and sales of the book were brisk. Four years later, the prestigious People's Literature Publishing House in Beijing produced a handsome box set of four of Jia's novels: *Fuzao* (Turbulence, 1988; winner of the Mobil Oil Pegasus Prize), *Feidu*, *Qin Qiang* (Northern Opera, 2005; winner of the prestigious Hongloumeng Prize), and *Gulu* (Ancient Kiln, 2009). Though Jia has hinted at an imminent abandonment of the writing life, he continues to publish big, popular novels.

❋

Ruined City is a brick of a novel, occupying nearly 500 pages of tightly packed Chinese characters (more than 400,000 of them) with indifferent punctuation, divided into neither chapters nor, for the most part, paragraphs. The absence of white space on the page can be daunting. For this translation, no chapter breaks were added, but paragraph breaks were inserted, especially for dialogue. The author approved the change.

Jia Pingwa writes in a semiclassical yet conversational and highly accessible style, paying little attention to nuanced verbiage or sophisticated narrative devices. There is an absence of irony and a paucity of humor, though it is present here and there, perhaps unintentionally. A repetitive use of terms and descriptions lends a slightly old-fashioned but not unpleasant feel for a Chinese reader, even now.

Some critics and scholars argue that, as Jia is well steeped in traditional literature, he set out to write a modern-day *Golden Lotus* (*Jin Ping Mei*), the Qing dynasty erotic novel. I have my doubts, for his descriptions of sex function as an indication of decadence, not as a quest for secret pleasures, as is the case in the classical novel. Sex is indeed a vital component of Jia's narrative, and is described in graphic terms, which is rare in mainstream Chinese fiction, especially in an atmosphere of lingering prudery and enforced modesty. His descriptions are, in fact, over the top, in places borderline absurd. He is said to have undertaken the descriptions of sexual activity by watching pornographic videos. One critic has commented that he either watched too few of them or understood too little.[3]

This leads to one of the most widely discussed aspects of *Ruined City*, the use of a series of blocks □□ □□ □□ followed by parenthetical notes that the author has deleted a number of characters/words during or following sex scenes. It has been called a gimmick by some, and has caused consternation over the missed descriptions by others. Jia himself had this to say about the technique: "When I was writing about sex, I wrote out a little bit, but then I didn't write any more, because I had to consider the national conditions, you know, so I thought I'd just write a little bit and that would be enough. And then I replaced the portion I didn't write with these boxes. When I handed the manuscript to the publisher later on, they deleted additional sections. So the number of characters listed in parenthesis as having been deleted is actually no longer very accurate."[4]

That could very well be the case. There is, however, another possible interpretation. Likely expecting that his new novel would be banned, in whole or in part, because of the descriptions of sexual desire and activity, Jia created his own excisions, either to foil the censors' anticipated action or as a parody, a mockery, of the process itself. I find this reading no less satisfactory than the author's explanation, essentially because the excisions follow, not replace, scenes of graphic sex and could hardly have added anything of substance or interest.

If *Ruined City* is neither a modern-day *Golden Lotus*, a voyeuristic and misogynistic (as some have claimed) exposé of late twentieth-century

China, nor a parody, what then is it? Jia's editor of the first edition of the novel, Tian Zhenying, has said succinctly that it "depicts the fall of a generation of intellectuals and the societal causes behind the decline of that society." This view is representative of many domestic critics and scholars, who see it as a portrait of the unhealthy ideological and mental state of intellectuals at the end of the twentieth century, a society in chaos, even a prophetic tale for all of China.

At the risk of overstating a nonrealist reading of *Ruined City*, however, I find it instructive to look at the characters who populate the novel. While one generally searches in vain for in-depth psychological probing in contemporary Chinese fiction, here the absence is exaggerated. Most if not all of the characters in *Ruined City* come across as unsavory stock figures who demand not to be taken at face value; frequently given to surprising bouts of weeping, apostrophic outbursts, unnatural dialogue, and irrational actions, they represent types more than individuated characters. Beyond that, lapses into fantasy, including a revocation of certain scientific principles, underscore the absurdities the author sees in contemporary society. If I am right, then our reading of the novel as one that tends to mock the genre and the state of contemporary urban society, at least to some degree, gains credence. I will leave final judgment on this score to the readers of the present translation.

One final note about names: Zhuang Zhidie's name has an obvious link to ancient China. Zhuang is the surname of the Warring States Taoist Zhuang-zi (fourth century BCE). One of the philosopher's most famous anecdotes is that he awoke one day after dreaming that he was a butterfly (hu-die; thus the -die in Zhidie) and wondered if he might actually be a butterfly dreaming that he was Zhuang-zi. The sly insertion of some of the philosopher's recorded aphorisms seals the deal. Beyond that, the "Zhou" in the name of the novel's second most important character, Zhou Min, is part of Zhuang-zi's formal name—Zhuang Zhou. While this may hint at an illusory quality to the novel in general, it may be best simply to attribute the choice to the author's fondness for Taoist traditions. The rest of the dramatis personae's names may well have been fashioned by Jia for allusive connections, but determining that would require a treatise of sorts, I'm afraid, probably with meager results.

In the preparation of this translation, I have suppressed the impulse to add a more modern touch to the narrative, simultaneously refraining from allowing it to seem quaint. Up-to-date twenty-first-century terminology or archaic terms and expressions would have rung hollow in a twentieth-century novel and might have further shattered the illusion that the reader is dealing with a Chinese author without intervention.

Throughout the translation process, I was rewarded with detailed responses to my many queries (I don't play mahjong, I've never had my fortune read by a Taoist, and I am unfamiliar with the specialized idiom of northern Shaanxi) from the author and one or more of his friends and associates. As always, I also am indebted to the wisdom and support of my wife, Sylvia.

HOWARD GOLDBLATT

NOTES

1. Joel Martinsen, "Jia Pingwa's Banned Novel Returns after 17 Years," August 4, 2009, *Danwei: Chinese Media, Advertising, and Urban Life*, http://www.danwei.org/books/jia_pingwas_abandoned_capital.php.
2. Yiyan Wang, *Narrating China: Jia Pingwa and His Fictional World* (New York: Routledge 2006), 252. Wang has done a superb job of analyzing Jia's novels up to 2005, especially *Feidu*, in terms of "cultural landscaping," "the sexual dissident," and "female domesticity." She translates the title as *Defunct Capital*, but when I asked Jia how he wanted it to be rendered, he said he preferred "city" over "capital," since the latter no longer applied, and asked for a term of destruction, not abandonment, as some critics and scholars have used, in the title.
3. A comment by Xie Youshun in an unreleased documentary titled *Feidu*.
4. Martinsen, "Jia Pingwa's Banned Novel Returns after 17 Years."

List of Characters

Ah-can	one of Zhuang's lovers
Ah-lan	Ah-can's sister
Aunty Liu	owner of the cow
Bai Yuzhu	a judge; consultant on the defamation lawsuit
Dai Shangtian	a book reviewer at the Writers' Association
Dazheng	the mayor's son; Liu Yue's eventual husband
Gong Jingyuan	a calligrapher; one of the "Famous Four"; the father of Gong Xiaoyi
Gong Xiaoyi	an opium addict; son of Gong Jingyuan
Gou Dahai	an editor at *Xijing Magazine;* a defendant in the defamation lawsuit
Hong Jiang	the manager of Niu Yueqing's Taibai Bookstore
Huang Defu	an advisor to the mayor
Huang Hongbao	the owner of the 101 Pesticide Plant
Huiming	a nun at the Yunhuang Temple
Jing Xueyin	Zhuang Zhidie's former love interest; plaintiff in the defamation lawsuit
Li Hongwen	a reviewer at *Xijing Magazine*; a defendant in the defamation lawsuit
Liu Yue	Zhuang and Niu Yueqing's maid; his lover; later the wife of Dazheng
Meng Jin	son of Meng Yunfang
Meng Yunfang	Zhuang's best friend
Niu Yueqing	Zhuang Zhidie's wife; owner of the Taibai Bookstore
Ruan Zhifei	one of the "Famous Four"; head of the philharmonic orchestra
Sima Gong	the judge in the defamation trial
Tang Wan'er	Zhuang's primary lover; Zhou Min's girlfriend
Wang Ximian	a painter; one of the "Famous Four"
Xia Jie	Meng Yunfang's wife
Zhao Jingwu	a friend of Zhuang's; Liu Yue's first fiancé
Zhong Weixian	editor-in-chief of *Xijing Magazine;* a defendant in the defamation lawsuit
Zhou Min	author of the article at the center of the defamation lawsuit; a defendant in the lawsuit; Tang Wan'er's boyfriend
Zhuang Zhidie	the main character in the novel; a famous writer; one of the "Famous Four"

Ruined City

SOMETHING STRANGE OCCURRED in the city of Xijing in the 1980s: When two devoted friends in search of a little recreation visited the tomb of the Tang concubine Yang Yuhuan, known as Guifei, the Imperial Consort, they wondered why so many visitors were scooping up gravesite dirt. They were told that since Guifei was known as an ageless beauty, if they took dirt from her grave and mixed it into their potted plants, the flowers would grow bright and beautiful. So the friends scooped up handfuls of dirt, took it home in their clothing, put it in a black earthenware pot they had kept for years, and left it there until they could purchase some fine flower seeds. Imagine their surprise when green sprouts broke through the surface a few days later, and within a month had spurted almost magically into a flourishing growth the likes of which no one had ever seen. They carried it into town to ask an old flower expert at the Yunhuang Temple what they had. He did not know. It so happened that Abbot Zhixiang was passing by at that moment, so they asked him. He just shook his head.

One of the men said, "I often hear people say that the abbot can divine the future by using the Eight Taoist Trigrams. Can you tell us how many shoots this flower will produce?"

The abbot told the second man to select a word.

Since he was holding gardening shears, he casually tossed off the word "ear."

The abbot said, "This is a unique flower that will bloom on four stems, but it will be short-lived."

The plant grew as predicted: the flowers looked a bit like peonies and a bit like roses, and of the four stems, one was red, one was yellow, one was white, one was purple, and all four exuded exquisite charm. Once word got out, people flocked to admire the flowers, and they left sighing in amazement. The friends were understandably pleased, one especially, who so cherished the rare plant that he placed it on his desk, as if to enshrine it, assiduously watering it and adding plant food, never stinting in his attentions. But after an evening of heavy drinking, he got up in the middle of the night and, feeling a need to water the plant, carelessly picked up a hot water bottle and killed it. Devastated by what he had done, he smashed the pot, after which he fell ill and was sick for a month.

Since this unusual incident revolved around a simple potted plant, it was not widely known, and was quickly supplanted by other news. But every resident of Xijing experienced an even stranger incident that summer, one that occurred at noon on the seventh day of the sixth lunar month, when a red sun shone brightly in the sky. The virtue of the sun is that people tend to ignore it when it shines, so no one in the city gazed skyward. The streets were no different than they were on any other day: ranking officials rode in chauffeured sedans, while people of means but no high position, unwilling to squeeze onto crowded buses, flaunted their money and climbed into taxis. It so happened that a VIP came to town in a caravan of police cars, sirens blaring as they forced private cars, taxis, and buses to slow down and move out of the way, and wreaking havoc on the flow of bicycle traffic. Unaffected pedestrians stepped on each other's shadow, but caused neither pain nor injury. As the shadows went from dark to light, they grew shorter, until they disappeared, seemingly in an instant. Bereft of shadows to drag behind them, the people stopped being people, or so it appeared, and reached behind them, looking doubtful. Someone gazed into the sky and cheered, "Look, there are four suns in the sky!" Everyone turned to look, and, yes, there were indeed four suns, all the same size, each one indistinguishable from the others, clustered in a "T" formation. In the past, the city had experienced both a lunar and a solar eclipse, but never four suns at the same time. People thought their eyes must be playing tricks on them. Another look and the sun had turned from red to white, bright as a flare. White like I don't know what. Then nothing. We cannot see in pitch darkness, but is that also the case when it is blinding bright? Not daring to start their cars or buses, some people honked their horns; others ran around as if they were not out on the street but were watching a movie when the film breaks and the screen goes blank, leaving only the soundtrack moving forward. If one person felt that way, just about everyone did, and they fell silent, deathly quiet, all but a man atop a wall who wanted to play one final note on a flute called the xun, but lacked the strength, like a gust of wind bouncing off a wall and disappearing. Mocking laughter greeted the flute player, and that reminded them where they were; suddenly unnerved by the silence, they screamed. Many fell into a state of absolute madness.

The bizarre situation lasted for about half an hour, until the four suns merged into one. When the people once again saw their shadows, they exchanged embarrassed looks and scattered. The confusion that followed occurred without a single traffic policeman in sight. An old man sat peacefully on a safety island. Dirty and unkempt, with a long face, he coolly observed the chaos around him. It was a look that people found so disturbing, so irritating, they wanted to call a policeman. But they did not see one anywhere, not until one named Su ran up, adjusting his helmet, and shouted at the beggar, "Pi! Fuck off!" using the coarsest term in the Xijing lexicon.

The old beggar responded by writing something on the pedestrian island with his finger. What he wrote was the single elegant, ancient character "Bi." In other words, Off you go! A smile spread across his face, eliciting raucous laughter from people who took note of what he was wearing as he stepped down off the island. His clothes had been fashioned out of a silk banner presented to the Yunhuang Temple by devout pilgrims. On his chest were the embroidered words "Every Wish," while the seat of his trousers, which were split up the middle and crudely sewn, sported two more characters: the left side of his buttocks read "Is," the right side read "Granted." The old fellow, exhibiting no sense of shame, opened his mouth and treated his audience to a bit of doggerel.

In the days and weeks that followed, it made the rounds in the city, and here is how it went:

One class of people is on the public weal, a life of leisure they proudly reveal.
A second class uses the wealth of others, and enjoys the protection of powerful brothers.
A third class contracts for large amounts, charging wasteful spending to expense accounts.
A fourth class lives on profits from rents, sitting at home to count dollars and cents.
A fifth class, the judges, whose courtrooms are used, profit from both accuser and accused.
A sixth class wields a surgical blade, filling pockets with cash from their trade.
A seventh class, actors on the stage, by comic routines make a tidy wage.
An eighth class, propaganda shills, turn slogans and chants into cashable bills.
A ninth class teaches in our schools, but where luxury is concerned are impoverished tools.
Society's masters stand high on the tenth rung, earnestly studying the life of Lei Feng.

After this began to circulate, people doubted that he was a beggar at all. At the very least, he must have been a teacher, they declared, since only a teacher could have managed to compose rhymes of that caliber, especially ones that mercilessly attack the first few classes of people yet expose the hardships of teachers. But that was just a guess. No one cared to probe further. In that year, as it turned out, Xijing welcomed a new mayor, a man from Shanghai who had married a Xijing native. For more than a dozen years, each of his predecessors had intended to make improvements in the old city, but after encountering daunting obstacles, they accomplished little and left office like flowing water. The new mayor had misgivings about taking office in his father-in-law's hometown, but as a public official, he had no say in where he was assigned. The question of where to start, what to tackle, arose on his first day in office. Fortunately, he had a wife who brought qualified friends and relatives on board as her husband's advisors. One of them, a young man named Huang Defu, offered a bold proposal. As the seat of government, a city that had seen twelve dynasties come and go, its cultural heritage was both its capital and its burden. Local officials and residents were mired in conservative thinking, which was why Xijing lagged behind coastal cities when it came to long-term economic development. The past few mayors had taken on too much, and because industry had stagnated and urban construction was deeply in debt, even hard work yielded meager results. Turnover was another problem, with each administration forced to leave office after no more than five years; such dramatic changes in personnel were a hindrance to long-term planning. Instead of continuing down the same path, he suggested, it would be better to adopt a new approach, one ignored by others: cultural development and tourism; that, in the short term, at least, would produce results. Inspired by this proposal, the new mayor, who was in no way ashamed to learn from subordinates, interviewed the young man for three days, after which arrangements were made for him to be transferred out of his teaching position to serve as the mayor's personal secretary. The mayor wasted no time in seeking appropriations from the central government, at the same time that he was amassing local funding in support of a project of unprecedented scope; it included refurbishing the city wall, dredging the moat around it, and building an amusement park, rich in local color, on the banks of the moat. He also rebuilt three city avenues: One with Tang dynasty architecture was designed for the sale of books, art, and porcelain. On a second avenue, styled after the Song dynasty, local and provincial snacks were sold. Local handicrafts, folk art, and specialty products were available on the third avenue, which boasted a mixture of Ming and Qing architecture. Unfortunately, the influx of outsiders introduced by the tourism industry had a negative impact on public safety, and people began referring to Xijing as a city of thieves, drug dealers, and prostitutes. This development bred a new form of disquiet among the local population. So when the unkempt old man appeared to entertain people with his doggerel, he was followed by a ragtag crowd of idlers, who shouted encouragingly: "Another verse, give us another one!" And so he did, two, in fact:

If I say you're all right, you're all right, whether you are or not.
If I say you're not all right, you're not all right, even if you are.

His listeners clapped their approval. Although the old man had not said who the target of his doggerel might be, they had no trouble figuring that out on their own. As it sped through the city, Huang Defu naturally got wind of it and placed a phone call to the police, ordering them to stop the old man from spreading rumors about the mayor. When he was taken into custody, they learned that over the past decade he had lodged repeated complaints with the government. Why? It turned out that ten years before, he had been a private schoolteacher whose principal unfairly kept him from being transferred to a public school. His appeal to the provincial authorities had been unsuccessful. So he had taken up residence in Xijing and appeared outside government offices on a regular basis to lodge complaints, both oral and written, and stage sit-ins. In the end, seeing no way forward and no way out, he'd begun to lose contact with reality and stopped lodging complaints. But instead of returning to his home, he wandered the streets. Since he had done nothing illegal, after ten days in custody the police put him in a car and dropped him off three hundred li from town. He was back within days, this time with a beat-up handcart, which he pushed up streets and down lanes as a junkman, regularly surrounded by idlers who wanted more of his doggerel. This time he declined, limiting his utterances to loud, long shouts of "Junkman! Collecting junk and scraps!" His voice was heard on the street every day, early and late. The other commonly heard sound came from the flute player atop the city wall. One resembled the howl of a beast, the other the moan of ghosts, two sounds echoing back and forth and drawing cries from hundreds and thousands of birds nesting in the bell and drum towers.

On this day, after pulling his iron-wheeled handcart around town for hours without picking up a single piece of scrap, the old man went to the square in front of the Yunhuang Temple to watch the qigong masters teach breathing exercises. When he spotted people crowding around a fortune-teller in front of a low wall, he walked over to see what the coming year might bring for him. "Old-timer," people said, "this diviner is a master from Mount Emei who predicts major events. He doesn't have time to worry about little people and their future." They elbowed him out of the way.

The taunts turned the old man's face bright red. Just then it started to rain, large drops that beat a tattoo on the earth, like coins falling from heaven, sending a cloud of dust into the air and turning the ground soggy, with bubbles forming and popping up here and there. The crowd dispersed. "A timely rain," the old man said as he abandoned his cart and ran to the temple gate, where he stood under the flagpole to keep dry. Either because he was bored or because his throat itched, he sang his doggerel at the top of his lungs.

He did not know that Abbot Zhixiang, who was sitting inside, heard him singing. Just inside the temple gate stood an unusual rock; most of the time it was nothing special, just a rock, but in inclement weather, the graphic outline of a dragon appeared on it. With the rain still falling, Abbot Zhixiang went out to look at the rock and listen to the words being sung: " . . . the officials get rich, the vendors prosper, the poor move aside . . ." He was lost in thought when a thunderclap sent an explosive rumble down onto the gate. He looked up and saw seven crisscrossing rainbows in the western sky, and was reminded of the day that the four suns had appeared in the sky. The thought occurred to him that something unusual was once again about to occur in Xijing. His prediction was confirmed the following day, when he heard on the radio that a relic of Sakyamuni had been discovered in the Temple of the Dharma Gate, no more than two hundred li from Xijing. The discovery of the Buddha's bone had rocked the mundane world, and that night, as the abbot sat in his meditation room, he had an epiphany. "These days," he muttered, "there are hardly any wolves, vermin, tigers, or panthers still in the world, for they have all been reincarnated as human beings. That is the source of so much evil. Meanwhile, great numbers of qigong masters and people with odd talents have arrived in Xijing in recent years. Maybe the heavens sent them to save humanity." The Yunhuang Temple had its own magical powers. With so many second-rate qigong masters and unique individuals coming down from the mountains, he could make a contribution. So he posted a flyer to announce that he was starting a qigong class in the temple, taking on students who wanted to learn elements of the exercise.

He held three sessions, each of them attended by a student named Meng Yunfang, who worked at the Research Institute of Culture and History and found little that did not interest him. Seven years earlier, a fad had swept the city prescribing red tea fungus as a cure-all and health tonic. Not only did he turn his home into a laboratory filled with vials of red fungus, he gave the stuff away all over the neighborhood, and in the process met a tea aficionado. He wound up marrying her. Husband

and wife soon after took up the laying on of hands, which they believed was a stronger cure-all than red tea fungus. That lasted six months, until the next fad came along—vinegar eggs. A drink made of chicken blood followed that, and like all the others, it caught their fancy. Unfortunately, the chicken blood produced an undesirable side effect: the wife's pubic hair fell out. None of the doctors could help, so when she learned that a neighbor had a secret remedy handed down from his ancestors, she sought it out. It did the trick, as the hair began to grow back. That particular neighbor, a year older than Meng Yunfang, was a former mahjong partner. When they met on the street one day, he greeted his benefactor with a cordial nod, only to be repaid with a short laugh. He went out and bought an expensive gift, telling his wife, "Since he fixed your problem, you can thank him with this." She returned from delivering the gift in high spirits, only to find a letter from her husband demanding a divorce. "Please sign this divorce decree," it said. "You are my wife, which means you are clothed in the presence of your father and naked in the presence of your husband. Whoever heard of a wife letting a perfect stranger see her privates?"

Six months after divorcing his first wife, he married a woman named Xia Jie and moved with her into a new single-story house separated from the Yunhuang Temple by a low wall. After the wedding, Meng spent most of his free time gazing across the wall at the temple, listening to the music as he watched the monks' activities. After joining the qigong sessions, whenever he heard the daily clang of a gong, he scaled the wall, spry as a monkey. On one occasion he was met by Abbot Zhixiang, who stopped him from running off by saying, "Don't I know you?"

Meng nodded. "The abbot has a wonderful memory. Apparently you remember me."

"Of course I do. Did that plant of yours die?"

"Yes," Meng replied, "and everything turned out just as you had predicted."

"What about your friend? Did he recover from his illness?"

"He did, some time ago. But if you knew he was sick, then you must be an immortal."

"I am nothing of the sort. If I were, I would have asked your famous friend to stick around for a friendly conversation."

Meng made haste to say, "I will bring him over to pay his respects to the abbot one of these days."

The very first qigong session turned Meng Yunfang into a devotee who never passed up an opportunity to spread the word that the exercises had endowed him with unprecedented qi. When friends called, he sat cross-legged to circulate the qi. He even tried to transmit it to his friends, then asked if they felt different. When they said no, it was time for an incantation, chanted with such fervor that he foamed at the mouth and broke out in a sweat. When that did not work, his friends had a good laugh.

"He really does possess qi," Xia Jie said. "Last night I woke up feeling bloated, so he used qigong on me. The next thing I knew, my stomach was rumbling, and I had to run to the toilet. He has stopped eating meat, doesn't drink alcohol, has quit smoking, and won't touch a leek."

"That's true," Meng confirmed.

His friends laughed. "So you turned into a monk by following one. What about sex? If you've stopped sleeping with your wife, then you have truly become a monk!"

Xia Jie laughed with them. "I'm waiting for his abstinence myself," she said as she looked at him out of the corner of her eye. He blushed.

Only Xia Jie and Meng Yunfang knew what she was referring to. During the time he was practicing qigong, Meng had met a nun from the temple named Huiming. A young woman of twenty-four, she had come to the Yunhuang Temple after graduating from a Buddhist college three years earlier, and the two of them had spoken on several occasions. Meng admired her for her extensive knowledge of Buddhism, and had read *The Compendium of Five Lamps* and the *Diamond Sutra*, upon which he was happy to expound. Huiming often went to see him when she encountered things she did not understand. As a result, she frequently showed up on her side of the wall around noontime and called out for Meng Yunfang, after which they engaged in long conversations. One moonlit night, Xia Jie came home to find Meng at the wall talking to Huiming; he had been standing there so long that mosquitoes were feasting on his exposed legs, and he was scratching one leg with the other foot, back and forth.

This side of the wall said, "Huiming, this essay is much better, but you need your rest."

"I am not tired," that side said. "Exhaustion comes from mental fatigue. I wrote this when it was quiet, and it made me happy."

This side said, "Is this the happiness of Nirvana? We are separated only by a wall, but live in two separate worlds. I envy you so . . ."

That side giggled. "You can be anything you want, anything but a monk. You are out there looking for peace and quiet, but you cannot find it. If you ever do find a peaceful and quiet spot, I am afraid you will be disappointed."

"Do you think so?" this side said.

"You cannot tell anyone what I said to you the other day," that side said.

"I know," this side said. "We are of one mind. My lips are sealed."

That side said, "Meng Laoshi, you are a good man. I have written a petition that I would like you to take to the mayor's office."

This side reached over the wall. "Stand on a rock and hand it to me. Oh, no, have you twisted your ankle?"

"No," that side said. Sheets of paper appeared atop the wall, which Meng grabbed, just as the board he was standing on snapped in two, sending him thudding to the ground. He banged his chin on a tile on the way down and sent it, too, crashing to the ground.

Xia Jie laughed as she watched the drama unfold in front of her. "Be a little more careful, Yunfang," she said. "I've only seen the first act of *Romance of the Western Chamber!*" Without looking to see if he was hurt, she carried a stool to the wall and gazed over it to the other side. The nun had already scurried away through the flowers, like an apparition.

That comment in front of all those people made Meng Yunfang blush. "Don't say any more," he cautioned her. "Buddhist affairs involve boundless beneficence."

The onlookers, who by now were totally confused, changed the subject to lunch. "Good sister," they said, "you supply the labor and we'll supply the capital!" Each of them handed five yuan to Zhao Jingwu, who did not mind the trouble. He took his basket to buy food and drink.

❉

Over a period of years, Tongguan County, four hundred li east of Xijing, had become home to idlers and ne'er-do-wells who complained about anything and everything, settling over society like a swarm of bottleneck flies. One of that crowd, a man named Zhou Min, looked on as those around him seeking government work made it onto the promotional ladder, and those looking to get rich were well along, with hundreds of thousands of yuan safely in the bank. He was still trying to find his way. As dusk settled in one afternoon, he was sitting around the house feeling bored. He tried to read but couldn't, so he went to a coffeehouse to kill some time, and from there to a dance hall, where he met a beautiful young woman. It was the first of many nights he spent in the same place, and she never failed to show up. Then one night he entertained a wild thought: maybe, he thought, she's the one for me. So, when the dance was over, he offered to see her home. She refused, but her refusal lacked conviction, which emboldened him. He gave her a ride to an out-of-the-way lane, and when she stepped down off the bicycle rack to say good-bye, she thanked him and said, "I'll be okay now." He stayed put, pulled her over, and kissed her. "I hate you!" she said tearfully.

"You excite me," Zhou Min said in response. "I can't help myself."

"I hate that I'm meeting you only now. Where were you three years ago?"

Zhou Min picked her up, sat her back down on the bicycle rack, and pedaled to a riverbank outside of town, where they jumped off the bicycle and began pawing and groping.

"I'm married," she said when they were finished. "I have a two-year-old child."

That was unexpected, but Zhou would not be denied. "I don't care, I want you. Marry me!"

Unable to get him out of her mind, the woman, whose name was Tang Wan'er, finally told her husband she wanted a divorce. He demonstrated his refusal by stripping her naked and beating her. When she did not show up at the dance hall that night, Zhou Min had a friend stake out her home, and when he heard what had happened, he waited till the husband left the house the next morning and took Wan'er someplace where the man would not find her. But Tongguan was so small that even the comings and goings of a fly, let alone a human being, did not go unnoticed. When Zhou Min went to see her on her fourth day in hiding, she told him she had spotted a friend of her husband's skulking around the place, obviously sent to find her. Deciding that Tongguan was no place for them, he hired a taxi, and he and Wan'er left for Xijing, where they rented a house and moved in together.

The couple took to the city like fish to water. After acquiring some furniture and whatever else they would need to set up house, they took in the sights—Huaqing Hot Springs and the Giant Wild Goose Pagoda; they even visited the Xijing Garden Hotel and Heavenly Horse Amusement Park. Born to be a tourist, she was captivated by the hotel's extravagant lobby and the beautiful clothing for sale. Wan'er was an avid reader, a woman with intriguing and unusual ideas about things. When they walked past the city's media tower, a gigantic clock announced the hour with loud musical chimes. "If someone were in the mood to kill himself," she said, "leaping from the clock tower would be a spectacular way to do it."

"That's not the way I'd do it," Zhou Min said. "I would hang myself from the clock itself. That way I'd go out with music, and in full view of everyone in the city."

Liking what she heard, Wan'er threw herself into his arms and told him that when she and her husband were arguing one time, she had played a serenade on the radio as a means of calming things down, but he had kicked the radio over.

"He's ignorant," Zhou Min said.

"He's all muscle," she said, "like a mule!"

Their passion cooled after a month or so, and their money was running out. To Zhou Min, this was what a man could expect from being with a woman. Wan'er was beautiful and glamorous, they were living in a big city, and yet none of this brought him the satisfaction he sought or helped him find what he was looking for. There were new movies to see, fashionable clothes to wear, and plenty of accessories to buy. What he lacked were new ways of thinking, fresh ideas. There were no changes in the morning sunlight scaling the city wall, the same flowers bloomed in the garden, and even though women now wielded more authority than their husbands did, they were still limited to one day—Women's Day—on March 8th. An eighty-year-old man could be a bridegroom, but he was still an old man. Zhou Min, who was now mired in depression, could not reveal these thoughts to Wan'er, and was reduced to making his way to the city wall in the mornings and evenings to play his flute. But that did not solve the problem of finances, so he went looking for work, and found it at the neighborhood Clear Void Nunnery, where several side rooms were being renovated. Since the workers were paid daily, he was able to buy a fish and half a *jin* of fresh mushrooms each day to take home for her to make dinner.

With his fair skin, Zhou Min stood out among the gang of laborers, so the on-site foreman put him in charge of purchasing materials. That meant he was subject to inspections by the nuns, which in turn brought him into contact with Huiming. In the wake of several conversations, he learned that she had arrived recently from the Yunhuang Temple. Although she had not been put in charge of the nunnery, she maintained a high degree of visibility and authority, thanks to her youth and breadth of knowledge; the other nuns deferred to her. Drawn to Huiming's good looks, Zhou Min went to see her whenever he could. One day he looked up from a book he was reading and spotted her waving to him from a wisteria trestle. He put down his book and rushed over.

"You are different from the others," she said. "What are you reading?"

"*Romance of the Western Chamber*," he replied. "The Putuo Monastery . . ." He stopped.

"Don't you think our Clear Void Nunnery compares well with the Putuo Monastery?"

Zhou Min took a look around and was about to respond when she smiled. She then continued in a more serious tone of voice: "The minute I saw you here, I knew you were no common laborer, and I was right, you are a reader. If you just read for fun, that's fine. But if you are looking for something more, a deeper meaning from books, I know someone you might enjoy meeting."

"That sounds wonderful," he replied. "But whoever it is, I wonder if he would be interested in meeting me. I would need your introduction."

"You are such a smooth talker, you could get your foot in any door in the city," she said as she wrote out the person's name and address and a brief letter of introduction. Overjoyed, Zhou Min turned to leave.

"Hold on," she said. "I'd like you to deliver another letter to him, this one from me."

Letters in hand, Zhou Min went to the address Huiming had written down. It was the home of Meng Yunfang, beyond the wall to the left of the Yunhuang Temple.

Meng gave Zhou Min a warm welcome, inviting him to tea, then peppering him with questions about what he was reading, if he had ever tried writing, and who he might know in Xijing.

Zhou Min, who was quick-witted, gave rapid answers, inspiration enough for Meng to invite him into his study, where they carried on a long and pleasant conversation.

Back home that night, Zhou Min described his day to Tang Wan'er, who said, "Xijing has never been an easy place to settle in, and we came here without knowing a soul. We're lucky you met that fellow. Now don't stop at one visit. Go see him often."

Zhou Min took her advice. Every few days he paid Meng a visit. At first he used Huiming's urging as a pretext, but as time passed, he began taking things along—a fish, some greens. Xia Jie was equally fond of Zhou, often telling him how impressed she was by his neat appearance and criticizing her slovenly husband in front of him. Within a month, Zhou was a regular houseguest, and he began asking Meng about the writing life. Meng, always the pedant, could expound on all sorts of things, from classical Chinese aesthetics to modern Western art, and all Zhou Min could do was nod his head and vow to take in everything his laoshi had to offer in hopes of improving his own talent. His work during the days was hard, but even worse, it left him little spare time. Since Meng was known around town, Zhou wondered if he might help him find a position at a newspaper or magazine office. That way he would have time to read and to write, and even when he was busy he would be surrounded by educated people, which would help him improve faster.

"There is plenty of talent in Tongguan," Meng said, "and the people there are unique in many ways." He smiled.

Not knowing what he was getting at, Zhou assured Meng that he would understand if he was asking too much. Finding a job was already hard enough, and finding one in an editorial office might be all but impossible.

"I can see that you're not fated for an ordinary life," Meng said, "and I'm not boasting when I say that I know someone at nearly every magazine in town. At the moment, they are all fully staffed, but if I put in a word for you, I wouldn't be wasting my breath. That said, to be part of Xijing's artistic and literary community, you need to be well informed. How much do you know about it?"

"How much do I know? I step out the door and I'm completely in the dark."

"I'll tell you. There are two types of special individuals called "xianren": one type is known as social xianren. They might have status in society, they might not; they might be employed, they might not be. For the most part they are energetic, spirited, capable individuals who like to meddle. They enjoy moving commodities around, they're good at mediating, they love to eat, drink, gamble, and go whoring, but they do not smoke opium. They pull scams, but they don't mug or rob people. They know how to create a disturbance and how to put one down. Xijing's fashion and food industries are in their hands, and our economic development depends on them. They move comfortably in legitimate circles and are in control of the underworld. They are represented by four individuals, their unofficial leaders, widely known as 'the Four Young Knaves.' If they like you, they will feed you their own flesh, but they will also turn on you without notice. Avoid them. Want to know how best to describe them? You can get a good idea by listening to their jargon. They don't call money cash, they call it 'handles.' A good buddy is a 'steel brother,' getting on with women is 'drilling a hole,' a beautiful woman is a 'bomb' . . ." Meng Yunfang was going to say more but stopped, seeing a smile on Zhou Min's usually diffident face. "You don't believe me?"

"No, I believe you," Zhou said, reminded of his Tongguan experience, pondering the difference between small-town and big-city Knaves: they might be of a different caliber, but their jargon wasn't all that different. "In today's society," he said, "if you can imagine it at home, it's bound to happen in real life, so I believe everything you say."

"That's enough about that crowd," Meng said. "Now I want to tell you about the second type: cultural xianren. There isn't a person in Xijing who hasn't heard of the Four Young Knaves. But the 'Famous Four' are even better known. If you have your heart set on becoming part of Xijing's literary community, you can't do so without knowing the Famous Four. The painter Wang Ximian is number one. He is forty-five years old, a former jade factory carver who began painting in his spare time, and became famous within a few years. He was recruited by the Xijing Academy of Traditional Art, but chose instead to go to the Giant Wild Goose Pagoda as artist in residence. The pagoda is an essential tourist attraction for foreigners, among whom his paintings are extremely popular, especially his albums. He can produce four or five small albums a day, at hundreds of yuan apiece, splitting the profits with the Pagoda management. His income far exceeds that of other painters. What sets him apart is his uncanny ability to copy the masters, from Shi Tao and Bada Shanren down to Zhang Daqian and Qi Baishi. Over the past couple of years, the value of Shi Lu's paintings has risen steadily, so Wang paints them in the master's style, so perfectly executed that even Shi Lu's family cannot tell they are fakes. As a result, the road to wealth has opened up for him; being a man who is particularly fond of women, he says that his passion for painting vanishes when there is no beautiful woman to mix the ink and arrange the paper. Last summer he invited several friends to join him on a trip south to Mount Wutai, ostentatiously hiring four taxis, one for women only. Once there, his lover lost a gold ring while swimming in a ravine pool, but when the other guests anxiously volunteered to dive in and look for it, he simply said, 'If it's lost, it's lost, forget it!' making a ring worth at least twelve thousand yuan seem like a piece of mud scraped from his skin. He reached into his pocket, took out a thick wad of bills, and handed them to her.

"For the next in line, walk down any street or lane in the city to look at the shop signs, and you will know the name Gong Jingyuan. During the Republican era, the shop-sign calligrapher everyone wanted was Yu Youren. But even at his peak, Yu was not as popular as Gong Jingyuan. Like Wang Ximian, he has to drive the women away, but he isn't burdened with Wang's infatuations. He has a good time with whoever comes along and quickly forgets her when it's over, which is why so many women call themselves Gong Jingyuan's lover, all of them women whose names he is unable to recall. Obtaining a piece of his calligraphy presents a problem, for when he gives one away he does not add his seal, thus making it virtually worthless. Adding the seal is his wife's business, and it is cash only. Fifteen hundred for one on paper, three thousand for a shop sign. She holds the purse strings. He doesn't even carry pocket change. The problem is, he's addicted to mahjong and can lose as much as a thousand yuan in a night. He covers his losses with calligraphy. He has been arrested three times for gambling, and each time the police let him out after he wrote calligraphy for them. There isn't a respectable hotel in the city that does not have one of his works on display, and none of them charges him for room or board. The managers treat him like the Buddha himself. The first question asked of a chef seeking admission into the city's Culinary Society is, 'Have you ever prepared a meal for Gong Jingyuan?' If the answer is yes, you have passed the first test. But if the answer is no, you are found deficient.

"The third person is Ruan Zhifei, head of the Western Philharmonic orchestra. He started out as a Shaanxi opera performer whose father had taught him such tricks of the trade as fire breathing, hair tossing, and tusk playing. But when the local opera began to lose its appeal, playing to dwindling audiences, he quit and organized a local song-and-dance ensemble with all of his opera performers. Singing tunes that others steered clear of and sporting costumes that rivals dared not wear, they toured the country for five years, playing to packed houses wherever they went; the money fell like snowflakes. But in recent years, as the popularity of song and dance performances has waned, the members of the troupe have drifted away in two groups, one moving to the countryside, the other opening dance halls in the city. Even at the unheard-of cost of thirty yuan to get in, those places are mobbed every night.

"All three of these individuals deal with the social xianren, but only when it suits their purpose. They rely primarily on the internal connivance of bureaucrats and the external support of foreigners.

"The fourth individual, on the other hand, lives a quiet, unassuming life. Although his wife runs the Taibai Bookstore near the Forest of Steles Museum, he neither has nor cares much about money, and is content to stay home and write about things that interest him. But the world moves in strange ways, and the less you want something, the more it attaches itself to you. Where those four are concerned, he is at the top of the heap and is the most accomplished; his fame is the most far-reaching. And he comes from your hometown—Tongguan."

Zhou Min was mesmerized by Meng's exhaustive narration, but when he heard that the man was from his hometown, he said, "You wouldn't be talking about Zhuang Zhidie, would you?"

"Yes, I would," Meng replied. "Which is why I said, 'There is plenty of talent in Tongguan, and the people there are unique in many ways.' When I saw how devoted you are to the desire to become a writer, I immediately thought of Zhuang Zhidie, the pride of Tongguan. You must know him."

"The name, of course. He once returned to Tongguan for a public lecture, but I learned about it too late. Tongguan is home to hordes of young people who love literature, thanks to his influence. I've seen him in pictures, but never in person."

"Of the Famous Four, Zhuang is the one I admire the most, and the one I am closest to," Meng said. "I'm sure I could help you find work in an editorial office, but I could run my legs off and not accomplish as much as a single word from him, for he is one of Xijing's leading writers. He drops by regularly for tea or something a bit stronger, so why not come over, say some Wednesday or Saturday afternoon, and you might run into him. I'll ask his opinion on which paper or magazine would be best."

Over the weeks that followed, Zhou Min visited Meng on Wednesday and Saturday afternoons, neatly dressed, his hair slicked down with gel. But while the house was always filled with writers, editors, painters, and actors, Zhuang Zhidie was a no-show. Having no luck getting hired on at an editorial office, Zhou was forced to stay on as a laborer at the Clear Void Nunnery to keep the wolf from the door, and he was losing hope.

One day Huiming asked him to deliver a message to Meng Yunfang, so he went for an afternoon of tea and talk, naturally bringing up Zhuang Zhidie. That was when he learned that Zhuang had been out of town for some time, news that Meng had received only that morning from Hong Jiang at the Taibai Bookstore. He was disappointed in Zhuang, whose reputation had continued to spread over the past year, but whose mood had worsened and whose temper had taken a bizarre turn. All that time away, and not a word to Meng Yunfang! Zhou Min sighed. But Meng handed Zhou a note and asked if he would be willing to look up someone in the Department of Culture. If he could get in to see that individual, there was a chance that he could land a position at the *Xijing Gazette*.

Zhou Min read the note and discovered that Meng had written to someone called Jing Xueyin, signing it Zhuang Zhidie. Meng's only response to Zhou Min's questions of whether Jing was a man or a woman and what he or she did was an enigmatic grin.

Not knowing what to expect, Zhou Min took the note to the Department of Culture. As evening fell, he returned to see Meng, who was in his study, dressed only in boxer shorts, sitting at his writing desk. He acknowledged the knock at the door but did not get up to open it, so his impatient visitor called out, "Meng Laoshi, it's me, Zhou Min." When Zhou heard footsteps, he waited until the lock turned, then rushed in and shocked Meng by falling to his knees in front of him.

Meng did not need to ask. "Got what you wanted, I assume," he said.

Zhou Min, whose face was red, turned and shouted to the door, "Bring it in."

A woman with large feet came in with a large traveling bag, from which she began taking things out and placing them on the dresser: a tin of Biluochun tea, two tins of vitamin C–enriched juice powder, a packet of shredded dried bamboo shoots, a bag of Ningxia wolfberries, and a packet of dried mushrooms.

"What's this, Zhou Min?" Meng asked. "All for me?"

"It's not much," Zhou replied. "You're working so hard on such a hot day, I thought you might like this. There is nothing here that will spoil a vegetarian diet. Thanks to your note, Meng Laoshi, I'm virtually assured of getting a job."

"I told you Jing Xueyin was the one to see. That may be where she works now, but she once worked in the Editorial Bureau. People are eager to do things for her."

Xia Jie, who had been asleep in the bedroom, called out from behind the curtain divider, "Zhou Min, you must have your head screwed on right! Your show of respect for Meng Laoshi is paying dividends."

With a deprecatory laugh, Zhou Min said, "Are you still in bed? Don't think I forgot you. I stopped at the Greenfield Jade Emporium to look at chrysanthemum jade bracelets. They had three, and I paid for one. But since they all had minor flaws, I told them to get me one that's perfect. It will be ready for pickup in three days. I hope you'll like it."

"You're quite the spendthrift," she said, "spending more than you earn."

This time Zhou Min just smiled.

Meng had already opened one of the juice powder jars and poured two glasses, one for himself and one for his guest; he was about to make one for Xia Jie when Zhou Min said, "I don't drink juice, so give mine to your wife."

"Whatever comes in my door belongs to me, and now I'm treating you," Meng said before taking a glass into the bedroom, leaving Zhou Min to sip his. Just then the door curtain parted, and the woman who had brought in the gifts motioned to him.

"What are you sticking around for?" Zhou Min asked out in the yard. "You've done your job."

"You owe me money."

"I already paid you."

"You paid for the merchandise, but I didn't carry it all this way for nothing."

"You expect to get paid for that short trip?" He handed her a ten-fen bill.

She refused to take it. "Do you think you're sending off a beggar? Even they get more than this for their trouble."

Zhou Min turned his pockets inside out to show that they were empty, sending her storming off muttering angry curses.

Zhou Min went back inside and said with a smile, "Miss Jing is a woman of class and elegance. The minute I laid eyes on her, I was so charmed I nearly decided not to give her the note. My palms were sweaty. She took me to the Editorial Bureau and introduced me to the editor-in-chief, even called the bureau chief out. I was told I'd get word in three days. She worked magic!"

"You don't know the half of it. She may be only a section head, but in the Department of Culture, with the exception of her boss, no one dares underestimate her. Your teeth will chatter when I tell you that the current deputy party secretary in charge of provincial cultural affairs once worked for her father, and the current Propaganda Bureau chief was her father's secretary. The old man has been reassigned from Shaanxi to an official position in Shanxi. He may not be here physically, but while the tiger may leave the mountain, as they say, its influence lingers on."

When Meng was finished, Zhou Min said, "Ah, now I know. If I'm not mistaken, Jing Xueyin was one of Zhuang Laoshi's old flames."

"How did you know that?"

"Once Zhuang became famous, anecdotes about him made the rounds in Tongguan. I used to think they were tall tales, but now I see they must be true. When she saw the note, she said, 'Zhuang Zhidie thinks too much of himself, sending a note instead of coming himself.'"

"What did you say to that?" Meng asked.

"I told her, 'Zhuang Laoshi is busy writing a novel, but he said he'd find time to come see you.' 'See me?' she said. 'An old hag like me?'" Zhou ended with an embarrassed laugh. "Meng Laoshi, everything seems to have gone so smoothly I'm worried that Zhuang Laoshi will be unhappy with us."

"That's why I was rushing to finish a review of his work."

Zhou Min expressed his gratitude, and they continued to chat until the clock struck midnight, when he said his good-byes.

Tang Wan'er knew that Zhou Min was out looking for work, since she hadn't seen him all day, so she warmed up the leftover noodles before taking a hot shower, rinsing out her mouth, and changing into a perfumed bra and panties to reward him on his return. But she waited and she waited, finally sitting up in bed to read. It was quite late when she heard footsteps at the door. She quickly lay down, covered her face with the book, and pretended to be asleep. When Zhou Min knocked at the door, it swung open on its hinges, unlocked. He saw that the bedside lamp was on, but she made no noise, so he carefully lifted off the book and saw that she was asleep. He stood there for a moment drinking in the scene, then leaned over and gently kissed her on the mouth. She surprised him by opening her mouth and clamping her teeth around his tongue.

"So, you're awake! What's the idea of lying here half-naked with the door unlocked?"

"I've been waiting here, hoping to be visited by a man with rape on his mind!" she said.

"Don't talk like that," Zhou Min said. "Can't I even be gone one day?"

"Well, at least you're aware that you've been gone so long!"

He told her that Meng Yunfang had written an introductory note to Jing Xueyin, and that the job was all but assured. Thrilled by the news, she got up and went into the kitchen half-dressed to warm up his dinner, then sat and watched him eat. When he was finished, she drew water for him to wash up, even before clearing the table. Off went the light, and the two of them climbed into bed to make love. □□ □□ □□ [The author has deleted 313 words.]

"What does Jing look like?" Wan'er asked afterward. "She's a lucky woman to be on such intimate terms with Zhuang Zhidie."

"You have nicer skin; she has wrinkles. And ugly feet. But she has a commanding presence and speaks with authority. She impressed me as a woman who likes to flirt."

Wan'er pushed his head away because of his smoker's breath. "Show me a woman who doesn't!" she said.

"Meng says she gets high marks from men, but that she has no female friends."

"I'm not surprised," Wan'er said. "She's obviously been spoiled by men, which of course boosts her ego. Sooner or later, most women like that turn into shrews. But a highborn woman with a decent upbringing can wrap men around her finger and give nothing in return. How does it go—wolves don't eat their young, and there's safety in numbers."

"You're quite a know-it-all, aren't you, you sly fox? But Tongguan is no Xijing. If she's what you say, how could a note from Zhuang Zhidie have such an effect on her?"

"Hard to say. But take my word, you don't want to get on the wrong side of a woman like that. People do things *for* her, and don't dare do things *to* her. Now that you've gotten some help, spend more time with Meng Yunfang. That way he'll be the one Zhuang Zhidie goes to see if he's angry that his name was used on the note."

Then Zhou Min told her about his plan to give Xia Jie a jade bracelet—one of Wan'er's, as it turned out—but only one. That was met with silence, so, he leaned over to kiss her body. She pushed him away.

"You bought those for me," she said, "and now you want to give one to a big-city woman with the sort of appeal you could fall for."

"Don't be silly," he said. "She dresses fashionably, but she can't change the fact that she's no longer young. Besides, we're only talking about a jade bracelet, and if I get the editorial job, I might find what I've been looking for down the line, so we can settle down in Xijing. Weigh the two against each other, and you'll see which is more important. But if you don't want to do it, I'll go out and buy a bracelet tomorrow."

"All right," she said, taking off one of her bracelets and placing it at the head of the bed before rolling over and going to sleep.

❉

Three days later, Zhou Min went to give Xia Jie the jade bracelet. Since Meng Yunfang was out, he raised the matter of the editorial office job. He was feeling anxious.

"If not for the monk," she assured him, "then it'll be done for the Buddha. Jing Xueyin will do what she can."

Recalling what Wan'er had said, he smiled and asked, "What is she to Zhuang Laoshi? Obviously they aren't married."

"Before Zhidie gained a reputation," Xia Jie said, "he was a nobody. Love is a strange beast. Not all married couples are in love, and not all lovers are married." She went on to describe Zhuang Zhidie's many entanglements, to Zhou Min's amazement. His heart raced as he heaved a series of sighs.

Back home that night, he gave Wan'er an elaborate account of the conversation. She was so delighted by what she heard that she asked for more. The only way he could satisfy her curiosity was to spice up the story. "We're in the middle of sex," he said, "and you want me to talk to you about someone else. Are you trying to be a second Jing Xueyin?"

"I was fantasizing," she said, "that I'm with Zhuang Zhidie!"

Zhou Min, deflated, stood there naked for several moments before reaching down and putting on his trousers.

As he'd hoped, Zhou Min received word from the editorial office to report for work. The news was like a rainsquall on parched summer land.

He went in loaded down with gifts, which he handed out to everyone in the office. After that, he started each day early and did not get home until late. He performed all sorts of odd tasks: making trips to the printers, delivering manuscripts, mopping floors, bringing coworkers water, pleasing everyone, high and low. An intelligent man, he spent his spare time reading manuscripts, and gradually got the hang of how to write. One day he showed the editor-in-chief, Zhong Weixian, a story he had written, taking the man by surprise.

"You can write?" Zhong said. "Why didn't anyone tell me?" Though the piece did not make it into print, Zhou's hidden talents had been unearthed, and from then on, instead of going to the city wall to play his flute each morning and evening, he bought and read books by Zhuang Zhidie, ferreting out from people everything he could about the man, which he then took home, to the delight of Wan'er. Once, as she rolled out dough to make dumplings, her full breasts in rhythmic motion, she said, "If you really can write, why not do a piece about Mr. Zhuang? There are so many stories about him floating around Tongguan, and you know what he's done in Xijing. You can try to get it published in the *Xijing Gazette*. Since a magazine's circulation is tied to celebrities, you could get famous by writing about a famous man. Writing about him can only increase his influence, and when he learns that his name was responsible for your getting the job, if that pleases him, he'll be grateful, and if it doesn't, it can't hurt you." Thrilled and excited by her suggestion, he took the rolling pin from her. Not even stopping to let her wash her hands, he led her into the bedroom for some coupling.

Zhou Min turned Wan'er's encouragement into a thirty-thousand-word article. Although he had yet to meet Zhuang Zhidie, a reader of the article might assume that he was one of Zhuang's closest friends, someone with intimate knowledge of his life, his creative genius, and the many women who populated his personal and literary world. To be sure, the richest, most florid, and most detailed portions of the article were devoted to Zhuang's relationship with Jing Xueyin, though she was not identified by name. Editor-in-Chief Zhong read the article with enthusiasm and decided to run it that month. As the date of publication neared, Zhou Min visited Meng Yunfang every day to ask if Zhuang had returned to the city. On one of those visits he learned from Xia Jie that Meng had gone with Abbot Zhixiang to the Temple of the Dharma Gate to view a Buddha relic. She informed him that Zhuang was back in town, and that he had phoned the night before. She wrote down his address and urged Zhou to pay him a call.

Zhou Min hailed a taxi and told the driver to take him to the headquarters of the Literary Federation on Beida Road. Halfway there, he told the driver to stop and let him out so he could walk the rest of the way to compose himself. When he got there, he saw a crowd at the gate and tensed up. Squatting down to rest, he stared at the simple metal gate, where a woman was carrying on a conversation and milking a Holstein cow into a porcelain mug.

A man shuffled out of the compound, stepping on the backs of his shoes. He was not tall, his hair was uncombed, and he was wearing a black T-shirt with yellow foreign words imprinted on both the front and back. The cow lowed loud and long.

"She's calling for you," someone in the crowd wisecracked.

"That's because she's afraid you people will drink all her milk. The woman brought her here for me, but you folks always drink first."

"In the month since she last saw you, sir, I've hardly been able to get her to move. And there isn't much milk. When we came to town today, she headed straight here, refusing to stop along the way, strangely enough, so I wondered if you'd returned. And here you are! But look how thin you've gotten!"

"What do you expect, with no milk to drink?"

"But you do have a paunch!" she said.

The man laughed and patted his prominent belly before lying down, taking one of the cow's teats in his mouth and squeezing. Zhou Min found this hilarious: *People in the Literary Federation sure are eccentric,* he was thinking. *It's strange enough to drink milk before it's pasteurized, but whoever heard of drinking it straight from the cow?* He overheard people discussing the man's paunch.

"Of course he's got a paunch!" someone said. "Just ask him where he's been."

So she did: "Where have you been, feasting on delicacies? A line in a piece of doggerel goes, 'An eighth class, propaganda shills, turn slogans and chants into cashable bills.' Were you off at a meeting?"

"Look at his T-shirt," said another. "In front it says 'Hans Beer,' and on the back it says 'Beer Hans.' There's the source of the big belly."

Pfft! The man lying under the cow exploded in laughter, spurting milk all over his face and neck. He stopped, handed the woman some money, stuck around long enough for a little banter, and shuffled back across the compound. She counted the money, saw that he'd overpaid her, and called out to return some of it.

One of the bystanders stopped her. "Maybe he drank more than you think," he said. "Besides, it ought to cost more to take milk straight from the cow."

"The other day," she said, "on South Street, a young man said he wanted to try that. Not only did he fail to get a drop, the cow peed all over him."

"He was lucky," someone said. "If his aim had been a little off, he could have wound up sucking something else!" That created another explosion of laughter. This time the woman punched the man and led her cow away.

The crowd dispersed. Seeing that both the woman with the cow and her customers had left the scene, Zhou Min stood up, pulled himself together, and walked toward the compound, just as the scowling old gatekeeper came out to shut the gate. A bicyclist rode up and stopped.

"What do you want?" she asked.

"I'm looking for Wang An," he said. "A lyricist who lives out back."

"Who are you?" she asked.

"Are you checking IDs now?"

"What if I am?" was her ill-tempered response. "A country has its laws, a family its rules. I'm the gatekeeper, so watching the gate is my responsibility."

"All right," the man said, "all right. I work at the Giant Wild Goose Pagoda Cultural Center. My name is Liu, first name . . ."

"I don't care what your first name is," she said. "I'll call him." She went into the gatehouse and blew into a microphone. "Any sound?" she asked.

"Yes," Zhou Min said, "there was."

"Wang An Laoshi, you have a visitor," she announced—twice, then a third time. The sound swirled around the compound. She stuck her head out. "He's not in," she said. "Come back another day." Then she asked Zhou Min what he wanted. He was about to tell her that he wanted to see Zhuang Zhidie, but changed his mind. *This old hag announces visitors like a whorehouse madam*, he was thinking. If Zhuang actually came out to see his visitor, how would Zhou Min introduce himself? And could he make his intentions clear in a brief exchange at the compound gate? So he went back to Meng Yunfang's home, arriving just as Meng was getting in. Meng offered to accompany him to the compound, but Zhou had a case of nerves. "Maybe it would be better," he said, "to wait till the magazine hits the stands. It would make things easier if he had a chance to read the article first."

But when he went home and told Tang Wan'er, she hit the roof: "What do you think you're doing, searching for the new world? You just don't get it, do you! Zhuang Zhidie is back in town, but you don't seem to be in any hurry to go see him. Do you plan to wait till he sees Jing Xueyin and blows up when everything is out in the open?"

Seeing what a mistake he had made, he thumped his head with his fists.

"How's this?" she said. "We'll host a meal in his honor."

"Do you think he'd come?"

"We'll get Meng Yunfang to invite him. If all goes well, he'll come. If not, that will be the end of your editorial office dream, and you won't have to suffer any more humiliation."

So Zhou Min went to talk to Meng, who then went to see Zhuang, and returned with the news that the invitation had been accepted, which thoroughly delighted the couple, who then busied themselves over the next few days getting ready. They settled on a date: July 13.

❋

On the morning of the thirteenth, Zhou Min went into the kitchen as soon as he was up. Since they were living in a temporary residence, they had few of the items they would need, so he went to a local restaurant and rented three bowls, ten large plates and five small ones, a bamboo steamer, and an earthenware pot. Back home, Wan'er swept the floor and the steps outside; she placed Zhuang Zhidie's novels and a collection of essays she'd bought on a table and asked Zhou where he had put the Tongguan map they'd brought from home.

"With all we have to do, what do you want that for?"

"To tack up on the wall," she said.

Zhou Min thought for a moment. "Aren't you the sly fox!" He pinched her on the bottom. With a yelp, she coquettishly lifted a corner of her skirt to show him the bruise, then announced that she'd done all she was going to do. Now it was time to get herself ready. As he was cleaning a fish, she modeled a red dress for him; she then changed into a black skirt, and wound up trying on everything—blouses, shoes, necklaces, stockings—one item after another.

"You're like a mannequin," Zhou said. "You'd look good in rags. Zhuang Laoshi is a highly regarded writer, whom we're meeting for the first time, so the simpler the better." After choosing a yellow outfit from the pile of clothes on the sofa, she powdered her face and then concentrated on her eyes and lips, finishing not long before Meng Yunfang and his wife arrived with a bottle of osmanthus liquor and a bag of apricots. "I said not to bring anything," Zhou Min said. "You shouldn't have done that."

Xia Jie poked him on the forehead. "The bottle is for Wan'er," she said, "and apricots are Zhuang Laoshi's favorite. I didn't think you'd be aware of his likes and dislikes. Where is she? I want to see our lovely little sister!"

Tang Wan'er rushed out to greet her guests. "You can look," she said, "but I'm afraid you won't like what you see."

"What's with this 'little sister,'" Zhou Min said disapprovingly. "She needs to call you 'shimu'—'teacher's wife.'"

"Please don't call me that," Xia Jie said. "She's every bit the rare beauty I thought she'd be." Lively chatter between the two women commenced: That's a lovely outfit. You're so young, what cosmetics do you prefer? Have you ever tried a breast-enlargement pump?

After a moment, Wan'er said, "Zhou Min, you're in charge. I'm going to play chess with Xia Jie." She picked up the chess pieces and board and went upstairs to the garret with her guest. The landlord had taken his family on vacation three days before, locking the three upstairs bedrooms but leaving open the terrace, which was furnished with a stone table and four drum-shaped stone chairs. They sat down and played, interspersed with conversation and an occasional glance at the street below.

Zhou Min walked up with an offering of tea, sweets, melon, and peaches. "Zhou Min," Xia Jie said, "I can't wait to see what delicacies you've prepared for us today."

"I'm afraid I'm going to disappoint you," he said, "since I'm not much of a cook. I just want to show my appreciation to you."

"And we didn't come expecting something grand," she said. "Just don't forget us after you've become famous." Then she shouted down to Meng Yunfang, "Hey, you, into the kitchen. None of that 'laoshi' business for you, sitting there like a wise, tea-sipping man."

"I do all the cooking at home," Meng said. "Do you really expect me to do the same when we go out? Zhuang Zhidie is the guest of honor, while I count for nothing." Having had his say, he got up to wash his hands, under the watchful eye of the giggling women upstairs.

Zhuang Zhidie was expected at ten o'clock, but there was still no sign of him by ten after. Meng had sliced the pork, fried the meatballs, soaked the wood fungus, pan-fried the fish, and stewed the soft-shelled turtle. "I gave him the right address," he said, "and this place is easy to find. I'll run out to the intersection and look around."

He stood at the sparsely populated intersection for a few minutes before barreling into the lane and heading to the Clear Void Nunnery, where there was no construction work that day. He opened the door, walked in, and was met by an elderly nun who asked him who he was looking for.

Master Huiming, he told her. She led him around back to a large hall, the interior of which was so cold that his sweat dried. And since he had come in out of bright sunlight, for a moment he couldn't see a thing. Eventually, a cot in a corner of the hall, surrounded by nylon mosquito netting, caught his eye. Someone was asleep there. Sensing the awkwardness of the situation, he turned to leave, just as the person woke up.

"Meng Laoshi!"

Meng Yunfang turned back. The sleeper was now sitting up in bed—it was Huiming. Her collar was unbuttoned and her face had a ruddy glow; overall, she looked quite fetching. She parted the netting, but remained sitting on the edge of the bed, barefoot. "Come, sit here," she said. "Just passing by?"

With an audible gulp, Meng said, "I had a lunch engagement."

"So you're not staying," she said, and then turned to the elderly nun. "You may continue with what you were doing." The nun smiled, then opened the door and walked out.

An hour later, Meng Yunfang walked out of the Clear Void Nunnery and trotted back to the intersection, where he saw a Magnolia motor scooter parked by the side of the road. It looked familiar, so he inspected it more closely. Some paint had been chipped off the right handlebar, and a large brick was tied to the rear seat. He looked around, and there, in front of a used-book stall, stood Zhuang Zhidie, who spotted him as he walked up. "Come here, Yunfang, look at this. You'll get a kick out of it." He pointed to a secondhand copy of *Selected Works of Zhuang Zhidie*, with Zhuang's signature and an inscription—"For Mr. Gao Wenxing"—on the title page above the date. That was accompanied by an imprint of his personal seal.

Feeling a sense of embarrassment for Zhuang, Meng fumed, "Who sells a book that was personally presented to him by the author without at least tearing out the title page? Is that all a book by Zhuang Zhidie is worth?"

"Do you know this Gao Wenxing?" Zhuang asked. Meng could not place the name. "He's one of Zhao Jingwu's friends," Zhuang said. "When he met me the other day, he told me what a fan he was and asked for one of my books." Zhuang then bought the book for what the seller was asking. Beneath the first inscription, he wrote "For Mr. Gao Wenxing—again." He added the date and where he had signed it: at a secondhand bookstall.

"Give it to me," Meng said. "Now it's really worth something."

"No," Zhuang said, "I need to send it to him."

"Then you might as well put a noose around his neck."

They retrieved the motor scooter and pushed it along. Meng told Zhuang that Zhou Min was nearly out of his mind waiting, and wondered why he was so late. Zhuang said that as he was riding past the eastern section of the city wall, he spotted a pile of used bricks. He stopped to dig through the rubble, and found the one that was now tied to the scooter. It dated from the Han dynasty. "Where else," he wondered aloud, "can you find an undamaged brick more than two thousand years old? This is the Clear Void Nunnery neighborhood," he said. Have you ever been there?"

Meng turned red. "Why would I want to go there?" he stammered. "Let's hurry."

Zhuang told him to go on ahead while he went to mail the book.

Meng returned to tell the others that Zhuang would be there soon, then went into the kitchen. The news flustered Tang Wan'er, who rushed downstairs and, keeping her voice low, asked Zhou if he thought her hair was glossy enough. He said she needed to tuck the stray strands behind her ears. She told him to let her know whenever they came loose.

"I'll signal by coughing."

Just as she went back upstairs to continue the chess game with Xia Jie, they heard the sound of a motor scooter.

"He's here!" Meng bellowed from the kitchen. He and Zhou Min ran to the gate.

Tang Wan'er looked out the window in time to see the scooter pull up and stop. A small man jumped down off the seat. He was wearing a dark red shirt over gray slacks and a pair of sneakers—no socks. She could not contain her surprise. "That's Zhuang Zhidie? I expected him to be a big man. And that's a woman's motor scooter." Strangest of all was that instead of taking out his comb to touch up his hair, he reached up and mussed it with both hands. She heard Meng introduce Zhou Min to Zhuang, who cordially shook Zhou's hand and commented on his slicked back hair. Then, after a quick look around, he wondered how they had managed to find this place. "It's so quiet!" he complimented them as he walked into the yard, with its pear tree and grapevines. "I'm like a bird; I live in a flat, and have no contact with Mother Earth."

To Tang Wan'er, the man seemed intriguingly casual for someone so famous, and that helped ease the tension. She waited till Zhou Min called her to come downstairs, but the minute she lowered her head, her Yunnan ivory hair ornament flew off and shattered at Zhuang Zhidie's feet. Zhuang and Meng looked up, heard gasps from the two women, and saw Wan'er's loosened hair cascade down. She quickly gathered it into a bun as she walked downstairs, finishing just as she stepped into the yard.

There were two women on the staircase: Xia Jie, in her forties, was in a red knee-length dress that exposed her muscular calves. Though heavily powdered, her face seemed somehow not quite clean. Tang Wan'er, in her mid-twenties, was encased in a tight light yellow dress that highlighted every curve. Though she did not have the oval face of a classic beauty, her skin was glossy under a light coating of powder. Her thin, arched brows almost seemed to dance, but the most eye-catching feature was her long, thin neck, like a piece of fine jade, encircled by a necklace that enhanced the beauty of her high collarbones. The sight got Zhuang Zhidie thinking: Meng Yunfang had said that Zhou Min had left house and home to elope with a woman to Xijing, and he had wondered what sort of beauty could have made him do that. Now he could see for himself, and there was no question that Xijing boasted few to match her.

Seeing Zhuang smile at her, Wan'er said, "I'm so embarrassed!" And yet she held her head high and, with consummate poise, reached out to shake hands. "It's a pleasure to meet you, Zhuang Laoshi," she said. "I can't tell you how fortunate we are to have you honor us with your presence. For a while I wasn't sure you would come."

"I may not go to many places, but I never miss a chance to meet someone from my hometown."

"Zhuang Laoshi, you haven't lost your Tongguan accent."

"What did you expect?"

"Most people come to Xijing and lose their accent within weeks. I assumed you'd be speaking standard Putonghua by now."

"Chairman Mao didn't speak it, so why should I?" That got a laugh out of everyone.

"Let's continue this inside," Zhou Min said. "It's too hot out here." Back inside the house, Zhou poured tea and handed his guest a cigarette, apologizing for the cramped quarters, which he said were not deserving of Zhuang Laoshi's status.

"There's no need to be so modest, Zhou Min," Xia Jie said. "You and Meng Laoshi look after the food, and I'll take care of our guest."

Meng and Zhou went into the kitchen, leaving Xia Jie and Tang Wan'er standing there, spraying jasmine perfume in the direction of the rotating fan.

"Come sit by me, Zhidie," Xia Jie said. "You were away so long, people had begun asking about you."

Zhuang smiled. "I thank my good sister for her concern," he said. "What have you been doing lately, choreographing a new dance routine?"

"I've been meaning to talk to you about that. The mayor has asked us to put on a new show, but nothing we've tried has worked. I'm losing hair over this."

"What do you need me for when you have Yunfang?"

"Him? His ideas are worthless. One minute he lectures us on classical Chinese dance, the next minute it's modern Western dance, and before you know it, he's the choreographer. He's got all the dancers up in arms. Come see for yourself. I trust your judgment."

"What are your themes?"

"We have three: 'Knocking down Sour Dates,' 'Bickering,' and 'Carrying Water,' all about couples who fall in love beside a well, followed by amusing scenes from their marriage. In the end the woman gets pregnant, and craves something sour."

"Not bad," Zhuang said.

"I'm happy to hear you say that," Xia Jie agreed, "but it needs more."

"Have you seen Tongguan's Chen Cuncai in the flower drum opera *Hanging a Painting?*"

"I've seen many of Dance Master Chen's performances," Tang Wan'er replied. "He's in his sixties and wears tiny shoes, yet he can leap onto the back of a chair, toss a paper ball into the air, and kick it before it lands. He was popular before Liberation. People in Tongguan used to say they'd rather watch Cuncai dance in *Hanging a Painting* than rule the nation."

"Opera is one thing, dance is another," Xia Jie said. Red-faced, Wan'er' sank down into the sofa with a perplexed look, more or less tuning Xia Jie out.

"You can put the chair-jumping skill to use," Zhuang suggested. "Have the water carrier jump onto the water buckets with both feet."

"Sure," Xia Jie enthused, "an excellent idea. She can jump onto the buckets, one foot on each, to show off both her talent and her new shoes. With the carrying pole still on her shoulders, she then walks with the buckets on her feet." She asked Wan'er to get some paper for Zhuang Laoshi to work out some sketches. Forced to stay out of the conversation, Wan'er merely filled their cups and walked out into the yard.

Zhuang Zhidie chatted a while longer with Xia Jie before excusing himself to use the toilet. He took a detour into the yard, where Tang Wan'er, looking bored, was standing under a grape trellis, dappled by its shadows. She smiled when she saw him approach.

"I can tell from your accent that you're from Tongguan's Dongxiang District," he said.

"You have a good ear. Have you ever been there?"

"Sure. It's where you get the finest pork and shredded tofu," Zhuang replied.

"How wonderful. I told Zhou Min that was exactly what I was going to cook for Zhuang Laoshi, and he laughed at me, saying most people don't like it."

"Good for you," Zhuang said as he eyed Wan'er, who in turn lowered her own eyes. He wondered aloud which grapes were still green at this time of year. So he jumped up to pluck one, but they were out of reach. Wan'er giggled. He asked what she was laughing at.

"People say Zhuang Laoshi prefers sour foods. I didn't believe that. I thought only pregnant women liked sour things. But you do seem to like them." Climbing onto a stool, she reached up, but the vine was too high, so she stood on her tiptoes and stretched like a bow, exposing the fair skin of her arm. Her sleeve slipped down, and Zhuang spotted a mole on her arm.

Zhou Min walked out from the kitchen with a plate of food. "What are you doing, feeding Zhuang Laoshi sour grapes?" he said when he saw what she was doing. "He won't be able to eat after that." Zhuang smiled and headed off to the toilet.

After washing his hands, he returned to a table laden with three cold dishes and several canned items. Naturally, he took the seat of honor. Xia Jie drank what she'd brought, Meng Yunfang enjoyed his almond drink, and Zhou Min raised his glass of baijiu. "Zhuang Laoshi," he said, "you are one of Xijing's most prominent individuals, but more than that, you are the pride of Tongguan. Thanks to you I found work in an editorial office, and I will never forget your kindness. Today I want to say that the way in which I landed the job was not altogether on the up-and-up. A note of introduction with your name on it was what did it. I hope you can forgive me for that. As for the article I wrote, I was still learning then, so don't laugh at me."

"What's done is done," Zhuang said, "so nothing more need be said. I haven't read what you wrote. Lots of people write things like that these days. They say they're promoting me, but they write to promote themselves. Someone once asked me to read a piece he'd written. I recommended that he not publish it, but he did anyway. People write not to write but to publish, so I've stopped reading all of it."

"I never thought Zhuang Laoshi could be so magnanimous," Zhou Min said. "To you!" He emptied his glass. So did Zhuang Zhidie. "Yunfang, have you really quit drinking?"

"Completely," Meng replied.

"What for?" Zhuang asked. "We draw our lessons from Buddhism and Taoism only in philosophy and aesthetics. Don't be like one of those old women who burn incense and kowtow to the gods. Besides, being a monk or a nun is just another occupation."

"That's where you're wrong," Meng replied. "No outsider can get the true picture. You can never master qigong exercises until you give up alcohol, meat, onions, and garlic. And you'll be discomfited if you eat them once you get the qi moving."

"Practice, practice," Zhuang countered. "Only true masters cultivate spiritualism and alchemy. Disciples and neophytes never move beyond practice."

Tang Wan'er chuckled, and when they turned to look at her, she gazed at the pear tree outside the window, draped in green leaves, a hole in its bent old trunk. Zhuang was taken by the look on her face. "Was there something you wanted to say?"

"I love listening to all this wise talk."

"Wise talk?" Meng sputtered. "All we do is argue, and our thoughts get more and more scattered."

"In my opinion," said Zhuang, "you always go to extremes. You said you were going to quit drinking, and you did. Well, I don't have that kind of willpower. Not even a drop? Really? This is genuine Wuliangye we're drinking."

"Not even if it's real Maotai," Meng replied.

Xia Jie had finished her drink and asked Zhou Min for a refill. "You're right, Zhidie. He has suffered from extremes all his life. He had gained a bit of fame by the time you came to Xijing, but in the years since, you've become a bright light, while he hasn't changed a bit. Instead of writing, he studies Buddhism and practices qigong all day long. He won't eat this, says no to that, until all I've got in my stomach is water, not a drop of grease."

"Then Meng Laoshi is missing out on the good life," Zhou Min said. "Businessmen enjoy good fortune without status. Meng Laoshi enjoys status without good fortune."

"Well said," Meng agreed. "Our Zhuang Laoshi has both fortune and status, and when you reach that point, you can have whatever you want."

With that comment ringing in his ears, Zhuang gazed at the sunlight streaming in through the window onto the food on the table. Dust floated in the sunbeams. He forced a smile. "I may have everything," he said, "but I seek perfection."

That surprised Meng Yunfang. "What did you say?"

Zhuang repeated himself: "I said I seek perfection."

"I can't figure you out," Meng said. "Believe me when I say I never thought you could spend so much time in a brewery. And I've noticed that your ideas seem to have undergone a change recently."

"I surprise myself," Zhuang said. "Am I adapting to society or becoming corrupt?"

"I'm not the one to answer that," Meng said. "I imagine it's no different than my infatuation with qigong and my willingness to stop drinking and become a vegetarian. It's all determined by the natural progression of life. After water is heated, the self-organized phenomenon of perfect symmetry will inevitably occur." Zhou Min and Tang Wan'er listened without quite understanding what the men were saying, as evidenced by their stiff smiles. "Tsk-tsk," Xia Jie reacted. "Comrade Meng," she said, "we've been invited to a meal, not an academic conference, so I think we've exchanged enough obscure talk."

"I'll stop," Zhuang said with an apologetic wave of his hand. "No more. We're here to drink." He picked up his glass and drank.

Only Zhuang and Zhou Min were drinking, which put a damper on the atmosphere. So Zhou Min suggested a few rounds of a finger-guessing game to spice things up. Zhuang begged off, but Zhou Min was relentless. Wan'er was tickled at how the two men refused to give in. "Zhou Min," she said, "stop treating Zhuang Laoshi as if he were one of your no-account friends. I'll drink with you, Zhuang Laoshi." Zhuang jumped to his feet and held out his glass.

"We've decided to stay in Xijing now that we've met you," she said. "Please take Zhou Min on as your pupil and teach him how to write."

"Now that Zhou Min works in an editorial office, I'll be the one seeking *his* help."

"Then here's to you," she said as she drained her glass. Her face reddened. Zhuang drained his own glass, and she followed him with another and yet another. When Zhou Min coughed to get her attention, she reached up and tucked some loose strands of hair behind her ear; she was getting more beautiful by the second. Zhuang spiritedly finished off three more glasses, and then, not giving an inch to Wan'er, turned the bottle upside down to show it was empty.

While the others laughed and carried on, Meng Yunfang went back into the kitchen, where he prepared three meat and three vegetarian dishes, then carried out a pan-fried fish with pine nuts, stir-fried pork kidney, frog meat, and a turtle that had been stewing in a clear broth. Xia Jie praised the turtle, claiming that whoever found the pin bone was in for good luck. In the West, she said, pin bones sell for five U.S. dollars as toothpicks. She split open the meat and placed a small portion on each diner's plate. Tang Wan'er picked at hers with her chopsticks until she found the bone. "Back in Tongguan I ate lots of Yellow River turtles, but they had a muddy taste. Your health is paramount, Zhuang Laoshi, so you can have my portion." She placed it on his plate before he could say anything.

Zhuang acknowledged her gesture by laying a portion on her plate. "This is the best part," he said. "You have to eat it."

Wan'er looked down and saw that he had given her the head—dark, long, and frighteningly ugly. She glanced at him out of the corner of her eye; his expression gave nothing away. She picked it up, put it in her mouth, and began sucking loudly. When Zhuang glanced her way, she blushed.

Xia Jie saw what was happening and was about to make a snide comment when Zhuang spoke up first. "Hey, I've got the pin bone!"

"Good luck seems to follow Zhidie," Xia Jie said. "Last New Year's I wrapped a coin in one of the dumplings I was making, and no one got it. Then he showed up. I tried to give him a plate of dumplings, but he said no. Finally I got him to try one, and, sure enough, that was the one with the coin."

Wan'er swallowed the turtle's head as the redness faded from her face. Not wanting to look at Xia Jie, she went into the kitchen to prepare the pork and shredded tofu.

As Zhuang drank, his head felt heavier and heavier. With the clatter of cooking in the kitchen, he said, "I can't stand it here with that aroma in the air. I must go see what she's doing."

"What's there to see?" Xia Jie said. "If you really want to see, get her to make it for you at your place. For now, sit there and let me toast you in thanks for your willingness to watch my new dance routine."

With a smile, Zhuang accepted the toast, but he sneaked a look past the open door to the kitchen, where Wan'er was busy at the stove.

After slicing the pork, Wan'er turned on the gas stove, and as the flames popped, she let her thoughts roam. She placed a small mirror on the chopping board, which allowed her to see Zhuang in the other room. *As far as looks go, he can't be considered handsome, but it's strange how after only just meeting him, I find him so appealing, looking better by the minute. Back home in Tongguan, Zhou Min impressed me as a smart, capable man who had some talent. But Xijing is, after all, Xijing, and next to him, Zhou Min merely looks clever.* By this point in her reverie, the oil had turned hot, and she hurried to dump in the tofu. But she mistakenly tossed in some wet ginger. *Pow!* Hot oil spurted out of the pan and spattered on her face. "Ow!" she cried out, dropping into a crouch in front of the stove.

At the sound of the cry, Zhou Min rushed in, pulled her hands away, and saw that her face was already beginning to blister. She grabbed the mirror and burst into tears when she saw herself. The others asked what had happened. "It's nothing; a little oil spattered on her face," Zhou Min answered as he led her into the bedroom and applied some ointment.

"Women these days are only good at having babies," Meng Yunfang said.

"Don't talk like that," Xia Jie chided him. "I haven't given you one yet." They laughed as Meng went into the kitchen.

"This is awful," Wan'er whispered. "I can't go out like this."

"Don't be silly," Zhou Min assured her, "Zhuang Laoshi won't care about something like that. I was surprised the first time I saw him. Remember I told you about that fellow who sucked milk right from a cow's teats? Well, that was him."

"Not caring for him isn't the same as not caring for you and me," she said. "For you it means being a slob, but for him it's more like poise."

Zhou Min went back to join the others. He split the chicken open and placed the head on Zhuang's plate. Zhuang in turn picked up a drumstick and laid it on Xia Jie's plate. Then he placed a wing on a plate and told Zhou Min to take it in to Tang Wan'er.

"Wan'er," Zhou Min said, "come out here. Zhuang Laoshi has put food aside for you."

She walked out of the bedroom. "I'm sorry, everyone," she said, keeping a hand over her face out of embarrassment.

"Sorry about what?" Xia Jie asked.

"It's disrespectful to show a blistered face," she said.

This woman is quite the flirt, Zhuang was thinking.

"With skin as fair as yours," Meng Yunfang said with a laugh, "a few blisters just make for another slight imperfection."

Wan'er sat down, the redness on her face refusing to retreat. She responded to Zhuang's gaze with a shy smile. Thanks to all the alcohol, his mind was beginning to reel. He excused himself to visit the toilet. By the time he was inside and had shut the door behind him, he had an erection. He couldn't pee, not now, and with his eyes shut, he was breathing heavily, an array of fantasies coursing through his head. With the arrival of the ejaculate, his head cleared a bit. He returned to the table and resumed eating, though he was no longer in such an upbeat mood.

The meal was over at four in the afternoon. Zhuang stood to say goodbye, telling Zhou Min, who tried to get him to stick around, that he had important business to discuss with Ruan Zhifei. So Zhou saw him out to the intersection and returned home, where he found Wan'er still leaning against the doorframe. She apparently didn't hear him when he called her name. "What's gotten into you?" he asked. He saw that the blister had flattened out a bit and was forming a scab.

"I didn't embarrass myself today, did I?" she asked with a pout when she regained her composure.

"Not a bit," he said. "You looked wonderful." He gave her a kiss. She let him, but didn't kiss him back. "Everyone had a good time," she said. "It was perfect. I'm just sorry that Zhuang Laoshi's wife couldn't make it."

"According to Meng Laoshi," Zhou said, "she stays home to take care of her ailing mother."

"Xia Jie says she's a real beauty."

"That's what people say. But you wouldn't expect Zhuang Zhidie to marry an ugly woman, would you?"

Wan'er sighed and went inside to sit on her bed, where she lost herself in her thoughts.

❋

Instead of returning to the Literary Federation compound that night, Zhuang accepted Ruan Zhifei's invitation to join the municipal leadership in reviewing a new program, helping to rewrite the script. When he got there, the actors roped him into a card game. It was late when he got up to leave, but Ruan talked him into going home with him to have a couple more drinks. He also wanted to show off his newly decorated apartment. Once there, Zhuang took no notice of that; he just drank and drank, recalling how he had once thought of Ruan as the dissolute head of an acting troupe, a leading figure in dramatic circles who had organized the troupe, and who was always surrounded by pretty girls. In reality, his actresses were like green persimmons, far from mature, and none had a face like Tang Wan'er's. He thought back to all that had happened earlier that day, and was pleased by how he had overindulged. He knew that Ruan's wife was not home. He was like the man who brought firewood home; she was like the woman who burned it. They had agreed not to interfere in each other's private life, the one condition being that they would spend Saturday nights together. So Zhuang took off his shirt and let the liquor flow, talking about everything under the sun until he was too drunk to keep going. Then he climbed onto an extra bed, where he snored the night away.

Sunlight was streaming in through the window when they awoke the following morning, and Zhuang was impressed to see how nicely Ruan had decorated his apartment. He proudly revealed that the wallpaper was imported from France, the tea-colored window glass made in Italy. He'd bought thirty-seven laminated decorative panels from Shanghai, which still wasn't quite enough. He took Zhuang into the bathroom to show off his tub, into the kitchen to show him the liquid gas stove, and into two small rooms to see the modular cabinets. One door off the living room was locked. "My wife's room," Ruan explained. "Wait till you see the unique Japanese chandelier." He took out a key and unlocked the door. Zhuang could not believe his eyes. Two people were fast asleep on a king-sized Simmons mattress: one was Ruan's wife, the other a man with slobber on his cheek. Zhuang had never seen him before and wondered if he was dreaming, but he heard Ruan say, "That's my wife . . . when did she get home? We were so sound asleep we didn't hear them come in." Zhuang did not know what to say, but he thought he was expected to say something. The more he tried, the more he was unable to think of anything.

"Who is that?" was all he could come up with.

"Let's just say it's me," Ruan said, before shutting the door and leading Zhuang back into his bedroom, where he opened a wardrobe with five shelves, crammed with women's shoes in all sizes. "I'm fond of women's shoes. Every pair you see comes with a beautiful story."

Zhuang wasn't sure what he meant, but he noticed that Ruan had sleep in his eyes. "Wipe your eyes," he said. *If he bought the shoes for women, why are they still here? Maybe for every pair he gives away he buys another, keeping some sort of record.*

Ruan handed Zhuang a pair. "Manager Zhu of the West Avenue Mall gave me these a few days ago. They don't have a number, and don't have a story. Give them to your wife. Don't say no."

Shoes in hand, Zhuang Zhidie walked out of Ruan's apartment and rode his scooter all the way to Guangji Road before recalling the payment voucher for one of his essays in his pocket. He turned and headed to the post office near the clock tower to get his money. It wasn't much, a little over two hundred yuan. Back on what was now a crowd-filled street, he checked his watch and saw that people were just getting off work. Threading his way to the parking lot, shoebox in hand, he asked himself why he'd foolishly accepted the shoes. He had to laugh. Then he had an idea. He went to the nearest telephone booth to call Jing Xueyin at home. A man answered. "Who's this?" he asked. Knowing it was Jing's husband, Zhuang hung up and tried her work number. He learned she was away visiting her parents. Patting the shoebox, he listlessly exited the phone booth and stopped to see what the posted newspapers on the kiosk had to report. A young man sidled up to him. "Want to buy some eyeglasses, friend?" he asked under his breath, opening his jacket to reveal a pair with hard frames hanging from his vest. "I won't lie to you, I stole them. Genuine crystal lenses, priced at eight hundred yuan at the store. I need money. You can have them for three hundred."

Zhuang looked into the sky, where the sun shone brightly. His eyes narrowed into a smile. He reached into his pocket, but instead of money, he took out one of his cards. "I won't lie to you, young man. I've been in your business, and that makes us soul mates. Here's my card."

The youngster took the card, read it, and snapped off a salute. "So you're Zhuang Laoshi! Today is my lucky day. I went to one of your lectures, but you're heavier now, with a bit of a paunch, and I didn't recognize you."

"You like to write, do you?" Zhuang asked him.

"I've dreamed of being a writer since I was a kid. The local paper published one of my little poems last year."

"Xijing is a remarkable place," Zhuang commented. "If a meteorite struck down ten people, seven of them would be fans of literature."

The young man walked off sheepishly, turning around every few steps to look back. Zhuang found it a bit comical and somewhat off-putting. When he came to a sundries store, he bought a set of Jingdezhen porcelain dinnerware, a spatula, a briquette stove, and a tea set with the two hundred yuan, and then told the salesclerk to deliver it all to Tang Wan'er at the address he gave him. After that, he rode his scooter to his in-laws' house on Shuangren fu Avenue.

Fifty-five years earlier, an eccentric by the name of Niu had lived on the bank of the Wei River in the northern outskirts of town. Coming and going like a shadow, he was adept at observing the constellations to see their effect on the world. At the time, General Yang Hucheng had ended his bandit career in central Shaanxi and become a powerful force in Xijing. He invited the eccentric Niu to be his aide. Unwilling to live in the city, Niu remained in his three-room cottage with its acre of anemic farmland, where he lived a life of ease, going into town when General Yang had something important for him to do. Soon thereafter, the Henan warlord Liu Zhenhua laid siege to Xijing. After meeting stiff opposition for eighty days, Liu tried the Japanese tactic of tunneling into the city.

The residents knew what the enemy was up to, but did not know where the tunnel ended, so at night they buried earthenware vats filled with water and regularly checked to see if they were disturbed. They were in a constant state of anxiety. The eccentric arrived, dressed in traditional garb, and after walking through the city, street by street and lane by lane, he rested on a boulder at the martial-arts school to smoke his water pipe.

"Dig here to create a lake," he said after twelve puffs on his pipe. Yang Hucheng was doubtful, but he had all the city's water brought over. The tunnel ended at the bottom of the lake, and when it broke through, all the water flowed out of the city. Liu Zhenhua was forced to retreat. A grateful Yang rewarded the eccentric with a house on Shuangren fu Avenue; but he chose to return to the bank of the Wei River, so his son moved into town. The largest of Xijing's four sweet-water wells was located in that lane, where the son created the Shuangren fu Water District, distributing fresh water throughout the city by the wagonload.

Zhuang Zhidie loved talking about this history. Whenever he entertained guests, he had his wife, Niu Yueqing, show them a photo of her grandfather and a plaque made of bone. He also took them to Shuangren fu Avenue and described how the Niu family had occupied an entire lane. His wife had criticized him in the past: "Why must you show off all the time? Are you mocking the Niu descendants as responsible for the family's decline? My mother had no sons. If she had, we would not have been reduced to owning a mere few houses."

"I'm not mocking anyone," Zhuang Zhidie said solicitously on one occasion. "The family may have declined, but the same may not be true for the son-in-law."

Niu Yueqing cried out, "Ma, did you hear that? Your son-in-law is saying that his fame is responsible for the Niu family prestige! I ask you, does he have the same renown that my father and grandfather enjoyed in their time?"

The old lady still lived in the house on Shuangren fu Avenue, refusing to move to an upstairs apartment in the Literary Federation compound, which forced Zhuang and his wife to travel back and forth between the two places. Every time he entered the street, images of the family's history filled his mind. He'd stand by the sealed-up well and stare down at the saw-toothed grooves worn into the stone platform by ropes, trying to imagine how it had looked back then. But his wife was right to criticize him, he thought.

The sun beat down mercilessly as Zhuang rode his scooter into the street, engulfed in stifling heat. Sweat ran into his eyes. A stray dog lay panting in the middle of the road, its tongue lolling. Zhuang swerved to miss it and ran into a wall, managing somehow to stay upright, though he scraped some skin off his left thumb. Zhao Jingwu was inside talking to Niu Yueqing when he heard Zhuang ride in through the gate. He ran out to greet him. "It's about time you got here." He took the brick from the scooter rack and carried it inside.

"Don't bring that filthy thing into the house!" Niu Yueqing complained.

"Look closer," Zhuang said. "It's from the Han dynasty."

"You've piled up so many of those in the other house that people can't get in the door; now you want to do the same here. You say they're from the Han; well, the flies in the house are from the Tang!"

Zhuang cast Zhao Jingwu a pained look, but said, "That comment is pure art. Your art cells don't catch fire till you're angry." He told Zhao to take the brick outside, tie it onto the back of the Magnolia, then come back inside.

It was an old house with large rooms, the walls and posts constructed of the best red pine. Though the carvings—portraits and nature images—were in bad shape, they attested to the original beauty of the place. The eighty year-old matriarch, who was in her bedroom behind a dividing wall, summoned Zhuang when she heard his voice. She had lost her husband at the age of fifty, and by sixty-three was getting senile. Two years earlier, she had slept for two weeks straight; people thought she was about to die, but then she came back around. Ever since then, she had been spouting nonsense about death and ghosts and acting crazy. The winter before, she had abruptly demanded that Zhuang Zhidie buy her a red cypress coffin. "You're in fine health," Zhuang had said. "You'll live another twenty years, so why buy a coffin now? Besides, underground burials aren't permitted in the city." She was unmoved. "I want a coffin as proof of my existence whenever I look at it." She refused to eat or drink as a threat. Unable to say no, he asked someone to purchase a coffin on Mount Zhongnan. The old lady took her bed apart and put the bedding into the coffin, where she began to sleep. That caused a rift between her and her daughter, who complained that people might accuse them of mistreating her. But Zhuang told his wife that the old lady was probably suffering from narcissism and that they should let her do as she asked. Strangely, once she started sleeping in the coffin, she took to wearing a paper mask when she went out, so enraging her daughter that she kept her mother inside as much as possible. Zhuang, always ready to tease, said the old lady had special powers, and that if he had them he could write magic realist novels by sheer intuition, without imitating a foreigner.

He went into her room, where the window was tightly shut and the drapes were drawn. He was sweating the moment he stepped inside.

"You think this is hot?" she said. "When I was young, it got so hot on the sixth day of the sixth month, when the sun was bright red, that people hung their bedding out to dry, along with the old folks' funeral garb. But your granddad walked out of the village under an umbrella without a word, so the villagers took in the laundry, some hurried, others slow, just before the sky opened up and rain pelted down. It's not hot today. If you think it is, it's all internal heat. Put some spit on your nipples and you'll cool down."

Zhuang merely smiled. The old lady spat on her finger and rubbed it on his nipples. A pair of chills entered his heart. He shuddered.

"Zhidie," she said, "your father-in-law came back a while ago, sat where you're sitting now, and told me he was upset. He can't abide his new neighbors, says they're always arguing and that their child is a handful, even comes over and steals food from them. I want you to light a stick of incense for him." A funeral photo of Zhuang's father-in-law stood on a table in the corner beside an incense burner filled with ashes. Zhuang lit a stick and looked up at a dust-filled cobweb in a corner of the room. He picked up her cane to knock it down.

"Don't do that," she said. "It's his favorite place to sit." Before Zhuang could say anything, she continued, "He came as soon as you lit the incense. Where have you been, damn you? How did you get here so fast?" Zhuang looked around but saw nothing. Smoke curled from the burning incense, rising like silk to the ceiling. She said that the old fellow was opening the box with the water district plaque. "That is the only antique that's been passed down," she said. "The mayor came to see it the last time he visited. Are you going to take it with you? If you do, what will I show him the next time?" She slipped the box, which she normally kept under her pillow, under her buttocks. That tickled Zhuang's fancy; he was about to say something when his wife called to him: "What are you and Ma talking about in there? You're free to leave when you're done talking, but I'll be afraid to go in there."

Zhuang left the room. "Mother has some strange tales to tell, and I think she's telepathic. The nineteenth is your father's birthday, though we haven't celebrated it for more than ten years, so this year buy some spirit paper for her to burn." He turned to Zhao Jingwu. "Something on your mind?" he asked.

"Not really," Zhao said. "I was just going to invite you to my place. It's an old-style courtyard dwelling, one of many that the mayor wants to tear down to build a gymnasium. This might be your last chance to see it."

"I keep meaning to go," Zhuang said, "but I can never find the time. Let me remind you that you promised me some antiques."

"No problem," Zhao said with a laugh. "Anything I drag out from under my bed will be as good as your wall bricks. Your wife needn't make lunch today. I'll treat you both to a lunch of hulutou, that soup with pig entrails. There's something important I want to talk to you about."

"Hulutou, on a hot day like this?" Niu Yueqing said warily. "It'll stink something awful. Count me out."

"That shows how much you know," Zhuang said. "It's a Xijing specialty. Although it's just steamed buns soaked in soupy intestines, the spices give it a unique flavor. The kind you get at Dongmen's Fushunlai is inferior. The genuine article is served at Chunshengfa in Nanyuanmen, where legend has it that the ancestral founder was given a recipe by the famed Daoist healer Sun Simiao. You've never tasted anything like it. It could work wonders on your chronic constipation. You need to structure your diet for what your body needs. You really should try it."

"Work wonders?" she replied. "Then why didn't it work on Jingwu?"

"What about him?"

"He complained to me a while ago that he had his eye on a girl who lives on Tangfang Street, but he was embarrassed to tell her how he felt, so he watched her go to work in the mornings and leave in the afternoons. He mooned over her for a month. Then three days ago, while he was waiting, he heard firecrackers. He went to see what the commotion was about, and discovered it was the girl's wedding—to someone else! Everything comes easy to Jingwu, everything but romance. Does he need to eat pig guts when he already has a pig brain?"

"Jingwu is unlucky in love, so what will work wonders on him is a woman," Zhuang announced.

Zhao laughed heartily and said he had decided to remain a lifelong bachelor. He stood up and took Zhuang by the arm.

"Don't leave yet," Niu Yueqing said. "Not till you've taken care of my business. Then you can stay away for three days and nights, for all I care."

"What business is that?" Zhuang asked.

"I bought Mother a backscratcher at the Zhuque Department Store this morning because she says she has fleas. How can she possibly have fleas? Your skin starts to flake as you get old. Well, when I got home with it, I was surprised to see that our neighbor, Aunty Wang, had given Mother a backscratcher that was nicer than the one I bought. I want to return it, but I'm not sure I can. What should I do?"

"How much can a backscratcher cost?" Zhuang asked her. "Aren't you overdoing it?"

"And who are you, the rich man Gong Jingyuan?"

"Your wife knows how to manage money," Zhao said.

"I have to. If not, we'd be poor no matter how much he earned," she said. "Zhidie is like a rake with no teeth, and I can't let the spending get out of control. Jingwu, I think that when I go to the department store, I'll need to tell them that I wanted to buy the backscratcher when I saw how well made it is, never dreaming that my husband had already bought one, also one of theirs. Does an old lady need two to scratch an itch? We have to work for every cent we earn, and having an extra one of these lying around would be wasteful, don't you think? So I'd like to return this one. If they refuse to take it back, I'll reason with them, stressing the need for fairness in business. If people these days are free to quit the Communist Party, who says you can't return a purchase? A young clerk might not listen, and if she argues with me, what should I do? Argue, I guess. My question is, should I be genteel, or do I use the coarsest language I know?"

"Let's hear the refined," Zhuang said.

"You people are using lame arguments, so go screw your old lady, you bastards, no-good sons of bitches!"

"You're so used to coarse language," Zhuang said, "that a slip of the tongue turns your genteel words coarse. Instead of 'screw your old lady,' you should say 'screw your mother.' Much more cultured."

"Jingwu," she said indignantly, "you see what kind of man your Zhuang Laoshi is? He's never taken my side in anything."

"Young people worship Zhuang Laoshi, he's their idol."

"I married a husband, not an idol. Those people have given him a big head. Not one of those youngsters knows that Zhuang Laoshi's feet stink, that his teeth are rotting, that he grinds them in his sleep, or that he farts while he eats, and won't come out of the toilet till he's read a newspaper from beginning to end."

Zhao laughed. "Here's what I think. If fighting with them doesn't work, ask to see their supervisor. If that fails, call the mayor on his private phone."

"That's what I'll do," she said. "I'll go now. Don't leave till I get back."

When she heard that Niu Yueqing was going out, her mother told her to put on some makeup, but Niu Yueqing ignored her and left. The old lady grumbled: "She won't wear a mask and doesn't like makeup. How can she let people see her real face?"

After Niu Yueqing left, Zhuang said, "In public I'm surrounded by admiring people, but here at home this is what I get."

"She's not so bad," Zhao said. "She's not terribly well educated, but you don't find many women that virtuous."

"When she loses her temper," Zhuang said, "she could give a rock a headache. But if she likes you, she'll stuff you with food even after you're full." Telling Zhao to stay put, Zhuang took the brick to the Literary Federation compound on his scooter.

When he returned, before he had even taken a sip of tea, Niu Yueqing came in and called her mother out for one of the still-warm stuffed buns she had bought. Her face glowed. "Guess what happened," she announced.

"Back so soon?" Zhao said. "I'd say they wouldn't take it back."

"They took it back!"

"See, you did it. You have to be tough to get by in the world," Zhao said.

"Not true," Niu Yueqing corrected him. "I went up to the counter, and when the clerk asked me what I was in the market for, I just stammered, couldn't say a word. She laughed and asked me if I was returning a purchase. I said yes. She took it, handed me my refund, and that was it."

"That was it?" Zhao asked, clearly surprised.

"That's what I'm saying. It couldn't have been easier. A bit of a letdown, actually."

No one spoke for a few minutes. "We often try to make complex matters simple," Zhuang said to break the ice. "But we also frequently do the opposite."

Niu Yueqing curled her lip. "Another object lesson from our writer."

The old lady complained about the blandness of the stuffed bun, so she took it back to her room to add some vinegar from a large vat. When she removed the cloth cover, the aroma flooded the room.

"What's that smell?" Zhao asked. "It's very strong."

"Did you stir the vinegar, Mother?" Niu Yueqing shouted. It had to be stirred with a clean paddle daily.

"No need," she replied, "it's ready."

"You make your own vinegar?" Zhao said.

"Your Zhuang Laoshi won't even taste the smoky vinegar they sell on the street. Nothing but white vinegar. So I made a vat of my own. It has a wonderful flavor, absolutely pure. I'll send you home with some."

"I'm not as picky as Zhuang Laoshi," he said. "I'll eat anything. But if you have pickled vegetables, I'll drop by someday to try them."

"You came to the right place," she said. "We have pickled cabbage, salted vegetables, pickled sweet garlic and chili peppers, whatever you like." At that, she fetched a plastic bag, filled it with a little bit of everything, and handed it to Zhao to take home.

Zhuang was talking about how they preferred the kind of food villagers eat when he was reminded of the shoes. He took them out of the scooter basket and handed them to Niu Yueqing.

"You bought these for me?" she said.

Zhuang did not tell her that Ruan Zhifei had given them to him. She did not like Ruan, thought he was a thug. So he told her that Xia Jie had given them to him the day before at Meng Yunfang's home.

"My goodness!" she said when she examined the black leather shoes with stiletto heels. "These aren't shoes, they're instruments of torture."

"I hate it when you talk like that," Zhuang said. "If they're instruments of torture, then why are all the women out on the street wearing them?"

Niu Yueqing took off her shoes and tried on the new ones. "You're always hoping I'll turn fashionable. Well, with these shoes, I won't be able to do a thing around the house. Are you willing to wait on me?" She stood up and complained of pain caused by the bulge in front. Born with wide, fleshy feet, she wore only flats, which drew a sigh from Zhuang Zhidie, who said that feet are a woman's most important feature. With unattractive feet, she loses three-tenths of her beauty. With a frown, Niu Yueqing said, "If I'm going to wear high heels, they have to be made in Beijing. I can't wear shoes made in Shanghai." Zhuang had no choice but to take the shoes back. Gratitude was one thing he did not want. He left with Zhao Jingwu, hanging the shoebox on his handlebars.

Zhao took advantage of Zhuang's good mood to tell him about an entrepreneur named Huang who had opened a pesticide plant in Shilipu on the south side of town and had come looking for him three times, insisting that Zhuang write an article about the plant. Length was no problem, and he could write what he wanted, so long as it was published. "How much did you get?" Zhuang asked Zhao with a laugh. "You let me pull up the stake so you can steal the cow."

"Oh, please," Zhao said. "I won't lie to you—he's a relative of my aunt. She came to me about this, but I put her off. But he won't stop hounding me. I see no reason for you to say no. You could knock something like that out by skipping one round of mahjong. I got him to agree to pay you five thousand yuan."

"I'll use a pen name," Zhuang said.

"No, you can't," Zhao replied. "It's your name he's paying for."

"My name is worth five thousand yuan?"

"You're a man of good character, and, unfortunately, these days that equals poverty. Five thousand is nothing to sneer at. You wouldn't get much more than that by writing a whole novel."

"I'll think it over."

"He's coming to my place today, so make up your mind now. Don't mention the money. I want him to pay up front. These people are rolling in the stuff."

They arrived at Zhao Jingwu's home, where a popcorn peddler had a fire going in his stove, sending smoke into the air in front of the gate. Zhao kicked the stove. "Are you trying to suffocate us? Can't you go somewhere else?" The soot-covered peddler rolled his eyes and was about to stand up to Zhao, but after he took a couple of steps, he swallowed hard and moved his stove away.

After the smoke cleared, Zhuang took a look at the address: 37 Sifu Road. The fancy arched gateway had decorative tiles and spiny glass ridges. Stone blocks carved with scenes and figures topped the towers. A detached protective guard on the frame, peeling black paint on the doors, and six missing metal fasteners marred the gateway. A pair of unicorns in relief decorated the high bluestone gate pier. Iron rings were inlaid in the outer walls, which were fronted by long purple stones. Seeing how intently Zhuang was looking everything over, Zhao told him that the rings were for tethering horses, while the long purple stones were known as mounting stones. In earlier days, rich families rode horses down the street; bells fastened to the reins rang out, and the hoof beats pounded rhythmically. It was a more impressive sight than officials riding by in cars these days. The carving on the gate pier particularly impressed Zhuang, who said that the residents of Xijing had excavated and restored just about everything else, but no one had paid any attention to the pier gate carvings. If he went around making stone pier rubbings, he could publish a book of them. He walked in through the gate and up to a screen wall that blocked the view from outside. The relief design was one of Zheng Banqiao's single-stalk bamboo paintings between a pair of scrolls that read

A stalk of green bamboo braves the storm
Like a brush that paints clouds in the sky

"This is the first time I've seen one of Zheng's single-stalk bamboo paintings," Zhuang said, clapping happily. "Why don't you make a rubbing of it?"

"They're going to demolish the house," Zhao told him, "and take this down. If you like it so much, why don't you preserve it?"

"The poem isn't bad," Zhuang replied, "but being carved into a gate screen gives it a bit of a bleak quality."

Once inside the compound, they faced three courtyards, each of which fronted an entryway, a corridor, and a bedroom with eight patterned windows. But a motley collection of residents had carved up the yard, with a tent here, a little shack there, and buckets of filthy water and trash baskets blocking every door. With difficulty, Zhuang and Zhao negotiated their way through, encountering residents in their underwear cooking a meal or playing mahjong on rickety tables in doorways, all turning to gawk at the new arrivals. The rear courtyard was a jumble, including side rooms, their wood-framed windows propped open by bamboo poles. A curtain hung over the doorway, which lay in the shade of a Chinese toon tree.

"This is where I live," Zhao said. It was dark inside, and it took some time before the pitted limestone-covered walls came into view. An old-fashioned mahogany table stood beneath the window, and behind it was a bed piled haphazardly with books and magazines. A thick layer of limestone covered the floor under the bed. Zhuang knew that was to protect against dampness. Zhao invited Zhuang to sit with him in two squat chairs, which Zhuang noted were exquisite. He heaved a sigh. "This is my first time inside one of these Xijing residential compounds," he said. "People used to say how comfortable they were. Now that they're home to so many families, I wonder what it was like to be the only residents in one."

"We were the only residents, but poor people were allowed to move in in the fifties, and once they were here, you couldn't get them out. The numbers mounted, all but destroying the place."

"So this place was yours. You never told me your family was wealthy."

"You won't believe it, but they weren't just wealthy. When the Eight-Power Allied Forces sacked Beijing at the end of the Qing dynasty, who do you think protected the Empress Dowager when she fled to Xijing? My grandfather. He was a famous Legalist scholar who served as the head of the Bureau of Punishments. The whole street was ours. When the allied armies attacked, he was one of the five pro-war leaders of the Qing court, a secret supporter of the Boxers. The allied armies were invincible, so the Empress Dowager fled west. The official Li Hongzhang stayed behind in Beijing to sign the Xinchou Unequal Treaty with the demonic Western powers, who demanded that the senior pro-war figures be severely punished, my grandfather included. They were to be hanged. The Empress Dowager was told to hand him over, but sixty thousand Xijing residents massed in front of the clock tower, saying that if she turned my grandfather over, she could no longer stay in Xijing. To appease the crowd, and to keep one of her ministers from falling into the hands of the Westerners, she allowed him to commit suicide. He swallowed gold, but when that didn't do the trick, he allowed himself to be smothered to death. He was fifty. After that, women in the family began selling off property to survive, until only this compound was left. You can see for yourself, these two chairs were the only things passed down to me."

"My!" Zhuang exclaimed. "Such a distinguished family history. Six months ago, the mayor organized a team to produce a book titled *Five Thousand Years of Xijing History.* I was responsible for the chapter on literature and the arts. After it was published, I read that the head of the Qing dynasty Bureau of Punishments had been a Xijing man, but I never dreamed he could be your ancestor. If the dynasty hadn't fallen, your grandfather would have lived his life out, and I'd have had a devil of a time trying to see you."

Zhao laughed. "And Xijing's Four Young Knaves wouldn't be the bastards we have now."

Zhuang stood up. Through the bamboo door curtain he saw a woman in red sitting on the steps across the yard rocking her baby in a cradle and reading a book. "The world is changing all the time," he said. "This is what a once-magnificent home has deteriorated into. Pretty soon even this will be gone. Tongguan is my ancestral home, and as one of the most strategic spots in the Central Plain, it has been the site of many glorious chapters in our history. But ten years ago, the county seat was moved, and the town became a wasteland. I went back not long ago and sat in one of the old buildings. I couldn't stop sighing. When I came back, I wrote an essay about it; maybe you read it."

"I did," Zhao replied, "which is why I invited you here today. Maybe you can write about this sometime."

The woman was now facing them, but did not look up. She was too caught up in her reading; only her long dark lashes and straight nose were visible. "She's lovely," Zhuang said.

"Who?" Zhao stuck his head out. "Oh, her. She's a maid for the family across the way, from northern Shaanxi. That part of the province has nothing to brag about but its women."

"I've been looking for a maid for a long time, but haven't found the right one. I'm not impressed with those at the labor market. Think she could find me one back in her village?"

"This one's articulate and mannered. If she worked for you, she'd treat your guests with courtesy. But people talk behind her back, saying that when her employers are away, she gives the baby a pill so it will sleep all morning. I don't believe it. I think the other maids in the neighborhood are jealous over her appearance and the affluence of her employers."

"Obviously a pack of lies. No girl would do something like that," Zhuang said.

The men sat back down after Zhao shut the door and began taking antiques out of a wooden chest to show Zhuang: ancient scrolls with calligraphy and painting, ceramics, bronze implements, coins, stone rubbings, and carvings, but what attracted Zhuang were eleven ink stones. They were also Zhao's most prized possessions. He had Duan stones, Zhao stones, Hui stones, and clear clay stones, all very old and all engraved with the users' names. One by one, he handed them to Zhuang to point out the color and pattern, to let him feel the texture with his fingers and tap them to hear the sound. He then told him the names of all the owners, original as well as later, and the official positions they held, what calligraphy and paintings they left to posterity, and what brought them fame.

"How did you get these?" Zhuang asked with surprise and envy.

"Some I collected a long time ago, others I bartered for. I paid three thousand yuan for that one."

"Three thousand? That's a lot of money."

"A lot of money? These days I wouldn't take twenty thousand for it. A month or so ago I visited the Lianhu District Museum. The city built a large museum and asked people to donate their artifacts. The district museum wanted to sell their undocumented odds and ends to put more money in the hands of the staff. I fell in love with this stone, which they offered to sell me for ten thousand yuan. We went back and forth, and since I know them, in the end I got it for three."

Somewhat doubtful, Zhuang picked up the stone to examine it closely. It was several times heavier than the other stones. He tested it with his teeth; it gave off a metallic ring when he held it up to his ear. He saw a line of characters on the bottom that read: "Wen Zhengming's fancy," the one-time property of the famous Ming painter.

"Jingwu," Zhuang exclaimed, "you're obviously an authority. If you forget me the next time you come across something like this, I'll never do another thing for you."

"Take it easy," Zhao said. "Someone told me that Gong Jingyuan's son, Gong Xiaoyi, an opium addict, has a fine ink stone he wants to sell as soon as his father goes abroad. I'll go see for myself. If it's the genuine article, I'll get it for you. I told you I wanted to give you something. How about these?"

Zhuang examined the two coins he was handed, turning them over and over. He laughed. "Jingwu, you devil, you can cheat other people if you want, but don't try to put something over on me. This Xiaojian Emperor four-zhu coin is valuable, but it was once a five-zhu Han coin, while this Jingkang Emperor coin is a common piece from the Song dynasty."

"I was just testing you. You know your business, so I'll give you something you'll like, something quite rare." Looking uncomfortable, he took out a small red silk bag and opened it. Inside were two bronze mirrors. He looked them over to decide which of them he would give to Zhuang, who saw that one was inlaid with two cranes carrying a silk streamer with mandarin ducks in their beaks, the other winged horses holding two ends of a streamer depicting a phoenix in their mouths. Thrilled beyond words, he took them both.

"They're a pair," he said, "you can't just give me one. Since you have a large collection of ink stones, I'll bring you one tomorrow to help you build your collection."

Zhuang was ecstatic; Zhao was not. "You can have them," he said, "but you have to get me one of Wang Ximian's paintings."

"That's easy," Zhuang said. "We'll go to his house, and you can tell him what you want him to paint. He'll even treat you to a meal." Zhuang walked over to the window with his mirrors to get a closer look.

There was a knock at the door. "Who is it?" Zhao asked. There was no answer. Zhao signaled Zhuang with his eyes to put away the mirrors, which he stuffed in his pocket while Zhao locked the chest and laid some well-thumbed books and periodicals on top of it. "Who is it?" he repeated. "It's me," came the response. Zhao opened the door. "Ah, it's our plant owner, Mr. Huang. Why so late? Zhuang Laoshi has been waiting to get something to eat. Our stomachs are rumbling."

Zhuang sized the visitor up. Short and thick, with a fleshy face, he was dressed in a white shirt and tie and carried a large satchel. Zhuang stood up and shook hands with Huang, who held on to his hand and said, "Zhuang Laoshi's fame is as great as a thunderclap, and today I finally get to meet him! When I told my wife I was meeting Mr. Zhuang, she laughed and called me a dreamer. I won't wash this hand so I can go home, shake hers, and let her share in the glory."

"I guess that puts my hand on a par with Chairman Mao's."

They had a good laugh over that.

"You're funny, Mr. Zhuang," Huang said. "The greater the man, the more amiable he is."

"I'm not great," Zhuang said. "I've just made a bit of a literary splash. But you, you're rich, and that gives you a louder voice."

The man was still holding Zhuang's hand, which was getting sweaty. "Hardly," he said. "I've read some of your work. I'm just a country boy from a working-class family. Money was once my enemy, but now that I have a bit, it still can't stand up to your reputation. I'm older than you, and if I may be so bold, I would like you to know that if you ever need anything, just ask. What's mine is yours. Business is good at the plant. Our 101 brand is in great demand. You'll get the grand tour when you come to see our operation."

"I've told Zhuang Laoshi what you want, so there's no need to beat around the bush. We're all busy men. He usually does not write things like you want. He's making an exception this time. Go ahead and make arrangements for us to visit the plant. There you can give me five thousand yuan. Publication guaranteed. We'll make it clear up front—five thousand words!"

Huang finally let go of Zhuang's hand and bowed deeply. "Thank you," he said, "thank you."

"When shall we come?" Zhuang asked.

"How's this afternoon?"

"That won't work. Let's make it, say, three days from now."

"Fine, I'll pick you up. Jingwu, I am so happy Mr. Zhuang is willing to do this for me. Let's go get something to eat. Where would you like to go?"

"Today's my treat," Zhao said. "We decided on hulutou."

"Isn't that a little too, you know—?" Huang said.

"It's fast and it's easy," Zhuang replied. "And the Chunshengfa Café is nearby."

"Okay, hulutou it is." He reached into his satchel and took out a bottle of Xifeng liquor, three jars of coffee, two packets of sesame candy, and a carton of State Express cigarettes, and handed it all to Zhao Jingwu.

Abashed, Zhao said, "I can't take all this. Here, Zhuang Laoshi, you take the cigarettes."

Zhuang pushed them back. "Foreign cigarettes are too strong for me," he said.

"Then keep them for yourself, Jingwu," Huang said. "Since Mr. Zhuang prefers Chinese brands, I'll bring him some Hongtashan cigarettes next time. Fighting over these little gifts makes me look tacky."

Zhao accepted the gifts, then looked at Zhuang and smiled. "I know you're hungry, but you don't drop by every day, so how about marking your visit with a piece of calligraphy? Just one. That won't keep you here much longer."

"You are a sly tiger. I know something's up any time I see you smile. But you already have everything, so why do you want a piece of my calligraphy?"

"I collect famous people's calligraphy."

So they set up a table and spread out a sheet of rice paper. Zhuang picked up a writing brush, but hesitated. "What should I write?" he asked as he cocked his head.

"That's up to you. Something you've recently come to understand. When your fame reaches the heights, people will want to study your life, and I will have primary material."

Zhuang thought for a moment, then wrote:

The wind dances gracefully when the butterfly comes
The person departs and the moon laments

"What does that mean?" Zhao asked. "The butterfly [*die*] in the first line is clearly from your name, and the moon [*yue*] in the second line is probably your wife, Niu Yueqing. I can figure out your use of 'gracefully' and 'laments,' but not 'comes' and 'departs.'"

Zhuang ignored him as he wrote in smaller characters on the side:

Zhao Jingwu asked me for this, so I copied some ancient lines. I know what I know and I know what I do not know. My words may not be worth a thousand apiece, but in three hundred years they will be cultural artifacts and can sell for eight hundred. If Jingwu has descendants, they will inherit tens of thousands.

That's it, I'm done. Zhuang herewith lays down his brush.

Zhao clapped in joy. "Terrific," he said with a laugh. "Definitely worth thousands."

Huang, the plant owner, salivated over the scene. "How about one for me, Mr. Zhuang? I'll have it professionally mounted and hang it in the main room." Without waiting for a reply, he began adding ink, splashing some on his hand when he pressed too hard. He ran into the yard to wash it off.

"He's washing off all my glory," Zhuang said softly. He and Zhao laughed. "Write one for him," Zhao said. "These wealthy upstarts are always in the market for a little refinement."

"Ah," Zhuang sighed. "People these days are transformed into experts in everything the day they become officials. Our mayor studied soil sciences in college, but now that he's in office, he delivers talks on industry at gatherings of industrialists, commerce at business meetings, and art and literature at cultural gatherings. And every word must be recorded."

"No matter how great his wealth," Zhao said, "for refinement he still needs you."

So Zhuang wrote:

> *There is no heavenly message for savage demons*
> *The moon is dark in the presence of starlight*

"Perfect!" Zhao complimented him as the bamboo curtains parted and a voice said, "Which of you is the writer Zhuang Zhidie?"

Zhuang saw that it was the young nanny from across the way.

While Huang was washing up outside, she'd asked him how his hand had gotten so black. He'd told her he had asked the writer Zhuang Zhidie for a piece of his calligraphy. It just so happened that the book she was reading was by Zhuang, so she stuck a pacifier into the baby's mouth and rushed over. This was Zhuang's first encounter with someone who called him by name without adding "laoshi," but for some reason he liked her straightforward nature. Looking into that pretty face, he said, "I'm Zhuang Zhidie."

The girl eyed him closely. "Liar. How could you be Zhuang Zhidie?" The startled plant owner gulped and cast a glance at Zhao Jingwu.

"What do you think Zhuang Zhidie ought to look like?" Zhao asked her.

"He has to be taller than you, about so tall." She held her hand up in the air.

"Ai-ya!" Zhuang exclaimed. "The price of everything keeps going up, everything but a man's height. I could never be Zhuang Zhidie."

Now pensive, she took a good look at him. And as her face reddened, she hastened to say, "I'm so sorry, I've offended you."

"You work for the family across the way, don't you?" Zhuang asked.

"I'm a nanny," she said, "so go ahead, laugh at me."

"Why would I do that? I said to Zhao Jingwu a while ago that you don't often see a girl reading a book while she's taking care of a baby."

"Well, if you don't find me undeserving, then you should give me a piece of your calligraphy."

"The way you say it, I can't refuse. What's your name?"

"Liu Yue."

"Another moon," Zhuang muttered before writing a couplet from an ancient poem:

> *In the wild the sky presses down on trees*
> *By the clear river the moon comes near people*

"You are a lucky girl, Liu Yue," Zhao said. "I laid out the ink, paper, and stone, but you get the poem. To pay for this gift, you must get a girl from your village to come work for him."

"Our villagers are too clumsy to serve someone as august as Zhuang Laoshi."

"Just seeing you tells me all I need to know about them," Zhuang said. "You will be able to find one for me."

"Then it will have to be me," she said after a thoughtful pause.

Zhao Jingwu couldn't have imagined that those words would come out of her mouth, and he tried to signal her with his eyes.

"That is precisely what I had hoped to hear," Zhuang said with a clap of his hands.

Encouraged by that statement, Liu Yue taunted Zhao Jingwu: "What were you trying to say with your eyes? I knew I'd be his maid the minute I discovered who he was."

"Impossible. You have a contract with the family across the way," Zhao insisted. "If you leave and they find out that I introduced you to someone else, I shudder to think what they'll accuse me of."

"It's not like I'm expected to marry into their family, is it?"

"How's this," Zhuang said. "Once you've fulfilled your contract with them, ask Jingwu to notify me."

⁂

Back on the street after lunch, Zhuang Zhidie commented that Liu Yue was too charming to be a country girl.

"She was a fast bloomer," Zhao Jingwu said. "When she showed up, she was dressed in handmade clothes, she kept her eyes down around people, and you couldn't get a word out of her. Then one day, while her employers were at work, she went into the closet and tried on the mistress's dresses, modeling them in the mirror. A neighbor spotted her and told her she looked like the actress Chen Chong. 'Really?' she said before bursting into tears. Why that made her cry, no one knew. When she received her first wages as a nanny, the mistress told her she should send some back to her family, since life was so hard for farmworkers. She didn't. Instead she spent it all on clothes. Clothes make the woman, a saddle makes the horse. Overnight she became a dazzler. Everyone in the compound said she did look like Chen Chong, and she grew livelier by the day. Her personality changed drastically."

Zhuang had tossed off his comment about hiring the girl because she had caught his fancy. "Are you serious?" Zhao said. "Don't make the mistake of hiring a maid and acquiring a pampered young mistress."

They spotted a lush persimmon tree in a private compound as they passed a narrow lane. A dead leaf whistling on the wind landed on Zhuang's right eye. "Jingwu," he said, "isn't the Clear Void Nunnery down this lane?"

"Yes."

"I met someone who lives nearby the other day. Why don't we see if we can all go for some hulutou?"

"Are you talking about the nun Huiming?"

"No, not her. She's a Buddhist, so she can't eat that."

"My mistake," Zhao apologized. "But since you have a new friend, I'd like to meet him."

"I'll go now and be right back." He rode off.

The sound of the scooter at the gate brought a full head of hair poking above the ivy-covered wall. "Zhuang Laoshi!" came the cry. He saw that it was a smiling Tang Wan'er and wondered how she had discovered his presence so quickly. Her powdered face disappeared amid the greenery. "Wait a moment," she said. "I'll open the gate for you."

He had arrived just as she was squatting in the toilet, looking at the watery smudges on the wall and imagining the people's faces they formed; for some reason, the image of Zhuang Zhidie floated into her mind, and she blushed. It was then she heard the motor scooter at the gate. She stood up, flustered. It was Zhuang Zhidie, of all people. She rushed toward the gate, nervously fastening the belt of her baggy trousers.

Zhuang watched her through a narrow opening. But instead of opening the gate, she ran back inside the house. The sight of her ample behind sluing from side to side sent a tingle through him.

Tang Wan'er hurriedly touched up her hair, added some rouge to her cheeks, and put on lipstick before rushing out to open the gate. Then she stood in the gateway, bestowing upon Zhuang the most fetching gaze she could manage. He looked into her eyes, in which a tiny human figure appeared. It was his reflection. "Is Zhou Min not home?"

"He left early this morning, saying he needed to go to the printers. Won't you come in, Zhuang Laoshi? You shouldn't be out in the hot sun without a hat." Zhuang experienced a moment of confusion. Should Zhou's absence be a disappointment or a cause for hope? Bag in hand, he walked in. Once inside, he sat down. She brought him tea and cigarettes and turned on the fan. "Zhuang Laoshi," she said, "we can't thank you enough. Most people never have a chance to actually meet you, while we've been the recipients of your favors."

"What favors might those be?"

"You gave us all this tableware, not only more than we can use now, but more than we'll be able to use once we get settled."

He had forgotten about having the things delivered. He smiled. "That was nothing. What I get for a short essay was enough to pay for everything."

She moved a stool up, sat down, and crossed her legs. "One short essay for all this? Zhou Min says that publishers pay by the word, punctuation included. Just think how much you could get for the punctuation alone in one of your books."

"No one would pay for a book with only periods and commas," he said with a laugh.

She laughed, too, as she raised the collar of her blouse, which had slid down, revealing a bit of cleavage. Zhuang's heart raced, and he made a conscious effort not to look there.

"I'd like to ask you something, Zhuang Laoshi. Do you fashion the characters in your books after real people?"

"That's a hard question to answer. I simply make up many of them."

"How can you create them in such detail? I've said to Zhou Min that Zhuang Laoshi is a man of rich and acute emotions, and his wife is lucky to have such a husband."

"She has said that if she comes back in another life, she does not want to be a writer's wife."

Surprised to hear that, Tang Wan'er paused, then lowered her eyes and said, "Then she doesn't know how lucky she is or how unpleasant it is to be to be the wife of a coarse, unrefined man." A tear fell from her eye, making Zhuang wonder about the woman's background. He had never seen her husband, but he could imagine what he must be like.

"You're a lucky woman," Zhuang consoled her. "I can tell that from your appearance. Believe me, you are not ill-fated. The past is the past. Things are fine now, aren't they?"

"What kind of life is this? Xijing is nice, but we need to settle down. You can tell fortunes, what do you see in mine?" She laid a fair hand on his knee. He took the hand and experienced strange feelings as he revealed signs of a woman's status based upon what he had read in a physiognomy text: a round, smooth forehead foretold high status, a wrinkled one low; a high nose high, a sunken one low; lustrous hair high, dull hair low; an arched foot high, a flat one low. The woman examined each of these on herself, and what she saw pleased her. What puzzled her, however, was what counted as an arched foot. Zhuang reached out but stopped before touching her and simply pointed to a spot below the ankle. She took off her shoe and raised her foot until it nearly touched his face. He was surprised by how lithe she was and noticed what a dainty foot she had. The transition from calf to foot was flawless, her instep so high it could accommodate an apricot. Her toes were as delicate as bamboo tips, starting from the long big toe and progressing down to the short little one, which was wiggling at that moment. Zhuang had never seen such a lovely foot, and he nearly let out a shout. After she put her shoe and stocking back on, he asked what size shoe she wore.

"A thirty-five," she said. "Too small for someone as big as me, all out of proportion."

With a laugh, he stood up. "Then these belong to you." He took the shoebox from his bag and handed it to her.

"They're beautiful. But they must cost a fortune."

"You expect to pay for them? No, they're yours, try them on."

Without stopping to thank him, she put them on and flung her old shoes under the bed.

Zhuang was in a wonderful mood when he returned to the restaurant, where Zhao and Huang greeted him not with open arms, but with a complaint for being gone so long and not bringing his new friend with him. He did not share their desperate hunger. He wanted a drink.

During the meal that followed, the three men drank a great deal. The top half of the bottle was accompanied by cordial, even affectionate, talk, while the bottom half brought out a more muscular dialogue. They ordered a second bottle and halfway through were ranting and raving. When they finished off the final half, marked by silence, it was late afternoon. Zhuang got up to leave.

"I'll see you home," Zhao Jingwu said.

Zhuang waved him off and stumbled out to the Magnolia. He climbed on and rode off, still sober enough to spot misspellings on shop signs along the way. He made it back to the house on Shuangren fu Avenue, walked inside, and immediately fell asleep, not waking till night had fallen and Niu Yueqing called him to dinner. He got up and sat on the edge of the bed. Not interested in eating, he said he would spend the night at the Literary Federation compound.

"You don't have to do that, you can spend the night here," his wife said.

Zhuang hemmed and hawed, saying he had an article to write.

"You can go if you want," Niu Yueqing said, "but I'm staying here tonight."

Zhuang understood what she was telling him, but he needed a quiet place to write. With a pained look on his face, he sighed and walked out the door.

The fading sunlight created a haze. Birds on the drum tower set up a din as wonton and kebab peddlers turned on lanterns and fired up stoves in front of the gate. Children crowded around an old man selling cotton candy. Curious as to how it was made, Zhuang walked over and watched the man spoon sugar into the spinning head and saw it emerge as fine, cottony threads. When he looked up, he spied Aunty Liu and her milk cow walking up to the gateway. After supplying milk to her regular customers, she and her cow usually rested until the night cooled enough for them to walk home. When the cow saw him, she mooed loudly, sending children scrambling away in fright. "You haven't bought any milk in days, Mr. Zhuang," Aunty Liu said. "Aren't you staying in the compound?"

"I'll be there tomorrow, and I'll wait for you." He walked up to the cow, patted her on the back, and struck up a conversation with Aunty Liu about how much milk the cow produced and what it sold for. She complained about how feed prices were going up, but not the price of milk, and on such a hot day she barely made enough to warrant coming into the city. The whole time they were talking, the cow stood there without moving anything but her head; she looked around, her tongue lolling, her tail slowly sweeping from side to side. "You can't earn anything if you don't come," Zhuang said, "and you still have to feed yourself and her. Look at her, standing there so composed, like a philosopher."

This casual comment got the cow's attention. There are people who say that dogs and cats understand human nature, but that cows do even better. A year earlier, Zhuang had stayed with Aunty Liu during a fact-finding trip to the suburbs. Originally a vegetable peddler, she had little skill in operating the scales, and was desperate. "Milk sold in the city is watered down," Zhuang said, "and people don't like that. But," he continued, "the demand is great and the sellers want to make a profit, so they add water. Customers complain, yet they continue to buy the milk. Why not get a milk cow, drive it into the city, and milk it there? You can demand a price that people will gladly pay. You'll definitely make a better living at that than by peddling vegetables."

Taking his suggestion to heart, she went to Mount Zhongnan and bought a milk cow, which, as Zhuang had suggested, she brought to Xijing, where he lay down beneath it every day and drank from her teats, earning the animal's immense gratitude. Now, whenever she saw him, she bellowed a greeting. So when she heard him say she was like a philosopher, she observed the city the way a philosopher would, although no one knew what she was thinking, since she lacked the ability to say so.

On this day, Aunty Liu led her cow over to the wall to rest. Zhou Min happened to be on the wall playing his flute, the slow, heavy strains lingering like a night wind outside a window, or ghostly moans in a graveyard. The sound had a chilling effect on her and the cow, though they listened with enjoyment. When the music stopped, they looked up at what resembled the paper cutout of a musician walking off slowly. Experiencing emotions that words could not describe, they sat with their heads lowered and fell asleep. The cow turned thoughtful as she lay on the ground chewing her cud:

When I was at Mount Zhongnan, I knew that the history of humans is tied up with that of cows. To state it differently, either humans evolved from cows or cows evolved from humans. But that's not how they see it. Humans say they evolved from apes. How could they possibly think that? They actually believe that creatures with asses as thick and as red as a face were their ancestors! Humans lie in order to have a clear conscience while keeping us enslaved forever. If this is a false accusation that can't be set straight, then let's reconsider: Cows and humans both descended from apes, following separate tracks of evolution, one that learned to speak and one that did not; speaking is how humans express their thoughts, while cows' thoughts are manifested in chewing cud. And that's it. Are cows, like fleas, so insignificant that they have no reason to exist in this vast, chaotic world? No, we are enormous creatures—large bodies, four strong hooves, and steely pointed horns fit for battle—and yet, in a world where humans are under assault by all other wild creatures, cows alone stand by them, cooperate with them, and do their bidding, all because of blood ties that approach the level of soul mates. But humans treat us the way they treat chickens and pigs, to be used as they see fit. As for the chickens and pigs, the humans must feed and take care of them in order to acquire their eggs and meat, while cows plow their fields, turn their millstones, haul their loads, and even produce milk for them to drink! Ah, you humans! You have conquered cows by forsaking fairness and with the invention of the whip.

The cow snorted out of both nostrils, creating hollows in the ground with each breath as she railed against the humiliation her species has endured. But then she raised her head, looked into the sky, and grew placid again, even releasing a long laugh. That laugh sounded to others like a long moo. What lay behind it was a reminder that of all the creatures on earth, only the cow is free of savagery, and only God and cows are silent. *As slaves of human beings, we differ from other animals by following humans on the path of a civilized society. How wonderful that being civil causes humans to employ a range of tricks, cleverness that ultimately backfires and leads them straight to destruction. So, then, who will take their place as masters of society? Cows, only cows. This is not empty rhetoric. Human history is full of examples of slaves who replaced their masters, isn't it? Besides, the bovine race has already begun assuming the appearance of human beings. Haven't you seen how people have taken to wearing coats, jackets, and shoes made of cowhide? Those are our spies. After infiltrating the world of humans, it is only natural that they yearn for their bovine race or remind themselves of their responsibility, covering parts of their bodies with cow things as a secret hint or an open display. As for me, this particular, prideful cow, my mission is of enormous importance, for I am the first to infiltrate this flourishing city in a cow's native state of being. In what other city does a cow walk grandly down the street?*

When the cow's thoughts reached this point, she was awash in gratitude toward Zhuang Zhidie. It was he who had suggested to the woman that she purchase a cow in a distant mountain town and bring it back with her, then take it into town to supply milk straight from the teats, and who finally uttered the comment "The cow looks like a philosopher." Powerful, rousing words worth their weight in gold, making her aware of her sacred mission. *I am a philosopher, I truly am. I must keep close watch over this city to evaluate the lives of its human inhabitants and serve as a bovine prophet during the transitional period between humans and cows.*

Around sunset on the nineteenth of June, Zhuang Zhidie brought a packet of spirit money back to Shuangren fu. Niu Yueqing had summoned a metalsmith to the compound gate to turn a pair of inherited silver hair ornaments into a new ring. Zhuang walked up to watch him work. A young man with a fair complexion, narrow eyes, and thin lips boasted about his family's skills as he pumped the bellows with his foot. He had laid the silver on a piece of wood and was melting it with an oil gun, turning it into tiny beads. That was a new sight for Zhuang, who had assumed that his wife was having a pair of earrings made. "If you use those hair ornaments whenever your mother has an attack of nerves," he said, "you will have to take them out of your ears and boil a pot of silver water for her to drink, won't you?"

"I don't wear earrings. Wang Ximian wears three rings, but you don't have even one. People will laugh and call you tightfisted and curse your wife for neglecting you."

"That's nonsense," he muttered before walking in to talk to her mother.

Once the ring was ready, Niu Yueqing cheerfully carried it inside and insisted that Zhuang try it on. He was busy stamping "RMB" onto the spirit money. With it stacked on the floor, he pressed both sides of an authentic bill onto each stack. Niu Yueqing laughed at him for taking his work so seriously, telling him he was putting a lot of effort into something that is used to express grief and sadness. The old lady reached over and pinched her daughter's lips shut and told Zhuang to make sure he did a good job of pressing the money down. If not, when the dead souls crossed the river, it would turn into useless money, known as iron currency. Niu Yueqing said, "You're talking about something that only applies to silver ingots and brass coins of ancient times. These days we use paper money, so if it turns into iron currency, that's a good thing, isn't it?"

With another cross word to her daughter, the old lady separated the stamped money into six piles and asked Zhuang to write the name of a deceased family member on each one. The father-in-law's pile, of course, was the tallest, followed by the old lady's parents, her uncle, and her elder sister. The final pile was for a sort of second mother to Yueqing, her so-called dry mother. Yueqing poked fun at her mother's sense of obligation to so many people as she slipped the large new ring onto Zhuang's finger. He struck a rich man's pose, leaning back on the sofa and swinging his foot up and down, the shoe balanced on the tip, as he tapped the arm of the sofa and complained that the shirt he was wearing was out of fashion, that he needed a new one.

"I bought you a red T-shirt just this morning, but was afraid you wouldn't wear it. Lao Huang in our office wears one. He's sixty-two, and it makes him look ten years younger."

"It won't go with these pants," Zhuang said. "People are wearing Hong Kong suit pants these days, and I need to get a pair. Then, once I have those, I will need new shoes, a new belt, new socks . . ."

"Enough already," Niu Yueqing said. "At this rate you'll be seeing a plastic surgeon to get a new face. And a new job, and a new wife!"

"Last year you traded a hair ornament for a gold tooth cap, and ever since then only nuggets of wisdom have come out of your mouth. What you say goes in this house. You wanted me to wear a ring, so you had it made." He laughed, took off the ring, and laid it on the table, complaining that she was always following the latest fad, and wondering what she wanted to turn him into.

That upset her. "What you're saying is that instead of kissing your ass I'm biting your balls, is that it? I try my best to make you look better, but you won't listen to me. So from now on, don't tell me how to do my hair or what to wear."

The old lady let them fight on, since she had discovered to her alarm that the old fellow was going to get money only in denominations in the hundreds, nothing smaller. "Won't that make it hard for him to buy things in the underworld?" So Zhuang picked up a stack of manuscript paper and stamped it with ten-, five-, and one-yuan bills, after which they took it all out into the lane to burn it-

It was pitch-black outside. Few cars or people were out on the street, which was dimly lit by a streetlight a few hundred yards away. The fire cast the flickering shadows of three ghostly figures onto the wall. Paper ash floated into the night sky, then settled to the ground. Zhuang and his wife knelt close to the fire at first, but moved back as it burned hotter and hotter, while the old lady began incanting the names of the dead, calling for them to come get their money, telling them to tuck it away safely, and urging them to spend it wisely but not to scrimp. They were to come tell her when it was gone. But a chill overcame Zhuang and his wife when they saw an eddy of wind swirl alongside the flames, which they quickly smothered with paper money, as a red light appeared in the night sky. They looked to the west. "Hungry ghosts are fighting," the old lady said. "I wonder which family they belong to. Damn your descendants for not giving them money. They're trying to steal from my husband."

Niu Yueqing shuddered. "What nonsense is that, Mother? It's a factory welding torch. What makes you think it's fighting ghosts?"

The old lady kept staring into the sky, and muttered something. Then she sighed. The old man was too quick for them, she was saying. He kept them from stealing our money. "Yueqing, does a pregnant woman live in number 10 over there?"

"They're colliers from Shangzhou. They made some money after coming to the city and sent for their families. One of them is pregnant."

"Those women have all had second or third pregnancies, despite the national family policy," Zhuang said. "The poorer people are, the more children they have, and that makes them even poorer. I don't know what they're thinking."

"I was at the hospital the other day," Yueqing said, "and the woman from number 10 was in the outpatient department. She said she wanted a doctor to check the position of her fetus. He wanted to check her abdomen with a stethoscope. When she undressed, he saw that her belly was so filthy, so black, he had to clean it with rubbing alcohol, leaving white streaks with each swipe. 'You should have cleaned up before you came

here,' he told her. She turned red. 'My husband's a collier,' she said." Niu Yueqing laughed. So did Zhuang Zhidie. "A reincarnated ghost," the old lady exclaimed. "The child's about to come into the world."

The words were barely out of her mouth when the bawl of a newborn baby pierced the air, followed by the sounds of running and pounding on a door. "Gensheng!" a man yelled, "She's had the baby! Let's go to Dongyang Street to buy wheat pancakes and a pot of rice wine. She's so hungry she could eat a cow."

Zhuang and his wife exchanged looks, wondering if maybe her mother knew what she was talking about. They looked back into the sky, turning somewhat fearful. Quickly burning what was left of the spirit money, they were rushing inside when a figure burst out from behind a parasol tree at the end of the lane. "Mrs. Niu!" she shouted, "Mrs. Niu!"

"Who is it?" the old lady asked.

"It's me." When she came close enough to be seen in the light of the fire, Zhuang recognized her as the Wang woman from the lane to the right. He snorted and went inside.

The Wang woman, a one-time prostitute at Spring Garden, had married a secretary to General Hu Zongnan and borne him a son who died in a motorcycle accident as a young man. A few years later, the former secretary died, leaving her, a childless widow, to live out her days alone, hard, lonely days. She had opened a private nursery in her spacious home two years before. Since she lived nearby, she visited often to gossip. Zhuang did not welcome her visits, for she was evasive, crafty, and sneaky. He complained that she was a bad influence on the children in her care, a comment that upset his mother-in-law and drew accusations of prejudice from Niu Yueqing. To be sure, Wang usually dropped by when Zhuang was not there, seldom when he was. Some six months earlier, she had wondered aloud why Zhuang and Niu Yueqing still did not have a child at their age, a comment that Niu Yueqing's mother found heartbreaking. She explained that her daughter had been pregnant the year after she was married, but because they were not ready to have a child, she had had an abortion. The second time, they had said that he wanted to wait till he was fully established before having a child, so that pregnancy was also terminated. Now they had everything they wanted, but she could not get pregnant. The Wang woman said she knew of a secret formula that guaranteed not only pregnancy, but the birth of a son. Thrilled by the news, the old lady passed it on to Niu Yueqing, who tearfully admitted that she desperately wanted a child, but that nothing had worked, and that Zhuang's potency was on the wane. She found it strange that he was virile when he didn't need to be, and impotent when he did. None of the many doctors they had consulted could help him, leading them to accept the fact that they would grow old childless. Niu Yueqing's mother fretted over this for days before coming up with a plan: they would go to the northern suburbs to ask the elder daughter of Niu Yueqing's "dry mother" to carry a child whom they would then raise as their own. A family member was preferable to raising a child by a total stranger. By sheer coincidence, the woman was pregnant when they divulged their plan to her, and she was beside herself with joy. The old lady had one condition: they would only take a boy, and she demanded that the woman submit to an ultrasound exam. It was a girl, so she aborted. Next the old lady took her to see the Wang woman, who told her what to do: she was to have sex three days after her period ended to get pregnant, then begin taking a patent medicine, one small spoonful in the morning, another at night, putting up with the bitter taste and ignoring the slight discharge. The old lady gratefully offered to pay for the bottle of dark, thick liquid, but Wang told her she need not pay anything till a baby boy was born. The medicine's most valuable ingredient was agar wood, which had to be imported. The woman told them she had some that had already been paid for, and was giving it to Mrs. Niu for her urgent need. They would have to buy enough to make another batch for the donor family. Niu Yueqing searched for agar wood, and Zhuang Zhidie was not happy to hear what she was doing. That led to arguments.

On this day, after watching Zhuang walk inside, Wang smugly announced to Niu Yueqing's mother, replete with gestures, "Did you hear the baby's cry in number 10? The collier's wife had three girls in a row before taking my medicine. Now she's had a boy. I've been at their house for days waiting for her to have her baby. Her husband said he might not let me go if she had a girl, and I said, 'If she doesn't have a son, I'll refund what you paid for the medicine. If it's a boy, it'll be the twenty-second birth from taking my medicine.' And there you have it, she had a son!"

"I believe you," Yueqing said, elated by the news. "I bought some agar wood."

"Did you?" Wang exclaimed. "Then don't forget me when you have your son."

Yueqing invited Wang inside for tea. "Another day," Wang said.

Her fear forgotten, Yueqing walked home down the dark lane to get her agar wood.

"Was that Wang woman talking to you about having a baby again?" Zhuang asked.

"Her medicine works," Yueqing said. "The collier's wife took it, and she had a son."

Zhuang asked how much the agar wood had cost her. Five hundred yuan, she told him, sending him infuriated into the kitchen for a bowl of porridge. As soon as he was finished, he climbed into bed under the mosquito net.

Niu Yueqing and her mother were in a good mood when they returned for dinner. They took a basin of hot water into the bedroom to wash up, and they told Zhuang that Hu Zongnan's one-time secretary had given the secret formula to his wife. Just before he died, worried about her spending the rest of her life alone, he divulged the formula to her as a means of survival. Zhuang said nothing. After washing up, Yueqing sprayed on a bit of perfume, got some hot water, and told Zhuang to get out of bed and wash up. He said he wasn't interested, so she lifted up the netting, took off his clothes, and said, "Maybe you aren't, but I am. The Wang woman gave me some of her medicine, so let's give it a try. I don't want to raise someone else's child if I can have one of my own. If this doesn't work, she can let us raise hers as our own without making it public. That way we'll have a future generation, someone you can nurture as a writer, and when he grows up, as the biological son of a relative, he won't turn his back on us."

"I've never liked that so-called sister of yours or her husband," Zhuang said. "Every time they're here, they complain about how they're living in poverty and ask us to help out. And the way she gets herself pregnant and then terminates the pregnancies tells me that they have their eye on our property."

She worked to get him aroused by washing his privates before they climbed under the mosquito net and turned off the light. He knew he lacked the needed potency, so he let his hands roam over her body. □□ □□ □□ [The author has deleted 111 words.]

"This time maybe it'll work," she said. "Say something. Tell me some stories, stories about real people and real events."

"How many stories do you think I have? If it works, it works; if not, that's because a great man comes by only once in a lifetime."

"You're known in Xijing, but Wang Ximian's fame is greater than yours, so how has he managed three sons, not to mention a rumored five-year-old out of wedlock?"

"If you didn't watch me so closely, I might have one of those," Zhuang said.

She had no response to that when, without warning, Zhuang had an erection. "Let's do it," he said.

"Not yet," she said. "Take it easy."

He went limp, and Yueqing pushed him off. "You've always got other women on your mind. Would you like to tell me how you expect to have a child out of wedlock?"

Zhuang was deflated; Yueqing was unsatisfied. She told him to bring her to orgasm with his hand, after which they rolled over and went to sleep. Not another word was spoken that night.

The next day, a tearful Niu Yueqing asked Zhuang to accompany her to her cousin's house with the patent medicine. He refused, so she stormed out of the house alone. He sat there awhile, until boredom set in, then got up to visit the 101 Pesticide Plant in the suburbs to gather material for the article he had promised to write. He got a bare bones tour, beginning with the owner telling him all about himself and ending with a quick look at the workshops. He knocked the article out that evening, and after he delivered the manuscript to the newspaper office, he experienced an urge to call on Tang Wan'er.

Zhuang had an attack of nerves when he reached the intersection in front of the Clear Void Nunnery. He didn't know whether Zhou Min was home, and even if he wasn't, the big question was how the man's wife would react to his visit. His talk with Ruan Zhifei that night had boosted his courage, but his experience with Jing Xueyin had eroded that courage. And besides, his impotence with Niu Yueqing in their marriage bed was deeply troubling—he was feeling less and less like a man. Yet just thinking about Tang Wan'er had the opposite effect, and he had to wonder what there was between him and the woman. The more he thought, the more confused he felt. He wavered for a while before finally entering a neighborhood diner, where he ordered a beer and a plate of smoked intestines. He drank alone. The bar occupied a space of twenty square meters or less, with unpainted dark brick walls. The countertop, made of heavy white wood, was lined with vats of alcohol, their openings covered with red cloth. Strangely, an old-fashioned wooden plow hung on the wall behind the bar, lending the place a rustic air. It was one of Zhuang's favorite places; it had a calming effect on him and often made him think back to his childhood in Tongguan. There weren't many customers that day. The first to come in after him were some peddlers who left their stands outside, keeping an eye on them while they chatted with the owner and sipped a glass of the strong stuff, making it last as long as possible. Then an old fellow stumbled in the door and stood wordlessly at the bar. The owner filled a glass from one of the vats. The man tipped his head back and drained it, then took some money out of his pocket, glared at the owner, and said, "Diluted it, didn't you?"

"Are you trying to put me out of business?" the owner complained. "If you do, who will wait on you three times a day?"

The man smiled and walked out. Quiet returned to the bar, with Zhuang Zhidie and an old man in the corner the only customers. The other man was wrinkled and gray, but his eyes were full of life. He was washing down a plate of salted soybeans with strong liquor. The way he held his glass between his thumb and two fingers told Zhuang that he was a cultured man. Zhuang frequently encountered old professors or veteran scholars from the research institutes in bars like this. They dressed simply and were quite convivial. Drunk young ne'er-do-wells were contemptuous of these men, mistaking them for retired laborers or mid-level government employees who had retired from active duty; angry that the older men were taking up their stools, the younger ones nudged them out of the way as they lined up to buy snacks to go with their drinks. Zhuang didn't recognize this particular old gent, but he was sure he was a man of wide experience and knowledge. He watched him as he drank, wishing the old fellow would look up and meet his gaze, but at the same time fearful that when he did, he would turn out to be one of those gifted individuals who could see deep inside you, someone to whom you might as well be transparent. But the man was oblivious to his surroundings as he picked up a bean and popped it into his mouth. He chewed for a moment, then picked up his glass and took a sip, enjoying the moment. Zhuang felt that he was wearing himself out, living a worthless, even base, existence. Strains of exquisite music drifted in on the air, getting louder. The bar owner ran to the door to see where it was coming from. Zhuang followed him. A procession of family members was coming up the lane to receive a relative's ashes from the crematorium. At the head of the lane, musicians were leading a dozen or so bereaved sons and grandsons who would accept the urn and perform the rites before turning to home, accompanied by music. Zhuang had witnessed a great many funerals, but he was moved by this music—properly funereal, yet relaxed, soft on the ear, quickly surging through his veins into all his joints, releasing his fatigue and melancholy and turning it into a long sigh. "What's that tune they're playing?" Zhuang asked the bar owner.

"It's an elegy adapted from a crying aria in a Qin opera," the owner replied.

"It's truly beautiful," Zhuang said, startling the bar owner, whose eyes expressed surprise.

"You're a strange one," he said, "finding a funeral melody beautiful. Even if it is, you can't play it at home. It's not just another popular song."

Zhuang let the comment pass as he returned to his table. A youngster with white-rimmed glasses had replaced the old man at the other end of the table. He was engrossed in a magazine, laughing softly from time to time. These days it was rare to see someone who could be so easily captivated by a world in letters, a thought that led Zhuang to muse that every essay in the world emerges from the pen of a writer and can play on readers' emotions. Knowing how he wrote his essays, his wife didn't think much of them. But other people's books could have her awash in tears.

The man smacked his lips, and Zhuang thought that one of the characters in what he was reading must be enjoying some good food. He let go of the magazine with one hand, picked up a pair of chopsticks, and plucked three pieces of smoked sausage off of Zhuang's plate, putting them into the mouth behind the magazine. A moment later the chopsticks reached out again to pick up two more pieces, so amusing and annoying Zhuang that he banged his own chopsticks against the table. The startled young man put down his magazine, and with an "Oh!" he spat the sausage onto the floor.

"Sorry. I'm so sorry. I ate from the wrong plate."

Zhuang laughed.

"What are you reading that has you so absorbed?" he asked.

"You wouldn't know, but this is about Zhuang Zhidie. Do you know who he is? I've read his works in the past but had no idea he's just like us."

"Is that so?" Zhuang said. "What does it say?"

"It says that Zhuang was a foolish child. In elementary school he thought teachers were the greatest people in the world. Then one day he went to the toilet and saw his teacher urinating. It was an eye-opener. 'Even teachers need to pee!' he said, as if they never needed to relieve themselves. Naturally his teacher glared at him, but didn't say a word, while Zhuang looked on and wondered out loud, 'Do teachers have to shake it, too?' Complaining that the boy had a low sense of morality, the teacher reported this to his father, who gave him a good beating."

"That is pure rubbish," Zhuang said.

"What do you mean, rubbish?" The young man said. "That's what's it says here. Don't you think great people can be great even in childhood?"

"Let me see that." Zhuang took the magazine and saw that it was the latest issue of *Xijing Magazine*, with an article titled "Stories of Zhuang

Zhidie," authored by Zhou Min. Was this the one he had spoken of? A quick read told Zhuang that it was all gossip, embellished and exaggerated to make for a lively, amusing read. *I ought to see what I'm like*, he told himself. So he read on and learned that Zhuang Zhidie was both generous and stingy, that he could give away a goat without a second thought, then turn around and demand that the tethering rope be returned, saying that he had only wanted to give away the goat, not the rope. Zhuang was wise and he was foolish; he was sure that Li Qingzhao was referring to the events of her wedding night when she wrote: "A gusty wind and fine rain last night / The taste of wine lingers after a deep sleep / I asked the one rolling up the screen / Only to be told that the crabapple was the same / Do you know / Do you know / The green should be growing but the red wanes." And yet he had trouble deciphering a train timetable. Zhuang could make you happy and he could embarrass you. He could tell you how to recognize a female fly by seeing where it lands; if it alights on a mirror, it is female, for even a fly wants to be pretty. When he is dragged over in a public place to have his photo taken, he can put on a miserable look and say he was a horse in his previous life, not a warhorse or a beast of burden, but a beribboned pony at a tourist site, where it is mounted for picture-taking. The sight could bring him to tears. As he read on, Zhuang came to the part about a romance from years before with a coworker at a magazine office; with many things in common, they were deeply in love, but ultimately parted ways owing to a strange combination of circumstances. Zhuang grimaced at the passage; the outlandish stories in the previous section were of no concern, but the romance should not have been mentioned so irreverently, since it involved another person. No name was given, but the outline of the story was clearly based on his relationship with Jing Xueyin. They had been very close, something he regretted now, but he hadn't touched her, not even a handshake, though the flame of desire had burned for years. But what was written in the magazine seemed to imply that they had done it all. Now they were both married, she with children, so how would her husband feel when he read this? How would Niu Yueqing feel? Everything in the article seemed based on real events and yet was at odds with what had really happened. Where had Zhou Min gotten his material? What bothered Zhuang most was how Jing would react after reading the article. She would likely think that he had given Zhou private information to demonstrate his allure. Would she then suppose that he was using a romantic dalliance to enhance his popularity? What would she do if her husband asked about it? Beset by worries, Zhuang put down the magazine and rushed over to the editorial office of *Xijing Magazine*, his desire to see Tang Wan'er gone.

❋

Zhuang had been an editor at *Xijing Magazine* twelve years earlier, when Jing Xueyin, a recent college graduate, was assigned to the Culture Department. A new desk, the fifth one, was placed across from his, overcrowding the editorial office, a former meeting room that had been repurposed. The head of the editorial office was Zhong Weixian, but Zhuang was the only one with true leadership qualities. Another senior editor, who had been hired at the same time as Zhong, was also a college graduate, and thus naturally would not take orders from him. The third person was Li Hongwen, a shrewd, resourceful, and articulate man who had been a great help to Zhong in his promotion to head of the editorial office. And yet Zhong had him pegged as a petty individual. Since it is always easier to deal with broadminded people than with petty ones, particularly those to whom one owes a debt of gratitude, Zhong made a point of conceding to Li whenever he could. The fourth person, a widow named Wei, was having an affair with the deputy head of the department, making her equally impossible for Zhong to lead. As for Jing, she called the deputy head "uncle" from the moment she arrived, since he had once worked for her father. As a result, Zhuang was the only editor whom Zhong could ask to do anything, so he was told to assist farmers during the summer harvest and to join the neighborhood disaster relief team after an earthquake. Zhuang had to fetch boiled water when he came to work in the morning and close up in the evening before he left. During his five years in the office, the high-water mark of his youth, he had cried bitter tears, cursing those people for their disdain and abuse; but after leaving, he came to see those years as critical, with his fondest memories revolving around Jing Xueyin. Thinking back, he viewed them as a bottomless sack of provisions that he carried with him during his passage through the world.

Now, twelve years later, the department head was still the department head, the magazine was still the magazine. The widow, on the other hand, had become the section chief in another office after marrying Deputy Head Yan. Jing had chosen administration over literary work and had been promoted to a mid-level leadership position. After considerable effort, Zhong Weixian, who had always been an old-fashioned man with limited prospects, finally became the new editor-in-chief, after triumphing over an editorial group that had run the magazine for three years and nearly driven it into financial collapse. Zhong never did trust Li Hongwen, though he found it impossible to do without him.

Zhuang arrived at the familiar old building and greeted acquaintances before heading to the editorial office. When he opened the door, the editors were all holding underpants. They did not have time to put them away before he walked in on them.

"Ai-ya!" Li cried out at the sight of Zhuang. "An early arrival is never as good as a timely one. Here, you can have these."

"Why are you all holding skivvies?"

A stranger came up to shake his hand.

"It's nice to meet you, Mr. Zhuang. I'm Wang Henian, a novelist. What do you think of our factory's products?"

"After a reorganization at the magazine, part-time writers began bringing in ad revenue," Li explained. "Henian is a good novelist. His factory is a small neighborhood concern, and since he can't afford to advertise, he gives us samples. These are anti-STD underpants. They can cure an STD if you have it and help prevent one if you don't."

"These are perfect for you guys. I, on the other hand, would need a pair that increases my sexual prowess," Zhuang replied, drawing laughter from everyone.

Zhong was laughing so hard his face shrank into a walnut. He took off his glasses to wipe away tears. "Come here, Zhidie," he said. "I've saved up some good cigarettes for you."

He opened his drawer and took out a box filled with cigarettes.

More than a decade earlier, when Zhuang had first taken up smoking, he had given Zhong a large box to collect cigarettes from part-time writers who came to Zhong with their manuscripts. Zhong did not smoke and had turned down the gifts until Zhuang stopped him, saying he would smoke the cigarettes for him.

"Zhong Weixian is old-fashioned," said Gou Dahai, an editor who had hired on after Zhuang's departure. "Do you think Zhuang Zhidie still wants those? Now that he's here, I'll take over." He dumped the contents of the box into his drawer and gave up his chair to Zhuang.

Zhuang sat down, and after some small talk began discussing the revamped magazine, a topic that involved them all. Confidence ran high over the contents, the cover design, even the ads for the first issue. The article by Zhou Min, in particular, had been promoted in posters in front of the post office as a special enticement. The editorial office had even decided to print additional copies and increase Zhou's fee.

"You're a popular figure," Li Hongwen commented. "As I said before, the only thing Cao Xueqin wrote was the novel *Dream of the Red Chamber*, but it has provided generations of scholars with a bountiful feast. Now you, Zhuang Zhidie, have reached the level of providing for others. Zhou Min's article is not long, barely enough for him to nibble at your toes. I wonder what I'd get if I wrote about you?"

"Nothing, at least nothing from me," Zhuang replied.

"All right, then one day I'll write a long piece and sign it with a woman's name. What will you do then? Probably let me have a bite of your tongue."

Zhuang laughed and said, "You can chew on my hemorrhoids."

Zhou Min, who had been quietly making tea for Zhuang, walked up.

"Zhuang Laoshi, this is my first article, so please don't be stingy with your views."

Putting the lighthearted banter aside, Zhuang said that he had come specifically because of that article, which he found somewhat troubling. Zhong tensed up.

"What bothers you about it?"

"Everything is fine except for the part about my relationship with Miss X. It was overblown, and there could be repercussions."

"I considered that," Zhong said. "I asked Zhou Min where he got his material, and he said it was all based on fact."

"It looks real, but the way it's written, it feels different. No names are mentioned, and yet the circumstances and images of the people involved are self-evident. You know that Jing Xueyin and I were close, but we never had a romantic relationship."

"So what?" Li interjected. "The woman in the article comes across as noble. What's wrong if you were in love? It's perfectly acceptable to have romantic relationships before marriage. Besides, now that you're a celebrity, she should feel honored to have had a fling with you. I'll bet she can't wait for the whole world to learn about this beautiful love story."

"Stop the nonsense, Hongwen," Zhuang objected. "I trust her not to raise a stink, but we are, after all, in China, where we must face certain realities. She's a wife and a mother, and a member of the leadership. No one will escape the fallout if something happens."

"What do you suggest?" Zhong asked.

"That you immediately send someone to Jing's house with a copy of the magazine and explain the situation to nip any potential problems in the bud."

"I've already been there," Zhou cut in. "She's not home yet."

"Go back as soon as she is," Zhuang said.

"Don't worry," Li said. "We'll take care of it. But not today. Stick around. Zhou can buy you lunch out of his fee, and the rest of us will get a share."

"No problem," Zhou replied. "My treat. I'll buy as many pork jelly buns from Cao's Damaishi Street shop as you can eat."

"I see Li Hongwen hasn't changed a bit," Zhuang said. "He's always looking to be treated, but never offers to treat anyone else."

"I can't help it. My wife holds the purse strings," Li said. "If you don't want Zhou Min to spend the money, then it's on you."

"How about a game of mahjong?" Gou Dahai said. "Winner treats."

"What do you say?" Zhuang asked Zhong.

"Go ahead as long as you don't play for money," Zhong said. "But you'll have to excuse me. I have something to attend to."

With a smile, Zhuang shook hands with Zhong and walked him to the door. Li closed the door after Zhong left.

"How's that for a boss?" he said. "See how clever he is with words? He has no objection to our game of mahjong, but he'll be blameless if there's a problem. That's true leadership quality."

"If he actually had that quality," Gou said, "he wouldn't still be an editor-in-chief, without making the grade of a section cadre."

"He's timid," Zhuang said. "He has dodged trouble his whole life."

After turning the desks sideways, Li took a set of tiles out of his drawer, while Zhou Min placed a cup of tea and an ashtray before each man.

"We have enough for a game," Zhuang said to Zhou. "So why don't you run over to the municipal newspaper for me?"

"What do you need?"

"Here's an article I've written about a local entrepreneur. Take it to Mr. Zhang, the head of the arts and culture section, and ask him to print it as soon as possible."

Zhou Min left in high spirits.

So Zhuang, Li, Gou, and a young editor named Fang drew lots for the seating. The results? Zhuang Zhidie in the east, Li Hongwen in the west, Gou Dahai in the north, and Xiao Fang in the south. Li wanted to change seats with Gou, saying that Zhuang was well heeled and today he was going to share his wealth with the rest of us. But Gou was such a poor player, he would inevitably feed him winning tiles.

"The problem isn't with Gou Dahai," Zhuang said to Li. "It's with you, since you were born under the sign of wood, while the north seat has water quality."

"So you know about such things," Li said.

"I know you."

Li blushed. "As I said, you have to lose today. How much do you have?"

Zhuang took off his shoes to show a ten-yuan bill hidden in each.

"Aren't you the sneaky one, Zhuang Laoshi," Gou said. "Who carries money in his shoes?"

"Money gave me a hard time back when I worked at the Department of Culture, so now I keep it under my feet."

"There are only two bills," Li said. "Will that be enough for my play?"

"Don't worry," Zhuang said, "I'll borrow the money to pay you if you beat me. But you should know that I'm an expert at grabbing knives barehanded."

Zhuang consistently picked up usable discarded tiles in the opening round, so upsetting Li that he cursed the tiles as ass-wipes. Though he didn't smoke, he demanded one of Zhuang's cigarettes to share in the man's good luck, but ended up coughing with watery eyes before he finished it.

At the mention of cigarettes, Xiao Fang asked Zhuang if he had smoked Zhong's cigarettes when they were colleagues in the Department of Culture. The topic of Zhong's cigarettes naturally led to talk about Zhong himself.

"How's he doing these days? Does his wife still come to the office?"

"That man has suffered plenty," Gou said. "On top of being labeled a Rightist for twenty years, he married an awful woman. She came here last month and, in front of everyone, scratched his face bloody."

"What can he do?" Zhuang said. "They were already living apart when we were together in the Department of Culture, and he panicked every time she came to see him. We encouraged him to get a divorce, but she wouldn't hear of it. I don't know how he's managed all these years, especially now that times have changed."

Li put out a tile, but changed his mind when Zhuang was about to pick it up. Saying it was a wrong play, Li took it back and offered a new one.

"I've got a secret, but you'll all have to promise to keep it in this room."

"Li Laoshi always has secrets," Fang said.

"Li Hongwen could have been a spy," Zhuang said. "He was the first to know when Deputy Head Yan of the Department of Culture was having an affair with the widow Wei. He actually spent four hours hiding in the toilet watching her room to discover what time the deputy head went in and when the lights were turned off."

"Didn't they get married?" Li said.

"They sure did, so what was the point of spying on them?" Zhuang asked.

"They have me to thank. They wouldn't have gotten married if I hadn't revealed their secret."

"All right, then. What's the secret about Zhong?" Zhuang asked.

"What do you think has kept him going all these years? He has his own spiritual support. He fell for a girl in his class when he was young. Soon after college he was labeled a Rightist, and later he heard that she suffered the same fate. Being a Rightist meant he had trouble finding a wife, so eventually he married his current wife, a woman from the countryside, through a matchmaker. Several years ago, he learned that the girl from his college days was still alive and teaching at a high school in Anhui. Not only that, she was divorced and lived alone. Zhong could not stop talking about her, even wrote her four letters. For some reason, he never received a reply. Maybe she's dead or maybe she's no longer teaching at the school. This might be nothing but gossip. But like a possessed man, he checks the mailroom every day to see if there's a letter from her."

"That must be where he was heading when he walked out," Fang said.

"I know where he's going," Li corrected him. "Another round of job rankings has begun, and he's trying to get the committee members to promote him to senior editor. A waste of time. Two years ago, Wu Kun was promoted to editor-in-chief, and the old man was passed over. This year they told him he wasn't senior enough. Ho!" he exclaimed, "I win." He turned over his tiles. It was a banker's win. He did the same thing three more times, and that made him even more talkative. He could not stop crowing about his wins or reproaching Gou Dahai for letting Zhuang pick up an "eight myriad" tile. He reminded everyone that they had to pay up at the end of the game.

"Li Laoshi frowns when he loses but turns into a chatty old woman when he wins," Fang said.

"So I'm your common enemy now. You're all jealous. Winning at a gaming table isn't everything it's cracked up to be. As they say, lucky in cards, unlucky in love. Hey, sorry, four of a kind," Li said, while taking a tile to play another hand. "The good luck keeps on coming. Too bad there's no bonus tile. Zhidie, I'm going to say something you may not like, but Zhong missed getting the rank of senior editor because of Wu Kun, who's tight with Jing Xueyin. She's the one you have to talk to."

Zhuang had his opportunities, but he fell a bit short of winning a round and had to borrow some money from Gou Dahai. Though he was looking at the tiles, he could not stop thinking about poor Mr. Zhong. It was hard to imagine how the old man had managed to survive all these years. He sneered when Li asked him to speak with Jing Xueyin.

"She's free to do what she wants. What right do I have to try to talk to her? Zhong isn't a young man, and he's still hoping to receive a letter from an old classmate?"

"There's more to the secret," Li said. "Have you ever been to his house? He has a fair number of performance-enhancement tonics. Now, he's been living alone for more than a dozen years, since he and his wife don't sleep together, and we've never seen him with anyone else. I think he's taking the tonics because the girl gives him hope. He's probably hoping to reconnect with her and enjoy a late-life marriage," Li said before suddenly shouting, "Got it!" He slammed the tile on the table, snapping it in two, with one half sailing out the window.

"Not so fast," Gou objected. "You need two for that, and you only have one."

"You saw the tile break in half!"

"So what?" Fang said. "You have only one in your hand and you need two. It's not a win."

Li went to the window to look for the broken piece, but to no avail. He asked everyone to pay up and was angry when Gou and Fang refused.

"This is not a banker's win, Hongwen," Zhuang said. "Do you expect the three of us to take off our pants and pawn our jackets to pay you?"

"Since you want to weasel out of paying up, I'm not buying lunch," Li said. "Let's just pretend I gave you the money, and you can buy your own lunches."

"No need for you to buy anything," Zhuang said. "I'll treat."

He borrowed another fifty from Gou and told Fang to get Zhong to go with them to lunch. Fang went, but Zhong was not in his room. So the four of them went to Damaishi Street for pork jelly buns, followed by a visit to a teahouse. It was dark when they split up.

On his way home, Zhuang thought about his terrible loss at the mahjong table. Li Hongwen had said lucky in cards, unlucky in love. His luck at the table had been lousy, so did that mean there was something romantic in store for him? He paused and, lost in thought for a moment, regretted not going to see Tang Wan'er earlier. Maybe he could go now. On second thought, it was getting dark, and Zhou Min might be home, so he headed reluctantly toward Shuangren fu.

A figure squatting outside the gate jumped to his feet and shouted when he spotted Zhuang.

"Junkman! Collecting junk and scraps!"

Zhuang laughed when he saw that it was the old man who spouted doggerel.

"You're still collecting scrap at this hour?" Zhuang said, as the taste of alcohol rose up with a belch.

Ignoring him, the old man pulled his cart down the main street and rattled off another bit of wisdom:

Getting drunk on revolution's brew, ruins the party's name, causes stomach woes true
So drunk his wife can only fume and stew, so she complains to the discipline crew
The party secretary says if asked to drink, you would, too.

❋

Zhuang opened the door. In the brightly lit house, his wife and Hong Jiang were sitting on the sofa counting money and punching numbers into a calculator. "It must have been a good month," he said when he saw the stacks of bills.

"A good month?" she said. "The shipment of Jin Yong's martial arts novels sold well at first, but we never anticipated that five more bookstores would open on the same street, all of them selling Jin Yong's novels. Business went downhill fast, since we couldn't get anything from our supplier. No matter how many times we count, this is barely enough to pay the two girls' wages and our taxes. Hong Jiang bought three bookshelves a few days ago, and we have no books to put on them. You're out there all day long. Why don't you check things out for us? Hong says that the Tianlai Publishing House in Hunan just published a book. What's the title again?"

"*Lady Chatterley's Lover*," Hong said.

"*Lady Chatterley's Lover* is in great demand, but we can't get copies," Niu Yueqing said. "Don't you know the Tianlai editor-in-chief? They're always asking you to write for them, so why don't you contact them tomorrow and ask them to send books?"

"That's easy," Zhuang said. "Hong Jiang, send a telegram in my name."

"That's what I've been waiting to hear," Hong said. "Most of the time, you complain that I use your name to cause trouble."

"Just my name. Don't tell them I own the bookstore."

"You're always so cautious. If we'd used your name for the bookstore, we could have had anything we wanted."

"I'm a writer. A writer writes. What would people think if they knew I owned a bookstore?"

"In this day and age, there's nothing wrong with a writer owning a business. Fame is wealth, and you shouldn't squander it. You can't get rich from writing alone. A novella is worth less than a single character written by the calligrapher Gong Jingyuan," Hong said.

"He has something else to talk to you about," Niu Yueqing said to Zhuang. "Go ahead, Hong Jiang."

"After running the bookstore for a year, I have a pretty good picture of the market. Writing books is not as good as selling them, and editing books is better than both. Many bookstores now edit their own books, either by buying a publishing house outright or by printing books illegally. Chapbooks are all about sex and violence, and there's no need for proofreading. With print runs in the millions, those people are getting rich. You know Xiaoshunzi on Zhuquemen Street, a stinking little shit who can barely read. Well, he hired some people to cut and paste erotic passages from other works and put out a book that made him a hundred and fifty thousand. Now he rides around in a taxi and eats exotic seafood at the Tangcheng Restaurant every day."

"I know all that," Zhuang said. "But that's not what we should be doing."

"I knew you'd say that," Hong said. "But there's something Shimu and I have talked about. A bookseller produced a martial arts novel by someone named Liu De. They're having trouble selling it and are offering it to us at half-price. I was thinking we could take it and change the cover. We can give the author's name as Jing Yong. I'm sure we'll make a bundle."

"How?" Zhuang asked.

"Jin Yong's books sell out. This one can't compare with his, but if we print the author's name as Jing Yong in cursive style, it will look like Jin Yong at a casual glance. If we're caught, we'll have every right to say the author's name is Jing Yong, not Jin Yong. I'll take care of everything, except for the hundred thousand that you and Shimu have to put up."

"As long as Zhuang Laoshi agrees, I'll get the money." Niu Yueqing turned to Zhuang. "Wang Ximian has invited us to a celebration for his mother's seventieth birthday tomorrow. We can go together. I'll borrow eighty thousand from him, and we'll make up the rest from our savings."

"So the old lady is going to be seventy? I thought she was younger than that," Zhuang said. "I agree, we should go, but how can we borrow money at a birthday party?"

They could not agree on what to do, so she sent Hong back to the bookstore.

"Are you going back to the compound tonight?" she asked him.

"It's too late, someone would have to get up to open the door for me."

"So you'd go if it were still early, is that it? What kind of couple are we, then?"

Zhuang quietly went to bed. She followed a while later, but they kept their distance from one another. Then they heard the weepy notes of a flute on the city wall.

"I wonder who's playing that," Zhuang said.

"Who's playing that flute?" she echoed, and they fell silent.

Zhuang hadn't wanted to voice his thoughts about the flute player, and he was surprised to hear his wife say the same thing. All he wanted was for her to fall asleep quickly, but he heard a rustling from her side. She nudged him and tried to take his hand, which was what he had feared. Turning his back in disgust, he ignored her, pretending not to have noticed her movements. After lying silently for a while, he felt bad about treating her that way, so he turned to fulfill his responsibility, only to hear her say, "You're not up for this, so let me help you while you tell me some stories."

Naturally, he tried to tell her stories he had repeated many times, but she wouldn't have it and asked for stories about real people.

"Where would I get those?"

"How about some of your experiences?"

"Like what? Like when the pigs at home are hungry, how can we sell the husks?"

"I'm just wondering why you can't do it all of a sudden. You must have serviced someone else."

"You watch me like a hawk, so how would I dare get near anyone?"

"No one? Weren't you with Jing Xueyin for years?"

"I didn't touch a hair on her head. I can swear to that."

"You poor thing. Why don't I find you someone? Tell me, who do you have your eye on?"

"No one."

"Don't think I don't know you. All you lack is the nerve. When I brought up Wang Ximian's birthday party for his mother, you happily agreed to go. That tells me you have your eye on his wife."

"So what if I do?"

She fell silent, which he mistook as a sign that she was asleep, but then she said, "Wang Ximian's wife loves to dress up. She's not a young woman, but she tries to look like one."

"She dresses well."

"For whose benefit?" she demanded. "Gong Jingyuan's wife said Wang's wife got around quite a bit when she was young. In the old days, when she worked as a salesgirl at a shopping center, she did it with a man after work behind the counter, and very noisily. When people looked to see what was going on, they saw her legs sticking up, so they banged on the door, but the two of them were oblivious. They hung on to each other until they were finished, even after people broke down the door and stormed in."

As she went on, she reached out to touch him and found his erection. So she guided him on top of her. □□ □□ □□ [The author has deleted 51 words.] She cried out and curled into a ball.

"So you couldn't hold out, either," Zhuang said.

"I didn't complain, so don't you. You're always saying you can't manage, but talking about Wang's wife got you excited. How can you expect me to last longer than you? You were born to be the master of the house, stretching out your arms to be dressed and opening your mouth to be fed, while I have to tend to every little thing in both houses."

"Stop the nonsense. How old are you, anyway? Look at Zhou Min's wife. She may be a few years younger than you, but after all she's gone through, there's not a wrinkle on her face."

That upset Yueqing. "So Wang's wife is not enough for you? Now you have to bring this one up. What has she gone through? Xia Jie told me that she ran away with Zhou Min."

"That's right."

"If she could run away from her husband, that can only mean she was the mistress of a house who did not have to do housework. That's what makes women so despicable. Once they're well dressed and well fed, the more a man treasures them, the more they're tempted to engage in illicit affairs."

"When was Xia Jie here?"

"This afternoon. She brought me a jade chrysanthemum bracelet, saying it was from Tang Wan'er, who felt bad that I couldn't make it to her dinner the other day."

"You see, she's nice to you, and yet you say unkind things about her behind her back. Where's the bracelet? Let's see what kind of jade it is."

"It doesn't fit my fat arm, so I put it away. When have I said something unkind about her? I'm just unhappy that every time you meet a woman somewhere, you come home and contrast my shortcomings with her virtues. People say you can go crazy trying to compare yourself with others. I wouldn't have all these wrinkles if I didn't have to worry about every little thing in this house."

That shut Zhuang up in regard to Tang Wan'er.

"You do work too hard, so why don't we hire some help? The other day, Zhao Jingwu promised to find someone for us. When that happens, you'll be the leisurely lady of the house, and you won't have to lift a finger. All you'll have to do is give orders."

That mollified her a bit. "You wait and see. I'll make my skin smooth and soft."

They talked for a while before she curled up in his arms like a kitten and fell asleep. Zhuang, on the other hand, wasn't sleepy, so after she started snoring, he quietly sat up and reached for a magazine under the pillow. Bored after a few pages, he lit a cigarette and waited for the flute to start up again. But there was no flute, and no shouts from the old junkman.

The next day, Niu Yueqing ordered a birthday cake from a bakery in the Guan Gong Temple and told the baker to decorate it with seventieth-birthday wishes. Then she bought some fine Suzhou silk, a bottle of aged liquor from Shuanggou, a package of cured mutton, two catties of brown sugar, and half a cattie of Dragonwell tea. Upon her return, Zhuang told her he didn't feel like going.

"You don't want to go? What do I say when Wang's wife asks why?"

"There will be too many people there, and I don't feel like dragging myself over and having to talk to them. If he asks, just tell them the mayor wanted to see me and I couldn't get away."

"They want you there to make the Wang family look good. He'll be upset. He might be willing to lend us the money, but what do I do if he isn't? Do you really not want to go, or do you think I'll make you look bad? If that's it, then I'll stay home."

"You think too much. I'll write a scroll for you to take along, and I'm sure that will make the old lady happy." Zhuang unrolled a sheet of rice paper and wrote: *The setting sun is unimaginably splendid / The human world values emotion late in life.* Then he told his wife to run along with it.

When she was gone, Zhuang considered going to Zhou Min's house, wondering what he might give to Tang Wan'er. After searching through the wardrobe, he found only some snacks and candy, nothing worth taking, so he went into Old Mrs. Niu's bedroom, where he found a piece of floral silk in her closet. The old lady kept him around to chat, going on and on about Yueqing's father coming to stir up trouble when it was barely light out. She told him she had asked the old man what made him so angry so early in the morning and he'd said, "Why won't you do something about them since I can't?"

"Who are they?" Zhuang asked.

"I asked him," she said. "I told him our son-in-law is a celebrity who sits at the same table as the mayor, so who would dare pick on him? He said it was the new couple next door. They fought and argued all day long, making so much noise he couldn't sleep and lost his appetite. I thought it over. He never lied. Since you're not going to the birthday party, go take a look. If there really are troublesome neighbors, plant a peach-wood stake on the spot."

When she finished, she went out into the yard and began slicing a peach tree with a knife. Bemused and annoyed, Zhuang helped her back inside before he carved three stakes with the promise of checking on the old man's grave.

He would have left after settling the old lady down if not for Niu Yueqing's cousin, who arrived from the countryside with a package of millet. The old lady was so pleased, her smile turned to sobs, saying how wonderful the woman was, always thinking about her. Mrs. Niu asked about the woman's father, with a litany of questions: What's he doing? Why hasn't he visited lately? People in the countryside are rich now, so he's forgotten about an old sister even though she doesn't plan to borrow money from him. The cousin quickly explained that her father had taken over the village's brick kiln. Though he was too old for manual labor, he had been a well-known stoker and was put in charge of regulating the fire's intensity. He simply could not get away at the moment.

"So he can't get away," Old Mrs. Niu said. "How did he find the time to come every three or four days to eat and drink and then leave with a sack of grain in the past?"

The cousin blanched at the reproach, prompting Zhuang to smooth things over by saying that his mother-in-law's brain was addled, which was why she talked nonsense all day long.

"How could I be upset over what she said? She was telling the truth. Life was tough back then, with so many children in the family. We were lucky to have Aunty's help." The cousin turned to the old lady. "Aunty, you have every right to complain about my father. He knows he hasn't been to see you in a long time. We're having a temple festival in ten days, and there will be an opera performance. He asked me to bring you back with me."

"Your brother-in-law here gets free tickets for shows at the city's Yisu Club, Sanyi Club, and Shangyou Club, so why would I want to go see a rural opera?" the old lady said.

"A theater performance is different from open-air. Besides, now that we're doing so much better, my father would like you to be our special guest. He'll even wait on you."

"I guess I should go. But you only invited me. Why don't you ask your uncle along?"

Color drained from the cousin's face as she stared at Zhuang.

"She's like that, talking about the living one moment and going on about the dead the next," Zhuang said.

"Sure, sure. I'll invite Uncle, too."

"This is what we'll do, Zhidie. You and your cousin go check on your father-in-law's grave. He won't go unless the new neighbors are punished."

Left with no choice, Zhuang stalled by saying that they should offer the cousin something to eat first. Saying she wasn't hungry, the cousin nevertheless sampled all the snacks and fruit that Zhuang brought out, while asking the prices of their refrigerator, tape recorder, modular cabinets, nightstands, and lamps. Her envy was palpable. When they were ready to leave, the old lady told Zhuang to go out for a while, for she had something to say to the cousin. He waited in the yard until the cousin came out with a red face.

"What did she say now?"

"She asked if I've taken the medicine Yueqing sent, and if I'm pregnant. She told me not to let my husband drink alcohol. I want my baby to have a good life here with you, but I'm worried he won't be smart enough to deserve your name."

Not knowing how to respond, Zhuang changed the subject, telling her some amusing anecdotes about the old lady's inability to tell the living from the dead.

"She's old, so it's not strange for her to be talking like that. For old people, there's no barrier between the human realm and the underworld, and we mustn't automatically think that what old people say is crazy talk. It happens in our village quite a bit."

Zhuang smiled unhappily. "I didn't expect you to sound like her."

They rode on Zhuang's Magnolia out the city's north gate and headed west toward an earthen trench next to a Han dynasty ruin. The heat made them sweat. After parking the scooter, they walked across a barren field and reached a ridge by the trench, where they saw a stone marker in the distance. The cousin began to wail.

"Why are you doing that?" Zhuang asked.

"If I don't, Uncle will be angry, and even the ghosts around his grave will laugh at him." She howled three more times.

Zhuang was surprised to see a new gravesite to the left of Yueqing's father's. Cogon grass had yet to grow on the mound, where rain-soaked white paper from funeral wreaths was scattered on the muddy ground.

*This must be the new neighbor the old man was talking abou*t. Zhuang's heart raced.

The cousin was muttering as she crouched down to burn paper money. He walked over to the ridge and asked a man digging dirt nearby who was in the new tomb. The man told him that a young couple and their child had been killed in an accident with a truck. Their kin had buried all three of them in one grave. The information so dismayed Zhuang that his face turned a ghostly white, as he now knew that the old lady had been telling the truth. He hurried over to plant a peach stake on the new tomb before dragging the cousin away.

After they returned, the old lady left for the countryside. Zhuang guessed that Yueqing would be coming back late after the party, so he scrounged up something to eat. As he thought back to what he had learned at the gravesite, he knew he could no longer treat the old lady's prattle as nonsense; instead, he racked his brain to recall all the strange things she'd said and wrote them down for closer examination. Meanwhile, the sky turned overcast and wind gusts rattled the window, a sign of an impending downpour. He shut the windows before going outside to gather the clothes and bedding drying in the yard. But no rain came after an hour, just surges of dark clouds accumulating and roiling in the sky, and changing shape every minute or so. Sitting alone by the window, he watched them for a long time as they grew in size and formed a figure that was nearly human, running with flowing hair. The figure's bare feet were so enormous he could almost distinguish upturned toes and detect their swirls. Amused, he tried to write down what he was seeing but could not find the words, so he took a picture before a sudden terror seized him. He turned to glance at the old lady's room, which increased his fright and unease, so he locked up and went to his apartment in the federation compound.

Niu Yueqing did not return that afternoon and was still out at nightfall. Around ten, someone came to the compound with a message: Old Mrs. Wang had insisted that she stay the night to play mahjong, so she was returning the favor by inviting Old Mrs. Wang and Wang Ximian's wife over the following day. They had both accepted the invitation.

"Am I expected to do the grocery shopping tomorrow morning?" Zhuang asked.

"That's what she said." The man handed him a shopping list.

Zhuang read the list: two catties of pork, one cattie of spare ribs, a carp, a tortoise, half a cattie of squid, half a cattie of sea cucumber, three catties of lotus roots, two catties of chives, one cattie of bean pods, one cattie of cowpeas, two catties of tomatoes, two catties of eggplant, two catties of fresh mushrooms, three catties of thick osmanthus liquor, seven bottles of Sprite, three catties of tofu, a half-cattie each of some Korean side dishes, two catties of mutton, one cattie of cured beef, five preserved eggs, one roasted chicken, one roasted duck, half a cattie each of cooked pork liver, pork belly, and smoked sausage. Also, he needed to bring from the Shuangren fu house a bottle of Wuliangye, ten bottles of beer, a pack of peanuts, dried mushrooms and wood ear, a bowl of sticky rice, a sack of red dates, and a handful of rice noodles. In addition, he had to buy a can of peas, a can of bamboo shoots, a can of cherries, a cattie of sausage, two catties of cucumbers, one ounce of thin seaweed, and three ounces of lotus seeds.

"What a pain," Zhuang said. "Why not reserve tables at a restaurant?"

"Aunty said you'd say that," the messenger said. "She asked me to tell you that this is for Wang Ximian's wife. You can enjoy gourmet food at a restaurant, but the ambience can't compare with eating at home, where you can have a real conversation."

She's convinced I have my eye on Wang's wife, I guess, he said to himself.

After sending the messenger off, Zhuang thought about inviting Meng Yunfang and his wife, along with Zhou Min and his wife. Since they were going to host a luncheon, that way he could prove to Yueqing that he wasn't interested in Wang's wife while giving Tang Wan'er a chance to see his house. With his mind made up, he called Zhao Jingwu and asked him to go shopping with him early the next day.

At the crack of dawn, he rode over to Zhou Min's house at 8 Ludang Lane. Tang Wan'er was up, working on her hair in front of a mirror. Zhou Min was crouching beneath a grape trellis brushing his teeth. With foam still in his mouth, he was beside himself with joy when he saw Zhuang walk in. His wife heard them and walked out, still touching up her hair. She blushed as she greeted Zhuang, and then walked to the side to wind her hair into a bun.

"Still fussing with your hair?" Zhou Min asked. "Why don't you get tea for Zhuang Laoshi?"

That brought her back down to earth; she rushed inside to make tea. The water was so hot, she had to switch the cup between hands as she brought it over. She sucked in air and shook her hands when she laid the cup down. She gave Zhuang an embarrassed smile.

"Did that burn you?" he asked.

"Not really." And yet she put her fingers in her mouth.

With a good night's sleep and careful makeup, her face was fair, her skin smooth. She was wearing a figure-hugging pink sleeveless blouse with a scoop neck over a super-short pencil skirt, showing off her slender waist and long, graceful legs.

"Are you going out today?" Zhuang asked.

"No."

"Then why you are so dressed up?"

"This is all I have. I just added some makeup. It's like this every day at home. I look better with makeup. And it shows respect for our visitors. I hope Zhuang Laoshi won't think I'm shallow."

"Why would I think that? That's how a woman should be. It's a great outfit."

His heart skipped a beat when he saw that she was wearing the shoes he had given her. She noticed his reaction and announced:

"Everything on me is five years old, Zhuang Laoshi, except for the shoes. They're brand-new. What do you think? Like them?"

That put his mind at ease, for he knew she was saying it for Zhou Min's benefit while letting him know that she hadn't told her husband.

"Not bad," Zhuang said. "Actually there's no such thing as a good or a bad outfit. It all depends on the wearer."

Zhou Min came in with a cluster of grapes he had just picked.

"She has a perfect figure for clothes. She bought these even though she has plenty of shoes, and they're the only ones she'll wear."

That pleased Zhuang enormously. *Why didn't she tell her husband where the shoes came from? And why had she lied so naturally to him? Does that mean she's interested in me?*

"Zhou Min," he said, "I came early to invite you two to lunch today. You have to put everything else aside. I've also invited the mother and wife of Wang Ximian, the painter, and Meng Yunfang and his wife. Now I have to go tell Meng and his wife and then go shopping for groceries."

"We don't deserve the honor," Tang Wan'er said.

"I accepted *your* invitation, didn't I?" Zhuang said.

"I'm sorry. We can't wait to get to know those people, and it's time we paid our respects to your wife. But there will be so many guests, I'm afraid we're not presentable enough. We'd make you lose face."

"We're friends, so no more talk like that. Wan'er, did you ask Xia Jie to give my wife a jade bracelet?"

"Yes, why? Wouldn't she take it?"

"That's not it. She didn't think she should have taken it, since she had yet to meet you."

"Oh, it's not worth anything. Zhou Min gave a bracelet to Xia Jie because Meng Laoshi introduced us to you, and I thought your wife should have one, too, so I asked Xia Jie to take one over."

Zhuang took out a cloth bundle.

"She asked me to give you this in return," he said. "I hope you like it."

She took it. "It's the thought that counts. I'd love it even if it were a lump of clay."

The opened bundle revealed an ancient bronze mirror, which drew a cry from her.

"Come take a look, Zhou Min."

"You're making it hard on me, Zhuang Laoshi," Zhou said. "This is a rare treasure!"

"It's just a nice thing to have, that's all."

She looked into it, saying she had heard of bronze mirrors and had always wondered how you could see yourself in one. She was surprised to see that it was as clear as glass, so she replaced a painted plate on the table with the mirror, on its stand, to admire herself.

"Now you're showing off," Zhou Min said.

"I was just wondering who might have owned this in ancient times and how she would have put on makeup in front of it," she said with a pout. "Zhou Min, you've been careless with the antique roof tiles I used to collect, putting them all over the place. You even broke one. Now, this mirror is a treasure, so don't you touch it."

"Do you really think I don't know what's valuable and what's not?" he said, with an embarrassed look at Zhuang.

"Why don't you deliver the lunch invitation instead of Zhuang Laoshi," she said, "and buy some gifts while you're at it? Maybe it's Zhuang Laoshi or Shimu's birthday."

"It's nobody's birthday. Food is secondary; the important thing is getting together with friends," Zhuang said.

Zhou got up to leave, and so did Zhuang.

"I'll go tell them, so you can stick around," Zhou Min said, "If you haven't had breakfast yet, Wan'er can go out for some rice and jujube cakes and some tofu jelly."

Zhuang sat down, saying he'd rest a while.

As soon as Zhou Min left, Tang Wan'er shut the gate.

"I'll go get some rice cakes, then," she said when she returned.

Suddenly Zhuang felt anxious. He got to his feet but then sat back down.

"I don't normally eat breakfast, but get something for yourself if you want."

"I won't eat if you don't," she said with a smile, her lively eyes fixed on Zhuang, which made him hot all over. The bridge of his nose was prickled with sweat, but he bravely returned her gaze. She then sat down in front of him on a stool, putting one leg in back and resting the other one limply sideways against it. With the toe of her shoe barely touching the floor, she wore the shoe halfway off to expose her heel as she tried to balance herself on the stool. Zhuang could not keep his eyes off the dainty shoes.

"These fit perfectly. Just wearing them refreshes me."

He reached out, made an arc in the air, and then pulled his hand back to cup his chin. She was quiet for a while before lowering her head and pulling her foot back.

"Zhuang Laoshi."

"Yes?" He looked up and met her gaze; neither of them could think of anything to say.

"Don't call me laoshi."

"What should I call you?"

"Call me by my name. Laoshi creates a distance between us."

"I could never do that," she said as she stood up, at a loss for what to do, before going over to fuss with the bronze mirror.

"Meng Laoshi says you're an avid collector of antiques. How could you bear to part with this mirror?"

"It makes me happy to see you enjoy it. Your surname is Tang, and this is from the Kaiyuan reign of the Tang dynasty, so it's more fitting for you to have it. You've only seen the smooth bright side. Now take a closer look at the decoration on the back."

She turned the mirror over to see a pair of mandarin ducks atop a water lily under the loop and mandarin ducks on both sides atop lotus flowers holding a ribbon in their beaks, while above the button were two cranes, their wings spread, their necks down, tugging on a sash with a heart knot.

Her eyes shone brightly as she read the description of the appearance and function of the mirror:

Reveals benevolence and virtue
foreshadows a long life
shows truth and beauty
highlights excellence and eminence
reflects dressing-table carriage
finds beauty in homeliness
displays blooming and withering
brightens like a full moon.

"Does this mirror have a name?"

"A bronze mirror with two cranes tugging a sash and mandarin ducks holding a ribbon."

"How could Shimu part with this?"

Caught off guard, Zhuang did not know what to say. She was blushing so much that her forehead was bathed in tiny beads of sweat.

"You must be hot," she said illogically, while getting up to prop open a window with a wooden peg. It was an old-fashioned window, with a nailed bottom half and a movable top. After several tries, she was unable to keep the peg in place, so she stood on tiptoes to fix it, stretching up and exposing her waist under the short blouse. He went over to help by putting the peg in place, but it slipped off, sending the window crashing down and causing her to scream in fright. When he reached out to steady her, she fell into his arms as if on a pulley. He turned her around, and they found each other's lips; they stayed that way for a long time, breathing hard through their noses, as if glued together. □□ □□ □□ [The author has deleted 23 words.]

Zhuang pulled away.

"Wan'er," he said, "I finally have you in my arms. I'm very fond of you."

"I'm fond of you, too," she said, as tears ran down her face. He tenderly reached out to dry them. Then he kissed them away. She giggled and pushed him away, only to have their lips meet once more, all their energy devoted to sucking. Before they knew it, their hands were roaming over each other's body; soon his hand snaked down, but her skirt was so tight, he could only tug anxiously at the waistband. She stepped back to unhook her skirt, and his hand slipped in; she was wet. □□ □□ □□ [The author has deleted 11 words.]

"I desperately wanted to touch your feet that day when I gave you the shoes."

"I could tell, and I hoped you would, but then you stopped."

"Why didn't you give me a hint?"

"I didn't dare."

"I was an idiot. I fell for you the moment I laid eyes on you and believed that we were destined for each other. You are the first woman I've ever really wanted, and I was intimidated. I knew that if you showed only a hint of feelings for me, my courage would know no bounds."

"But you are a famous man, and I was afraid you wouldn't find me desirable."

He carried her limp figure over to the bed and took off her skirt, then rolled her stockings down to her knees. It felt like stripping the tender bark off a spring willow, as he had done as a child back in Tongguan, or removing the outer layer of a green onion when her ample white legs came into view. She wanted to take off her shoes and her stockings, but he said he liked her with her shoes and stockings on. He stood beside the bed and raised her legs. □□ □□ □□ [The author has deleted 379 words.] She moaned the moment he entered her and started moving, a new experience to him, so arousing his desire for conquest that he still had not come after prolonged thrusting, to his surprise. Her face was flushed red and her hair disheveled when she sat up.

"Let's change positions," she said. She got up and leaned against the bed.

Zhuang stared at a mole on the left side of her buttocks, but was panting too hard to speak. She stopped and took off her shoes and silk stockings. □□ □□ □□ [The author has deleted 213 words.] He watched her squirm through drunken eyes; his lips twitched, his eyes rolled back, and he cried out. □□ □□ □□ [The author has deleted 50 words.]

When he finished dressing, she was still curled up, as if dead, so he went over and laid her out straight before sitting down across from the bed to smoke a cigarette and feast his eyes on the alluring sleeping figure. She opened her eyes to look at him and laughed soundlessly, as if embarrassed; she was too weak to get out of bed, which reminded him of the lines of Tang poetry about the Imperial Consort who looked weightless after bathing in a hot spring. He realized that it was not about getting out of the bath, but about the sight of a woman after sex.

"You were amazing," she said.

"Really?"

"I've never enjoyed it like that before. You really know how to make love to a woman."

Immensely proud, he said earnestly, "You're only the second woman I've had, after my wife. Today was special. I've never performed like that before. Honestly, I come too soon every time with Yueqing. I thought I was finished, that I was not a man anymore."

"If a man is impotent, it's his wife's fault."

He was so touched by her words that he rushed over to take her into his arms and burst into tears.

"Thank you, Wan'er. I won't forget you as long as I live."

She lifted him up and called out softly, "Zhuang-ge, my elder brother."

He could only murmur a reply.

"It'll be better if I call you Zhuang Laoshi."

"Are you pitying me?"

"I've been calling you that all along, and it wouldn't be good if I suddenly stopped. So I'll keep doing that when there are people around, but in private I'll call you Zhuang-ge."

They fell into each other's arms again and kissed for a while before she got dressed. After tidying her hair, she reapplied her eyeliner and lipstick.

"I'm yours now, Zhuang-ge. Wang Ximian's wife, whom you've invited today, must be as pretty as a fairy. Will I look shabby when I go to lunch?"

"I invited you so you could gain some confidence."

"But I'm still worried."

"What's there to worry about?"

"Will your wife welcome me to your house?"

"That all depends on how you deal with her."

"I should be all right, but I'm not sure. She'll probably laugh at my clothes."

"That's a nice outfit. If we had time, I'd give you some money to buy something fancy and trendy."

"I won't take your money, but I'd like you to help me choose an outfit."

She opened her wardrobe and tried on every piece she owned. Growing anxious, Zhuang waited until she chose a black dress, and then, after holding her in his arms for one more kiss, he rushed home.

When he got home, Zhao Jingwu had been there with the groceries but, unable to get in, had left everything outside. Zhuang opened the door and was hard at work when Niu Yueqing came home with Wang's wife. When she saw him squatting in the kitchen cleaning a fish, Wang's wife yelled out, "Ai-ya! How fortunate to have a renowned writer cleaning a fish for me."

"Zhidie, that's enough showing off. Our house is no match for yours, my dear, so you'll have to find a clean spot to sit. Zhidie will entertain you while I go into the kitchen."

"Where's Ximian?" Zhuang asked. "Why isn't he here yet? Is he coming with Old Mrs. Wang?"

"Ximian had to go to Beijing today. He bought the ticket days ago, so he can't get away. Old Mrs. Wang promised to come last night, but she had a headache this morning, probably because we had so much fun. We played mahjong late into the night, and it must have tired her out. She said she couldn't make it after all, but to send some of the good food over later, a sort of token of her presence."

"That's too bad. She's been never here."

"It's good she's not here," Wang's wife said. "I'll feel more at ease. With her around, we'd have to watch what we said."

"You're alone today," Niu Yueqing said with a smile. "Just make yourself at home and do or say whatever you want."

Niu Yueqing slipped out of her heels, put on an apron, and sent her husband and Wang's wife into his study.

"You've lost weight," Zhuang said after getting her settled. How come?"

She touched her face and said she'd lost so much weight that her face was losing its shape. Zhuang replied that she was thinner, but that actually improved her looks. Was she on a diet?

"Why would an old hag like me be on a diet? I've been suffering from a lack of energy since the beginning of the year. I experience chills and I catch cold easily, but no medicine works. Earlier this month I went to see an herbal doctor, who said there is no remedy for my illness, that I'm like a pot of water that will never boil. It's the aftermath of bearing a child. He said I needed to get pregnant again so my body could have a major tune-up. How am I supposed to do that? I couldn't even if I wanted to."

"People often say that if you try hard at fifty-nine, you can have a baby at sixty. You're not too old. I'll get you permission if you really want another child."

"You're younger than us, why don't you have one?"

Zhuang blushed, though it had only been a casual question. Niu Yueqing heard them when she left the kitchen to get some spices from a room opposite the study, so she parted the curtain and said, "That's a good point. We've decided to have one. Zhidie was busy with his career before and afraid of the distraction a baby would create. But now it's obvious that the house is too quiet with just us two adults. I asked him when he'd be done with his essay writing, since he's already gained a bit of undeserved fame."

"That sounds right," Wang's wife agreed, while Zhuang could only feign a smile. Niu Yueqing gave him a lacerating look.

"You're such an idiot, Zhidie," she said. "You've been talking so much, you forgot to offer her something to eat."

Zhuang hurried to get some fruit for Wang's wife before realizing he should call Zhao Jingwu and ask why he had left. They needed help in the kitchen.

The loudspeaker in the yard croaked three times, followed by a voice: "Zhuang Zhidie, you have guests."

"Who could that be?" Wang's wife asked.

"That's so annoying. It's Mrs. Wei, the gatekeeper. She takes her job seriously, and that's fine, but she calls me to greet guests as if I were a prostitute waiting for her john."

Amused by what he had said, Wang's wife's face crinkled with a smile. Zhuang was about to go downstairs when Niu Yueqing said from the kitchen, "We have important guests today, so turn everyone else away. Just have the old lady say you're out."

"I also invited Meng and Zhou Min and their wives."

Niu Yueqing paused.

"You and your plans. All right, then, the more the merrier. But Meng Yunfang talks nonstop," she whispered. "How will we be able to ask for a loan with him around?"

"Why don't you ask her now?"

"Why must you avoid difficult issues? You're like a turtle hiding its head!"

Zhuang left with a laugh. Niu Yueqing brought a kettle to the study, where she added hot water to Wang's wife's tea. She then broached the subject, and Wang's wife agreed at once to lend them the money. Before long, footsteps sounded on the staircase, followed by Meng's raspy voice.

"Where is Wang Ximian's wife?"

The women stopped talking and came out of the study. Meng was standing by the door.

"It's been a year since I last saw you," he said. "People were saying you're showing your age, but you actually look younger than Xia Jie, with fresher, softer, tender skin. Are you making us all old before our time? Now I know how Wang Ximian can be so creative: his source of inspiration is forever young."

"Listen to you. I'm just glad you're not saying bad things about me," Wang's wife said. "Why not swap with Old Wang if you're interested in me?"

Meng turned to his wife. "Sounds good to me, and you're probably even more eager to swap than I am. You'd have a better life with him, since he gets thousands for a painting."

Xia Jie glared at her husband, but said with a smile, "Wang could never be interested in me, and you, you would be a perfect cook for his wife."

Wang's wife playfully pinched Xia's mouth, and the two women horsed around like children. Meng kept his eyes on Wang's wife as he sat down to have some tea.

"Since you don't believe me when I say you look young, I'll ask Zhidie to note the blaze above your head."

Startled, she asked, "I have a blaze above my head?"

"All animals have them. The size and brightness indicate the length and strength of vitality."

"You probably didn't know that Meng Laoshi is studying qigong," Zhuang said.

"I heard that, and I'm intrigued," Wang's wife said.

"There's nothing intriguing about it. I now have a complete grasp of *Plum Strategy of Change* and *The Sixty Heavenly Stems*, and I've read *The Compendium of Imperial Prophecies* three times. I've also given three talks on *The Book of Changes* and am now focused on *Master Shao's Magic Numbers*, a book that is a storehouse of knowledge. Once I have a total understanding of the book, I will be able to know, in great detail, what people were in previous lives, what they will become after their death, who their parents were, when they were born, whom they will marry, and whether they will have sons or daughters."

"If you're right," Zhuang said, "then everything is predestined and there is no need to work hard."

"Of course there's predestination, but that doesn't exempt us from striving hard. I have given the question considerable thought and can say that we can achieve total fulfillment in life precisely by exerting ourselves. There are few original copies of *Master Shao's Magic Numbers* circulating inside or outside China, and though there is a book to unlock the secrets in it, it's nearly impossible to find a copy. It took me considerable effort, but I have finally deciphered two numbers out of a six-digit series. Don't make light of this, because this has stumped even Master Zhixiang at the Yunhuang Temple, and the book seems to take possession of everyone who studies it."

"Yunfang, enough with your rambling already. Your job today is to cook, as usual," Yueqing said to him.

"You see, this is my fate. Even if I became the nation's chairman, I'd still have to cook for members of the Politburo," he said on his way to the kitchen.

After Meng left, Wang's wife said to Zhuang, "Why didn't you tell me, Zhidie?"

"Tell you what?"

"What do you think? I'd have brought it today if you'd mentioned it yesterday at the house."

"It's just one of Yueqing's crazy ideas, but thanks for helping."

Baffled by their talk, Xia Jie asked, "What are you talking about? It sounds so secretive."

Zhuang did not reply.

"Don't say anything, Zhidie," Wang's wife said. "We'll see each other tomorrow by the third pillar of the Dongxiang Bridge at Lianhu Park. Whoever gets there first stays until the other shows."

"Right, and the same code word," Zhuang said.

"A secret tryst. I'm going to tell Yueqing," Xia said with a pout, knowing that they were joking in order to change the subject, as if she were a stranger. Without revealing her feelings, she asked him why Zhou Min and his wife weren't there yet and whether he had a Five in a Row game set, vowing to beat Tang Wan'er this time. Before she finished, she heard someone at the door. She went to open it. "You little tart, how dare you put on airs! What took you so long, arriving even after Zhuang Laoshi and his wife? Did you have a bit of fun at home before you left?"

She opened the door, and there stood Zhao Jingwu, with a blushing, pretty girl holding a bundle. Quickly covering her mouth, Xia called out to Zhuang Zhidie, who was equally surprised when he saw who it was.

"I'm reporting for duty, Zhuang Laoshi," the young woman said.

Completely unprepared, Zhuang froze on the spot.

"Liu Yue came to see me a while ago, saying she had quit her job and wanted to come to your house," Zhao said. "I told her to wait for another day, since you're hosting a luncheon today. But she was happy to hear that, since she knew you could use some help. I had to agree with her, so here she is."

Taking the bundle from Liu Yue, Zhuang led her into the kitchen to meet his wife.

"Look who's here, Yueqing. Remember I told you about finding some help? Well, Jingwu has brought us some today."

One look at Liu, and Yueqing broke out in a big smile. "What's this, a beauty pageant?"

"Please show me what to do, Shimu," Liu Yue said, put at ease by Niu Yueqing's comment. She gave her a quick appraisal. Her new mistress had a medium build and was a bit on the heavy side, with her hair fashionably short and pulled together with a cheap plastic hair band; she had a large, rather square face, a straight nose, big eyes, and some light brown facial spots.

"What's your name?" Niu Yueqing asked.

"Liu Yue."

"I'm Yueqing and you're Liu Yue. What a coincidence that we both have a 'moon' in our names."

"That means I was destined to work for you," Liu Yue said.

Visibly pleased, Niu Yueqing said, "That's our karma. You can see now, Liu Yue, this is our house. The work isn't terribly hard, but we have lots of visitors, and there won't be a problem so long as you keep your eyes on everything and receive the guests properly. People are strangers outside, but once you're in here, you're family. Your Zhuang Laoshi is busy running around all day, so the two of us will stay indoors like sisters."

"I feel like I've fallen into a bed of roses. But I'm a country girl, uncultured and inattentive, and I'm afraid I'll make mistakes receiving important guests. I won't mind if they complain about me, but I wouldn't want to damage your family's reputation. So I'm going to treat you like my own dajie, my big sister, the same as a grownup in my family. You must teach me. Let me know when I fail to measure up. You can curse me, even hit me if you like."

That thrilled Niu Yueqing. Liu pulled her hair into a ponytail before rolling up her sleeves to wash the vegetables. Niu Yueqing stopped her.

"Don't be in such a hurry. You've just arrived, and you haven't even had time for your sweat to dry. I won't need your help yet."

"You really are a dajie. I'm not a guest here. I was eager to come today precisely because I knew you'd have a house full of guests, and there's work to be done. Otherwise, why am I here, to enjoy the festivities?" Liu said.

"Then you should at least get some rest first," Niu Yueqing said.

Zhuang took Liu Yue out to meet the others, all frequent guests at the Zhuang home, before showing her around. Liu noticed that the main wall of the large living room was taken up by calligraphy in a black glass frame done by the man of the house, which read "God Is Silent." It looked familiar, and after a mental search, she realized that it was from one of Zhuang's books. The original phrase was longer: "Ghosts look hideous and God is silent." Without the first phrase, it fit better in a living room and demanded rumination, which made her marvel at how uniquely different writers are. The wall by the door was lined with four screens carved with soaring phoenixes, next to a black Hong Kong–style oval table with two high-back black chairs on each side. Under the calligraphy was a sectional sofa of Italian leather. The south side of the room was taken up by a black four-shelf stereo cabinet and a squat glass and chrome stand with a TV set above and a VCR below. A light-colored floral silk cloth was draped over the TV, next to which was a black ceramic vase from Yaozhou containing a bouquet of plastic flowers, adding a liveliness to the room and highlighting the understated elegance of the contrasting black furniture and white walls. Liu Yue sighed over the refined taste of an intellectual family, so unlike her previous employers, whose house was filled with gaudy colors. To the south of the living room were two bedrooms, one of which, for the master and mistress, had a beige wool rug and two single Simmons beds, each with a low nightstand. A bronze-colored modular cabinet was placed along the wall facing the door, while a row of low cabinets stood by the window with floor-length fuchsia-colored silk curtains around an air-conditioner. A large wedding photo hung between the beds. Behind the door was an exquisite glass frame with a colorful mermaid print. What interested her most were the twin beds. There was a question in the look she gave to Zhuang, and it was not lost on him.

"The beds can be put together if desired," he volunteered.

She giggled, drawing Wang's wife and Xia Jie from the study. She blushed from embarrassment. After Zhuang made the introductions, Xia led Liu into the study.

"You're no maid; you look more like a princess. Where are you from?"

"Northern Shaanxi."

"I've heard it said that Qingjian is famous for its flagstone, Wayao Fort for its coal, Mizhi for its women, and Suide for its men. You must be from Mizhi."

"You are really smart," Liu said with a nod.

"Your master is the one who's smart," Wang's wife said. "Just look at his study."

Liu Yue checked out the room. Every wall of the modest-sized study was filled with floor-to-ceiling bookshelves, leaving room only for the door and a window. The top two tiers were reserved for an array of antiques in various sizes, heights, and quality. Liu recognized some earthen jars from the Han dynasty, plus pottery containers for grain and silkworm cocoons and pottery stoves from the Eastern Han dynasty, as well as tri-colored glazed horses and colorful figurines from the Tang dynasty. She did not know the origin of the other objects, which included ancient jars, bowls, Buddha's heads, and bronze plates. The lower seven tiers did not have glass doors with hidden locks, and the books on them were unwrapped, exposing their eye-pleasing colors. Every shelf had about four inches of empty space to hold all sorts of roof tiles, stone axes, rocks in odd shapes, wood carvings, clay sculptures, dough figurines, bamboo weavings, jade objects, leather cutouts for puppet shows, paper-cuts, and the twelve zodiac animals carved in walnut, along with a pair of grass sandals. The curtain was raised at the window, in front of which stood a large desk. A bronze bust of the master sat in the middle of the desk, flanked by a tall pile of books and paper. Brushes, ink stone, paper, and ink were strewn across a table by the bookshelf next to the door, while scrolls of various lengths protruded from a large blue-and-white ceramic vat beneath the desk. In the middle of the room and in front of the sofa was a low table of the type commonly found on brick beds used by country folks; it was made of passable wood but was finely crafted. Atop the table was a coarse city wall brick that supported a large, heavy-looking bronze incense burner; alongside the burner was the figure of a Tang dynasty chambermaid, her hair piled high above a brightly rouged face with upwardly slanting eyes and long, slender eyebrows. She was full-figured, with a lavender shawl draped over a short red jacket. Her hands were folded in front, and a smile seemed about to appear on her handsome face. Liu Yue smiled at the figure.

"She looks like she's moving," she said, a comment that pleased Zhuang Zhidie.

"Liu Yue has fine instincts to be able to sense that."

He lit a stick of incense and put it in the burner, sending a tiny column of smoke rising through the three openings to the ceiling, where it roiled like white clouds. "Take another look now."

"The more you look at her, the more it feels like she's flowing toward you."

"This is clearly fate," Xia Jie said. "Look, doesn't the maid resemble Liu Yue? You could almost say the facial features were modeled after her."

Liu Yue had to agree. "I was modeled after her," she said. Suddenly overcome by shyness, she leaned quietly against the door.

"You're home alone with your dajie, Liu Yue, so you can come here to read any time you like," Zhuang said.

"Your study is like the emperor's audience hall, and commoners are seldom allowed in," Xia Jie said. "It was because of Sister Wang that I was lucky enough to spend some time here. But Liu Yue gets special treatment the moment she arrives."

Zhuang blushed. "Well, she's family now."

That only made Xia Jie less willing to drop the subject. "Oh, so she's family now. That sounds so intimate." She went up and whispered to Zhuang, "You're getting a maid, not a concubine. So be careful."

He was so embarrassed, his face turned red as a cinder. Liu Yue had not heard what was said, but she could tell it was something about her that embarrassed her master.

"I can read," she said, "but I could never learn to be a writer. It would be enough for me to breathe in the air here when I come to clean the place."

"You can clean the place, but don't kill the mosquitoes," someone said from the doorway. "They suck Zhuang Laoshi's blood and become learned. We'll be well-read if they bite us."

Everyone in the study turned to see a rare beauty at the door in front of Zhou Min, who was grinning from ear to ear, holding a package of gifts. Zhuang jumped to his feet but could find nothing to say. The young woman gave him a quick glance.

"Sorry we're late, Zhuang Laoshi," she said with a tiny laugh. "Will you introduce us?"

Energized by her words, he took the gifts from Zhou Min while ushering them inside to make the introductions. When he mentioned the famous painter Wang Ximian, Wang's wife complained, "Just tell her who I am. I don't want to enjoy favors because of my relationship with Wang Ximian." She reached out to shake Tang Wan'er's hand and continued, "I can't believe that anyone could be so fair, so lovely. If I were a man, I'd fight to the death to have you."

Tang was unnerved by the comment. The light went out of her eyes, and her face darkened; she did not recover until Zhuang introduced her to Liu Yue. Without another look at Wang's wife, she chatted with Liu Yue, even taking the girl's hands. Then she removed a red hairpin for her.

"I don't know why," she said, "but I feel close to you, as if we've met somewhere. Be sure to open the door when I come to pay a call on Zhuang Laoshi."

"You are Zhuang Laoshi's friend, and I'm sure you'd complain to him if I dared to refuse you. I would lose my standing here," Liu Yue said.

Xia Jie, who had been quiet, cut in: "Are you finished, you little tart? I've been waiting for you to play chess."

"You'll just have wait, then," Tang Wan'er said. "I'm going to pay my respects to his wife first."

"I should help out in the kitchen," Liu Yue said. "I'll go with you." In the kitchen she said to Niu Yueqing, "The guests are here, Dajie. Why don't you take a break and entertain them while I help Meng Laoshi?"

Zhou Min introduced Tang Wan'er to Niu Yueqing, who was brushing the ashes off her clothes. She froze at the sight of the radiant young woman. Liu Yue was a pretty girl with fine features, while Tang Wan'er had deep, small eyes and a narrow forehead, though her skin glowed. The hair at her temple, which was combed back, was so thick it almost looked false to Niu Yueqing; but a second look told her that she had been born with beautiful hair.

"So you're Tang Wan'er. We haven't met, but I've heard your name so many times, my ears are getting calluses. I've been asking Zhidie to take me to meet you, but I could never get away. Being with a celebrity means I'm kept busy while he's occupied from dawn to dusk, and yet I'm not quite sure what I've accomplished. On the other hand, I'm like a legless crab, so what else can I do but run around for his sake? As the saying goes, a woman depends on her man. She eats his food, so she goes where he goes."

"That's only half the saying," Meng said. "She eats his food, so she goes where he goes and fondles him in bed at night."

"You and your filthy mouth!" Niu Yueqing protested. "Don't forget you're a teacher to Wan'er, who is of a tender age. You compromise your dignity by saying things like that."

"She called me her teacher when we first met, but I'm not really her teacher, am I? We become equals once we get to know each other better. Didn't Zhidie refer to me as a teacher before he became famous? And now? Two years ago he started calling me Old Meng, last year it became Yunfang, and now I'm his cook. And you say Tang Wan'er is of a tender age? In fact, she has plenty of experience. Last month, on the way to Huayin County in the Mount Huayin foothills, where I was to give a talk on *The Book of Changes*, the bus made a late stop to let the passengers off to use the toilet. A youngster started to relieve himself as soon as he stepped down. When a mother and her daughter got off after him, she blocked the girl's view. 'You're disgusting,' she said. "Don't you know enough to stay out of sight when you're peeing?' The boy replied, 'Old Aunty, you're old enough for me to be a little boy to you, so what's the big deal?' The woman's daughter sneered, 'You say you're still a boy? Who are you fooling? Not with that tool. You must think I don't know anything?'"

Niu Yueqing picked up a broom and smacked him over the head before dragging Tang Wan'er out of the kitchen. "Ignore him. He's just running off at the mouth."

After sitting down with Wan'er, Niu Yueqing thanked her for the jade bracelet as she recalled Zhuang's comment about the absence of wrinkles on Tang's face. She took a closer look, and indeed there were none, so she asked her what she used on her face. "You've met Mrs. Wang, haven't you? Well, she told me to put cucumber slices on my face for fifteen minutes during the day and egg whites at night to tighten the skin and reduce the appearance of wrinkles."

"I don't use any of those," Wan'er said. "I'd rather eat the cucumbers and eggs. That's for people with money and leisure. I just use whatever cosmetics I can lay my hands on."

"I can't compete with natural beauty, no matter what I do. Besides, I have to take care of the house. It's not my nature to worry about my looks, even if I did have the time."

"You are an exemplary wife," Wan'er said emphatically. "You say you live for him, but everyone knows that his accomplishments actually owe a great deal to his superb helpmate. People out there refer to you as Zhuang Zhidie's wife, as a sign of respect and honor."

Wang Ximian's wife heard every word in the study and, annoyed, said to Xia Jie in a low voice, "That little tart is mocking me. What have I ever done to her?"

Xia Jie smiled and whispered to her the story of Wan'er and Zhou Min's elopement.

"Oh, my, I had no idea. I didn't mean what I just said. What a heartless woman, running off like that. Leaving her husband is one thing, but how could she bear to leave her child, her own flesh and blood?"

The talk went on like that until two o'clock, when Niu Yueqing set the table. Meng Yunfang laid out eight cold and eight hot dishes, four with meat and four without, plus a variety of alcoholic and non-alcoholic beverages, before getting everyone to take their seats after washing up. He announced that he would not sit with them, because of the alcohol and meat on the table; instead, he would enjoy his vegetarian fare in the kitchen.

"We thank you for your hard work, then," they said, raising their glasses in a toast. Zhuang toasted Wang's wife, Xia Jie, Zhou Min, Tang Wan'er, Zhao Jingwu, and Liu Yue.

"Me too?" Liu said. "I should be toasting you."

"We make no distinction for age or seniority at this table," Zhuang said.

"Even so, I should be last. You should toast your wife first."

"We have never toasted each other," Niu Yueqing said.

"Then you should do it today. Make it a cross-cup toast, like newlyweds at a wedding banquet," someone said.

"All right, then. We're an old married couple, but we'll do it for you," Niu Yueqing said as she looped her arm, cup in hand, through Zhuang's arm, which was met with laughter. Tang Wan'er laughed soundlessly as she cast an unhappy glance at the meddlesome Liu Yue, who was laughing merrily, her eyes on Tang, who ignored her and looked away to see a fly above a flowerpot on the windowsill. It flitted over and landed on the tip of Zhuang's ear. With a cup in his hand and his arm linked with Niu Yueqing's arm, he could only shoo the fly away by shaking his head. It stayed put. *If there is such a thing as divine intervention,* Wan'er mused, *let the fly land on my head.* To her amazement, it did just that, drawing a private smile from her as she sat motionless. Zhou Min saw the fly and blew on it, sending it flitting back and forth over the table, so upsetting Tang that she gave him a blistering look. Xia Jie, who was taking everything in, said, "After seeing the old married couple have their cross-cup toast, the young couple ought to do the same."

"Let's not complicate things. Let Zhuang Laoshi and his wife drink their toast," Tang said with a smile. She reached out to shoo away the fly, which had landed on a plate of pig's feet, sending it straight into Niu Yueqing's cup.

When Niu Yueqing looped arms with her husband, a dark shadow flickered between Tang Wan'er's brows. She was jealous. She noticed that although Niu Yueqing was getting on in years, she had the face of someone born into good fortune. She had heard that Zhuang's wife was a beauty, which was true, and yet she thought that all those fine features looked uninteresting on her face, like expensive ingredients that may not be tasty when cooked together. Then she thought some more about her own features; her skin was fairer, but her eyes were smaller, her nose was not as straight, and her mouth was bigger. But when everything was put together, her features overall looked better than Niu Yueqing's. Everyone froze when the fly fell into the hostess's cup, everyone but Tang, who was buoyed by the occurrence. "You should have a larger cup, Shimu," she said with a smile. "Here, take mine."

She swapped cups with Niu Yueqing, emptying the contents of the contaminated cup under the table. After finishing her toast with Zhuang, Yueqing was grateful to Wan'er and brought a bottle to refill her cup.

"These people all know each other, Wan'er, so I don't have to take care of them. You and Liu Yue, on the other hand, are new, so make yourselves at home. I'll be upset if you don't."

"Of course I will," Wan'er said. "Here's to you, Shimu. Since you couldn't make it to our place last time, I'll have you over in a few days."

They drank to each other. Not much of a drinker, Niu Yueqing felt her face burn after a couple of cups. Wan'er stopped her before she could go into the bedroom to check herself in a mirror.

"That red is more becoming on you than if you'd put rouge on your cheeks."

The women reached their limit after three rounds, while Zhou, Zhao, and Zhuang were unaffected.

"You're here today to drink, so don't disappoint me," Zhuang said. "Let's play a drinking game. We'll follow the old rules by taking turns reciting idioms."

"This is all new to me," Liu Yue said.

"New how?" Tang Wan'er asked her.

"Before I came here, I often wondered about life in an intellectual's house. Now that I'm here, I realize that you say all sorts of things, like ordinary people, but then you act differently at the table. When I went to dinners in the past, I saw people play finger-guessing games or a game of the weak fighting the strong. I've never heard of an idiom game. How does it work?"

"It's simple," Zhuang replied. "The first person offers an expression, and the next person has to use the ending to begin a new idiom. Homophones are acceptable. We keep it going until someone fails and has to drink a penalty."

"I'll get Meng Laoshi to play for me," Liu Yue said.

"You young people all have at least a high school education, Liu Yue," Niu Yueqing said. "So you should be able to follow along. I'm the only one who won't be able to."

Meng heard the exchange and spoke up from the kitchen, "As the saying goes, sleep with the master and you'll learn the tricks. So you have no excuse."

Niu Yueqing cursed Meng, as Zhuang announced the beginning of the game by offering the first expression, "Honored guests fill the hall," followed by Zhao, who said, "The hall is all gussied up," followed by Zhou Min's "Upward and onward," followed by Liu Yue's "Onward with Lord Ye, who loved dragons," followed by Xia Jie's "Dragons brought relieving rain," and by Wang's wife's "Rainy days are over."

"That won't do," Xia Jie objected. "'Rain' and 'rainy' aren't the same. Besides, you made it up."

"That's all right; it's acceptable." Zhuang said.

Tang Wan'er was next. She looked stuck and was deep in thought, her eyes fixed on Zhuang. Suddenly she said, "Over my dead body."

"Good," Zhuang said.

Next came Niu Yueqing, who said, "Body, body, body what? Bodyguard."

Everyone laughed, and someone said, "Bodyguard doesn't work. Drink up."

Niu Yueqing downed a cupful and started a new round. "I have one. Body and soul. Let's use that, body and soul."

Zhuang said, "Soul searching," followed by Zhao's "Searching high and low," Zhou Min's "Lo and behold," Liu Yue's "Behold the power of one," Xia Jie's "One of these days," Wang's wife's "Days of our lives," and Tang Wan'er's "Lives and deaths." That startled Zhuang, which made Tang laugh. The others joined in. She offered a new one, "Lives of fire."

"Good," Zhuang said.

"Good means not bad," Niu Yueqing said, to which the others objected. "That's not an expression. Drink up and we'll start over."

"Didn't I say this is not for me? Now I'm going to finish that bottle all by myself. Tang Wan'er comes before me and keeps giving me hard ones. I'm going to sit somewhere else."

"Come sit next to me, Dajie," Liu Yue said. "I will give you easy ones, and Tang Wan'er can make it hard on Zhuang Laoshi."

Niu Yueqing got up and sat next to Liu Yue. "Let me start again," she said. "Good fortune abounds like the open sky," followed by Xia Jie's "Sky's the limit," and so on. Yueqing was stumped again and picked up her cup to drink. The others commented on the hostess's honesty, but she was drinking all the liquor meant for the guests. She laughed as her body went limp; she grabbed the edge of the table, but her legs carried her body down.

"She's drunk." She was already on the floor. Some of the guests rushed over to offer tea and vinegar, but Zhuang said, "She'll be fine when she sleeps it off. Now that the hostess got drunk first, whoever loses must drink up—no exceptions. Xia Jie, it's your turn."

After finishing the vegetarian meal he'd made for himself, Meng Yunfang came out of the kitchen.

"What's the matter with you all?" he said. "What's with all those inauspicious expressions? I'll tell you what, you all take care of yourselves by picking up your cups and drinking toasts to each other. Then I'll bring you some hot food and rice."

They stood up and downed their drinks, their faces as red as peach blossoms, all except Zhou Min, whose face looked washed out. Meng brought out a table full of hot food, and when they had eaten their fill, he served a fish soup with dried longans. As everyone reached out with their spoons, Zhuang said, "Yueqing's performance today was the worst, so naturally she had to get drunk. Now we vote for the best performance and let that person have the first taste of the delicious soup."

"We won't object if you want Tang Wan'er to enjoy the soup first, so we can skip your little scheme," Xia Jie said.

"I didn't do as well as Xia Jie," Tang Wan'er said. "As a playwright and drama director, she has a ton of expressions in her belly."

"Oh, so that's what's in there. I've always thought her belly was a bit too big and told her to get up early each day to exercise," Meng quipped.

Xia Jie went over and pinched her husband's ear. "So you think I'm fat, do you? Got your eyes on some willow-waisted woman? You'd better come clean now."

With his ear in his wife's hand, Meng continued to eat. "It's a sign of love when this wife of mine hits me or yells at me."

"Let me see which of the men here has the biggest ears," Wan'er said, with her eyes on Zhuang. The others smiled knowingly. Pretending not to have heard her, he gave the first scoop of soup to Wang Ximian's wife instead of to Wan'er. Wang's wife dabbed her lips with a perfumed handkerchief when she was done. She put down her bowl; Wan'er and Xia Jie followed suit and put down theirs. Liu Yue got up to hand everyone a small plate of melon seeds before gathering up the dishes to wash in the kitchen. Zhuang told the guests to do whatever they pleased, including taking a rest in the room across from his study or reading in the study. Wang's wife asked for a glass of water to take her medicine, saying she had had too much to drink and would rest for a while. Xia Jie wanted to play a game of chess with Tang Wan'er, insisting that Zhou Min come along as their referee. Zhuang and Meng went into the living room.

"I want to talk to you about something, Zhidie," Meng said. "You gave the material from Abbess Huiming to Defu, who received the mayor's approval. Now that the nunnery has its property back, they're planning an expansion, and Huiming has been put in charge. She's immensely grateful to you and asked me several times to invite you to tea."

"That Huang Defu is a decent fellow. He should be invited to the nunnery, too."

"Of course, that would be great. I'm just not sure he'd go," Meng replied.

"He'd have to go if the invitation was from me."

"There's one more matter, an important one, that could be taken care of if he went. The nunnery also wanted to reclaim the area to the northeast, but it currently has a five-story building that houses many families. The mayor did not plan to return it to the nunnery, since it would be difficult to relocate the residents. Huiming has agreed to that decision, with one request about an empty three-room unit. She would like to have it serve as temporary lodging for their secular visitors, but the mayor was reluctant to agree. I've given it some thought. If he would give it to the nunnery, who would then let us use it, that would be ideal for anyone who wants a quiet place to write or paint for ten days or a couple of weeks. We could even meet there regularly, as a sort of literary salon. Wouldn't that be great?"

Zhuang was animated by the suggestion. "Sounds ideal. I'll talk to Defu. It shouldn't be a problem." He lowered his voice. "But you mustn't tell anyone but writers and artists. Don't forget that. Not even my wife, or she'd tell visitors to go see me there if I decided to use the place to do some writing."

"Got it," Meng said.

"I want your help in something else. Are you really familiar with hexagram divination?"

Meng responded with a swagger, "I'm not very good at the ancient occult theories, but I'm an expert in the common hexagram divination."

"Keep your voice down. Do one for me if you really know how."

"What happened? Why do you need divination?" Meng asked quietly.

"You don't need to know now. I won't tell you if nothing happens with what I'm thinking. But if it does, then I'll need your help."

Meng said they'd need milfoil, the most effective medium in divination. He had a bunch that someone had brought back from Henan for him, but he'd have to go home to get it.

"Are you looking for an excuse because you're really not that good?"

"All right, then, I'll use matchsticks instead." Meng removed forty-nine matches from a box and told Zhuang to put his palms together. He told him to randomly divide the matches into two piles, then he moved the sticks around some more and gathered them up. After taking away the odd one, he told Zhuang to divide the sticks into two piles again. The process was repeated six times, during which he was chanting an incantation the whole time—Yin, Yang, Old Yin, Young Yang. Eventually he looked up at Zhuang and said, "What's this all about? It's very complicated."

"You tell me; you're the divination master."

"Judging by what's been happening in recent years, I'd say your star is on the rise and shines so brightly it could blind anyone, but this is clearly a stagnation symbol. Tell me when you were born."

Zhuang told him.

"You were born under the water sign and that's fine. But if what you want to know about is an object, which is wood 木 oriented, put that in a box, 口, and you get the stagnation symbol 困. If what you want to know about is a person 人, put that in a box and you get the sign for imprisonment 囚."

The color drained from Zhuang's face, as he said, "Naturally, it's about a person."

"That would give you the sign for imprisonment, either jail or sanctions. But luckily you have water in your karma, which, when put alongside the symbol for imprisonment 泅, means you can swim away and be rescued. However, you will be rescued only if you can keep yourself afloat. If not, you could be in serious trouble."

"This is all rubbish," Zhuang responded, before getting up to refill Meng's teacup, his mind filled with trepidation.

⁂

Xia Jie and Tang Wan'er played three rounds of chess, and Tang lost each time. But she refused to accept defeat and insisted on playing more. Then a cry sounded in the bedroom. Zhuang had just added water to the teapot and put it on the stove when he heard it, so he plopped the teapot down carelessly, dousing the fire and sending steam swirling in the kitchen. With no time to pick up the pot, he ran into the bedroom, where a sweat-drenched Niu Yueqing was sitting on the rug atop the bed mat that had slid down with her. By then everyone had crowded into the room to see what was wrong. Still frightened, Niu Yueqing said, "I had a bad dream."

The others breathed a sigh of relief and laughed.

"You nearly took our souls with you. Not even the meal you treated us to pays for what you just did to us," someone said.

Embarrassed, she got up off the floor and tidied her hair at the mirror. "It was a terrifying dream."

"What was it about? The Japanese devils coming to your village?" Meng asked.

"I don't remember now."

The others laughed again; she shook her head.

"I do recall bits and pieces. It seemed like Zhidie and I were on a bus when we saw smoke. Someone was shouting about explosives and everyone was jumping off, including us. We ran. He was so much faster, so I told him to wait up, but he wouldn't. Eventually I reached a cliff and was safe; then he came up to say we were lucky to escape. I refused to talk to him, since he'd cared only about himself when we were in trouble."

Wang's wife and Xia looked over at Zhuang.

"What are you looking at me for? Do you think I'm really that bad?"

They all had a good laugh, and Niu Yueqing added: "So I shoved him away, and guess what: I pushed him off the cliff."

"Great. So you got even. He left you behind, so you pushed him off the cliff," Xia Jie said. "In my opinion, you were embarrassed about getting drunk in front of your guests and falling asleep, so you made up a story to save face when you woke up."

"I was scared witless, don't make fun of me. I wasn't really drunk. I'm good for another round."

"We all know what you're good for," Zhuang said. "It's not every day that we're all together, so why don't we take some pictures?"

Tang Wan'er was the first to concur. Zhao first took a picture of Zhuang Zhidie and Niu Yueqing, after which Wan'er stood behind the couple and rested her head on Niu Yueqing's shoulder.

"One of the three of us. Just like this."

Photos of various combinations followed, and they quickly finished a roll of film. After enjoying the lively scene for a while, Zhou Min got anxious and left, telling his hosts he shouldn't spend too much time away from the office, since he was new there.

His face was burning from too much alcohol and from his rush to get to work now that he was already late. He stopped midway to buy a bottle of sour plum juice, which refreshed him. Groups of people were gathered in the yard talking about something when he reached the office. Being a newcomer, and a temporary hire at that, he had made up his mind to form a solid base from which to begin a new life. He was fast on his feet and amiable in his speech, treating everyone with respect.

"Speak of the devil," someone said. "That's him."

Zhou smiled and started to walk away when someone came up to him.

"You're quite something, Zhou Min."

"Not really," he said. "I still need help from all of you."

"You're too modest. Is that something you got from Zhuang Zhidie? He's always telling people he has nothing to write about, and yet he can produce a novel after disappearing for only a few days. The more you praise his work, the more he says he just knocks it out. To be honest, he may be a good writer, but he has yet to give us something the people in this office want to read first and then argue about. This article of yours is explosive."

"Have you all read it?" he asked.

"We have. Even illiterate Old Shi in the boiler room asked someone to read it to him. We hear that Jing Xueyin did not go straight home after getting off the plane, that she and her husband went to see the department head. She was crying and made a scene, though we had no idea why. She looks so prim and proper every day, but now we know she once tried to seduce a writer! But why didn't she marry him? Because she thought he wasn't a good match. Now she regrets her choice, and her shame has turned into anger now that the truth is out. She can't recognize a person's true worth, so she lost the gold ring. All she knows is how to climb the official ladder, just like her parents."

Zhou stormed up the stairs before the man was finished. He opened the door to the office and saw that everyone in the editorial section, except Zhong Weixian, was there, screaming and cursing.

"Are we in trouble?" Zhou asked.

"We won't go if that's what the woman wants." Li Hongwen was still fuming. "She's only mid-level leadership, what can she do to us?"

"Just because her old man was a high-ranking cadre doesn't mean she can lord it over us like that," Gou Dahai said. "She should look at the reactions of the masses. Our magazine is for society at large, not for her alone."

Zhou realized that Jing Xueyin had been to the editorial office to vent her anger, and that this was something that would not easily be smoothed over.

"When did she come back? Zhuang Laoshi said that we should keep an eye on her return schedule and take a copy of the magazine over to explain to her the moment she got back. Did anyone go?" he asked.

"When the magazines arrived yesterday afternoon, Wu Kun grabbed one as if it had been sent down from heaven, and then he went to see Jing's husband last night. Who knows what evil wind he stirred up, but the husband came to see the department head early this morning. Then he returned with his wife after her plane landed. The guy kept saying that as Jing's husband, he was taking the matter very seriously even if no one else was. Hell! Who knows what was going on with Wu Kun and his wife, but he puffed out his chest as if he were a real man."

Zhou felt like a deflated balloon, while the good food and liquor he had consumed at lunch rose up. *You see a ghost when you're afraid of ghosts*, he said to himself. *A rope breaks at the weakest spot*. He realized not only that he had caused a major headache for Zhuang, but that, as a temporary hire, he might not be able to keep his job.

"Where's Mr. Zhong?" he asked Li.

"The department head summoned him."

Zhong returned a short while later, and when he saw Zhou, he said: "So there you are."

"I'm so sorry I've let everyone down, Mr. Zhong."

"Nonsense. This is not about who you've let down. Now that it's come to this, there's no need to assign blame. We must think about our writers and the magazine first. Besides, this impacts Zhuang Zhidie's reputation. He's a celebrity, and we need for him to submit manuscripts in the future." When Zhong took off his glasses, his eyes were bloodshot. He rubbed them but failed to remove the sleep in the corners before putting the glasses back on.

"I know all this, but now it's gotten out of hand. Jing came at noon to raise hell, but I refused to acknowledge any wrongdoing on our part, so she immediately went to see Lieutenant Governor Qu, who is in charge of cultural affairs. He turned the matter over to the propaganda chief, who sent her to our department head with a letter that included three directives: One, the author and the editorial office must admit that the romance between Jing and Zhuang was pure fabrication and slanderous gossip that seriously damages Jing's reputation, and they must apologize to her in person, in addition to clarifying the matter at a department meeting. Two, the magazine will be suspended and restructured, while the issue will be recalled. An announcement in the next issue will publicize the serious lack of truth in the article and forbid any reprinting. Three, the author will not be paid for the article and will receive no bonus for the present quarter."

"What kind of leadership is that?" Li was outraged. "Did he investigate before giving these orders? And the department accepted the judgment?"

"Who would dare argue with the order, no matter how unhappy they might be?"

"They're afraid of losing their jobs," Gou said. "So the magazine will do what they say. You have to speak up, Zhong Weixian. You're not afraid of losing your position, are you? It's a shitty position anyway, not even at the section level, more like a county head."

"No need to get angry, everyone. Let's calm down and think this over," Zhong said. "Tell me the truth, Zhou Min. Is everything you wrote in that article true?"

"Of course it is."

"There's no law against a romantic liaison before marriage," Li said. "Besides, it's between two consenting adults. I can't guarantee that what Zhou Min wrote is absolutely true, but then who can say it isn't? Jing Xueyin was adamant in her denial, so she will have to present proof that it isn't true. The article said she gave Zhuang Zhidie an antique pottery pot, which I've seen in his study. Does she want to deny that, too?"

"Give me a cigarette," said Zhong.

Gou fumbled in his pocket before producing a cigarette and handing it to Zhong, who was not a smoker. He lit up, took a drag, and immediately started coughing. "I'm going to present our objections to a higher authority and try to get the three directives rescinded. Don't say anything if anyone mentions the article; just pretend it's no big deal. But I want you all to come to work on time every day so we can put our heads together if necessary." He went to his new office. On his way out, however, he banged his head against the door, stumbled, and knocked over a spittoon in a corner, sending its filthy contents all over the floor.

"When your luck stinks, even a fart will hit you in your heel," he cursed.

Li Hongwen laughed. "Watch where you're going, Old Zhong." He shut the door and continued, "Zhuang Zhidie is a true genius in his writing, but a perfect idiot when it comes to women. Jing Xueyin probably made a fuss because nothing happened between them; or she wanted Zhuang to ravish her but he didn't, so she's borne a grudge all these years. Now that her feelings for him have been exposed, she blows up."

"Ravish is the right word. But why was she upset when he didn't ravish her?" Gou asked.

"You're still single, so you wouldn't understand," Li replied.

"I've had more romantic relationships than you," Gou said.

"But they all came to nothing. Have you ever thought about why? If you don't ravish a woman you're in love with, she'll think you aren't a man. Got that?" Li said.

"You have experience in this, Zhou Min. What do you think?"

Zhou thought it over and nodded.

"If Zhuang Zhidie had ravished Jing Xueyin years ago, would she be raising hell now, even if she weren't married?" Li was talking a blue streak when a knock was heard at the door. He shut up and went to open the door. It was Zhong Weixian.

"I thought of something we must be careful about," Zhong said. "Over the next few days, if you run into Jing, make sure to be nice and don't say anything nasty. Don't react even if she tries to provoke you. If we do, it will only make things worse."

"You were a Rightist, you can do that," Li said. "I can't."

"I've always gone along with you, but this time you have to listen to me," Zhong said as he walked off.

"That's really uncalled for, Hongwen. The old man is in such terrible shape, you shouldn't be making things even harder on him," Gou said.

"I think you'll have to get more involved or get Zhuang Zhidie to work on this," Li said. "Old Zhong can't make things worse, but he can't make them better, either. He's been weak his whole life, but he's now become a real coward, and we'll be in serious trouble if we pin our hopes on him."

Disconcerted by what he heard, Zhou Min wanted to ask for advice, but Li sat down and took out a bottle of hair tonic to rub on his scalp. He asked Gou if he saw any new growth.

"Maybe three new strands," Gou replied as the crackle of firecrackers sounded outside.

Zhong ran in. "Who's setting off firecrackers?"

Li, Gou, and Zhou all ran to the balcony, but Zhong said, "Dahai, you go check it out. It would be too obvious if all three of you were out there. Everyone in the Department of Culture is watching us, you know."

Gou went to take a look and came back to say, "The second window on the west side of the third floor. When they saw me looking down, some people held up a newspaper that said 'Bravo to the Magazine.'"

Zhong's face darkened. "Those people never liked Jing Xueyin and questioned how she was qualified to be promoted to mid-level leadership, but the department ignored them, so they're using us to vent their anger." He told Gou to go down and stop them before they caused any more trouble. Li offered to go instead. He quickly returned, looking pale, as he told everyone that Wu Kun had taken his bureau chief to watch the fireworks display, raising a fuss about the current state of the Department of Culture. Wu Kun even complained that the previous editorial committee had been disbanded in vain, since the new team had failed to promote stability and unity. Zhong was outraged.

"Even if the magazine is shut down, that fucking Wu Kun has no chance of landing on his feet. Give me a cigarette."

Gou Dahai didn't have one to give him, so he went to the door to pick up a cigarette butt, but they were all soaking in dirty water.

Niu Yueqing went to Wang Ximian's house for the cash. Wary of walking around with that much money, she asked Liu Yue to go with her. As a precaution, they changed into old clothes. Niu Yueqing put the money under some cabbage leaves in a shopping basket; Liu Yue walked three steps behind, gripping a rock so tightly that her palm was sweaty. They walked down East Avenue, past the post office near the clock tower, where a billboard advertised "The latest issue of *Xijing Magazine*, with an exclusive exposé of a secret affair by the celebrated writer Zhuang Zhidie." Niu Yueqing stopped, crouched down, and set the basket between her legs. She told Liu Yue to buy a copy. She began reading and was soon breathing hard, her face dark. Not knowing what was in the magazine, Liu Yue knew better than to ask. They went home, but Zhuang was still out, so Niu Yueqing went to bed alone, so rattling Liu Yue that she didn't know what to cook. She went in and asked Niu Yueqing.

"Anything," was the answer.

What exactly was anything? Liu Yue decided to make fried millet cakes, her best dish—stir-fry some shredded potatoes and add half a pot of rice with dates. Night had fallen when she was finished, so she sat down in the living room, but was quickly bored. She stepped outside for some fresh air, just as Zhuang rode up on his scooter.

He was returning from the camera store, after passing the two-hour wait for the film to be developed by watching four old women play cards by the side of the road. All of them were wearing glasses, and they interrupted their play by talking to someone across the street, a big-boned woman with high cheekbones and a pointed mouth. She was drying persimmons on the mat in front of her door. They smelled bad to Zhuang, lacking a sweet aroma. When one of the old women saw Zhuang looking across the street, she blinked and said: "You don't think she looks like much, do you? But she's a rich lady who plays cards in her free time with money she keeps stuffed in her bra. She has piles of money in there."

"What does she do to have so much money?" Zhuang asked.

"She's from Mount Zhongnan. She rents this storefront to sell dried persimmons dusted with talcum powder that she passes off as a powdered sugar."

"That's terrible," he said. "Won't that cause diarrhea?"

"No one stops her. Want to ask her about it? Ma Xiangxiang," she shouted across the street, "this comrade wants to talk to you."

The ugly woman stopped to look at Zhuang. "Want some dried persimmons?"

"The sugar on your persimmons looks awfully white. Could it possibly be talcum powder?"

"What do you do?"

"I'm with the Writers' Association, the Zuoxie."

"Zuoxie, oh, a shoemaker," she said, mishearing his words. You guys all take shortcuts with your shoes. I bought this pair last week, and the front's already come unglued."

"Not a shoemaker. I'm a writer. You know what a newspaper office is, don't you? Well, Zuoxie is like that."

The woman picked up the tray of persimmons, turned around, walked inside, and locked the door behind her, making all the old women laugh.

"What's not fake these days?" one of them said. "Do you believe you can bite your own ears?"

"I think I could if I had a ladder," Zhuang replied.

"Ah, so you're a clown. I'll show you how I do it." She opened her mouth to reveal two rows of shiny white teeth, which she nudged with her tongue into her hand and put around her ear. Zhuang laughed.

"Cosmetic surgery is all the rage nowadays," she said. "You can have fake eyebrows and fake noses. I even heard of fake breasts and fake buttocks. You can't tell what's real and what's fake on the girls walking around these days."

The humor and witty comments kept Zhuang around for a while before he checked his watch and saw that more than two hours had passed. He said good-bye and left for the camera shop. As he walked away, one of the women said, "He could be fake, too."

Zhuang overheard her comment and began to wonder. Recalling what he had done with Tang Wan'er, which seemed like a dream now, he had the nagging feeling that he might not be Zhuang Zhidie after all. If he was, how would a coward like him have the nerve to do something so daring? If he wasn't, then who was he? He paused to light a cigarette, and for the first time in his life, he noticed that the shadow of his cigarette smoke was not grayish-black, but dark red. Abruptly turning his head, he saw an elongated figure jump to the base of a wall, a sight so startling it gave him goose bumps. But when he looked closer, he realized it was his shadow, cast onto the wall by the reflection of sunlight from the opened glass door of a store. Not a man who was afraid of ghosts or the supernatural, he was nonetheless scared by his own shadow. He looked around to make sure that no one had seen his jittery state before rushing over to pick up his photos. He had another shock when he looked at the pictures of himself with Niu Yueqing and Tang Wan'er. Everything in his living room—the table and chairs, even the jade carving on the screens—had come out nice and clear, but the people were so faint they might as well have been invisible. Tang Wan'er and Niu Yueqing looked like disembodied heads set atop two pairs of shoulders. Everyone else looked the same in all the other photos. He asked the clerk what had happened, only to be scolded for bringing in negatives like that, complaining that it could ruin the shop's reputation. Not daring to say more, Zhuang walked out, only to find that he could not start his scooter; he had no choice but to push it home, feeling quite dazed.

When Liu Yue saw him, she asked where he had been. He told her he had gone to have the photos developed. She asked to see them, complaining that she wasn't photogenic. Zhao Jingwu had told her that a photo alone would not be enough in seeking a husband, and that she had to meet the man in person. Zhuang was reluctant to show them to her—she was too eager—so he put her off by lying that they weren't ready. Her excitement dampened, she lowered her voice to tell him that Niu Yueqing was so upset over a magazine that she'd gone to bed. Feeling suddenly drained, he put the photos out of his mind and took the magazine to read in his study. He emerged a while later, smiled at Liu Yue, and said softly, "Get her up for dinner."

"I don't dare."

He paused before walking into the bedroom.

Niu Yueqing was asleep, wrapped in a terrycloth blanket, with a rush fan over her face.

"Why are you in bed at this hour?" Zhuang shook her. "Get up, it's dinnertime."

She ignored him. Zhuang tugged at her again. She rolled onto her back, but her eyes remained tightly shut. Liu Yue was standing at the door, stifling a giggle with her hand.

"Yueqing. Stop pretending to be asleep," Zhuang said. She didn't move. As if to see whether she was breathing, he put his hand under her nose. She snapped into a sitting position.

"I didn't feel any warm air," he said with a laugh, "so I thought you were dead."

"You wish!"

"Go check the weather, Liu Yue, and see why it's suddenly windy and rainy on a clear day."

"The sheets are drying on the balcony," Niu Yueqing said.

Liu Yue laughed as she disappeared into the kitchen. Realizing what Zhuang had been getting at, Niu Yueqing also laughed, but quickly frowned and cursed him: "You really know how to stir up trouble, don't you? Are you proud of your past? Are you trying to prove how carefree you can be by showing off a romantic liaison with a famous person?"

"You must have read the article by Zhou Min," he said. "It's pure rubbish. You know all about what happened between Jing Xueyin and me."

"Then why did you allow him to write it?"

"I had no idea he was going to write about this. You know I never read articles like that. I just thought he was new in town and could use me as his material to get started. I would never have allowed it to be published if I had known this was what he had in mind."

"Yes, he's new, so how did he come to know so much?"

"Maybe he heard Yunfang and others gossiping about me."

"But that could only have come from you. She's the daughter of a high-ranking cadre, and you were probably bragging about an affair with her to bolster your image."

"Do I need her to raise my status?"

"Now I see. You didn't end your relationship with her, and now you talk about it for vicarious gratification." Niu Yueqing was getting progressively angrier and was soon in tears.

Liu Yue ran in from the kitchen when she heard them arguing.

"Don't be upset, Dajie. There's no need to be unhappy. Zhuang Laoshi is a celebrity, and things like this happen to famous people all the time. It's no big deal."

"You make it sound as if it really did happen, Liu Yue," Zhuang said. Niu Yueqing smiled as she took the girl in her arms.

"Liu Yue is new here and is right to laugh at us for fighting."

"We often bite our tongues, and every couple fights," Liu Yue said. "With my previous employers, the husband had a woman outside, and someone told the wife. She said she didn't care, so long as the money he earned came to her, not to anyone else."

Niu Yueqing laughed as she pinched the girl's mouth.

"All right, you're not angry anymore, so let's eat," Liu Yue said.

"It doesn't really bother me, it's just that your Zhuang Laoshi's reputation will suffer. But I know he's not like that. He may be an adulterer in his mind, but he doesn't have either the nerve or the muscle to actually do something. I don't believe anything people say about him. What really bothers me is how he can brag when he's in a good mood without any regard for the consequences." There were more tears. Liu Yue was about to say something when they heard a knock at the door. Quickly drying her eyes, Niu Yueqing signaled Zhuang to go into his study.

"Who is it?" she called out.

"It's me, Zhou Min."

Niu Yueqing opened the door with a smile. "Didn't you go home after work? Well, you came at the right time, you can join us for dinner."

Zhou said he had gotten off early and had eaten at home. He was in the habit of strolling by the city wall in the mornings and evenings, so he had stopped by on the way. Zhuang came out of the study and said he was glad that Zhou had dropped by. He invited him to stay for a fried millet cake. Zhou begged off, so Zhuang put a tape into the cassette player for Zhou to enjoy some music while he sat down with Niu Yueqing and Liu Yue for dinner.

When Zhou heard that it was a recording of *The Butterfly Lovers*, he asked Zhuang whether he enjoyed folk music.

His mouth full, Zhuang just nodded.

"I have another tape," he said a moment later. "The quality is poor, but it's wonderful music." He changed the tape. Deep, slow, lingering music spread out like water.

"That is an instrument called the xun. Where did you get it?" Zhou asked.

Proudly, Zhuang replied, "Have you noticed that someone often plays the instrument in the mornings and evenings on the city wall? One night I went out and recorded it from a distance, which is why it sounds fuzzy. But if you close your eyes and imagine you're there, you'll feel as if you were in a primitive world, with pining ghosts and will-o-the-wisp sparks.

You enter a pitch-black ancient forest and can hear a dewdrop rolling slowly down a branch, where it hangs precariously before crashing to the ground. You sense something fearful and mysterious, but can't suppress your fervent desire to explore. You walk deeper into the forest, where you see miasma surging, followed by spiky rays of sunlight slanting in through the tree branches and miasma. But you can no longer find your way back." Zhuang was so caught up in his narration that he laid down his rice bowl.

"Is that a lyrical poem, Zhuang Laoshi?" Liu Yue asked.

Zhuang saw Zhou lower his head. "Doesn't it make you feel that way, Zhou Min?"

"That's me playing the xun, Zhuang Laoshi."

Zhuang let out a soft cry, his mouth hanging open. Niu Yueqing and Liu Yue stopped eating.

"I was just playing it to pass the time. I never expected you to hear it. But if you really like it, I will make a better recording for you another day. What I don't get is, you're a celebrity now and can have anything you want. Whatever you set your mind on will be yours, and yet you like xun music." When he finished, he took a small black clay object from his bag and told them that it was a xun. Zhuang, who had heard the sound but never seen the instrument, took it and marveled over how unique it was. He asked Zhou where he had bought it, adding that he had inquired at a musical instrument shop, but the salesperson did not even know what a xun was. Zhou Min said it was an ancient instrument that few people played these days. He had studied with an old folk musician in Tongguan after hearing the man play. Later, when he came to Xijing, he dug the instrument out while he was working at the Clear Void Nunnery; he was the only one who knew what it was, so he kept it out of sight before he went up to the city wall to practice, playing whatever came to mind. They carried on a spirited conversation.

"I don't know why," Zhuang said, "but here's some music I really like. I bought a tape of it. I'll play it for you. It's quite intense." He put it in the tape deck, from which emerged funereal music. Niu Yueqing came up and stopped it. "Who ever heard of enjoying this?"

"Be patient and listen. You'll like it when it begins to speak to you," Zhuang said.

"I'll never like it. People are going to think someone in our family died when you play that."

With an unhappy smile, Zhuang turned off the cassette player and sat down to eat.

"So Zhuang Laoshi is henpecked?"

"I'm not. It's just that she's not cowed by me."

Niu Yueqing ignored his response, so he muttered, "This is good porridge." He laid down his chopsticks and asked Zhou if he was free to go see Meng Yunfang.

Zhou looked uncomfortable as he hemmed and hawed. "Actually, I do want to talk to you about something, but I'll wait until you're done eating."

"I'm done, so go ahead."

"I thought I'd repay your kindness with some of my own, which is why I wrote the article. I wanted to promote you, and never expected to cause so much trouble. Jing Xueyin has raised a fuss. The higher-ups in the department may come to you for verification, so I'm here to see what you have to say."

"Zhuang Laoshi and I have read the article," Niu Yueqing said, sending Zhou into a minor panic.

"So you've read it, too, Shimu?"

"Don't go looking for trouble when everything is fine," she said. "And don't be afraid if trouble arises. If anyone should be raising a fuss, it's me, not her. Zhuang Zhidie did not write that article, but shouldn't she at least keep Zhuang in mind? Like they say, show some respect to Buddha if not to the monk. Don't past feelings mean anything to her?"

Ignoring what Niu Yueqing said, Zhuang frowned and asked Zhou to give him a detailed account of what was happening at the department and the magazine. "I said repeatedly that you must go explain things to her the moment she came back." He sighed. "Why didn't anyone pay attention? Now that she's raising hell, her enemies will gossip and gloat over the situation. And then there's Wu Kun, who's adding fuel to the fire, using her husband to pressure her. Self-esteem requires her to complain; otherwise, people would take her silence as an admission. Now that she has created such an uproar, they probably won't let it quietly pass. No one has ever been able to get an advantage over her. As someone who has been a proud person all her life, she can't just back down, like a stone rolling downhill."

"Now that the woman has turned hostile, why look at it only from her perspective?" Niu Yueqing said. "Subjectively speaking, there's nothing bad about the publication of Zhou's article. What you just said could make many people lose heart and cause a ripple effect."

Zhuang felt anger rising inside, but he held his temper and said, "So what do I do?"

"If someone from the department comes to check with you, all you need to do is insist that everything in the article is true," Zhou said. "You can even say—this probably is something Shimu would not like to hear . . ."

"Go ahead, say it," Niu Yueqing said.

"You can say you and she were intimate, but that the article stopped short of saying so. This is common in romantic liaisons—he said, she said, where are you going to find a witness? Once the water is muddied, no one can clear it up."

Zhuang jumped to his feet, looking very stern. "How could you come up with such a nutty idea? This is not about taking responsibility for your own words, but about having a clear conscience."

"Don't ever say that, Zhou Min," Niu Yueqing added. "Unlike you and me, Zhuang Laoshi must think about his status in society. If that got out and was passed around, he would be no different than a hooligan and one of Xijing's idlers. And what would I say to people?"

Zhou's face reddened at the reproach. He slapped himself, saying that he must have lost his head to come up with such a repellent idea. He was so inexperienced, he had been scared witless when he learned of the directives from the Provincial Office, and he begged forgiveness from Laoshi and Shimu. Still irate, Zhuang grabbed a teacup and put it up to his lips before realizing it was empty; he put it down and looked away. Niu Yueqing came over to pour tea for both of them.

"No need for that, Zhou Min," she said. "Zhuang Laoshi understands, so no more talk about forgiveness, all right? It upsets us when you go on like that."

Looking contrite, Zhou said, "I'd never say that to anyone else. What do we do, then?"

"I don't know," Zhuang said. "But I'll never admit that she and I were in love."

"That's all in the past," Niu Yueqing said. "I don't care whether you were in love or not, because it happened before we met. I didn't want to say anything, but you two did not have a clean break. It went on after you and I were engaged. I wasn't blind, I saw everything. I even told you not to see her again, but you were always defending her, even though it hurt my feelings. I thought she was a noble person who had strong feelings for you, but now we know that she could push you over a cliff or down a well."

"Are you finished?" Zhuang said. "You're only making it worse."

"You probably think I'm jealous, don't you? I just feel sorry for you."

Liu Yue tried to smooth things over while Zhou blamed himself.

"I've put up with a lot," Niu Yueqing said, "but I'm disappointed that you're not angry or upset with her even now. How can you explain your relationship if it wasn't love?"

"We were comrades, friends," Zhuang said.

"If that's the case, then why didn't what was in the article happen between you and someone else at the magazine?"

"We were just closer than most comrades and friends."

"I'll go along with whatever you say. But are you being realistic? What was written reeks of a true romance, so the magazine and Zhou Min will suffer if you insist upon your denial. Then what will people say about you? They'll say Zhuang Zhidie can sacrifice friends who support and promote him on account of a woman."

"Are you forcing me into an admission?"

"You treat something considered trash by others as treasure, which can only mean you're still thinking about her. So go ahead and do whatever you want." She turned to Zhou and said, "Go tell Zhong Weixian and the others that you all deserve to suffer because you wanted to promote Zhuang Zhidie. You should pack up your things and return to your job at the nunnery tomorrow." She got up and went into the bedroom.

Zhuang paced the living room with a sour look on his face, while Zhou looked on blankly, unsure of what to do. Pained by the sight, Liu Yue went into the kitchen and brought out a plate of plums for Zhou Min, who did not want one, despite her insistence. They went back and forth until Zhuang came over, picked one up for Zhou, and took one for himself.

"Here's what I think we can do. You insist that what you wrote was based on truth, and you can even say it came from me. But I didn't say it was between Jing and me; it was based on what has happened between me and all the women I've known. What you wrote could be about Jing Xueyin, but it could also be about someone else entirely. It was a realist piece based on the principles of literary creation. You gathered material, generalized and summed up what happened between me and all those women, and then represented the scenario through this symbolic image called X. Would that work? That way you can be free of responsibility, no matter what accusations they hurl at you."

Zhou thought over the suggestion. "All right," he said, "that's what I'll do." He bade them good-bye and left.

Niu Yueqing knew that Zhou had left when she heard the door open, so she called out from the bedroom, "In here, Zhidie."

Zhuang opened the door to see his wife leaning against the bed as she wiped her face with facial cleanser.

"You're amazing!" he said. "Instead of dealing with Zhou Min's mistake when he was here, you decided to go off on something else. What will he think of me now? He's going to say I'd sacrifice him and others in the magazine."

"Would you have come up with that idea of yours if I hadn't?"

"What do you know about Zhou Min? We have just met, after all. I wasn't too happy when he used my name to get a job at the magazine, and now he's stirred up so much trouble, and yet you're on his side. What can I say to Jing Xueyin when I see her?"

"Oh. So you're still thinking about seeing her?"

With a curse, Zhuang shut the bedroom door and went into the living room to smoke. He heard the faint sound of a xun. When it finally stopped, he told Liu Yue, who was dozing on the sofa, to go to bed, while he stayed in the living room and inserted the funereal tape in the player. Keeping the volume low, he turned off the light to immerse himself, body and soul, in a state that even he found hard to explain.

❋

Over the next few days, Zhou Min left early in the morning and returned home late at night, not straying from the magazine. At home he had little time for Tang Wan'er. Always itching to go somewhere, she complained that they hadn't been to the Sheraton Dance Club for a long time, but he kept putting her off. She told him that Zhuang Laoshi had opened a bookstore to the left of the Forest of Steles Museum and said they should go check it out, see what sort of books they stocked, and show Zhuang Laoshi that they cared about what he was doing. Zhou replied impatiently, "I don't have time for that. You can go if you want." He did nothing but play the xun on the city wall and sleep. Upset, she ignored him. When he left for work in the morning, instead of going out on her own, she stayed home and tended to her appearance, putting on perfumed rouge and painting her brows thin and smooth. She kept her ears pricked, thinking it was Zhuang coming to see her every time the metal ring on the door made a noise. When they had made love that first time, she was elated that the barrier between them had been removed. As she thought about how she was now his, her face burned and she got hot all over from arousal; when she saw how the people passing by the door outside looked indifferently at the pear tree, she laughed coldly as her anger rose: *Just you wait, one of these days you'll know what I mean to Zhuang Zhidie. Then I'll watch you come fawning over me and embarrass you until you look for a place to hide.* But it had been so long, and Zhuang had not shown up again, so she vented her anger on herself by mussing her hair and by pressing her lips on the mirror and the door to leave red circles. That night, the moon was as bright as water. As usual, Zhou Min went to the city wall to play his xun. Wan'er shut the gate and went in to take a bath. Then, draping her nightgown over her naked body, she went out and sat on the lounge chair under the pear tree. Utterly lonely, she thought about Zhuang Zhidie: *Why don't you come? Were you, like all the other men, just satisfying a sudden urge that day and put me out of your mind once it was over? Did you simply want the memory of another woman added to your list of conquests? Or, as a writer, did you merely use me as material for something you were writing?* She thought some more, and as she savored the memory of that day, she retracted her earlier thoughts. He would not be like that. The look in his eyes when he first saw her, his timid approach, and his madly urgent behavior when they were together gave her the confidence that he was truly fond of her. Her first sexual encounter had been with a manual laborer, who had forced her down on the bed, and that had led to their marriage. After the wedding, she was his land and he was her plow; she had to submit to him whenever he felt like cultivating his land. He would climb on with no preamble and finish before she felt a thing. With Zhou Min, she naturally enjoyed what she hadn't had with her first man, but Zhou was, after all, a small-town character who could never compare with a Xijing celebrity. Zhuang had started out shyly, but once he entered port, he was immensely loving and tender; his many tricks and techniques had finally taught her the difference between the city and the countryside, and between one who was knowledgeable and one who was not. She came to know what makes a real man and a real woman. She touched herself as she followed this line of thought, until she began to moan and groan, calling out to Zhuang. She was writhing and squirming on the chair. □□ □□ □□ [The author has deleted 37 words.] The chair creaked and inched slowly toward the pear tree; squinting at the moon through the branches, she fantasized that it was Zhuang's face. As she flicked her tongue, she wrapped her legs around Zhuang until she was up against the tree trunk, where she moved, rocking the tree and swaying the moon, until one final, forceful push of her body before she went limp. Three or four pear leaves circled above her and then settled onto her body. Exhausted, she remained in the chair, lost in thought, so weak it felt as if all her bones had been removed.

"You're still up?" Zhou Min remarked when he returned from playing the xun.

"Yes." Without getting up, she brushed the leaves off her body and adjusted her nightgown to cover her legs. Zhou cast a bored look at the moon. "The moon is pretty tonight."

"Yes," she said, wondering what Zhuang was doing at that moment. Was he reading in his study or was he already in bed? *Zhuang-ge*, she said silently, *I must be away from you for now, for I have to be with another soul under these eaves. Keep your door open so the wind can blow in your direction and maybe startle you awake, possibly because of the soft noise. But don't move, my Zhuang Zhidie. Close your eyes and let us begin our conversation.*

When Zhou saw her still lying there after he had washed his face in the kitchen, he said, "Why aren't you coming to bed?"

"Stop annoying me!" she said angrily. "You talk too much. Go to bed if you want." She shuffled in her slippers out to the gate.

"Are you going out? It's late," he said.

"I can't sleep. I'm going to buy some ice cream at the street corner."

"In your nightgown?"

In her simple white nightgown, she disappeared through the gate and walked out to the lane.

Instead of buying ice cream, she borrowed the store's phone and called Zhuang's house. Liu Yue answered. When she asked who was calling, Tang Wan'er wondered why Liu could not recognize her voice. She asked after Zhuang and his wife.

"Ah, it's you." Liu Yue was happy to hear Wan'er's voice. "It's late. Are you all right?"

"Everything is fine," Wan'er said. "I was just wondering if there's any heavy-duty work that needs to be done at your house, like bringing charcoal home, carrying rice or noodles back, or changing the liquid gas tank. Zhou Min is strong, he can do all those things." Then she heard Liu Yue call for Niu Yueqing, who asked who was on the phone. Liu Yue told her about Wan'er and her offer, and Niu Yueqing picked up the phone.

"You're so considerate, Wan'er. Thank you very much. Why haven't you come to see us?"

"I'd like to, but I don't want to bother you while Zhuang Laoshi is writing."

"He's not home. He's attending the Municipal People's Congress. He won't be back for ten days. Come on over."

"I will." Feeling better, she wondered if it would be easier if she went to see him. After putting down the phone, she kicked herself for not asking where the meeting was being held.

Zhou Min came home early the following evening, and began writing something after dinner. She went up to take a look, but he covered it with his hands, so she walked away and moved the TV into the bedroom to kill some time before going to bed. She saw that there was a special report on the meeting of the Municipal People's Congress. Seeing Zhuang Zhidie on the screen, sitting on the stage, she fantasized how wonderful it would be if she were Mrs. Zhuang Zhidie. When the news reached Tongguan, where people saw Zhuang on TV, they would be talking about her, and anyone who knew her would no longer be critical. Instead they would be speechless with envy. What would the worker who was deprived of a wife say? If he knew she was with Zhou Min, he'd come after him because Zhou was no better than him in terms of status and reputation. But if she were Mrs. Zhuang, the worker would be so ashamed of his unworthiness that he would ask for a divorce on his own. This train of thought prompted her to touch herself again, and soon she was wet. When Zhou was finished, he put away his pen and paper and came into the bedroom. But they had nothing to say to one another; they turned off the lights and went to sleep. She was in the habit of sleeping naked and curling up like a kitten in his arms. He had complained about the uncomfortable sleeping arrangement and wanted to sleep in separate cocoons. She objected vehemently. On this night, though, she made a cocoon for herself, and was startled awake when she realized that he had climbed out of his cocoon and wriggled into hers.

"I'm tired." She pushed his hands away.

Deflated, he stopped and returned to his side, but now, unable to sleep, he sat up and sighed. She ignored him, so he turned on the light and picked up a book, then threw it to the floor and sobbed, which disgusted her even more.

"Idiot. Why are you crying in the middle of the night?"

"I have so much on my mind, and yet, instead of comforting me, you pick a fight. People say a man's home is his safe harbor, but this broken ship comes home to be battered by the wind and waves."

"You call this home? Women depend on their men. I followed you here, abandoning a stable life, my child, my reputation, and a job. But we're always on the move, with no idea how we'll make it through the next day. The road ahead is shrouded in darkness. How can this be called home? And I'm always being scrutinized. The other day, when Wang Ximian's wife humiliated me in front of everyone, you didn't so much as let out a fart, let alone defend me. Now you want me to comfort you? Recently, you've left early and come home late every day, leaving me alone here with no one to talk to. Who's here to comfort me?"

"I shoulder all my troubles because I don't want you to worry, and yet you're unhappy with me."

"What troubles could you possibly have? You're a literary figure now, with a carefree life."

He told her about the trouble caused by his article. "If we were still in Tongguan, I would get my buddies to beat up that woman, but that tactic won't work here. Zhuang Laoshi helped me get the job at the magazine, but now that there's trouble, he's a no-show. He insisted it wasn't a romance so he could please both sides, but that woman is a force to be reckoned with. If I pressure him, he might say that what I wrote was simply not true. In the end, he could turn out to be the one who made me and then broke me."

Apprehensive about what she was hearing, she got up to pour him a glass of water, noticing that he did look gaunt. But she was annoyed when he put his arms around her. An uncharitable thought flashed through her mind: That wouldn't be so bad. If he lost his standing in Xijing's literary scene, she would have more opportunity to be with Zhuang Zhidie. She struggled out of his arms and went back to her cocoon.

"Don't blame Zhuang Laoshi. He probably has his own problems."

"I just hope he doesn't abandon me. But I've thought about it and planned my own way out."

"What is it?"

"For now I'll follow his plan to say that what I wrote was true, but that it was a generalization, not about a particular woman. If he sides with her and claims that what I wrote was false, then I'll say I got my material from him. I will have my interview notes as proof that I simply wrote down what I heard."

"But you never interviewed him. You got your material from gossip."

"I know what to do," Zhou assured her.

She did not respond, but her heart was racing as she turned off the light and slipped down into her cocoon.

Zhou Min rushed off to the magazine early the next morning, while Wan'er snapped on the TV, for she knew there would be a rebroadcast of the news from the night before.

Zhuang's face appeared again. After memorizing the location of the meeting, the Gudu Hotel outside the south gate, she made herself up nicely and headed for the hotel. As expected, the entrance was decorated with colorful flags and an enormous red satin banner hung from the rooftop: "We Warmly Welcome the Representatives to the Municipal People's Congress." The main entrance was locked, while men with "Security" armbands guarded a side door. No one but the attendees was allowed through. Over the metal railings, she could see a row of vehicles out in the yard where the representatives were taking an after-lunch stroll. Some were picking their teeth as they took coupons to the guardhouse for cigarettes. On this side of the railing, a crowd was in an uproar over something. Intrigued by the noisy scene, she tried to push her way through, when someone stepped on her heel. She stopped unhappily to wipe her shoe with a tissue. Then she saw three greasy-haired women and a rough-looking man pressed up against the railing. The man was holding a sheet of white paper over his head: "We plead with the People's Representatives to hear our grievance." Under the large print was some text in small characters explaining their grievance. The three women got down on their knees when they saw the representatives in the yard. "We want to see the mayor. Let us meet with the mayor," they shouted tearfully. The security men came up to drag them away, but the women held on to the railing; their shirts rose up to expose filthy dark bellies and shriveled nipples.

"Why won't the mayor see us?" they demanded. "If the officials refuse to help the people, they should go home and help their wives take care of the children. I'll bang my head against this railing if you don't let go of me."

They let go of her. "Go ahead, make a scene. We'll see what sort of storm you can kick up." They walked off to the side to smoke.

As Wan'er looked on, more and more people crowded up. Many of the men had their eyes on her instead of the protestors, and she knew she looked more beautiful than ever in contrast to the three ugly women. Unburdened by shyness, she calmly slunk over to the side door. The guard did not stop her until she had stepped inside.

"Where's your card, comrade?"

"I'm not one of the representatives. I'm here to see Zhuang Zhidie."

"I'm sorry, but the rules of the meeting do not allow non-attendees in. I'll get someone to bring him out to see you." He relayed the information. Before many minutes had passed, Zhuang walked up.

"Ah, what a surprise!" he said happily.

"Take me inside. I need to talk to you."

Zhuang said something to the guard and then led her into the yard. "You're too conspicuous," he said. "I'll go up first. It's room 703. Don't go to the wrong room." He spun around, and, without looking back, entered the building. She followed him to the room. He shut the door and lifted her up. Quickly realizing what he had in mind, she did not resist; instead, she wrapped her legs around him. With her arms around his neck, she appeared to be sitting on his hands.

"You were so cautious a while ago, but now you're getting a little crazy."

He just laughed. "I can't get you out of my mind. I even dreamed about you last night. Guess what happened? I was climbing a mountain the whole night with you on my back."

"You must be exhausted."

He laid her on the bed and touched her all over, like kneading dough. She giggled.

"I can't move. If I did, I'd drip all over the bed."

Aroused, he swallowed hard and started undressing her. She stood up and did it for him, saying she wanted to wash off the sweaty smell from the walk. Zhuang went into the bathroom to fill the tub for her, while he calmly took off his clothes to wait by the bed. When his patience had worn thin, he opened the door and found her standing naked in the tub, her long hair falling over her shoulders, holding the showerhead in one hand and cupping her breast with the other. He rushed up to her, and she went limp as she dropped the showerhead. □□ □□ □□ [The author has deleted 112 words.] With her head lying against the side of the tub, and her hair spread across the floor, she let him leave four bite marks on her neck.

"Don't get my hair wet," she cautioned.

He got up, turned off the water, carried her over to the bed, and laid her down. She took a long look into a large mirror on the wall above the head of the bed. "Look at you," she said with a laugh. "Is that what a writer looks like?"

"What should a writer look like?"

"More refined."

"Very well, then." He lifted her legs to gaze at her down below, so embarrassing her that she tried to fight him off. "Don't. Stop that." But she was unable to say more as she felt something leak out. So he put a blanket under her head so she could see herself in the mirror and covered her mouth with his when she began to moan. They were both breathing hard. □□ □□ □□ [The author has deleted 500 words.]

When she heard him say she had a mole down there, she looked for it in the mirror, while imagining how much he loved her. The worker in Tongguan had never noticed the mole, nor had Zhou Min. Nor even had she.

"Is it good to have a mole there?" she asked.

"Good, maybe. I have one there, too." He showed her.

"That's wonderful. We'll be able to find each other no matter where we go," she said. "Is the door locked? No one will come in, will they?"

"*Now* you're worrying about the door? I'm not sharing with anyone, so no one will come in."

She remained in his arms.

"We had sex the moment we came in the room, as eager as a couple of teenagers. Actually, I came to the meeting to talk to you about something. Zhou Min's article has caused you trouble, hasn't it?"

"So you know about that? I told him not to tell you. I didn't want you to worry, since there's nothing you can do. Why did he have to tell you?"

Repeating what Zhou Min had told her, she asked if it was true. He nodded.

"I may live with him," she said, "but I'm yours. You'd better watch out for him."

"What about him? Does he know about us?"

He fell silent when she told him about Zhou's plan B. A derisive laugh escaped from him.

"Are you upset with him? Are you going to punish him? I came to tell you this so you could be on guard, not for you to punish him. Zhou Min is smart, and sometimes he can be too smart for his own good, but he's not a bad person."

"I know that," he said.

Her cheeks twitched as tears streamed down her face, prompting him to ask her what was wrong.

"Maybe we're destined for each other, or maybe the karmic connection between Zhou Min and me is broken. But I can't stop thinking about you. I've never wanted someone so much in my life, not even as a teenager. I'm so preoccupied I can't do anything. Now I know what's meant by sleeping in the same bed but having different dreams."

"It's been like that for me, too," Zhuang said. "Don't cry. It's bad for you at a time like this. Stop crying, won't you?" He dried her eyes tenderly, as if she were a child.

"I'll listen to you. I won't cry. But I must tell you what's on my mind or I'll die from holding it in. The bolder I become in order to be with you, the more it frightens me. How can I keep going like this, always afraid? Zhuang-ge, I want to marry you. I mean it. I want to marry you." She went on without waiting for his reaction. "I want to marry you; I want us to be husband and wife for the rest of our lives. I'm not good at anything in particular. I don't have residency in Xijing, let alone social standing, and I probably wouldn't be as good at taking care of you as Niu Yueqing is. But I can say that I'd make you a happy man, because I can sense that you're different from most men. You're a writer who needs to be on the lookout for creative inspiration, while most people, including your wife, can only tend to your physical needs; they lack the ability to constantly change themselves to bring you something new. I realized the moment I met you that you are the serious type. I could see that you were despondent, and I understood why you seemed dispirited even when you smiled. Why do you find me attractive? I guess there are many reasons, and one of them exposes the fact that you are sexually repressed. I don't think I'm a bad woman who is intent upon seducing you and breaking up your family; nor do I have designs on your property and fame. What is it, then? Maybe people would say that you're a man who prefers the new to the old and that I'm a wanton woman with loose morals. But that's not true. All humans are born with a desire to pursue beauty. For a writer, it's simply an expression of creativity to abandon the old for the new, something impossible for the average woman to understand. That's why Niu Yueqing said she wouldn't want to marry a writer in her next life. I'm confident that I'm better than other women in this respect. I know that I can constantly adjust myself to fit your need for new, fresh experiences. That doesn't mean I would erase myself in the process; on the contrary, it would make my life more interesting and enjoyable. Conversely, you would never tire of new experiences while I'm enjoying life. The purpose of a woman's existence is to contribute to beauty, and once that's accomplished, you will have an even greater ability to display your talent. I get excited when I think about all this; I'm so keyed up, but I often wonder if it's even possible. I wouldn't be so confident if I hadn't met you. You're a ray of sunlight that has made me shine brightly. Am I getting fanciful? Am I overselling myself? Sometimes I remind myself that you're married and that your wife is a pretty and a capable woman. Worse yet, you are so famous that you're not Zhuang Zhidie for yourself any longer; you belong to all of society, and even a hint of something out of the ordinary can create trouble. Can you take that risk? Could you bear up under that sort of trouble? If it came, my love for you would be your downfall. So after that first day, I told myself that it was a one-time fling and that I mustn't allow myself to get in any deeper, and I should just treat you as a friend when we met again. But I can't control myself. Zhuang-ge, don't laugh at me for saying this. Let me finish. How this will end, whether or not you want to marry me, is beyond my control. I just want to tell you to your face, because it will make me feel so much better." She lay motionless, face down, when she finished. Her revelation had caught Zhuang by surprise, but it only made her more endearing. He took her in his arms and looked into her eyes. A sudden sadness sent his tears flowing.

"I wouldn't dare laugh at you, Wan'er. I can only thank you. You've had all of this on your mind, but do you know how unsettled I've been? When I first arrived in this city a decade ago and saw that wonderful clock tower, I vowed to make a name for myself. I worked hard to achieve a bit of fame, but at great cost. I often thought that Xijing, this big city, meant nothing to me. What here truly belonged to me? Nothing but my name, that was all. My name, and yet it was often used by others. When I went out, there were people who worshipped me and fawned over me, but I didn't understand what I had done to deserve their attention. Were they mistaken? Was it simply because of the articles I'd written? What were they, anyway? I knew I had made a name for myself without achieving much. I wanted to write something I was happy with, but I couldn't, not at the moment. That made me ashamed, something others mistook as a sign of modesty. What did I have to be modest about? I was tormented by a pain I couldn't share with anyone, since no one would have understood. Meng Yunfang is my best friend, but I couldn't talk to him about this because he said I complained too much. Niu Yueqing is a good wife, and in other people's view I should thank my lucky stars to have found a wife like her. But she's not someone I can share my thoughts with, either. I was often depressed, so naturally I didn't talk much at home, which made her wonder what was wrong with me. As a result, she griped about trivial household matters. It was my fault that we quarreled. The more we fought, the less we communicated with each other. Just think, how was I supposed to write something good under those circumstances? With no inspiration, I felt anxious. I blamed others and I blamed my fate, so I wound up agitated and irritated. I wondered if I had used up all my talent and was finished. My health had suffered for a year or more. My nerves were shot, and my sex drive was nearly nonexistent. That was when I met you. I can honestly say that I've known a fair number of women, but they were all mere acquaintances. Some of the people around me take delight in talking about sexual indulgence, but it's not something I condone, for I can't imagine how anyone can do that without an emotional attachment. I would rather masturbate than have random sex and just walk away. I don't know why my heart stirred when I met you, and I have no idea where I found the nerve to do what I did. I think you're wonderful. You hold an attraction I can't describe. It's like cadence to sound or flame to fire. You're a real woman. What I'm most grateful for is your acceptance of my love. You make me feel like a man again when we're together. You stir up surging passions inside me, making me feel that I'm not finished yet, that I still have some good stories left to write. But I have to mourn the fact that we met too late. Why didn't you come to Xijing earlier? And why didn't I meet you back in Tongguan? I've also thought about marrying you, even about how our lives would be if we were a couple. But what about reality?

I don't like it when my fame becomes a burden, but I have to think of my reputation. A huge storm would erupt if I were to ask for a divorce now. What would people in leadership positions, or my friends and family, think of me? What would Niu Yueqing do? Unlike ordinary people, the trouble for me would not end in two weeks or even two months. Wan'er, I'm telling you this so you can understand how difficult this is for me. I'm not trying to sweet-talk you; I'm just telling you what's on my mind. But I can tell that we will eventually succeed. I want you to remember this: Please wait for me. I will marry you sooner or later. You must trust me."

She nodded. "I trust you, and I will wait for you."

He kissed her. "Give me a smile."

She did. They collapsed onto the bed again, and he climbed on top of her.

"Can you do it again?" she asked.

"I can, and I will." □□ □□ □□ [The author has deleted 517 words.] Then they heard someone calling out in the hallway, "Time for the meeting. It's meeting time."

He checked his watch; it was five past two. "We can't," he whispered. So they got up and quickly dressed.

"I'm the first speaker at the afternoon session."

"Who would imagine that you'd be giving an important talk just moments after you've had sex? When you appear on TV tonight, many people will see you and say, 'Look, that's my idol, Zhuang Zhidie.' But not me, for I'll be saying to myself that I know how big that thing in his pants is."

He bit her neck playfully. "I'll leave first," he said. "You wait till the hallway is empty."

After he left, she brushed her hair, redrew her brows, and touched up her lipstick, then straightened up the bed. She waited until all was quiet outside before slipping out like a leaf on the wind.

❋

Over the next three days, while the meeting was in session, Tang Wan'er came twice, with the promise to come again. Zhuang was overjoyed and in high spirits, no longer bothered by worries over his writing. He ran into Huang Defu at the dinner table on the third night, and was shocked to see how thin he had become. Huang's face, which had once been so fair, had turned sallow and as parched as wax, and there were dark circles under his eyes. Zhuang asked him if he was ill.

"Exhaustion."

Zhuang mentioned the request to convert the unit at the nunnery into a literary salon and his need of Huang's help to talk to the mayor. Huang did not turn him down, but insisted that he not be in too much of a hurry to get it done because the mayor had a million things to tend to at the moment, all important matters that meant he had no time for minor requests like Zhuang's.

"How much time could it take the mayor? Does it require a written report and a study group? A word from you will take care of it. Doesn't this meeting give the mayor a perfect opportunity to rest?"

"What can I say about you writers? Do you think the mayor can rest during the meeting?" Huang took Zhuang aside and continued in a low voice, "This meeting makes everyone more tense than a battle. Every night when the meeting is in session, he and his chief of staff drive out to the countryside and to all the districts in the city to get a sense of what's going on and to talk to the people in charge. He's been giving clear instructions when he can and hints when he can't. He hasn't had a good night's sleep in five days. Things get complicated during the sessions. The original plan was to replace the chairman of the People's Congress, but some people have secretly gotten together to reelect him. It might work, and that would not be good. The mayor very likely will get a second term, but it would look terrible for him if he got only a simple majority of the votes. Are you aware of all this?"

"How could I be? The meeting appears to me to be very much aboveboard. Who knew there could be so many complexities?"

"It's all right that you writers know nothing about politics, but think about this. You want me to talk to the mayor about the nunnery unit right now. Well, that's no problem if he's in a good mood. But what if he's not? He could simply find a reason to turn you down, and you could never bring it up again. I'll wait for the right moment to bring it up, so don't worry. I won't forget it."

The man sounded sincere, but Zhuang decided to drop the matter. When he saw the mayor smiling and shaking hands with some of the representatives in the hall, instead of going up to greet him, he went up to his room to read.

On that afternoon, the chairing committee told the representatives to hold small discussion groups. The staff delivered the three newspapers that had been ordered specifically for the meeting. The speakers continued to talk while the representatives read the news. Zhuang opened the provincial paper to the arts and culture section before moving on to the municipal paper, in which the first two pages were taken up by reports on the meeting. Nothing interesting there, so he moved on to the third paper, *Weekend*, where a headline grabbed his attention: "Tardiness at City Hall; Only half show up for work in the first half-hour." A reporter had conducted a surprise survey by standing at the entrance to City Hall and determining how many employees arrived within the first ten minutes, how many twenty minutes later, and how many half an hour later. Several bureau chiefs and deputy mayors did not arrive on time. There were whispered discussions in the room, where the topic shifted from the mayor's report on city government performance to debates over the newspaper report. Zhuang listened for a while but was bored by all the complaints, so he went to his room to call home and see if anything urgent had come up. Liu Yue picked up the phone. "Who's calling?" she asked—twice. Zhuang was about to tell her when he heard the sound of laughter in the background; he remained silent so he could hear who was there with her. "Idiot," Liu Yue complained, and hung up. Zhuang dialed again, only to have her say, without waiting for him to identify himself, "Wrong number. This is the crematorium." She hung up again. He was so angry he dialed again and shouted into the phone the moment it was picked up.

"Is this how you answer the phone at home, Liu Yue?"

"Oh, it's you, Zhuang Laoshi!" she said when she heard his voice. "There have been so many calls for you. I tell them you're not home, but they keep calling back. So Dajie told me to tell callers they've dialed the wrong number. I didn't expect to miss your call."

Still upset, Zhuang said, "Who's there talking to her?"

"It's Hong Jiang. He came to see you. Do you want to talk to him?"

Hong Jiang came to the phone. After hemming and hawing, he told Zhuang that the books had been printed two days before. He had distributed them to booksellers, and they were selling well. He went on and on, but when Zhuang failed to respond, he said: "Did you hear what I said, Zhuang Laoshi?"

"Yes."

"We made a killing this time. I did a rough count. We could reap a net profit of thirty thousand from an investment of a hundred thousand. Judging by what's happening now, I think we'll need to do another print run of ten thousand copies in ten days. I'm wondering if we should do something to show our appreciation to Mr. Jia of the Post Office Distribution Section. He's someone we need to treat well, since, in addition to the official channels, he has an underground distribution network. If you agree, could we meet today or tomorrow?"

"I'm busy. Why don't you talk to Shimu?" Zhuang said and hung up. He spread out the bedding to sleep until dinnertime.

After dinner he went into the yard, but Tang Wan'er was not there. A Qin opera was staged that night for the attendees, many of whom were strolling in small groups. Someone called to Zhuang to come with them; he responded with the excuse that he had to go home for some out-of-town guests. When the operagoers had all left, he went back to his room to wait for Wan'er. Then he thought he ought to have something for her, so he bought a pack of chewing gum at the gift shop. He was barely back inside when Huang Defu knocked at his door.

"The mayor is looking for you."

"Really?"

Zhuang went with Huang to a suite on the second floor. They saw the mayor sitting on a sofa, smoking a cigarette. He rose when he saw Zhuang.

"Here's our famous writer. Since you're here, why haven't you come to see me?"

"You're a busy man, I didn't want to bother you."

"I might not see others, but how could I say no to you? Defu mentioned your request, and of course you have my support. People say I focus so much on cultural affairs that I ought to be the culture chief, not the mayor. Since that's what they think, I really ought to do something for the intellectuals. You can have the unit at the nunnery, and don't forget to tell me about future activities if you think I'm a worthy audience."

"Thank you so much, Mr. Mayor." Zhuang jumped to his feet. "You really have your finger on Xijing's pulse when you focus on culture. When cultural activities set the stage, economic development has a place to put on a show. This is not about culture alone. I don't know much about other areas, but I know your accomplishments are well known and highly regarded in cultural and artistic circles."

"Give him the key, Defu."

Huang took out the housing authorization and a key. "The mayor has thought of everything. He said you'd have to go see different people if you applied for the authorization yourself, and he didn't want writers wasting their time, so he had me take care of it earlier."

Zhuang was moved as he took the key.

"Come see me in the future if you folks need anything," the mayor said. "I know about Xijing's four celebrities, but I've only met two of them, you and Ruan Zhifei. Defu, pick a Sunday and get all four of them together for a meal so I can get to know them."

"That would be wonderful," Huang said. "Throughout his life, Premier Zhou Enlai befriended cultural figures, saying a major statesman must have friends who are writers and artists."

"They're all city treasures," the mayor said. "As the ancients said, officials come and go, but the yamen is ironclad, there forever. I may be the mayor today, but I'll be a nobody tomorrow when I step down. But you're different. With your good works, you will leave a glorious legacy."

"You're too modest, Mr. Mayor," Zhuang said with a smile. "What we do is ephemeral. When I was at Liufu Street, I saw them building a water-storage unit, and on the wall a sign had been painted: 'Remember the mayor every time you drink the water.' I was deeply moved; what leaves a glorious legacy are practical contributions to the people. Hangzhou's Baidi and Sudi levees, as well as the Zuogongliu in Gansu, are the perfect examples."

The mayor laughed, obviously pleased.

"The area around Liufu did not have tap water, and the residents had to take pots and jugs to places three li away to get water, which was a huge burden in the summer. The people were very unhappy about it. When I learned about the problem, I demanded an explanation from the heads of the city construction bureau and the water company. Of course they pleaded all sorts of practical difficulties. That really angered me. I told them I didn't care how many excuses they had. How can a modern city like Xijing still have an area that is not supplied with tap water? I told them to make water available in ten days. If I didn't see tap water on the eleventh, I'd fire them. Guess what, tap water was running by the ninth day. Thousands of people clanged gongs, banged drums, and set off firecrackers that day; they even wanted to make a plaque to be delivered to City Hall. I told Defu to stop them from doing that and said to myself that the people are simply wonderful. They won't forget you if you really care and do something for them."

"This is a great topic," Zhuang said. "We should get someone from the Writers' Association to write about it."

"No, please don't do that. I don't want to take the credit. But I do have an article here, not by anyone in this office, which they showed me for approval. I think it's quite well written. I've been told that the provincial paper is going to publish it, but I don't know when. They tell me there's a terrible practice that requires that you know someone even to publish in party newspapers. That's outrageous." The mayor took out the manuscript and handed it to Zhuang. "Why don't you have a look?"

Zhuang took the manuscript.

"Defu, why don't you and our celebrity writer go read it in your room? I have a meeting with the party secretary in three minutes. I will come see you in your room when I'm free, Zhidie. You're in 703, aren't you?"

"Just give me a call and I'll come down to see you."

Zhuang and Huang went into the adjoining room. "Go ahead, you read it first," Huang said.

The article was titled "The mayor takes command as a vanguard of reform," with the subtitle "New trends in the Xijing City Hall." It was a rebuttal to the criticism in *Weekend*.

"Did you read the article in *Weekend* today?" Huang asked. "It's a political maneuver. Articles like that should be published in the city paper, but they chose to print it in *Weekend*, making their objective clear—they want to malign the work of City Hall before the election. That article has had terrible repercussions, and our investigation shows that it was written by people working for the chairman of the People's Congress. We rushed this one out this morning and decided to print it in both the provincial and the city papers. There's no problem with the city paper, but the provincial and city papers have a history of not working well together. We have no control over the provincial paper. You know people there, so you should talk to them and get their assurance that it will appear tomorrow as headline news. You can decide who you need to work on, and don't worry about money. We can come up with ten or twenty thousand, or more, to buy the spot if necessary."

"I do know people over there, but is there time to get it into print by tomorrow?"

"The election is the day after tomorrow, so it has to be tomorrow," Huang said. "It's all up to you now. A car has been ordered, and I'll go with you."

"All right, then," Zhuang said. "It's too late to see the editor-in-chief. The head of the layout section is the brother of a friend of mine. I will ask him to insert this in place of something else." Zhuang wrote down some names of people for whom gifts would need to be bought. Huang told an aide to purchase items such as rice cookers, toasters, and game consoles. "We're not coming back if the article doesn't appear tomorrow," Huang added, when he noticed the look on Zhuang's face. "Are you busy tonight?"

"Not really. Wait for me here while I go to my room for my satchel."

"I'll go with you. You're such a celebrity that people will stop you if you go up alone."

"Then I won't go," Zhuang conceded with a private groan.

They did not make it back that night. Zhuang's friend was out of town, so they went to see the head of the layout section and handed over the gifts. The article was accepted, but they had not anticipated that the deputy editor-in-chief, who was on duty that night, would read the mock-up.

"Who wrote this?" he asked. "Why do the contents differ from what was printed in *Weekend?* What exactly is going on at City Hall? We have to be careful."

The layout section head returned to his dorm, where Zhuang and Huang were waiting. They went to explain the situation to the deputy editor-in-chief, who replied, "One of you is a senior secretary at City Hall, and the other is a celebrity writer. So of course I trust you. We can run the article, but it may not make it tomorrow. How about the day after tomorrow?"

"That won't do." Huang said. "Why can't you print the one it replaced the day after tomorrow?"

"We've already delayed it three days. They sponsored one of our calls for submissions, and the head of the factory has been here three times to complain."

"Is an item from some factory more important than one from City Hall?" Huang complained. With a combination of reason and threats, he cajoled the man into agreeing to a ten thousand yuan payment. The article was going to make it into print. When they were done, Zhuang thought about Tang Wan'er, who had been waiting for him all this time; he urged Huang to return to the hotel with him, but Huang insisted that they wait to see the final copyedits so he could proofread. The two men dozed in the section head's office until the copyedits were ready. Huang wanted the headline to be in a larger font, which displeased the section head, who said the typesetters were losing patience. So Huang went out to a night market and bought several cartons of cigarettes, one for each worker in the printing room. He also bought a roasted chicken and a bottle of liquor to share with the deputy editor-in-chief and the section head. The liquor loosened the tongue of the section head, who complimented Huang on his dedication to his job, saying that young men like him were a rarity these days. The man was so enthused that he offered to write an editorial note, and did so. Aided by alcohol, he wrote a flowing note and replaced a short news item with it. Immensely pleased, Huang handed over his business card and wrote down the section head's phone number, repeatedly telling the man to come see him whenever he needed help. It was after midnight when they had the freshly printed paper in hand; Zhuang was so sleepy he could barely lift his head. Dawn was about to break by the time Huang dragged a sleepy Zhuang into the car to return to the hotel.

Zhuang woke up as the car was passing the nunnery, and said they ought to take a look at the unit while they were in the neighborhood. Huang went up with him to the fifth floor, where they opened the door to a living room plus a three-room unit. It was on the highest floor, so it was quiet. Huang promised to have the Gudu Hotel send over some used furniture, including easy chairs, a desk, a chair, and a bed, along with bedding. Being mostly poor writers and artists, none of them could afford to spend their own money on items like that. Zhuang was thanking him when they heard some people clamoring downstairs, "One more. Give us another one." Obviously a street artist had set up a stall downstairs. They went down and were surprised to see a group of youngsters surrounding the same old junkman, who was rattling off doggerel:

His hair is a mess as a teen
At twenty, a babe in his arms is seen
In his thirties, a promotion gives life a sheen
In his forties, a muddled and downcast mien
In his fifties, retired and back home to stay lean
In his sixties, to raise fish and flowers he's keen
In his seventies, he helps China achieve a glorious scene.

With a frown, Huang shouted, "What nonsense are you spouting there, damn you?"

The old man looked up. "Nothing, I didn't say anything."

"I'll have the police chase you out of town if you keep doing that."

Quickly donning his straw hat, the old man scurried off with his cart, raising his hoarse voice along the way to shout, "Junkman! Collecting junk and scraps!"

Zhuang, who was still coming down from the second floor, missed a step just as he was about to say something to Huang; he fell, rolled down the stairs, and sprained an ankle.

❋

Three nights and one cast later, he left the hospital, able to hop on his good leg, and returned to the house on Shuangren fu Avenue. His mother-in-law, who was still away for the temple celebration, sent someone back with a message that she wanted to spend more time in the countryside and would return when it cooled off. Niu Yueqing had the messenger stay for a meal while she put some changes of clothes for the old lady in a bundle. Then she gathered up some of her and his old clothes, some socks and hats, and said, "You're not going to wear these anymore, Zhidie. Why don't we give them to my cousin? They don't mind used clothes in the countryside."

"Do what you want." Zhuang looked unhappy.

As she walked the man to the gate, she picked up a pack of cigarettes on her way out for him to smoke on his journey home.

"Why the long face when I gave away those old clothes?" she asked when she came back in. "You embarrassed me in front of a stranger."

"Who's embarrassing whom? When did you ever talk to me before giving things to your relatives? You always do it in front of people, so how could I say no?"

"Am I the only one who gives things to relatives? Listen to your conscience when you say things like that. Don't people from your family in Tongguan come here all the time? Sightseeing, going to a doctor, doing business, pursuing a court case, you name it. We put them up and feed them, and have I ever mistreated them? Your mother's brother and your aunt's son-in-law come to borrow money and never ask for anything less than two or three thousand. I give them the full amount, plus change, knowing full well that we'll never see the money again. It's like throwing meat buns at dogs, but have I ever said no? Do you know why young girls in Xijing these days don't want a husband from the countryside? To avoid that kind of trouble."

"Are you finished?" Zhuang flung out his hands. "I have enough trouble already." He struggled out of the chair and went into the bedroom on crutches. Niu Yueqing's anger faded once her husband had stormed off, and after a momentary pause, she called out for Liu Yue to pour a glass of sour plum juice. She motioned toward the bedroom with her lips, signaling for the girl to take the juice in to Zhuang. But when Liu Yue was heading that way, Niu Yueqing took it from her and walked in, while the girl stood by the bedroom door.

"Why are you doing that?" she asked.

"You think I'm being shameless, don't you?" Niu Yueqing said. "A woman can run as far and fast as she wants, but sooner or later she'll run into men."

"You'll just spoil him even more. He won't drink that."

But he drank it down. "I did that because of the fantastic thing you just said."

"What did I say?" Niu Yueqing asked, immediately deflating him.

"I know," Liu Yue said. "It was about a woman running into a man. Zhuang Laoshi loves things like that and thinks they're good enough to be written down. If you curse him with these phrases in the future, he won't be mad."

❁

Aunty Liu, who delivered milk, had come to the compound more than once without seeing Zhuang, so she asked around and learned that he had hurt his foot and was staying at Shuangren fu. The next time she came to the city, she made a point of walking the extra distance to deliver his milk and brought along a large pumpkin. Applying the meat to an injury, she said, was an effective cure for a sprain. Grateful for her kindness, Niu Yueqing tried to pay for the pumpkin, but Aunty Liu wouldn't hear of it. Then, when the tofu vendor walked by, Niu Yueqing wanted to buy some for the woman.

"I don't eat city tofu," she said. "It upsets my stomach."

"Allergic?" Zhuang asked.

"No. City tofu has gypsum and doesn't taste as good as tofu from the countryside. I've heard that city tofu makers add old gypsum that the bone and joint ward tosses over their wall."

Zhuang laughed. "I guess I should save the plaster on my foot, then."

"I know you're saying this as a way to turn down my gift," Niu Yueqing said. "So how can we thank you?"

"Ai-ya! There's no need to thank me. It's my good fortune to get to know you. When I came into the city a few days ago, the area near East Avenue was closed and sirens were going off. I was told that a Beijing official was in town, so no one was allowed to cross the street until the official's car had passed. I walked on with my cow anyway, and a pockmarked policeman railed at me, 'You can't cross, not you and not your cow.' So I said, 'Comrade, I'm delivering fresh milk to Zhuang Zhidie.' 'Zhuang Zhidie?' he said. 'Is that the writer?' I said, 'Of course it is.' He snapped off a salute and said, 'Go ahead. Please tell Mr. Zhuang that a policeman named Su is a fan of his.' So I crossed the street with my cow, having gained an enormous amount of face. You know, eight hundred, even a thousand yuan is no match for that kind of honor."

"Is that the truth?" Liu Yue asked.

"I wouldn't lie to you."

Liu Yue smiled at Zhuang. "Oh, I remember something else," she said, arching her brows. "Hong Jiang called the day after you went to the hospital and said you've been invited to serve as an advisor to four community factories. You won't have to do anything except write about their products and submit work reports. They'll pay you a thousand a month."

"Hong Jiang loves meeting strangers. He can make friends at a urinal. I wonder how he's used my name this time. What would I be doing for them?"

"That's what I asked. He said that intellectuals are in great demand; in the old days, bandits all needed advisors, and now community factories are following suit in order to make more money." She slapped Zhuang on the back, knocking a gadfly to the floor. "So many people around, and yet they picked you."

"That gadfly must not have been a lover of literature or the head of a factory," Zhuang said, making everyone laugh.

They continued to talk until it had gotten late, and Zhuang strained to get down to drink milk from under the cow. Intrigued, Liu Yue said she wanted to try, too, but the cow stamped a hoof the moment she was on the ground and brushed her face with her tail. That hurt, and when Liu Yue tried to get out of the way, her jade bracelet hit the floor and broke. Her face fell. She said it had cost her a month's salary at her previous job. She picked up a broken brick to hit the cow, but Zhuang stopped her.

"I could tell it was inferior jade and not worth much. Your dajie has a jade bracelet that's too small for her thick arm. I'll get her to give it to you."

That brought a smile to the girl's face. "This ill-mannered cow doesn't move when you drink her drink. Maybe you were connected in a previous life."

"Could be," Zhuang said. "You broke a bracelet because of the cow, so maybe you owed her a small debt in your previous life."

Though it was only a casual comment, it appeared to bother Liu Yue, who was glum the rest of the day, distracted by the possibility that she and the cow could have been karmic enemies. After dinner, she went to the city wall, where she gathered a large basket of wormwood, purslane, and splendens grass to feed the cow the next morning.

"You're a good person, Liu Yue," Niu Yueqing said. "We're destined to be sisters. I can't bear to see anyone suffer, either. Whenever there's a funeral, I tear up when I hear the family members cry. If a beggar comes and I don't have anything ready to eat, I'll go buy some steamed buns for him. Early last summer, three migrant wheat reapers came down from Mount Zhongnan, but couldn't find work. One rainy day they curled up under an eave at the entrance to the lane, so I had them spend the night here. Zhuang Laoshi laughs at me, says I was born to be poor."

"Impossible," Liu Yue said. "You're more fortunate than most people. Even Aunty Liu, the milk woman, told me that the mistress has the look of a goddess, with your broad face, straight nose, and bright eyes."

"He meant that I won't enjoy great fortune."

"That's probably true. Before I came here, I imagined the kind of rare delicacies you ate at home, but after I arrived, I was surprised to find that you like simple dishes. You don't chop and stir-fry your vegetables; instead you boil them. Even us country folk don't eat them that way."

"It's the most nutritious way to cook vegetables. Everyone knows that Zhuang Laoshi prefers corn gruel and boiled potatoes, but no one is aware that I add Korean ginseng powder to his food every day."

"You don't lack for money, so why don't you wear fashionable clothes? And you use far fewer cosmetic products than my previous employer."

"Zhuang Laoshi nags me about that." Niu Yueqing smiled. "And now you. Do I really look that frumpy?"

"It's not that. You're at an age when it's important to make yourself look nice. With what you have, you only need to put in ten percent effort to look a hundred percent better."

"I don't like to keep changing my hairstyle or put on makeup so I can look like a stage actress. Zhuang Laoshi says I never change, so I asked him why I needed to. I gave up a career to be a good homemaker. He wouldn't be able to write in peace if I dressed up like a vixen and, like the fashionable women out there, spent my days shopping at the mall, strolling in parks, drinking coffee at hotels, and doing disco at a dance hall."

Unable to respond, Liu Yue changed the subject. "Do you read Zhuang Laoshi's novels, Dajie?"

"I've read a few, but they don't draw me in."

"I've read every one of them, and I think he's best at describing women."

"People do say he's good at portraying women, making them look like goddesses. Earlier this year an editor from Beijing asked him to write for them, and she said the same thing, with a comment that he's a feminist. I don't know a thing about feminism."

"That's not how I see it. I think he's very detailed in his psychological portrayal of women. I think I read something similar to what you just said. In his descriptions, women are beautiful and kind, while men are simple on the surface but have complex inner worlds and are very cautious. That can only mean he's sexually repressed."

"He's sexually repressed?" Niu Yueqing said with a laugh before jabbing at the girl's forehead. "How should I put it? You silly girl, what do you know about sexual repression? You've never been married, let alone been in love. Let's talk about something else. Spray some water on the grass you gathered and take it to the bathroom to store in the shade. Otherwise it will wilt in the yard under the hot sun and won't be fresh and tender for the cow tomorrow."

"Talk of cows," she said when she returned, "unsettles me. Something bizarre once happened in our village. When a man named Zhang Laizi's father was alive, they were doing so well he lent eighty yuan to Laizi's maternal uncle. One day, Laizi's father was crushed to death while digging a hole. Laizi went to his uncle to get the money back, but his uncle denied ever borrowing the money. That led to an argument. His uncle swore that he would be reborn as a cow if he had borrowed money, so Laizi left without the money. In March of the same year, the cow at Laizi's house gave birth to a calf, and the moment the calf was born, someone came to tell him that his uncle had just died. Laizi knew that the calf was his uncle's reincarnation and was very sad. He raised the calf with great care, never taking it to work the field. One day he took it to the river for water. The cow stopped when they met someone from a neighboring village carrying clay pots. Laizi said, 'Why are you stopping, Uncle?' The man was puzzled why Laizi had called the cow 'Uncle.' When Laizi explained, he learned about the uncle's death and shed a few tears, for he had known him. To their surprise, the cow kicked over the man's carrying pole, breaking all the pots. Laizi asked the man how much they cost so he could pay him back. The man told him the price was forty yuan, but said, 'There's no need to pay me. I borrowed forty yuan from your uncle, and he has demanded payment for the debt.' Dajie, the cow made me break my bracelet, so did I really owe it something in a previous life?"

"Even if you did, you're all square now, aren't you?" Niu Yueqing replied. "You heard what Zhuang Laoshi said. I have no use for that jade bracelet of mine, and you can have it." Niu Yueqing went to get the bracelet and put it on the girl's wrist. It fit perfectly, as if it were made for her. From then on, Liu Yue often rolled up her sleeve to show off her fair arm.

The next morning, after Liu Yue helped Zhuang drink milk at the gate and fed the cow the fresh grass, Niu Yueqing left for work. Zhuang stayed behind to chat with Aunty Liu and watch the cow enjoy the grass. Liu Yue went inside and, with nothing to do, got a book to read in the study. When he moved back, Zhuang had asked her to bring over a large number of books from the apartment in the Literary Foundation compound. Liu Yue had left all the antiques and other objets d'art behind, taking only the clay figurine, which she placed on the desk in the study. Now that she thought she might have owed the cow something, she recalled how, when she first arrived, people had commented on her resemblance to the figurine. To her, it could have been a different kind of karmic connection, which prompted her to come look at it daily. She was soon engrossed in the book. When Zhuang came in, she got up to go into the living room.

"Don't worry," Zhuang said. "Go ahead and read. I can still write."

She sat back down to read but could not get back into the book. She liked the feel of the study at that moment: one person writing and one reading. The thought made her blush. She looked up at the figurine, with its hint of a shy smile. She admired her doppelgänger and, envying the figurine, said to herself, *I can only read near him for a while, but you're with him from the moment he comes in.* She gave the figurine a pouty smile.

"What are you two talking about, Liu Yue?"

"Nothing." She was embarrassed.

"I could hear you talking with your eyes."

Now her face was as red as a peach blossom. "Instead of concentrating on your writing, Zhuang Laoshi, you were eavesdropping."

"Ever since you came, people say this figurine looks like you, and it does feel as if it's alive. When I come in to read or write, I always sense that she's looking at me. Now a living Tang figure is sitting here, so how am I going to focus on my writing?"

"Do I really look like her?"

"The mole between your brows is the only difference."

Liu Yue reached up to touch her forehead, but couldn't find the mole.

"Is it ugly?"

"It's a beauty mark."

She laughed, but quickly stopped with a shrug of her shoulders. "I have another one on my arm," she said with a twinkle in her eye.

Reminded of the moles on Tang Wan'er's body, Zhuang was distracted. Liu Yue rolled up her thin silk sleeve, which was loose enough to expose her arm, fair and well formed, like a section of lotus root. She raised it to check the mole on her elbow, giving him a good view of her lush armpit hair. He took her arm in his hands.

"You have a lovely arm, Liu Yue." He bent down to give it a wet kiss. Right then the sound of children cheering came through the window, as a kite rose up into the air.

❋

When the cow saw Liu Yue come with an armful of grass, she rewarded her with a grateful look. To the cow, the young woman and the house seemed familiar. It took several nights of reflection before she recalled her former life, also as a cow, when she was one of the thirteen water-carrying beasts working for the Water Bureau at Shuangren fu. The woman had been a cat at the bureau. One day, after the cattle returned with 104 receipts from delivering 52 buckets of water, the cat took two of the receipts to play with at the wall while the owner sat down to smoke and then doze off. The receipts were lost, incurring punishment for the cattle and their owner. Later she was sold to someone in Mount Zhongnan, where she was reborn, again as a cow. Lured by a fish, the gluttonous cat was skinned and turned into a neck warmer before being reincarnated as a human being in the northern Shaanxi countryside. Chewing the cud is a form of contemplation for cows. It differs from human ruminations in that it allows them to go back in time to recapture, though not always clearly, early images. This difference between humans and beasts means that cows know more than humans, which is why they do not need to read. Humans, on the other hand, remain in a state of ignorance after birth, knowing only how to eat and drink; they go to school to learn, but by the time they know how to think, they are nearing the end of their lives. Those who come after them repeat the process, going to school to dispel the ignorance of their own age, which explains why humans never grow big and tall. The cow wanted to explain all this to humans, but unfortunately was unable to use human speech. Oftentimes humans cannot recall what happened in the past, and after something has taken place, they open their thread-bound books to read "How can there be such astonishing similarities in history!" They sigh. The cow had to laugh at the pitiable humans.

Now, after the cow had enjoyed the tender grass, Liu Yue led her out of Shuangren fu Avenue, and as they walked down a lane, the cow shooed away gadflies with her tail and began to think again. In this life she had been born as a beast of burden deep inside Mount Zhongnan, and everything in the city still felt strange, even though it had been here for quite some time. What is a city? Just a mountain of concrete. Everyone in the city complains that there are too many people, saying the sky is getting smaller and the land narrower. Yet people in the countryside want to escape into the city, and no city resident would give up residency and walk out through one of the four city gates. Are humans really that debased? They create a city to hem themselves in. Mountains have their ogres and waters their spirits, so what demons does a city have? What makes people leave their harmonious, amiable villages, where everyone knows the nickname of everyone else's grandpa, and people all know who owns every chicken on the ground? What makes them come to a city with its single-family units, where people shut their doors when they get home, ignoring everyone outside? With so many people out on the streets, people inhale each other's breath; the buses are crammed full and the theaters are jam-packed, but people just stare at each other, total strangers. They are like dirt that forms a clod in your hand but falls through your fingers when you open it; the more you try to bring it back together with water, the more it scatters. People from places with an ocean or a river want to swim in man-made lakes at a party, while those who come from mountains climb fake hills. What is laughable is that they suffer from heart, stomach, liver, and nerve problems in their square or round or trapezoid concrete structures within the confines of four city walls. Forever vigilant in regard to hygiene, they wear facemasks, produce soaps to wash their hands and feet, invent medicines and vaccines, brush their teeth, and put condoms over their male organs. And they seem to wonder what it is all about. Research is conducted, meetings are held, leading to the conclusion that the population must be reduced, so they promote the idea of a powerful bomb that will kill off everyone but their own families.

All this made the cow laugh, which was manifested in the form of a sneeze, something she did every day. Then she resumed her contemplation, going back and forth with her thoughts. Occasionally she hit upon the idea that she didn't really understand humans, while wondering whether her inability to deal with this overcrowded city was due to the fact that she wasn't human and didn't have city residency. She was, after all, a beast of burden, with a wild streak, a large capacity to digest grass, and a substantial body with no need for clothing. Yet she firmly believed that humans were just one of the beasts that had populated the earth back when the world was in primal chaos. At the time, there was a correspondence between heaven and earth, between all animals and heaven and earth, when humans and animals were equal. Now humans were among the most populous species, along with flies, mosquitoes, and rats, and were different from other animals solely because they built cities like this. Sadly, however, they had built a city that made their species move in reverse, turning into them selfish, petty, narrow-minded creatures whose fingernails were not strong enough for anything but cleaning their ears. Their intestines, too, grew shorter, with one section becoming a useless appendix. Snobbery made them look down on other animals, oblivious to the fact that the creatures in the mountain forests and the rivers were silently anticipating the impending doomsday annihilation. Moreover, the cow had always sensed that this city would be leveled one day, as she realized on quiet nights that it was sinking, either because so much water was being drawn every day or because the pressure of increasing numbers of people and buildings was affecting the movement of the earth's crust. But completely unaware, the humans continued to pile cement on top of the land and to ceaselessly draw water from underground. Hadn't some of the eight rivers that circled the city and gave the residents so much pleasure already dried up? Wasn't the Giant Wild Goose Pagoda, the city's landmark, slanting so much it was about to topple? When that day came, the city would sink into the ground, while the water from the Yellow

River could turn the place into a marsh; either that or it could be drained of water, overgrown with wormwood. Then and only then would humans truly see the error of their ways; they would know how wrong they had been, but they would have already become fish and tortoises in the marsh or wormwood-eating cows, sheep, pigs, and dogs. They would understand how wild animals were one with heaven and earth, and know that they must find a new way to survive in the world.

Thinking about this made the cow's head hurt. She was walking down streets in a haze, with the satisfying feeling that she was a philosopher, though she rued the insufficient intelligence she had been given, for her thoughts were so jumbled that her head ached from prolonged contemplation. Sometimes her soul would leave her body, giving her the illusion that she was pulling a plow from the Western Han dynasty or the early Tang period, searching in vain for a field as she stared uncomprehendingly at the constantly moving heels of shoes, while she was hemmed in by little cars that looked like dung beetles. She had to sigh over her lack of wisdom and her uncontrollable tendency to lose concentration. Hence, as Aunty Liu took her down a path outside a park wall, she decided to turn and gnaw on wild jujube thorns. Humans ate hot peppers for their spiciness, and cows chewed on date thorns for the prickliness. Aunty Liu was so upset, she kept hitting her with a switch.

"Get moving. Come on, it's getting late."

It was taking Zhuang Zhidie's injury longer than expected to heal, so Niu Yueqing would not let him move around after changing the dressing. She talked to the elderly gatekeeper and to the families on either side of the lane outside Shuangren fu, asking them not to give out Zhuang's address and to tell visitors he was not home. In private, she also told Liu Yue to keep the phone off the hook so no calls could come through; that bothered Zhou Min more than anyone. One afternoon he came to tell Yueqing about the three directives from the head of the Propaganda Section at the Department of Culture, as well as their decision that Zhou and someone from the magazine must apologize to Jing Xueyin. He and Li Hongwen had gone. Jing had received them, her head held high as she painted her fingernails. When she was finished, she inspected her nails but did not say a word. Zhou spat on the floor, opened the door, and walked out. When Li reported their visit, the department head said, "Well, she can ignore you if she wants. We don't have to do anything about the other directives, just the third one, which requires us to publish a formal announcement in the next issue. You go write a draft, and I'll check it later."

Zhou Min had gone to see Zhuang about the wording, but he had been at the People's Congress that day, and Zhou was not allowed into the Gudu Hotel. Since he was running out of time, he penned a draft with Zhong Weixian the following morning. The department head sent the draft for Jing's approval, which she refused to give, complaining about the ambiguous language and demanding that the words "grave inaccuracy and malicious slander" be added. Zhou and Zhong naturally would not concede, resulting in a stalemate. The department head then handed the draft to the Propaganda Section for their judgment. Zhou went to the Literary Foundation compound and to Zhuang's house a few more times, but each time was told by the gatekeeper that he was not home. He phoned both houses and became suspicious when he always got a busy signal, wondering if Zhuang had decided to wash his hands of the matter. If Zhuang, a celebrity with many connections, turned his back on Zhou, then he would be done for. He silently cursed Zhuang at home.

Tang Wan'er had something else on her mind. She was worried that Zhuang had been avoiding them because Niu Yueqing had learned about her visits to Zhuang's hotel room. She recalled that when she had stealthily appeared outside his room that afternoon, the door was ajar but Zhuang was nowhere in sight. After waiting half an hour, she had to leave, so she walked up and down the hallway before going downstairs and sneaking into the alley, where she checked to see if the light was on in the third window. She waited two hours, until her neck was sore and her feet hurt, but the window remained dark; finally she turned and went home in dejection. They had agreed on her visit, so why wasn't he in his room? Somehow their tryst must have been exposed, or Niu Yueqing had gone to the hotel and forced him to return home every night. Either that or the hotel staff was gossiping when they cleaned Zhuang's room and found long hairs and curly pubic hairs on his sheets and in the tub. With her mind occupied with these thoughts, she was so lethargic she stayed home several days in a row, wedging herself into the bed or a chair as she read a book called *A Collection of Great Classical Essays.* Included in the book was "Six Chapters of a Drifting Life" by Shen Fu, and "Reminiscences of the Plum Shadow Studio" by Mao Pijiang, about his life with the famed courtesan Dong Xiaowan, along with a section on women in "Idle Sentiments and Occasional Thoughts" by Li Yu, with which she began. She was puzzled by the section about the critical trait of deportment until she read the argument that fine deportment can enhance the allure of an unattractive woman, while poor deportment can detract from the charm of a pretty one. Deportment for a woman is like a flame to fire, like brightness to a lamp, or luster to jewelry. It was an eye-opening revelation. *Isn't deportment what we call style?* she said to herself, confident that she definitely had that. She then fell head over heels for Dong Xiaowan in "Plum Shadow Studio," and compared the talented Mao Pijiang with Zhuang Zhidie. Mao was the romantic sort; so was Zhuang. Did that mean she was a modern-day Dong Xiaowan? Could anything be more wonderfully coincidental, since there was also "wan" in her name? She cocked her head and, sensing that Dong Xiaowan was drifting gracefully toward her, smiled sweetly. Then she gazed out the window at the pear tree, thinking how beautiful it was in the spring when it was covered in simple white blossoms, and in the winter when it was blanketed by thick snow. She would be inside listening to the snow while Zhuang walked down the snowy path to wait for her; he must look as white as the tree. Being summertime, there were no blossoms nor any snow, and the leaf-covered tree looked emaciated, as sparse as her life. Engrossed in her dreamy state, she read on. When she read about rain, she got up and walked into the yard, where she found, to her surprise, that rain was falling. Gazing at the pear tree in the lonely rain, she was convinced that it was Zhuang Zhidie's avatar. So had he come here to wait for her long before she'd moved into this place? She wrapped her arms tightly around the tree for a while before going back inside, where she let a raindrop fall from her eye onto the open book.

The day dragged on until night. It was late, and Zhou Min was still not home. The sound of a bell from the nearby nunnery made the night seem colder than usual. A gust of wind whistled through the paper covering a broken windowpane, making her heart race as she imagined Zhuang pacing outside. She raced out in her slippers, her hairpin falling out as she flew down the stone steps, which sent her hair cascading down over her shoulders. She tried to pick up the pin, but gave up after several unsuccessful attempts. She went to open the gate—not even a shadow was out there. Looking left and right, she wondered if he might be waving to her from a dark corner; eventually, as if in a daze, she made her way back inside, realizing that it was just the wind playing tricks on her. When she finally collected herself, she accepted the fact that Zhuang Zhidie had not come and, after being absent for many days, might never return. She choked up, and with tears on her cheeks, she sighed over her sad fate. Once she started sobbing, she couldn't stop, and soon she was howling, as a pent-up longing for her son sought release. A quick calculation told her that he would be three years old in three days, which prompted her to open the door and go out again, unconcerned about whether or not Zhou would be back. She flagged down a pedicab driver, offering him three yuan to take her to the post office near the clock tower so she could send a telegram to Tongguan. After sending her son a message reading "Happy birthday to my boy," she sobbed all the way home and went to bed.

Upon his return late that night, Zhou was greeted by a dark house with no dinner prepared for him. He turned on the light and pulled back the blanket to ask her what was wrong. Puzzled by her eyes, as puffy as rotten peaches, he saw the receipt for a telegram to Tongguan by her pillow. He demanded an explanation, so enraged that he slapped her. Leaping off the bed naked, she grabbed his hair and spat out angrily, "How dare you hit me! That motherless child is about to turn three years old, and even the worst mother should be able to send him a five-word telegram!"

"Do you have water for brains? Or is that a pig's brain in your head?" he demanded. "What good is a telegram? When he gets it, he will check to see where it came from and will know it's Xijing. Were you planning for him to know where we are?"

"So what if he knows?" she said. "Xijing is as big as the ocean; how is he going to find us?" She looked at her face in the mirror, and seeing the red marks from his hand, she reached up and pulled hair out of his head.

"You're fearless, aren't you?" she sobbed. "Why are you afraid he might find you? You're scared of him. A gutless coward like you should never have seduced his wife into running away with him and sneaking into Xijing like thieves. I don't mind roaming like this, but how dare you hit me? He never touched a hair on my head, but you, you're a heartless brute. Why not hit me again, why not kill me?"

Seeing her swollen face reminded Zhou of how hard it had been on her, wandering around with him. Filled with regret for his cruelty, he got down on his knees and wrapped his arms around her legs to beg for forgiveness, while using her hand to slap his own face. An expert in sweet-talking women, he managed to stop her crying by showing that he hated himself for his actions. As she wiped away her tears, he went up, put his arms around her, and kissed her, then tickled her to make her laugh as proof that she forgave him. She was so ticklish, he had once joked that it was a sign she'd had many admirers. Zhuang Zhidie had also tickled her, digging in the more she laughed. She could not stop laughing, which put his mind at ease as he went to the kitchen to make dinner. He brought some food for her before they went to bed in peace and harmony.

Over the days he was shut in at home, Zhuang sensed an invisible shadow looming over him. He felt like complaining, but could find no excuse; unable to leave the house for any sort of diversion and enjoying no visits from old friends, he could only pass the days reading. But he forgot what he read almost immediately. All he had for amusement were chats with Liu Yue. By then they were closer than just a domestic helper and her employer. He asked her to sing, so she sang a folk tune called "Holding Hands."

When you hold my hand, I want to kiss your mouth;
holding hands and kissing, we walk down the alley to the south.

The tune made Zhuang's blood run hot, while she, her face red, ran into the old lady's room and shut the door. Zhuang limped over and called out to her when he couldn't push the door open, "Keep singing, Liu Yue."

"It's a bad song. I shouldn't sing it," she said from inside.

"It's all right if you don't want to sing. But why don't you open the door?"

She was quiet for a moment. "You must think I'm being bad."

"I never thought of you that way," he said, still trying to open the door. She quietly pulled the latch when he gave the door a push, sending him to the floor when it burst open. His face twisted in pain, scaring her so badly that she squatted down to check him out.

"It's my fault," she said gravely. "Dajie will be mad at me when she comes home. She'll send me away."

He pinched her buttocks. "How would she know? You won't go if I don't want you to." He tugged at her, making her stumble and nearly step on him. She tried to move her foot but ended up sitting on his neck, with her belly almost in his face. He wrapped his arms around her legs, startling and embarrassing her. "That's better. Let's have a good look at you."

He looked up, and through her loose blouse he could see a pair of large, fair breasts with tiny maroon nipples, the color of red beans.

"So you don't wear a bra?" he said, reaching under her blouse. She squirmed to stop his hand from going further. □□ □□ □□ [The author has deleted 25 words.]

"You've had so many women, why would you be interested in a maid from the countryside? You know I'm a virgin." She pushed his hand away and stood up to go into the kitchen to cook. His face red, Zhuang lay on the floor and reproached himself for projecting his longing for Tang Wan'er onto the girl. He was besieged by shame and guilt, when Liu Yue began to sing again in the kitchen:

When the big red fruit was peeled, people talked about me and you.
Names were besmirched, though nothing happened between us two.

That night, when husband and wife were chatting in bed, the topic naturally turned to Liu Yue.

"Why was she wearing my shoes today?" Niu Yueqing asked. "I didn't notice at first. She quickly changed into slippers when I came in, and her face was red."

"She washed her shoes in the morning and had nothing to wear to go out grocery shopping, so I told her to wear yours. She probably forgot to change after she came back. She has a nice figure and looks good in anything. You have so many shoes, why not let her have those?"

"Buy a new pair if you want to give her shoes. I've only had those for two weeks, and, besides, we'd be giving her used goods."

"What a nice person you are. I'll give her some money to buy a pair tomorrow."

"You're so considerate," she said. "Something's been bothering me all day. This morning on my work to work, I stopped by a candy store on Zhubashi Street. The shopkeeper stared at me. 'Aren't you the wife of the writer Zhuang Zhidie?' she asked. I said, 'Yes, I am. Why do you ask?' She said she had seen a picture of us in a magazine and asked if we had recently hired a maid. I said, 'Yes, a smart, pretty girl from northern Shaanxi named Liu Yue, a radiant girl no one would assume was from the countryside by the looks of her.' 'Don't judge a person by her looks,' she said. I asked her what she meant. Had Liu Yue bought candy and walked off with more change than she deserved? She said that Liu Yue had worked for her and caused her a great deal of trouble. She said, 'I hired her at a labor market to take care of my child. But somehow she heard about your family and asked to leave. I couldn't keep her if she insisted on leaving, and all I asked was for her to wait until I found a replacement. Then one day I came home after work to find my child crying and the girl nowhere in sight. There was a note on the table saying she'd left. She had made it into a better family, while I had to stay home to care for the child for two weeks. I lost my bonus, but she walked off with two weeks' pay.' I said nothing, because I couldn't be sure that the shopkeeper's story was credible. If not, it would be a false accusation. But that still made me uneasy. What do you think?"

"Liu Yue can't be that bad. Maybe she was so good at her job that the family didn't want her to leave. Now that she's gone, they're jealous of us and are trying to drive a wedge between Liu Yue and us."

"That's what I thought, too. Being so pretty, so neat and tidy, she can easily make people like her. It's one thing for me to treat her well, but you need to be careful. Don't get too cozy with her."

"I'll let her go tomorrow if that's how you feel."

"You're just saying that because you know I don't want her to leave." She moved close to him, saying she wanted to make love, but he complained that it would be too much for him with his bad foot. She straightened out her legs. "All right. But don't forget you owe me." She lay back down and fell asleep.

The next morning, she went to work as usual. Her cousin called her at the office. Niu Yueqing asked how her mother was doing. "She's fine. She had a bowl and a half of rice porridge with red beans for breakfast, only half a bowl of rice for lunch, but with plenty of odds and ends. My husband caught three fish in the Wei River, which we saved for her. The children were not allowed to touch them. For dinner we steamed two eggs for her, to go with a glass of fresh milk. Aunty has put on weight, and her skin is brighter. All she worries about is the vat of vinegar, since it has to be stirred. She asked me to tell you not to keep the lid on it all the time. Oh, and she complains about not having a radio to listen to opera." Niu Yueqing said her mother was an opera fan who had spent much of her time at the theater when she was young. She went on to tell her cousin about life at home—the vinegar was fine; the old lady's shoes had been washed and dried in the sun; Granny Wang had come several times and brought over a yellow stomacher. Niu Yueqing ended the report by telling her about Zhuang's foot. It so happened that one of Niu Yueqing's superiors would be going to the Wei River at noon to buy some cheap mutton for the staff, so she hurried back to the compound to pick up a Walkman and two opera tapes for him to take to the Deng Family Fort, where he would deliver the package. But by the time she got home, her mother was there. When Yueqing's cousin had told her mother about Zhuang's foot, the old lady had insisted on coming back to Shuangren fu without delay. Unable to change her mind, the cousin had brought her home on the bus. After checking on Zhuang's foot, her mother grumbled about Liu Yue not folding the blanket neatly, placing the bottles incorrectly on the table, putting too much water in the flower pots on the windowsill, and for sweeping away a spider's web on the wall. Liu Yue didn't dare say anything. At night, Liu Yue slept in the same room as the old lady, who continued to use the coffin as her bed and started talking around midnight. At first the girl thought she was talking to her, so she pretended to be asleep. But the old lady kept on, almost as if she were having an argument with someone, softening her tone to reason with the other person one moment, then hardening her voice to frighten the listener the next. She even threw her pillow at the door. Liu Yue couldn't see a thing in the darkness, and she was so scared that she got up and went to knock at the other door. Zhuang and his wife got up to ask her mother if she'd had a bad dream.

"They all left when you called out. I did my best to talk them out of it."

"Who were they?" Niu Yueqing asked.

"How should I know? I saw several of them come in with clubs, and I knew they were here to hit Zhidie's foot. I have no idea where they came from or why they wanted to hit my son-in-law's leg, since we haven't done them any harm."

"Mother was talking about ghosts again," Niu Yueqing said. Liu Yue's face was pale. "No more, Mother," Niu Yueqing said. "You scare us every time you go on and on like this."

"Let her talk," Zhuang said. "Did you manage to stop them, Mother?"

"They were evil spirits, so they wouldn't listen to me. Go see the abbot at the Yunhuang Temple tomorrow and get some paper amulets. The city is overrun with evil spirits, and only the monk can subdue them. When you get them, paste one above the door and burn a second one, then put the ashes in some water and drink it. Your foot will be fine."

"I'll go tomorrow. Now you go back to sleep." He told Liu Yue to go back to bed, but she decided to sleep on the living room sofa.

Niu Yueqing went to work the following morning. Liu Yue woke up with puffy eyes after a virtually sleepless night. Following a breakfast of milk, a flaky pastry, and one or two other items, the old lady dug up a piece of cloth to make another mask. Liu Yue offered to help, but she did not like the girl's needlework, so Liu Yue went to talk to Zhuang in the study. When she heard them talking, the old lady looked at them over the top of her glasses.

"Zhidie, didn't you say you'd go to the Yunhuang Temple?"

"I know." He went to the bathroom, and when he returned to the living room, he sat down to watch Liu Yue hang a newly washed curtain over the kitchen door. She had on a pair of heels she had bought with the money they'd given her the day before, and the sight of her without stockings was strangely charming. In her tight black shorts she strained to hang the curtain on the doorframe, stretching her body and highlighting her graceful figure.

"You look really nice in those shoes without stockings, Liu Yue," he said.

"I don't have hairy legs," she said, still struggling with the curtain.

"Do they pinch your toes?"

"I have narrow feet."

"Your dajie has big feet and thick toes, so her shoes usually lose their shape after a week, but that's nothing compared with some of the people I know. Xia Jie has a hammertoe and can't wear heels at all, even medium height. Have you noticed how she always hides her feet when she sits down?"

The girl raised her leg to take a closer look. Zhuang took the foot in his hand and, pressing his face close, sniffed the leather and the fleshy fragrance of her foot. With her hands still on the doorframe, she quickly lowered her foot, but not before Zhuang managed to give it a peck. As she stood there, she experienced a ticklish sensation so strong that it even turned her face red. Feigning nonchalance, Zhuang told her he liked the style of her new shoes, which settled her down.

"For a man, you're very attentive to women's feet and shoes. People would find that hard to believe."

"A good farmer makes sure to plant his seeds at the edge of his plot, a good dishwasher always cleans the rim of a pot, and a woman's beauty shows in her head and feet. So long as you have nice shoes, you'll look terrific even in rags. Tang Wan'er knows this, which is why she's so meticulous about her hair. But she's lucky to have thick, healthy, long hair, with a light yellow tint. Have you ever seen her in the same hairstyle twice? Why do you always wear your hair in a ponytail?"

"Because I don't have a small purse, and none of my summer shirts or skirts has a pocket. So when I go out and take a handkerchief to wipe my sweat, I have to tie it to my skirt or to my hair for easy access."

"Why didn't you tell me? I'll give you money to buy a purse. I've recently discovered why women carry purses. I used to think it was to carry money, but it turns out they contain nothing but handkerchiefs, tissues, and cosmetics. "

Liu Yue laughed.

"It's getting late, Zhidie," the old lady said when she heard them. "Why aren't you going to the temple?"

He winked at the girl.

"I'm leaving now." He grumbled about why Niu Yueqing had told her mother about his foot injury and then agreed that she should come home. She was probably worried that something might happen if he was home with nothing to do but chat with Liu Yue. The thought depressed him; his scalp tingled and he felt itchy all over. Deciding to call Meng Yunfang and ask him to pick up a couple of paper amulets at the Yunhuang Temple, he realized that the phone was off the hook.

"I was wondering why there haven't been any phone calls while I've been stuck in the house. Turns out the phone was off the hook. Liu Yue, did you do this?"

Unable to lie, the girl told him it was Niu Yueqing's idea, which sent him into a rage.

"Resting? Resting peacefully? Why didn't she simply send me to prison?"

"I have to do what she wants."

"What she wants? What she wants is for me to break both of my legs; then she'll be happy."

"She's just being considerate. That's unfair to her."

"She is good at making sure that others are fed, warm, and in good health, but she will never understand that some people need more than that to stay alive. Don't be deceived by her carefree attitude. She actually has a bit of a mean streak and is on guard against everyone."

"Including me?" Liu Yue asked.

Without responding, he put one hand on the wall to support himself as he walked into the study, where he sat down to stew in anger.

Meng came over later that morning with the amulets, as promised. He expressed his unhappiness that Zhuang had not told him about his bad foot. Though they were like brothers, Zhuang had been keeping his distance, not thinking that there was anything Meng could do to help. He hurried to explain that the sprain was not so bad, but that it would take time to heal. If he had told Meng, it would only have caused him undue worry; besides, he hadn't told a soul.

"What undue worry?" Meng said, still upset. "I'd have brought you tonics like royal jelly and longan extract. They're not expensive."

"When have you ever brought anything with you?" Liu Yue asked snidely. "You load up on food and drink every time you come. Zhuang Laoshi told you about his bad foot when he asked you to get the amulets. So what did *you* bring for the patient?"

"Stop picking on me. I didn't bring him anything, but I'm going to give you something." He tapped her on the top of her head. With a shriek, she cursed him, saying he would not meet with a good end, that he'd get what was coming to him.

"You're right. The son by my first wife, when I lived in the countryside, joined the army five years ago, and he's a platoon leader. He wants to be promoted further, to a company or regiment commander, but he wrote last month to say that the army is going to deactivate him and told him to go back where he came from. My son said, 'They're all common soldiers, sir, and they can go back where they came from, but I'm a platoon leader.' The regiment commander said, 'It's no different for platoon leaders.' So my son said, 'I'll follow your order if it's the same for everyone, but I came from my mother's belly, and I can't go back, since she's dead.'"

"That sounds like a son of yours." More or less appeased, Liu Yue smiled. "How many wives have you had? Dajie said your first wife was from the city and that your son is only eight or nine. How could he be in the army?"

"You don't know, Liu Yue, but he also divorced another woman in the countryside," Zhuang said.

"I've been married three times, and each wife has been younger than the one before."

"No wonder," she said. "That's the source of all those wrinkles."

Zhuang glared at her. "So what will your son do?" he asked Meng.

"I know the executive county head in my hometown, so I called him, and he promised to find a job for my son at the county level. You won't believe what I'm going to tell you. I asked if I should come with Zhuang Zhidie to talk to the district commissioner, who was a classmate of Zhuang's, and he said, 'Are you trying to force my hand by bringing in a big gun?' 'So you know Zhuang Zhidie, do you?' I said, 'Not only do I know him, I was the witness at his wedding.' 'Zhuang Zhidie is a celebrity,' he said, clearly pleased, 'and I must do whatever he wants. Our policy doesn't allow us to give your son a job, and I won't use the back door. If I did, someone could file a complaint. Instead I will deal with it out in the open, telling people that your son is a relative of Zhuang Zhidie's, and that we must find him a job. I'd promise to do that for anyone whose relative makes as many contributions to society as Zhuang Zhidie.'"

"You're always cooking up something, and I'm the one who's in trouble if there's a problem," Zhuang said.

"It's just that you're so famous," Meng said. "When the county head comes to Xijing, I'll bring him here, and you can entertain him as a favor to me."

"Ai-ya!" Liu Yue remarked. "You not only come here alone to eat, but now you want to bring other people with you."

"Why not? Here, look at this." Meng took out a medicine pouch and told Zhuang to put it up against his navel.

"What kind of a crazy idea is that? I injured my foot, and you want me wear this on my belly?"

"You never believe me. What does a writer know about health products? As the mayor suggested, a street for magic health products has been created in the eastern part of the city, where twenty-three companies are selling their wares. This one is called a magic health sack. They also sell magic brain caps, magic kidney belts, magic power bras, and magic virility underwear. I hear they're working on magic socks and shoes and hats, as well as magic cups, belts, pillows, mattresses, chair cushions, and so on."

"That's enough. This is not a good sign. I wonder who gave the mayor that terrible idea. When society went downhill during the Wei and Jin dynasties, qigong practice, alchemy, and the search for an immortality elixir became trendy. So now it's health products."

"Why are you worried about that?" Meng said. "If there's a seller, there's a buyer, and when there's a buyer, there's more to sell. Besides, it aids Xijing's economic development."

Zhuang shook his head and changed the subject:

"I've been home all this time and no one's been by. But there's something I want to talk to you about." Zhuang asked Liu Yue to leave them alone, to which she replied with a pout, "Is it something sordid you don't want me to hear? I'm going to tell Dajie."

"Be a good girl and go on out," Meng said. "I'll bring you a magical power bra in a few days."

"Shut your filthy mouth!" she said. "Have your wife wear it first."

"Listen to her," Meng said. "My wife tried one, and now she has the nipples of a young girl."

"Liu Yue is still young, so watch what you say," Zhuang cautioned. He continued in a soft voice after the girl was gone. "I talked to the mayor about the upstairs unit at the nunnery, and he has agreed to give it to us, along with a set of used furniture. Here's a key. Go take a look, but I have to stress that you mustn't mention it to anyone, especially Niu Yueqing or your wife."

"Great!" Meng was overjoyed. "You are, after all, a celebrity, unlike us insignificant people with no sway. We should write a piece for the paper to let people know how much our mayor values culture."

"Go ahead, write one, since we'll likely need more help from him in the future," Zhuang said. "Now that we have a place, let's think about the kind of activities we want to hold there, who should and can be invited, and who absolutely shouldn't be allowed in. But no matter what, you and I must be the only two with keys. We can host our first meeting after my foot gets better."

"Why don't we start off by having Huiming give a lecture on Zen Buddhism? There's a type of futurology that's really hot these days. I've had a look at just about every book on the subject, domestic and foreign. But she has new views from the perspective of Zen. She thinks the world of the future will or ought to be a Zen energy field and that advanced humans should follow Zen philosophy. I've been thinking about that myself, and I could write something now that we have a quiet place. When I'm home, Xia Jie is always nagging me about one thing or another. They say that Zen requires peace and quiet, but up till now I haven't had a quiet place to go."

"The greatest peace comes with true Zen, when your mind is calm. What matters most is a transcendental state of mind, but when did you ever put aside everything in the mundane world? And you have the nerve to talk about Zen? I think you're getting unhappy with your latest wife. If you don't change, you could marry ten times, and every one of them would nag you."

"Impossible," Meng said with a laugh. "I'm no celebrity, so where am I going to meet that many women?"

"You're in a league of your own."

"You're too career-oriented to have a carefree life." Meng said with a snigger. "I've thought a lot on your behalf. You've accomplished so much more than the average writer, but can you guarantee that your work will enjoy long-lasting fame, like that of Cao Xueqing and Pu Songling? If not, even a minor section head can enjoy a happier life than a writer. Buddhism focuses on dharma, of which there are thousands of different kinds. Different professions experience dharma in their own way, whether it's a general, a farmer, a thief, or a prostitute. When you look at it that way, being a general doesn't make you noble, nor does being a prostitute make you humble, since everyone is equal."

"I know all this, of course," Zhuang replied. "I said long ago that being a writer is only one way to earn a living. But personally speaking, writing is all I know, so all I can do is write the best work I'm capable of."

"If that's the case, there's no need for you to live such an austere life. Nowadays in this chaotic society, if you don't use the power you have, it will soon become useless, and if you don't exploit your fame, your hard-earned reputation will have been achieved in vain. You don't need me to tell you how those in power use their authority for personal gain. You've seen enough yourself. But let me tell you about our next-door neighbor, an old man who made a killing in business. Like an old cow that prefers tender clover, he married a young woman, with the view that a rich man needs to have his way with women before he becomes incapable of enjoying the good things in life. On my way over here, I walked by his house. He's been bedridden for three days. Through the window I heard his young wife ask him, 'What would you like to eat?' The old man said, 'Nothing.' 'What would you like to drink?' she asked. Again he said, 'Nothing.' So then she asked, 'So do you still want to do it?' The old man said, 'You'll have to help me up.' You see, he's not too sick to know how to enjoy himself."

"Enough of that," Zhuang said. "Have you seen Zhou Min and the others lately? Why hasn't he come to see me? I feel like there's a cloud looming over me. Yunfang, I've felt it since the beginning of the year. I get jumpy easily."

"Do you think it's some sort of premonition?"

"Nothing bad is about to happen, is it?"

"Well, now that you mention it, there is something. You didn't say anything about it, but Zhou Min did, and I've been waiting for you to bring it up with me. Since you trust me, I will tell you what I think. It's a minor incident, but it has far-reaching consequences. You're so well known that your every move can have serious repercussions. Zhou Min has been in a bad way, and you have to help him out."

"Do you think I haven't? Don't listen to him," Zhuang said. "How about his wife?"

With a wily smile, Meng lowered his voice and said, "I knew you'd ask about her."

"You and your smutty mouth. Stop the nonsense," Zhuang said with a stern look.

"I wouldn't dare. I've been to their place, but I didn't see her. Zhou Min says she isn't well. That little fox is as happy as a flag in the wind and a fish in the waves. There's nothing that could lay her up. But I do wonder why the heartless woman hasn't come to see you. Zhuang Zhidie does not easily fall for someone, but now that he has his eyes on this woman, why doesn't she, someone without a city residence card, grab hold of him? Why stay away?"

Picking up a piece of soft candy, Zhuang stuffed it into Meng's mouth to shut him up.

❊

After lunch, Zhuang went in to take a nap, but he couldn't stop thinking about what Meng had said. He had been unhappy with Tang Wan'er for not coming or calling over the past few days, and now it turned out she was ill. What was ailing her? Could she have fallen ill from thinking too much after he had failed to show up at the hotel and her calls could not get through? People's thoughts tend to run wild when they are not feeling well. He wondered what such a hot-blooded woman might be thinking about him as she lay in bed. As his thoughts drifted to events at the hotel, he became so aroused he found his crotch was wet. He took off his underwear and went back to sleep naked. When he got up later, he handed his underpants to Liu Yue to wash.

Liu Yue knew what the crusty white spots were and was thrown into a state of confusion. Zhuang's wife had not been home at lunchtime, so who had he been thinking about that had caused him to make those stains? Or had he dreamed about someone? That day she sang "Holding Hands," he had put his arms around her, and she might have become a woman if she had loosened up a bit. She was being shrewd, unsure if he was truly fond of her or was merely using her to satisfy a passing desire. *As a celebrity, he's met plenty of people and seen a great deal. If he really cares for me, I'm young enough to become the mistress of the house, and he'll treat me well if that doesn't work out. He'll give me a positive reference if I seek a good job, maybe even a husband, in Xijing. But if he is so spoiled by his fame that he thinks he can have any woman he wants, I'll mean nothing to him and will be the big loser.* Now, looking at his underwear, she did not know if she was the cause of it, but it helped her see through a famous man she had idolized, to the point that she was no longer in awe or afraid. Instead she felt closer to him.

When the washing was done, she hung it up to dry in the yard before returning to her room, where she sized herself up in the mirror. Surprised to find herself prettier than before, she was pleased. She tugged at the front of her blouse to send her unbound breasts jiggling, and was reminded of her visit to the public bathhouse with Niu Yueqing a few days before; Niu's breasts sagged like persimmons on a winter branch, which had thrilled Liu Yue. She flashed a fetching smile, then heard a knock at the door, a light tap that she initially mistook for the wind. The sound was repeated, so she went to the door and put on the chain before opening it. Zhao Jingwu was standing there. He winked and tried to enter, but had to pull his foot back when he could not get through the narrow opening with the latch on.

"What's your hurry?" Liu Yue said. "You knocked like a civilized man, but you're acting like a thug trying to rush in like that."

"Is Laoshi home?"

"He's taking a nap. Want to sit down and wait?"

"You've gotten prettier in the past few days, Liu Yue," he whispered. "And look at those pretty clothes."

"Dajie gave me my first month's pay on my second day, so I went out and bought these. With the visitors they entertain, I'd embarrass Zhuang Laoshi if I wore shabby things."

"Why, you're even wearing a chrysanthemum-patterned bracelet!"

"Don't touch it."

"Are you ignoring me now that you've flown up to a higher branch?"

"Of course I'll have to thank you for making the introduction."

"How will you do that? With what?"

The girl giggled and slapped Zhao's frisky hand.

Zhuang asked who the visitor was. Zhao identified himself as he smoothed his hair at a mirror.

"Come on in, Jingwu." Zhao entered the bedroom to see Zhuang lying in bed.

"How's your foot, Laoshi? I ran into Meng Laoshi before lunch, and he told me about it. I know how hard it can be when a bad foot keeps you from moving around, especially with nothing to occupy your mind. So here I am, ready to chat. And I've brought you some things to help you pass the time." Zhao took out a fan and a plastic bag holding a folded painting. He opened the fan. Zhuang saw that it was exquisite, with delicate, evenly spaced ribs, slightly yellowed paper sprinkled with tiny gold specks, and a rivet in the shape of a little gourd. The front had a landscape painting in the style of Bada Shanren, nothing special there, but the back was filled with concise, superb handwritten script. A quick read showed that it was not the usual poetry or lyrics from the Tang or Song dynasty, but the final resolution of the Communist Party's general line of socialism. It was signed by one-time party intelligence chief Kang Sheng, who had stamped the script with two of his seals.

"Is this really by Kang Sheng?" Zhuang sat up.

"I know you like antique vases, so I wrote to a friend. He promised to give you one, saying he'd be in Xijing at the end of the month. Unfortunately, he got in trouble last week when two small Buddha statues he had bought for sixty thousand yuan were confiscated. I wonder where they came from to be so expensive. They were being transported to Xijing from Hanzhong in a taxi that was stopped when it reached Baoji, and he was taken away by the police, along with the statues. Two days ago someone from his family came to see me, saying that they'd heard from the police. The statues have been confiscated, naturally, and he can either spend seven years in prison or pay a fine of a hundred thousand yuan. They have to let the police know which they've chosen in three days. Of course, they would prefer to pay the fine. They've already spent a hundred and sixty thousand, so a hundred thousand more would mean nothing. What worries them is that the police may not let him go after they pay the fine, so they've asked me to find a way to smooth things over with the police. They gave me this fan, saying it's not an antique, but that it can pass as an object from a modern-day palace. Kang Sheng was, after all, considered a traitor to the Communist Party, and now that he's dead, this ought to be worth something. He gave it to Liu Shaoqi before the Eighth National Congress. A former opponent of Liu, Kang tried to ingratiate himself once he saw that Liu's star was on the rise. He wrote the text on this fan to get on Liu's good side."

"This is terrific," Zhuang said. "Kang Sheng was a pretty good calligrapher."

"Of course. He was considered a master. I know you appreciate good calligraphy, so you can keep it."

"A gift must be repaid with a gift in return, Jingwu. Look around, and if you see anything you like, you can have it."

"I don't want anything except a few of your handwritten manuscript pages."

"I'm not a Nobel laureate, so I can give you a bundle of them."

"I just want a few. Look, I have something else for you. I'm sure you'll like it." Zhao opened the plastic bag to reveal a large ink painting, *Climbing Xiyue's Mount Hua* by Shi Lu. With an unusual composition and unrestrained brushwork, it was bold and imposing. Recognizing right away that it was a later work, executed after Shi suffered a mental breakdown, Zhuang could not stop admiring it. He read aloud a line of tiny writing on the side: "If you want to see into the distance, you must climb a high building."

"Shi has truly lost his mind. His calligraphy has the feel of inscriptions on ancient stones and bronze, but he made a mistake copying the Tang poem. In Wang Zhihuan's original 'Climbing the White Stork Tower,' it was 'If you want to see to the distant horizon, you must climb another high building.' But Shi has dropped 'horizon' and 'another,' and now the inscription makes no sense."

"He's a painter, not a writer. Maybe after dropping the first word, he thought it wouldn't look good to add it on the side, like they used to do, so he decided to omit the second one, too. That's a vivid demonstration of his mental state. This painting was cheap; I bought it from a woman in Lintong for three hundred. I could easily get forty or fifty thousand if I sold it in Guangzhou."

"Really, that much?"

"I'm an expert on this subject. Right now, Shi Lu's paintings fetch the highest prices in the south, and they sell for as much as a hundred and twenty thousand yuan overseas. Do you know how Wang Ximian did so well financially? He did it by faking Shi Lu's paintings to scam the foreign tourists. I know someone in that business who worked with Wang before, hawking fake paintings. After a recent fall-out with Wang, he came to see me about a joint gallery. You can't make much money selling paintings by famous or lesser-known painters in a gallery. The key is to sell fake works. We could have someone fake the paintings, and then you could write a line as a foreword or a colophon. I'm sure we'd make a killing."

"But they'd clearly be fakes. With my colophon, it would be a huge loss of face if we were found out."

"Not true. If we were found out, we'd simply claim that we were tricked into believing they were genuine. If we had known they were fakes, then why would you have shown how much you treasured them by writing a colophon? You only decided to sell them because you were short of money. These days no more than two or three out of every ten murder and arson cases are solved, so what we do would be of no significance to the authorities, who would not have an easy time proving they were fake. An expert would buy them even if he knew they were fakes. You know why? Because they'd still be valuable, though not as valuable as the genuine articles. Besides, you're a celebrity and a renowned calligrapher, which would make them collectible. Don't turn your nose up at all that money and choose instead to make a pittance by slaving away at your desk."

"You make it sound so easy, but I'm not convinced. Something like that takes time. Where would the gallery be? Just for appearance's sake, you'd need to hang a few pieces by well-known artists, and I can only supply a few."

"I've already looked into that. There's an empty storefront suite next to our bookstore. We'll buy it and turn it into a gallery, a perfect companion for the bookstore. You don't have many scrolls from famous artists, and that's fine, because I have some back home. We could also find a few more over the coming days. Did you know there's a major work in Xijing that has yet to make an appearance?"

"What is it?"

"According to the family of that friend of mine, the owner of the fan came to Xijing three months ago to ask Gong Jingyuan's grandfather to write a script for a stele. When it was done, the man returned with a piece of Mao Zedong's calligraphy, which was a partial copy, only a hundred and forty-eight words, of Bai Juyi's long poem 'Everlasting Sorrow.' Each character is big, about the size of a rice bowl. When he took it to the house, Gong Jingyuan was out, so his son, Gong Xiaoyi, accepted it on his behalf and reciprocated with four scrolls he'd sneaked out of his father's collection. Now, Gong Xiaoyi is a good-for-nothing opium addict, so he wanted to sell Mao's calligraphy for a high price to buy opium. I don't suppose it's sold yet, and I think I know how to get it. If we had that, we wouldn't have to worry about not having enough to show in our gallery."

"You're quite the wheeler-dealer. What you're saying sounds all right, but I can't do it. Why don't you go talk to Hong Jiang."

"Who needs you to do anything? All I want is an okay from you. Hong Jiang is all right, but he can be impulsive. I know how to deal with him, so you needn't worry."

When they were done, Zhuang asked Liu Yue to see Zhao out.

"Jingwu, what were you talking to Zhuang Laoshi about?" she asked when they were outside. "You look so pleased."

"We're going to open a gallery, Liu Yue, so be nice to me and I'll hire you as an official greeter. You won't have to be a maid, cooking and doing the washing for others anymore."

"Have I not been nice to you?" she said. "There's no sign of a gallery, and you're already giving me a hard time. You'd probably order me around like a slave if you were Zhuang Laoshi."

He gave her a playful punch, and got one from her in return. They went back and forth a few times until she gave him a kick in the pants.

"Was that family mad at me when I left?" she asked.

"Of course, and they cursed me, too. They're telling anyone who will listen that you fed their child sleeping pills to make your job easier. Did you do that?"

"That boy was a reincarnation of a wailing ghost. He started crying the minute he woke up. Don't tell them I work here; they might make a scene and ruin my reputation."

"I won't tell. But you're a living person, not an object, and you have to leave the house for things like grocery shopping. How can you be sure that someone from that compound won't spot you and tell the family? If they come to see me, I'm not the police and I can't stop them."

Her face darkened. "Aren't you always bragging about all the people you know? Why don't you get some friends from the underworld to scare them a bit? You take care of it for me. And don't even think about coming back here if you say yes but then do nothing."

"You're using your employer to bully me."

After Zhao left, Liu Yue stood at the lane entrance, and before long, Niu Yueqing returned from work. When she saw the girl standing there sucking on her finger, she asked her what she was doing. Liu Yue told her she was about to go home after seeing Zhao Jingwu off. Niu Yueqing cautioned her that a young woman should not stand at the lane entrance like a flirt. As they talked, they saw Zhou Min and Tang Wan'er riding up the street on their bikes.

"Hey, you two, golden boy and jade girl," Niu Yueqing called out. "You're always out and about, without a care in the world. Which dance hall are you going to today?"

Wan'er got off her bike. "We're on our way to Shimu's house. We heard from Meng Laoshi that Zhuang Laoshi injured his foot. I was so worried, I wanted to come right away, but Zhou Min asked me to wait until he was off work. Is it serious?"

"Wan'er, you're such a smooth talker. When you meet me you say you're coming to visit. If I hadn't spotted you, I'm sure you'd be off to a dance hall. Otherwise, why dress up so nicely just to come to our place?"

"That's not true. Other people may not care about Zhuang Laoshi's injury, but we do. I always dress up, no matter where I go, not just to your house. Looking nice is a sign of respect to the people you're visiting." She put her arm around Liu Yue affectionately, which prompted the girl to take note of Wan'er's new style, a perm that draped across her shoulders. Niu Yueqing was all smiles. "I was unfair to you. Come have dinner with us. Liu Yue and I will make Shaanxi noodles."

"We've already eaten," Zhou Min said. "Wan'er and I had dinner with Chief Editor Zhong. We had mutton dumplings in sour broth at a diner. Why don't you go back home, and we'll be along in a moment. Mr. Zhong went home to get something after dinner, and we've agreed to wait for him here, since he wouldn't be able to find your house."

Niu Yueqing returned home with Liu Yue, who went straight to the kitchen to make the noodles, while Niu Yueqing told Zhuang that Zhou Min and Tang Wan'er were coming over with Mr. Zhong, who had never been to their house. He had always phoned about manuscripts. If it had been to inquire about Zhuang's injury, since they weren't close friends, he would have asked Zhou to send his regards. Besides, it was dark out, so why would the old man come all the way out here?

"Zhou Min must have talked him into coming," Zhuang said. "It's about that article. Zhou Min got the idea that I wouldn't listen to him, so he's trotted out Mr. Zhong to get my attention."

"He may be smart, but that's the sort of thing small-town people would do," Niu Yueqing said before taking fruit to wash in the kitchen.

Before long, the three visitors arrived. Zhuang limped to open the door, and Wan'er helped him back inside to sit on the sofa, before putting a stool under his injured foot so he could stretch his leg. "Does it still hurt?" she asked tearfully when she removed the gauze and saw the swollen ankle. Seeing that she had forgotten herself, Zhuang secretly pinched her arm to stop her hand, and tossed her a towel to dry her tears.

"I feel terrible having someone your age come all the way to see me," he said, looking at Chief Editor Zhong. "You can come any time you want, Zhou Min, but why must you drag Chief Editor Zhong along?"

"Even if you didn't want me here, I would come as soon as I heard about your injury. You agreed to have Zhou Min's article appear in the first issue, and we will want to publish one of yours in the future. An editor relies on the support of writers and readers. I can feel secure in my job only with your help."

Now that Zhong had brought up Zhou's article, Zhuang decided to skip the small talk and get straight to the point.

"I spent ten days at the meeting, where I hurt my foot, so I couldn't check things out at the magazine. How is everything now? Zhou Min didn't come by to fill me in."

"I did," Zhou Min said, "but since you were at the meeting, I had to turn over the announcement to the department for approval by the Propaganda Section."

"Here's how it looks now," Zhong said. "Jing Xueyin insisted on adding the words 'grave inaccuracy and malicious slander' to the announcement, but I couldn't accept that. I said to the department head, 'I was labeled a Rightist for twenty years and was in charge of the magazine for three years after my rehabilitation before Wu Kun schemed to replace me. Now that I'm the editor-in-chief, do you think I care about the title? Worst-case scenario, I'd step down and be a Rightist again. What would our readers think about our redesigned magazine if we didn't stick to our principles and rushed into punishing people or publishing an announcement? What kind of credibility would the magazine have then? How are we going to express our determination to protect the rights of writers?"

A usually cautious, timid man, Zhong sounded particularly firm when he was keyed up, which impressed Zhuang and Niu Yueqing.

"Chief Editor Zhong has been toiling over this day and night," Zhou Min said. "Without his firm stance, who knows how many people would be laughing at me and at Zhuang Laoshi. It doesn't matter in my case, since I'm like the man who doesn't have to be careful when he pees if his pants are already wet. But we have to think about Zhuang Laoshi's reputation."

Without responding to him, Zhuang told Liu Yue to fill Mr. Zhong's cup. The girl, who was having a great time sharing ideas about hairstyles with Tang Wan'er in the study, came out to pour more tea before getting Niu Yueqing to go back inside with her.

"The announcement is still at the Propaganda Section," Zhong said. "I've been calling for three days, asking for a decision, either a formal letter or for the announcement to be returned with a comment. But they say the deputy governor for cultural affairs, who has to read it, has been too busy. They told me we'd hear from them soon. That worries me. It would be wonderful if the deputy governor accepted what we wrote, but my hands will be tied if he listens to that woman and consents to her request for the added language before giving his approval. I might be bold enough to argue with the head of our office, but not with the deputy governor."

Zhuang fell silent, his head down.

"Here's what I think," he said after a moment. "I'm not worried about the magazine with you in charge. I could go see someone in the Provincial Office. Zhou Min, I'll write a letter for you to the secretary-general of the Municipal Party Committee. He and the deputy governor are in-laws. Go see him and ask him to speak to the deputy governor. We don't expect them to be on our side. All we want is for them to remain neutral and not favor one side over the other."

Zhou Min was so elated he stopped eating the apple he was holding.

"I didn't know that Zhuang Laoshi had such a connection. Would that woman have been so arrogant if we'd exploited it?"

"Good steel must be used only for a sword. Important connections like this should never be exploited except when absolutely necessary."

Zhuang remained silent as he lit a new cigarette from the one he was smoking, sending smoke spreading along his cheeks into his hair and making it look as if it was on fire.

After he finished the second cigarette, he asked Niu Yueqing to talk with Mr. Zhong while he went into the study to write the letter. Tang Wan'er and Liu Yue were still in there, chattering away, but when he came in, Wan'er turned to ask how he had injured his foot. She said she had had the same dream every night, one about him riding down the street on his scooter; he didn't stop when she called to him, and she wondered how he could go so fast. The dream turned out to be the opposite of reality, since Zhuang actually had injured his foot.

"I did go too fast," he said. "I twisted my ankle when I ran out of my room to take care of the mayor's requests. Isn't that something? I'd agreed to meet with someone that night to talk about art, but the person ended up making the trip in vain. I wonder if that person is mad at me." He looked at Wan'er, who cast a glance at Liu Yue before saying, "You're a celebrity, so it's no big deal if you can't keep your word. That person was obviously not lucky enough to have that conversation with you. No need to worry that the person might have gotten bloodshot eyes from waiting."

"I wouldn't mind if the person cursed me," he said with a smile. "We know each other well enough that cursing is a sign of affection and slaps mean love. The next time we see each other, I'll let the person bite off a piece of me."

The veiled talk had Liu Yue in a fog. "Why are you spending so much time talking about some other person?"

"I'll stop," he said. "Wan'er, I heard you've been under the weather."

"Achy heart," she said, her eyes bright.

"Ah, does it still ache?"

"Not anymore."

"But be careful." Then he turned to Liu Yue. "Go into the old mistress's room and get a bottle of vitamin E from her drawer."

"So you're worried about Wan'er, but no one so much as made a noise when I had a headache last night."

"What nonsense is that?" Zhuang said. "You snored all night long, so how could you be sick? Are you jealous of someone's ill health? Be careful or you might fall seriously ill."

"You heard her snoring all night?" Wan'er asked. Liu Yue flashed a charming smile before walking out. She was barely out the door when Zhuang and Wan'er turned toward each other and stuck out their tongues, snake-like. She rushed over to hold him tightly as tears ran down her cheeks. She sucked on his lips. Zhuang tried to put his tongue in but was too nervous to manage it, so instead he pinched her arms to disentangle her before Liu Yue returned with the vitamins. Sitting in a chair, shaded by the lamp and complaining about a pebble in her shoe, Wan'er wiped her tears away and bent over to remove her shoe. She took the bottle. "So all I get is medicine, Zhuang Laoshi."

"You ingrate," Liu Yue said. "This is not bitter medicine."

"It doesn't matter if it's not bitter; it's still medicine, and all medicine is toxic."

"Zhuang Laoshi has to write something, so let's leave him alone," Liu Yue said as she dragged Tang out of the study.

When the note was finished, Zhuang thought about Wan'er; they hadn't seen each other for some time, and now that she had finally come, there were so many people around that they could not find a private moment to talk. He had wanted to arrange a time to meet, which was why he had sent Liu Yue away, but Wan'er had used the opportunity to kiss him, rendering his mouth useless for talking. He quickly scribbled a note, which he would try to sneak to her before emerging with the letter for Zhong Weixian to read and hand to Zhou. They had more tea, and when the water boiled on the stove, Liu Yue shouted from the kitchen that she was cooking the noodles. Zhuang asked the guests to stay for dinner, but Zhong declined with thanks, saying he had to be going. With his bad eyes, he would have trouble riding his bike home at night. He got up to leave, followed by Zhou Min and Tang Wan'er, who told Zhuang to take good care of himself. Niu Yueqing stopped her, saying she had some mung beans for Wan'er to take home to make porridge, since the young couple probably did not have much at home. She begged off, but Niu Yueqing insisted and forced the sack into her hand, adding that mung beans' cooling effect was especially good on hot summer days. They went back and forth with obvious affection. After walking Zhong Weixian and Zhou Min to the gate, Zhuang turned to look at Wan'er, who was still chattering with Niu Yueqing and Liu Yue; he was sure the two women would walk her out, and he would not be able to pass her the note. Then he saw Zhong and Zhou Min unlocking their bikes, and that gave him the idea to roll up the note and insert it into the keyhole on the lock of Tang Wan'er's red bike.

As she walked with Niu Yueqing and Liu Yue, Zhuang, who was talking to Zhong Weixian at the gate, called Niu Yueqing over to say good-bye to the old man. Niu Yueqing walked to the gate, while Wan'er went to her bike and discovered the note inside the keyhole. Immediately realizing what it was, she took it out, smoothed it in her pocket, and read it as she bent over to unlock the bike. It said, "Come by at noon the day after tomorrow." Hiding it in her palm, she was overjoyed as she pushed the bike to the gate, where the visitors shook hands with Zhuang and his wife. When it was her turn, in addition to making sure he could feel the note in her hand, she scraped his palm with a finger. They exchanged smiles.

Niu Yueqing was oblivious to what went on, but not Liu Yue, who saw everything.

❋

Zhao Jingwu and Hong Jiang were busy making preparations for the expansion of the bookstore; they worked on Young Knaves Number Two and Number Four in the city to buy the next-door storefront and obtain an operation license. As everything was coming together, they spent several days making connections and forging friendships with relevant personnel at the Industrial and Commercial Bureau, the Tax Bureau, the Utility Bureau, the Environmental Sanitation Bureau, the Public Security Bureau, and the Subdistrict Office. After a roasted duck dinner at the Xijing Restaurant, they hosted another banquet at the Delaishun Restaurant, where they all enjoyed a soup made of cow, donkey, and dog penises, followed by all-night mahjong games. The two made sure to lose more than they won. All these activities helped to reduce the distance between them, to the point that they were calling each other brother. Hong Jiang was in charge of the funds for the expansion. The martial arts novels by Jing Yong had brought in a hundred and twenty thousand yuan, so he took eighty thousand to Niu Yueqing, along with the receipts for her to repay the debt to Wang Ximian's wife. Niu Yueqing returned forty thousand to him, telling him to talk to Zhao Jingwu about the gallery. Hong Jiang then told her there was still fourteen thousand yuan outstanding, all owed by retailers outside Xijing. The amounts owed by each were not large enough to warrant a personal visit, since the expenses for travel and room and board would cost pretty much the same. All he could do was write to them, but it was likely the money would be lost. Without going into detail, Niu Yueqing could only curse the debtors, complaining about how times had changed, and that people were no longer trustworthy. She took out several hundred yuan for his monthly salary. Saying it was too much, he insisted on returning fifty. In fact, he had already collected the outstanding debts, because the retailers had not been allowed to cart away the books without paying up front. He had given the money to a distant relative to open a junk station in Wangjia Lane by the east gate.

The walled area there was Xijing's famous "ghost market," where the city's junk was bought and sold every day after dark and before sunup. Funny thing was, it was called the ghost market because of its hours of operation, but the area did have an eeriness to it. It was low to begin with, and the section of the moat outside the gate was the deepest and widest, with the most vegetation, shrouded in fog in the morning and at dusk. The streetlights were dim, and the people at the market usually talked in low voices. Dressed in tattered clothes, with disheveled hair, they rushed about, casting shadows on the moss-covered city wall by the streetlights that were sometimes oversized and sometimes diminutive, a sight both gloomy and scary. Early on, the market had been the gathering spot for junk collectors to sell their wares to people who needed parts—a pedal wheel or chain for a bicycle, a burner tile or a hook for a gas stove, masonry nails, broken windows in need of repair, a section of water pipe, faucets, chairs, used planks to replace the leg of a bed, plywood, house-painting rollers, caps for hot water bottles, springs for home-made sofas, burlap sacks, and the like. People went there for daily necessities they could not find at state-run or privately owned stores, or because they could get things cheaper there. But as the size of the market grew, those frequenting the area were no longer limited to the ragged country folks who came into the city to collect junk, or the teachers and government employees who dressed in four-pocket shirts and wore their hair parted down the middle, combed back or crew-cut. Gradually mixed in were men in baggy shirts with baggy pants, tight shirts with tight pants, baggy shirts with tight pants, and tight shirts with baggy pants. They brightened up the place, peppering their speech with an argot that no one could understand. Women with blood-red lips and blue eyes or girls with full breasts and prominent hips ran their stalls. These fashionable types changed their looks constantly, wearing three-inch, chopstick-thin stilettos one day and slippers revealing chubby white toes with scarlet nails the next. As for the men, they might sport light brown hair down to their shoulders in the morning and show up in the afternoon with their heads shaved. They were often heard bragging about the name-brand items they wore. Believing that the addition of the new group raised their status and value in the city, the original buyers and sellers in the market basked in the prestige at first, but soon they realized that the newcomers were nothing but hooligans, rascals, thieves, and pickpockets, people who sold brand-new bicycles, wheelbarrows, and three-wheelers cheaply, or dealt in items the old-timers had never seen before, such as rebar, cement, aluminum ingots, copper rods, all sorts of pliers, wrenches, electric cables, wire, even broken manhole covers with the words "urban construction" still visible. Soon more junk shops opened up in the narrow Wangjia Lane, not far from the ghost market, including the one run by Hong Jiang's relative. Business was good from the get-go; the proprietors reaped impressive profits by reselling the junk to state-run junk stations or directly to factories and township industries in outlying counties. Niu Yueqing and Zhuang Zhidie, and even the three female bookstore clerks, were unaware of Hong Jiang's secret venture.

A large sum of money was needed to expand the bookstore and add a gallery, far more than the forty thousand yuan from Niu Yueqing. The revenue from earlier book sales helped, but not enough. Hong Jiang's idea was to form a board of directors for the gallery, offering each member space at the door to display ads for their business, with the added incentive of an annual gift of two paintings by famous artists. When member businesses organized an activity, the gallery would invite renowned painters and calligraphers to liven things up with demonstrations. In fact, what Hong Jiang had in mind was simply business sponsorship, or, to put it bluntly, asking the businessmen for donations. After a discussion with Zhao Jingwu, Hong Jiang went to see Mr. Huang, the owner of the 101 Pesticide Plant.

Since this was their first meeting, Hong introduced himself and praised the efficacy and quality of 101 Pesticide. He went on to say that he could sense that Huang was a prototypical modern entrepreneur the moment he met him. Huang's nose was dripping; he had a cold. "Is this for corporate sponsorship?" he asked. "How much?"

"Do you get a lot of that?"

"Like locusts," Huang said. "I have no idea how they know I have money, but they'll say anything to get some of it out of me."

"That's because, one, your products have a great reputation," Hong said with a laugh, "and two, the article by Zhuang Zhidie has had a tremendous effect. But you must be on guard so as not to be swindled. I'm here to see you because, one, I'd heard of you but had never met you, and I'm always on the lookout for new friends; and two, on behalf of Zhuang Zhidie, I want to use our newly opened gallery to promote your plant." He produced a copy of the rules regarding the nature and responsibilities of the board and the qualifications of a board member. Huang took it with a smile and, like a schoolchild reciting a text, read the rules word for word: "Minimum membership fee is five thousand, parenthesis, at least five thousand, parenthesis. Ten thousand will make the member eligible for vice chairman of the board. There is no limit to the number of vice chairmen. The chairman of the board will be Zhuang Zhidie, the celebrated writer."

When he finished, Huang looked up open-mouthed. His son, who was doing homework in the yard, came in with a book.

"Dad, what's this character?"

"Don't you know that one? It's ocean, as in ocean liner," Huang said after looking at the book. "Let's say it three times together so you'll remember."

"All right."

"Ocean, ocean, as in ocean liner," Huang said, followed by his son's "Liner, liner, as in ocean liner."

"No, it's ocean as in ocean liner, not liner," Hong chimed in.

"Go on, get out of here. You don't pay attention in class and then come home to confuse me." After shooing his son away, Huang turned to Hong, "That's all there is to it?"

"It's a privilege to share a bench with cultural celebrities. Do you plan to be a plant owner forever? Why not become a real entrepreneur?"

Huang chuckled. "Let's go inside." After inviting Hong into the house, he offered his visitor cigarettes and tea. He asked if Zhuang Zhidie had moved recently, if his father-in-law had recovered from his illness, and if, as planned, he had lasered off the mole on his chin.

"No need to test me, Mr. Huang," Hong laughed. "But that was quite clever of you. If I were a scam artist, I'd say what I thought you wanted to hear and be exposed, like the wolf pretending to be Little Red Riding Hood's grandmother. Check this out. Doesn't this seal look exactly like the one on the scroll hanging on your wall?" Hong handed him the bloodstone seal and let him press it on a piece of paper. They were identical.

"Zhuang Zhidie left this seal at the bookstore, originally for a book signing, but he had to attend the People's Congress and then he injured his foot. So we stamp it on the title page of his books, which are selling faster than ever. He'd have come in person today if not for his bad foot, which is why I came with this seal. It represents Zhuang himself; you can trust me on that."

"Of course I trust you. And I don't need to examine the seal carefully; would I trust a seal if I didn't trust you? Don't police often break cases of people making fake government seals?" Then he asked, "How did Mr. Zhuang injure his foot? Is it serious?"

"It happened a while ago and still hasn't healed completely. The mayor himself personally called a professor at the hospital affiliated with the medical school to prescribe something, but it hasn't helped."

"Folk remedies can sometimes put famous doctors to shame," Huang said. "He might have already recovered if I'd known earlier. I know someone whose family has many secret remedies for contusions and sprains. One plaster will take care of the injury."

"That's exactly what he needs. Let's ask him to check Zhuang out, and then you'll know if I'm the real the thing or not."

They left to call on the man at his house, from where the three of them took a taxi to Shuangren fu Avenue.

⁂

After removing the gauze on Zhuang's foot, the folk practitioner pressed down on a spot near the ankle, leaving an indentation that took a while to disappear.

"What so-called professor did that?" Huang said angrily. "More like a beast feasting on socialism. Just wait. Dr. Song here will put a plaster on your foot, and tomorrow you'll be able to run and jump on the city wall."

"Please don't call me that," the man said. "I'm not a doctor."

"You're one of those people who'd rather die than ask for help, like carrying a gold bowl to go begging. Why don't you quit that lousy middle-school job with its terrible pay and open a private clinic? That way you could enjoy life. Take good care of Mr. Zhuang, and when his foot is healed, a celebrity like him could easily get you a license to practice."

Zhuang asked why he was unable to practice. Huang said the man did not have a license and had to settle for a middle-school kitchen-supervision job, while writing prescriptions privately.

"You should be able to put your special skills to use," Zhuang said emotionally. "Of course, you'd need a license from the Board of Health, and I don't know anyone in that office. But I do know Mr. Wang, the neighborhood office director, whose cousin is a bureau chief at the Board of Health."

"Did you hear that, Dr. Song?" Huang said. "What is a celebrity? A celebrity is not an ordinary person. We must strike while the iron is hot, as they say, and ask Mr. Zhuang to take us to see Director Wang, so he can contact the bureau chief. Your Buddhist master can lead you through the door, but the personal cultivation is up to you. After today, you can go see the man yourself; no need to bother Mr. Zhuang again."

The good news was clearly more than Song had hoped for, but he hesitated. "Could it possibly work? And how can we ask Mr. Zhuang to make the trip today?"

Zhuang was not happy with the way Huang had appropriated his mention of a connection, but he was endeared to the honest-looking Song when he saw the embarrassed look on the man's face. These days, in his view, doctors of Western medicine applied tests to see what was wrong with a patient, while practitioners of Chinese medicine boasted that they could cure anything. Earlier, when Song had looked at his foot, he had not said that he could guarantee a recovery, which told Zhuang that he had confidence in his healing abilities, and that he had not been able to get a license because he was poor at social networking. So Zhuang agreed to go with them. Song got up to use the bathroom, and Zhuang offered the toilet at his house, saying it was the sit-down type, much more comfortable than public toilets.

"Well, that's precisely my problem," Song said. "I'm not used to sit-down toilets." So Liu Yue walked him out to the gate and pointed to the public toilet. Song was gone a long time, so Huang talked to Zhuang about the production at his plant, with effusive thanks for his article. Hong naturally brought up the gallery board of directors, but Zhuang told him to talk to Zhao Jingwu. Huang was about to say more when Hong cut in, "You're sweating, Mr. Huang. Why don't you go wash your face?"

With an embarrassed look, Huang wiped his face with his lapel. "Fat people can't take the heat," he said as he walked off to wash up at the sink, followed by Hong, who whispered, "Please don't mention the board around Zhuang Laoshi. You heard me say that he gave me full authority to take charge. His injury has put him in a foul mood, and he would criticize my ability to get things done if you brought it up with him."

"Why don't you give me a copy of the bylaws? I'm short on cash this month, but I'll come see you next month with the money."

Hong handed him a copy, along with his business card. Song finally returned with a plastic bag filled with two cartons of Hongtashan cigarettes, two bottles of Hongxifeng liquor, and packages of sweet puffy rice snacks and sesame crackers.

"I thought you were going to the toilet," a surprised Zhuang said, "not to buy gifts. I can't accept them from someone who came to take care of my foot."

"This is our first meeting, and it was impolite of me not to bring something," Song said, red-faced. "Besides, you've agreed to take me to see Mr. Wang. My meager gifts can't possibly repay you for your kindness."

"Take them," Huang said, "just take them. Dr. Song will be rich once he opens his clinic."

"All right," Zhuang said. "We'll take these to Mr. Wang." But Song objected, and they went back and forth until Zhuang agreed to keep one carton of the cigarettes. Song went out to hail a taxi while Huang and Hong helped Zhuang out into the lane, where they all piled into a taxi heading to Shangxian Road. When they got there, Mr. Wang was busy with someone at the neighborhood office and invited them to take a seat; he offered them water.

Wang's visitor was a woman wearing a pair of white-framed glasses. She sat with her legs crossed at the ankles, tightly gripping a small purse on her knees. "Mr. Wang," she was saying, "I'm extremely grateful for your concern and trust. I was so moved by your willingness to give me the task that I was still awake at three this morning. My sister thought I was involved with a man at that hour."

"Doing what?"

"How should I put it? You see, my sister is worried about my marriage prospects, and she thought I might have a boyfriend."

"The head of your factory said you didn't have a boyfriend. Do you have one now?"

"On the day I graduated, I vowed not to marry until I'd made a name for myself. Mr. Wang, that is why I cherish this opportunity. At three this morning I came up with several possible plans. Should we adopt the Tang or the Ming-Qing style of architecture? I'm wondering if I could incorporate some elements of modern Western architecture, so it would look like an urban sculpture *and* a practical space for public use."

"Don't be in such a hurry to decide that. I'm confident you'll do a fine job. I brought up your name when we were discussing candidates and stood my ground when the others objected. Now I can see I was right to pick you. But let me give you some advice: you must also think about your personal life. It's hard to believe that a pretty girl like you is still single. You must have set the bar too high."

"As I just said, I won't consider marriage until I've accomplished something." That elicited a frown from the director, who reached back to punch a sandbag hanging on the wall behind him. There was even a pair of boxing gloves next to the bag. Looking somewhat startled, she adjusted her glasses.

"Is the director a boxing fan?" she said.

"It helps me let off steam," he replied. "I understand when you say you won't get married until you've accomplished something. There are so many things to make a person unhappy these days. I assumed the directorship five years ago, and I still have the same job. How could I not be unhappy? But what can I do when I'm upset—beat someone up, kill someone? And who would that someone be? So I stay home with my old lady, who nags me if I even raise my voice to speak. That's why I bought these boxing gloves, so I can punch the bag to vent my frustration."

Zhuang sympathized with the man. He could not agree more.

"That's a great idea," Huang blurted out. "My wife wins every fight. If I slap her once, she answers with two. As a man I have to let her have her way. Besides, she won't back down if I don't hit her hard enough, and I'm afraid I'd hurt her if I hit her too hard. I'm going to buy one of these." He got up, walked over, and put on the gloves. He tried a few tentative punches. The woman had stood up to leave when the director was talking to his visitors about boxing.

"Don't go yet. There's more we need to talk about."

"I'll go to the toilet," she said. "Where is it?"

"There's no toilet on this block, but if you go out the back door, you will find one to the left of Shangli Road. Just follow the flies."

She smiled at Zhuang and the others as she walked out, but came back for her purse.

"There are bricks by the back door. Take a couple to stand on out of the dirty water."

The moment she was out of sight, Hong whispered to Zhuang, "She looks like a woman of means."

"I'm not so sure," Zhuang said. "The purse looks expensive, but all she had in it were tissues."

"A pretty woman like her shouldn't have trouble finding a rich husband," Hong said.

"She is pretty, isn't she?" Director Wang said. "The best-looking worker at the candle factory. Just look at her face with its rosy glow, like a peeled egg soaked in rouge."

"She doesn't look like a factory worker. What are you working on?" Zhuang asked.

"Writers have eagle eyes," he said. "She majored in architectural design at a vocational school, but then couldn't get a job assignment upon graduation. How could she, when architectural graduates from regular colleges at the provincial and city levels can't find them? So she was sent to the candle factory. Now forty-eight streets in the city do not have public toilets. At the People's Congress, the mayor discussed projects that would benefit the residents, and toilet construction was one of them. I gave her the job of designing a toilet for this block." Wang turned to Zhuang. "I haven't seen you for ages. What has our celebrated writer been working on? When will you write something about us?"

"No problem. I'll come for a tour whenever you want, but I'm here today to ask a favor." Zhuang told him about Song's situation, and asked Wang to talk to his cousin.

"How can I say no to someone like you? Now that we've met, Dr. Song, you can come back some other day to describe your situation. I'll take you to see my cousin."

Song nodded over and over, like a chicken pecking at rice. The woman returned and stopped at the door, where she stomped her feet loudly.

"I told you to take bricks," Wang said. "Why didn't you?"

"I did, but there was a long line, and they got too heavy, so I threw them away. Luckily I'm wearing high heels. If not, my feet would be soaked."

"The line shouldn't be long now. The longest lines are in the evening after the TV shows or in the morning when people first get up. Many husbands line up for their wives and vice versa, giving the impression that these are unisex toilets. What's funny is, sometimes passersby think the people are lining up to buy something that's about to go up in price, and they'll line up, too."

That got a laugh from everyone.

"You have a back door," the woman said, "but other people have to take the long way around. A single visit to the toilet made me realize how important my task is, Mr. Wang. But we need to talk about the location.

I looked around. There's a restaurant to the north, so the toilet can't be built there. To the south is a shop, next to a public faucet, and a toilet can't be placed by a source of drinking water. The only workable site would be somewhere in the middle of the lane, but there's a barbershop there whose owner protested that his family depends on it for their livelihood. He would fight anyone to the death who dared try to take the site away from him."

"How many lives does he have to give?" Wang said, and the woman fell silent.

"You don't sound like a local," Zhuang said, finding her student-like demeanor captivating.

"I'm originally from Anhui," she replied.

"Ah-lan, meet an old friend, Zhuang Zhidie, a writer."

She uttered a cry, but quickly blushed at her inappropriate reaction. "No wonder I thought you looked familiar when you walked in, but I couldn't recall where I'd met you. Thanks to Mr. Wang, now I remember, I've seen you on TV."

Zhuang smiled. "So you're from Anhui. Where in Anhui?"

"Suzhou. Have you ever been there, Zhuang Laoshi?"

"No, but it reminds me of someone. I wonder if you know her. A college student back in the 1950s, labeled a Rightist, a talented, pretty woman. I only know that she's widowed and that she lives in Suzhou. I don't know where she works."

"Are you talking about the girl who was close to Mr. Zhong years ago?" Hong Jiang asked.

"You know about that, too?"

"Zhou Min told me about the quirky old man. How can he be so lovesick at his age? He keeps writing to her but gets no response, typical unrequited love."

"You don't know what's going on, so don't speak ill of him." Zhuang turned to the woman. "Do you know her? Do you know anything about her?"

She considered his question and then shook her head softly.

"When did you leave Suzhou?"

"Seven or eight years ago."

"Do you still have family there?"

"I have two sisters. One is here in Xijing with me, but our older sister works in Suzhou's postal and telecommunication office. I can ask her to track down the woman."

"No need. She might not be in Suzhou at all. She could be dead, for that matter. I have a different favor to ask, if you're willing to help."

"What is it?" Ah-lan asked. "I'd be honored to do something for you."

Zhuang handed her one of his cards. She said she had no card to give him. There was a phone at the factory, but the workers were not allowed to use it, so he could only contact her by calling her sister's house. She added that she had been staying with her sister while her dormitory was being relocated. She wrote down her sister's address, name, and phone number. Zhuang thanked her and added, "I'll look you up when the time comes."

Growing impatient at the prolonged conversation between Zhuang and the woman, Wang hit the punching bag, a signal that was not missed by Zhuang, who said to Song, "That's that, then. Mr. Wang is willing to help, so you can come back someday to go see the chief with him. Mr. Wang has a lot to do today, so we should be leaving."

They stood up.

"Leaving so soon? Well, then, come back any time you're free. If you ever need a fourth for a round of mahjong, give me a call and I'll be there."

As they walked to the door, Ah-lan took out a diary for Zhuang's autograph.

"What's the point?" he asked, but he signed anyway, so elating the woman that she missed a step as she was walking them out.

"Have you twisted your ankle?" one of them asked.

She hadn't, but one of her heels had broken off, and she was red from embarrassment.

"Look at you," Wang said. "Just look at you. What were you doing?"

"This is so embarrassing," she said. "These are new shoes, so how could the heel break off so easily?" She stood up and hobbled along on the uneven heels. Wang offered to buy a new pair for her at the store at the intersection, but she declined.

"No, I can't let you do that. It's no big deal. My brother-in-law can repair shoes." She picked up a brick to knock the heel off the other shoe and put both heels in her purse, before looking red-faced at Zhuang and his friends. "So long."

The taxi dropped Zhuang off first. As the night ended, he found he no longer needed the crutches, though his foot still hurt a bit. Everyone was happy for him. The old lady attributed the improvement to the efficacious amulets. The next night, Liu Yue was fast asleep when she heard the old lady say, "The amulet quelled the evil spirits, so stop making a scene. The maid is here. Do you want her to laugh at you?" Liu Yue thought they had a visitor, but when she opened her eyes, there was nothing to see but flickering moonlight.

"Are you seeing things again, Aunty?" she asked the old lady, who sat up in her coffin.

"So, you're awake. Have you been awake for a while?" Without waiting for a reply, she scolded someone and flung one of the shoes she was holding. Then she laughed. She habitually slept with shoes in her arms. "Your soul stays with you if you sleep with your shoes," she said. "When you're asleep, it's like being dead, but not really. Your soul leaves you to circle above your head. Your dreams are your soul. You can't dream if you don't cradle your shoes, and if you don't dream, your soul will leave. That is real death."

Liu Yue did not believe her, but she didn't dare touch the shoes. Often the old lady would fall asleep watching TV, cradling them in her arms. Liu Yue would never try to wake her; instead she would wave her hand in front of the old lady's eyes. When she got no response, she would carry the old lady, shoes and all, to her coffin bed. Sometimes the old lady would be awake, and when Liu Yue waved her hand in front of her face, she would say, "I'm awake, but don't forget to leave the shoes in my arms if I fall asleep."

Having seen her throw a shoe, she asked what was happening.

"Your uncle is here. He was standing by the wall and I hit him."

Breaking out in a cold sweat, Liu Yue snapped on the light, and saw nothing at the wall but the wooden peg she had put up earlier that afternoon to hang her clothes on. The old lady got up and walked over to touch the peg, saying it was something that had belonged to her husband. She wondered out loud why it had turned into a wooden peg.

"Where did the old fart get that kind of energy?" She pulled out the peg and tossed it out the window. "No harm if a dog gets it," she mumbled.

When day broke, Zhuang went out to the gate for some milk and listened to Zhou Min play the xun at the city wall. After a prolonged period of immobility, he was happy to be walking again, so he went over to the city wall, but Zhou had left. He stood there, looking at the red bricks in the morning sun, before heading home to ask Liu Yue, "Has anyone come by?" "No one," she said. "Any phone calls?" "No."

"Why isn't she here?" Zhuang murmured, and Liu Yue was reminded of his behavior with Tang Wan'er a few days before. She wondered if they had made a date for her to come over that day.

"Are you talking about Tang Wan'er?" she asked.

"What makes you say that? Zhou Min went to see the secretary-general, and I was wondering what happened. He hasn't come by to bring me up to date, and he hasn't sent Wan'er."

So he is waiting for her, Liu Yue said to herself. "I think she'll be here," she said to him. When there was no sign of Tang, he went to his study to write a letter.

At ten-fifteen, Tang showed up. "Liu Yue," she called out softly at the door. She smiled, her white teeth sparkling. Liu Yue was doing laundry; with her hands covered in suds, she looked up and saw that Tang had a new hairstyle and was wearing a loose purple dress.

They're having an affair, she said to herself as jealousy welled up inside, but she smiled. "You must have been in a hurry, Wan'er. Look at the sweat on your neck. Anything important? Zhuang Shimu isn't home, but Laoshi is in the study. Why don't you go on in?"

"Shimu is out? I thought she'd be home. I came to visit her."

"She has an ear infection that has affected her hearing. You'd have to raise your voice to talk to her, making conversation impossible. You wouldn't have enjoyed the visit." Glancing at Tang's rising chest, she reached out and touched her breast. "Such a pretty color. Where did you get it?"

Liu Yue pinched Tang's nipple while pretending to comment on the dress. It hurt, so Wan'er pushed the hand away. While this was going on, Zhuang walked out of the study to greet Wan'er. They sat down to talk.

"Stay for lunch," he said. "My wife is always saying you don't get enough to eat at home, and she wants you to drop by for a meal now and then."

"There's no need for that," she said. "We have everything at home."

"We won't make you pay for your food," he said, turning to Liu Yue. "Go buy some pork and some leeks. We'll have dumplings for lunch."

"It's about time I went to the market," Liu Yue said, picking up her shopping basket.

As soon as she left, Tang Wan'er ran into Zhuang's arms with tears in her eyes.

"You're crying again. Don't cry."

"I miss you so much. I thought these three days would never end."

They hugged and kissed madly. She reached down between his legs. When he gestured toward the bedroom, they pulled apart. He looked in through the slightly open door to see the old lady sleeping in her bedroom; closing the door softly, he went into the study, followed by Wan'er, who tiptoed in and closed the door quietly. They immediately began undressing.

"You're not wearing underwear."

"To save you time."

He sat her down in his leather chair, raised her legs, and kissed her down below. □□ □□ □□ [The author has deleted 42 words.] The more she squirmed, the more he was aroused; he kept kissing her and felt an itch on his back. He asked her to scratch him. "It's a mosquito. A mosquito in broad daylight?" She began scratching his back. "Who do you think you're biting? Who, who do you, you think, you—you—oh, oh." She stopped, her eyes rolled back, and her body stiffened. He felt a surge of warm liquid. □□ □□ □□ [The author has deleted 33 words.] Zhuang stood up and smiled. "What does it taste like?" she asked. "Here, taste it." He put his mouth on hers, then stepped down and stretched out his leg, only to land on her with a shriek.

"What's wrong?"

"My foot."

"Don't put any weight on it," she said.

"It'll be all right." He was about to begin again when she said, "Let me do it." She got up to give him the chair. □□ □□ □□ [The author has deleted 25 words.]

"Don't make any noise," he said. "The old lady is sleeping in the next room."

"I don't care." She continued to moan and groan, so he handed her a handkerchief to stuff in her mouth. She bit down. □□ □□ □□ [The author has deleted 18 words.]

"Hurry up and get dressed. Liu Yue will be back soon," he said.

She put her dress back on, combed her hair, and wiped her sweaty face. She asked how her lipstick looked. It was completely gone, of course. He applied a fresh coat, and when he was done, he raised her skirt to write something on her thigh. She did not put up a struggle, letting him write while she powdered her face in a mirror. When he finished, she looked down to see what he had written. "Worry-free hall," she read.

"That's the name of a study, isn't it?" she said.

"Why don't I write it on a piece of paper with a brush and paste it up in your house?"

"People are fascinating. We have a head that brings us worries, but we have these parts to help rid us of problems. Have you had enough?" she said.

"Have you?"

"I have. I'm so satisfied it should last me a week."

"Me too. I don't know what I'd do without you," he said.

"Then why don't you marry me as soon as possible?

He lowered his head, with a pained look.

"Let's not talk about that. It's a blessing to love and be loved, don't you think?"

"Yes," he replied. "But I still want to say, wait for me. You must wait for me."

They went back into the living room, where they talked until Liu Yue returned and went into the kitchen to prepare the dumplings. Wan'er looked at her watch.

"Ai-ya," she said. "It's getting late. I should go home to make lunch for Zhou Min. He's been going to see the secretary-general the past three days, but hasn't seen him yet. He said that if he fails to see him again today, he'll go to the man's house and wait on his doorstep." She got up to leave.

"I won't keep you," Zhuang said. "Didn't you say you wanted a book?" They went into the study, and Liu Yue, worried they would take the book she was reading, put down her knife and followed them. The study door was ajar, but the curtain was down; two pairs of facing shoes, the high heels standing on top of the others, were visible under the curtain. She spun around and went back to the kitchen. A few moments later, she heard Tang call out. "I'll be going now, Liu Yue." She watched as she walked out, not making a move to see her off.

After walking Tang out, Zhuang returned to the kitchen to help with the vegetables. He asked Liu Yue the price of pork. Without replying, Liu kept chopping noisily. "Be careful not to cut your hand," Zhuang said, sensing that the girl was on to them. But he knew she would say nothing even if she was sure, so he let her be. Suddenly exhausted, he went to his room for a nap.

After finishing the fillings, Liu Yue thought about her own feelings for Zhuang, who had said so many nice things to her. But his heart, it appeared, was with Tang Wan'er. That was deflating. Then she told herself that Zhuang could have a relationship with her as easily as he had with Tang. But was she exaggerating her own importance, or was she thinking too much? She had rejected him once. Wasn't that how Tang Wan'er got in ahead of her? Now she was angry with Wan'er.

"Shameless bitch," she cursed silently. "Remembering to cook for Zhou Min after what you did!"

She came out to speak to Zhuang, and when she saw him napping, she speculated that they must have been engaged in something while she was out grocery shopping. If she had any evidence, she would tell Shimu. She went into the study but could find nothing suspicious, nothing but three sheets of writing paper. It was a love letter to "Dear Ah-xian" from "Meizi, who loves you." She snickered at their correspondence. The letter had yet to be sent when the woman came over, so he must have shown it to her. A careful study of the significance of the code names revealed nothing, so she laid the sheets on the floor to make them look as if they had been blown off the desk by the wind, before walking out and closing the door behind her.

When Niu Yueqing came home from work, she told Liu to get Zhuang up for lunch.

"Zhuang Laoshi must be so engrossed in writing that he forgot the time. Why don't you go get him?"

Greeted by an empty study, Niu Yueqing grumbled about the open window and the paper on the floor. Picking it up, she started reading and stood there until she finished. Liu Yue picked that moment to walk in.

"Time for lunch. Why are you sitting here? You don't look too well."

"Did you receive a letter today, Liu Yue?"

"No letter, but Wan'er came. Is something wrong?"

"No, I'm just curious," Niu Yueqing said, as she put the letter in her pocket and went in for lunch. Liu Yue went to the bedrooms to call Zhuang and the old lady. When he came out and saw Niu Yueqing eating, he said, "You started without waiting for Mother?"

"Why wait for her? She may have to go begging one of these days."

"You may have had a bad day out there, but don't take whatever it is out on us."

"Who am I taking it out on? Who's there for me to do that to?"

Zhuang frowned at her unreasonable outburst. "You're deranged."

Slamming down her rice bowl, Niu Yueqing got up and stormed into the bedroom to cry. When her mother came out, she asked Liu Yue, "Did you do something to upset her?"

"Would I dare do that?"

"Then why are you crying?" The old lady scolded her daughter. "What kind of problems do you have? Everyone says this is a fine family, and if it falls short, it's just that you don't have children. Now even that's not a problem, since your cousin has promised to give us one. Who knows, she might be pregnant already. Where there's a sprout, it will surely grow, won't it? The wind blows and a child grows. You have to start setting things up now, telling people you're pregnant. Then no one will be the wiser when the time comes for the switch."

"No more of that, please, Mother," Zhuang said.

"What are you crying about, if not children? You have all the food, clothes, furniture, and status you could ask for right here. When I go out, people treat even me differently. Has Zhidie mistreated you? You're still young, and yet he has hired a helper so you don't have to trouble yourself with grocery shopping, cooking, and laundry. What do you have to cry about?"

"He's so good to me," Niu Yueqing said from the bedroom, "just wonderful. I slave for this family, do everything I can to protect it, but my sentiments can only warm his body, not his heart."

"What's the matter with you today?" Zhuang said. "Why are you spouting nonsense?"

"*I'm* spouting nonsense? You know what the matter is."

"I know what the matter is," the old lady cut in. "You're living in bliss, but you don't know it. How can Zhidie not know you're good to him? He just keeps it inside, so you won't hear sweet talk from him."

"He reserves all the nice things for others, so of course he has nothing for me."

"Watch what you're saying. I see with my own eyes that he works hard, entertaining guests when they come and sitting down to write the moment they're gone. Doesn't he do that to earn money and fame for your sake? With a foot injury like that, any other man would just lie around, but not him. He spent the whole morning in the study."

"Sure, he can write. Of course he writes. Of course he's not tired. Actually, writing energizes him," Niu Yueqing said as her tears flowed, so enraging Zhuang that he put down his bowl and lay down on the sofa. Liu Yue went into the bedroom with food, but Niu Yueqing refused to eat, so she went to Zhuang Zhidie. He suspected her of saying something to his wife, so he snapped at her, "I don't want anything. I've got a belly full of anger. Go eat by yourself." Now Liu Yue was upset. She went into the old lady's room to cry.

Silence hung heavily over the house that day and night. The next morning, when Zhuang got up, he recalled his plan to go see Ah-lan, so he went into the study for the letter. It wasn't there. He asked Liu Yue about it. She pleaded ignorance. When Niu Yueqing came out of the bedroom, her hair uncombed, she said with a sneer, "Did you think things through during the night?"

"Think about what? I was too angry to think."

"Of course you're angry with me, Ah-xian," Niu Yueqing said.

"Ah-xian? Who's that?" Liu Yue asked.

"You have no idea how many pennames your Zhuang Laoshi has taken. And besides the pennames, he even took someone else's name. Ah-xian, isn't that sweet?"

"Where did you get a name like that, Zhuang Laoshi?"

It finally dawned on Zhuang that his wife had seen the letter, and why she had caused a scene the night before. His mind now at ease, he decided to make an issue of it. "So you've seen the letter?"

"You ought to be more careful and keep your secret communications in a safe place. Now that you know I have the letter, I might as well ask you which classmate she is. When did you hook up with her again? What have you written in previous letters? The Jing Xueyin affair has caused enough trouble. Who knew there'd be another one? Who's Meizi?"

"Keep your voice down. Do you want the neighbors to hear you?"

"Yes, I do. I want everyone to know that the celebrity may be worshipped like a god outside, but he's a common charlatan."

"The newspapers all say that you and Laoshi have a happy marriage, rooted in deep love, Dajie," Liu Yue interjected. "You must have misunderstood him."

"Deep love? Love has made me blind."

Zhuang waited for her to finish before saying in measured tones:

"Now, listen carefully. Ah-xian is not my penname, nor was it a name given to me. It's the nickname of Mr. Zhong at the magazine. Who's Meizi? She was his girlfriend back in college." He followed up with a detailed explanation of Zhong's past and current situations, adding his encounter with Ah-lan in Director Wang's office. "Mr. Zhong has been supportive of me over this article incident," he concluded. "I understand how he feels, and sympathize with him, so it occurred to me that I might be able to bring him some comfort in his old age. I adopted a woman's voice and changed my handwriting to send him a letter, but it can't be mailed from Xijing. I'm going to give it to Ah-lan, who will then send it to her sister to be delivered back to Xijing. This is what's going on. You can go ask Zhou Min if you don't believe me."

Both Niu Yueqing and Liu Yue were speechless when he finished, yet it still sounded too fantastic.

"So Zhuang Laoshi is a procurer, Dajie," Liu Yue said.

"Of course I'll ask Zhou Min," Niu Yueqing said. "You must have had similar feelings in the past to be able to write something so sweet and tender, even though this one is for Mr. Zhong."

"I'm a writer, after all. I wouldn't deserve to be one if I couldn't imagine that kind of emotional state."

Niu Yueqing handed him the letter. "I'm glad that's all it is. But why did you behave like that? I was upset, and all you did was scowl, refusing to say a word to me. I can't be sure if what you just said is true. Even if it isn't, you'll be able to make it sound credible to talk me around. Women can't resist sweet talk."

"How did you manage to see the letter?" he asked.

"Liu Yue told me to go to the study, and there it was, on the floor."

"I put a paperweight on it, so even a wind could not have blown the pages to the floor."

"I saw it first," Liu Yue said smugly. "I didn't want him to do something foolish, so I left it on the floor for Dajie to see."

"Liu Yue did the right thing," Niu Yueqing said. "You have to tell me about such things in the future."

"So we've got a spy." Zhuang was furious.

Liu Yue, remorseful over being too clever and for overstepping the bounds of what was expected of her, offered to deliver the letter, but Niu Yueqing said she'd do it on her way to work.

Deeply angry with the young maid, Zhuang gave her the cold shoulder all morning. He complained about the unfriendly tone she used when answering the phone.

"You said no phone calls for you this morning."

"But you should have asked who the caller was and what it concerned. Instead, you picked up the phone and said, 'He's not in.' You sounded angry."

There was a knock at the door. She went to let the visitors in. It was three aspiring writers coming to ask Zhuang for advice.

"Would you please tell us how to write a novel, Zhuang Laoshi?"

"What can I say? Keep writing, and you'll know at some point."

"You're being too modest. You must have some secret methods, Laoshi."

"No, I really don't."

But they would have none of it and left unhappily an hour later. The moment they were gone, Zhuang lectured Liu Yue for not saying he wasn't home and costing him valuable time.

"How was I supposed to know they were unimportant?" She shed private tears in the kitchen. A few hours later, there was another knock. It was Zhou Min.

"Laoshi isn't home," Liu Yue said.

"Yes, I am," Zhuang called out from the study when he heard who it was. "Come on in."

Zhou Min was upset with Liu Yue for lying to him, which led to more tears.

Zhou was no sooner in the study than he began grumbling to Zhuang as he handed him the letter. He had run around for three days and never managed to see the secretary-general, who, as Zhou found out only when he went to the man's house that morning, was at a meeting at the Lanniao Hotel. Zhou had gone to the hotel, where the meeting was in session and the man was at the rostrum. Naturally he couldn't ask for the man to come down to talk to him, so he waited, thinking that nature would call at some point. It took two hours of waiting, but the man came down, and Zhou followed him into the toilet, where the secretary-general squatted down over one hole and Zhou took the one next to him. Not knowing how to begin, Zhou hemmed and hawed for a while before finally asking, "Are you the secretary-general?"

"Yes."

"I've seen you before."

"Oh."

"Have you ever seen a tiger?" Zhou asked.

"No, I haven't."

"I haven't, either."

The secretary-general wiped himself, got to his feet, and pulled his pants up.

"I need to speak with you, sir," Zhou said when he saw that the man was about to leave.

"Who are you? I don't know you."

"No, you don't. But here's a letter. You'll know what this is about when you read it."

The man took the letter with one hand to read as he adjusted his crotch with the other. "What's our writer friend been up to lately?" He handed the letter back.

"Writing, of course." Zhou replied.

"That's good. Writers must write."

"Zhuang Laoshi does nothing but write."

"That's what everyone says. I believe it. I never expected him to be interested in politics."

"He knows nothing about politics," Zhou said.

"Is that right? I seem to recall that he spent a night at a newspaper in order to get an article published. You're a friend of his, so tell him not to become someone's weapon. We all have our ups and downs, like the Yellow River changing its course every thirty years. Other people can pack up and leave if things aren't going well, but not him. He's a fixture in Xijing."

They walked out together. The secretary-general made no more mention of the letter.

"How about the deputy governor in charge of cultural affairs?"

"Are you suggesting that I commit the error of using a back door?"

❋

When he heard Zhou's story, Zhuang felt as if he'd been smacked in the head. He tore the letter to shreds and cursed: "What kind of goddamned leader is he? I went to the paper, so what! How did I wind up offending the chair of the People's Congress? By not realizing the extent of their network, that's how. Am I playing politics? No, but if I were, I wouldn't take any shit from him. The Yellow River changes its course every thirty years. Is the chairman of the People's Congress staying within the bounds of his authority? The secretary-general is in the same camp, and when his boss loses power, he'll go after the mayor. What kind of secretary-general is he to dump it all on me? I'm not interested in an official position, I just want to make a living with my writing. Is he powerful enough to snap my pen in two?" Zhuang furiously shoved his ashtray away, sending it gliding across the glass tabletop; it fell on top of a vase under the bookcase and smashed it. Alerted by the noise, the old lady rushed in and began scolding when she thought they were arguing. Unable to defend himself, Zhou Min walked out silently. Liu Yue came in to pick up the pieces.

"Keep your anger in check," she said to Zhuang. "Aunty thought Zhou Min was at fault, and he's crying in the living room."

"You stay out of this, and keep your mouth shut."

She slammed the door shut behind her.

After sobbing for a while, Zhou Min decided to go back into the study to cheer Zhuang up.

"Please open the door, Zhuang Laoshi," he said. "We can talk about what to do next."

"I'm not going to take all that abuse. What is a secretary-general, anyway? I'm going to write to the mayor."

"Then write to the deputy governor, too, and I'll go see him."

"No, we won't see anyone. We will wait for instructions from high up. What are you afraid of? I stand to lose more than you do."

Not daring to say more, Zhou stayed a while longer before leaving for home in dejection.

When she came home that evening, Niu Yueqing walked in to find her mother burning incense in the bedroom, Liu Yue sobbing in the living room, and Zhuang playing his mournful music on the cassette player. The study door was shut, and he would not come out when she called him. She asked Liu Yue what had happened, and after hearing the explanation, she went to knock on the study door again. When the door opened, she launched into a litany of complaints about being kept in the dark about such an important matter. He was a writer, after all, and had been told by the mayor to go to the paper. The politicians were scheming, so what did that mean for her family? She shifted her vilification to the mayor, reasoning that he must have sold them out. Otherwise, how could their adversary know so much? Or could it have been Huang Defu? She ended her tirade by cursing the secretary-general, calling the man a pig and a dog, someone who would wind up in front of a firing squad sooner or later. But she wasn't quite finished. She lamented how appalling the world had become. You never knew when you might offend someone, she said. It was like carrying a basket of eggs onto the street—you're afraid of people bumping into you, but they don't care. She went on and on, calling Jing Xueyin a horrible woman, and railing at her husband for grandstanding. Well, he had gotten more than he'd bargained for.

"Enough already! Stop annoying me," Zhuang roared as he pounded the sofa. "Are you giving me advice or handing me a rope to hang myself?"

Niu Yueqing was stunned into silence. She and Liu Yue went into the kitchen to make spicy ramen, her husband's favorite.

An aspiring young writer had recently made his appearance in Xiliu Lane near the city's north gate. Looking old for his age, he worked in a factory electrical room. His shift gave him a day off every three days, enough time to run a small business had he wanted to. But he wanted only to write. Few people in Xijing outside Xiliu Lane had heard of him, however, since he had published very little, even though he had used more than a dozen pennames, for all of which he'd had seals carved from Lantian jade by artisans. When his neighbors walked by his window and saw him writing, coughing from his low-quality cigarettes, they mocked him as a typical writer. A few years earlier, he had visited Zhuang, who had recommended his work to the editor at the city paper, an acquaintance of Zhuang's. Two of the young man's short stories were published. He went to see Zhuang every couple of weeks, either to pay his respects or to talk, but he was embarrassed to keep going after nothing more of his was published. Over the past two years, a bookseller had been asking him to write something with plenty of sex and violence, and he had written two stories purely for money, the payment for which totaled several hundred yuan. Feeling that he had shamefully compromised himself, he felt even less worthy to pay Zhuang a visit. Later, a relative came in from the countryside to look for work in the city, and spent the night at the writer's house. Once there, he rode a three-wheeler to Jixiang Village on the south side, where he bought a load of fresh vegetables from a wholesaler and hawked them in the city. He earned at least thirty yuan a day. Seeing how tough life was for the writer, he tried to get the young man to join in, but the writer begged off. After making enough money and several friends, the relative moved into a house on North Ring Road. He continued to sell his goods in the daytime and played cards and drank with his friends at night; soon he had enough money to bring his family in from the countryside. The writer's wife was so envious of their lifestyle that she constantly berated her husband for his lack of prospects. One day the relative came to see the writer while his wife was haranguing him. The visitor mentioned a government-owned steamed bun shop on North Ring Road; it had been contracted out to someone who had just quit and left the spot vacant. He asked whether the writer was interested. "If you are, I'll have my wife help you out, and we can consider it a partnership. It looks to be a profitable enterprise. The previous proprietor steamed fifteen hundred catties of buns a day, but we won't do that much. We can steam between eight hundred and a thousand, enough for us each to net about a thousand a month."

"I'll do it," the writer said. "She nags me so much I can't write anything at home anyway, but I've never steamed a bun before."

"The place already has a license, and this sort of business requires no connections at government offices. We'll just sell the buns until we run out. You can continue your shifts at the factory every other night, and my wife and I will steam the buns; you don't need to know how to do the work. All you have to do is be there."

So the writer took his bedding to the shop to make it easier to travel between there and the factory, which meant he could stay away from home for ten days in a row.

His change of heart elated his wife, who eagerly hoped he would give up writing so they could have a normal marriage. To her surprise, he came home on the eleventh day riding a three-wheeler loaded with his bedding and four sacks filled with steamed buns.

"We lost money," he said.

"How is that possible?" she asked. "Everyone else does fine, why can't we?"

"When you're born to do something, you can't change your destiny. You complained when I wrote, but look what we got for five hundred yuan—four bags of steamed buns after ten days of hard work."

He hadn't known until he arrived at North Ring Road that his relative had rented a place in a horse-and-wagon shop compound. Vegetable vendors and colliers from the countryside occupied the row of dilapidated buildings; the steamed bun shop was located across from the horse-and-wagon shop. On the day they opened, they used eight hundred catties of flour to steam the buns, which turned out yellow and too hard, because they had used too much baking soda. The vendors refused to buy them, as did the neighborhood residents. When they tried again, using only five hundred catties of flour, they ended up with buns that were still not white enough and were hard as rocks. Why did the same kind and amount of flour produce white, spongy buns at other shops? They went to ask a cook, who revealed the many secrets behind steaming buns, which included adding yeast, powdered laundry detergent, and chemical fertilizer, after which the buns were smoked with sulfur. But he refused to say how much of the extra ingredients to add, and how and for how long to smoke the buns. Though the writer sneaked over to other shops to watch how it was done, when he returned to try a third time, his relative's wife complained that they would have to sell off what they had already produced in four days or they would lose their investment. Besides, who could be sure that the third time would work? So they went around hawking the buns, but with minimal results. Only the colliers and vegetable vendors bought their buns, and they could only consume so many. The writer suggested that they sell them to a pig farm at twenty fen a cattie, but the relative's wife could not bear to do that. "If that's what you want to do, count me out," she said tearfully. "We'll split them. I'll take my share back to the countryside to dry them in the sun and eat over time." So the young man put in a second five hundred yuan and received four sacks of steamed buns in return. Naturally, that subjected him to another tongue-lashing from his wife, but in the end, they still had to deal with the buns.

"The buns taste all right, even though they don't look so good," she said. "It would be a shame to sell them to a pig farm, but how will the three of us finish them on our own? Why don't we give them to friends and family in exchange for some goodwill? You have your mentors and friends, like Mr. Pang at the city paper and that Zhuang Zhidie."

"You want me to give these worthless things to Mr. Zhuang?" he grumbled, but he was reminded of Ruan Zhifei, who, as he knew, was having a dormitory renovated for his band. He could sell the buns cheaply to the migrant workers at the job site. So he went off to see Ruan, but to his disappointment, the construction was finished and the workers had left. Feeling sorry for the man, Ruan called up some people he knew to see if the kitchens at their workplaces could buy some. At one point, he reached Niu Yueqing at work. She had been trying to find a way to cheer her husband up when the call came. Feeling genuinely sorry for Zhuang's mentee, she said to Ruan, "All those people who dream about becoming a writer can't live a normal life. Tell him to come see me this afternoon. I'm afraid our kitchen won't buy the buns, but I'll take them all. You don't have to say what I'd do with them; just tell him our kitchen bought them."

"You put me to shame with your compassion and generosity," Ruan said.

"You don't have to do anything for him, since he's just an acquaintance. But Zhidie has been his mentor."

"What has Zhidie been writing lately? He hardly leaves home, as if he's on a spiritual quest. When will he consider stopping? Won't you let him come enjoy the entertainment here? I have a favor to ask him."

"Sure. Come over and invite him to the show. He's been in a bad mood lately, and nothing pleases him at home. Some entertainment with an old friend might cheer him up."

With the favor in mind, as well as Niu Yueqing's request, Ruan picked up Zhuang that day to have lunch at the Tanghua Hotel, after which they returned to Ruan's office on the ground floor of his house. It was a medium-sized three-story building whose second and third floors were rented by the band. Three rooms on the first floor had been turned into a large rehearsal studio, while the remaining rooms were used as offices and temporary guest rooms. After a few cups of Bashan's Yunwu xianhao tea, Ruan asked Zhuang if he would be interested in watching a show that afternoon at a factory auditorium in the eastern suburb. One of the factory's products had won second prize in Beijing, and the provincial government was hosting a celebration, for which Ruan's band would perform. Zhuang asked if the program was the same as one he'd seen earlier, and decided not to go when Ruan said it was pretty much the same, just with different performers.

"I was hoping you wouldn't want to go," Ruan said, clapping his hands. "I have to be there with my band, but you can stay here. I'll get you something good to drink and some cigarettes, and you can write an article for me." He told Zhuang that the members of his original troupe were undergoing a professional evaluation. Ruan had taken unpaid leave to start his own band, but he had to undergo a professional evaluation with his troupe, since it could not be done with a band like his.

"With what you're doing, why do you need the title?"

"Money is important and so is a professional title, because it gives you status. In our society these days, power and status can be turned into money. Take you, for example. Now that you're famous, you can get published easily, and when that happens, you get paid. Am I right?"

"I get my status from my writing. What sort of professional title does a drama troupe provide?"

"I was once in charge of costumes. Just eliminating sweat stains on costumes is enough to write an article to get an advanced professional title. You know, when the performers sweat onstage, their costumes can't be washed afterward. The common method is to spray alcohol on them, but you can still see the stains after they dry, plus wrinkles. My secret was to fold the costume after spraying alcohol and leave it in the trunk, where the alcohol slowly evaporates to clean off the sweat stain."

"You need an article for that?" Zhuang laughed. "I can't write that."

"It's not much, I know, but I'd earn a few hundred less if I didn't know the secret. As far as I can tell, no one in the country who's in charge of costumes knows this technique."

"Why don't you apply for a patent?"

"I'll try performance if I can't make it in costume," Ruan said.

"What performance are you qualified for?"

"None, but I have unique tricks, passed down by my father before he died, though the troupe would not assign me a role so I could prove it. Take handling the fan, for instance. A fan onstage isn't meant to cool you off; it has a specific purpose. It started out as a prop, then became formulaic before handling it became an artistic skill."

"Are you going to tell me how each role has its style of handling the fan?" Zhuang asked. "Like the person in the martial arts role waves the fan in front of his belly, a scholar waves it around his chest, a monk over his sleeves, an old man by his beard, a blind man in front of his eyes, and a teacher on a stool, while a clown role stretches his arms with the fan to shoulder height."

"So you know all that?"

"And those are your tricks?"

"All right, you know the fan. How about the hair? Do you know about 'straightening,' 'tossing,' 'driving,' 'turning,' 'twisting,' 'spiraling,' and 'skyrocketing'?"

"No."

"Of course you don't. You don't know handling the fangs, either. Actually, it isn't just you, but no one in Xijing's Qin drama knows. Why doesn't anyone stage *Zhong Kui Marries Off His Sister, Muddy River,* or *Underworld Judgment* anymore? Because no one can master the skill of handling the fangs."

Zhuang had never heard of handling the fangs; he didn't even know what it meant. "You know how to do that?"

"Of course I do. Could you maybe write something about that?"

"How am I supposed to write about it if I've never seen it done? Even if you haven't had a chance to perform it onstage, you can practice on me, and what I write might be helpful to your title assignment."

Ruan was saying he would need pigs' fangs but had no idea where to get them, when he smacked the back of his head before running to his bedroom on the third floor, where he got a handful of yellowed paper.

"Great, perfect. Here's a description of different performances with fangs."

Zhuang took it and saw that the text was accompanied by illustrations.

"My father wrote this years ago, private notes he never showed anyone but me. Why don't you make some changes and turn it into an article? You have to help me this time. You can stay here and take a nap now, then work on it in the afternoon. I'll treat you to some snake gallbladder liquor tonight."

"I can do that," Zhuang said with a smile. "You're quite a character in Xijing, but who knew that you've been involved in schemes like this."

Ruan laughed. "You write for fame and posterity, but I'm not that ambitious. I'm a living ghost striving for something better; great if I make it, but all right if I don't. If I dress, it's a fur-lined coat; if not, I go naked."

In the afternoon, Ruan led a group of stylish men and women to the performance while Zhuang sat down to rewrite the fang-handling techniques after a nap. He had agreed to the task as a distraction to forget his worries, but he got hooked after a careful reading of the worn pages, even learning a few things, like the three body parts required to handle the fangs—the tongue, lips, and cheeks. A performer has to master the skills of lifting, moving, and controlling. The fangs can be placed either together or side-by-side. The different types of motions include swirling the fangs around in the mouth with the tongue; pointing the fangs up toward the eyes; moving only one set of fangs; making both sets protrude from the mouth; bringing the sets together; separating the sets; moving the sets to the corners of the mouth; pointing the sets down; and pointing the fangs down and moving them back and forth.

Ruan had still not returned by the time Zhuang finished, so he decided to go out. He walked down a narrow lane and arrived at a nearby market.

The market was jam-packed and deafeningly loud. After walking around for a while, he spotted a collier who was carefully piling coal against a wall, leaving the pieces loosely stacked. Then the man took his cart to a noodle shop, where he haggled with the shop owner, who wanted to weigh his goods. The collier insisted on selling the whole load, so the shop owner went over, gave the cart a violent shake, and reduced the pile by half. With the scam exposed, an argument ensued, which soon turned physical. In the end, the collier's dark face was white with flour, while the shop owner's fair face was black with coal powder; both were bleeding. Bored by the scuffle and feeling chilled, Zhuang looked into the sky, where clouds roiled and were turning darker by the minute. Rain was likely, so he started back. The wind blew, sending people scurrying and creating chaos at an intersection, where a woman was bent over picking out a pig's heart and lungs at a pork stand. She was tall and slender, dressed in a dark green skirt that accentuated her buttocks as she leaned forward. Afraid that the wind would blow her skirt up, she had tucked the hem up between her thighs; her legs were crane thin, and she was wearing high heels. *Conical buttocks usually define an ugly woman when she bends over,* Zhuang said to himself, *so a woman with such a beautiful behind must be quite pretty. On the other hand, an alluring figure from behind sometimes turns out to have a regrettable face. How will this one turn out?* He walked past her and turned to look; it was Wang Ximian's wife, a discovery that made him laugh out loud. When she heard the laughter, she looked up.

"It's you, Zhidie," she cried out. "What are you doing here? How did you know it was me?"

"I was just wondering where this woman came from. She was so pretty, and yet she was buying a pig's heart and lungs, so I figured that her husband must be a good-for-nothing bastard. How could I know I was cursing a friend?"

"These are for our cat. We can't eat this stuff." She laughed. "I haven't seen you for ages. Meng Jin's mother told me you hurt your foot, and I was actually thinking about coming to see you tomorrow. But here you are, running around."

"I did hurt my foot, but it's fine now," Zhuang said. "Who's Meng Jin? And how did his mother know about my foot injury?"

"That's Meng Yunfang's son. Meng Jin must have heard it from his father and gone home to tell his mother."

"So you've been to their place. How's she doing?"

"Well, that's a long story," she said, taking the package from the butcher and paying him before turning to say, "Come over to our place. Ximian left for Guangzhou again, so it's only the old lady and the maid. I'll make you some wontons, and you can meet my cat."

"I'm at Ruan Zhifei's place, writing something for him. He's not back yet, so I need to let him know." As he spoke, loud thunder exploded, making both of them jump.

"It's going to rain. After the summer drought, we really need it," she said. People in the market ran like a swarm of bees. The wind picked up, kicking up dust. Wang's wife squinted and lowered her head to spit it out.

"It'll rain any minute now. What do you say we go over to Ruan Zhifei's house to escape it?" The words were barely out of his mouth when coin-sized raindrops pelted down on them, sending them sprinting for the lane, where they ran bent over in sheeting rain. Since she could not keep up with Zhuang, he reached back to drag her along, nearly picking her up, for she was surprisingly slight. By the time they reached the office, they were soaking wet.

They sat down. Thunderclaps came in waves, the sky quickly darkened, and white light flashed outside the window, where the sky looked ink-splashed. The next clap sounded as if it had come from the yard out front. The door and windows shook, followed by the sound of something falling off the wall. Zhuang was about to turn on the light, but he changed his mind at the possibility that electricity could travel through the ground wire. Instead, he lit a candle on the table.

"Afraid?" he asked her.

"Why should I be, with you around? If the thunder dragon came, it would take us both," she said as she picked up a towel to dry her hair. Her dress was drenched, plastered to her body and shiningly thin, giving Zhuang a clear view of her curves. Noticing that he was watching her, she blushed and tugged at her wet dress before moving over to sit in the shadow cast by the candlelight.

"Did you say you went to see Meng Jin's mother?" Zhuang asked. "How's she doing? I haven't seen her in years."

"A woman without a man is like a legless crab, and her son has turned out to be quite a troublemaker, another Meng Yunfang. When I ran into her the other day on the street, she looked worn out, and was crying the minute she opened her mouth. I asked, 'Why haven't you found someone else after all these years?' Through her tears she said, 'Who would want a forty-year-old widow with a son? Not the young ones, for sure, and older men either are too old or have a child of their own. Meng Jin's a handful already. I can't afford to have another one, and what would I do if we didn't get along? He could team up with Meng Jin and cause all kinds of trouble.' I promised to help her find someone, and as luck would have it, I asked around and learned that one of my neighbors has a relative, an engineer whose wife died two years ago. With the children working out of town, wouldn't that be a perfect match? I was going to talk to her about him today."

"You're a good person. I recall that she has a flat nose and might not make a good first impression. We'll see which the engineer values most, appearance or living a good life."

"Hard to say. I told him the same thing when we first met, and he said, 'I'd count my blessings even if she wasn't as pretty as you.'"

"If she had half your looks," Zhuang smiled, "Meng Yunfang wouldn't have wanted the divorce."

"You're mocking me. I might have had passable looks when I was younger, but now I'm old and in such poor health that I'm skin and bones."

"Not true. I often compare you to Yueqing, and she usually says, 'Wang Ximian is rich enough to buy an elixir for his wife to keep her young.'"

She laughed, but quickly teared up, throwing Zhuang into a minor panic. "Everything I said is true. You are a bit on the thin side, but I think you should stop thinking of yourself as a pot of water that never boils. Listen to the doctors, but don't believe everything they say. The way they tell us about all the germs in the air, you'd think we should never open our mouths."

"Ximian did buy tonics for one thing or another, but I know the cause of my illness." Her eyes reddened as she sniffled. Deciding to drop the subject, Zhuang went to get her a towel. "Is Ximian going to Guangzhou for another of his exhibits?" he asked. "He's crazy. After taking the north by storm, does he now want the south?"

"Not an exhibit. He's there to talk about the sale of a painting. You may already know this, but he's had health problems in recent years, too."

"What's wrong with him? He's dark and thin, but he's spryer than me sometimes."

"He's really not well. He has hepatitis B, but his liver's all right. He's just a carrier."

"How come no one knows about this?"

"He doesn't want anyone to know. He takes medicine, but it's a disease that can't be easily cured. Let me tell you something that will make you laugh. We haven't kissed for several years now. And when we do it, which is maybe once or twice a month, he wears a condom."

Not entirely convinced, Zhuang wondered if Wang was indeed ill or just pretending. If it was true, he'd be harming himself as well as all the women he was rumored to have something going on with. His wife was in her sexual prime, and people were saying how lucky she was, when she was in fact suffering.

"I told him to stay home and rest, since he's not feeling well, but he still spends half a year away from home, sending me money every month. Yes, we're financially set now. Money can buy a house, but can it buy a home? It can buy medicine, but can it buy health? Money can buy fine food, but can it buy an appetite? Money can buy entertainment, but can it buy happiness? Money can buy a bed, but can it buy a good night's sleep?" When she was done, she turned to look out the window, where it was pitch-black with continuing rumbles of thunder and gusty wind with its accompanying rain. She sat up.

"I shouldn't have told you these things, Zhidie, and this is hardly the place to do it, either. I've often thought about visiting you, but I always change my mind and turn back. Why should I disrupt your peaceful life? When I ran into you earlier, I wanted you to come meet my cat. I'm like a cat now. Who would have expected that a rainstorm would bring us here to have this conversation? Now I've said so much, I might as well use this opportunity to fulfill one of my long-term wishes."

"What is it? I haven't visited you, either. I don't feel as if I've been much of a friend, now that I think about it. I'll do better from now on, especially if you need my help."

"Do you mean that?"

"Let thunder strike me dead if I'm lying."

"Don't say that. I would rather die if thunder struck you. You'll laugh when I tell you this. When I was younger, I once went to a literary forum in Xijing where you were giving a talk. I had never seen you before, but for some reason an idea crept into my mind—I'm going to marry him. Later, after I met you, I tried to find ways to see you, but I couldn't ask you in person. So I asked a friend to tell Jing Xueyin about me and asked her to talk to you. She sneered and replied, 'Where did she get the idea to come to me?' I was puzzled when my friend told me about her reaction, but then I heard that you and Jing were an item. I was so upset, I could have kicked myself. Then I learned that you and Jing broke up and you married Niu Yueqing, and I cried. After that, I went to your house once and met Niu Yueqing. When I saw how pretty and talented she was, I gave up and married Wang Ximian. Now we're both older, and after what we just talked about, I've decided to tell you this. You don't have to say anything. I'm at peace with myself now that I've finally done what I've always wanted to do."

He sat blankly, too shocked to speak. His lips quivered. His heart filled with remorse and deep emotions as he thought back carefully over the years since they'd met.

"Don't say anything," she repeated, "I don't want to hear it."

In the end, a sigh represented all the things he wanted to say to her.

They sat quietly for a while before there was noise in the staircase, followed by a shout from Ruan Zhifei: "You're still here, Zhidie? Ah, you're a real friend." He came in, and Wang's wife got up. "Zhidie is a real friend," she said to Ruan, "but what about you? You asked for his help but didn't stick around or feed him, walking off like that. You'd have had to pay someone to watch your house, wouldn't you?"

"I said he was a true friend, but I've changed my mind. If you hadn't been here, I doubt that he'd have stayed this long."

Zhuang got a towel to help Ruan dry his hair and told him he had run into her at the market earlier that evening and had come to Ruan's place to get out of the rain. They hadn't had anything to eat yet. Ruan apologized, saying that the factory had hosted a dinner after the performance. He wanted to leave but they wouldn't let him, so he had to stay in order not to offend the host. Then he shouted upstairs for one of the performers to go get some takeout.

After they ate, Ruan read the article that Zhuang had written and was enormously pleased. He brought out some liquor, but Wang's wife said she had to head home, and Zhuang said the same thing. Ruan asked them to wait till the rain stopped, offering to hail two taxis for them. After they had finished half a bottle, their faces turned red and shiny, but it rained on, while the rumbling thunder intensified.

"Why must you insist on going home in such a downpour?" Ruan asked. "One of you can sleep in this office, and the room next door is vacant, with clean bedding."

"That's fine with me, but I don't know about Mrs. Wang," Zhuang said.

"Ximian isn't home, and I'm used to coming and going on my own. I just can't leave that cat behind."

"That's easy. I'll call both of your places for you," Ruan offered. "Niu Yueqing asked me to get Zhidie out of the house, so she won't accuse me of getting him involved in any monkey business. With you, Mrs. Wang, I'll call Ximian's mother and ask her to take care of your cat. How does that sound?"

"Please tell her not to forget to feed the cat tonight. There's a fish in the fridge. She can give the cat half of it."

"Ai-ya, you're feeding a cat like it was a husband," Ruan said as he went upstairs to place the calls.

When he came back down, they resumed their conversation and finished the bottle. It was late, and Ruan's head was getting heavy.

"Don't stay up too late," he said as he asked who would take it. Zhuang took a look and said the bedding looked cleaner, so she should take that one. Ruan told them where the toilet was and where they could get water, and then wobbled his way up the stairs. Before long, it was quiet. Zhuang went to get some water for himself, and then brought some for Wang's wife.

"Here, wash up and go to bed. It's a cool night, great for sleeping. I'll knock on your door in the morning, and we can have mutton cakes at Laosunjia."

He went back to the office, closed the door, and wiped himself down before going to bed. A good drinker, he had finished half the bottle, but not only did he not feel the effects of the liquor, he was tense. He lay in bed listening to the rain for a while before his thoughts turned to Wang's wife. Over the decade since they'd met, he had always been fond of her, but he had never allowed his feelings to go any further, treating it more like a secret one-sided admiration. After what she had told him earlier that night, he was surprised to learn that the feeling had been mutual. Reminded that she didn't want him to say anything, he rolled over, forcing her out of his mind; but the more he tried, the harder it was not to think about her. How could he not? Despite himself, he compared her with his wife, with his mistress, and with Liu Yue. All that comparative examination got him so aroused that he had an erection. Without turning on the light or lighting the candle, he put on his clothes and got off the bed to pace the room for a while before opening the door to stand in the hallway. Feeling listless, he went to the toilet, but nothing came, so he returned to knock on her door.

"Who is it?" Wang's wife asked.

"It's me," he said, leaning against the door with his eyes closed.

"Is everything all right?" she asked. "Just a minute."

A light shone through the transom window, which was pasted over with newspaper. He heard her walk up to unlatch the door.

"Come in," she said without opening the door. So he pushed it open and saw her sitting on the bed, her blouse draped over her shoulders and a terrycloth blanket covering her lower body.

"Did you hear the cat crying upstairs and think it might have reminded me of my cat?"

"I—" Zhuang stammered as he closed the door and walked over to the bed, not sure what to do next. She understood what was happening.

"Zhidie—"

He bent over to hold her head in his hands and whispered, "I can't sleep. I—" He put his wet mouth over her thin lips. She put her arms around him and twisted around, bunching up the blanket to reveal that she was wearing pink panties. She looked like a mermaid. Zhuang climbed onto the bed with his shoes on, but she cooled off at that instant and stopped him with her hands.

"No, Zhidie, we can't do this. You'd be cheating on your wife, and I wouldn't be able to face my husband."

Zhuang wouldn't listen, but she quickly wrapped herself up in the blanket and looked at him with pleading eyes. He froze. She reached out to smooth his clothes and asked him to sit at the head of the bed.

"I fell in love with you and don't think I'll ever stop, but we can't do this. If you do love me, let's wait till we're both old. I don't mean to curse my husband, but if he dies before me, and Yueqing before you, then we can be together. But if we both die before them, then that's our fate. We can't escape our destiny and shouldn't force the issue. Otherwise, if we don't stop here, life will be difficult, since you and Ximian are both famous, and after only one night as husband and wife, we'd continue living with our spouses with a sense of remorse." She finished with a sad smile as she dried his tears, before reaching into her bra and bringing out a coin tied to a cotton thread.

"You saw this earlier, didn't you? I wear gold rings, gold earrings, and gold bracelets, but no gold necklace, not because I don't have one, but because I can't bear to part with this coin. I took it from your windowsill that time I went to your house to take a look at Niu Yueqing. I wanted to wear something of yours since I couldn't have you. Ximian knows nothing about this. Now I'm telling you, and I want to give it back, but not as something I'm returning. I've been wearing it for over a decade now, so it has been infused with my sweat, oil, and body odor to become an important part of me. I'm giving it to you so you'll know what I'm like." She took the necklace off. He put it around his neck and started to walk out tearfully, holding the coin in his mouth. When he got to the door, he stopped and turned to look at her. She laid her hands on her belly with an agonized smile.

"Are you in pain?"

"It's my stomach, an old problem. It goes spastic when I get agitated. It's all right. Go on back to sleep."

He wanted to say he'd massage her abdomen for her, but instead he fumbled in his pocket before producing the magic health sack from Meng Yunfang.

"Here, put this on."

She nodded with a smile and took the sack, then watched him open the door and walk out.

Over at Shuangren fu, Niu Yueqing, Liu Yue, and the old lady went to bed early on the night of the thunderstorm. At some point Liu Yue was startled awake by a loud thunderclap; to her it was like a fireball whirling in the sky before falling onto their rooftop and smashing the glazed roof tiles into pieces. When she was at home back in northern Shaanxi, she had seen a dragon snatch people. That was also on a day when thunder crashed, and she heard the villagers shouting, "The second mistress of the Hao family in the east has been taken by the dragon." She ran over to see. Mrs. Hao, a woman with a fair face and a slender figure, was lying by a locust tree that had been split down the middle; its top half was resting in a pond, still smoking. The woman had turned into a five-foot-long charred log, a recently whitewashed canvas shoe the only thing that was still intact. When Liu Yue heard the thunderclap right above the roof, she wondered if it had come for her. Sticking her head out from under the blanket, she looked outside to see if a fiery red ball was about to break through the window.

"Aunty," she called out, "Aunty. How can you sleep so soundly tonight of all nights? I'm so scared."

The old lady didn't make a sound. Liu Yue tried again; still nothing. It appeared to her that the dragon had taken the old lady instead, and she was dazed, feeling that all the dragons had come to Xijing at the same time to snatch away Wang Ximian's wife, Meng Yunfang's wife, Jing Xueyin, and Tang Wan'er, who was taken while washing her privates, which were rotten and filled her tub with bloody water. Liu Yue screamed.

It was a terrifying scream, especially coming so late at night. Niu Yueqing ran from her bedroom into the living room and turned on the light. The girl had crawled, stark-naked, in there and stared at Niu Yueqing as she said, "The dragon is snatching people, Dajie. The dragon is snatching people, and Aunty is gone."

Niu Yueqing went into their bedroom, and indeed the old lady's coffin bed was empty. She then went to the kitchen, the toilet, and the study, but there was no sign of her anywhere. "Check her shoes," Niu Yueqing said. Her shoes were gone, so they opened the door and ran into the yard. It was still raining, and in between the flashes of lightning, they saw the old lady kneeling on a stone, praying, palms together. Still naked, Liu Yue rushed over, picked up the old lady, and brought her inside. Niu Yueqing followed. She found her mother a change of clothes, then draped a thin blanket over the younger woman.

"It's pitch-black outside, Mother. Why did you go out there? Were you trying to get struck by lightning?"

"They were having a fight in heaven. I was worried it would get out of hand and spread to our city."

"A fight in heaven?" Liu Yue asked unhappily.

"Demons fighting demons. It was terribly violent, and everyone in the city was watching. Wicked gawkers just wanted to enjoy the scene, and no one wanted to pray."

"Who's out there on the street?" Liu Yue said. "Ghosts more likely."

"Right, it's ghosts. There are more ghosts than people in the city now. People die and become ghosts, but ghosts never die, so they crowd into each other."

The girl turned pale.

"Ignore her, or the more she talks the more frightened you'll get," Niu Yueqing said to Liu Yue, before turning to her mother. "Go to bed, Mother. Everything is fine."

The old lady grumbled unhappily as she changed out of her wet clothes, but she would not let go of her wet shoes as she lay down in bed. Niu Yueqing told Liu Yue to go to sleep, too, adding, "Are you becoming as deranged as she is, Liu Yue? When you don't see her in bed, get up and look around. If she's not in the toilet, then go look for her in the yard. Where could she go? Why were you screaming about dragons snatching people? You've been to school and ought to know that lightning strikes are caused by static electricity. It's not a dragon snatching people."

The color had returned to the girl's face by then, and she looked sheepish, though still afraid. "I don't know why, but I thought it was a dragon that was snatching people."

"You must have been dreaming, so you screamed when you woke up to find Mother gone."

"I'm not sure now."

The thunder died out after midnight, but the old lady did not go back to sleep. Liu Yue was getting drowsy, but before she fell asleep, the old lady poked her with her cane. "Someone's knocking at the door, Liu Yue."

The girl cocked her head to listen. "There's no one there. Who would come at this hour?"

"Someone is knocking."

The girl got up to open the door, but saw no one. "No one's out there." She went back to bed and slept awhile before the old lady called out again, "Listen, someone's at the door."

She got up again to open the door: still no one, not even a breeze. When she got back inside, she lay down without a word. At about four in the morning, the old lady sat up.

"Who's that?" she asked. "Who's out there?" She called out to Liu Yue, who pretended to be asleep by snoring loudly. The old lady came over to pinch her nose.

"How can you sleep like that?" she groused. "Someone's at the door."

Liu Yue sat up and said, "Do you not want me to get some sleep just because you can't? Who's knocking on the door? It's a ghost." She scared herself so much just by saying it that she pulled the blanket over her head and lay back down.

"You call yourself a maid? More like a young mistress of the house. You won't even open the door when someone's knocking."

Upset by the comment, Liu Yue got up angrily. There was still no one there. But instead of going back into the bedroom, she lay down on the sofa in the living room.

When day broke and Niu Yueqing got up, she was shocked to see the girl sleeping on the sofa looking tired, with dark circles under her eyes. After hearing Liu Yue's explanation, she said, "Mother is losing it again, I'm afraid. When Zhuang Laoshi returns today, I'll have him sleep in her room, since he likes to hear her talk about the ties between humans and ghosts. You can sleep in my room."

Zhuang came home early that morning and asked where Niu Yueqing was. Liu Yue told him she'd gone to work. Zhuang wondered why she was working on a Sunday, so Liu told him that she was helping someone out with leftover buns, relating the story about how Zhuang's mentee was having trouble selling the buns he had steamed, how Niu Yueqing had told the man that her office kitchen would buy them and that she would pay for them herself, and how Niu Yueqing was now trying to get the four sacks of buns delivered to a glue manufacturer.

"Another kind deed," Zhuang said before going to see the old lady, who naturally started ranting about the events of the night before. His interest piqued, he asked for details, telling Liu Yue he wanted to write a series of magic realist novels, which meant nothing to the girl, who made a pot of tea and sent it into the study. Zhuang was barely into the third sheet when he heard the old lady tell Liu Yue that someone was knocking on the door. She went to the door, but the old lady stopped her from opening it.

"Don't," she said. "Last night I thought it was someone I knew, but you said no one was out there, so it must have been a demon. Why keep knocking at our door? Don't open it. No matter what, don't open the door." Then she shut the windows in her room and drew the curtains before shutting her daughter's bedroom door and telling Liu Yue to shut the kitchen windows. She refused because she was cooking, and that led to an argument. Frustrated, she went into the study to talk to Zhuang, who went to talk to his mother-in-law.

"On a hot day you have to keep the windows open, Mother, or the house will be too stuffy."

"Won't that thing come in through the window if it can't open the door?" she asked, keeping her voice low. "Hot, you say? How hot can it be?" She licked her finger and touched Zhuang's nipples under his shirt, but when she moved on to Liu Yue, the girl blushed and held her hands in front of her chest.

"There's no need to be afraid in broad daylight," Zhuang said. "Come on, I'll go with you to see who's knocking. If it's a demon, I'll cut it down to size." He took an exercising sword down from the wall.

The three of them walked up to the door, and Zhuang opened it. Nothing stirred on the other side. The old lady took a careful look and fixed her gaze on the door.

"See there!" she called out. "Those really are ox demons and snake spirits, straight from the Cultural Revolution."

"Where? What?" Liu Yue asked.

"That's an ox and that's a snake, a two-tailed snake," the old lady said. "What's this? I've never seen anything this strange, with two horns and eight legs. This one's human, with long teeth. Another human here, with a pig's head."

Zhuang saw nothing, but a chill rose inside when he recalled the photos they had taken together.

"It's obvious to me, why can't you see anything?" the old lady said. "They must have imprinted their shadows on the door when they came knocking. Can't you see them either, Liu Yue? Can't you see the images? Can't you tell that this door is thicker than it was before? It's thicker with all those layers of their shadows."

With a shake of his head, Zhuang could tell that the old lady was sliding back again. He was also thinking that those defective photos must have resulted from a problem with the camera or a mistake in the developing room. Liu Yue, who was watching him the whole time, was relieved when she saw him shake his head. "The door *is* thicker, Aunty," she said with a giggle as she looked away.

"Yes, it is, Mother," Zhuang echoed. "Now stay inside and don't worry. Nothing can happen with Liu Yue and me here." He returned to his study and resumed writing.

The old lady was agitated the rest of the day, going frequently to the study to tell Zhuang that someone was knocking again or that they should not open the windows. He was clearly annoyed, and when his wife came home, he told her that he could not get anything done at home. She went in and complained to her mother, only to have the old lady insist that they go see the monk in the temple for another amulet. Zhuang phoned Meng Yunfang, who came over with a paper amulet, which he pasted on the doorframe. Meng told Zhuang that Huiming had drawn the amulet, not Abbot Zhixiang at the Yunhuang Temple.

"Tomorrow is Huiming's first day as the head of the nunnery. She asked me to invite some writers and artists to take part in the festivities. Want to come along?"

"So Huiming is taking over."

"That little nun is very accomplished. She can do pretty much anything she wants to. If she were in politics, she could very well be a vice mayor."

"I'm actually worried that she'll return to secular life one day." Zhuang smiled at Meng.

"What do you mean?"

Zhuang just smiled, then changed the subject. "Let me have the key," he said, lowering his voice. "I'm going over there to write."

"That place is wonderful. There's no one to bother you. I made another key, so you can keep this one."

"I'm going out with Meng Laoshi," Zhuang said to Liu Yue. "I may be back tonight, but if not, I'll be at his place. Tomorrow morning the new head of the nunnery will assume her position, and we're invited to attend the celebration. Tell your dajie that I have to attend, since the city's leaders will be there."

After walking through the gate, Meng asked, "Why won't you be back tonight?"

"That's none of your business."

"What do I do if Yueqing calls and asks to speak with you?"

"Just tell her we're working on an article. Did you finish that one for the mayor?"

"It's done. I already sent it to him for his approval."

"He'll know all about it once it's published."

They said good-bye, and Zhuang headed straight for Tang Wan'er's house.

She was packing when he surprised her by striding in, proof that his foot had healed.

"You came as soon as your foot was better," she remarked with a clap of her hands. Zhuang went up to kiss her. "Where else would I go for my first stop?"

After making him a cup of coffee, Wan'er stuck her head out the door to look up and down the street.

"Come sit down and talk to me. What are you looking for?"

"Zhou Min went to buy toothpaste. Why is it taking him so long? When he comes home, I'll send him out to buy a roasted chicken."

"I don't want any roasted chicken. I want tongue."

"You're so bad. I'm not going to give you any." She looked at him out of the corner of her eye. "We can't today," she said softly. "He'll be back soon. He said the magazine is sending him on an overnight trip to Xianyang to help sell the latest issue. An order from on high told them to destroy all copies of the magazine. About eighty percent were sold to retailers, so they're sending people out of town to help sell the rest and avoid a huge loss of revenue."

"When will he be back?"

"Tomorrow around noon. I said, 'Why not spend another day in Xianyang and take in the sights?' but he said it was Mr. Zhong's idea, and that could cause problems if people in the Department of Culture got wind of it."

"This is a godsend. Come to room 13 on the fifth floor in the building to the left of the nunnery. I'll wait for you there."

"Whose house is that?"

"Ours when we're there." He got up to leave. After he left, she washed the coffee mug and hastily put her stuff in a bag before searching in the wardrobe for her new skirt.

❋

At dinner that night, Liu Yue said to Niu Yueqing, "Is Zhuang Laoshi really not coming home again tonight?"

"He can go wherever he likes over the next few days. Meng Yunfang is such a show-off that your Zhuang Laoshi has to spend the night whenever he's there."

"Does Meng Laoshi have a big enough place for that?"

"Who cares?" Niu Yueqing sighed. "We've run into some bad luck this year, with all sorts of unpleasant things. His birthday is next Wednesday. In our family, we only celebrate my mother's birthday. But this year I've been thinking about a celebration. Maybe the festivity of a birthday party can wash away the bad luck."

Sensing Niu Yueqing's determination, Liu Yue added her thoughts: "It's so weird. The magazine was only trying to promote Zhuang Laoshi, and Zhou Min wanted to repay his kindness. How could a simple article cause so much trouble with Jing Xueyin? Before that was over, he hurt his foot in a fall, but he has never had a single accident on his scooter. Most people recover quickly from something like that, but he hobbled for days and days. Then the trouble with the secretary-general came just when his foot was getting better. Don't you think that's weird? The old mistress's odd behavior is nothing new, but Zhuang Laoshi has changed. He's no longer as easygoing as when I first got here."

"You need to understand that all these problems have put him in a bad mood. It's normal for a writer to be moody. And he's the sensitive type, which is why he can act like a child even in his forties. We've been married for over a decade, so I'm used to it. I'm just glad he doesn't smoke opium or fool around outside, so we have to tolerate some of his problems at home. That day you and I wrongly accused him of infidelity because of the letter, he was boiling mad. But the angrier he got, the more secure I felt. Being married to someone like him, I have to be both wife and mother."

A good wife, but a bit foolish, too, Liu said to herself. "People often say the wife is the last to know when her husband is having an affair," she said to Niu Yueqing. "You're his wife *and* his mother." She smiled. "But you also have to be his daughter and his courtesan."

"What nonsense is that? A wife is a wife. How can she be a courtesan? What kind of man would he be, and what kind of woman would that make me? If anyone outside heard what you just said, they'd surely look down on our family."

Liu Yue stuck out her tongue and said, "I know nothing. Just some rubbish."

"You know too much, and often what you shouldn't know. You little tart, whoever marries you will be tormented to death within a year."

After dinner, she told Liu to get a pen and paper to write out a guest list for the birthday party. When she finished, Niu Yueqing checked the list: Wang Ximian, Gong Jingyuan, Ruan Zhifei, Meng Yunfang, and Zhou Min and their wives, Zhao Jingwu, Hong Jiang, Niu Yueqing's cousin and her husband, Mr. Wei, the deputy chair of the League of Writers and Artists, Ding at the Artists' Association, Wang Laihong from the Dancers' Association, Zhang Zhenghai of the Writers' Association, as well as Mr. Zhong, Li Hongwen, and Gou Dahai from the magazine. More than two tables.

"Will the banquet be held at a restaurant or here at home? I can't cook for that many people."

"The ambience at home is better," Niu Yueqing said, "and of course you won't have to cook. My cousin's husband is a chef who will do the cooking, while old Meng can take care of the noodles and buns. You and I will take handle the invitations and the shopping."

They proceeded to look up everyone's number in the phone book and wrote them all down for Liu Yue to call; Niu Yueqing would personally invite those without phones. Then they moved on to the shopping list for food, cigarettes, and liquor, as well as utensils and a coal-burning stove that needed to be purchased.

A melodious call sounded beyond the door: "Junkman! Collecting junk and scraps!"

"The junkman is here, Dajie. Let's sell him the empty bottles and old newspaper under the rear window so the house will look neat and clean when the guests arrive."

Niu Yueqing nodded and went with her to bring out the scrap. In the light from the streetlamp at the entrance, they saw the old junkman lying face-up on the straw mat in his cart smoking, clearly enjoying himself as he puffed and blew smoke rings.

"Isn't it a bit late to be collecting scrap?" Niu Yueqing asked.

Without looking at her, he blew a smoke ring and said, "It's late, have any scrap?"

Liu Yue burst out laughing.

"Why are you laughing?" Niu Yueqing chided. "Silly girl."

"We have so many worries, but look at him, he's enjoying life. I've heard he's good at making up doggerel. Let's ask him to sing." She turned to the old man, "Hey, sing for us and we'll sell you this scrap cheap."

Still ignoring the women, he exhaled a column of smoke that rose up to the streetlight, where it dispersed like a cloud and highlighted mosquitoes.

"You sleep on a springy mattress, but it feels like a straw mat; I sleep on a straw mat, but it feels like a springy mattress. Two cranes soar in the clouds."

Liu Yue chattered something in response to the strange words.

"Be more serious, Liu Yue," Niu Yueqing said. She turned to the old man. "You've worked hard today. Where will you stay tonight?"

"I stay where the wind stays."

"It's late. Have you eaten?" Niu Yueqing asked.

"What you ate I ate."

"Go inside and bring out a couple of buns, Liu Yue."

Reluctantly, she went inside. Without thanking her or stopping the girl, the old man jumped off his cart to weigh the scrap and counted out the money. Niu Yueqing wouldn't take it, but he kept counting.

"Everyone says you're good at making up doggerel, old uncle. I have a favor to ask," Yueqing said. He abruptly stopped counting. Seeing that he was listening, she gave him a brief description of her husband, who worked on cultural propaganda and had had an article published to help someone one out during the People's Congress election. The former chair was not reelected, and now people were plotting against him. She wondered if the old man could come up with something to spread around that would help her husband appeal the injustice. He did not respond. Liu Yue came out with the buns and handed them to the old man, who offered the coins with one hand and took the buns with the other. Niu Yueqing still would not take his money, so the coins littered the ground as he left with his cart. Niu Yueqing sighed, wishing she hadn't wasted an explanation on him, but just as she was about to enter the yard, she heard the old man reciting words, one by one, from the far end of the dim alley.

"What's he singing?" Niu Yueqing asked. "That's not what I asked for."

Liu Yue said it was wonderful. Back inside, she waited until Niu Yueqing went to bed before going to the study to copy down the ditty. As expected, it turned out to be quite well known in Xijing's literary circles. Here was what she had:

> *Fangzi* (房子 house), *guzi* (谷子 grain), *piaozi* (票子 money), *qizi* (妻子 wife), *erzi* (儿子 son), *sunzi* (孙子 grandson), 庄子 Zhuangzi, 老子 Laozi, 孔子 Kongzi.
> After a lifetime of buzz, leaving nothing but a chin with fuzz, *huzi* 胡子.

When she was done, she undressed and climbed into bed with Niu Yueqing, who was still awake. She touched the girl's smooth, supple body. "You have a nice body, Liu Yue."

The caress tickled the girl. They chatted a while before one of them said, "Time to sleep." They soon drifted off.

The thunderstorm from the night before had cooled things off. Liu Yue had not slept well the night before, and she was exhausted. She slept soundly on this night. Yet she thought she heard something in her dream, and it might have been real. It sounded like someone moaning and whining, clearly not caused by pain; it was fast one minute and slow the next, high one instant and then low; sometimes as rapid as the hoof beats of a horse running down the street, or rain beating down on a sandy beach, at other times as leisurely as an old ox plowing a rice paddy or a kitten licking starchy paste. She didn't know why, but she went limp at the sound, her arms leaving her at first, followed by her legs, and finally her whole body; there was nothing left but her beating heart, as her body soared, flying up into a shiny white cloud before thudding to the ground. She woke up, exhausted beyond words and drenched in sweat. Strange how comfortable she had been a moment before. Then, feeling a coolness between her legs, she reached down and found that she was wet. She was wiping it with the sheet when she heard Niu Yueqing moaning beside her.

"Are you having a nightmare, Dajie?" she called out. Niu Yueqing opened her eyes. She lay in a partial daze for a moment before she said to the girl, feeling a sense of shame, "No. Have you been awake the whole time?"

"I was asleep, but I thought I heard a noise, a strange one, and it felt like a current ran through me."

"I think I heard that," Niu Yueqing said, which puzzled them both.

"It must have been a dream," Niu Yueqing said, echoed by Liu Yue: "Yes, we must have had the same dream."

"You woke up before me, Liu Yue. Did you hear me talking in my sleep?"

"You were just whining. I woke you up because I didn't want you to be frightened by a bad dream."

"I'm fine. It couldn't have been a bad dream. Go back to sleep," Niu Yueqing said and got up to use the bathroom. Then Liu Yue went in and saw Niu Yueqing's panties soaking in the tub, a sight that immediately told her that she and Niu Yueqing had experienced the same thing.

❋

The Clear Void Nunnery had been built in the Tang dynasty, when, people said, it was much larger and grander, with many more monks, nuns, and worshippers than the Yunhuang Temple. Half of the structures had been destroyed in an earthquake during the Chenghua reign of the Ming dynasty, in the second half of the fifteenth century, and it had never recovered its former glory. Renovations were focused only on the remaining buildings. It suffered an even worse fate during the Cultural Revolution, when most of structures were seized by factories in the surrounding areas, while the three dozen monks and nuns dispersed. By the time religious practices resumed, an extensive search for the former monks and nuns revealed that some had died and some had resumed secular lives; only five nuns survived, living in five different villages in three neighboring counties outside Xijing. Talked into returning, they hobbled back, only to see a sight that had them wailing: the Buddha's image had been destroyed, the halls and rooms had collapsed or had leaking roofs, and weeds had overtaken the compound. A dozen wild doves flew out from under the offering table, which was littered with their droppings. As the saying goes, if you can't do it for the monks, at least do it for the Buddha. Still possessing a strong belief in their faith, they thought it was the Buddha's will to have them survive all the tribulations in order to guard the temple, so they shaved off their gray hair and donned their black robes. Although contributions from worshippers were meager, and they were forced to rely on a subsidy from the city's Ethnic Affairs Commission, at least the melodious bells were heard again in the mornings and evenings. After several years of work, the main hall was restored, the Guanyin Bodhisattva statue was repainted, and the east and west meditation rooms were renovated, but they lacked the funds to work on Shengmu Hall behind the main hall, while the factories and the local residents who were occupying the land had yet to be removed, leaving the temple territory in the shape of an upside-down gourd. None of the aging nuns could read; they knew only how to burn incense and pray. When they tried to recite the sutras they had learned years before, they could only manage to recall parts, which made them laughingstocks to the monks at the Yunhuang, Wolong, and Lihua temples. After graduating from a Buddhist seminary, Huiming was put up at the Yunhuang Temple for a short stay, just as the Buddhist Association sent over some young nuns from the Qianfo Temple on Mount Zhongnan. Upon her arrival at the Yunhuang Temple, she decided she would like to go to the Clear Void Nunnery one day, after seeing that the Yunhuang Temple was a large place with both monks and nuns, some of whom were eminent or near-immortals. As a newcomer, she knew little about the Clear Void Nunnery, so she declined when the Buddhist Association expressed a desire for her to go there. However, she began taking part in the Clear Void Nunnery's affairs, helping to draft plans for recovering land and to write applications for funding. When everything was taking shape and she had gained some sway, she put in a request to move, but not initially as the head. Instead, she showered respect on one of the old nuns by serving as her assistant, while plotting to have the older nun one day make a fool of herself and expose her incompetence. Soon Huiming had gained the trust of all the other nuns, who backed her when it came time to replace the old nun. Huiming then employed all her skills and went where she had to in order to build up a network. She was able to obtain a large sum of dedicated funds to give Shengmu Hall a speedy restoration and a new coat of paint in the rooms. As it would take time and effort to remove the illegal occupants, she pored over Xijing's gazettes and found a reference saying that the temple was rumored to have been where the Tang Imperial Consort, Yang Yuhuan, had become a nun. It was a providential discovery, and she made more than a dozen copies to send to the Provincial and Municipal Ethnic Affairs Commissions and the Buddhist Association. In addition, she asked Meng Yunfang to draft a report on the religious and historical importance of the ancient site where Yang Yuhuang had once been a nun, finally alerting the mayor to hold a meeting with the relevant religious offices, the factories, and the housing authorities. The occupiers were asked to relocate, the sooner the better. In the end, all of the temple's land was recovered, except for the five-story residential building. With this impressive accomplishment behind her, she launched a restoration of the main gate. It was not the traditional arch with wood and stone carvings, but displayed grandeur comparable to the Yunhuang Temple; it received cheers from the nuns and admiration for Huiming from everyone in the Buddhist realm. Like a flower blooming in a breeze, she naturally took this opportunity to work on the relevant authorities, and eventually was promoted to head of the temple. An auspicious date was chosen for her to take over.

After a night of abandonment to sexual pleasure, Zhuang and Tang rose at eight, their faces puffy. They massaged each other's face before a quick breakfast consisting of a thick spicy soup with meatballs at the Hui People's Market. Then, pretending to have just rushed over, they sat and talked outside the fence at the temple's main gate. Inside was the new gate, whose eaves were draped with a horizontal red satin banner that read: "Assumption Ceremony for the Head of the Clear Void Nunnery." On the spacious steps under the eaves were tables covered with white cloth, on top of one of which was a microphone wrapped in red cloth; two rows of five hard-backed chairs had been placed at the side. Tall pillars were hung with couplets that read: *Buddhist thoughts are like clouds; the clouds rise to the mountaintop; the clouds are farther away when you get to the mountain peak / Buddhist teaching is like a moon; the moon is in the water; the moon reflects deeper when you part the surface.* A crowd had gathered on the ground at the base of the steps; there were monks in dark robes and Taoist practitioners with topknots, but most were guests and police sent to maintain order. A row of sedans sat beyond the fence. Glancing at the license plates, Zhuang was surprised to see the mayor's car, and he sighed with admiration over Huiming's ability. Residents who knew about the celebration but did not have an invitation and a permit to enter sprawled across the fence to peer inside. Vendors selling all sorts of food and sacrificial paper and candles set up stalls in the alleys, where they shouted for customers. Zhuang looked around but did not see Meng Yunfang; he wondered who else Meng had invited. Then he went to buy a string of candied hawthorns, but Wan'er complained that it wasn't clean. Instead she wanted to eat "mirror cake," a type of sticky rice cake that had long been absent from the street markets. The vendor was an old man who sat in front of his stove, high atop a canopied three-wheeler that looked more like a peddler's stand than a moving vehicle. A horizontal board with the name of the snack written in ink was on the canopy, while the slender posts on each side had inscriptions: "Original rice and original juice made with original skill" and "An old family and an old man carry on an old name."

"Great," said Zhuang when the old man removed the lid on the steamer to show them two cakes with bamboo sticks in them. "One will be enough. None for me," he said.

"Oh, so you're not a lover or a paramour? I'm so sorry," the old man said. "Then the wife will have one."

Wan'er gave Zhuang a look, and they both smiled.

"What can you tell us about the cake?" Zhuang asked.

"It's called a mirror cake because it's about the size of a hand-held mirror, also symbolizing perfect harmony. During the Tang dynasty, it was a special treat sold at courtesan establishments, and later in the old society it was sold at theater entrances and amusement parks. It's not so popular anymore, but it's like drawing a lot: if a couple comes up and buys only one, then the woman must be the wife, a comrade, or a close friend. If a couple buys two, then they must be lovers or paramours. It never fails."

"But isn't that incorrect?" Zhuang asked. "With two to form a union, the woman has to be the wife, representing perfect harmony between husband and wife, isn't that right?"

"Yes. As the ancients said, a wife cannot compare with a concubine, a concubine cannot compare with a prostitute, and a prostitute cannot compare with a secret lover. These days, nine out of ten couples manage to hang on to their marriage. But I'm just joking. Just joking."

They walked away.

"Why didn't you buy one and try it?" she said. "Don't you think we can be together forever?"

"The old man was just wisecracking to get more business. You can't believe what he says. If you do, then buying only one means that the woman is the wife, and that's a sign that we'll be husband and wife in the future."

She was greatly pleased by what he said. Just then they heard someone calling out to them: "Hey, you two. Out for a stroll?"

Startled, she turned and stepped to the side, as if they were strangers. It was Meng Yunfang.

"What's taken you so long?" Zhuang said. "I ran into Tang Wan'er at the intersection and told her to get Zhou Min, since you've invited us to the ceremony. She said he wasn't home and she didn't want to come, but I got her to stick around." He turned to her: "Wan'er, ask Meng Laoshi if he invited you."

Knowing what he was getting at, she smiled. "I don't believe you. Meng Laoshi wouldn't invite me."

"I did," Meng said. "If I'm lying, I'm a dirty dog."

Soon Li Hongwen and Gou Dahai from the magazine and Dai Shangtian, the book reviewer at the Writers' Association, showed up on their bikes. They greeted each other before Meng led them to the entrance, where he talked to the police and showed them inside. Being familiar with the temple grounds, Meng told them about the place as they walked along: the flagpoles outside the entrance were from a certain time in the Song dynasty, and the entrance, which faced the gate on the city wall, had excellent fengshui. They passed the entrance and came to a large area with a pond in the center. A fountain in an artificial hill spewed water into the pond. People tossed in coins, saying that good luck would come to anyone whose coin floated on the surface. Wan'er pushed her way through to take a look; she tossed in some coins, but they all settled to the bottom. Unhappily, she reached into her pocket for more, but there were none; she turned to see a yellow banner with long colorful ribbons on each side tied to a flagpole behind the pond. Zhuang was standing there reading the writing on the banner, so she went over to ask him for some coins. With his eyes still on the banner, he struck a match to light his cigarette and told her get some from his pocket. After getting what she wanted, she rested her hand inside his pocket and held his ample penis.

"Stop that! This is a Buddhist spot," he said.

She gave it a squeeze and it began to harden. "So you're reverent, are you? Then why are you getting hard?" She laughed and walked off with the coins.

Meng came up and said to Zhuang, "That's not worth reading. I wrote it myself." He dragged Zhuang to the rear, as Tang finally kept a coin floating on the surface. But with no one she knew there to cheer her, she pouted and walked off. She was happy to see statues under the veranda on both sides; the Bodhisattvas seemed familiar, but she couldn't name them, with their pretty faces, round as a full moon, and their soaring brows and graceful eyes.

"Tang Wan'er, are you looking at beautiful statues or are you trying to see if you're prettier than they are?" Meng called to her.

She ran over looking displeased, but was laughing by the time she reached them.

"You do look like them when you frown," Meng said, "but that smile is too pretty, it ruins the resemblance."

"You spout nonsense wherever you are," she said. "It's disrespectful."

"I know more about Buddhism than you do. An ancient master once said that the Buddha is nothing but a dead wooden stake."

As they talked and walked, Li Hongwen saw Zhuang look into a row of sutra halls and bedrooms. "Are those rooms for the nuns? Do they sleep alone or in pairs?"

"Why do you care how they sleep? Go check in at the reception desk," Meng said.

Li Hongwen turned to Zhuang and said, "The nuns do sleep together. So, do you think there are lesbians among them?"

Zhuang didn't reply. A nun walked by, dressed in a long gray robe, looking graceful. Li stuck his tongue out and exclaimed how pretty she looked with her head shaved.

"You'll probably shriek in admiration when you see the abbess later," Zhuang said.

A crowd had gathered at the registration area when they arrived; an old nun was sitting behind a desk covered with writing brushes, ink, and a book with rice paper pages. Meng introduced Zhuang to her, eliciting cries of surprise from her and several nearby monks. Huiming came out through a small round door, which drew a gasp from Li Hongwen, as predicted by Zhuang, who reached out to shake her hand; she responded with a Buddhist greeting and invited them inside. It was a small, clean compound, with two rooms to the north; she led them into one. They were served tea.

"We are honored by your visit," she said to Zhuang. "I was worried you might not accept my invitation."

"How could I stay away from something this important? Congratulations."

"Why don't you go meet the provincial and municipal leaders?"

Before Zhuang could ask who they were, she took him into a suite with a circle of black straight-backed chairs with apricot-yellow cushions. Cigarettes and used teacups were strewn across the top of a black lacquered tea table inlaid with strips of patterned Lantian jade that sat in the middle of the room.

"Let me make the introduction, honored leaders. This is the celebrated writer Zhuang Zhidie."

"We all know who he is," they said, reaching out to shake Zhuang's hand. He knew some of them—the chair of the Provincial Ethnic Affairs Commission, the head of the Bureau of Civil Affairs, Huang Defu, and the secretary-general of the Municipal Party Committee. After shaking hands, Zhuang walked up to Huang Defu.

"Is the mayor coming?" he asked.

"He had an important meeting and sent me as his representative."

"I saw his license plate and thought he must be here. Getting all of you here is quite a coup."

"This is the temple's first major event."

"What great thing are you working on these days?" the secretary-general asked, but Zhuang ignored him and continued his conversation with Huang.

"How are you doing?"

"Fine. How about you? How's your foot? I hear it was healed by an unlicensed doctor."

"Yes, he was really good. Two plasters and I'm fine." Zhuang turned to see the secretary-general lean forward, ready to shake his hand. But, still pretending not to notice him, Zhuang said something to Huang before going back to his seat. Picking up his cup to sip tea, Zhuang glanced at the secretary-general out of the corner of his eye; the man was still standing there, his outstretched hand suspended for a while before he curled his fingers and said to someone beside him, "It's Wednesday today; it'll be Thursday tomorrow and Friday the day after."

Zhuang spotted Meng waving to him from the door, so he walked over.

"Huiming is busy today. She said she can't receive everyone properly and asked me to take care of you. She gave me six coupons for a meal here after the ceremony. They serve vegetarian fare, but the dishes are unique, so you may want to try them."

"Too many people and too much going on to enjoy a good meal. Why don't we go for some spicy noodles? They can cool you off on a hot day like this," Zhuang offered.

"Sounds good. I'll take them to see the congratulatory scrolls. It's about time for the ceremony to start. Want to come with us? You'll have to sit onstage with the leaders."

"That secretary-general is here, too. I ignored him earlier, but I'd be out of bounds if I ignored him when I'm up there with them. What will the ceremony be like?"

"First a brief gathering at the entrance, with music and firecrackers, followed by Master Xingyun of the Famen Temple, who will announce Huiming's assumption as abbess. Then will come speeches by the leaders and representatives from various temples and religious sects. The assumption ceremony in the Buddhist tradition will take place last."

"I'm not going to the gathering, but I will stick around for the ceremony."

"I'll go tell them to look around on their own, and we'll meet at the gate later. Wait for me at the hall. I want to show you something you will definitely like."

Zhuang went to Shengmu Hall to look at the statues. A large ringed cauldron, filled with incense ash, stood in the front, behind an iron rack more than a dozen feet long, into which holes were drilled at four-inch intervals. Swarms of worshippers were burning incense and lighting candles to fill the holes, sending soft red wax dripping everywhere. The air was too acrid for Zhuang, so he walked out to look at the small pavilions on either side of the hall. He first went to the one on the east, where a stone stele detailed how Yang Yuhuan had become a nun here before she was chosen to enter the palace, and how Emperor Xuanzong of the Tang dynasty had come here to worship the Buddha and burn incense. He smiled, knowing that it had all been made up by Meng Yunfang, and walked across the pavilion to the west. Just then, Meng came over with Wan'er. Her face was even lovelier from the sweaty heat; she said she had been to every hall, and asked him why there were so many monks at a nunnery, not to mention an orchestra whose members were all monks and nuns. Did they play musical instruments?

"There are only thirteen nuns here, not enough for a major event like this. The others have come from temples," Meng said. "I borrowed the orchestra from Ruan Zhifei. They dressed up like monks and nuns to show their respect for the solemnity of the occasion. Based on your train of thought, there will be lots of 'affairs' here with so many monks in a nunnery."

"Is the stele in the pavilion your work, Meng?" Zhuang asked. "It's a bald-faced lie. What proof do you have for Emperor Xuanzong's visit?"

"What proof do you have that he didn't come?" Meng retorted while leading him to the pavilion to the west. "Look at this, this is the real thing. The nunnery once had a rare beauty who became a nun."

Zhuang took a closer look at the smaller stele and read the inscription:

Epitaph for Ma Lingxu, a nun from the Shengwu Temple at Dayan

Drafted by Li Shiyu, Vice President of the Board of Punishments, and inscribed by Liu Taihe, a commoner

The Taoist lady is called Lingxu, surnamed Ma, from Weinan. With tender skin and a graceful manner, she had a unique aura, a pure heart, and a gentle nature, sparkled like a mirror, and was as fragrant as an orchid. She could roll her long sleeves seven times, and her exquisite singing lingered for three days. She strummed an instrument and sent cranes dancing, played a bamboo pipe to make a dragon sing. Although she learned to sing from tutors, she was so talented that she put the girl from Wu to shame and demoralized the girl from Han. Her fame was not limited to that place, for she was well known in the south also. Things changed in the world, and her heart ceased to beat. Leaving the world, she was included in the roster at the celestial palace. A woman made up for the one she loved, she sought to be with the gentleman. Of the thirteen shrines in the Tianbao reign, she was enshrined in the Kaiyuan Temple, returning to Master Dugu on the first day of the lunar year during the Shengwu reign. The pure jade was pinned back on the robe, while the green pine stood alone. Knowing the past like the deities, I could tell the secrets behind everything. But things did not turn out the way I wanted, and I spent three years with no results. My heart knew where it belonged, and a glance was good enough. Pleasant talk and laughter to accompany my friend went with the zither. Before the month was out, she died without suffering an illness. As the gentleman said, "A splendid appearance with no substance is a great regret." Twenty years have passed. My father, Guangqian, was the Xiuning County Head at Xinzhou. He celebrated good deeds and outstanding people, and asked me to draft these humble words to commemorate the lady. The epitaph would read:

Such a graceful lady, her beauty like the spring. Could it be jealous enough to snatch away her life at such a young age? She would be the clouds on Wushan and the goddess at the Luo River. I do not know where she is, and can only ask the deities.

Established on the 22nd day of the first lunar month in the first year of the Shengwu reign.

"Such beautiful prose!" Zhuang exclaimed. "It makes me wish I could have met the lady in the inscription. Years ago, when I went to the Luo River, I was reminded of 'Ode to the Luo Fairy,' and was so moved I cried in the wind. After reading the stele, I felt as if I had met her or that she was right in front of me. The poor lady was such a beauty, and yet she suffered terribly. It makes me sad."

Seeing him so emotional that his eyes turned red saddened Tang Wan'er.

"Zhuang Laoshi sounds like he was reciting a Shakespearean sonnet," she said with a pouty smile. "It's too bad he wasn't born back then, or she would be Mrs. Zhuang."

Still enthralled, Zhuang said, "No, that wouldn't happen, but I would definitely want to meet her." He went to buy some incense and placed it in front of the stele, making Wan'er even more jealous.

"Zhuang Laoshi is such a romantic soul," she said, "that the lady could sense that even after death. But there are so many great women, in ancient times, now, and in the future. Zhuang Laoshi could not have been born in ancient times; nor can he live long enough into the future. Even now, pretty women are as numerous as the clouds, so which one will he love?"

Zhuang blushed at her words, suddenly realizing that he had been too caught up in the beautiful tale and had said too much. Music sounded at that moment, drawing all the worshippers and tourists away from the hall to the entrance.

"Hurry, Mother. The abbess is going to assume her position," a woman shouted shrilly.

The three of them followed along, wondering how Huiming would make her entrance. They saw a fat-faced, big-eared monk in a red cassock who was holding a jade tablet and chanting as he walked to the front. Behind him a nun carried an image of Buddha, and another was banging on a wooden fish, followed by four younger nuns in two rows with lotus lanterns. Then came Huiming, draped in a gold-foiled cassock and wearing a pair of black cloth shoes with slightly elevated heels. With a solemn expression, she looked serene with her bright eyes and white teeth in a rosy-cheeked face above a graceful neck. She walked slowly and effortlessly, seemingly floating like an immortal. Eight monks playing instruments and four nuns brought up the rear, a magnificent contingent approaching Shengmu Hall. Li Hongwen, who was with the other onlookers, ran along to keep Huiming in his field of vision. Tang whispered into Zhuang's ear, "Look at her. Isn't she the Miss Ma from the stele?"

"Maybe she is. The nunnery is a fantastic place."

"I will come here one day," she said.

"You think you could live in a place like this?" He slyly poked her.

When the contingent entered the hall, the onlookers crowded against the entrance, blocking Zhuang and the others, who could only hear the music and chants.

"I'll go find someone to let us in." Meng headed toward the entrance, just as the crowd parted to open a passage. The contingent was inside paying respects to Shengmu; the actual ceremony would be held at Daxiong Hall. The contingent went to both pavilions, where they burned incense and knelt to worship, then moved to the front to pay respect to the various Bodhisattvas before heading to the main hall. The officeholders had been taken ahead of time to the main hall, where they sat against the wall to watch. Meng tried to get Zhuang to join them, but he refused. The contingent entered the hall. Once again, the crowd surged around the entrance, and no one could see a thing with all the heads bobbing in front of them.

"Forget it. We won't see much even if we're in there," Zhuang said.

"Then where do we go? There's no place to sit," Meng said.

"Let's go out back and have a drink."

"Good idea," Meng said, clapping his hands. He called the others together and led them out through the gate. They turned down a lane to reach the building, and went up to number 13.

On the way up to the fifth floor, Meng gave everyone a description of the room, while trying to come up with a name for the place. When he opened the door, he saw that Zhuang had already hung two large characters framed in glass facing the living room wall: *Seeking Imperfection.* To fit the circumstances, he announced, "This is our salon, which we will call the House of Imperfection Seekers." The name was unanimously approved, for the notion of seeking imperfection seemed both elegant and meaningful.

"We can let the magazine's writers revise their work here," Li said.

"No, this is for our activities only," Zhuang said. "And we won't accept outsiders during our weekly get-togethers. I brought you here today because you're all tired, but please don't go around telling people about it, or we'll lose a quiet place to work."

He brought out the bottle of liquor and two packets of peanuts he had bought at the shop downstairs, telling them to sit wherever they wanted and make themselves at home.

"You can bring food and drink here, but once you're here, you must talk about literature and the arts," Meng said. "Let's begin."

"Literature isn't like business," Gou Dahai said. "You can't just start talking. Why don't we drink and chat for now, and maybe at some point the topic will emerge?" He opened the bottle and, because there were no cups, poured its contents into the bottle cap to pass around. Wan'er, who was sitting by herself on the bed, said, "I don't drink."

"Why not? Are you having your period?" Meng asked.

"Nonsense. I'm not a writer or an editor, so I can't talk about literature or art," she said as she fluffed up the bed pillows. She found a long hair and quickly picked it up.

"Well, you don't want to talk about literature or art, but you are a work of art, so we'll talk about you."

"Your mouth stinks the moment you open it. I won't call you laoshi anymore."

"How's this?" Zhuang cut in. "Let's each tell a story and then rate them at the end. Those who tell good stories will be safe; those with terrible stories will be fined three drinks."

"I know what you're up to," Meng said. "You want to hear our stories and then use them as material for your novels."

"So what?" Gou said. "Didn't Pu Songling have a studio for idle chat?"

"Pu Songling didn't work as fast as Zhuang Zhidie," Meng said. "About a third of his writing material comes from me, and I've never been paid. But I will tell another story today, with a price tag attached. Zhidie, will you pay for it?"

"After this, I'll treat everyone to a bowl of noodles."

"All right," Meng said. "This is a true story. Do you know the low-lying area near Gongde Gate? The residents there are mostly from Henan. The Yellow River flooded often before Liberation, so the people from Henan who had fled to Xijing threw up tents and sheds and never moved back home. More and more people from Henan settled there, which is why the area is called the Henan Special District. There aren't many sheds anymore; they've been replaced by single-story houses, but space is so limited that an entire family lives in a single room, with a window to the left and a door to the right. And that's how our story takes place. One day a new couple moved in. The woman was so pretty, so tender you could draw water if you tapped her skin, and naturally the man could not get enough of her. They had sex several times that night, and he wanted to do it again in the morning, making their neighbor uneasy over the noise. You see, the neighbor was a bachelor. The couple naturally repeated the activity the second night, after which the woman needed to pee. Women like to pee at such times."

"You need to wash your mouth out before telling stories," Tang Wan'er said.

"All right, then. I'll try a more refined story," Meng said. "A hospital admitted a patient with appendicitis and needed to have his pubic hair shaved. An old nurse started shaving, but then a call came for her, so a young nurse took over. When it was done, the two nurses went to wash their hands at the sink, and the old nurse said, 'The youngsters these days all love tattoos, but this one is weird. He has a tattoo on his thing that says "spring up."' The young nurse said, 'No, it says "spring water in the river flows up."'"

No one caught the joke at first, but then Tang punched Meng. Dai Shangtian was totally lost. "What does that mean? Why did one see two words and the other see seven?"

"You're so dense," Meng said. "Tang Wan'er knew right off. If it were you and me, there would always be only two words, but if she were there, there would be seven."

They all laughed. "Now back to the first story," Zhuang said.

"The added story was free, of course," Meng continued. "So the woman went to pee and walked back to her place, but it was dark, and all the buildings looked the same, so she opened the door and went straight to bed. But guess what? She had entered the bachelor's room instead. The bachelor, who was already having trouble sleeping, got worked up when he heard the woman peeing outside. When she climbed into his bed, he knew she was in the wrong house. But he said to himself, *Why pass up something good that drops right in your lap.* He put his arms around her and began humping. 'You're amazing,' she said. 'You just did it, and now you can do it again.' The bachelor said nothing, but was breathing as hard as an old cow, arousing her suspicion. She reached out to touch his head. He was bald. She let out a cry, got out of bed, and walked back to her own place. Her husband asked her if she'd peed a riverful. She sobbed, saying she had done something terrible. He was outraged when he heard her explanation and stormed out of the house. But he walked into the room on the left. Oh, I forgot to tell you that they left their doors open in the summer for ventilation. The occupant of the room to the left was an old man, whom the husband beat the hell out of. End of story."

"That's it? What happened next?" Li asked.

"Of course there was a huge to-do, even involving the police," Meng said. "That prompted the residents in the area to lodge a complaint with the mayor, asking for a solution to their housing problems, or, they said, there would be more stories like this one to bring shame to Xijing. Didn't you notice how the low-lying areas are under reconstruction?"

"That's a funny story. You don't have to drink," they said.

"All of Meng's stories involve sex," Li said. "I'll tell you one that won't offend Wan'er. You know that we've been long-time residents of Xijing, and that I have lots of uncles on both my mother and father's sides. These days, networks are all the rage—the mountaintop network, the group network, the alumni network, networks for people from the same area and networks for secretaries. All but the worthless network for relatives serve a useful function. Now that the rural areas are closing in on the city, most of our officeholders have worked their way in from the rural areas, while hardly any of the old residents occupy official municipal positions. There are eighteen families in my clan, with thirty-six children. Half of them have been sent to other counties and can't come back, while the remaining half are all on society's bottom rungs. I can't count on their help, not even to find a child-care center for my kid. And yet I have to go see them with gifts come holiday time. Earlier this year, over New Year's, I bought a box of snacks and my wife said, 'With so many relatives, who are you giving that to?' I told her not to worry. On the first day of the lunar year, I gave it to my maternal uncle. That afternoon, my first maternal aunt sent her kid over with a box of snacks, which I re-gifted to my second maternal aunt, and so on. I was on a virtual carousel, not having a moment's peace to eat and sleep. You visit relatives to fulfill a responsibility, and you can leave after you hand over your gift. We started back to work on the eighth, didn't we? Well, that night my wife's brother-in-law came, the last of my relatives. He left a gift and went home before I came home. When I got back, I thought it looked familiar. The price tag was still on it: three yuan thirty, which was what I had written on it when I bought it. He re-gifted it right back to me. How's that for a fine piece of reportage?"

"Interesting, but not quite up to snuff. Drink up." So Li drank. "Not interesting enough for you? All right, I'll take that. Now I'd like to see what you have to offer."

It was Dai Shangtian's turn. "I can't tell stories," he began, "so I'll drink."

"You're a book reviewer, which gives you an advantage. You have to tell us a story," Zhuang said.

"Our housing wasn't assigned by my workplace. My wife works at a bank, and she gets housing, so I live with her as her dependent. It's a high-rise, and we live on the tenth floor, which means I'm often out of breath after climbing the stairs. One day I looked for my key but realized I had forgotten to lock the bike, and the key was still in the lock. Oh, I forgot to tell you that I keep the door and bike keys on the same key chain."

He stopped. They waited for him to continue.

"Go on," they urged.

"I'm done."

"You can't get away with that," Wan'er said. "We want another one."

"I often wonder," Dai said, "why I only deal with four or five people in a large city like Xijing. At home, I'm my parents' son, my wife's husband, and my son's father. Away from home, I'm friends with you and my officemates. So what really belongs to me? The only thing that's truly mine is my name, and yet I never call myself by that name. It's always someone else who uses it."

"Drink up," Meng said. "That didn't sound like a story at all."

"What he said makes me sad," Zhuang said. "We can't punish him. Your turn, Dahai."

"What I'm going to tell you is not really a story, and I can't verify it, either. I heard it from someone else. You know how many fake goods there are these days, and I've always thought that those in power would be spared. But last Sunday my sister told me about an old Xijing official who hosted a banquet for his comrades. To show off his success, he held it at a high-end hotel restaurant. They ordered Maotai, which the hotel manager brought out. They tasted the first bottle; it was a fake. So he brought out another bottle, and it too was a fake, as was the third one. The manager was clearly embarrassed. 'What's a hotel like this doing with fake liquor?" the official grumbled before sending his secretary to his house to bring back a bottle of his own Maotai. They opened it, and everyone got a glass. Guess what? It was not only fake; it was just water, tap water."

"It must have been a bribe," Meng said. "Maotai is so expensive, no one can afford to give the real thing, but nothing gets done without a gift, hence the fake. Zhao Jingwu told me he did something like that once. Everyone's heard the story Dahai just told us, and if not, they can imagine it. But this bottle is the real thing, and you have to drink, Dahai."

"I did say it wasn't a story," Dahai said, red-faced. "It's just a detail you might find useful in your writing." He took a drink.

"You people didn't like what I just told you, either, but it contains some gems," said Li Hongwen. "But I must tell you that I've used it in one of my stories, so don't you use it, Zhidie. You're so famous that if you copy me, the readers will actually say I copied you."

"It didn't interest me anyway," Zhuang said. "Here's my story. Earlier, I went to use the toilet at the nunnery. The holes were all taken, and more people were waiting in line. One of the squatters smiled at me, and I tried to figure out who he was. A fan of literature? A member of the audience at one of my talks? Or someone who had seen my picture in my books? I walked over to him, but he ignored me. Then I realized that he was straining so much, his face had contorted into a smile."

They laughed.

"You're mocking us," Wan'er said. "You made us laugh so we'd all look like that guy. But you've demeaned yourself, a famous writer telling that kind of joke."

"Nothing wrong with demeaning oneself. In fact, the best way not to embarrass people is to demean yourself and get a good laugh over it. In the past we said 'say cheese' to get people to smile when taking their photos. In the future, why not say 'strain'? How do you like that little item? It's copyrighted, so you can't use it."

"No deal," Meng said. "Whatever is said here today is open to all. Salon means to share ideas, give each other inspiration, and help with creative writing."

"Now I know how to be a writer," Wan'er said. "You use my ideas and I use yours. Like fish in a tank, I eat what you spit out and you eat what I spit out, which turns the water fetid and the fish stinky."

They fell silent at this comment before Meng laughed.

"Wan'er is amazing," he said, "stripping away all our writers' skins. I recommend that we seek some sort of breakthrough. I wanted to invite Huiming to give a talk on Zen, but she's busy these days, so we'll have to wait. If you're interested, I could share some knowledge on qigong. In *Master Shao's Magic Numbers*—"

"We'll pass on your 'numerical divination,'" Zhuang interrupted. "Wan'er isn't a writer or an editor, but she's more intuitive than the rest of us. As an outsider, she can see us more clearly than we see ourselves. Let's listen to her."

"I have nothing to say."

"Of course you do," Meng said. "Go on, so we can go get something to eat."

"You want to hear something clean or off-color?"

"You know both?" Li asked. "Then off-color, of course."

She looked around and broke up laughing. "Look how you all perked up when I mentioned something off-color. Sorry, but I don't know anything like that. Being from a backwater, I'm still learning about big-city life, but I did hear something the other day. Why don't I sing it for you?"

"Great!" Zhuang said. So she began:

Dust swirled on Qin's eight hundred li of land.
Thirty million people roared in singing the tunes of Qin.
Filling a bowl with long noodles pleases everyone.
Not adding spices and chilies makes them grumble.

They clapped when she was finished.

"She's a real Shaanxi resident, a true portrait of Shaanxi people," they said. "Where did you hear that, Wan'er?"

Raising his cup, Zhuang said, "The most engaging person today is not us literary types, but her. She's so much better than the rest of us. The lyrics are terrific, and so is her singing. I propose that we reward her with three cups. If anyone else wants to drink, we can take the bottle along when I treat you all to some spicy noodles."

They stood up to urge her to drink. She could not stop smiling; her face brimmed with delight. After downing the first cup, she said she would stop there and asked Zhuang to drink the second one for her, with an offer to toast him with the third. Zhuang clinked the bottle with her cup. She held her head high when she'd finished, her face like a peach blossom.

❋

After visiting several markets and stuffing the refrigerator, Niu Yueqing counted the days and decided not to buy seafood. Instead, she decided to purchase a set of red clothes for her husband. She went to a department store on South Avenue and, with a woman's attention to detail, pored over the merchandise without finding anything to her liking. She then headed to the City God Temple Market. Built during the Song dynasty, the temple's gate was still intact, but the grounds had been renovated and turned into a narrow street. Parallel lanes spoked out on either side, so that all the shops faced each other, a perfect image of a willow leaf that has been dried until only the ribs remain. Each was a specialty shop, selling miscellaneous items like needles and thread, buttons and ribbons, shoes for bound feet, felt hats, mahjong tiles, spittoons, and chamber pots. Six more lanes had opened up in recent years for shops selling objects related to traditional customs and lifestyles: candles and spirit money for the dead on Tomb-Sweeping Day; long red ropes for hanging apples for horseplay at weddings; swaddles for newborns; funeral kerchiefs for mourning sons and grandsons; sets of red clothes and belts for middle-aged men's birthdays, to drive away the bad and summon the good; bamboo steamers for date cakes at temple celebrations in Dongcheng District on the eighth day of the fourth month; wooden molds to create patterns for fried cakes; small galoshes for little old ladies; black satin hair nets with glass baubles; and large tin kettles for brewing thick liquor over charcoal fires in the last month of the year in Xicheng District.

Niu Yueqing went to the shop selling red clothes, where she asked if any of them were available in one hundred percent cotton and whether anything had a Buddhist symbol printed on the back. She complained about one for its crude needlework and another for not being well stitched. Lucky for her, the salesclerk was patient and good-natured. Looking at the clothes strewn across the counter, Niu Yueqing said, "I'm picking out a dragon robe for an emperor's enthroning ceremony," and laughed at her self-mockery.

Emerging from the lane onto the street, she was surprised to see Gong Jingyuan, who now had a significant paunch.

"You're still looking young." Gong smiled broadly. "And you still have the figure of a young girl. I'm so envious of Zhidie. You must get old and look ugly quickly to make me feel better about myself." Slapping his protruding belly, he said he was no longer presentable. Niu Yueqing patted his belly and said it added to his charm at that age, which so elated him that he thanked her for perking him up. As they jested, Gong noticed the red clothes in her hands and wondered why she would want to wear something that flashy.

"I'm glad I ran into you, it saves me a trip," she said. "Wednesday is your friend's birthday, and I want to invite you to be part of the celebration."

"That's wonderful! I'll bring a set of mahjong tiles, and we'll play non-stop for a day. Did you invite that Mr. Ruan? Tell him to bring some members of his troupe, will you? We'll make it a big celebration. Need me to bring a chef? I can get you one from any hotel in town."

"No need to bring anyone or anything; just bring your mouth. I will be unhappy if you follow the old practices. But do bring a set of tiles if you want to play mahjong, since we don't have a good set at home."

"Guess what I'm here to do?" Gong asked, then answered his own question: "Buy a good set of mahjong tiles."

They went their separate ways after some more banter. It was nearly dark when Niu Yueqing got home, where Liu Yue had already put food on the table. Niu Yueqing's cousin's husband was sitting at the table, and next to the sofa were a bag of potatoes, two pumpkins, and some newly picked daylilies wrapped in a bandana. He hadn't eaten yet, preferring to wait for Niu Yueqing and Zhuang Zhidie. After a brief greeting, Niu Yueqing said, "Zhidie has been out and about for a few days. Since he's not home, it's likely that he's already eaten elsewhere. So we won't wait for him."

She had barely finished speaking when Zhuang walked in the door.

"We were just talking about you," the cousin's husband said.

"We haven't seen you in ages," Zhuang said genially. "I hear you won a contract for the kiln, so you must be doing well."

"You make money without working for it, or you work hard without making any money. I could fire bricks all night long, but what I make doesn't amount to one of your punctuation marks. I busy myself all day long without much to show for it. I received a message about some planned affair, so I told her I would pass up a chance to mine gold to come over. I brought some local produce."

"I'm not in business and I'm not building a house, so what planned affair are you talking about?" Zhuang was puzzled. "It must be that she missed you and wanted you to visit."

"You're less open and honest than Yueqing. You won't invite country cousins to come for a meal, is that it? Well, I'd be here even if you didn't want me to be, and I'll bring the whole family, plus Aunty's relatives and friends."

The man looked too serious to be joking, so Zhuang turned to his wife. "What's this all about?"

Niu Yueqing just smiled.

"You're always running around, never worrying about what goes on at home," Liu Yue said. "Now you've even forgotten your own birthday."

Zhuang's face darkened as he gave the red clothes a shake. "Am I about to turn seventy or eighty? We never celebrate Mother's birthday, so why celebrate mine?" He turned to the cousin's husband. "Don't listen to Yueqing. She's just looking for something to do. Go ahead and eat. I've already eaten."

He went into his study.

The cousin's husband had planned to speak with Zhuang at the dinner table, but when he saw the unhappy look on his face, he changed his mind and said to Yueqing in a low voice that when her cousin received the potion to produce a son, she was told to try it for a month. But she'd caught a cold that had lasted three days, and then he'd had to leave home to collect a debt owed by a kiln customer. He was away for two weeks, and they'd missed the window of opportunity when he got back home. He wanted to know if they could get more of the potion from the old lady. That upset Niu Yueqing: *That potion cost several hundred yuan. How much could the outstanding debt have been? It's true, you didn't have to agree to help, but when you did, you needed to keep your promise, since other people are affected by your failure to do so. How could you be so careless?* But things being the way they were, she could not say anything unpleasant; besides, they were relatives, and she needed their help.

"I'll ask," she said. "This potion has to be treasured. The eagle wood alone cost me five hundred yuan."

"I promise I won't go anywhere next month, no matter what," he said. "I won't touch any alcohol, either."

"You must keep it a secret," Niu Yueqing whispered. "Don't tell anyone. Let me know when she's pregnant, and I'll take her some nutritious food. Don't say anything negative, don't let her do any heavy work, and don't argue or upset her. When the time comes, I'll talk to someone I know at the city hospital, and they'll send a car to pick her up."

He nodded. "Of course. We'll do as you say."

"And don't tell Zhidie that she had to take more of the potion," Yueqing said before going into the study. "Come have a drink with him, even if you don't want to eat. I'm going out to buy her a pair of sandals. I'll be right back."

Zhuang walked into the living room with a bottle of liquor, wearing a smile.

Rushing out of the house, Niu Yueqing first went to Granny Wang's, where she bought another potion for five hundred yuan, then headed to a shoe store to buy sandals. When she got home, her cousin's husband and Zhuang had drunk half a bottle. Putting the shoes and potion in a plastic bag, she said to her cousin's husband, "Here are the shoes. Be careful on your way home." She signaled to him with her eyes. Knowing what she meant, he said, "I will," before saying good-bye. Realizing that he hadn't been very cordial, Zhuang felt bad about what he had said earlier, so he walked the cousin's husband out to the end of the lane. After the visitor was out of sight, his displeasure with Niu Yueqing's plan for his birthday flared up again, so he went to the park outside the west gate to listen to some street performers sing a Qin opera. On his way home, he spotted a taxi coming out of their lane; the passenger looked like Gong Jingyuan's son, so he asked his wife when he walked in the door, "Was Gong Jingyuan's son just here?"

"Yes. Everyone says the young man is an opium addict, and his face did look like a tattered sack. He said his father had urgent business that required him to make a trip to Lanzhou early tomorrow morning and told him to send a gift over. I offered him tea, but he wouldn't drink it. His nose was running, so he was off somewhere to smoke opium. Ai! I wonder what he was in a previous life, and why he's here now to bring ruin to the family."

Zhuang took a look around and saw a large birthday cake and a fancy paper tote bag with "Luxurious satin comforter cover" printed on the side.

"So you told Gong Jingyuan, too?"

"I ran into him on the street this afternoon and mentioned it in passing. You can't say no when he has his son bring over a gift, can you?"

"I told you I don't want a birthday celebration, so why are you accepting gifts?" Zhuang fumed. "You do like to show off, telling people without checking with me. Did I just become an emperor or a new father? Haven't I lost enough face over the Jing Xueyin fiasco? Now you want to have a celebration in the midst of this foul atmosphere, which will give people a reason to laugh at me? Return the gifts to the people you've told. If you don't, I'll stay away that day."

Niu Yueqing was speechless.

The old lady came out of her room.

"I don't like to meddle in your affairs, but what you just said was deplorable. I was already unhappy, with everyone waiting for you to come home for dinner, and then, when you finally show up, you say all those things to your cousin's husband. Are you intentionally insulting my relatives? I should be the one who objects to Yueqing's plan for your birthday celebration. Your father came this morning and mocked me for having an unfilial daughter. I told him I'm old and must depend on her, and that in the end we have to look to our son-in-law for help. A son-in-law is like half a son, so you are a son in two families. I don't like to complain about you two, but now you're unhappy over a relative creating a foul atmosphere? Is that a complaint about my poor relatives? This house once produced a famous person, and the Water Board would have been as powerful as the yamen if Xijing hadn't brought in tap water."

Zhuang helped the old lady back to her room and told Liu Yue to make her a glass of orange juice. "What are you talking about, Mother? I was just unhappy that Yueqing made plans without consulting me, and that she has no understanding of how irritated I am these days."

"You're irritated?" Niu Yueqing said from the living room. "I'm your wife, don't you think I have a reason to be irritated? We've had so much bad luck this year, I thought a birthday celebration could chase the bad away. But what do I get? Nothing but a warm cheek bumping up against a cold behind. You say awful things that cut into my heart like a knife. I've put up with it so long I've gotten used to it. But now you've embarrassed me in front of my cousin's husband, making me lose face and all standing in the family. You're always talking and laughing outside the house, but once you're home, you do nothing but scowl. Over the past six months, you've become a different person. You're tired of me, aren't you? Everyone says I have a good life at home, but no one knows that I'm not a wife, I'm your maid, your slave."

"Dajie, there's nothing wrong with being a maid, and it's not being a slave," Liu Yue piped up from the kitchen, where she was scrubbing a pot. "Is that how you see me, as a slave?"

"You stay out of this," Niu Yueqing said.

"Only bad things happen when you curse someone," Liu Yue said, "so it doesn't bother me, but this time, the less you say the better. You have good intentions, but Zhuang Laoshi isn't being unreasonable. If you want to have a birthday celebration to chase away bad luck, why not just invite a few friends over? But you want to make a big splash. Our place is small to begin with, and it would be torture on a hot day. Besides, people may think that Zhuang Laoshi has something else in mind."

"Hear that?" Zhuang said. "Even Liu Yue knows better than you."

Niu Yueqing, who had no way to vent her anger, blew up when she heard Liu Yue's comment, followed by Zhuang's ridicule. "I know I'm no match for Liu Yue. She doesn't like to cook, so she's happy that no one ever eats in this house."

"I spent all morning in three markets," Liu Yue said. "And do you hear me complaining? Did I say anything about my feet getting bigger from all that running around? I'm a maid, born to cook for others. So don't say I don't like to cook." Liu Yue had always taken Niu Yueqing's side, so what she said this time made Niu Yueqing feel that she had spoiled the girl. Why else would she talk to her like that? Reaching the peak of her anger, Niu Yueqing said, "Then you're a fence-sitter. What did you say when I discussed the celebration with you? Now he doesn't want one, so you side with him. He's your laoshi, a celebrity. People say that once a woman's husband treats her badly, everyone else will do the same. That's so true. What do we do now, Liu Yue, since you know better than I do? Come on, tell me. What do we do?"

Liu Yue began to cry. Zhuang, who was sitting there looking stern, saw that and realized that she was, after all, an outsider. But he also wanted to aggravate his wife.

"No need to cry, Liu Yue," he said as he banged the table. "Let her do what she wants. One of these days, you'll come back to the compound and cook for me alone."

"All right, then," Niu Yueqing said. "Since you make enough money to hire a maid, you can do what *you* want. You're ganging up on me. I can't criticize my husband and I can't say a bad thing about a maid, so what status do I have in this house? I've brought shame to my ancestors." Now she was crying, which increased Zhuang's anger. But before he could blow up, the old lady came out on unsteady feet. Liu Yue went up to help her, but she pushed the girl away and pointed her finger at Zhuang. Her lips quivered, but not a word came out. Zhuang turned, opened the door, and walked out, heading for the apartment in the Literary Federation compound, where he would spend the night.

Zhuang chose not to return home from the apartment; Niu Yueqing chose not to join him there. Given the standoff, the birthday party was canceled. Liu Yue's outburst that day had created a rift between her and Niu Yueqing, a development that secretly pleased her, as she had been waiting to see Zhuang's wife make a fool of herself. She started paying more attention to her appearance. One day, when some fans of literature dropped by, she received them properly, without looking too humble or too haughty. A while later, she gathered up some papers Zhuang needed to attend to—important letters, requests from newspaper editors, and invitations to various social functions—and handed them to Niu Yueqing. "These are all pretty urgent, Dajie. Do you want to deliver them, or should I go?"

Niu Yueqing, surprised by how the girl's mind worked, wondered if maybe Liu Yue was more capable than she. "I don't want to see him."

So Liu Yue went to the compound. Zhuang was naturally happy to see her, taking note of how neatly she had arranged the letters and documents, how bright her clothes were, and how nicely she had made herself up. Taking her hand, he chatted with her for a while, then asked her to make something for him to eat before she headed back. Thereafter, she traveled between the two places. Niu Yueqing was upset with Zhuang, but he was her husband, after all, so she did not voice her view on Liu Yue's trips; rather, she bought what he liked to eat and quietly left it in a basket for Liu Yue to take along.

During this time, Tang Wan'er also made several visits to the compound, frequently enough that the guard, Granny Wei, could remember the young woman with the lovely eyes and easy smile. Once she even asked Zhuang if Tang was an actress, prompting him to change their meeting place to the House of Imperfection Seekers. On this day, the sun came out after a brief rain, turning the air humid and stiflingly hot. Zhuang waited at the house for Tang, but she didn't show. So he took out a pair of binoculars they had bought together to enjoy a view of the city and trained it on a building across the way. It was the dormitory for female workers at an embroidery factory. Eight young women with pretty eyes and nice teeth stayed in one room. They had likely just gotten off work, for they were washing up, dressed in shorts and bras. Three of them were engaged in horseplay. Engrossed by the scene, he was surprised to see a sheet of newspaper held up to the window with large words in ink: "Shame on you." Red-faced, he lowered the blinds and went back inside, where he spotted a note under the door. He picked it up and saw that it was from Tang, who had slid it in earlier that day. He had overlooked it when he came in.

"Good news: Zhou Min says the deputy governor in charge of cultural affairs has stepped down and that the head of the Propaganda Office wrote 'To be resolved by the Department of Culture' on the announcement, so the magazine has stuck to their decision to print it as written. Jing Xueyin objected, and Zhong Weixian said that in that case they wouldn't print it. So it doesn't appear in the latest issue." She had added: "I can't come today. A friend of Zhou's came from Tongguan with news from home, and Zhou Min and I have to feed him. I stopped by on my way to buy groceries. Forgive me."

Zhuang let out a sigh. So the deputy governor was out. *What good timing. Niu Yueqing wanted a birthday celebration to drive out bad luck, but how can a birthday do that? And now something good has happened without a celebration. What a shame Wan'er can't be here; otherwise we would drink a toast to that.* He fantasized about what they would do, and as his fanciful thoughts took flight, something stirred between his legs. He took off his clothes to take care of himself. □□ □□ □□ [The author has deleted 48 words.] He reached the height of his fantasy and came; then, when he wiped it off with the note, he discovered more writing on the back: "Bad news: Zhou Min said that Meng Laoshi has gone blind in one eye."

Zhuang was staggered. He quickly dressed, washed his face, and rushed out, heading for Meng's house.

Meng had indeed lost sight in one eye. It was a highly unusual circumstance: everything looked fine on the surface, and he felt no pain or itch. He just could not see with that eye. Not in the least upset, he said with a laugh, "I found out yesterday morning when I woke up. I went to the doctor, but the exam didn't show anything. Zhidie, don't try to pull one over on me anymore, because I'm now a one-eyed wonder."

Feeling sorry for the man, Zhuang said that one visit wasn't enough, that Meng should go see more doctors.

"Not even the King of Medicine, Sun Simiao, with his magical healing powers, could do anything. You know why this happened? I've made some progress in my study of *Master Shao's Magic Numbers*. Let's give it a try."

He took a leather case out from under a table. It was filled with three thread-bound books. "You were born at eight o'clock on the evening of July twenty-third in 1951, weren't you? Now, wait. I'll come up with a series of numbers, and you can look them up in these."

Zhuang was in a fog as Meng wrote out three four-digit numbers. Following the instructions, he flipped through the books to come up with three poems:

One: *Cut up goose down when a northern wind blows*
Plum blossoms in snow and the bamboo is brighter than ever
The birthday is the seventh month of the intercalary year
And he was born on the twenty-third day

Two: *The lost wild goose misses its flock, and tears fall freely*
The siblings have different spans of life
Three brothers, each has his own destiny
One suffers a blow and loses his life early

Three: *Father was born in the year of the boar and died young*
Father and mother are constantly at odds
With the two parents, he loses the father first
While he will see longevity enjoyed by his mother

Speechless after he read the three poems, Zhuang cried out: "I can't believe there's such an incredible book. Everything about my life is recorded there."

"You didn't believe me when I told you about it before." Meng closed the book and continued. "This is the most magical of the many books derived from *The Book of Changes.* It was lost for millennia, and even some of the finest practitioners of divination have never heard of it. According to Abbot Zhixiang, the Huangcheng Library in Xijing once held a copy. Kang Youwei came to visit, asked to see rare treasures that were scattered around the city, and walked off with a few pieces. When the library and the Yunhuang Temple found out that he'd taken an ink stone and a volume of sutras, they wrote to the provincial military governor, who sent a man after Kang. He rode his horse all the way to Tongguan before catching up with him and demanding that he return the stolen items. The incident shook up the whole country. But later they realized that one book was also missing, and after checking the catalogue, they learned that it was *Master Shao's Magic Numbers*, a long-sought-after book that no one was able to find. They knew Kang must haven stolen it. No one knew what happened to the book after Kang died. Two years ago, someone with unusual talent in Taiwan claimed to have a whole set of the magic numbers, but he didn't have the decoding system; he traveled to thirteen provinces in search of it, but wound up empty-handed. I've got it right here."

"You sound so mysterious, but I don't hear you making any noise about it."

"You think I'm the type that makes noise all the time? It depends on the matter at hand. I'm telling you now, and you must keep it a secret. This book originally belonged to a sixty-two-year-old man in the northern suburbs who never told how he came into possession of a copy. I've heard he's a Manchu, a descendant of the main branch of the red banner, so the book must have come from the Imperial Palace. For several decades he hid it from everyone, and he worked hard on the decoding system for eighteen years, with no success. I met him at Abbot Zhixiang's place, and after we'd gotten to know one another, he let on about the book and asked me to work on it. I've only gotten the first step solved. Now I can change birth dates and years into four-digit numbers, but all I'm able to tell you is when you were born, your parents' zodiac signs, the number of siblings you have, and your wife. Beyond that, there is what you were in your previous life and will be in the next one, in which years you will meet with calamity or great fortune, on which day you will make or lose money, and your official position and rank. But I don't know how to decipher these. The book's first page says, "Revealing the heavenly secrets will cause you to lose your sight and hearing." I lost sight in one eye after taking this small step toward solving the secrets."

Zhuang was dismayed by what he heard.

"Don't read any more," he said.

"How can I not?" Meng said. "You can keep your eyesight if you don't understand this book, but human eyes can only see the mundane world. You lose your sight when you read this book, yet you can see into the future. Which is more important? So I was actually happy when I couldn't find a cause for my blindness, because I knew that I'd managed to read and understand a tiny bit of the magical book. I was even more energized when I returned from the hospital. I studied day and night, but unfortunately I haven't been able to make more headway."

Zhuang had to agree with his friend. "Well, you do enjoy doing this. Why don't you check on my marriage?"

Meng spent quite a bit of time calculating before coming up with another four-digit number. When they looked it up in the book, they found:

A phoenix graces the dead tree in front of your house
Fortunes in life must be pursued but none are real
It is best to put aside the short term and go for the long
Others will gossip about everything you do.

"What does that mean?" Zhuang asked. "It looks like it's about Yueqing, but then not quite."

"I can't tell you, either."

"Have you looked into the people we know?"

"Look at this one." Meng took a piece of paper from the book and handed it to Zhuang, who read it but understood nothing.

"This is about my wife, and it's dead on," Meng said. "She's destined to marry twice. As for others, I don't know their birth dates and years, so I can't look into it."

"Here, let me give you three people. The first is Tang Wan'er, who was born between nine and eleven on the third night of the third month in 1957. The second is Liu Yue, born between five and seven in the morning on the twenty-eighth day of the twelfth month in 1963. And the last is

Wang Ximian's wife, born between five and seven on the eighth night of the last month in 1950."

Meng looked them all up. Strangely, each of them had only one four-digit number, and the poems did not meet the style of regulated poetry, as had Zhuang's.

Tang Wan'er:

The lakes and the ocean are places of great leisure
Dip in a rod and hook to fish amid mist and ripples
The affair is over, but not others
The yin could have it but not the others.

Liu Yue:

Happy go lucky but will it last
After obtaining the pearl under a majestic steed
It is soon lost in the water.

Wang Ximian's wife:

Worrying heart
Pitiful cries
Round after round of vexations
It is over, but not quite.

"Why don't any of these say anything about their marriages?"

"I may need a different set of numbers to look that up. This is all I could come up with, having only their birth dates and years."

Zhuang was saddened by the lack of information, but he told himself, *It's better this way. Wouldn't it be terrible if I knew it all? If everything is predestined and Niu Yueqing and I will not be together in the end, it would be fine to continue dealing with her the way I do now. But what if she and I are fated to grow old together? It would be all right if Wan'er and I are to marry, but if she were to marry someone else, how could I keep loving her when I knew she would belong to someone else in the end? And then there's Liu Yue, as well as Wang Ximian's wife, and perhaps others in the future. Based on* Master Shao's Magic Numbers, *everything was settled before I was born, and that means what I have, all my accomplishments, my fame, and my entanglements with the women around me, have been preordained. Then what excitement awaits me?* He regretted looking these things up in the book.

"It's better that you can't find those. Don't look up anyone we know, and don't tell anyone what happened today."

"Yes. Otherwise, you'd know too much and could lose your ability to speak, even if you didn't go blind. Unlike me, you are at the peak of your career. So enjoy life."

"How am I supposed to do that?" Zhuang shook his head.

About an hour later, Xia Jie came home, drenched in sweat, and plopped down on the sofa after briefly greeting Zhuang. Saying she was dead tired, she asked Meng to light her a cigarette, which he did.

"You've started smoking?" Zhuang asked.

"I have to enjoy what you men enjoy. What are we eating today, Yunfang? Is lunch ready?"

"Zhidie is here, and we had a lot to talk about, so I didn't have time to cook. Why don't you make us some noodles?"

"You've been sitting in a cool house all morning and now you ask me to cook? No."

"Okay. I'll go buy some noodles." Meng walked out with a container.

"You must think I'm a tyrant in this house," Xia said to Zhuang the moment Meng left. "I've refused to do anything around the house lately. He's obsessed with that *Master Shao's Magic Numbers* and is getting weird. He never listens to me. In the past, Abbot Zhixiang was like a god to him, and then he went on and on about the nun Huiming. Now he's found another idol after meeting a doddering old man in the northern suburb. He's the type who would die without someone to worship."

Zhuang laughed. "So has he stopped being an advisor to the magic health products factory?"

"He stopped that long ago. Look under the bed, and you'll find a pile of magic sacks. When he was writing up product information, he said the sacks contain musk, borneol flakes, and tiger penis. I asked him how a factory could get that many tiger penises for all the sacks they make each day. A tiger can have only one, and how many sacks could it fill? Are they raising tigers under beds or catching them on Mount Changbai up north? Aren't they afraid the police will accuse them of killing nationally protected rare animals?"

Zhuang laughed. When Meng returned with the noodles, he asked what was so funny.

"Don't tell him," Xia said to Zhuang. "We're laughing at laughable people."

Meng did not press them, and they sat down to eat. After lunch, Meng wanted to go out with Zhuang, so annoying Xia that she ignored them. Meng perked up once they were out of the house. He asked Zhuang to give him a ride to Xiaoyang Village in the northern suburb, where the old man lived. He once again described the mystical old man who had spent years traveling all over China, searching out true masters of divination and ferreting out the decoding system for *Master Shao's Magic Numbers*. Meng added that he owed his own access to the secret code to a ditty by the old man, who had in turn learned it from an old woman who specialized in phrenology. Intrigued by Meng's description of the old man, Zhuang sped toward the north side.

A small building stood at the entrance to Xiaoyang, a medium-sized village. When they arrived, a young couple was standing on the balcony, where the woman was breastfeeding a baby. The man said, "If you don't want it, Daddy will take it." He leaned forward and noisily sucked a mouthful. "What a shameless daddy you have," the woman said to the baby. Then she amused the child with a little ditty: *"Twenty-third, offer sacrifices to the kitchen god. Twenty-fourth, sweep the floor. Twenty-fifth, grind beans for tofu. Twenty-sixth, steam the buns. Twenty-seventh, kill the rooster. Twenty-eighth, paste paper-cuts on the window. Twenty-ninth, seal the grain vat. Thirtieth, stew a pig's feet. On the first day of the new year, kick out your feet.* Zhuang could not stop looking at them. "They're the old man's son and daughter-in-law," Meng said. "They're just having some fun. Don't stare."

"I was listening to the nursery tune. The second part is terrific. But why stew pigs' feet on the thirtieth and kick out your feet on the first?"

"On the thirtieth, you boil water to wash your feet, clip your toenails, and put on new shoes. Then, on the morning of the first, children kowtow to their elders, and they kick out their feet when they do that."

"That's wonderful! And it sounded especially good in her Henan accent."

Meng looked up at the balcony. "Where's your father?" he asked.

"Inside," the young man said.

Meng led Zhuang into the yard and went up to a room on the ground floor on the north side, where an old man sat drinking tea. Instead of getting up, he merely moved a bit so that they could sit down. Then, after handing Zhuang a tea-stained mug, he turned to whisper something to Meng. Zhuang was surprised to find the room shrouded in darkness, and noticed that it did not have a single window and that it smelled bad. Thread-bound books littered the old man's bed and table.

"This is my cousin," Meng said. "He's okay, you don't have to lower your voice."

"Have a cigarette," the old man said as he glanced at Zhuang. Not finding any on him, he leaned forward to grope through a pile of bedding, where he found a pack, which he tossed to Zhuang. "I traveled north of the Wei River three times," he said, still in a soft voice. "The man simply refused to show it to me. On my fourth visit, he said I couldn't see it because that would be the same as buying it. I said I'd buy it and asked him how much. He said he needed two hundred thousand to build a house. I told him I didn't have that much, but I could offer forty thousand. 'Not enough,' he said, and started haggling. I upped my offer to forty-five thousand. That was all I could come up with. Two days ago I went back in the afternoon, but he had changed his mind. I spent the whole night talking to him. I said, 'You don't have the book, so what are you going to do with the twenty-three lines of decoding rhyme?' He said, 'You're right, but you don't have the rhyme, so your book isn't even as useful as a traditional dictionary.' He was right, too, of course, so I offered to give him a photocopy of the book when I had it all decoded. He finally agreed the following morning. I handed over forty-five thousand yuan, and he produced a small pamphlet, wailing and calling himself an unfilial son who gives away a treasure passed down by his ancestors. He cried so hard he doubled over." The old man brought out a small camphor case, from which he retrieved a four-page handwritten notebook and whispered something to Meng.

"It's all right," Meng said. "He'll give me a ride home. I'll be back as soon I make some headway."

"You don't need to come back. But I might come see you tomorrow afternoon."

After the two men walked out, Meng asked, "So, what do you think of him?"

"I'm not a fan of people like that. Too secretive."

"He was guarded against you. I wouldn't tell him your name, so he ignored you."

"Now you're going to lose sight in your other eye," Zhuang said.

"I can't really tell if the rhyme is the real thing or if I'll be able to use it. And if I lose my sight in both eyes, I'm afraid Xia Jie will leave me."

"I thought you checked her fortune and saw that she'll only remarry once."

"She'll be mean to me even if she does stick around. You'll have to come see me more often when that happens."

"Of course. If that's how she turns out, I'll deliver you to the nunnery. Hasn't Huiming always been good to you?"

"Things are different now that she's the abbess. For funding, I introduced her to Huang Fude, and now she runs to him if she needs something. When she sees me, she says Amita Buddha, all prim and proper, like a true Buddhist adept."

"Of course she's a true Buddhist adept," Zhuang said with a laugh. "I've always been worried that you'll ruin that for her."

Meng laughed but said nothing. Troubled by something, Zhuang nearly rode the scooter into a roadside ditch. He was thinking of Huiming in her gold-foiled cassock. When they reached the north gate, Zhuang was surprised to see railroad tracks. "Isn't this Daobei?"

"Yes, it is."

"Where's Shangxian Road?"

"Go east after you we pass through the gate. It's not far."

"Good. I'll take you to meet a woman I know."

"So you keep a woman here," Meng said.

"You and your dirty mouth," Zhuang said, before telling him about Zhong Weixian and Ah-lan's address. "Now that we're here, why not ask her if the letter has been posted and find out how things are in Suzhou."

Meng praised Zhuang for his thoughtfulness. They soon reached Shangxian Road and turned down Puji Lane.

They had no idea that people from Henan congregated on the west side of Shangxian Road. The moment they entered Puji Lane, they felt as if they were in the passageway of a large building—both sides of the street were packed with houses tall and short, with either one or two rooms. Cooking stoves, earthen vats for water storage, and trash baskets were lined up under each windowsill, which made it difficult for passersby to avoid bumping into things. The street was too narrow for three people to walk shoulder to shoulder; in fact, you had to turn sideways when passing another pedestrian, and you were so close you could smell a cigarette or garlic on the other person's breath. Zhuang looked for a safe place to park the scooter. "Put it over there, it'll be fine," an old woman playing cards at the entrance said. "Thieves don't come here. This isn't Xijing."

"That's strange. Does a police chief live here?"

"Police chief? Not even a regular policeman would want to live here," she said. "See how narrow the lane is? Where's a thief going to hide with all the facing doors and windows? And then there's us. We have a card table on this end of the lane and a mahjong table on the other. How's a thief going to get out?"

"A lane of people like one big family. That's wonderful," Zhuang said. "Do you know where a sister of Ah-lan lives? She's from Anhui."

"Anhui? We don't have anyone from Anhui."

"Isn't Mu Jiaren's wife from Anhui?" a second woman offered.

"Why didn't you say she's the wife of someone from Henan? Of course we know Mu Jiaren's wife. She has a sister who's been staying with her for quite some time. They're the two flowers of this lane. Where are you from? Are you relatives or old school friends?"

"Coworkers," Meng said.

"Number 27. Don't forget. It's 27, next door to 29. Don't walk into the wrong house. There are newlyweds in 29. They're in bed now, and wouldn't be happy for you to walk in on them."

They started off down the lane, laughing.

"The Mu family is very strange," the old woman's voice followed them. "The men in every generation are simpletons, but the wives keep getting prettier."

The heat was like a steam bath as they walked along checking house numbers. They spotted a half-naked woman with shriveled breasts, tangled hair, and signs of prickly heat on her forehead, which was covered by a thick layer of white face powder. She was standing in front of a window with tightly drawn drapes.

"Ah-gui, are you dead, Ah-gui?" she called out, but no sound emerged from inside until a woman replied, "Ah-ah-ah-gui-is-not-not-in-in-in!"

Zhuang was puzzled by the response. Then the woman outside said, "Oh, you say Ah-gui is out? How can that be? Why did you have the drapes closed? Aren't you afraid you'll get prickly heat on your bellies? Oh, well, go back to what you're doing. I'm going home. When you're done, have Ah-gui lend me some yam paste to make noodles."

Zhuang realized why the woman inside had talked in that voice, and the realization brought a smile to his face. They walked out to the middle of the lane, where they saw a man squatting outside number 27 doing laundry.

"Is this number 27?" Zhuang asked.

"It is."

"Does Ah-lan live here?"

The man looked up at them. Just then a voice came from inside the house: "Who's that out there? Yes, Ah-lan lives here."

The man nudged his basin aside to let them pass. They went in and saw a large bed, on which sat a woman in pajamas who was clipping her toenails. She had small, slender, pretty feet with red nail polish. She looked up. It wasn't Ah-lan. Meng took out his card and handed it to her. "This is Zhuang Zhidie, the writer. He knows Ah-lan."

The woman slipped off the bed and looked almost furtively at Zhuang before crying out, "Ai-ya! How could such an important person be here in our house today?" She picked up a shirt and hastily put it on. "Please, have a seat. Jiaren, come see who's here. Why are you standing there? Hurry, bring some water. This is my husband."

Mu Jiaren, his hands covered in soapsuds, turned and smiled, displaying very white teeth against a very dark face.

"Just look at this husband of mine. All he knows how to do is wash and scrub at home. Totally worthless. Please don't laugh at us."

Mu blushed, adding a red tint to his dark face. Embarrassed, he could only stammer, "You won't do the washing, so I have to."

"Listen to you," the woman said. "If you were as talented as Mr. Zhuang, I'd wait on you day and night so you could write. You wouldn't have to worry about a speck of dust."

"Do you really think I'm that special?" Zhuang said. "I often cook and do the washing at home."

"That's ridiculous. If so, it's your wife's fault. Housework might wear her out, but physical fatigue is nothing compared with mental exhaustion."

Mu Jiaren brought them tea and moved with a smile to the side, where he sat while his wife waved a fan to create a breeze for her guests, complaining that their house was too small and that they had no electric fan. Her husband, a draftsman for the city's construction brigade, often worked at their table while their child did his homework on her sewing machine table. An electric fan would have blown everything all over the place. Zhuang took the fan from her to cool himself, since it embarrassed him for her to do it.

"So you're looking for Ah-lan," she said. "I'm her second sister, Ah-can. She told me what happened when she got back that day, but I didn't believe her. Where did she find the luck to meet a celebrity like you? When she took the letter out, I had to believe her. She said your wife gave it to her for me to send to our elder sister. Why did you want her to send it back to Xijing?"

Zhuang told her the story behind the letter. "Any news from Suzhou?" he asked.

"My sister wrote to say that a woman named Xue Ruimei, a teacher at a middle school, had been labeled a Rightist for decades. She died three years after she was rehabilitated."

Zhuang's heart ached at the news, for she had been Zhong Weixian's moral support all these years. Zhong would surely fall apart if he knew she was no longer alive. "Don't tell anyone about this, Yunfang. And you, too, Ah-can, please keep it a secret. Even a passing comment could kill Mr. Zhong. Obviously I'll have to keep writing to him as Xue Ruimei and ask you to send my letters to your sister for her to send back with her address on a new envelope. Otherwise he would keep writing to Xue's old address. His previous letters must have been lost, since they weren't returned. He'd be suspicious if his letters were returned again."

"I can't say no to such a kind-hearted person," Ah-can said. "When it's ready, you can bring it to me or I can stop by your house to get it."

"I can't ask you to make the trip. Ah-lan's workplace isn't far from my house, so I'll give it to her."

"That's fine, too, except she hasn't been at the factory much lately. She's running around all day long. She's supposed to be designing a public toilet."

"Is she still working on that design?" Zhuang asked.

"Who knows? It's only a public toilet, but she's spent so much energy on the design, you'd think she was drawing up a blueprint for the Great Hall of the People. Over the past few days, she's been saying that Mr. Wang asks to see her often but has yet to settle on a design. She's been so worried that she's lost her appetite and just goes upstairs to be alone when she comes home."

Zhuang noticed a ladder in the corner; it obviously led to a second floor, where Ah-lan lived. "It's probably cooler up there," he said.

"Are you serious? It's like a hothouse," Ah-can said. "There's a window that could be opened to allow in a breeze, but she has to shut it because two bachelors live across the lane. You can't stand up straight inside, and it's dark. I make cold bean soup for her every day and tell her she ought to get married. Marry someone successful, and you won't have to suffer at my house any longer, I tell her. But she says she wouldn't be able to accomplish anything if she were married in her current state, for that would mean the end of her career. Ai! I was more ambitious than her as a girl, but I ended up with nothing to show for it, and life goes on."

Outside, the washbasin was blocking a man with charcoal on a three-wheeler, who called out for them to move it. Mu Jiaren ran outside to push it out of the way and carried in a bucket of dirty water to make room for the vehicle to pass, after which he took the bucket back out. With nothing else to do or say inside, he went back to his washing. Ah-can told him to go buy some takeout so they could treat their guests. Zhuang quickly declined her offer, which offended her. "Do you think we're too poor to offer you something to eat and drink? Or is the place too dirty for you?' She even laid her hands on Zhuang's shoulders to keep him in his seat and, while she was at it, flicked off some dirt from the back of his collar.

So they stayed, drinking and eating the usual things—pork liver, shredded pork belly, pig's ears, bamboo shoots, and mushrooms. Ah-can also cooked a medium-sized fish. When she was frying the fish on the outdoor stove, the aroma spread through the lane, causing the children in the room across the way to cry out for fish. Zhuang looked out and saw an old woman making noodles; she too was stripped to the waist, her sagging breasts hanging almost all the way down to her waist. She had two children on her back. "What fish?" she grumbled. "Can't you see that Aunty Ah-can has guests? Have this instead." She reached down with her floured hand and flung her breasts over her shoulders. Surprisingly, the children grabbed them and began sucking. Ah-can quickly filled a bowl with rice and a few pieces of fish and went over with it. She came back and whispered, "You'll probably laugh at the way she looks, but I heard she was a true beauty as a younger woman. Those breasts alone had men salivating. Two of the men even crossed the line. But now she's old and doesn't care about her appearance. Besides, this place is so hot she couldn't keep any nice clothes on her anyway."

When they were finished, they chatted some more before Mu did the dishes and got ready to go to work. Zhuang and Meng got up to leave also, but Mu stopped them, "What's the hurry? I'm on night shift and have to leave, but you two stay and talk some more. Stay for dinner, and we'll treat you to a Henan specialty, spicy noodles."

"We can't keep eating like this," Zhuang said, "or you won't have anything for us next time we come."

"I know what you're thinking. You don't think it's proper to stay when my husband is out, do you?" Ah-can said. "If their conscience is clear, a man and a woman can sleep in the same bed with nothing to fear."

Zhuang and Meng blushed so deeply that even their necks turned red; they couldn't leave now. After Mu left, she asked them how they got there and where they parked. When told it was a scooter, she asked Meng to go out and wheel it over, in case the old woman went home and there was no one to keep an eye on it. As soon as Meng stepped out, she fixed her bright eyes on Zhuang and said, "Tell me the truth. Do you really need to leave, or do you think it's improper to stay?"

Zhuang laughed and said, "You're such a straightforward person that even though we're meeting today for the first time, I feel like I've known you for a long time. Like an old friend."

"Truth always pleases the ear. You have no idea how happy I am about your visit. Stay awhile if you don't think this place isn't good enough for you. I'm going next door to borrow a pack of watermelon seeds to nibble on." She left.

"What do you think of her?" Zhuang asked when Meng walked in.

"A born beauty with a great personality."

"I don't meet women like her very often. She's more poised than Ah-lan and less girlish than most women. It's a rare quality for a woman, like a knight without the airs of a swordsman or a monk who doesn't look like a temple attendant."

"She's caught your fancy, I see," Meng said as Ah-can walked in and handed them each some watermelon seeds.

"Ah-lan will be home late," she said. "Why don't you write a letter for Mr. Zhong here, and I'll post it to my sister tomorrow. Given Mr. Zhong's situation, one more letter could add another year to his life."

"I'm glad you feel that way," Meng said.

"Of course. All you have to do is put yourself in his shoes. I'm young, but I have no one to write to, nor anyone to write to me."

"That's impossible for someone with your looks and temperament," Meng said.

"That's what everyone says. But my looks and temperament were my downfall. When I was younger, I set my heart on the sky, but in the end my fate has turned out to be worth less than a sheet of paper. I didn't meet people who were better than me, and I couldn't get rid of the deadbeats. I'm not as lucky as you."

"We're all the same," Meng said. "Mr. Zhuang receives lots of letters, but they're mostly from people seeking writing tips. I've never heard him mention any girls."

"It's probably because Mrs. Zhuang is so pretty that the girls stay away after assessing their own looks."

"You're right, she is quite good-looking."

"That's good," she said with a smile.

"What's good about it?"

"I'd feel bad if you said she wasn't pretty. You see, I'm sure that meeting Mr. Zhuang is a personal highlight for all women, but they probably can't tell you why. Now, if they heard that his wife was ugly, they would think he had low standards and there'd be no point in falling for him."

"That's an interesting way of looking at it. Usually when a woman falls for a man, she can only hope that his wife is ugly enough for her to have a chance."

Zhuang waved his hands, complaining about the direction of their conversation. "It's too bad Ah-can has to live around here," he said.

"Nothing bad about that. Haven't you noticed that many great women marry men who aren't their equals? People often say that gold is gold even if it's buried in the ground. Of course I'm not gold, but even if I were, what's the use in being hidden? Iron isn't worth much, but it can be turned into pots for cooking, and become more valuable than gold. My greatest comfort now is my son, a great kid, good-looking and smart."

"Where is he?" Meng asked.

"He's in middle school. He comes home late because they offer after-school classes. My hopes are all on him now. I want him to go to college and then get a doctoral degree so he can go overseas and make a name for himself."

Troubled by her talk, Zhuang cut in, "You're still young. You should be living for yourself. Pinning all your hope on your son could—"

She smiled stiffly and looked down. A layer of dust caught her attention, so she picked up a rag and wiped it away. "You're right, of course. But you don't understand." She gave a short laugh. "I once told Ah-lan about going hungry in Xinjiang. She said she'd gone hungry once, too, but that was when she was on a business trip and had to skip meals while she was traveling. Me? It was not knowing where my next meal came from. We were so poor, we couldn't scrape together a handful of rice. We both went hungry, but in totally different circumstances."

"I see," Zhuang said.

Meng thought he got the drift of their conversation, but all he was sure of was that Zhuang and Ah-can had a lot to talk about. So he said he would take the scooter into town on business, and Zhuang could stay to write the letter. He would be back in a couple of hours. Without waiting for a response, he walked out and rode off on the scooter.

Meng's departure made Zhuang uneasy.

"You can write that letter now, can't you?"

"Yes."

She brought him a pen and paper, pushed everything on the table to the side, and invited him to sit down, saying she wouldn't bother him. She would sit and read. Unable to get into the mood, he tore up the first few openings. Offering him some sunshine, she opened the drapes and fanned him from behind so the heat would not bother him. He told her there was no need for that. Finally getting the inspiration he was looking for, he started writing, with so much feeling he seemed enthralled. After reading for a while at the head of the bed, she quietly watched him as he wrote. A long time passed before he finished and turned to see her staring at him. She seemed not to be aware that he was looking at her. "I'm done," he said.

Startled out of her reverie, she blushed, knowing she had been distracted. "Really? So soon?"

He was surprised to see her blush, for she hadn't been at all shy until then. She walked up and asked, "Could you read it to me?"

"Sure. Listen and tell me if it sounds like a woman's voice. I'm worried he might be able to tell it's a fake."

So he read it, all three pages, and when he was done, he looked up to see a tender, fair hand with slender but nicely shaped fingers, her pinkie and ring fingers pressing down on the table while her middle and index fingers quivered. He realized that she had moved over to stand next to him, resting one hand on the table and fanning him with the other. He peered into the face looking down at him; her eyes were glazed over, her cheeks flushed.

"What do you think?" he asked.

"For a while I thought it was written for me."

Impulsively, he called out hoarsely, "Ah-can."

"Yes." She began to sway. He reached up with the hand holding the pen, and just before that hand touched her waist, he tried to stand up. Halfway there, the face above him fell on his. The nib of the pen left a spot of ink on her white blouse. They fell into each other's arms, knocking over a rattan chair.

"This was my best letter ever, Ah-can. And all because of my feelings for you."

"Really? You really like me?"

He tightened his arms around her and gave her a passionate kiss, feeling there was no need to say more; he wanted to let his strength and passion convey his sympathy and attraction.

"What must you think of me?" she said, still in his arms. "You must think I'm too easy, but I'm not. I'm really not. I really can't believe that you're fond of me. I was thinking that it would be a beautiful experience if we made love. I would like to have such a beautiful experience at least once in my life."

Making him sit down, she repeated that she was a good woman, a reputable woman. She had been a good student, but her family background was so bad that she had been sent to Xijiang to defend the border. There she managed to find a man, Mu Jiaren, with whom she had been transferred to Xijing a few years back. Her life had been difficult and exhausting; she was insignificant, but she had a lofty mind and wasn't ugly, with a nice figure and a fair complexion. She had let no one but her husband look at and admire her body.

"I believe you, Ah-can. You don't have to say any more."

"I want to. I want to tell you everything. I want to be transparent before you. I want you to look at me and tell me if you like what you see. I'm going to surprise you." She took off her blouse, her pajamas, her bra and panties, even kicked off her slippers, and stood naked before him. But instead of drinking in the sight of her body, he wrapped his arms around her and teared up, despite himself. She reached out to wipe his tears. "I didn't frighten you, did I?"

Wordlessly, he gave his body to her after she lay down on the bed. "You really are fond of me, aren't you?" she said softly. □□ □□ □□ [The author has deleted 411words.] She pulled him down, and he detected an unusual fragrance.

"I smell good. Mu Jiaren has said so and so has my son. Smell me down there. That's where it's best."

He lowered his head and did detect a warm fragrance; he felt enshrouded in misty clouds. □□ □□ □□ [The author has deleted 22 words.] Grinding her teeth, she called out in pain, and he stopped, afraid he might hurt her.

"Do whatever you please, as long as it feels good. When I was pregnant, the doctor said my pelvis is narrower than most women's and that I might have trouble giving birth."

He began again slowly; she shook her head with a smile. They kept up the talk until he said he was about to come. She told him to pull out first. □□ □□ □□ [The author has deleted 51 words.]

"I'm not wearing an IUD, and I don't want to get pregnant." She put her arms around him. They lay together that way, and then her face twitched and tears ran down her face.

"Do you regret what we did, Ah-can?" Zhuang said as he tried to get up. "It was my fault. I shouldn't have done it." She sat up to hold him and bring him down to lie next to her. "No regrets. Why would there be? I was thrilled. I want to thank you. Really, I can't thank you enough. You satisfied me, not just physically but psychologically, too. You have no idea how depressed, how dispirited, I've been. I thought my life was over, but now I know that you care for me. I don't want anything from you, not your money or your help. I have regained my will to live just knowing that a celebrity like you finds me attractive. I envy your wife. Having you proves that she must be someone who can be successful in whatever she does. I'm jealous of her, really, truly jealous. But please believe me when I say I would never want to replace her. I wouldn't dare think about that. Please don't worry about what we did today. I would never cause you any trouble or become a burden."

It was the first time a woman had ever said anything like that to Zhuang. He sat up and dried her tears. "I'm not as good as you think, and am ashamed to hear you say so." He sat there staring blankly.

"Don't be like that. I don't want you to be like that." She put her arms around him and laid her head on his chest. They sat quietly for a while before she asked softly, "Would you like a cigarette?" She reached over and took one from a case at the head of the bed. Putting it in her mouth, she lit it and then put it in between his lips. He removed it and said, "Could I smell you again? I want your fragrance to mask my stink."

She lay down, submissively as a cat, and he knelt to smell and kiss her from head to toe. Then he gave her the address of the House of Imperfection Seekers, adding that he would like to see her again. She tearfully agreed.

❋

The village at the foot of Xijing's Giant Wild Goose Pagoda had an unusual name, Yaobao, or Divination Fortress. Every one of its residents was a drummer. Their ancestor was said to have been a drummer in the Qin emperor's army who later settled in the area. In order to commemorate their ancestor's accomplishment and enforce clan unity, they passed down drumming skills and the performance of drum music from a court dance that originated in the Tang dynasty. Their ancient customs also included a drum festival on the second day of the second lunar month, the traditional holiday when the rain dragon raised its head. A village elder would carry an apricot-yellow flag and lead several hundred drummers in a parade. On this day, the shops in town, seeking good fortune, tied yard-long satin cloths to the flag-bearer's head when the procession reached their shops, while tens of thousands of firecrackers were set off, creating an earth-shattering din. In recent years, as things changed, the villagers had continued their tradition, but turned drumming into a livelihood. Whenever peasants-turned-entrepreneurs from the southern suburb wanted to promote a new product or celebrate high sales figures, they would hire the drummers from Divination Fortress to play. So in addition to enjoying the drum parade, the residents within the city wall would know from the sound that another peasant had made enough money to show off, and they would surge onto the street to watch.

One Sunday, the drum music sounded again on the street, more spectacularly than ever. Niu Yueqing and Liu Yue, who were winding yarn at home, were agitated by the drumbeat. Liu Yue, who was holding out her hands in the shape of an elongated box, could not concentrate, so Niu Yueqing said, "Can't you sit still, you little monkey?" She put the yarn away and told the girl to get her high heels for her so they could go out and take a look. After freshening up, they went out onto the street, where a huge crowd blocked their passage. Taking Niu Yueqing by the hand, Liu Yue climbed over the pedestrian railing and threaded her way through the traffic. Niu Yueqing struggled out of the girl's hand to look a bit more refined and shouted, "Why are you walking so fast, Liu Yue?

Afraid you might miss your bridal sedan?" Niu Yueqing had thought that Zhuang would be back home within a few days of his spiteful move to the Literary Federation compound, and was surprised that he had stayed away so long. Her attitude had begun to soften, but she refused to go there for fear of losing her dignity as a wife. Life at home had become tedious. Then she recalled her husband's complaints about her lack of attention to her appearance, so she went out and bought some new clothes and gave her nearly new used clothes to Liu Yue. She was wearing heels with pointed toes, which pinched her feet soon after she went out to watch the drummers; she cursed the girl for walking so fast. Liu Yue came back and walked more slowly beside her. "I've never seen anything like this. Back home, we also have drum music during the New Year's celebration, but they never beat the drums so fast or so loud. My heart is racing."

"You don't just watch the drummers; you have to look at the people who watch the drummers. It's more fun that way," Niu Yueqing said.

Liu Yue began paying attention to the people on the street, who were all nicely decked out. Soon she realized that many of them were looking at her.

"Dajie," she whispered, "you're so pretty that everyone is looking at you."

"Me? What for? Who would want to look at an old hag? It's you they're watching."

Though dressed in hand-me-downs, Liu Yue had such a nice figure that she looked good in anything. She was young, and the clothes fitted her better than brand-new ones. She could see that Niu Yueqing was right, that she was the focus of the onlookers' attention; instead of looking around, she stuck out her chest and raised her head high, checking out of the corner of her eye.

"Don't stick your chest out like that," Niu Yueqing said, making the girl giggle.

By the time they had pushed their way through to a spot beneath the clock tower, the drum band was arriving from East Avenue, drawing a large crowd. The two women jumped onto the stone ledge of a fountain outside a hotel, and saw three three-wheelers traveling side by side under a gigantic sign with gold lettering: "Greetings to the Residents of Xijing from Huang Hongbao, Owner of the 101 Pesticide Plant." Behind the sign, a swarthy, heavy-set man rode on another three-wheeler, grinning from ear to ear and waving to the onlookers. He was followed by four rows of three-wheelers: cymbal players stood on the outside vehicles, clanging on brass cymbals fastened to their hands with yellow ribbons; the vehicles in the middle carried large drums edged with burnt-black tacks. Everyone on the team sported a red-edged yellow sash that hung from the right shoulder across the body. The sashes also had a message: "Good News Heralded from the 101 Pesticide Plant." With three loud clangs, the players raised their cymbals, which flashed brilliantly under the sun. The drummers, in the meantime, beat their drums three times on the inside and three times on the outside, then twirled their sticks in the air and held one up before dropping it to start again. The onlookers cheered and applauded the performers as they moved in unison, the drums and cymbals playing off each other in rhythmic fashion.

After watching awhile, Niu Yueqing said, "Look at that dark, ugly guy acting like Chairman Mao inspecting the military. People can do just about anything they want to these days, so long as they have the money. I know him. He's been to our house."

"I thought he looked familiar. Now I remember. He looks so smug now, but he couldn't kowtow enough to Zhuang Laoshi," Liu said, and then let out a loud scream. "Ai—"

"Why are you screaming like that?" Niu Yueqing said.

"Isn't that Tang Wan'er?"

Niu Yueqing took a closer look. Yes, it was Tang and Xia Jie among the crowd, two beauties in fashionable clothes, very eye-catching. Tang looked around when she heard the scream and spotted them. "Liu Yue! So you're here with Shimu. Is Zhuang Laoshi with you?" Tang and Xia squeezed their way over and jumped onto the ledge, where they held hands and draped their arms around each other's shoulder, laughing the whole time. They were an attractive sight to begin with, and now their laughter drew looks from even more people, including a group of idlers who grinned at them. Quickly averting their eyes, they heard one of the men say, "Xiao Shun. Did you hear me, Xiao Shun? Have you lost your soul?"

"Look, four bombs," another one said.

"What's a bomb?" Liu Yue whispered to Xia Jie.

"He's saying you could stun him."

Liu Yue poked Wan'er in the waist and said, "You're the bomb. You dressed up so nicely today. Who are you doing it for? So pretty!" She then removed one of Tang's hairpins and stuck it in Niu Yueqing's hair, who removed it and saw that it was a tasseled ivory pin from Dali, Yunnan.

"So Zhou Min bought one for you, too, Wan'er," she said.

Tang blushed.

"It looks so much better on you. Your Zhuang Laoshi bought one for me two years ago when he went to a meeting at Dali. It was too big, too flashy. I can't wear something like that, so I put it in a chest. I thought it was only sold in Dali, but obviously it's also available in Xijing." Niu

Yueqing stuck it back in Tang's hair. Tang gave Liu Yue a playful kick. Liu Yue jumped off, lost her footing, and fell to the ground. After dusting off her gray harem pants, she went back up to join the others.

"You don't care about your things, do you?" Tang said. "You don't even bother to pick up all the goodies you left behind."

Liu looked down at the ground and asked, "What goodies? I don't see anything."

"You dusted all the beady eyes off your pants!"

The others paused a moment before laughing.

"Wan'er is a clever little fox," Niu Yueqing said. "That's a funny way of putting it. I'm afraid you've drawn more eyes than any of us."

The music halted at that moment, as brochures with product information settled onto the heads of the onlookers like snowflakes. When they reached up for them, the many hands looked like trees in a forest. Liu ran over to catch some as the performers donned masks resembling aphids, wood lice, moths, and flies, all strangely shaped and terrifying. They started singing:

We are pests, we are pests. 101—it kills, it kills us. Kills us, kills us all.

The music resumed when they finished, and the cycle repeated itself, making the onlookers cheer as they crowded forward. Chaos erupted. A woman cursed, "Who's the shameless thief that took my purse? Pickpocket! You think people from the countryside have money? Thief! 101 Pesticide is rich, but not me. I only had fifty yuan for a trip into the city, and you had your eye on it. You city people, you stole my money. You'll die a terrible death."

"If a thief took your money, why curse the residents?" someone in the crowd said.

"You city thief, when your wife eats the food you buy with my money, she won't give you a son and your dog won't have her pups," the woman continued.

"That's great. Now you're part of family planning. Xijing is teeming with thieves, and you should take better care of your money."

"Who says I didn't? Several youngsters crowded around me, in front and behind, and they even reached for my breasts. I just thought the young men had never seen anything like it, so I let them. I'm a mother of three, and those weren't made of gold or silver. Who knew those damn kids wanted my money, not my breasts. They should be taken out and shot, or cut to pieces."

The people who heard her howled with laughter.

"My anger has made me lose my head," she said. "What was I saying?" She crouched down as the crowd surged again.

"There's a lesson for you," Xia Jie said to Tang Wan'er. "You're going braless today, aren't you?"

"It's too hot in the summer to wear one," Tang said, as Liu Yue ran over.

"There's something here by Zhuang Laoshi, Dajie."

"Let's see what he wrote." Wan'er grabbed the brochure and read aloud.

"Stop that. What a disgrace to have his name on this. That Huang guy probably didn't warn him," Niu Yueqing said as the people around them pointed and whispered. She heard a man say to someone next to him, "See them? Those are the wives of the writers."

"Which ones? Where?" several people asked in unison.

"The one in the middle, in a green qipao, that's Zhuang Zhidie's wife."

Niu Yueqing's heart skipped a beat as she said to herself, *He must know me, but I don't know him. If he knows me, he should come say hello. Why hasn't he? Why is he gossiping like that? Is he making fun of me because he knows that Zhidie and I had a fight?* She turned to the others.

"Let's go. Let's get away from these gawking eyes."

They got down off the platform and headed toward South Avenue.

"Since we're not going to watch anymore, why don't we go to my place for a game of mahjong?" Xia said. "It's not far."

"Liu Yue and I have to get back. We've been out too long already."

"I had you in mind when I made the suggestion," Xia Jie said. "You're always so busy, you can never get away. Now that you've found the time and are in the mood to come out, you must stop by my place. Wan'er, Liu Yue, we'll carry her if we have to."

"All right," Niu Yueqing laughed. "I'll treat myself today."

The four of them breezed down several lanes before reaching Meng's house.

Once inside, they washed their sweaty faces, and Tang borrowed some of Xia's cosmetics for a touch-up. A table was set up, dice were cast to determine the seating order, and they sat down to their tiles.

"Where's Yunfang?" Niu Yueqing asked. "Practicing qigong at the Yunhuang Temple?"

"Who knows? He's studying Shao Yong day and night. He's already lost the sight in one eye and probably will wind up losing it in the other."

The other women all knew about Meng's eye, so they joked about who would look at Xia's pretty face if he were completely blind.

"If that happened, I'd bring a man over. He wouldn't be upset if he couldn't see." Xia's comment left the others speechless; they didn't know what to say to her. Niu Yueqing heard someone selling fresh milk outside.

"It sounds like Aunty Liu, Liu Yue," she said. "Go see if it is."

She went outside. Aunty Liu had brought her cow.

"Out selling milk at this hour, Aunty Liu?"

"Oh, it's you, Liu Yue. What are you doing here? I went to North Avenue this morning to deliver milk and was stopped on the way home. I couldn't get through no matter what."

"Tie your cow up here and come in. Dajie is inside playing mahjong."

Without waiting for a response, Liu tethered the cow to a purple pagoda tree and led Aunty Liu inside, where she was greeted by the three women.

"This place is too nice for someone like me."

"Don't worry about that. It's a friend's house. We buy milk from you most days, but it's late today, so don't be in a hurry to go home. Stick around for a game. We'll have lunch here. Niu Yueqing dragged Aunty Liu over to the card table. A lifelong mahjong fan back home, Aunty Liu was happy to be invited by these urban ladies and could not wait to play a round. And yet, despite the honor, she was worried they might be betting more than she could afford. Touching her pocket to get a feel of how much money she had earned selling milk, she knew that if she lost it, she would have wasted a trip into the city and, worse, might wind up owing them money, which would make her a laughingstock. So she begged off. Knowing what was on her mind, Niu Yueqing said: "We play small, one yuan, maybe half that, a round. Here, you play a round for me. You can keep what you win, and I'll pick up the losses."

"Zhuang shimu is too rich already," Tang said, "so we're going after her today,"

Aunty Liu sat down. "All right, I will play a round for you. My hands smell, so I'll just play one round."

When Niu Yueqing stood up, Liu Yue said: "Take my place, Dajie. I have to go to the compound to make lunch for Zhuang Laoshi."

Feigning ignorance, Wan'er said, "Is Zhuang Laoshi staying at the compound?"

Niu Yueqing ignored her and turned to Liu Yue. "Don't worry about him. He comes and goes as he pleases. He just doesn't think we can do the same."

"Did they have a fight?" Wan'er asked Liu Yue. "Are they living apart?"

"Not really," Liu Yue whispered and then turned away. Curious about what was happening between Zhuang and his wife, Tang was peeved at the girl's response, but she knew better than to show her displeasure. Yet as she moved her tiles, she could not stop wondering, and ended up playing a wrong tile. Liu Yue snapped it up and kissed it.

"I'm too good a feeder," Tang said. She got up and asked Niu Yueqing to play for her, saying she would deposit her poison in the toilet. When she walked out the door, she saw the cow lying on the ground, motionless except for her tail, which she was swishing back and forth to chase away insects. Tang made a secret pledge: *Zhidie keeps asking me to wait for him, so did he find an excuse to fight with his wife, or was it just a common quarrel? If it's for me, let the cow moo once; if not, then nothing.* She watched for a while, until the cow cocked her ears and let out a snort, not a moo. With no way to tell if she was the cause of the fight, she turned around unhappily.

"Ai-ya, it's you, Zhuang Laoshi!" she called out shrilly. "I didn't expect to see you here. As they say, the road turns when the mountain won't."

When the women inside heard her shout, Niu Yueqing pushed her tiles away. "Don't tell him I'm here," she said as she went into the bedroom and lowered the curtain. That was all the proof Tang needed that they really had had a fight, which elated her. She gestured to the other women with a smile and said, "Come, sit here, Zhuang Laoshi. Shimu is here. Now, where did she go?"

The others decided to go along. "When Shimu heard you were here," one of them said, "she went inside to 'get pretty for the one who pleases her most.'" They struggled to keep from laughing. So did Tang, who said, "Leaving already? After you heard that Shimu is here?" She walked into the yard and slammed the door shut, prompting Niu Yueqing to curse from the bedroom, "Let him go. Don't stop him. Let him go, and he'll never have to see me again if he doesn't want to." She seemed about to cry, which the other women found laughable. Xia Jie and Liu Yue went into the bedroom to drag her out.

"It's all Wan'er's fault. How could Zhuang Zhidie just show up like that?" Xia Jie said. "Wan'er, come, kowtow to Shimu to apologize."

Clearly in high spirits, Tang swayed in and actually got down on her knees in front of Niu Yueqing, who could not suppress her amusement despite her anger. Pinching the girl's lips, she said, "You little tart. You ought to go out on the street to sing 'We are pests'; I will use 101 to kill you."

After they had played four rounds, Meng Yunfang came in with a child, Meng Jin, the son from his previous marriage. When Meng told him to greet the aunties, the boy, without looking at the women, said, "How are you, Aunty Niu, Aunty Tang." Then he went into his father's study to look at some books. Xia Jie was unhappy but decided not to say anything. Meng was clearly in a good mood, and told everyone to stay for lunch, then went into the kitchen to cook. Feeling the need to be a good guest, Aunty Liu went out with five mugs to get milk for everyone.

Niu Yueqing said she didn't drink freshly squeezed milk and summoned Meng Jin, who drank it down in one gulp.

"Look how big he's grown and how much he looks like his father," Niu Yueqing said.

"Yunfang and I have fought over this countless times," Xia whispered to her. "We had an agreement when we were married. The court gave the child to his ex-wife, and I didn't mind if he wanted to care for him, but he was not to spend time in this house. He agreed, but now he brings the kid back all the time. When I mentioned it, he promised to stop doing it, but the moment I'm out, he brings him here to eat and drink whatever we have. Today he thought I'd be out and, you see, he brought him back again."

"Well, he is, after all, Yunfang's son. Let him bring the child here if he wants to. How much can a little boy eat?"

"It's not how much he eats. When I divorced my first husband, the court awarded me our son, but Yunfang has never warmed to the boy, though he doesn't treat him badly. But when he brings his son back, he showers him with love and ignores us, which makes my son feel terrible."

Niu Yueqing did not know what to say beyond trying to make peace: "Try to be fair-minded with the two boys, and I'll talk to Yunfang. Now that the two of you are married, both sons should be treated equally. He should not favor one over the other."

Tang moved over when she saw them engaged in an intimate conversation, prompting them to change the subject and talk about the weather.

Liu Yue was still worried about Zhuang when they sat down to eat. "I wonder what Zhuang Laoshi is having for lunch."

"Something good, I'm sure," Meng said. "I ran into him on the street earlier, and he said he was going to the magazine office. He'll either treat them to lunch or they'll treat him."

After lunch, Aunty Liu said her stomach was full but her cow's was still empty, and she needed to get home. After she left, Meng played four rounds with the women before the party broke up.

❋

As she walked home with her cow, Aunty Liu regretted having stayed so long, all for a free lunch. Her cow needed to be fed. Then there was her baby son, born outside state family planning, who was home in the care of her mother-in-law. Her breasts ached, but she could not find a secluded place to deal with that. Seeing that the front of her blouse was already wet, she found a public toilet and went in to squeeze out the milk. As she followed along behind Aunty Liu, the cow started out walking spiritedly, but before long, she lowered her head to think her many thoughts. Back when Aunty Liu was playing mahjong and having lunch, she had lain under a tree. When people who had been watching the drum procession left the area near the clock tower, vehicle and pedestrian traffic flowed like water down the lane, past the cow, which had a clear view of the people's feet and the kinds of shoes they wore. Why have humans created high heels with pointed toes for feet that were made for walking? Why do they think that is attractive? In her view, it was cows, bears, and cranes that had pretty feet. Humans admired and were envious of the powerful beauty of a bear's paws or the sturdy straight legs of a crane, but they did not understand that those feet were beautiful not for beauty's sake, but for the need to survive. As she continued this line of thought, she felt pity for humans, whose standards of beauty had regressed. They do not run barefoot on sand or in brambles, but eight or nine out of ten of them have corns. Are they reaching the point where they will have to hobble along supporting themselves with their hands on a wall? In her mind, the worst developments were motor vehicles and elevators in high-rises. Everything is modernized. And look at the things they eat and the clothes they wear. And yet they lose sleep when they are bitten by a mosquito and have stomach trouble after eating a bowl of undercooked noodles. The bowls and chopsticks at food stands must be disinfected over and over; they need an umbrella when it rains and a scarf in the wind. They turn on air-conditioners in the summer and heaters in the winter. Humans are more fragile than a blade of grass. They brush their teeth every morning and night, so weakening the teeth that they avoid sour, sweet, hot, or cold food. They even use toothpicks! The most laughable, in her mind, were the so-called modern artists who displayed sculptures and murals on the street. What do they think they are doing? Nature has already provided everything out there. Can a painter create elaborate patterns to mimic the clouds? Can modern artists show the uniqueness of a wall after the rain, even the colors and images formed in a cesspool? And what is the deal with those martial arts practitioners along the city moat? Martial arts—*wushu*—sounds nice, but humans have turned it into a mere show with no substance. They watch TV at night. There is this thing called the Olympics, a congregation of the best athletes, who could never outrun a common gazelle in a hundred-meter dash. The Banpo people in Xijing were the ancestors of humans, the real humans. They might not have been able to run as fast as those athletes, but they were certainly better at combat. Humans have regressed to the point that they pale in comparison even to the Qin terracotta soldiers—shorter in height, with thinner waists. But humans want to look trim, so there are waist tightening belts and pants for sale, even slimming creams and tea. They have a clever brain, but that brain is precisely the cause of their regression. The cow finally realized what a city really was: a place where regressed humans congregate after they can no longer adapt to nature and the universe, when they are afraid of the wind, the sun, the cold, and the heat. If a human were put on a vast prairie or on a high mountain cliff, he would not be the equal of a rabbit, even a ladybug. The cow's head hung even lower at these thoughts, and she heard a passerby say:

"Would you look at that old cow. What a stupid animal!"

The cow was not upset; she snorted, laughing at the man. They don't understand that the wisest men often appear to be dimwitted. Seeing that the cow was not angered by the comment, the passerby walked up and poked her in the rump with a broken branch and slapped her on the ear. "See, she doesn't dare move," he said.

She opened her eyes and stopped. Frightened by the motionless cow, the man said, "Watch your cow, lady." At that moment, she wished she could storm into every house in one night and assault the city's women to invest the human race with strength and a wilder nature. The cow did have that urge one day, when an old man turned on his radio to listen to *Journey to the West*, the tale of a monk who retrieves the sacred Buddhist texts and fights demons with the help of Monkey, Pigsy, Sandy, and their White Horse. Convinced that modern people can only enjoy the spectacle, not the classical author's meaning, the cow wanted to shout: It's not about a master and his four disciples, but about the idea that only through their combined effort can nature be conquered and the sutras obtained. But what can humans do now that they no longer have Buddhism in their hearts and have lost the spirit of the monkey, pig, and horse?

❋

Zhuang Zhidie had a free day, so he put the finishing touches on a series of magic realist fiction he had recently completed and sent it off to a newspaper, before heading off to the editorial section of *Xijing Magazine.* He had yet to learn of Zhong Weixian's reaction after receiving a letter from Suzhou, and was worried that he might have seen through the ruse. He walked in and saw three desks pushed together for the editors to eat a Western-style buffet lunch.

"This is an example of 'Heaven invites when man will not.' We're celebrating a victory today and have agreed not to invite any outsiders, but then you show up. So we'll just have to eat less," Li Hongwen said when he saw Zhuang.

Zhou Min got a chair for him. "They said we ought to celebrate with a lunch," Zhong Weixian said. "I'm fine with that, but then they wanted Western food and had to eat it in the building. So we ordered this from the Xijing Hotel. Now that you're here, we must all share in hardship and in good fortune. Everyone, let's toast our writer."

Zhuang downed his first glass. "I got you all in trouble, and it was through concerted efforts that we are here today, so I'd like to say thank you."

"I was the one who got the magazine in trouble," said Zhou Min, "and got Zhuang Laoshi involved. I want to apologize to everyone."

"No need for apologies or thanks. If anything, we ought to thank the deputy governor in charge of cultural affairs," Li said, and they had another toast to that.

After lunch, Li collected the plastic containers, intending to string them together and then hang them out the window. Zhong Weixian did not like that idea, considering it unsightly, but Li said he wanted it to be harsh on the eyes of Jing Xueyin and Wu Kun. In his view, they were being magnanimous by not setting off firecrackers and flashing slogans.

"What did the other side say about not printing the announcement?" Zhuang whispered to Zhong, who was sitting beside him.

"She raised hell in the department head's office, and Wu Kun pressured the higher-ups, claiming that she could not explain herself to her husband. They said she had always been the dominant member of the family, but now he could hold this over her head and had become a brute, making life so hard on her that she tried to take her own life several times. Who believes that nonsense? No one. Li Hongwen even said he saw Jing and her husband shopping at a mall arm in arm."

"Do you really trust Li to tell the truth?" Zhuang asked.

"Even if we don't," Zhong said, "she wouldn't consider suicide; she's not the type. It's all because of that meddling Wu Kun, who's using Jing to attack me. She doesn't understand that."

Zhuang said nothing in response. Then Gou Dahai came in with a pile of magazines, newspapers, and letters.

"Is there a letter for me?" Zhong got up.

"No," Gou said.

"No?" Zhong sat back down. "Maybe one's stuck in between." He flipped through the mail but found nothing. Then Gou took a letter from his pocket.

"I knew you'd ask about letters," he said. "You owe me a meal. If you say no, I'll open this in front of everyone."

"Don't do that," Zhong said with a red face. "I treated you last time. Do you really expect me to do it again? How many people am I going to have to feed the next time I get a letter?" He reached out, grabbed the letter, and shoved it into his pocket.

"What's so important about that letter?" Zhuang asked.

"They're just having fun with an old man," Zhong said. "A letter from a friend."

"Come tell us when you'll send us one of your manuscripts, Zhidie," Li said. "Mr. Zhong has to go to the toilet now." That got a laugh out of everyone but Zhuang, who was confused. "Going to the toilet right after lunch? It looks like the import and export firms are right next to each other."

"He's going to read the letter!" Li said. "He went to the toilet when the last letter arrived, and stayed there so long I thought he'd passed out from holding it in. So I walked over to take a look. The door was shut and he was inside crying."

Zhong was too embarrassed to stay, so he went with Zhuang into the hallway. They chatted for a while. Noticing that Zhong did not invite him to his office and that he kept touching his pocket, Zhuang knew that he was eager to read the letter, so he left. When he turned the corner in the hallway and spotted a toilet, he went in. He shut the door of the stall, and saw that it was crammed with graffiti and drawings, not much different from other toilets all over China, except for one phrase: "Class A cultural relic for preservation—the site where Zhong Weixian reads letters and sheds tears." Zhuang felt like laughing, but a sense of sadness made him pull up his pants and walk out.

When he returned to the federation compound, he saw that Liu Yue had not come to cook for him. He sat down to write another letter for Zhong. After he finished it, he thought about how the letter was a fake, and yet Zhong treasured it so. An old man like that could not forget the love of his youth. What about him? He and Jing Xueyin had once been so close, and now they were mortal enemies. A loathing for Zhou Min rose up inside when he recalled how happy he had been at the lunch celebration. He wondered how Jing felt at that moment. Wu Kun had said she wanted to take her own life, which was unlikely, but it was inevitable that she would be having trouble at home. Feeling sorry for he, he decided to write her a letter, but he tore it up halfway through and started another one, this time to Jing and her husband. He told them he hadn't read Zhou's article and would not have approved it if he had, adding that the author was simply inexperienced and had no intention to slander. Zhuang hoped they would believe and forgive him. He finished the letter by stressing that he would never forget the care and concern she had shown him in the past. Now he could only apologize again for the problems it had caused her and her family. What he could do was insist that there had been nothing romantic in their relationship. He felt calmer after writing the letter. He lit a cigarette and played the funereal music tape that Liu Yue had brought over for him. Later, when dusk arrived with its red sunset, he walked out with the two letters, planning to give Zhong's letter to Ah-lan the next morning. But he was confused and posted both letters. Standing at the mailbox, he could have kicked himself over his relationship with Jing Xueyin. He had been naïve, too self-deprecating and timid. What would things be like now if back then he had been the way he was today? Thumping himself in the chest, he wondered if he had acted correctly. Suddenly feeling nauseous, he threw up loudly, making passersby cover their noses. He looked up and saw someone with an urban sanitation monitor armband eyeing him with a summons book in hand. Zhuang was so mad he went over to a sewer drain, but he couldn't bring up anything more.

He went home, feeling light-headed, and knocked on the door, before realizing that Niu Yueqing wasn't at this house. Quietly opening the door, he went in and stood blankly in the living room, as a sense of loneliness gripped him. He could write letters on behalf of Zhong Weixian's love life and he could testify about Jing's family life, but he had no idea what to do when it came to his own marital problems.

Someone knocked on the door. He thought it might be Liu Yue, but, no, it was Tang Wan'er, to his surprise.

"You poor thing. Shimu and Liu Yue had an enjoyable day eating, drinking, and playing mahjong at Meng Laoshi's house today, while you were here all alone."

"I have my music." He played the tape again.

"Why do you listen to this? It's so depressing," she said.

"Only music like this can comfort me," Zhuang said as he took her hand and sat down on the bed with her. He gave her a mirthless laugh and lowered his head.

"Did you two have a fight?" she asked. He didn't respond. Tears ran down her face, which she buried in his chest as she cried. Feeling even more agitated, he reached out to dry her tears before taking her hands and stroking them as if they were made of rubber. They fell silent for a while, before she reached for the bag behind her and took out its contents: a vitamin C fruit drink, a pack of fried cakes stuffed with leeks and sauce, three tomatoes, and two cucumbers that had been washed clean and put in individual plastic bags.

"It's late, and you probably haven't had anything to eat," she said softly

She watched him as he ate. When he looked up at her, she smiled but did not know what to say, though she wanted to say something.

"Xia Jie told us something really funny," she recalled. "A man from the countryside went to North Avenue but couldn't locate a toilet, so he found a deserted wall and relieved himself. Seeing a policeman come over just as he was pulling up his pants, he took off his straw hat and laid it over the excrement, keeping his hand on the hat. 'What are you doing?' the policeman asked. 'I caught a sparrow,' the man said. The policeman wanted to remove the hat, but the man said, 'Don't do that. Wait till I buy a cage.' He ran off, while the policeman cautiously kept his hand over the hat. Isn't that funny?"

"It is. But why are you talking about shit while I'm eating?"

"Oh, no! I—" She slapped her forehead and laughed as she went to the kitchen to find a napkin, her long legs ending in high heels. Zhuang wiped his lips with the napkin when she came back. "I never noticed how gracefully you walk, Wan'er."

"So you've noticed," she said. "My left foot splays out a bit, and I've been trying to correct that by walking straight."

"Walk for me again."

She turned around, walked a few steps, and smiled back at him, before opening the door to the toilet and going in. When he heard the sounds from inside, like spring water flowing down a gully, he got up, walked over, and opened the door. She was sitting on the toilet.

"Don't come in here. It smells."

But he didn't listen. Instead, he picked her up in the seated position and carried her out of the toilet.

"I can't today, I'm having my you-know-what."

He checked, and indeed there was a sanitary napkin in her panties. "But I want to. I want you, Wan'er. I need you." So she agreed. They laid out a thick layer of paper on the bed. □□ □□ □□ [The author has deleted 100 words.] Bloody fluid fanned out on the paper; bright red blood snaked down along her porcelain-white legs.

"As long as you're happy, I'll do anything. I will bleed for you."

Avoiding her eyes, he pulled her head to his chest and said, "I'm ruined, Wan'er, washed up."

Startled, she struggled to look up at him, detecting the heavy smell of cigarettes and alcohol. She reached out to remove a whisker the razor had missed. "Are you thinking about her? Were you pretending I'm her?"

He didn't say a word, merely paused briefly in his heavy breathing. She could tell. But he wasn't thinking only about Niu Yueqing, he was also thinking about Jing Xueyin. At that moment he could not explain why he had been thinking about them and why he treated Wan'er that way. But reminded by them, he turned her over as if crazed; with his arms on the bed to support himself, he entered her from behind without looking into her eyes. □□ □□ □□ [The author has deleted 300 words.] Blood dripped noisily onto the paper, creating a plum flower pattern. It was impossible to say if he despised the woman under him, or if he despised himself and the other two women. He collapsed on top of her when he came and lay there as funereal music continued to swirl around the room.

They lay in bed exhausted, as insubstantial and languid as waterlogged adobe bricks. Their eyes closed, neither said anything, and before long Wan'er dozed off. Some time later she opened her eyes to see him still on his back smoking a cigarette. She looked at his crotch and sat up when she saw nothing between his legs. "Your—"

"I cut it off," he said calmly.

Startled, she spread his legs to check and found that he had tucked it between them. "You scared me," she said with an irritated laugh. "You're terrible."

He smiled and said he was starting on a new work, which he had been planning to write for a long time. It was to be a long novel. "Wan'er," he grabbed her shoulder, "I want to tell you something, and you must understand. Everyone has issues, but mine are worse than most. I must write, for only that can free me. But writing a novel requires time and peace, so I must leave all these activities and people, including you. I'm going out of town. I can't write anything if I stay here in the city. That would be my downfall."

"You finally said it. I've been waiting for you to say that. You once told me that I inspired your creativity, but you haven't written much lately. I was also wondering if I've been greedy and disrupted your peace. But I have no willpower, and I can't stop myself from coming to see you, and when we see each other, we—"

"It's not your fault, Wan'er. It's precisely because of you that I want to write a great novel, and I desperately need your support and encouragement. I'm telling no one but you. I will write when I get where I'm going. Will you come if I ask you to visit me?"

"Of course I will, as long as you need me."

He kissed her again and licked a spot under a rib where he found a patch of ringworm, but she stopped him.

"It'll get better once I lick it. See, it's almost gone after I licked it only three times."

She lay still to let him kiss the spot like a dog.

❉

He could not reach any of his friends who lived in neighboring county towns, so he decided to go see Mr. Huang, the owner of the 101 Pesticide Plant, in a suburb. Huang had told him once that he had many rooms in his house, perfect for writing, adding that his wife, who did not work, was a great noodle maker. Leaving a note to say he had "gone away to do some writing," Zhuang got on his scooter and left. He reached Huangzhuang at noon. Huang Hongbao lived in a newly built multistory walled house. The building closely resembled a traditional brick structure, with a round mirror on the roof ridge, soaring eaves made of carved bricks, red lanterns at the ends, a heavy door made of tong wood reinforced with steel bars, and a horizontal board inscribed with "A Family of Farming Scholars" above the door. There was some meandering writing in chalk on the half-open gate panels. Zhuang went up for a closer look. One panel had "Acutely Smart," the other "Smartly Acute." Having no idea what they meant, he looked in through the gate and saw a large yard and a high entryway. The house had three stories, each with five windows and a balcony with a balustrade decorated with four-season nature scenery. It was in an L shape, with a row of single-story structures connected to the wall to the left; a tall chimney rose above one of them, which marked it as the kitchen. A stone path linked the yard entrance to the front door. Nothing hung from the clothesline stretched above it.

Zhuang coughed, but got no response, so he called out, "Is Mr. Huang home?" Still no response. As he pushed the gate open, he heard a roar; a brown creature leaped out, accompanied by the sound of clanging metal. He saw a wolf-like dog whose leash was tied to the wire overhead. Though restrained by the leash, the animal, which was only a few feet away, growled like a wild animal. Startled, he backed up to the gate just as a woman walked out from the kitchen. She looked at the visitor through red, puffy, somewhat glassy eyes. "Who are you looking for?"

"Mr. Huang, the plant owner. Is this his home?" The woman spat into her palm and smoothed her messy hair, which was so thin her scalp showed. He knew it must be Huang's wife. He was balding, and so was she. The graffiti on the door must have been a vandal's prank.

"I'm Zhuang Zhidie, from the city. Are you Mrs. Huang? You don't know me, but Mr. Huang and I know each other quite well."

"Of course I know you. You're the one who wrote an article for 101. Come in." But the dog refused to back down, incurring a string of insults from the woman, as if they were being directed to a human. She went over and pinned the animal's head between her legs, then smiled and invited Zhuang inside. He walked toward the main door of the three-story building, but the woman called out, "Over here. We live on this side." She ran off to open the kitchen door. The house had three rooms, with a half-wall in the middle—three wood-burning stoves on one side, a kang, a sofa, a reclining chair, a TV, and some other household objects on the other. When he sat down to smoke, the woman set some water on to boil, making a loud noise with the bellows and filling the room with smoke.

"Don't you use a gas stove?" he asked.

"We have one, but I think it's dangerous. A wood stove gives a stronger flame. Besides, it doesn't feel like cooking if I don't use the bellows."

That made him laugh. "Is the building rented?"

"No, it's unoccupied."

"Then why do you live on this side?"

"I prefer single-story houses, and sleeping on the kang is so much better because it doesn't cause me back pain. He smokes all night long and needs to spit, and a brick floor is better than a carpet."

She brought over a pot of boiled water; instead of tea, it contained four poached eggs. As he ate, Zhuang mentioned Huang's earlier invitation and the purpose of his visit.

"That's wonderful. You can do your writing here. You'll be my advocate. I probably would have looked you up anyway if you hadn't come."

He smiled, knowing that she had no idea what his writing was all about; instead, he asked if Mr. Huang was at the plant and when he would be back.

"He'll be right home now that you're here. I'll send for him." She asked if he was tired, and said if he was, he could go upstairs for a nap. She led him over to the three-story building, where they entered a room furnished with an oversized desk surrounded by armchairs. To the left was a staircase with bamboo and orchids painted on the handrail spindles. She showed him the second and third floors, where every room was carpeted and had a bed with a canopy frame, poorly constructed but carved with brightly colored fish, insects, flowers, and birds. The mattresses had been placed on the wood frames in such a way as to show off the gold-plated aluminum edges. A wall mirror was painted with a dragon and a phoenix, with two ribbons. There were also a shoe brush and a backscratcher. A thick layer of dust coated the floors, the beds, and the desk. Thumping the bedding, she cursed the smokestack at the village refinery; like a crematorium, it brought disaster to the villagers. "With ash flying the way it does, a bride could pee black for three years," she complained.

"You're in fine shape financially. Not even the mayor can afford to live in such a big house." Zhuang secretly laughed at the furnishings, so typical of newly rich country folk.

Sitting him down on the edge of the bed, she told him how happy she was that he had come. She had heard from her husband that he'd be coming and that his favorite food was cornmeal noodles. Why would he want something even the peasants refused to eat? Could he have such a poor palate that he can't enjoy cuttlefish and sea cucumbers? He wanted to explain to her, but found it impossible to do, so he just smiled.

"How do you write? You must write me into your work so everyone will know I'm his wife."

"But you *are* his wife."

Her face crinkled, a horrendously ugly sight that startled him. Then she began to cry.

"I helped him build up 101, but he stopped loving me once he got rich. I'm not ashamed to tell you this. He could wrap his arms around me when he needed me, but push me off a cliff when I was no longer useful to him. He was so wretchedly poor in the old days that if he'd been lying in the road, people would have covered him and walked off. I was the one who was willing to marry him, and I even gave him a child. It was his fate that he couldn't keep the second one, but he blamed me for scalding the baby to death. Now, you be the judge. I was boiling water in a wok, and when I ran out of firewood, I went out to the yard to get some. When I returned, there was no baby. I looked inside the wok, and the baby was in there! He'd been playing on the kang next to the stove and had fallen in. Was that my fault? Now he complains about my blackened teeth and short, stocky figure. I was born this way, and he didn't complain when he married me. Now when we're in bed, he looks at a movie pictorial, working away on me while looking at the slutty women in the magazine. So I said women are all the same, and that spot isn't all that different from the eye of a dead pig. He said a man fucks a woman but looks at her face, and he said I have a disgusting face. We fought over that, really fought, so he walked out and refused to come home. He wants a divorce. Tell me, how can I agree to a divorce? He'd make my life not worth living, so I'm not going to make it easy for him, either, not as long as I'm alive. I'd never let those sluts into this house. Not one of them will ever sleep on one of these springy mattresses."

His scalp tingled as she went on, and he knew it would be impossible to write here, no matter how delicious her cornmeal noodles might be. He stood up.

"How could Mr. Huang do something like that? I just came to look around. I'll come back another day to write about you."

He walked out into the yard and started up his scooter.

"Ai! Why are so impatient? Can't you wait a second?"

Even after he had pushed the scooter to the road outside the village, he could still hear her shouting to someone at the gate, "See him? That's a man who writes books. He's here to write about me and speak up for women. Ai-ya! Don't go in there; that's where the writer left his footprints."

He rode all the way to the south-side city gate, grumbling about the lack of a quiet place. A weakness washed over him when he went through the gate, as he wondered where he should go, to the compound or Shuangren fu Avenue, or maybe Wan'er's house. After a few moments of indecision, he parked his scooter and went up to the city wall, where he paced listlessly. He wished he could run into Zhou Min and ask the man to teach him how to play the xun. Zhuang was convinced he could learn to play it. But the city wall was deserted, not even a bird in sight. Wild grass had overtaken the spaces where the large square bricks met, making the wall look like a fine rug with a green-and-white checked pattern. Walking along the parapet, he saw lovers cuddling in the woods outside the wall. Watching out only for people around them, they were oblivious to the pair of eyes above the city wall. Zhuang looked at them as if they were animals in a zoo; he kept walking with the hope of gaining a clearer view until he reached a corner of the wall. Birds soaring in the sky abruptly disappeared into the wild undergrowth as if sucked into a void. Feeling calmer, he wanted to see where they went to rest and why the area attracted birds from the city. Then he spotted someone sitting there; it had looked like a rock at first, but he quickly realized it was a man. So someone else was searching for peace and quiet? Moved, he was about to go up and introduce himself when he discovered that the man was masturbating. He lay back with his legs out before falling backward into the reeds, where he groaned, startling the birds into flight. Flustered, Zhuang did not know what to do, so he just stood there; when he gained his composure, he spun around and took off running, castigating himself for not leaving sooner. His stomach churned, and he knew he was going to throw up. Supporting himself with one hand, he climbed down off the city wall in time to retch yellow liquid onto the ground. Darkness filled his eyes when he was done. He wondered if they were playing tricks on him or if he was delusional. There was water in the marshy reeds all year round. Could he have seen his own reflection? At that moment, the junkman came out of a deserted lane near the city wall, pulling his cart and shouting in an undulating voice, "Junkman! Collecting junk and scraps!" He walked toward Zhuang, chanting a bit of his doggerel:

When drinking, never get drunk over one bottle or two;
When playing mahjong, never get sleepy after three days or four;
When dancing, never make a mistake over five steps or six;
When fooling around, never shy away from seven women or eight.

⁂

After mailing a letter at the post office, Zhong Weixian returned to his office, where he marked that day's date with a red pen on his calendar and added an exclamation mark. He had just made tea and taken a sip when the head of the Department of Culture sent over a document. After one look, Zhong's face turned ashen. He placed an immediate phone call to Zhuang's house. Liu Yue, who answered, mistook Zhong for Meng Yunfang. "You can tell me what this is about," she said. "I'm his secretary."

"Secretary?"

Realizing her mistake, Liu Yue panicked and called Niu Yueqing over.

"Is that you, Mr. Zhong? Zhidie's not home. Is there something I can do?" She glared at Liu Yue, who stuck her tongue out. Niu Yueqing's face fell as she said urgently, "Tell him to bring it over."

She hung up and collapsed into the chair.

"What's wrong?" Liu Yue asked.

"Go to the compound and bring your Zhuang Laoshi here immediately."

"I haven't seen him lately. I don't keep up with his comings and goings. He wasn't there this morning. He left a note saying he'd gone somewhere to write. God knows where he is."

"Where could he be? Go check again. If he's not there, ask old Mrs. Wei, the gatekeeper, if he said anything to her. If not, go to Meng Laoshi's, then to the bookstore to ask Hong Jiang."

"Well, then, I'll have a tour of half the city."

"This is no time to be clever with your tongue. Go on now. Take a taxi if you're tired. I'll wait for Zhou Min here." Niu Yueqing gave her thirty yuan.

She went in to change clothes and took Niu Yueqing's monthly bus pass from her jacket before walking out with her own purse.

With the thirty yuan, she bought a pair of stockings and, adding some of her own money, a pair of white leather sandals and some dark sunglasses. Seeing she still had three yuan left, she went into a snack shop and ordered a dish of rainbow ice cream. She took off her old shoes and put on the stockings and the new shoes. Wearing the sunglasses, she grumbled as she ate the ice cream, "What could be so urgent that I have to run all over town? She was upset when I complained. I probably wouldn't have gotten the thirty yuan if I hadn't." Noticing a young man at the next table looking at her, she boldly returned the gaze, under the protection of her dark glasses. She was swinging her crossed leg. The man smiled, exposing bright red gums, and beckoned her with a curled finger. Suddenly frightened, she got up to leave. The young man followed her out. Ducking into a shop, she thought she had shaken him, but he was waiting for her when she came back out. "Drill a hole, miss."

She had heard about streetwalkers and their secret code with potential johns, "drill a hole." She broke out in a cold sweat. Forcing a smile, she said, "Are you from Guangdong? Ai-ya, you have a piece of leek in your teeth." The man turned red from embarrassment. While he was checking his teeth in the store window, she jumped on a bus. The door shut the moment she was aboard. Leaning against the window, she saw the man turn to look for her, so she gave him a charming smile, pointing at herself with her right thumb and then wagging her pinkie before spitting on it.

No one was in when she reached the compound. The gatekeeper had no idea where Zhuang was. She wondered if he had left another note, so she went inside, but she found nothing but a copper coin hanging over the bathroom faucet. She looked at it, fell in love with it, untied it from the thread, and put in her pocket. She left the apartment and boarded a bus to Meng Yunfang's house. He was dressed in baggy shorts. He told her to wait while he rode his bicycle to see if Zhuang was at the House of Imperfection Seekers. Not finding anyone there, he returned home.

"Where did you go? Why did it take you so long?"

Knowing he mustn't give her the address, he didn't answer. Liu Yue now had to pin her hopes on the bookstore. When she got there by taxi, she saw that the space next door was being remodeled and knew that it was the planned gallery. She asked the workers if Zhao Jingwu was there, and was told that he'd gone out to buy building materials. Mistaking her for Zhao's girlfriend, the workers drooled as they plied her with questions. "Disgusting!" she said and went into the bookstore. Hong Jiang wasn't in, so she took the stairs to the second floor, where Hong lived next to two storage rooms. It was quiet, except for a cat licking a bowl of paste. She kicked open the door to Hong's room and found him in bed having sex.

"Well, well. Doing that in broad daylight, are we?" she said.

Hong quickly pulled up his pants and dragged a sheet over the girl before shutting the door with one hand and covering Liu Yue's mouth with the other. What bad luck to see something like that. She brushed Hong's hand away, sat down to pick up a newspaper, and covered her eyes. "Despicable. Just despicable."

"Good sister, please don't tell Laoshi or Shimu about this. I'm begging you."

"Trying to sweet-talk me, are you? Who's your sister? Let's not worry about Laoshi and Shimu yet. You have to deal with me first. If we were in the countryside, you'd have to give me two yards of red satin to ward off bad luck. Besides, I'm still unmarried."

Hong opened a drawer and took out a stack of bills.

"Trying to buy my silence?"

"Please take it, good sister. I'd be worried if you didn't. I know you don't make much each month. Come see me if you need any help. I'm a man of my word."

"I won't take it. But if you're worried, put the money in the bank and give me the deposit book. Has Zhuang Laoshi been here?"

"I'll give it to you tomorrow. No, he hasn't."

"Do you know where he is?"

"I have no idea."

She got up to leave, but changed her mind and walked over to the bed to pull the sheet back. "Let me see who the lucky girl is." She didn't know the owner of the tender white flesh under the sheet, but she noticed a large mole on one cheek. She committed that to memory.

Niu Yueqing was waiting for Liu Yue and Zhou Min. Zhou Min didn't show, but Tang Wan'er came. It turned out that Zhong Weixian had called Zhou in to read the document, and was told to make a copy for Zhuang. Zhou Min's jaw dropped when he read it. It was a notice from Jing Xueyin, claiming that she would be taking legal action, since the department had failed to follow the directives from the head of propaganda, and that the magazine refused to publish an announcement. She had turned in a statement of charges to the District Court, which refused to take the case on the grounds that it was outside their jurisdiction, since Zhuang

Zhidie, one of the defendants, was a member of the People's Congress. The case was then turned over to the Municipal Intermediate Court. The defendants included Zhou Min, the author of the article; Zhuang Zhidie, the source of the material; Zhong Weixian, the editor-in-chief of *Xijing Magazine*, which provided the space for publication; Li Hongwen, the final reviewer of the article; and Gou Dahai, the initial reviewer. The Department of Culture did not receive the statement of charges, but was given a photocopy of Zhuang's latest letter to Jing and her husband, with sections of the letter highlighted in red. Without a word, Zhou left the office, but instead of going to see Zhuang at Shuangren fu, he went to a beer bar and ate forty skewers of barbecued mutton, washed down with four bottles of beer, before stumbling his way home. Wan'er had gone out that morning to pick up a bottle of nail polish. She was applying it after carefully filing her nails when Zhou came into the yard and leaned against the door with a smile.

"Are you drunk?" She grew suspicious. "Seriously?"

He slid down the doorframe to the ground and threw up. Chickens in the yard came to peck at his former stomach contents, themselves swaying and falling down drunk. Incensed, she tried to pick him up, but he was too heavy, so she grabbed him by the arms to drag him inside. He held on to the pear tree and swore: "He sold me out! He sacrificed me because of a woman. He's despicable. Ugly. He's not a man."

"What are you talking about?" she asked. "Who sold you out for what woman?"

"Our laoshi, the one you adore."

Her heart raced, but she retorted angrily, "What are you talking about? How did he sell you out? What woman? How did I wind up here with you? Am I supposed to belong to you just because I have no legal protection?"

He glared at her until he was overcome by dizziness and could not clearly hear what she was saying; he saw her red lips flapping and her red-nailed fingers flailing before he passed out, dead drunk.

She stood there, disgusted at the sight of the wretched man, wondering what she had seen in him to make her follow him here. *The day has finally come*, she said to herself. *It's finally here.*

She had wanted to leave him for some time, but had stopped herself each time she was about to tell him that. She was worried that he would find out about her and Zhuang from someone else, which unsettled and frightened her. But now that he knew, she was surprisingly relaxed. After taking a look at the sun beating down with its fiery rays, she squatted down to say to the sleeping Zhou, "Our karmic connection has run its course. Go ahead and sleep, and when you wake up, I'll tell you everything. Don't blame me, since I never really belonged to you."

A roll of paper in his pocket caught her attention, so she took it out and cried out at the first sight of its contents. She ran inside and read it three times, realizing that he hadn't found out about her and Zhuang. It must have been a result of Jing Xueyin's lawsuit or of the letter Zhuang wrote to Jing and her husband. What came to mind initially was why Zhuang still could not cut ties with Jing even at a moment like this. He had repeatedly told her that he and Jing had never been in love, so where had the emotional attachment come from? He had done everything with Wan'er and had told her everything, but was that other woman still on his mind? What kind of woman could infatuate him like that? Putting the document away, she managed to get Zhou Min inside and lay him down on a sofa before dashing off to the compound to see Zhuang, unaware that he had left the city. She changed her mind halfway there. As resentment toward him welled up, she decided to use Niu Yueqing to cut things off between Zhuang and Jing.

After reading the document, Niu Yueqing said, "Mr. Zhong called and said he'd send Zhou over with this. I was dying from worry. Where is he?"

Recalling Zhou Min's drunken tirade earlier, Tang now realized that he harbored so much resentment against Zhuang that he had intentionally delayed sharing the document. She thought about how close she had come to contributing to the delay, and was happy she had made the right decision to come here.

"Zhou Min was outraged at that woman when he read the document. Does Jing Xueyin want to see Zhuang Laoshi sent to jail? He felt so bad he was crying at home, saying he was too ashamed to see Zhuang Laoshi."

Niu Yueqing was touched. "There's no need to cry. The threat of a lawsuit can't put anyone in jail." Liu Yue came in at that moment, startling them with her new look. "How can you think about dressing up at a time like this?" Niu Yueqing said. "Where is he?"

"I couldn't find him."

"Did you look for him, or did you go shopping?"

"Where would I get the money to buy anything? I ran into someone I knew from home. She works in a hotel, raking in several hundred a month. She thought I looked shabby, so she gave me a pair of shoes, some stockings, and the glasses."

"You don't look shabby," Niu Yueqing said. "Why compare yourself to a hotel employee? You see them every day at the train station looking for business. They work in the hotel during the day. Who knows what they do at night?"

Knowing that she didn't need to say anything, Liu Yue took off her shoes and rubbed her feet, sending the jade bracelet rolling around her arm. Tang saw that it had been one of hers, intended for Niu Yueqing, but somehow it had made it onto Liu's wrist. As feelings of jealousy rose inside, she embraced Liu Yue and said: "I see we're like sisters. We have identical bracelets." She held out her arm to hold the bracelets together. Liu Yue was pleasantly surprised and slipped the bracelet off Tang's wrist for a closer look. "Like me, you only have one. It would be nice to have a pair."

Niu Yueqing, who heard the exchange, did not want the story behind the bracelet revealed, so she flipped through the document and asked: "Have you read this, Wan'er?"

"I have. Zhuang Laoshi really should not have written that letter. He did it with the best of intentions, but see what he's getting in return? It will be used as evidence in court, and there's nothing he can say to defend himself."

"Men are like that. The nicer you are to them, the less they care about you. Whatever they can't have is the best. He believes there is always candy inside a wrapper, but this time there was actually a time bomb."

"Every man's the same," Liu Yue said, "hankering for the six flavors when he has his fill of the five grains. Flowers in the family garden never smell as good as those outside."

Wan'er blushed. "Zhuang Laoshi isn't like that. He can't get enough of the fragrance from Shimu, the flower at home, so how could he have time for anyone outside?"

"What are you saying? What would people think if they heard you? So vulgar," Niu Yueqing said. Without asking Tang to stay longer, she instead asked Liu Yue to move back to the compound with her and wait for Zhuang's return. Having given the document only a quick read, Liu Yue was apprehensive and secretly chastised herself for dallying on the street so long. Now she understood why Niu Yueqing was unhappy with her.

"I may be just a worthless maid in this house, Dajie, but I am, after all, a member of this family. Why did you hide such an important matter from me?"

"I was so anxious when I told you to look for him, I didn't have time to explain things. Aren't I showing you the document now?"

"So you really want to move back, then? After holding out all these days, you're going to blink first. In the future, instead of controlling his temper, Zhuang Laoshi will vent his displeasure on you and me."

"I can't help it that I'm his wife. At such a critical time, I can't keep fighting with him. If he winds up in jail, I'll be the one to deliver food to him. That's my fate. I can't share in his glory, but I'm fated to be his partner in misery. All our fights end with my admitting defeat anyway."

They left together, Tang Wan'er going south, the other two north. But before Tang walked off, Niu Yueqing called her back. "Since Zhou Min didn't come, I guess he's unhappy with your Zhuang Laoshi. When you get home, tell him not to be upset and to please be more understanding, for Zhuang Laoshi is in a tight spot. At moments like this, we must stand together. If he goes down, we will, too, but as long as he's around, Zhou Min will have nothing to worry about." When Niu Yueqing finished, she told Liu Yue to go inside to get a bottle for Tang to take home for Zhou Min. Tang stopped her. "I know all that. I wouldn't go along if Zhou Min was disrespectful. There's no need to get any liquor for him."

The two women felt so close they were on the verge of tears, and parted ways only after holding hands for a moment.

Niu Yueqing continued to watch Tang as she walked out of the lane and disappeared from sight.

"Let's go," Liu Yue said.

"Yes," Niu Yueqing said, then added, "What do you think of Tang Wan'er, Liu Yue?"

"What do *you* think?"

"She has a good heart."

"As long as you think she's a good person," Liu Yue said.

When they reached the apartment, Zhuang, who had returned to take a bath, was dressed in his pajamas, turning the house upside looking for something. He had realized during his bath that the coin around his neck was gone. The string was made of nylon, not likely to break, and he wore it like a necklace, which could only mean that he had taken it off and put it somewhere before the bath. But he couldn't find it in the bathroom or in the bedroom. He was drenched in sweat from the search, but stopped looking when Niu Yueqing and Liu Yue came in. Quietly he made himself a cup of tea to drink alone. Ignoring the cold shoulder, Niu Yueqing told Liu Yue to prepare some noodles, while she went inside to make the beds in each bedroom, wipe down the tables and chairs, spray some perfume, and light some sandalwood incense, making the place clean, bright, and cozy. Then she changed into a soft satin qipao and put on some makeup before sitting down beside him. She took out a pack of State Express cigarettes and handed it to him. "What a temper you have. You should have made some sort of noise when we came in, even if Liu Yue and I had been beggars."

"What's the matter with you?" Zhuang cast a puzzled look at his wife.

"Me? What's the matter with *you?* Don't look angry. Come with me to help Liu Yue cook."

In the kitchen Liu Yue smiled at him, while Niu Yueqing returned to the living room.

"What's wrong with her?" Zhuang whispered.

"The well has fallen into the bucket! You won. You're a celebrity, so who could out-wait you?"

Zhuang pinched the girl's mouth. "Don't be so clever. You will realize how nice I was when your husband starts finding fault with you."

"We'll see who finds fault with whom."

He studied her figure in the short, tight skirt and her impossibly pretty legs, highlighted by the nude-tone stockings. "You look nice in stockings."

"Poor me. Dajie was angry with me for buying these."

"You're not poor. What happened to the money I gave you a few days ago?"

"It wasn't very much, and I'm saving it to buy a down coat for the winter."

He poked her in the waist. "You're getting cleverer by the day."

She shrieked. Niu Yueqing, who was clearing the dining table, asked from the living room, "What's wrong?"

Liu Yue banged her knife on the chopping board and said, "I cut my fingernail."

"Be careful. Don't cook one of your nails into the noodles."

Zhuang ate three bowls of noodles, after which his forehead resembled a steamer.

"Are you finished?" Niu Yueqing asked him. "I'm going to show you something. Liu Yue, bring his cigarettes so he can smoke while he reads."

When he was finished, he sat motionless for a long time before sneering and wiping the tabletop with the document.

"Liu Yue, your dajie did a nice job with her makeup today. It would have been even nicer if she'd used less rouge."

Niu Yueqing and Liu Yue were shocked. When it came to the serious matter that had kept them running around all day, he was treating it as if it were nothing.

"I'm glad you're not angry," Niu Yueqing said. "But don't treat it as a lark, either. Now, since this doesn't seem to bother you, I have two things to say to you. I'm your wife and I have to bring them up, even if they displease you. First, why did you have to write Jing Xueyin such a letter? It shows not only that you still have feelings for her, but that it was a foolish move. You should never have written something like that at a time like this, no matter how much you feel for her. Do you honestly believe she's as tenderhearted a person as I am? You're being nice to her, and see what she does in return? It's all right for her to photocopy the letter as court evidence, but Zhong Weixian told me she's made copies for the provincial and municipal leadership, the Women's Federation, the Standing Committee of the People's Congress, and all the cultural and art organizations. How they must be laughing at you. From what I've heard, she's going around telling people that you pursued her years ago, while she couldn't have cared less about you. You deceived yourself into thinking that she liked you. Won't the letter serve as further evidence of her claim once it goes public? I don't want to say more about this, or you'll think I'm jealous. I can ignore it when outsiders mock me, but have you given a single thought to your wife? Second, you're a celebrity. As the saying goes, the tall trees catch the wind, but you know that tall trees can also block the wind. It's different for Zhou Min, an ant that anyone could easily pinch to death. He was the one who caused all this, but you must remember that he didn't mean to. If it weren't for Jing Xueyin and for your tendency to brag for momentary gratification, this article would only serve to promote you and spread your fame. You helped Zhou Min find a job, and if you were to abandon him on account of her now, his anger would erase everything you've done for him. Besides, others won't regard you favorably. You have to be aware of what kind of person he is. He was not a reputable character, and his old habits could return to betray him even though he tried to turn over a new leaf. He already bears grudges against you. Earlier today, when Zhong Weixian called, he said he asked Zhou Min to rush the document over. But he didn't. It was Tang Wan'er who did, and who knows what he said to her. You need to figure out why he chose not to see you about this important matter."

She was being clear and logical, but he remained motionless after hearing her out. "I was going to write a novel," he said at last, "but I won't if you say no."

❋

Zhuang called Meng Yunfang over that evening and had him ask Zhou Min, Hong Jiang, and Zhao Jingwu to come with him. After discussing various strategies, they reached the conclusion that they could no longer depend solely on the people at the magazine. They had to work on the Municipal Intermediate Court to reject the lawsuit. Zhao said he knew a judge named Bai Yuzhu, who might not be in charge of the case, but would help out if he could. Zhuang told Zhao and Zhou to go see Bai at his home right away and report back on the results, no matter how late it was. Niu Yueqing put together a large parcel of gifts for the two men to take along.

"I'll pay for these," Zhou Min offered.

"No need to worry about trivial matters like that," Niu Yueqing said. "We may have to spend money in other areas, and you can pitch in then."

After Zhao and Zhou left, Zhuang said, "Don't look so sad, it's no big deal. We'll play some mahjong while we wait for them to return."

Zhuang, Meng, Niu Yueqing, and Hong sat down to play, while Liu Yue served them cigarettes and tea. Her eyes were fixed on Hong, who said: "See my jacket over there, Liu Yue? Check the pocket and get me some change, will you?"

She went to the coat tree and searched his pocket for the deposit book. It had her name on it, with an entry of three hundred yuan. Putting it in her pocket, she said: "Is that all, Hong Jiang?"

"Not enough? It's plenty."

"How much?" Niu Yueqing asked.

"Twelve yuan."

Hong winked at Liu and said with a laugh, "I'm good at grabbing a knife barehanded."

Liu came over to watch him play. "Grab a knife barehanded? I think you're going to lose. People say lucky in love, unlucky in cards. You're not going to win anything."

"Tiles worth eighty thousand, that's a winner," Meng Yunfang announced. "I wonder which girl has been caught in Hong Jiang's web this time?" Hong blushed and played the wrong tile. Criticizing his terrible play, Liu Yue slapped him on the head.

"Hong Jiang is a bookstore manager. He's good-looking and dresses well, so how could all the girls not fall for him? Of course he's lucky in love."

"Don't spoil his Hong Kong hairdo, Liu Yue," Meng said. "Like women's feet, men's heads should be looked at but not touched. I thought you had your hooks into him. In my view, it's hard for him to find a good girl. That's just the way things are. Handsome guys can't get pretty girls. I don't think Hong Jiang's wife is as good-looking as Liu Yue. So then Liu Yue would have trouble finding a handsome husband. This is what we call 'A guy with a limp gets to ride a fine horse.'"

Liu Yue was so put out that she pounded Meng with her fists. "An ugly mind goes with an ugly look."

Niu Yueqing criticized Liu Yue for saying that.

"It's my fault," Meng said. "I've let her say whatever she wants, and now she doesn't know her place."

"You're always doing divinations, Yunfang. Why don't you see what will come of Zhao and Zhou's visit?"

"I will need my equipment for that. You don't have the perpetual calendar, so I can't convert the dates."

"I have a coin. Why don't you use that?" Liu Yue took a shiny copper coin on a keychain out of her pocket to show him. Zhuang stared at the coin and said, "Let me see that." She refused. Niu Yueqing played a tile and asked her husband to make his move. With his eyes still on Liu Yue, Zhuang reached for the tile from the end of his line, prompting Meng to hit him on the hand. "Be careful. Don't go to the ladies' room when you want to use the toilet."

Zhuang regained his composure and looked at the tiles carefully.

"How many times do I have to flip the coin?" Meng said. "How about this? Yueqing, give me a three-digit number off the top of your head. I'll use 'Master Zhuge's Pre-Battle Divination Method.'"

"Three-seven-nine," she said.

Figuring the numbers with his left hand, Meng said, "'Minor good luck.' Not bad."

Niu Yueqing's face lit up. "Good. Now watch me win. Playing mahjong requires a lot of energy. You see, I won. I'm going to be the 'lord' now."

Meng was upset. "Go ahead," he said before shuffling the tiles. "You can be the sow for all I care." A cat was meowing in the yard, making one bleak sound after another. Hong asked if they had a cat. He told them to keep it away from feral cats when it was in heat. He added that he had a Persian he'd bring over in a few days.

"How could we have a cat?" Niu Yueqing said. "I don't like cats or dogs. It's the neighbor's cat, a big headache for me, because it attracts feral cats that meow nonstop."

"Ai-ya! I took the lid off the vat of pickled vegetables to let in some sunlight this afternoon, but I forgot to put it back," Zhuang said as he ran out onto the balcony and called out to Liu Yue, "Come help me move the vat so the cat won't take our vegetables."

When she came out, he shut the balcony door and asked in a low voice, "Where did you get that coin?"

"I found it in the bathroom. It looked so nice I tied it to my key chain."

"It's mine. Give it back."

"Yours? There was a string attached to it, and I've never seen you wear anything around your neck."

"I've been wearing it for a long time. I don't take it off. But how would you know?"

"I've never heard of a man wearing a coin around his neck. You look so angry. Could this be a token of love from some woman while we were staying at Shuangren fu?"

"Stop the nonsense," he said as he grabbed her hand and reached into her pocket. When he took the coin out, she tried to snatch it away, so he put it in his mouth with a smug look. In the meantime, the other three players had finished laying the tiles out. Impatient for him to return to play, Meng called out, "How hard can it be to move a vat? Are you playing or not, Zhidie?"

He went back inside, the coin secure in his pocket. "This is a fine year for pickled vegetables, Yunfang. I'll put some in a plastic bag for you."

Zhao Jingwu and Zhou Min returned around midnight, saying they had managed to see Bai Yuzhu. Bai was not going to be the convening judge, but he knew all about the charges, which had everyone at court talking. Naturally, they all had different views. The statement had originally been sent to the criminal court, but it was transferred to the civil court because of the absence of a criminal element. Both the presiding judge and the trial judge, Sima Gong, were Bai's friends, and he would talk to them about dismissing the case. He had kindly suggested that they see Sima Gong first, and even went with them. Sima was aloof, so they told him that Zhuang had wanted to come see him personally but was stricken with a stomach problem on the way there and had returned home. They also told him that Zhuang had asked them to see Sima on his behalf and had sent along a copy of one of his books. Zhou had come up with that idea and had bought the book at a night market stall. He had then signed Zhuang's name. After leaving Sima's house, they went back to see Bai, who said he had wanted to meet the hugely famous Zhuang Zhidie, but had never had the opportunity. He was happy that he could establish a friendship with Zhuang's friend over the case. He went on to tell them what a fan of Zhuang's works his son was. The young man, a soldier in charge of divisional public relations, had written some stories and essays and could use some guidance from Mr. Zhuang.

"We can't help him with other things, but this is no problem," Niu Yueqing said. "You can all help the young man publish his works."

"Yes." Zhao took out four manuscripts. "Judge Bai gave us these things his son has written, saying the army has a stipulation that five works published by provincial or municipal presses can earn a soldier a third-class merit, and three by the national press will earn him a second-class merit. His son sent him these four, hoping to get them published in Xijing. Bai has been trying to find an entrée into the publishing world. So we brought them back, boasting that we can guarantee publication."

"That's good," Zhuang said. "So go ahead."

"We can't do it," Zhao said. "It's up to you."

"All right, leave them with me. I'll take a look at them tomorrow," Zhuang said with a laugh. "What else does he want?"

"He said that Sima Gong is a bit eccentric," Zhao said. "He's reserved and he doesn't smoke, drink, or play mahjong. Bai could work on him to help us, but it would be much harder than with others. He does, however, have a fondness for calligraphy and paintings, which he collects. Bai said we should try to acquire a scroll for him. I agreed to give it a try. Why don't we go see Gong Jingyuan's son one of these days and get that one by Chairman Mao? That would pretty much seal the deal."

They decided that Zhou Min should get to know Bai Yuzhu better, through frequent visits to the man's house, while Zhuang read the articles and found a way to get them published in a hurry. Zhao and Zhuang would go see Gong Xiaoyi about the scroll. Once they got it, Zhuang would pay Sima Gong a personal visit. It would be best if they could invite Sima and Bai out for dinner. Zhou would talk to Bai to see if that could be arranged. When the plan was settled, Zhuang said, "We ought to see if there's a listening device under the table." That got a laugh.

"This is probably how a coup d'état is plotted," Meng said.

"And maybe a Politburo meeting. A few people talk something over at someone's house, and national policy is formulated. I once read an article about Mao Zedong meeting with Zhou Enlai and Liu Shaoqi at his house about national affairs. They talked late into the night after a bowl of noodles. Liu Yue, why don't you make us each a bowl of noodles?"

She went to the kitchen and almost immediately brought out seven bowls of noodles. They sat down to eat before dispersing.

Zhuang did not get up until the noon the following day. He read the articles, which got him cursing. They were terrible, filled with errors. They gave him such a headache that he crumpled them up and tossed them into the toilet. Niu Yueqing fished them out and told Liu Yue to dry them on the balcony. Zhuang went out onto the balcony with a broom and swept the pages over the railings. Seeing her husband's mad behavior, Niu Yueqing was on the verge of tears. "They're not yours. What do you care about their quality? All we need is to get them published."

"Who would publish crap like that?"

"So you don't want to win the lawsuit?"

Breathing hard, Zhuang sat down. Then he got back up and went in search of two of his own unpublished essays. "I'll go to talk to people at the culture and arts section at the provincial paper. We'll put his son's name on these and get them published first. What kind of writer am I? Do I call myself a writer?" He stumbled out the door and slammed it so hard the house shook.

The essays appeared two days later. Zhou Min bought copies of the paper and gave Bai Yuzhu one. Beside himself with joy, he asked when the other two would be published. When Zhou relayed Bai's question, Zhuang flew into a rage. "Aren't two enough for him? No more. I won't do it again. Even if I won the lawsuit, I would still be the biggest loser."

Zhou dared not say a word, while Niu Yueqing got a tongue-lashing for offering her view. She decided not to talk back; instead she tried to make Zhou feel better before going to see Meng Yunfang in hopes that he could talk Zhuang around. Then she was worried he would be mad at her for doing that. She felt exploited and shed secret tears.

Liu Yue stayed to cook for the couple while making two trips a day to prepare meals for Niu's mother, who was suffering from her old problem again, complaining that the doors were getting thicker and that the shadows etched on the door came alive every night. She wanted Zhuang to come burn them. When Liu Yue said he was too busy to make the trip, she argued with the girl, saying that Zhuang was her son-in-law, not someone under Liu Yue's thumb, and that she wasn't his wife. That so upset Liu Yue that she did a terrible job cooking, wishing the old woman an early death. She would have given her sleeping pills for a few quiet days if not for her fear of potential health problems. In the end, the old woman walked to the compound with the help of her cane and got Zhuang to come out with her. Though the street wasn't particularly crowded on the road to Shuangren fu Avenue, she complained that it was so packed she could hardly move. Then she pointed to three people sleeping on the street and said they were so skinny she could see their ribs. Zhuang looked, but saw nothing.

"Mother must be seeing ghosts."

"I can't tell the difference, so maybe they are ghosts," she said as she thrust her cane around as if fighting her way through a crowd. Zhuang thought she might have a point; if everyone turned into a ghost after death, wouldn't there be more ghosts than humans by now?

When they reached Shuangren fu Avenue, she told Zhuang to strip the shadows off the doors. Of course he couldn't do that, so she said: "Just stand there. You're a celebrity with lots of energy, so everyone is afraid of you. You've given me the courage to do it myself." She picked up a knife and began carving the door. She said she removed one layer at a time, until she had taken twelve layers off. Holding the strippings as if she were cradling them, she went into the kitchen, where she lit a match to burn them, even asking Zhuang if he could hear the crackling sounds. Suddenly she shouted that a pair of human feet had run off—she had cut them off a cow that had grown human feet. They fled after she chopped them off, so she ran around the house to chase them out. Eventually she got the feet out the door. She had worked up a sweat, but was finally able to sleep peacefully. Zhuang, on the other hand, had trouble sleeping that night, for there seemed to be human feet all over the room, dancing in a variety of styles and leaving footprints on the floor, the walls, and the ceiling. He seemed to have followed the pattern, walking deeper into it until he could no longer get out, since the prints kept changing. He was startled awake, bathed in sweat. He saw no footprints on the floor or on the walls when he turned on the light. The old woman's talk about footprints must have affected his dream, he told himself. Unable to go back to sleep, he sat outside her bedroom to smoke. She slept holding a pair of tiny shoes in her arms, as the dreary sound of a xun started up, like sobbing ghosts and howling wolves.

Zhuang had now spent a few days at Shuangren fu, but Niu Yueqing did not dare come to take him home. Instead she talked to Meng Yunfang, who suggested that she let him stay with the old woman. He also offered to write two more essays and find a venue for their publication. After Zhuang got over his anger, they would see if he was willing to go to Gong Xiaoyi for the scroll. Niu Yueqing waited daily for Zhou Min to update her on the developments; in the meantime, she entertained Zhao Jingwu and Hong Jiang on their daily visits. Her biggest headache was Bai Yuzhu, who, after being invited over once by Zhou Min, began dropping in regularly at mealtime or late at night. Sometimes he even brought along a group of book lovers who worshipped writers. Niu Yueqing forced a smile as she made tea and offered them cigarettes. By the time the guests had left, she could not stop yawning, so exhausted she could hardly move. Liu Yue swept the floor, reciting her litany of complaints: the visitors tossed their cigarette butts on the floor instead of using the ashtrays; after they spat, they rubbed it in with their shoes; she'd make a pot of tea for one visitor, but he would take a sip or two and then more visitors would arrive, requiring her to make another pot and waste the tea leaves; and they left urine on the rim of the toilet.

Zhou Min was visibly thinner, and his face resembled a porcupine after several days without a shave. He could not stop complaining, saying that Bai Yuzhu had asked about the scroll several times already. So Niu Yueqing urged Meng and Zhao to talk Zhuang into going to see Gong Xiaoyi. He finally agreed to go. One night he and Zhao went to see Gong Xiaoyi, who was in, luckily. Though he was Gong's only child, he and his father did not get along; Gong Jingyuan had bought a separate place for Xiaoyi so he could avoid being annoyed by the sight of his son. Xiaoyi was a decent host, offering his visitors cigarettes and tea.

"Why have you come, gentlemen? My house is a mess. Try to find a clean place to sit," Xiaoyi said as he covered the chamber pot under his bed with a newspaper. The house was a pigsty and smelled like piss. Zhuang opened a window before he sat down on the edge of the bed. Xiaoyi sat down on a rattan chair, but was soon sprawled over it; no matter how hard he tried to sit up straight, he ended up curling into the chair, yawning, with teary eyes.

"Have some tea, gentlemen. I have to use the toilet."

He spent a long time in the bathroom, and at one point Zhao and Zhuang detected a pleasant fragrance; even the wilted leaves of a potted plant perked up. They exchanged a silent look. Eventually Xiaoyi emerged from the bathroom, looking like a different person, his eyes sparkling.

"Did you smoke some opium, Xiaoyi?" Zhuang asked. "Why don't you show us? We've never seen what it looks like."

"So you know?" Xiaoyi said. "Well, you gentlemen are not strangers, so I'll show you." He displayed a lump that looked like black dirt, saying that he put a small ball in a cigarette to smoke. He had run out of heroin, the best stuff. He offered the opium to Zhao and Zhuang, who turned him down.

"You're writers, gentlemen, can you contact some government offices for me?"

"What for? Is there something we can do?"

"All the fake stuff out there that harms the consumers. The fake heroin raises blisters and makes users' hair fall out."

"Why don't you write that up and I'll send it to the police?" Zhuang said. "They can launch an investigation."

"You're joking," Xiaoyi said with a laugh.

"I have something to say to you, Xiaoyi, though you've probably heard enough. You can eat and drink anything you want, so why must you smoke opium? Your father has told me he worries about you. People treat you differently. It's an expensive and, most importantly, harmful addiction. You're still young. Don't you want to get married?"

"I'm not upset by what you say. I know you worry about me, but you don't know how wonderful it feels. After I smoke, I can have anything I want and do anything I like. To be honest with you, I hate my father. He's so rich, he can lose two or three thousand a night at a mahjong table, but he hardly gives me anything. I hate Xiaoli, a girl I dated for five years and slept with, because she up and left me. I hate my boss, who spreads rumors about me. For giving me the job, he got ten scrolls from my father, and yet he fired me without a second thought. I know the more I smoke, the harder it is to quit, but I can achieve my dreams and aspirations only after smoking opium. Don't try to stop me. You have your way of life and I have mine. You're probably like my father, who is so well known that the mere mention of your name can cause a tremor, but I'm sure I live a freer life than either of you. But believe me when I say I will never be a social pariah. I don't steal, rob, rape, or kill. I would never harm anyone. I'm my father's son, and he'll have to treat me as a son no matter how unhappy he is with me. His works are worth enough for me to smoke for the rest of my life."

"Of course. That's why Xiaoyi is so lucky," Zhao said. "I know you have some of your father's works with you. I also heard that someone from Hanzhong gave you a long scroll of Mao Zedong's calligraphy. Is that true?"

"You're amazing, Brother Zhao. You know everything about me. Did you mention that to my father?"

"We're brothers, I would never betray you. Liu Yezi and Fatso Wang have long wanted to stop supplying you with opium, because they're afraid your father will sue them if he finds out about them. Wasn't I the one who talked to them?"

"You're a real friend, Brother Zhao. Chairman Mao's calligraphy is excellent. The moment you see it, you will know it was from the hand of someone destined for greatness. I do have the scroll."

"Great. I'm going to be frank with you. I came here today with your Uncle Zhuang to have a look at it. He's a writer who doesn't care about calligraphy, but he's writing an article about Mao Zedong's poetry and calligraphy, so he would like to get his hands on the real thing. When he mentioned that, I said it was no big deal, because Xiaoyi has one. I told him that personal loyalty is so important to Xiaoyi that he'll give it to you. He has no use for it."

"I wouldn't take it without giving something in return," Zhuang said. "Come to my house, Xiaoyi, and take whatever you like."

"Mao's calligraphy is surely much more valuable than one by some governor. On the other hand, it's not a cultural relic, either. But can you sell it even if it is a cultural relic from the revolution? You'd have to turn it over when the government saw it, and you wouldn't get a cent for it," Zhao said.

Xiaoyi just snickered.

"What are you laughing at?" Zhao asked.

"You're not strangers, so I'll tell you the truth. I can let you have anything by my father, but not this scroll. Someone offered five thousand for it, and I wouldn't sell. I also love Chairman Mao. He's no longer alive, but he's still a deity, and anything by a deity can help ward off evil spirits at home."

Zhao looked over at Zhuang, who shook his head, so Zhao said: "Well, if that's the way you feel, we won't press you. But you can't let your Uncle Zhuang leave empty-handed. Why don't you give him some of your father's scrolls?"

Xiaoyi brought out an armload of calligraphy from a cabinet and selected three that had been turned into scrolls. "This is my fund for opium. You have no idea how strictly my father controls things. It wasn't easy to get my hands on these."

"I owe you, Xiaoyi. I'll speak with Liu Yezi and ask her to give you a good price when you buy from her." Zhao wrapped the three scrolls in newspaper, tucked it under his arm, and walked out with Zhuang.

⁂

After the two men left, Xiaoyi took a long wooden case from the cabinet and opened it to look at Mao's calligraphy, before wrapping it back up and locking the case, which he then put at the bottom of the cabinet. *Zhao Jingwu has brought Zhuang Zhidie for this*, he said to himself, *which can only mean that the calligraphy is a true treasure.* He would sell it only if absolutely necessary. Opium prices had been going up steadily, and he would need to sell the scroll when he ran out of money. The thought of opium triggered his craving, so he took out his only packet of heroin and dumped the powder onto aluminum foil. He lit a match to heat the underside of the foil before using a paper tube to suck it all in, followed by an orangeade to keep every tiny whiff of the heroin from escaping from his windpipe. Then he lit a Marlboro and lay down to smoke; he was soon in a different world, where he fantasized the arrival of Xiaoli.

"You're here, Xiaoli. Where have you been? I thought you'd never come to see me again."

"I miss you. I miss you so much. But you didn't come for me," Xiaoli said with a pout before pressing herself up to him; rubbing her breasts against his face and reaching for his crotch, she said she wanted to eat that sausage. Xiaoyi took off his clothes and then hers. She wanted everything done for her, insisting that he undress her. She was wearing a lot. He took off one item after another and then another, until finally a petite figure emerged. They tried different acrobatic positions. He asked her if she had ever been on a boat. She said no, so he dumped a sack of soybeans on the bed, spread them evenly, and placed a board on top. They then got on the board and started in, making the board roll back and forth. But she climbed off the bed and her expression changed; she looked like a savage dog. Xiaoyi blew up.

"So you don't want to make love with me, is that it? Did you come with that guy Zhu something? How is he better than me?"

"Yes, I screwed him the moment you walked out the door. He's better than you. He's a superman, and it was wonderful beyond words."

He picked up a knife and threatened to kill her. She said go ahead, so he killed her with one flick of the knife. She fell, her snowy body still writhing on the floor, while the gush of blood split into two streams like branches and flowed over her nipples. When the blood reached her thighs, it appeared to be blocked and rose up to form a ridge. He pricked the ridge and created a white path for the blood to flow down. Then he plunged the knife into her chest and plucked out her heart. *So, Xiaoli, your heart is as hard as a rock.* She screamed and died. One spot on her dead body was still stirring, impossibly beautiful, and her scream was so exciting that he laughed and laughed over the pleasure it brought.

Back home, Zhuang unrolled the scrolls and saw that they were among Gong Jingyuan's best. Unable to bear the thought of giving them all to Sima Gong, he took two out and handed them to Zhao Jingwu for the future gallery. Zhuang fretted over his visit to Sima, saying he had never asked for anyone's help that way, and he felt debased somehow. Zhao told him he had to go, reminding him of the tale of Han Xin, who had burrowed into a man's crotch when he was down and out. You have to lower your head when you're under someone's eaves. Zhuang preferred to go with Meng Yunfang, who was good at small talk and could help prevent an awkward silence. On the night before his visit, Zhao went to get Meng, but he wasn't home. His wife said he had gone to Bai Yuzhu's house, because of the lawsuit. Bai's mother suffered from back pains, so Meng went with Mr. Song to examine her. When Zhao returned with the information, he and Zhuang went to Bai's house, where they found Meng and Song. Having just massaged the old woman's back, Song was writing a prescription under a lamp and asked Zhuang if his foot had recovered. Zhuang expressed his gratitude, stomping his foot and praising the efficacy of Song's plasters. He told him he hadn't experienced any pain over the past five days. Bai, who had been to the compound five times but had always missed Zhuang, was naturally happy to meet him, boasting that with his involvement, everything would be fine with the lawsuit. After a few words of gratitude, Zhuang took out the scroll by Gong and asked if that would work as a gift to Sima. What would they do if he refused?

"Why wouldn't he accept it?" Meng said. "This isn't something extravagant like a refrigerator or a TV, nor is it cash. It's only natural for a literary person to give calligraphy as a gift. It's actually an act of refinement. You won't lose face by giving it, and he won't be embarrassed to take it. He can even tell everyone who gave it to him. He'd never be accused of accepting a bribe and would in fact be honored. I'll go with you if you're not comfortable going by yourself."

"I came here precisely to ask you to accompany me."

"Why don't you stick around here while I go to his house to check things out. If he has visitors, then of course you don't want to go. If he's alone, then I'll chat him up to gauge his mood. It would be risky to go if he's worried about something. Everything will be easier if he's in a good mood."

"Good idea," Meng said. "We'll wait for you."

When Bai left, Zhuang asked Song if he had gotten his license and if he'd seen Director Wang.

"I've wanted to come see you, but I thought you might know already. I didn't want to bother you."

"What is it?' Zhuang asked.

Song went to the kitchen to wash his hands and motioned to Zhuang to follow him. In the kitchen, Song shut the door and said, "Do you really know nothing about what happened to Wang? Remember the woman who drew up the designs?"

"I do. I haven't seen her for a long time."

"She had a nervous breakdown."

Zhuang was so shocked, he nearly cried out. "How? How could she have a breakdown? Did someone tell you or did you see it yourself?"

"I didn't see her, but I know it's true. You see, I went to Director Wang's office three times, but he was always busy. He told me to come back, and eventually we settled on a date. When I went that day, I had barely opened my mouth when a woman came in. She told Wang she was Ah-lan's sister, and that Ah-lan had suffered a breakdown and said she had shamed herself, so her sister came to ask him what had caused Ah-lan's illness. 'She had a breakdown?' Wang said. 'What about the design?' Ah-lan's sister took out a piece of clothing and laid it on the desk to ask him what it was all about. I took a close look and saw that it was a pair of women's underpants with the crotch clearly cut open with scissors. 'You see, I'm busy today,' he said. 'Why don't you go home and come back in three days.'" Song stuck his head under the faucet, drank some water, and gargled before spitting out the water. "When I went back three days later, Wang wasn't there. His neighbors told me he was in the hospital. I thought I'd buy a gift and go see him, so I asked them what was wrong with him. They laughed. Then they told me the whole story. It turned out that Wang had used the design for the public toilet to keep Ah-lan coming to see him. The girl was too eager for the work to see through his evil scheme. One day she went there, and Wang told her the plan had been settled and they needed to celebrate. He got her drunk and then laid her down on the desk and took off her clothes; he was in such a hurry that he cut open her underpants. He took advantage of her, and she was frantic when she woke up. But he said he'd tell everyone it was consensual if she dared make a scene, because she had gone to his place on her own. Ah-lan had to swallow her anger, but the more she thought about it, the more outraged she got, so she told her sister. Her sister was enraged, cursing the girl's naïveté and her single-minded focus on the design. Ah-lan suffered a nervous breakdown when she thought herself into a dead end. When I ran into her sister that day, she was there to see Wang, who knelt down to beg for her forgiveness. But she had a plan for revenge. She softened her tone and forgave him, even smiling as she said he should have gone to her, a married woman, instead. Why pick Ah-lan, a virgin, who would have trouble finding a husband? Emboldened by the sister's words, Wang also noticed that she was prettier than Ah-lan, so he went up and put his arms around her, without meeting any resistance. He was so thrilled, he told her he'd get a divorce and marry her. Ah-lan's sister went to his house the following day and said to his wife, "I love him and he loves me. We've been together three years, so please make it easy for us." She sat on their bed when she finished, even pouring herself a cup of water. She was incredible. Her demeanor and imposing air so stunned Wang's wife that she was speechless. Then she stood up and said, 'Remember my name, Ah-can. Only Ah-can is qualified to be the mistress of this house.' She strode out after that, leaving Wang's wife to wail. The wife went to the office, where Wang was presiding over a meeting, and stormed in to drag him out by the ear. She yelled at him in the yard, calling him a scoundrel who kept a mistress and even let the mistress humiliate her in her own house. The couple got into a fight in the yard. When Wang went to see Ah-can that night, she smiled at him the whole time, asking him to kiss her. He did, and she bit off part of his tongue. Finally realizing that she had been planning revenge all along, he covered his mouth and ran off.

"Mr. Zhuang, what's wrong? Is it your heart?" As he went on, Song looked up and saw that Zhuang's face was drained of color. With his eyes shut, he was leaning against the wall; he slid to the floor. Panicking, Song called out to Zhao and Meng, who were startled by what they saw. They laid Zhuang down on the floor and massaged his chest until he opened his eyes. "I'm okay," he said as he sat up. Zhao brought him some water, while Meng said, "What were you talking about, Dr. Song? He was fine a moment ago. What happened?"

"I was sharing some gossip and never expected this to happen."

Everyone breathed a sigh of relief when they saw color returning to Zhuang's face after he had some water. Saying he might suffer from heart problems, they urged him to get a checkup at the hospital.

Bai returned a while later to say that the leader of their compound was at Sima's house, and they should wait until the man left.

"Well, they might not be done chatting for a while, and it's getting late. Old Bai, why don't we come back to see Mr. Sima another day?" Zhuang said.

Zhao told Bai about Zhuang's possible heart problem, so after thinking it over, Bai said, "That's fine, too. Your problem must have been caused by worry. Take it easy. Didn't I tell you I'd take care of it? If I can't even help you with this, then I'd have been a judge in vain all these years." He walked them out and gave Zhuang a hug when they were saying good-bye, telling them to call him before they came next time. He'd have a camera ready to take a photo with everyone as a cherished memento.

When they returned to Zhuang's house, Zhao mentioned Zhuang's episode to Niu Yueqing. She and Liu Yue were so frightened they were soon crying. Saying that Zhuang had never had any heart trouble, Niu Yueqing got some sugar water for him while Liu made ginger tea. They asked him what he would like to eat, but he said he just wanted to sleep, and went to bed. After the visitors left, Niu Yueqing quietly got undressed and lay down next to her husband. Zhuang woke up, so she asked him how he felt. He said he was fine.

"I won't worry as long as you say you're fine." She curled up in his arms and said, "Your heart is as hard as stone. You would probably continue to ignore me if it weren't for this urgent matter. See how much weight you've lost. The trouble you had earlier has probably been caused by worries. Men need to be broad-minded and not let things bother them. No matter how serious something is, it will blow over. What do you say?" Zhuang put his arm around her. When she pressed her body tightly against him, she detected something hard, so she groped around and found the coin.

"Where did this come from? Is it such a treasure that you have to wear it?"

Zhuang hemmed and hawed before saying, "Isn't it nice enough to wear?"

"A man shouldn't wear something like this. It must have been a gift. I've been leaving you alone these days, and some shameless slut must have gotten you hooked on her."

"Don't frighten yourself with scary stories again," Zhuang said. "Ruan Zhifei called me to come by the other day and said that a qigong master sent his qi on the coin to help ward off evil spirits and maintain good health. Ruan gave it to me."

"Nine out of every ten things Raun Zhifei says are lies. He had to make up a fantastic story just to give you this. So why did you suffer heart trouble even with it around your neck?"

Wanting to change the subject, Zhuang told her about Ah-lan and Ah-can, which naturally had Niu Yueqing cursing the director. But she also criticized the way Ah-can had handled the matter. She was, after all, a woman, and should never hug or kiss a man, even for vengeance.

"You don't understand," Zhuang said.

Niu Yueqing grumbled to herself that he had fallen ill because of the two sisters. He wouldn't have been like that over passing acquaintances, even if he felt sorry for them. "I don't understand. But you do, I see. So tell me how you understand her."

Zhuang snored softly, pretending to be asleep.

❋

For three days, Xijing was under the assault of torrential rain that was as white as dense strands of hemp hurled down from the sky. It was dark even at noon. Water nearly covered people's feet in housing compounds and residential buildings, flowing over doorsills and into houses when it didn't drain fast enough, while the water taps stopped running. People learned that a section of the road outside the west gate had collapsed and broken a water pipe. When Liu Yue took a bucket out to catch rainwater on the balcony, she'd barely left it out before it was filled, but half the water had sloshed over the sides by the time she brought it inside. It was like catching the contents of a cascading waterfall. With too much to do, but unable to leave the house, Zhuang discovered that he had seven boils on his back, though they didn't hurt. Niu Yueqing was worried, but he said that they might have been caused by the humidity. He applied some menthol ointment. She worried about her mother and the house at Shuangren fu. The phone wasn't working when she tried to call, so she decided to go over with Liu Yue, but the girl wouldn't let her go out in the rain and offered to head over there herself. The loudspeaker at the gatehouse, which had been silent for days, suddenly came back to life with "Testing, testing—."

"A visitor on such a rainy day?" Niu Yueqing said, and, before she finished, Old Mrs. Wei's voice sounded in the yard, "Zhuang Zhidie, you have a visitor. Come see your guest."

The color drained from Niu Yueqing's face. He asked her what was wrong. She responded, "My heart races every time something unexpected occurs."

"I'm going downstairs anyway," Liu Yue said as she put on her rain slicker and rain boots, "so I'll go take a look. I'll send whoever it is away if it's not important and let him in if it is." She ran downstairs. Someone was standing in the rain, drenched from head to toe. It turned out to be the junkman. Ignoring him, Liu Yue said to old Mrs. Wei, "Who's looking for Zhuang Laoshi?"

She pointed to the old man.

That was strange.

"Are you looking for Zhuang Laoshi?" she asked him.

"I want to see Zhuang Zhidie, not Zhuang Laoshi. I don't have a laoshi."

Liu Yue laughed and asked, "What do you want? You can tell me."

"You once gave me two steamed buns," he said after taking a look at her.

"Good memory. But you don't have to thank me."

"I'm not going to thank you. I want to complain. The stuff stayed in my stomach and made me so bloated I couldn't sleep that night."

"So you've come in the rain to complain about me?" She walked off.

"You can leave if you want, but your laoshi will still have boils on his back."

Stunned, Liu Yue halted, wondering how he could have known about the sores. "What did you say?"

"Old Mrs. Niu at Shuangren fu asked me to deliver a message on my way. She said her old man came home several times but didn't enjoy a single good meal. Neither his son-in-law nor his daughter came, so he lashed the son-in-law's back with a whip."

"She doesn't have an old man. He's been dead for ages. The old lady is getting muddle-headed again. I'm actually going over there. Where are you headed, Grandpa?"

"Where am I going? The streets are deserted on a rainy day. So I'd be the governor if I went to the Provincial Office, and the mayor if I went to the Municipal Building. I'd be the police if I stood on the traffic platform, and a rich man if I walked into a restaurant. You're going to Shuangren fu? Well, get on my cart. I'll be the driver, and when we get there I'll be your master."

"You really can talk," Liu Yue said. "See, I'm getting on your cart, all right? But I feel terrible being taken places by someone your age."

"Then I'll get on and you pull the cart. I'll be an official in a sedan."

"I can't pull the cart," she said, while he took off running slowly down the street with the cart.

"Are you getting dizzy?" he asked.

"No."

"Then you were born to be taken around, as an official's wife if not an official."

She was so amused she laughed. But rain poured into her mouth the moment she opened it, so she tightened the slicker around her. When she noticed that the weedy hair on the old man's head was plastered in clumps, while his gaunt, bony back was visible under his soaked shirt, Liu Yue felt bad and offered her rain slicker to him.

"You were born unlucky, then."

"Why is that?"

"If not, why did you offer me your rain slicker? I've been running around Xijing for years, and everyone treats me like a madman except those who sleep under the city gate at night."

Liu Yue fell silent as a myriad of emotions welled up inside.

The flooding was worse on the streets, which were like rivers. Manhole covers had been removed to help the water drain, but it was actually gushing out from some of the openings, and was nearly knee high. Taking a detour, the old man drew her attention to the scenes along the way—that wall has collapsed; that utility pole fell and broke the line because the ground beneath it has turned soggy. She saw cars stuck in potholes, and a truck and a van stalled on the street after a collision. It looked like the truck had been trying to pass but had rammed into the van. The junkman laughed and she asked, "What you laughing about?"

"What do you think the truck was trying to do?" he asked her. "Everything in the world is sentient. The truck was attracted to the van, so it went over for a kiss and got into trouble. Many good things can only be watched, not touched. Like grabbing a piece of burning coal—you'll burn your hand."

She took another look, and it did look like what he said, which made her laugh. But that dismayed her. The old man pulled the cart along like an ill-behaved monkey, picking up a broken plastic basin here and a shoe there. Tossing the shoe onto the cart, he said it looked new, so it must have flowed out from under someone's door. Too bad there was only one. Why couldn't a color TV or a bundle of RMB have flowed out instead? She laughed again. The old man said he wasn't crazy, but he wasn't far off. Suddenly he shouted, "Junkman! Collecting junk and scraps!"

"I'm on your cart, so does that make me junk?"

"My throat hurts if I don't shout."

"Why don't you recite one of your poems for me if you don't want your throat to hurt?"

He turned to look at her for the first time since she'd gotten on. A smile creased his wrinkled face, giving him an innocent look in the pouring rain. "You like those, too?"

"Yes, I do," she said. He took off running; the iron wheels rolled more easily in the water than on dry land, splashing water to the sides as they tore down the street, while his voice sounded in her ears.

Central government leaders travel in flight.
Provincial and municipal leader from limos alight.
County and township leaders ride in Jeeps so bright.
Peasants ride "East Is Red" tractors on the right.
The citizens ring their bicycle bells at night.

He turned his head. "What's your name, young lady?"

"Liu Yue."

And Liu sits at water dragon height.

"I don't want you playing with my name," she complained. "I don't like it." But he ignored her and repeated the lyrics. When the pedestrians standing under eaves to stay out of the rain heard him, they quickly picked up the lyrics. Liu Yue could hear people they had passed singing at the top of their lungs, a pack of howling wolves, each ending the line with "And Liu sits at water dragon height."

An unhappy Liu Yue jumped off the cart and fell into a puddle. But the junkman, oblivious to what had happened, continued to race down the street.

⁂

When Liu Yue got to the house on Shuangren fu Avenue, it was a chaotic scene. The street and its lanes were teeming with clamoring people, young and old, all ducking under eaves with bundles of various sizes and small electrical appliances wrapped in plastic clothes, rain slickers, and plastic wraps. Police were shouting at residents; some were taken away, while others put up a vigorous resistance. A group of people rushed into the old woman's yard, demanding that someone place an emergency phone call. Liu Yue's first thought was that something had happened to the old woman, so she stormed inside to find the house filled with people. The old woman was sitting with her feet up on the rattan chair by the door. Liu Yue ran over and put her arms around her. "Are you all right, Granny?"

"I'm fine. Your grandpa stayed with me all day yesterday and came back today. None of you were here, so he was angry and said he'd whipped his son-in-law. He might have beaten him too harshly. I'm worried he's hurt your Zhuang Laoshi badly."

"Nothing like that has happened. He just has a few sores on his back."

"What are they if they aren't lash marks? When I was young, there was a carter at the Water Board called Liu Dayu, who spent his salary in brothels and gambling dens instead of on his parents or in finding a wife. One summer when there was thunder and lightning, his back was black and blue, punished by thunder. Your Zhuang Laoshi refused to come over after the whipping. Is he waiting to be punished by thunder?"

"He's busy, so I came instead."

"Your grandfather said his son-in-law wouldn't come, and he was right about that. So he took it out on me, asking me to fry cakes with peppercorn leaves. It's pouring out there, but the old man forced me to pick peppercorn leaves in the yard, and the wall toppled. Don't you think that's strange? The wall fell on their side and killed Shunzi's hunchbacked mother. You know what Grandpa said? He said he knew why the wall fell on that side; he saw a ghost pushing it, and he smiled at her when she looked up, so she pushed it over onto her. The old man is such a scoundrel." The old lady fumed. Someone in the house who caught a few of the words she said asked, "So it wasn't the rain that caused the wall to collapse? Who pushed it over?"

"She says it was a ghost," Liu Yue cut in. "Granny can't tell the difference between the human world and the underworld, so don't believe her. If you do, you can ask her about Grandpa, who's been dead for decades. Ask her where he is now."

The old lady frowned, grumbling about how Liu Yue was a counterrevolutionary who was always contradicting her. "I asked your grandpa if he's still being a playboy over there, and he got mad at me. We had a fight. He didn't leave until these people came in to use our phone, saying the smell of strangers gave him a headache." The people around them laughed, now aware that the old woman was weak in the head. Finally someone was able to get through on the phone and shouted at the others, "The mayor is coming with some people to help us. He's also going to bring a crew of TV reporters, newspaper journalists, even the writer Zhuang Zhidie." They cheered at the good news and ran out the door.

"With such heavy rain, why does the mayor have to bring him along?" the old woman said. "And to do what? Pump the water out? Grandpa couldn't get him to come even after lashing him, but he'll race over when he's summoned by the mayor. The mayor is an official and so is your grandpa. He's a chief working for the City God."

"I think the mayor wanted him to come so he could write something about this."

"Well, then you go out and take a look. When he comes, make sure to bring him back to burn some spirit money for Grandpa."

Without a word, Liu Yue changed into dry clothes and went out with an umbrella to see what was going on outside.

The wall had indeed collapsed. A large latrine pit on the other side of the wall belonged to Shunzi's family. Bricks and rocks had fallen into the pit, causing the human waste to overflow. Next to the pit was a pile of loose bricks. Liu Yue had known that the area was low and that the Zhuang family house had been built on a raised foundation, but she was surprised to have a full view of the lowland houses by simply looking over the wall. The structures on that side followed no rules, with houses built according to the lay of the land; but every house had a tall earthen doorsill to prevent flooding. The crisscrossing lanes slanted in one direction, so water eventually flowed to the center of the lowland and formed a large pond. With three days of rain, a pump to divert the water from the pond to the underground storm drain could not drain it quickly enough; water had surged into nearly half the houses. She jumped through a crack in the wall and saw that Shunzi's mother had yet to be put in a coffin and taken to the crematorium. She was covered by a white sheet and laid out in the house. It was dry inside, but water was about to reach the steps in the yard. Shunzi's wife and their fat little boy, both wearing white cloths around their heads, were burning spirit money under the table set up for the body. They had stopped crying, with so many disaster relief helpers around. Shunzi was building a mud levee at the entrance of the yard with one hand and scooping out water with the other.

"It was raining," he said to some friends who had come to check on them, "so I didn't go out to set up my cigarette stand. I went to bed, and the more I slept, the sleepier I got, like the fatigue I've accumulated over the summer finally caught up with me. Then a crash startled me awake. I said to myself, 'What's fallen this time?' I came out and saw that the wall by the latrine had collapsed. People all around had walls crumple or eaves give in, so it was no big deal. I'd take care of it when it cleared up, I thought, and I went back to bed. But then I couldn't sleep, wondering where my mother was. She slept in that small room across the way. She had a hunchback, but her hearing was sharp, and she always came out to look around when she heard a noise. She'd call out to me or my son, saying that something had happened to so-and-so's house and telling us to go check it out. But why hadn't she made a sound after the crash of the wall? I told my son to see if she was in her room. He came back to say she wasn't there. I thought she might have gone out to look at the flooded lanes, so I went back to bed. Then I had to pee, so I got up and walked over to the latrine, where I saw my mother's tiny shoes floating in the pit. I panicked and immediately got down to remove the bricks, and I saw one of her hands. She was buried alive when the wall fell on her as she was using the latrine. That damned mayor. He spent money and time building cultural streets and art streets, but he wouldn't spend anything on houses for us. Let the rain come to destroy all the houses around here. He should be here when everyone is dying under crumpling walls, shouldn't he?"

"Don't talk like that," someone said. "Don't you watch the news? The mayor has been running around the past few days helping people in the disaster areas. I heard that three hundred houses collapsed in the lowlands north of the west gate and that twelve people died. Someone has called the mayor. He'll be here soon. So no more talk like that. He's serious about helping, and will surely send relief supplies and money. He's only human, and he'd be so unhappy to hear what you just said, he might give us only half a million of the million we deserve."

Shunzi nodded as he carried over two figurines a neighbor had bought for him. He tearfully went inside to place them on the table, where he knelt and wailed like an old cow.

Unable to stand the sight of people crying, Liu Yue walked off, tramping through muddy water. Stumbling along an uneven road surface, she traced the sounds of vehicles and human noises from a distance, her mud-splattered pants legs getting soggy. Then she saw someone shooting street scenes with a video camera. There were many clusters of people, some carrying pumps and other shouldering tarps, all rushing in the same direction. She spotted Zhuang Zhidie and walked over to tug at his shirt. "You're here, Zhuang Laoshi."

"The mayor asked me to take a look. I couldn't say no. Is the old lady all right?"

"She's fine. She wants you to burn some spirit money for Grandpa, saying he came back today."

"How can I get away to do that? After I'm done here, I'll probably have to go to the lowland area north of the west gate."

She turned and walked away, but came right back and whispered, "Which one is the mayor?"

He pointed to a tall man who had joined a group of residents at the entrance to the lane. "It's a tough job," she said.

"Of course it is."

"I've seen a thief being beaten, but not how a thief eats." That drew a glare from Zhuang, who walked off to join the group of people.

The rain stopped that evening, but Zhuang did not go home. The special topic on that night's TV broadcast was a disaster relief report from the mayor to the residents. He said the city was simply too old, and that municipal construction projects had incurred a substantial amount of debt. After rebuilding four lowland areas, the government would work hard to secure funding to rebuild the lowland areas north of the west gate and around Shuangren fu Avenue.

Zhuang was put up at a hotel, where he worked all night with reporters sent by the Propaganda Department to write about the disaster relief effort. Focusing on observations of the disaster and plans for rebuilding the lowland areas, they produced a report of more than ten thousand words that was published in the municipal paper two days later. When it was time to check out of the hotel, Huang Defu came on behalf of the mayor and hosted a banquet to reward their effort. It was a sumptuous meal, but they were too tired to have much an appetite, so half the food went untouched.

"Do you have a cat at home, Mr. Zhuang?" Huang said. "Why don't you take the fish home? Then we won't be wasting food."

That reminded Zhuang of Wang Ximian's wife, so he put the fish in a plastic bag and, after leaving the hotel, headed for Juhuayuan Street.

Wang's house was a two-story structure he'd remodeled in a traditional compound. In front of the house stood a large willow tree that provided shade for half the yard. Ivy with sturdy vines and dense leaves was planted all around, giving the house the look of a lush green haystack. Zhuang rang the bell, but no one came to the gate, so he pushed it open. He walked in, but still no one came out, not the maid nor Wang's mother. The stone steps were covered in moss, and a leaf had fallen with its stem stuck in the moss, quivering in the breeze. To him, the rain had turned the yard gloomy and chilly, instead of imbuing it with serenity. As he wondered where everyone was, a cat came out; it stopped and sat down three steps away to watch him with its bright eyes. Then it swished its tail and walked back inside. Zhuang knew that it was the pet belonging to Wang's wife, so he followed it inside. Instead of pausing in the hallway, the cat started up a spiral staircase, turning toward him halfway up. He took the staircase to the second floor, where he looked into the room facing the stairs and saw Wang's wife leaning weakly against the head of her bed. She smiled at him. Putting down the bag, he walked in and asked, "Are you not feeling well?"

"I'm not well enough to go downstairs, but I knew it was you when I heard your footsteps in the yard. Where were you? How did you know I was ill?"

"I didn't. What's wrong? Have you seen a doctor?"

"My back hurt two days ago when I got up in the morning. The maid said I had boils on my back. I ignored them. But they hurt badly last night, and my back has gone stiff. So she took me to the hospital this morning. The doctor said there was pus, so he opened them up, cleaned them out, and applied some ointment. They no longer hurt, but I'm drained of energy."

"Let me see what they look like."

"No need for that. My once-smooth back is now an ugly sight," she said, shifting to make room for him to sit on the bed.

"Is Ximian away again? Where are the maid and the old lady? Have you eaten?"

"He's still in Guangzhou. The old lady and the maid might have gone to the post office to send him a telegram. Help yourself to some water."

Saying he wasn't thirsty, Zhuang added, "That's strange. I've got boils on my back, too, but they don't itch or hurt. Yours seem to be much worse."

She was visibly surprised by what he said. "Is that right? What a coincidence. You're not saying it as a joke to make me feel better, are you?"

He unbuttoned his shirt to show her. Yes, seven boils lined up like the Big Dipper. She froze at the sight, seemingly lost in thought. When he turned around to button his shirt, she said, "I see you're still wearing the coin."

"Yes."

She lowered her eyes as tears fell, a stirring sight that rendered him incapable of saying or doing anything. Then he spotted her tiny foot under a thin embroidered blanket, resting limply sideways. After reaching out to cover her foot with a corner of the blanket, he let his trembling hand stay on it. She dried her tears and smiled sadly. "What did you bring me?"

He removed his hand and said, "I just checked out of a hotel. Here is some leftover fish for your cat."

"You're wonderful. You remembered my cat. He hasn't had any fish for two days. Leftovers are fine. Can you give it to him now?"

Zhuang opened the bag, but he couldn't find a plate for the fish; then he recalled the newspaper in his pocket, so he took it out and spread it on the floor. The cat meowed with delight when he put out the fish.

He chatted with her for a while, but the old lady and the maid were still not home. When he got up to leave, she couldn't walk him out, so she held the cat in her arms and said, "You must remember him." The cat meowed, as if it understood what she'd said. "Walk him out for me, would you?" she said. The cat jumped out of her arms and walked toward the stairs. Zhuang picked it up and said, "No need to walk me out. Stay here and keep your mistress company." With his eyes on her, he gave the cat a loud kiss on the head.

He was exhausted when he got home. Niu Yueqing gave him a royal welcome and told him to take a nap, while she read the report in the paper. She came in while he was in bed. "Bai Yuzhu called for the second time a while ago, saying we can't put it off any longer. You must go see Sima Gong by tonight at the latest. So get a good nap and go over later this evening."

Zhuang lay in bed, but he couldn't sleep; he kept thinking about Wang's wife and her desolate life. He felt sorry for her. Nothing had happened between the two of them, and yet he felt an emotional attachment to her;

they even had boils at about the same time and in nearly the same spot. What kind of karmic connection was it? Feeling keyed up by the thought, he dressed and got out of bed. He asked his wife what she thought about the report and told Liu Yue to boil some water so he could invite Meng Yunfang and Zhao Jingwu over for tea. Then he took out a box. "Take a look at this. Do you know what kind of tea it is? It's Maojian from Junshan, a gift from the mayor." He made a cup for himself first and let Niu Yueqing take a look. Half the leaves floated to the top, each the thin, slender, pointed tip of a curled leaf, standing straight as a miniature forest. When the leaves sank to the bottom, layers of light green mist rose up, permeating the room with a subtle and pleasing aroma.

"I've never seen tea this fine," Niu Yueqing said.

"Call Meng Yunfang, Zhao Jingwu, and Zhou Min and his wife so we can all have a taste."

"I read once about Huo Qubing, who was at a battlefield near the Hexi Corridor when the emperor rewarded him with a vat of liquor," Liu Yue said. "He poured the liquor into a spring so every man in his army could have a drink. The spot was later named Qiuquan, 'Liquor Spring.' Now the mayor has given you this packet of tea, and you invite friends to share it. You might as well put the leaves in the water tower so the whole city can appreciate a special favor from the mayor."

"Are you mocking me for overreacting to the special favor? Don't be jealous. The mayor gave me the package, not you."

"Don't underestimate me," Liu Yue said.

"It's all right if you want your friends to share the tea," Niu Yueqing said, "but there's no need to get Tang Wan'er involved. She's a woman and can't tell the difference. Like me. I enjoy the smell of fine leaves, but they all taste puckery and bitter to me."

"You're typical of the Guanzhong people, who drink tea only when you're thirsty. Or it could be that the water in Guanzhong is strong in alkaline and tea leaves are added to mask it. The water in the south is good, which is why people there are particular about their tea. Tang Wan'er is from Tongguan, but her family was originally from southern Shaanxi, so she knows how to appreciate tea. The last time I visited Ah-can at her house, she offered me tea from the Yangxian Tea Farm in Jiangsu. It was fine tea, and I swallowed it, leaves and all. I even grabbed a handful to chew without water. The fragrance lingered for days."

"Eating the leaves in the tea?" Liu Yue said. "You sound like a farm boy."

"You're from northern Shaanxi and even less qualified in tea appreciation. You may be well read, but do you know why they always say 'eat tea' in ancient books? That's because ancient Chinese ground up the tea and added water to make a tea paste to eat. Or they sprinkled the powder on their rice. But you gulp it down like a cow drinking water."

"Well, we're cows, and only high-class people like you eat tea. But I'm wondering why a tea connoisseur like Ah-can would do what she did," Liu Yue said.

"You know Ah-can? What has she done?" Zhuang asked.

"She came here yesterday afternoon. I'm worried what people in the compound would think of us if they knew it was her."

"She was here yesterday? What did she say?" Zhuang asked.

"Liu Yue doesn't know when to shut up," Niu Yueqing said, "just like Meng Yunfang, saying things without thinking. Ah-can *was* here. You've been telling me how pretty she was, but she had dark circles under her eyes! She said her sister had gone crazy; the hospital said she was incurable and recommended sending her to a psychiatric hospital. She asked you to go see her sister before the girl was sent to the hospital today."

"What else did she say?"

"What else could she say? She told me what happened between her and Director Wang," Niu Yueqing continued. "Would you believe that she had a chunk of the man's tongue wrapped in paper? It was shriveled up and smelled bad. She said she'd gotten a divorce—"

"Divorced?" Zhuang yelled out. "What was she thinking? And why didn't you go see her sister? What did you say to make her feel better? Why didn't you ask her to stay awhile?"

"I got rid of her."

"What do you mean, you got rid of her?"

"Now everyone knows there's a woman in Xijing who bit off a man's tongue. Director Wang is a sex fiend, but if his tongue was bitten off, that can only mean that they kissed. Who knows what else they did? I've heard a different story. The sisters were fighting over Director Wang. The younger one lost and went crazy. Her older sister was sleeping with Wang and blackmailed him, asking for money. He wouldn't give in, so she bit off his tongue. She's the kind of woman who disgusted her own husband so much that he divorced her. She wants you to visit her sister, and you're actually thinking of going? We have guests here all the time. It would ruin our reputation if you let her stick around. What if some gossip ran into her here and spread rumors about us?"

His face a steely gray and his chest heaving, Zhuang said, "That's enough. You're famous for your compassion, and this time you did just great. You got rid of her. Did you shoo her out with a broom? Why didn't you use a cleaver? She's a loose woman, so how can you show people you're honorable if you don't just kill her?"

Niu Yueqing was stung by Zhuang's unjust insinuation. "You're mad at me because I got rid of her? I'm not honorable? What have I done to disgrace you? You know who I did it for? You think I'm a mean woman, don't you? All these years, when beggars have come to our door, have I ever not given them something to eat or drink? When we don't have anything in the house, I go out and buy food for them. But I can't tolerate unsavory women, and I will not allow someone like that to soil our floor."

With a sarcastic laugh, Zhuang got up and went into the study to pick up the scroll with Gong Jingyuan's calligraphy. When he came out, he made a point of coughing and spitting on the floor. "Now it's soiled. Everything is dirty, everything but you. You're clean and you can stay clean forever." He opened the door and walked out without bothering to close it behind him.

"See that, Liu Yue?" Niu Yueqing said. "I mean nothing to him. The more I try to please him, the unhappier he is with me. Why is that? Can you tell me? He's always so considerate of others, afraid to hurt this one or upset that one, but he has absolutely no regard for my feelings. Tell me, why is it so hard to be the wife of a famous man?" She broke down.

Zhuang tore down the street on his scooter. Muddy puddles remained in the lanes and in front of shops, while the street centers had dried out from traffic, leaving a film of dust. He could not imagine how Ah-can had been able to find his house when the area was flooded. She had obviously had her mind set on finding him and asking him to go visit her poor sister. He wondered how she had related her sad story to Niu Yueqing, who ended up sending her away. She must have been heartbroken as she walked down the stairs. Did she cry as she told her sister about the visit after she got home? The more he thought about it, the more jumbled his mind became. He felt a deep loathing rising up for his wife, for the vile Wang, for the mayor, the head of propaganda, and Huang Defu, who had kept him back to write the report. He rode his scooter all the way to Shangxian Road before it dawned on him that Ah-can wouldn't be living in those squat, narrow houses now that she was divorced. She was going to admit her sister into a psychiatric hospital, so she might be there. He turned and headed toward the hospital. As he was negotiating the weedy, muddy path leading to the mental ward in the outskirts, he saw a figure walking toward him, head down, but he didn't pay her much attention until his scooter splashed her and he turned his head to apologize. It was Ah-can. He called out to her and came to a screeching halt. She looked up and stared at him blankly before bursting into tears and running into his arms, smearing his clothes with mud and tears.

"I wasn't home, Ah-can. I really wasn't home. I just learned that you went to see me," he said as he dried her tears. She stopped crying, took a step back, and took out a compact mirror to compose herself. "Did you hear what happened to me?"

"I did." She teared up again. He turned his scooter around for her to climb on, saying he wanted to see Ah-lan. She told him there was no need, for that was no place for a normal person to spend much time in. After being there for only a short while, she said, she thought she'd lose her mind as well. Besides, Ah-lan had just been admitted, so the doctors probably would not let her out again so soon. He looked up wordlessly at the sky, filled with an indescribable sadness. Turning the scooter around again, he said, "Let's find someplace where we can talk."

"You don't think I'm unworthy?"

"I wouldn't have come if I felt that way."

She got on the back of his scooter, and when he started the engine, she said: "I would have gone to your house again today if you hadn't come. I wanted to see you one more time, even if your wife cursed or struck me. Where are you taking me? Someplace where there's no one else but us, I hope. I want to be with you. I want to tell you something."

Now it was his turn to weep. His tears dried quickly in the gusty wind coming at him, but his face was quickly wet again from new ones. He did not turn his head or wipe them off, as they seemed to have created gullies on his face, deep indentations like those made by a rope on the edge of a well.

When they reached the House of Imperfection Seekers, he asked for a detailed account of what had happened, adding his objection to her vengeance on Wang after Ah-lan had her breakdown. She said she hadn't planned it that way. She had gone to the District Office to see someone in charge of community affairs, but was told that they couldn't care less about such matters at a time like this, not to mention the fact that there were no witnesses. What conclusion could they draw based on hearsay? They even told her that Director Wang had a fine record in community affairs, with fine performance ratings in developing both collective and private enterprises. It was precisely because he was an effective leader that he worked tirelessly to build public toilets for the district. These days the people in leadership positions were often accused of malfeasance and corruption, either taking bribes or engaging in illicit affairs. They had launched a few investigations, but in the end no one had been punished. With the advent of reform and opening up, the sense of morality and the old system of values had begun to change; what had been once been considered out of bounds was now viewed as acceptable or was ignored, which led to many cases of false accusations. The lesson the leadership had learned was to discipline those who were at fault and defend those who must be protected. She was even told that they would try to understand what had happened between Wang and her sister, but they should also check to see if she was Wang's mistress. Having a mistress was in fashion, and Ah-lan was old enough to have known better. Besides, it had occurred in Wang's office, not in Ah-lan's room. Ah-can said that her heart sank when she heard that, and she decided to take matters into her own hands, realizing that filing a complaint was useless. She wanted revenge. But what could she do with a vile person like that? She had only the pitiful methods available to a woman.

Reminded of his lawsuit and the related troubles, he put himself in her shoes and sighed over her situation. But he was still unhappy that she hadn't come to see him earlier. "Since it's come to this, we need to think about what to do next. Wang's reputation may suffer, but he could be transferred to a community affairs office in another district if he can't stay here. I hear he's been spreading rumors to slander you and Ah-lan, so you should file a complaint against wrongful accusations. Here is a piece of calligraphy by Gong Jingyuan. Give it to whoever's in charge. I'll go see the mayor, who may listen to me."

"Let's let it go," Ah-can said. "I don't have any more fight in me. As an ordinary woman, I failed to protect my own sister, though I tried. Now I've gained the reputation of a loose woman. My confidence is gone, particularly after the humiliation I suffered at your wife's hand in your house. I'm tired, simply exhausted. What else can I do? Would managing to remove that bastard from office and sending him to jail make up for what Ah-lan and I suffered? At least I've vented my anger. I was the one who asked for the divorce. Mu Jiaren isn't a smart man, but he's a decent one. The passion was long gone from our marriage, but I didn't want what happened to have any negative effects on his life. I'm telling people he wanted a divorce so he can maintain his dignity as a man. I never dreamed I'd see you again, but you came looking for me, and with heaven's blessing we ran into each other on the road. I'm so grateful to you. I have only one request, and please don't laugh at me. If you're willing, I'd like to get naked and sleep with you, with a clear conscience. Could you give me a baby?"

They both had moist eyes as they held each other tight. They swallowed each other's saliva and tears when they kissed and made throaty sounds. Ah-can struggled out of his arms.

"Let's not cry anymore," she said with a laugh. "No more tears so we can be happy together. Wait for me here. I want to be pretty for you one more time." She went into the bathroom, took a shower, brushed her teeth, and combed her hair. Then she sat in front of the mirror, took her eyebrow pencil from her handbag to paint her brows, and powdered and rouged her face. He wanted to come in to look at her, but she locked the door. After what seemed like a long time, she walked out naked, a brilliant glow on her impossibly beautiful face. He came up and held her.

"Let me dance for you," she said. "I won third prize in an amateur contest at my workplace." She spread her arms and began a graceful dance, doing all she could to show off her fair, tender body, before flitting toward him. □□ □□ □□ [The author has deleted 995 words]. For a very long time, a different kind of human passion burned inside them. They forgot all their pain and worries as they recalled the language employed in all the classical texts and even uttered the words themselves. Abandoning themselves to wild movements, they felt as though they had been blown high into the sky and exploded into pieces above the clouds. Or as though it were sunrise on the summit of Mount Hua, and they had leapt over the cliff as the light of Buddha shot through the boundless nebula in the canyon below. They tried every move and position, including those by foreigners on videotapes, those by the ancients portrayed in the sex manual *Sunü Classic*, even those by wild beasts and domestic animals, and then they created their own. They reached orgasm at about the same time, and amid the screams, Ah-can said: "Do it. Come inside me. I want a baby. I want your baby."

It came like roaring water from the Yellow River, erupting like an enormous geyser. Then they lay as if dead, like beached fish, quietly, as if hundreds of years had passed, while the rays of the setting sun slanted in through the window to glide slowly over their bodies. They smiled at each other.

"What do you think the baby will look like?"

"Pretty. Like you."

"I want him to be like you."

They were in each other's arms again. □□ □□ □□ [The author has deleted 221 words.]

"How sweet it smells," he said with a smile.

She reached out to pick a strand of hair from his lip before applying lipstick to her own lips to kiss his body, repeating the process until it was covered in red circles, as if bedecked with medals or red suns.

It was late at night when they parted.

"I want to thank you one last time," she said.

"One last time?"

"Yes. I won't come to see you again, and don't you worry about me. Promise me you'll forget me. I don't want anyone to be aware that you know me, so I won't taint you."

"I can't do that. I will look you up no matter what your situation is. I want to see you."

"Look out the window," she said with a smile. "It's so dark out."

He turned to look. It was pitch-black, only a single star in the distant sky. "That star must be above Mount Zhongnan." He looked back at her and saw a bloody gouge on her cheek. The hair clip in her hand was smeared with blood. Stunned, he moved closer to check the wound, but she picked up a bottle of ink and poured some into her palm to cover half of her face. There was a smile on the exposed half. "This may leave a scar when it heals. If not, the ink will spread and stay there forever. I've been pretty and now I want to be ugly. Don't come to see me again. I will ignore you if you do." He slumped to the floor, watching as she opened the door. She was nearly out the door when he reached out. She stopped him.

"Don't get up. Just watch me go like this. You must forgive me for no longer being able to forward letters for Mr. Zhong. I'll write to my older sister, and you can send them to her. I'm leaving with your baby now. It's yours, and you'll be able to see him one day. What are you crying about? Don't you want to see me leave happily?" She turned and walked down the stairs, each step accompanied by the echo of her shoes. In all, he heard seventy-eight of them.

⁂

He returned home at eleven that night, in a daze. Niu Yueqing wasn't home, and an unhappy Liu Yue was quick to complain. He had agreed to see Sima Gong that night, so Meng Yunfang and Zhao Jingwu had come and waited for him. In the end, Niu Yueqing had to go with them on his behalf. As they were leaving, they realized that the calligraphy by Gong Jingyuan was gone and recalled that Zhuang had gone out around noon with a roll of something. In the end, Zhao had to go over to the gallery and retrieve another scroll.

"Where have you been?" his wife asked.

"I found Ah-can."

"Is Ah-can more important than the lawsuit?" She was indignant.

"Of course," he said coldly and went into the bedroom. But he quickly returned with a blanket before lying down on the sofa in his study.

⁂

In the meantime, Meng Yunfan, Zhao Jingwu, and Niu Yueqing went to see Sima Gong. He was courteous to them, offering them tea and cigarettes before expressing his views on Gong's calligraphy. But then he said, "Bai told me about Jing Xueyin's lawsuit. I read the complaint, and Jing and her husband have come to see me. She's not merely a stylish woman, but a highly competent one. I could tell she still has strong feelings for Zhuang Zhidie. I get the sense that she could not explain herself clearly to her husband, and being that she's the daughter of a high ranking cadre, everything had been going her way with no setbacks before this fiasco. The magazine and its author, as well as Zhuang Zhidie, have yet to apologize and express regret, so she had no way out, which is why the matter has escalated to the point that no mediation is going to work. The best solution would be for her to withdraw the suit, but that's unlikely. I decided to take a passive approach, not saying whether I would prosecute or not. I thought that if I could delay for a while, maybe she would calm down enough to withdraw her suit. But she has repeatedly gone to see the chief justice and the presiding judge, demanding to know why the case hasn't been recorded. This afternoon the presiding judge told me that it had to be recorded, and now it has."

Niu Yueqing was speechless.

"Can't anything be done to pull it back?" Meng asked.

"That's impossible, unless you can make the presiding judge change his mind. But his official position will not allow him to retract his decision."

Feeling her chest tighten, Niu Yueqing began to cry, though she quickly dried her tears. She started sniffling.

"Is your sinus infection bothering you?" Meng asked. "Here's a tissue."

Knowing she had behaved improperly, Niu Yueqing said, "I'll get some." She went into the bathroom to cry some more, dried her tears, and composed herself before rejoining the others. Sima handed her a piece of candy. She took it with a smile. With the candy in her hand, she said to him, "Please go ahead, Comrade Sima."

"Recording the suit doesn't mean the plaintiff will win. The result will have to wait until the court launches a full investigation and reaches a judgment based on provisions of the law. Zhuang Zhidie isn't here, but you can tell him to get ready. When he receives a copy of the complaint, he must write a convincing rebuttal statement. This is how it will proceed. It won't look good for me to keep you long. Now that I have the case, I must avoid excessive contact with both sides in my house. Please take Gong Jingyuan's calligraphy with you." When he finished, Sima got up to watch TV in his bedroom.

"Why don't you walk the uncles and Aunty out?" he said to his son.

They had to leave. After a brief discussion in the hallway, they turned and headed to Bai Yuzhu's house. After hearing about their visit to Sima, Bai could not stop complaining.

"What have you been doing all this time? Even in a rainstorm, I twice saw a woman waiting outside the court to talk to the presiding judge. I asked who she was and was told it was Jing Xueyin. But look how long it took you to move. Mr. Zhuang should have gone, too. Everyone is equal before the law, and the same goes for a celebrity. If you lose the suit, his reputation will suffer."

"You're right, it's our fault. But because of the flood, the mayor asked Zhidie to write a report, and he couldn't make it back home in time. The mayor summoned him again tonight. Of course he'd have come. He'll definitely come see you and Mr. Sima in a few days. Mr. Sima was courteous to us, but what he said frightened me."

"He's in charge of the suit, so he said what he had to say. He couldn't express any clear bias toward either side. He'd be in serious trouble if he did so and the other party filed a complaint. I'm going to say something I shouldn't: the law is based on the legal code, but it's enforced by people."

"We're friends, old Bai, so we're counting on you. The suit has been recorded, but you're the only one who can talk to Mr. Sima when it comes to the final judgment."

"Please tell Mr. Zhuang not to worry. No matter what the outcome is, I'll do my best."

"How can you say 'No matter what the outcome is'?" Niu Yueqing said. "That has plunged my heart back into a bottomless pit."

Bai fell silent. "Let's do it this way, then," he said. "I'll prepare some food and invite Sima Gong over for a drink. Of course he knows about our relationship. If he refuses to come, it must mean that he thinks it's a tough case after reading the complaint, and that the prospects are dim. If he's willing to join me, then there will be hope. When he's here, I will offer him Gong's calligraphy. If he declines to take it, then it's hopeless, since he wouldn't want to be embarrassed by taking your gift and then ruling against you. If he accepts it, the odds of a positive outcome will be sixty percent. If he takes the calligraphy and we have a bit to drink, I will certainly ask him about the case. We may have a problem if he clams up because he's unsure or is leaning the other way and doesn't want to be frank with me. If he's willing to talk about it, he'll be seeking my view, and the odds of getting a good outcome will rise to eighty to ninety percent."

Niu Yueqing could not stop praising Bai's strategy.

"Ah! You're an expert in the classical novel *Water Margin*, old Bai," Meng said. "You sounded just like Granny Wang showing Ximeng Qing how to seduce Pan Jinlian."

"My favorite is actually *Romance of the Three Kingdoms*."

Niu Yueqing told Zhao to go buy some food and liquor at the night market. Bai said he already had plenty, but Niu Yueqing insisted on handing the money to Zhao, who soon returned with three bottles of Wuliangye, some tripe, pig's tongues, pickled pig's feet, preserved eggs, and a chicken roasted in five spices. Bai told them to wait downstairs and that he would signal by opening and closing a window. When Sima arrived, he would open the window, and then he would shut it when the judge accepted the calligraphy. When the window was opened a second time, it would mean that he and Sima were talking about the case. They could go home with assurance when the window was shut one last time.

So the three of them went down to wait by a wall across the street, fixing their gaze on Bai's window. As expected, it opened, and they smiled. Then came the anxious wait for it to be shut. But it remained open; meanwhile the number of pedestrians dwindled. They heard people arguing in the nearby night market as it escalated into a fight. Meng turned to watch until he lost interest. "You're young, Jingwu," he said, "and your neck doesn't get sore so easily. So you watch the window while I shut my eyes and get some rest." He took off a shoe to sit on, resting his bare foot on the other shoe; he lowered his head and was soon snoring. About twenty minutes later, a figure flashed past the window and shut it. Zhao shook Meng. "Meng Laoshi, Sima Gong has accepted the calligraphy." No response from him.

"He's tired," Niu Yueqing said, "let him sleep. You can doze off too if you want."

"I'm not sleepy. Meng Laoshi has only one good eye, and it must be tired after doing the work of two all day. He deserves some rest."

"What kind of rubbish is that, Jingwu?"

"So you weren't sleeping?"

"I was keeping that eye open. Did you hear anything?"

"They're not fighting anymore."

"Listen closely. It sounds like Zhou Min playing his xun at the city wall."

Niu Yueqing and Zhao listened carefully; they heard soft xun music.

"Zhou Min has been feeling terrible lately, so he goes up there to play every night. But why must he play the xun, with its sad, bleak sound. The more he plays, the more ill-fated it makes me feel," Niu Yueqing said.

"He's the restless type," Meng said, "with high ambitions but lousy luck. I've studied his facial features. He has a mole on the bridge of his nose. Anyone with that is destined to spend his life alone; he could accomplish something spectacular, or he could also end up in a terrible mess."

"I share your feelings," Niu Yueqing said. "When he seduced Tang Wan'er into running away with him, he ruined a family. Then he stirred up trouble soon after arriving in Xijing. I don't want to say he harbors ill intentions, but he's brought us a lot of grief. Let's not talk about him. They've been up there drinking for quite some time. Could Bai have gotten so drunk he forgot to mention the case?"

"He wouldn't do that. Forgetting his promise is one thing, but messing things up for us is much more serious," Zhao said. "Zhuang Laoshi isn't your average defendant, not to mention the fact that they're drinking our liquor. You can tell people's fortunes by looking into their faces, so why don't you read mine, Meng Laoshi?"

"I won't do that, but I'll tell you one thing: you've been suffering from constipation."

"How did you know?"

"So you really do know fortune-telling?" Niu Yueqing asked.

"Of course. I used qimen divination. Look where you're sitting. We all picked a spot at random, but you chose to sit under the utility pole. Doesn't the round bulb look like that thing of yours? But the shade has been smashed, probably by a kid's rock, which is a sign that you're having trouble down there. I can also tell you that the resident in the house to the left is a bachelor. Why? Because that locust tree in front is bare, with no branches or leaves. I could sense that the moment we got here. Go ask him if you don't believe me."

Zhao got up and said, "The light's on in the house. I'll go check it out by pretending to borrow a match." He was about to walk off when he cried out, "The window is open."

Niu Yueqing was elated. "Old Bai is amazing. We'll have to do more to thank him later." She added, "Don't go there, Jingwu. If you verify that he's a bachelor, that would only make your Meng Laoshi even more smug. But if he's wrong, he'll pout. Why don't you two go have some roasted octopus in the night market?" She handed Zhao forty yuan and urged them to go. Forty minutes later, she came to the night market and said to the man selling fermented rice, "Give us three bowls, with three eggs in each bowl."

Meng and Zhao knew immediately what had happened. They joined her, and each had a bowlful.

It was two in the morning by the time Niu Yueqing returned home. Liu Yue was sitting in the living room with a book, but her head was drooping. Niu Yueqing took the book away, then tapped the girl on the head with it. "Dreaming about someone?" she said.

Liu Yue laughed as she stood up to get some water. Niu Yueqing told her to bring her a razor to trim a corn on her foot. When the girl returned, she cut very carefully. "It's so thick!" she said. "It's the fault of high heels. Men only know that women look pretty in heels; they don't have a clue as to the kind of suffering we go through. It sends shooting pains to your heart." Finally she managed to slice off a huge piece without drawing blood. Niu Yueqing put on her slipper and tried her foot on the floor. "Is he home?" she whispered.

"Yes, he's sleeping in the study."

That elicited a sad sigh from Niu Yueqing. "Let him. I don't have the energy to deal with him. Wait till he's on the defendant's stand, and we'll see how pompous he can be." She went into their bedroom and locked the door from the inside.

When Zhuang was washing up the next morning, he learned that Niu Yueqing had left for work. He asked Liu Yue if she had said anything. Nothing, she told him. Zhuang phoned Meng Yunfang, then sat in his study to drink, feeling glum. The postman came at around three in the afternoon and delivered a notice from the court, including a copy of the complaint and a request for a rebuttal. Zhuang was told to wait for the court's notice regarding an inquest and trial date. He read the first three pages. It was Jing Xueyin's handwriting, but the tone was clearly someone else's, which told him that someone was helping her strategize and adding fuel to the fire. He cursed three times before reading on to see the five people listed in the suit: Zhou Min, followed by Zhuang Zhidie, Zhong Weixian, Li Hongwen, and Gou Dahai. Zhuang was the second defendant, but the charge against him was the longest, with the most sarcastic terms, painting him as a relatively well-known figure with a sordid soul, an ingrate who sold out friends, and a despicable man who fabricated romantic conquests without regard for others' reputation. Zhuang felt his face burn, knowing full well that Jing had torn their former friendship to shreds and that he was totally worthless in her mind. He was hurt by the unfairness of it, and his self-esteem suffered a serious blow, as rage rose up inside him. After downing half a bottle, he staggered out the door. He was going to Zhou Min's house. Zhou, who had also received the notice from the court, was drinking, too, so Zhuang sat down to drink with him. Zhou told him that a copy had also been sent to the magazine office, where they had studied the tone and concluded it was by Wu Kun, who specialized in this kind of thunderous statement and vociferous claim. Zhou added that someone had once seen the woman doing something unsavory with Wu Kun, but her husband trusted him.

"Stop talking about her. Not another word," Zhuang shouted as he smashed his glass and fell down, dead drunk. He was still in a stupor at lunchtime, so Tang Wan'er went out to phone Niu Yueqing, who hung up. "I can't control him," was all she said.

Tang was piqued. *Maybe you can't control him, but don't accuse me of getting him drunk in my house*, she grumbled to herself.

She returned home and moved Zhuang into bed with Zhou Min's help. Zhou needed to go to the magazine office to check on new developments, so he told her to stay home and watch Zhuang to make sure he didn't fall off the bed.

Tang shut the yard gate the moment her husband left. Zhuang, still inebriated, was sweating profusely, so she unbuttoned his shirt before sitting down by the bed to read *Dream of the Red Chamber.* But she had a hard time concentrating, distracted by the wonderful sound of him breathing evenly on the bed while she was reading. The pear tree outside the window creaked under a gentle breeze, and a mouse appeared in a ceiling baffle. It watched them with its bright, beady eyes for a long time before sliding down the lamp pull cord and landing on the blanket at the head of bed, where it disappeared in a flash. She was immediately plunged into a dreamy state in which she mistook the man sleeping on the bed for hers. In her mind, he had fallen asleep by listening to her read the novel aloud. "You're so bad," she said. "I read until my throat is parched, and you fall asleep." Putting down her book, she crawled over and kissed him on the lips. He didn't stir. Struck by an idea for a prank, she took a writing brush and began painting his body, turning his nipples into a pair of eyes and his belly button into a mouth. She turned up the corners of the lips to create a smiling face. "What are you smiling at? Don't laugh at me." She added a string of tears under each eye, and the face looked to be laughing through them. He was still asleep when she finished. "Why aren't you awake? You're faking sleep." But he was in fact fast asleep, and she wished he would stay that way forever, as she got the idea of untying his pants and taking out his tool to play with. □□ □□ □□ [The author has deleted 26 words.] Soon she felt heat rising between her legs. When she got up to look at the stool she'd been sitting on, she saw a round wet spot and abandoned all reason. □□ □□ □□ [The author has deleted 53 words.] With her shoes off, her legs moved back and forth on the floor, and just as she was overtaken by the sensation, a bang on the back of her head sent her jumping to her feet, her face drained of color. She turned around, but there was no one behind her. Zhuang was winking and smiling at her when she turned back; she covered his eyes before getting onto the bed, where she sat on top of him and put him inside her. "You're shameless," he said.

"Don't talk. I want you to be drunk," she said as she put her mouth over his. He rolled on top of her and rocked like a wolf, working hard while pinching, biting, and nibbling at her. "I'm drunk. I'm still drunk."

It was getting dark outside when he collapsed on the bed and sighed repeatedly. "It's dark, Wan'er," he said.

"Yes, it is. Why is the day so short?"

"Did you put a love potion in the liquor? This is the first time I've ever been that drunk. I have to go home now, but how can I walk on these rubbery legs?"

"Don't go home. It's dark and you can sleep here. It's sleep no matter where you spend the night."

"What did you just say? Say that again."

"It's sleep no matter where you spend the night."

"That's a wonderful phrase. It makes you a poet, Wan'er."

She reached over his head to get a pair of panties from the closet. After putting them on, she smoothed her hair. "Really? Well, you're the novelist, so I'll be the poet. We can spend the night chatting when Zhou Min comes back. Do you really have to go home for a night of intimacy with your wife?"

"I'll sleep in my study. I have no more love in me, and a loveless person lives in darkness as black as the night."

"Then I'll give you light." She reached over to pull the lamp cord, but the switch popped twice without turning the light on. "Power outage again. This happens too often in Xijing. If I were the mayor, I'd fire the head of the Electricity Board. No power. I'll light a match for you." She struck the match, and they smiled in the dim flickering light before it went out. She struck another, but it went out right away. Before she could start again, he said, "I just called you a poet, and now you're going to turn yourself into a poem. Stop that. Don't waste matches. Where's Zhou Min? Did he go to work?"

"He did. He goes out to play his xun every night. It's late and he's still not back, so it must mean something's up at the office. You can get dressed while I make us some soup."

"Forget the soup. He'd be suspicious if he came back and saw us in a dark house."

"If you leave now, you might run into him at the gate. Then there'd be plenty for him to be suspicious of. Let's do this: Put on your clothes and go back to sleep. I'll lock up and go out. We'll pretend I locked you in for the afternoon. I won't come back until he returns."

Joking that she was more devious than any man, he took a roll of bills out of his pocket. "If you're going out, why don't you buy yourself a new outfit? The shopping malls don't close before midnight. I've always wanted to buy you something, but was worried it might not fit. So go get it yourself."

She refused the money and he grunted unhappily, so she took it and walked out, locking the gate behind her.

Zhuang spent the night away from home. Zhou Min returned and woke him up before Wan'er came in with a new outfit, to Zhou's displeasure. She offered to cook something as an apology to Zhuang Laoshi. After they ate by candlelight, Zhou asked Zhuang to stay for the night, while calling Meng over for a game of mahjong.

"You're all so dissolute, how can you call yourselves literary figures? I thought we'd be talking about literature tonight, but now you're getting the mahjong tiles out."

"Why does playing mahjong make us dissolute?" Meng, who had just arrived, asked. "Hu Shi said, 'Reading makes one forget mahjong, and playing mahjong makes one forget reading.' In my view, both reading and playing mahjong make you forget all your troubles. Zhidie and Zhou Min got themselves into a whole lot of trouble by reading and writing, so how are we supposed to forget our troubles if we don't play mahjong?"

They ended up playing all night. When day broke, Meng invited Zhuang to his house, where he spent three days. Once they went to a gathering of painters at a hotel, where the manager treated everyone to a sumptuous meal, then entertained them with pop singers. *These artists live such a carefree life*, Zhuang said to himself. *This must have been what it felt like when the ancients went on outings with courtesans.*

"Have you noticed that singer?" Meng whispered. "Isn't she a charmer? When she laughs, the tip of her tongue quivers between her teeth. That is so sexy. When we meet at the House of Imperfection Seekers, we should invite these singers along."

"Your eyes are bad, so you ought to close them and get some rest," Zhuang said. Meng was so upset he pinched Zhuang on the leg. After belting out some songs, the singers left with twenty yuan each as payment. The hotel manager then put up a table, laid out paper, ink, and brushes, and held his hands together politely to say, "You're all celebrities and it's a rare opportunity for you to grace my humble establishment. I'm also a lover of great calligraphy, so do you mind?"

"I thought the hotel provided a quiet place for artists to gather for casual conversation," Zhuang whispered to one of the artists.

"Painters are actually more popular than writers, but the eggs are the reason you feed the hens. So we're more unscrupulous than writers in the end."

One at a time, the painters went up to knock out a quick painting, then took out a seal to stamp the piece. "It upsets you to have to do it, yet you come prepared with your seal?" Zhuang whispered.

"We all know what's expected when someone invites us to a meal."

Zhuang sat idly by with a smile, but before his smile disappeared, the manager came to ask him for his work. When Zhuang told the man he didn't know how to paint, the manager said he wasn't hoping for a painting. "You're a writer and calligrapher, so why don't you write epigrams on their paintings?"

Zhuang had no choice but to write a few lines on each painting before leaving a thumbprint, since he didn't have his seal with him.

"That's even better. It's the real thing, no one can fake it."

After mingling with the painters, Zhuang went with Zhao Jingwu to the house of an antique collector to see his collection, to the opera, where they cheered the actors, to a snack street for something to eat, and to the Yunhuang Temple to watch Master Zhixiang teach qigong. More than two weeks went by like that, and then he received a subpoena indicating the first court date. A quick check told him it was less than two weeks away, so he gave up his outside activities and went home to wait. Zhou Min and Zhong Weixian came to see him several times to go over the contents of their rebuttal. They hired five lawyers, each of whom required a personal visit from Zhuang, since they were taking the case because of him. For them, it was a boost to their legal career to defend a celebrity, whether they won or lost. Zhuang had to smile and be cordial to them, but a problem arose regarding what they all should say. The lawyers first did an analysis of the purpose behind Jing Xueyin's suit: under normal circumstances, a woman should feel honored to have an entanglement with a celebrity. So was it possible that Jing was stirring up trouble for publicity? Zhuang immediately nixed that idea and told them Jing wasn't that kind of woman. They then argued that if they discounted that possibility, the only way to win would be to confirm the existence of a former romantic relationship. One of them criticized Zhuang for writing that stupid letter and asked him to declare in court that he had concealed the truth and had written it purely to smooth things over so as to avoid further confrontation. Now that the other side had resorted to legal measures, he must reiterate and reconfirm their romantic past. When he heard that recommendation, he knew that the lawyers had been influenced by opinions offered by Zhou Min, who would emerge guilt-free if they followed this line of logic, since the court would think that Zhuang had supplied the material for the article. What made it hard for him was how he could bring up the nonexistent affair to Jing's face. Even if he could force himself to lie, he would have violated her right to privacy, since it was a private matter he had bragged about and agreed for someone to write about when both he and Jing were married. Besides, if the court were to question the time when what was printed in the article had taken place, it would appear that he had been seeing Jing while he was dating Niu Yueqing and after he married her. Jing's husband would never let her off the hook, and Niu Yueqing would feel sordid. Zhuang refused to agree to that line of defense and insisted on his original idea.

"Zhuang Laoshi is such a decent person," Zhou Min said with a cold smile. "He's always the soft-hearted one."

That upset Zhuang. "I'll wash my hands of the whole matter if you insist on approaching it this way. I'll tell the court that what was written in the article wasn't completely groundless, but it was embellished and exaggerated. I didn't write the essay, nor did I read it beforehand. I never talked to you about any of this, and I hadn't even met you yet when you wrote it. My rebuttal would be, I should not be a defendant. If my rebuttal is rejected and I'm found guilty, I will go to jail."

They were both scowling, so Meng stepped in to mediate, telling them to cool off and think it over before they met for another discussion. Meng then took Zhuang out with him.

"It's no big deal, so why get upset? What can they do to you if you lose the case? Your fame comes from your works, so your reputation can't be ruined so long as you continue to write good works. If you ask me, the greatest pity would be losing a paramour you've known for years. You don't love women. If you did, I could be your pimp and get you eight or ten any time you wanted. You've been to lots of entertainment spots recently, and you've seen how happy other people can be. Why don't you emulate them? I'm going to take you somewhere today I'm sure you've never been, and it'll be an eye-opener."

"I've been pretty much everywhere but to the brothels near the train station."

"So the suit has been a wake-up call for you, and now you *do* want to go visit them?"

"Listen to you. You seem to know everything. If you're so good, go get me one."

They went to Meng's house, where Meng told Xia Jie to go with Tang Wan'er for a game of mahjong with Niu Yueqing.

"Good idea. I was bored stiff. But I have one condition: Don't bring Meng Jin over when I'm gone," she said before changing clothes and leaving with a roll of bills.

"She doesn't like Meng Jin here?" Zhuang asked.

"You have no idea how many times we've fought over this. He's my son. Is there a father who doesn't love his son? But he's very smart, and you know how smart kids tend to make mischief. His mother can't control him, and she's worried he'll turn bad, so she wants me to rein him in. But the moment the boy is in the house, Xia Jie hurls veiled abuse and scowls at me." Meng fumed as he stuck his head under the faucet for a drink of cool water. "Let's not talk about that. I wanted to show you a good time so you'd forget your troubles, but now I'm ranting about my own troubles. Why don't you take a rest here while I go see Hong Jiang about something. Don't lock the door."

Zhuang was napping when he heard a knock at the door. He thought it was Meng, so he said, "Come on in. The door isn't locked." But it was a woman with a heavily powdered face, two tiny eyes, and boldly painted brows. After looking around the room, she asked, "I'm looking for a Mr. Meng."

"Who are you? Where are you from?"

"Are you Mr. Meng?" With a laugh, she swayed her way into the room, looking at him out of the corner of her eye. She sat on the edge of the bed and stopped him when he tried to get up and get dressed. Then she stripped. "You sure know how to enjoy yourself, waiting at home instead of going out for the fun. I thought maybe you were a cripple."

When she was nearly naked, Zhuang saw a magic health sack around her waist. Finally realizing what was going on, he silently cursed Meng Yunfang for sending him a prostitute. He studied the woman's figure, which was average except for her full hips. She wore a thong, the back part of which was buried between her cheeks, while the front had an embroidered pink lotus flower. Keeping the thong on, she said, "Why don't you come to bed? It's for an hour, so when the time's up, I'm done whether you are or not." She pulled back the blanket, got into bed, and took off her thong under the blanket. At a momentary loss as to how to react, he said, "Let me see that flower on your panties." He pulled the blanket away. She was holding her legs tightly together. *So a woman like her knows to be shy*, he thought to himself, as a strange desire rose inside and he reached over to spread her legs. With her legs apart, she said, "Don't look. Let's get on with it." When he took a closer look, he was stunned by what he saw. There were sores all around her genitals, and one spot that seemed to be rotting away, apparently caused by a sexually transmitted disease. Gripped by fear, he pushed her off the bed and had her put her clothes back on. "Take your business elsewhere, all right?" He tossed her thirty yuan. "Go on now."

She whimpered as she picked up the money and looked at the bills before laying them down on the edge of the bed. "I've been paid already. On my way over, I thought I'd get you to pay me, too. But when I got here and saw you, I realized that I've never seen a man so attractive and told myself that I wouldn't leave after an hour. I wanted to have fun with you for two or three hours with no extra pay, never expecting that you wouldn't think I'm worthy of you, just someone you paid for sex. Well, you can keep your money." She got dressed and walked out.

Unable to get back to sleep, Zhuang felt sorry for the woman. Soon Meng came in to say, "You're done already? Why was she crying?"

"You're a whoremonger, Meng Yunfang. How could you send a woman like that?"

"To help you forget your troubles." Meng laughed. "I'm not interested, and I don't have a lot of extra money or troubles like you. Look here. I did get myself a set of boxing gloves and a sandbag, like that Director Wang. That's enough for me. Nowadays, who doesn't go whoring once he has the money? With prostitutes you pick up on the street, you don't have an emotional investment, so it can't affect your marriage. You pay for play, no worries. So what are you mad at me for?"

"Did you see the condition she's in? It's rotting away. Did you want me to be infected?"

Meng rued the forty yuan he had paid before saying with a laugh that it was Zhuang's bad luck to meet someone like that on his first try.

"She ruined my nap *and* my mood. Now you have to stick around. Didn't you say there's a place I haven't visited yet? Now I'm ready to check it out."

"You say you've been everywhere. You turn your nose up at the train station hotels, and I don't have the connections to get you into Zhongnanhai." Then it came to him: "An emporium!" he said emphatically. "Do you know what that is?"

"No, what is it?"

"You'll see. I said you've never been to this place, and it's true."

Instead of riding his bicycle, Meng climbed onto the back of Zhuang's scooter and pointed the way as they headed to the north of the city. It turned out to be a large trading post dealing in rare domesticated animals and fowl, cultivated flowers, birds, insects, and fish, along with water and food vessels, plus animal feeds and supplements. Visitors and idlers swarmed to the place, carrying bags and baskets, until it nearly burst at the seams. It was hundreds of meters long, a noisy, thriving place of business.

"So this is an emporium," Zhuang shouted to Meng.

"Don't shout, or people will spot you as a greenhorn. Take a good look around. It might appear to be teeming with shady dealings and turmoil, but in fact it's well organized and ordered based on unwritten conventions. There are people from all walks of life and backgrounds, local hooligans and gangsters, small merchants and peddlers, profiteers and minor criminals."

They walked in, and indeed, the merchants, brokers, and peddlers were hawking their wares and shouting at friends while keeping a close eye on their territory. Confined to a small space, they handled their own business, rarely arguing with each other. The first spot they entered was a fish market, where large aquariums edged in gold with aerators stood in front of each stand. Aquatic plants glimmered under flickering lights, while graceful tropical fish swam up and down, displaying silvery, scaly bodies. After looking them over, Zhuang said happily: "See how happy the fish are, like they have no worries."

"Want some? Set up an aquarium and you'll become a fish yourself."

"People seek peace in noise and noise in peace. When we watch the fish here, I envy them, but if I took them home, I'd think fish were better than people. I'd be even more annoyed at being jealous of fish, with nothing to distract me."

After the fish came the crickets. Zhuang owned several cricket jars passed down from earlier generations, and he had caught a few crickets by the city wall, but he had never seen such ornate jars. Picking up a dark green one for a closer look, he praised the design and the inlaid descriptions on the side: "King Cricket with a Golden Head" and "Invincible General." The owner was all smiles. "Want to buy one?"

The two friends smiled without answering, erasing the smile on the vendor's face. "Please move to the side, then, gentlemen, so you won't stand in the way of people who want to do business." He turned to two new customers with a cordial greeting and handed them a jar. "Magical Heaven-Sent Insect," he called out.

Bending over to remove the lid and examine the insect, the two men smiled broadly, bent down for a closer look, and asked the price. The vendor took of his straw hat and reached into the jar with both hands. One of the swarthy men gaped in surprise.

"Now you'll see its quality." The vendor dropped the insect into a box the size of a rice bowl. Zhuang and Meng cocked their heads to watch, while everyone around them held their breath. Immediately there was a thumping noise as two crickets were locked in battle, following a well-orchestrated format of attack and defense. One of them cunningly feigned defeat and faked a retreat, but then sneaked around to attack from the rear. Zhuang was captivated by the fight when Meng tugged at his lapel.

"You like things like this?" he asked.

"Guess what just occurred to me?"

"What? Were you still sighing over the woman with the festering sores?"

"I was thinking that humans have developed from crickets, not apes. Maybe crickets are our ancestors."

"Then why didn't you ask the man the winning cricket's official rank?"

They moved on to the dog market, where Zhuang had his eyes on a longhaired shih tzu, a lovely animal with a leonine head and pretty eyes. When it saw them, it sat up on its hind legs and greeted them with its front paws together.

"The dog looks a bit like Tang Wan'er," Zhuang said.

"Since you like her so much, why not buy the dog and give it to her? But if you want my opinion, I'd say men should not keep cats and women should not raise dogs. Let's go to the flower market. You can get her a potted canna lily. It's strange she doesn't have a single plant in her house."

"No more talk about flowers. I'm getting a headache. We did a terrible job caring for that pot of unusual flowers, so what business do I have buying a canna lily? Besides, I asked her why she doesn't plant flowers in the yard, and she said hers never live long, no matter what she plants. The flowers are jealous of her and she's jealous of them."

"The little tease is always saying things like that. Women all have the same problem. Xia Jie often tells me that so-and-so is fond of her or so-and-so is interested in her, but it's all meant to show me that someone else is in love with her if I'm not. So I say to her, that's great. If someone gives you an opening like the eye of a needle, you send a gust of wind the size of a bowl through it. She gets angry and starts crying."

Zhuang smiled and turned to look around. "Is there a pigeon market?"

"You want to raise a pigeon?"

"It's the only bird I like, so I'd like to get one for Wan'er."

"I see. That must have been her idea."

"What do you mean?"

"There's no phone at her house, so she can have a messenger pigeon."

"Only you could think of such a scheme."

Meng took him to the pigeon market, where he checked out the birds by feeling their necks, tugging at their wings, examining their color, and looking at their toe rings.

"Are you buying a pigeon for her or picking a consort for yourself?"

Zhuang finally settled on one and walked away feeling terrific. He spent another night at Meng's house, away from his own home at the compound.

⁂

When she learned that Zhou Min and Zhuang had had a falling-out, Wan'er was furious with Zhou, but only told him not to ruin a friendship.

"Even if you lose the job because Zhuang Laoshi can no longer watch out for you, and you can't stay at the magazine, don't forget that he was the one who gave you the job in the first place. Besides, he's like a tall tree with deep roots, so he's Jing Xueyin's match. If you get on his bad side and he begins to ignore you, you'll be the one who's lost even if you win the suit."

Zhou calmed down after hearing her out, for he had to agree with her. So he brought out his xun and, looking at what was written in a notebook, played softly, a strange tune that was alien to her ears. When he tired of that and went out for a walk, she looked at the notebook, surprised to see it was not musical notations but a poem he had written:

I traveled everywhere and visited everyone. I looked everywhere but couldn't find a place for my soul to settle. I got a new woman, but she'd been married before. I stayed in a brand-new house, but it had only old furnishings. Moving from a derelict town to a bustling city, I met only old men and hear nothing but the ancient past and present. Mother, you gave birth to this son of yours, but when will new ideas begin to sprout in his head?

Realizing that he had been playing his xun while reading the poem, she felt sorry for him and shed a tear, followed by a sigh. But she was put out by the line "I got a new woman, but she'd been married before." *So you're unhappy that I was married before,* she said to herself. *You knew about that beforehand, didn't you? I threw away a stable life because of you, but this is what you think of me.* The more she thought about it, the angrier she grew, and she couldn't wait for him to return to explain himself. She sat down angrily by the window, but then changed her mind. *Forget it. I no longer care for him, so what's the point of getting mad and arguing? If we break up, he might feel he has nothing to lose, particularly with the lawsuit. What if he were to go off the track at court? Wouldn't that make things worse for Zhuang Zhidie?* Eventually, she decided to hide the notebook for the day Zhou found out about her and Zhuang. If they had a fight and decided to break up, the notebook would be her best defense for a counterattack. Then she took the bronze mirror from the bedside table and put a string through the hook to hang it high on the living room wall. She knew Zhou needed to be mollified for now, so she went to Meng Yunfang to see if he would talk some sense into Zhou Min. Meng agreed and came over with the pigeon.

"Zhuang Zhidie wasn't really angry," Meng said to Zhou. "He said what he did that day for the sole purpose of winning the case. He was an innocent bystander who got dragged into the suit. If this were anyone else, he would have sued you already. But no, he stands by you, and in fact has turned an old paramour into an enemy. What do you have to be mad about? Look here. He's not petty like you; he actually bought you two a pigeon."

Taking the pigeon from him, Wan'er laid her face against it. The white feathers perfectly matched her complexion, making her eyes a more alluring black and the pigeon's red beak even brighter.

"Which one is fairer, Meng Laoshi, me or the pigeon?"

"You know I have only one good eye, so what can I see? Let's wait until Zhuang Laoshi comes and have him take a look. His eyes are sharp."

A look of slight intoxication appeared on her face when she said, "Meng Laoshi, do you believe that Jing Xueyin was Zhuang Laoshi's lover?"

"Stop that nonsense," Zhou Min said. "You ask too many questions."

She was thrilled to learn that Zhuang had bought the pigeon for her and hadn't bought anything for anyone else at the emporium. When she was alone, she had many fanciful thoughts and spent a lot of time in front of a mirror. When she was done, she would smile seductively and call out softly, "This smile is for you, Zhuang-ge." She would then lose control and satisfy herself with her hand. Over that period, Zhou Min had wanted sex, but she had put him off, claiming she wasn't feeling well. When she could no longer say no, she told him to hurry and washed herself repeatedly afterward.

"Have you lost your sex drive?" he asked her.

"I'm getting old."

"They say a woman is like a wolf in her thirties and a tiger in her forties. How old are you now?"

She smiled and changed the subject. "I have an idea. To make up for the argument you had with Zhuang Laoshi, why don't we invite him over for a meal? The human heart is made of flesh, and he'll forgive you if you take the initiative and make some concessions."

Reminded of the headache from the lawsuit, he hemmed and hawed without saying yes or no before going out into the yard, where he fanned himself to cool off.

A few days later, when Zhong Weixian asked Zhou Min to get in touch with Zhuang, he offered to have everyone meet at his house. After agreeing on a time, he returned home to inform Tang, who was thrilled by the news and said she would get something really nice ready. But she could not decide what to make, so she went out with a flashlight that evening. Zhou asked where she was going, to which she replied, "You'll know when I get back." She went all the way to the woods by the moat, where she turned on her flashlight to catch cicadas that had just emerged from near the roots to climb up the tree trunks. After mating in the trees, the cicadas dropped their eggs onto the ground, and the newly hatched cicadas climbed up the trunks to grow wings. They were particularly tasty and nutritious when stir-fried.

Zhou waited until midnight, when Tang returned, her hair a mess and torn socks on her muddy feet. She was carrying a plastic bag filled with live cicadas. "What crazy idea is it this time?" With a smile, she said she had run into a man along the moat who had followed her. She was ready to give him all her money if he came near her, but fortunately a group of people came by, and he went away. "He didn't want your money," he said.

"What did he want?" she asked "Any chance he could have gotten it?" She poured salt water into a basin and plunged the baby cicadas in to get rid of the muddy smell.

"Why aren't you coming to bed?" Zhou asked.

"Go to sleep; don't wait for me."

"Wan'er, Wan'er." She knew what he wanted and ignored him. She tiptoed into the bedroom once he began snoring.

The next day Zhuang and Zhong came by at the prearranged hour. Zhou Min brought out some liquor so they could drink and talk. When Zhong said they didn't have anything to go with the liquor, Tang emerged with a smile and a plate of golden fried young cicadas, so alarming Zhuang that he covered his nose and mouth. Upset by his reaction, she said, "Isn't this up to your standard, Zhuang Laoshi?"

"How could anyone eat this?" he said.

"They're delicious. People in my parents' village drool over them. I made a special trip last night to catch them in the woods by the city moat."

"You people from southern Shaanxi will eat anything in the air but airplanes and everything on the ground but straw sandals," Zhuang said.

"Won't you give it a try?" she said, picking one up with three fingers and feeding it to him. An unusual fragrance filled his mouth, and the more he chewed, the better it tasted. That brought a smile to her face as she placed those three fingers in her mouth to suck on the oil. "Now you know how good they are." She smiled and continued, "You're always eating long noodles and cornmeal-nugget soup. I'm going to train you to be a gourmand."

"Train. That's a fine word," Zhong Weixian said. "I've never heard of a woman training a man. I once read that a woman is like a piano, and that a good man can produce beautiful music on it, while an awful man can only pollute the air with noise."

"That's a good line," she said. "But I read that a man is like a horse, and a woman is the rider who can determine whether the horse is good or bad."

"That's enough," Zhou Min said. "Don't you know who Mr. Zhong is? Why show off for him?"

"Mr. Zhong doesn't pay my salary, so I needn't be humble, like you." They joked for a while before Zhong asked Zhuang if he knew the people in charge of assigning job titles at the Provincial Office.

"I do, but not well," Zhuang said.

"As long as you know them, they'll listen to you. I have a favor to ask. The business sections at the Department of Culture have been given two high-ranking posts for the coming round of job title assignments. But there are two editorial offices, one for *Xijing Magazine* and the other for *Xijing Drama World.* With so many editors, it's like more wolves than meat and will end up creating rifts among the intellectuals. I wouldn't have to ask for help if I hadn't been condemned as a Rightist. But I wasn't an editor during those years. I was in charge of a magazine for a while after my rehabilitation before I was removed from the position. I didn't have anything to do for several years. Now I've finally been promoted to editor-in-chief, and yet the very first issue under my editorship got us in trouble. So the department has refused to give us one of the titles. I went to see them and was told that there weren't enough. Which is why I'd like you to talk to the people in charge of the assignment and see if they could give the department one more title. I'm old and frail, and who knows how long I have. It really doesn't matter to me if I get a high-ranking title. But it's a government perk for intellectuals for which I'm qualified. Those people use the job title to put me down, so I plan to fight for it to show them. What do you think?"

"Of course, absolutely. If they think you're not qualified for a high-ranking title, then why did they make you the editor-in-chief of such an important magazine? I'll go talk to them over the next few days and see if they can give us an extra title specifically for you."

"There's no need for that. It'd be easier if there were just one more title. I wouldn't complain if they acted without bias against me and the assignment committee deemed my job performance to be below their standard."

"If you're not up to their standard, then I'm afraid no else in the department could be."

"I'm touched that you agree. I was worried you might laugh at me for using a back door for this."

"Wasn't your problem caused by my troubles?"

"Now that you mention it, I will tell you and Zhou Min something, so you can both be prepared. Li Hongwen has changed completely since we received the notice from the court about a rebuttal. Gou Dahai was the first reviewer of the article and Li the second, so now he has adopted a defeatist tone, saying we'll definitely lose the case; he even tried to shirk responsibility by arguing that Gou Dahai said in his review that it was a great article, but he asked me to be the final reviewer since he thought it involved personal privacy. He said I confirmed in my final report that it should be the featured article because the contents were factual and the writing was elegant. In fact, Gou wrote the first review, Li wrote the second, and I wrote the final report, and we all had the same view. He showed us his copy of the report, and there was nothing in the second review column. Dahai and I suspect he forged the report. Dahai wanted to take the form to the police for authentication, but I stopped him. I told him not to bother with Li's attempt to duck responsibility. He was the second reviewer, so how much blame can fall on him if we lose the case? As the magazine's legal authority, I will bear the heaviest responsibility."

"No wonder Li Hongwen was smiling when he went to greet Jing Xueyin yesterday," Zhou said.

"A lawsuit isn't a covert revolution, so why would he turn on good friends like that?" Zhuang said. "You never know a person's true colors until something happens."

Zhou Min's face reddened when he heard Zhuang's comment; he called out to Wan'er to make some noodles. Zhong took out his rebuttal for Zhuang to read and whispered to Zhou Min, "Do you know where I can find a rental in the city?"

"Don't you have a place here?" Zhou asked.

"It's not for me. I invited an old schoolmate to Xijing, someone I haven't seen for decades. I need to find a good place. I'd like to rent it for a week or ten days."

"Then a rental place won't do. You'll need to book a room in a hotel."

"Where am I going to get that kind of money?"

Zhuang, who was listening to them as he read the rebuttal, felt his heart skip a beat, wondering if Zhong was trying to find a place for the woman in Anhui. Ah-can's sister had forwarded three of Zhong's letters from Suzhou, and in each one Zhong had expressed his desire for her to come visit him to fulfill their life-long dream. They'd been in love all these years, so why not spend a few days as husband and wife? After this bold request, he asked if he'd gone overboard, if he sounded unsavory. In his forged reply, Zhuang wrote that that was what "she" was thinking, what she had been hoping for, if not for the fear that she would not have a place to stay in Xijing. It had to be a secret. People approved of a young couple living together, but for older folks it would be considered an illicit affair, and no one would understand. She would come when everything was ready in Xijing.

"I can help you out with that," Zhuang said. "When is your friend coming?"

"I don't have a specific date yet. I think I'll wait till after the case is over and I get the job title assignment, though I'd like to find a place as soon as possible. I need to remind you that you and Zhou Min are the only two who know about this. Please promise not to tell anyone else."

Zhuang had to kick himself, knowing that his recent responses were going to cause problems. He knew he'd have to write another letter in a day or two to tell Zhong that she had broken her leg while going downstairs and would have to postpone the trip. As he worked out the details, he had trouble looking Zhong in the eye and decided not to talk about the case, either. When he saw Wan'er walk in with the noodles, he complimented her on how tasty they looked. He ate fast; soon he was done and put down his bowl.

"You were saying how good the noodles look, Zhidie, so why don't you have some more?" Zhong asked.

"I had a late lunch, and I'm not particularly hungry. I'm done, but take your time and enjoy the noodles."

"I will. It's been a long time since I've enjoyed such delicious handmade noodles." As steam rose, Zhong removed his fogged-up glasses before having another bowl. Then he took out his dentures to rinse them in clean water. "Zhou Min is so lucky. He can have these every day if he wants."

When they were leaving, Zhou and Tang walked them to the gate.

"Thank you for this pigeon, Zhuang Laoshi," Tang said, holding the bird in her hands. "It's so sweet, it talks to me during the day and sleeps with me at night."

"You're like a little girl," Zhong said. "How does the pigeon talk to you?"

"It looks at me when I'm talking, like it can understand me," she said. Then she turned to Zhuang. "Are you still not going home? You've been away for days. When I went to play mahjong at your house, I saw how much that pained your wife. Why don't you go home and take the pigeon with you? Keep it for a few days so it will get to know everyone there. Then you can let it go; it knows this place by now."

Meng had said he'd bought the pigeon to use as a communication tool. Apparently, she had the same idea. "I'll do that," Zhuang replied cheerfully. He took the pigeon home for Liu Yue to look after.

After Liu Yue began caring for the pigeon, Zhuang bought millet for it every day. A few days later, he tied a short note to the ring on the pigeon's leg, inviting Tang Wan'er to the House of Imperfection Seekers. The letter arrived safely, and she showed up on schedule; they shared a pleasurable time, an experience that made Tang treasure the pigeon even more. For a while after that, whenever Zhou Min was away, she sent the pigeon with a note asking Zhuang over. Emboldened by then, he invited her to his house one day. After reading the note, Wan'er sent the pigeon back with her reply, and then took extra time getting ready. But their affair was doomed to be exposed that day. Liu Yue was putting clothes out to dry on the balcony when the pigeon flew back; puzzled by its speedy return, she spotted the note on the ring. She took it from the pigeon's leg and read it.

"I've long wanted to come to your house. I will feel like the lady of the house when we make love there." Liu recognized Tang's handwriting.

"I always thought they had an unusual relationship," she said to herself, "but I didn't realize it had developed into this. Who knows how many times they've already had sex. The mistress is totally in the dark, and I've been blind to what they've been up to."

She replaced the note and went into the kitchen.

"Zhuang Laoshi, the pigeon is calling for you."

He went outside, caught the pigeon, and read the note, then let it fly off before he returned to the kitchen.

"The pigeon? Didn't we let it out earlier? Liu Yue, my wife went to Shuangren fu today because her cousin came with her family to visit the old lady. There are too many people for her to cook for all of them. Why don't you go give her a hand? You don't have to worry about me here at home. Meng Laoshi just called to say an editor has come from Beijing for manuscripts and is staying at the Gudu Hotel. He wanted me to go with him to see the man. We'll eat at the hotel."

You fooled me in the past with stories like this, but no more, she said to herself, but to him she replied, "All right. You're a grown man acting like a little boy who prefers to eat out as long as others pay. But don't be too greedy and eat too much. They pay for your food, but you'll have to pay for your health if you don't watch what you put in your stomach." She opened the door and left.

Liu Yue did not go far, though. She roamed the streets for a while, her mind a jumble of unhappy thoughts, and came back when she expected that Tang Wan'er would have arrived. Instead of knocking at the door, she went next door and, pretending to have forgotten her key, asked to use their balcony to get back inside. The row of houses had connecting balconies, separated by low walls, which she had climbed over before when she locked herself out. Once inside, she tiptoed into her room before hugging the wall and slinking over to Zhuang's bedroom barefoot. The door was ajar. She heard soft, wanton laughter inside. □□ □□ □□ [The author has deleted 52 words.]

"Get dressed," she heard Zhuang say. "Liu Yue's such a scatterbrain she might turn around halfway and come back for something."

So you gossip about me to butter her up. Liu was piqued. *When was I a scatterbrain?*

"No," Wan'er said, "I want more."

Liu thought they had to have finished already, so Zhuang must have given her something belonging to the mistress, and she was complaining about not having enough. She peered into the room and saw Tang lying naked on the bed holding Zhuang in her hand. □□ □□ □□ [The author has deleted 55 words.]

"No more. You're always saying I beg you to do it, so today I want you to beg me."

"I won't beg you. Just touch me some more, please."

So he bent down to suck on her breast as he reached between her legs, making her writhe and ask him to mount her. He laughed but refused. She was soon moaning and groaning.

"Please, I beg you. How much wetter do you want me to be before you'll take me?"

Liu Yue's eyes glazed over when she spotted the glistening dampness between Wan'er's legs. Something was pressing uncomfortably down below, and then it flowed out. She wanted to flee, but her legs were frozen to the spot. She kept watching as Zhuang mounted Wan'er. □□ □□ □□ [The author has deleted 473 words.] Wan'er let out a scream, her head rolled back and forth, and she clutched the bed sheet with both hands, wadding it out of shape. As if drunk, Liu Yue crumpled to the floor and bumped into the door. The noise alarmed the people inside. Seeing that it was Liu Yue, Zhuang covered first Wan'er, then himself with the sheet. "What are you doing here? What in the world are you doing here!" he demanded.

Liu Yue got to her feet and ran off.

"Liu Yue!" Zhuang shouted as he looked for his pants. "This is terrible!" he said. "She'll tell Niu Yueqing."

Wan'er took the shirt he had picked up from him. "What makes you think she'll do that?" She pushed Zhuang, still naked, toward the door, silently urging him to go after Liu, who by then was in her room, leaning against the foot of the bed, breathing hard.

"Are you going to tell, Liu Yue?" Zhuang asked.

"No," she said.

He went up, wrapped his arms around her, and started taking off her clothes. She briefly tried to stop him, then let him take off her pants. Seeing how wet her panties were, he said, "I've always said that Liu Yue didn't understand, while all along she's been a ripe persimmon." They came together on the side of the bed. □□ □□ □□ [The author has deleted 31 words.]

"Why is there no blood? You aren't a virgin, Liu Yue. Who was your first?"

"No," she said, "you're wrong." She writhed on the bed, unable to control her body.

Tang Wan'er, who was at the door watching them the whole time, went over and put her arms around Liu Yue when she and Zhuang finally separated.

"Liu Yue, you and I are real sisters now."

"How could I ever dream to be your sister? Who'd have even noticed me if I hadn't seen you? He did this simply to shut me up." She was besieged by regret. Wanting to win him on her own at first, she had taken the moral high ground when Zhuang had tried to get on her good side. She teared up when she realized she had been sacrificed for their sake.

"You're a rare treasure, Liu Yue. How could I not be fond of you? I'm always on your side. It's just that you're so watchful, I'm afraid that my wife has told you to spy on me."

"You think she'd trust me? She's usually on her guard with me, too. Whenever the two of you have an argument, she vents her anger on me."

"Don't mind her. Just blame everything on me when there are problems from now on, all right?"

"You're household help," Tang joined in, "not a slave. If it gets really bad, just go find another employer, and when she has to take care of everything herself, we'll see if she still throws a fit."

"Don't give her any of your bad ideas," Zhuang said. "Why does she have to leave? I'll arrange something for her when the moment is right."

That made Liu even more despondent, and she began to sob. Seeing her cry like that, Zhuang and Tang knew they could not console her for now, so they went back to the bedroom to get dressed.

"What lousy luck to have her see us like that," Tang said.

"It's all right. At least we don't have to watch out for her anymore."

"I know what you're thinking," she said. "You're falling for an even younger girl. I was watching you earlier; you didn't have to have sex with her to shut her up. You're her employer. All you had to do was scare her a bit. Do you think she'd dare go around talking about it? But no, you had to actually do it. Even if it was necessary, couldn't you just have humored her? Did you have to be so eager, so intense? She *is* fresher and younger than me, so you probably won't want me anymore."

"I can't believe it. You're the woman who told me to go to her, and now you don't want me to say anything."

"I have to tell you this, though. She has an aura of calamity. I noticed when you were in bed with her that she didn't have a single pubic hair. People are always saying that a woman without pubic hair is a white tiger, a sign of calamity. A man whose chest hair extends all the way to his back is a black dragon. Great fortune will visit a man who's a black dragon when he meets a white tiger, but disaster will fall on a man who's not. You had sex with her today, and I'm afraid that may be trouble in the future. Be careful."

Her words sent a chill down his spine. After seeing her off, he mixed some brown sugar in water and took the glass to his study to drink.

❋

But Zhuang did not heed Tang's advice. After the first time with Liu Yue, he had sex with her again and again. A close examination verified that the lovely creature was indeed a white tiger, but her secret spot was such a luscious mound, bewitching as a peach blossom when opened and a piece of flawless jade when closed, that he forgot all about possible disasters or calamities. A bit more money came her way with the attention from Zhuang, which in turn made her think quite highly of herself. Taking the missus less seriously, she disobeyed Niu Yueqing on several occasions, and nothing Niu Yueqing said to her made a difference in her attitude. One day, before Niu Yueqing went to work, she told Liu to buy pork and leeks for dumplings, and not to stuff a coin in one of them for fortunetelling. Liu said she would do it, but ended up buying mutton and fennel, and placing a two-fen coin in one of the dumplings. At lunch, Niu Yueqing asked why she had bought mutton, since the gamey taste made her nauseous. Liu Yue insisted that the mutton was not gamey, even went so far as to gulp down one of the dumplings without chewing in front of Niu Yueqing. That led to an argument, which Niu Yueqing more or less lost, so upsetting her that she went to nap without eating. Liu Yue sent an invitation to Tang Wan'er via the pigeon, and when she arrived, Liu told Niu Yueqing that she had invited Tang over to cheer her up. Before Niu Yueqing had a chance to chat with Tang, Liu Yue brought out a bowl of dumplings.

"Big Sister Wan'er, Dajie doesn't like these, and I don't want to throw them out. Why don't you have some, unless you think I've poisoned them?"

Tang took the bowl from her and, saying they didn't smell gamey, took a bite, only to chip her tooth. She opened her mouth, and a coin clinked into the china bowl. Liu had her hands all over Tang. "You're the lucky one," she said, "with a strong life force. I ate more than you but didn't find the coin, and here you find it with your very first bite." She pinched Tang between the legs.

The sight of the two women having so much fun annoyed Niu Yueqing, but she could say nothing, and that caused her to belch and suffer shortness of breath. Worse yet, feeling unclean, she began washing her hands with soap, cleaning every crease, including under her nails with a tiny brush, over and over, often for half an hour.

Liu Yue started going out more and more, as if she could not bear to stay home. Every time she went grocery shopping, she took the opportunity to window-shop, watch a movie, or play video games at an arcade.

"Liu Yue," an unhappy Zhuang said one day," you've changed."

"Of course I have. With something of yours in me, Liu Yue is no longer a pure Liu Yue."

What really upset Niu Yueqing was that Liu Yue was always coming home with a new blouse or a different hairstyle. When she asked the girl where she had been, Liu always had an answer.

"I didn't see you send money home this month," Niu Yueqing said. "Obviously, you spent it all on yourself. Don't you think about repaying your parents for all it cost them to raise you?"

"They say they never have enough money. I've been away for a while now, and they've never come to see me, yet they expect me to have found a gold mine for them here. How much do I make a month, anyway?"

That effectively shut Niu Yueqing up.

When she came home from work one day, Niu Yueqing walked into a house full of young women, all heavily made up, crossing their legs alluringly or twisting their hips as they drank. When they saw the mistress, they gulped in surprise and left noisily.

"Who were they?" Niu Yueqing asked Liu.

"All girls from my hometown. Did you see how well they're doing? They've long wanted to visit the writer. Everything in this house was new to them. I treated them to a bottle of wine because I wanted us to look generous in their eyes."

"Does this look like a tourist destination for shady characters? Who knows what they do in those hotels, but in any case, we're not running a brothel," Niu Yueqing said.

"What gives you the right to call them prostitutes? If they are, then I am, too."

Liu's retort made Niu Yueqing furious. "You learn from the people you're with. You changed after meeting them. You're a different person. Go check yourself out in the mirror and see what you look like."

"I don't need a mirror. I can see myself in my own pee. I'm a prostitute, all right? I *am* a prostitute. This house is more like a whorehouse than those hotels."

"What did you say? Why are you cursing my house?"

"Do I dare curse your house? If I did, how would I make any money pimping?" She banged her teacup down on the table, sending it sliding into the teapot, which crashed to the floor.

"Well, well." Niu Yueqing jumped to her feet. "Now you've started smashing things. This isn't your house, not yet, and you have no right to break things."

"I'll pay you back. I'll pay you for the teapot, and for the bottle of wine we drank." She sobbed all the way back to her room.

❋

On the same day, Zhuang Zhidie assumed a woman's style and wrote Zhong Weixian to say that an injured leg had made the trip to Xijing impossible. After sending it, he went to the Performance Evaluation Office and spent the morning talking to the man in charge, who insisted that he could not increase the quota; he could do nothing unilaterally, since quotas were decided at meetings. All he could do was contact the Department of Culture and ask for a fair hearing. He immediately placed a call to the chief of the department. Zhuang listened to the conversation and complained that Zhong's name had not been mentioned.

"How could I mention anyone's name? It's unwise for someone in a supervisory position to interfere in personnel issues in the office he oversees. If he does, he risks an outcome that is the opposite of what he wants."

Zhuang returned home in a low spirits. Before he had a chance to vent his displeasure on Niu Yueqing and Liu Yue, he heard them quarreling as he reached the stairs. A crowd was eavesdropping in the hallway outside his apartment; they quickly and quietly dispersed when they saw him coming. With mounting anger, he walked in and shouted to stop the two women, before scowling and asking Niu Yueqing what was going on. Seeing how cross he was, Niu Yueqing softened her tone and told him about the women Liu had invited over.

"We live in professional housing, where our neighbors are all intellectuals. When she invites shady characters over to eat, drink, dance, sing, and raise hell, what will our neighbors think of us? I talked to her about it, and she threw a temper tantrum. She even smashed a teapot."

Zhuang went to Liu's room to talk to her. After sleeping with him, Liu thought she had become his favorite, so she defended herself with her head held high, spraying him with spittle. He had planned to scold her a little and let the whole thing drop, but her inflexible attitude told him that Niu Yueqing might grow suspicious, for it did not seem normal for a domestic helper to behave that way with the head of the household. As he tried to hide any sign of their relationship, Niu Yueqing showed up at the door to the room.

"You see? If she treats you like that, how do you think she behaves with me? Does she even act like a domestic helper? She's more like my own mother!"

Zhuang slapped Liu gently. She froze momentarily, staring wide-eyed at him, and when her status in the home finally became clear to her, she slumped to the floor and banged her head until her forehead bled. Husband and wife fell silent at this violent reaction; they brought a bandage for her forehead, but she fought them off, wailing as she tore at the door.

"Do you plan to go screaming into the courtyard?" he demanded sternly. "Listen to me. Don't even think about coming back if you go out bleeding like that."

Unable to go outside, Liu went into the bathroom and opened the faucet all the way to let the water gush.

Zhuang phoned Meng Yunfang and asked him to go ask Tang Wan'er to hurry over. She arrived dressed to go out, and was shocked when he told her about the fight. She was, however, pleased to learn the reason behind the quarrel; she went to the bathroom and got Liu Yue into her room to smooth things over.

A while later, Zhuang led Tang to his study, where he asked if she could take Liu Yue home with her to let the girl cool off.

"She did deserve to be punished," Tang said softly, "but you shouldn't have hit her in the face. No one could have seen if you'd spanked her till her behind was black and blue."

"I didn't do it. She banged her head on the floor."

Tang laughed. Then she kicked a chair to make a creaking noise so she could give him a loud kiss before walking out to say good-bye to Niu Yueqing. She managed to get Liu Yue to go home with her, while Niu Yueqing, still stewing in anger, refused to get up to see them out. So Zhuang walked the two women to the door and took out ten yuan for a taxi. Refusing to take his money, Tang pointed at his face with a barely concealed smile before walking down the stairs with Liu Yue. Puzzled over the reason behind Tang's smile, Zhuang went to splash some water on his face in the bathroom and saw in the mirror a faint red mark on his left cheek. He quickly washed it off. The house felt too quiet when he was done. A sadness rose up inside when he saw the few laundered garments floating in the tub. He took them out to dry on the balcony before going back inside and saying cheerlessly to Niu Yueqing, "Happy now? You have what it takes to bring a man so much good fortune."

"So it's my fault? She learned her bad habits from those women from her hometown and will become a prostitute one of these days if nothing changes," Niu Yueqing said.

"Don't talk like that! What was she like before? She turned bad after coming to work here. It's you who indulges all her whims."

"That girl doesn't know what's good for her. I treat her well, and that's gone to her head; she does whatever she wants, any way she likes. She'd shit on my head if she could get away with it!" Using her complaints about Liu Yue to vent her unhappiness on her husband, she added, "She wouldn't treat me like that if you showed me some respect. When your man looks down on you, even the pigs and dogs move in."

"Are you finished?" He stormed into his study and slammed the door.

After Liu Yue spent the night at Tang Wan'er's, Zhuang told Niu Yueqing to go see the girl. She refused. Liu Yue returned on her own. Without saying much, she went into the kitchen and started cooking, a sight that removed the anger from Niu Yueqing's face. She behaved as if nothing had happened. Starting that night, she ate with them at the same table. When she finished, she asked without looking up, "What do you want for the next meal?"

"Up to you," Zhuang said.

"How do you make 'up to you'?"

"Then how about braised noodles with tofu?" Zhuang said.

That was what they had next.

After having the same thing for several meals in a row, Niu Yueqing decided to write down what she wanted for the next meal before going to work in the morning. She put the note on the dining table, where Liu Yue saw it, but while Niu Yueqing was changing into her work shoes, Liu Yue shouted at the door to the study, "What do you want for the next meal?"

"Didn't she write it down and put the note on the table?" Zhuang asked.

"Rice with something chicken." She picked up the note. "Zhuang Laoshi, I'm not educated enough to know if it's stewed chicken or what."

"You work for a writer, and you don't know if that's stewed chicken?" he said from inside the study.

"No, I don't. If I did, I wouldn't be working here."

Niu Yueqing was so annoyed she snatched up the note and tried to pinch the girl's lips, making her giggle. Zhuang came out and saw them.

"Good, good. Now you're back to being sisters again."

Though Niu Yueqing was still angry, she had to laugh. "Liu Yue," she said, "you don't act anything like a maid."

"That's my problem exactly," the girl laughed along with her. "I came with you because you were so nice to me. I'm not a maid."

"I'll tear out your tongue if you ask Zhuang Laoshi what to eat again," Niu Yueqing said, before going out the door and walking downstairs. She stopped and shouted up, "Liu Yue, bring me a handful of watermelon seeds, will you?"

The girl grabbed a handful of seeds and took them down for Niu Yueqing, who walked off to work, cracking seeds along the way. Liu Yue went back into the living room and sat down with some seeds of her own before heading over to the study.

She looked inside. "What are you writing? Why don't you open the window a crack? You're disappearing into a cloud of cigarette smoke."

"Leave me alone. I'm writing a rebuttal."

Feeling bored, she went to her room to sew buttons on a shirt, but fell asleep before she was finished.

Zhuang felt jumpy after an hour of writing, so he called the magazine office to ask for Zhou Min. When Zhou picked up the phone, Zhuang told him to relate what had happened at the Performance Evaluation Office to the editor-in-chief; Zhou was to stress to him that Zhuang would personally go see the head of the Department of Culture. After the call, he felt like snacking on something, so he went into the kitchen, where he spotted a plate of plums on the table. He picked one up and ate it, and, wanting to share some with Liu Yue, he called out to the girl, but got no response. So he went to her bedroom. She was lying on her back; a button on her open blouse had been sewn on, but she hadn't had time to cut off the thread on the needle. The skin below her bra looked fair and tender. Zhuang laughed and, unable to resist, unhooked her bra and untied her skirt so he could quietly feast on her pretty body. □□ □□ □□ [The author has deleted 38 words.] Afraid that he might wake her up, he rubbed a plum gently on that special place, and, to his surprise, it opened up to catch the plum, presenting a remarkable sight. Laughing silently, he gently backed out of the room to resume his writing in his study, and promptly forgot about it.

At around ten o'clock that morning, someone knocked at the door. He went to answer it; it was Mr. Huang, the plant owner, drenched in sweat and looking harried.

"Ai-ya. I was afraid you might be out. Great, you're home. I made you three curio cases and brought them over in a three-wheeler. They're downstairs, but don't worry. I'll carry them up for you."

"Why did you do that? You shouldn't have gone to so much trouble. Wait, Liu Yue and I will give you a hand."

"I can't let you help," Huang said as he walked downstairs. "Just Liu Yue will do."

She was half-awake when Huang knocked on the door. Then she heard Zhuang opening her door, so she shut her eyes and went back to sleep. When she then heard someone calling her to move something, she got up and ran for the bedroom door, realizing that her blouse was unbuttoned and she wasn't wearing her bra and skirt. A stuffed-up sensation down below caught her attention. She shrieked, and that reminded Zhuang of what he had done earlier. He shut the door and walked over.

"You're so bad, Zhuang Laoshi."

"What's Laoshi done now?" He feigned ignorance. "Ai, Liu Yue, what have you put down there? Trying to pickle a plum?"

"Right," she said. "A plum in sugar water. Want some?"

He went up and pressed her down to retrieve the plum, but he had to part her labia to get to it.

"It's not clean," she said when he was about to put it in his mouth.

"Every part of Liu Yue's body is clean." He took a bite before she snatched the remaining piece and put it in her mouth. They giggled.

"You're teasing me with this prank," she said. "Would you do that with Wan'er?"

"I wanted to share some plums with you, but you were asleep. You looked so fetching, I couldn't help myself."

"You don't love me anymore," she pouted. "I'm just a servant to you. She was mean to me when we argued, but instead of saying anything to her, you slapped me. No one's ever done that to me, not even my parents."

"How else could I have given her a way to save face? You were in the wrong, and you got sassy when I came home. If I hadn't slapped you and she suspected us, what do you think she would do to you? And now you're mad at me."

"Why didn't you say even a word to her?"

"She is, after all, the mistress of the house. I didn't say anything to her in front of you, but do you know what I did after you went to Wan'er's? Nothing physical, but our hearts grew more distant, while my heart is now closer to you after the slap."

"Liu Yue is a fool, and you're trying to fool her," she complained.

Plant owner Huang knocked again, so she quickly dressed and went out with Zhuang to open the door and help Huang and another man move the cases inside. He had already worked up a sweat; his shirt was dripping wet.

"Liu Yue, maids at the prime minister's house are more powerful than a county official. You work for a writer, so that makes you one, too. Mr. Zhuang doesn't have to come help me, but you should. No matter what anyone says, I'm one of the city's outstanding agricultural entrepreneurs."

"Didn't you notice that I had something in my eye that made it water?" she said before going downstairs to help with the second case.

When all the cases were in, Liu Yue went into the bathroom to wash her hands and wipe her privates with a towel, singing a tune the whole time she was in there.

"You have such a nice voice, Liu Yue," Huang said. "Why don't you come out and sing for us?"

She stopped singing. After emerging from the bathroom, she made tea and carried out the plums from the kitchen. Huang said he couldn't eat anything sour, that just looking at tart fruit made his teeth hurt.

"Too bad for you," she said. "If you don't want them, Zhuang Laoshi will eat them all. He loves the things."

After picking one out for Zhuang, she dusted the curio cases and pointed out where they should go.

"I hope you like them, Mr. Zhuang," Huang said. "A man like you, who has made so many important contributions, must have a case or two. You can't display all your antiques on bookshelves. I had these made long ago, but I couldn't find the time to come into the city until this morning, when I brought my wife to the hospital in a truck."

"The hospital? Is she all right?" Zhuang asked. "She looked fine when I saw her."

"Speaking of that, why didn't you stay? If you'd written your book there, I could have preserved the room as a cultural relic and turned it into an exhibit hall in the future. You've seen my wife, who is not a very presentable woman. She loves to talk and is lucky her mouth is made of flesh and blood. If her lips were made of clay, they'd have broken into pieces long ago. Women, especially those in the countryside, have no vision. She knows nothing about my career, let alone my aspirations. She is definitely not my soul mate. With a wife like that, I don't even feel like talking, but she won't give me a minute's peace. She's always nagging me about one thing or another, constantly raising hell, and now she's gone and drunk pesticide, a whole mugful. What could I do but send her to the hospital?"

"Pesticide?" Zhuang was stunned. "Mr. Huang, you're in big trouble. That's like poking a hole in the sky. You should be at the hospital, not bringing me curio cases."

"When I took her to the emergency room, the doctor said the husband should stay away in cases when a couple has argued and the wife takes poison, because she won't cooperate with the doctor if she sees her husband. That made sense to me, so I left a woman there to help out, and here I am. So what if she dies—I didn't strangle her. I carried out my responsibility as a husband by taking her to the hospital."

Liu Yue stopped dusting and stared at Huang wide-eyed.

"Why are you looking at me like that, Liu Yue?" Huang asked.

"Who's staring at you? I was born with big eyes."

"Your pretty big eyes are like two eggs."

"And I have fair skin, like bleached flour."

"Put some things together for me," Zhuang said, noticing her unfriendly tone. "I'm going to visit Mrs. Huang at the hospital. She treated me well when I was there."

"You want us to go together?" Huang said. "All right, then. I can show the people at the hospital what kind of friends I have."

Picking up the gifts that Liu Yue had put together, Zhuang said nothing as he got ready to leave.

"There's no need to take anything along. Who knows, she may be gone by the time we get there."

"Why must you say things like that?" Zhuang hissed.

They left together.

When they arrived at the hospital, they were surprised to see that she was sitting up eating noodles. Huang was so stunned his mouth hung open. "You, you're fine. You're actually eating?"

His wife threw the bowl at him. He dodged, and the bowl smashed on the floor. "You'd rather I was dead, wouldn't you? Well, this old lady of yours isn't going to die, so of course she'll eat. She's not going to leave all that money to a man with warts on his you-know-what."

"She's getting brassy because you're here," Huang said to Zhuang. "This is a case of an earth deity unworthy of being a god, and a woman unfit to be called human."

As he ran to the emergency room to find out what had happened, his wife asked Zhuang to sit down and shouted for another bowl of noodles, plus one for Mr. Zhuang. He begged off. "How did you get better so quickly? Did the doctor pump your stomach? If so, then you shouldn't eat anything right away."

"No pumped stomach for me. I told them I was drowsy and thought I was dying, but I felt fine when I lay down in bed. Really fine. I was just hungry."

"I see. You were just trying to scare Mr. Huang. You didn't take the pesticide, did you?"

"The doctor had the same reaction. He said I claimed I'd drunk pesticide so I'd be taken to the hospital. If I hadn't sat up to tell them I was fine, they'd have pumped my stomach, maybe even operated on me. I wasn't trying to scare him; I really wanted to die. He brought that slut home with him, and to make sure she didn't sleep with anyone else, he shaved off her pubic hair. 'Now that I've shaved you down there, no one will sleep with you,' he told her. I walked in on him while he was doing that, and he had the balls to say, 'I'm hiring her to be my personal assistant. You're no match for her. Can you write, can you perform calculations? Do you have fair, smooth skin like her?' I was so furious I drank a whole mugful of pesticide."

"What good would killing yourself do? But it's strange that you're still fine after drinking that much pesticide. Maybe you were fated to be his wife!"

"I don't know what happened. Maybe my stomach is different from other people's. The doctor was curious enough to ask the woman staying with me to go fetch my mug. They're going to analyze the chemical components of the pesticide. They have it now."

A while later Huang came back, looking listless and dejected. Zhuang asked him what was wrong, but instead of answering him, Huang told the man with him to take his wife back in the truck. She refused to go, so he went over, picked her up, and stuffed her into the truck. The man drove away, leaving Zhuang bewildered. Huang led him over to a corner and, unexpectedly, wept.

"Mr. Zhuang, I really need your help now." He got down on his knees. Zhuang reached out to help him up, but he stayed where he was.

"I won't get up unless you agree to help me."

"What are you doing? Just tell me what's going on. Of course I'll help you if I can. It doesn't look right for a man your age to kneel like that."

"You have to keep your word." Huang got up. "If you don't, it'll be me, not my wife, who will commit suicide."

"What's going on?"

"When I went to the emergency room to ask them how my wife had recovered so quickly, one of the doctors said, 'What kind of pesticide did she take?' I said, 'I'm Huang Hongbao, and she took 101, No. 101

pesticide from my plant.' Then I gave him my business card. He looked at it and asked me how much of the stuff I'd sold. I said a lot. He said, 'That's good,' and led me into the hospital director's office. The man was writing something when I came in, and he said, 'Our analysis shows that the pesticide your wife took contains no toxic components. We've already notified the relevant city government office that No. 101, the heavily promoted pesticide, is a fake, and we must stop peasants from being deceived by it.' Mr. Zhuang, how would I know it's a fake? I thought it was toxic when it was put together. Otherwise, why would my own wife use it to commit suicide, and why would I be so scared and take her to the hospital? But now that this has happened, I'll be done for if it's publicized. It will be the end of 101. You have to help me. Can't you write another article to talk up the power of the pesticide? I'll quit once I've made a little more money. Just a thousand characters will do, so long as it comes out in a paper with influence. I'll pay you ten thousand for it. I promise. Ten thousand yuan." He was so incoherent, it took Zhuang a moment to understand what he was saying. At first he was amused, but then panic set in. If the pesticide was really a fake, then what about his first article? What would the city leaders say? What would society at large think of him? Zhuang pushed Huang back down to the floor.

"You're getting what you deserve," he said. "All you had on your mind was money. Your plant was all you cared about. You didn't give a thought to the mayor or to the law of the land. You could have faked anything but pesticide. Do you realize how badly you've screwed up, how much trouble you've caused people? The farmers buy pesticide to kill pests, but it turns out that you're the pest. A gigantic pest." Zhuang was relentless. Huang let him rant. When he was finished, Zhuang was exhausted.

"What's the use of getting mad at you now? I was blind to befriend you. Here's what I think: I won't write that article, but you have to hurry over to the city government office and talk to the people in charge. Tell them what happened and write a self-criticism if you have to. Don't even think about keeping your title as outstanding entrepreneur; you can count your blessings if they don't shut your plant down."

"I'll do what you say. I don't care about being an outstanding entrepreneur anymore, but once people know about my wife taking the pesticide, who will want to buy 101, even if they don't shut me down? What's the point of keeping the plant? How am I going to make a living? The storehouse will be full of useless pesticide. What do I do then?"

"You're asking me?"

"But I'm on your board, Mr. Zhuang," Huang said.

"What board are you talking about? I wrote an article for you, and now you're hanging on to me like a drowning person grabbing someone's legs."

"I paid four thousand yuan to be on the board of the art gallery. Hong Jiang came to me on your behalf. Are you denying that?"

Zhuang silently cursed Hong.

"What about Hong Jiang? You cheated people but didn't expect to be scammed by Hong, did you? Go sue him if you want, but don't try to hang this one on me."

"That's not what I had in mind. I'm in a jam and need some advice, that's all." He whimpered. Zhuang couldn't say anything at the moment, so he lowered his head and smoked a cigarette. Then he laughed.

"You've got an idea, don't you?" Huang asked urgently.

"Your wife brought on all this trouble, so let her go and spread the word."

"Let her spread the word?" Huang fumed, "If I don't divorce her this time, you can call me the illegitimate child of a teenage nun!"

"If that's what you have in mind, then we have nothing to talk about."

"So you mean—" Huang was puzzled.

"Since everyone will soon know about your wife's failed suicide, you might as well use that as a pretext for a different kind of publicity, the more the better. While you're doing that, add some more components to the formula before telling people that your wife didn't take 101, but a newly developed product, 102, or 202, or whatever you want to call it. You tell them it was specifically produced for the benefit of families throughout the world. You see, ninety percent of the families these days are barely coping, especially those who have gotten rich in recent years, men who either keep a mistress or sleep with prostitutes. Even those without money can't avoid having lovers. Everyone is having affairs, and only the experts can keep it hidden. But even with them, how can a family live in peace? As the saying goes: For a day without peace, invite some guests; for a whole year without peace, build a house; but for a lifetime without peace, take a lover. When that happens, the betrayed spouse will raise hell, and that's where your pesticide will come in handy. If she takes it, her husband will be frightened into inaction, and no one will die. Can you imagine the demand for something like that in today's society?"

Huang smiled broadly.

"Mr. Zhuang, you are truly brilliant. This is the second time you've come to my rescue. But how do I go about making that public? If I mention the function of 102, everyone will know its function is only to scare someone, that it's not a real pesticide. Who will want to buy it?"

"That all depends on how you sell it. You have to be secretive. If you tell a man, then you can't let his wife know, and vice versa. You must promote it personally at government offices, where there are few couples working side by side. Many of these offices have private clubs for hen-pecked husbands. Why don't you go see them?"

Grabbing Zhuang's hands, Huang insisted on taking him to dinner. Zhuang declined, so Huang hailed a taxi, tossed a wad of money at the driver, and told him to take Zhuang home.

That night, Zhuang stayed in his study to work on the rebuttal. At eleven o'clock, as usual, he prepared to bed down, but the blanket had been taken back to his bedroom earlier, when Liu Yue was tidying up. So he stepped into the bedroom for the blanket before Yueqing went to bed and shut the door. With her pants off, she sat in bed flipping through a pictorial magazine. When she saw him going for the blanket, she said: "Are you sleeping in the study again?"

"I have to work overtime on the defense, and I don't want to bother you."

"Bother me, you say? Am I forcing you to sleep on the sofa?"

"That's not what I said. Why are you still awake?"

"So now you're worrying about my staying awake? Do I still have a husband or not? Why do I spend every night alone in this bed?"

"What about me?"

"You can write. Who knows what you're writing anyway," Niu Yue-qing said. "It's not the same thing."

"I told you already, I'm writing a rebuttal."

"So you can have a good time reminiscing about what you did with Jing Xueyin years ago."

"That's nonsense. I'll show it to you."

He went to get the unfinished statement for Niu Yueqing, who read a few pages before saying, "Go sleep there, then."

"Why can't I sleep here?" He tossed the blanket he had been holding to the side. "I want to sleep here."

She ignored him, but did not object when he got undressed. He crawled into bed; she poked him on the forehead.

"I hate you. I don't want to have anything more to do with you. You can come out in the open and ask for a divorce if you find me so unattractive, but don't kill me slowly like this."

"Stop that. I came here to sleep. Why can't you ever say anything nice?" He climbed on top of her. □□ □□ □□ [The author has deleted 117 words.]

"Don't kiss me." She tossed her head back and forth. "Your mouth stinks of cigarettes."

He stopped moving.

"Are you just humoring me?"

"You really know how to kill a man's desire."

She fell silent, but with her mouth still clamped shut, she complained about pain. He reached out to pull the cord on the lamp.

"Why did you turn off the light? I've asked you to in the past, but you wouldn't, saying it was more exciting to see. Now you turn it off. Is it because I'm no longer exciting to see?"

He quietly turned the light back on, and when he was in the mood again, she said, "Did you wash up? Or did you climb on top of me without washing up?"

So he got up, went to the bathroom to wipe himself clean, and started over, but it didn't work. He told her to change positions, but she asked where he had learned all these tricks, forcing him to go back to the old way. Now nothing worked, no matter how hard he tried.

"Forget it," Niu Yueqing said with a sad face.

Feeling a hint of remorse, he was sorry. "I'm impotent," he mumbled. "How could I become impotent just like that?"

"When have you been potent over these years? You can hardly get it up and barely give me any pleasure at all. With the way you are, you have the nerve to complain about me this and me that, and all the while you can't keep your eyes off other women. They wouldn't be as tolerant as I am. They'd kick you out of bed."

Zhuang held his tongue. Breathing loudly, he turned his back to her. She turned him around to face her.

"Don't fall asleep yet. I have more to say to you."

"What else do you want to say?"

"What are your feelings about Liu Yue?"

Unsure what she was getting at, he decided not to respond directly.

"What about you?"

"We have trouble with domestic helpers. Every time we hire one, things are fine at first, but then they slowly deteriorate. Look at this one. She makes herself up like a princess and loves to shop. She no longer does a good job in the kitchen, and she argues with me at the slightest provocation. Should we let her go?"

"Do you want to fire her?" Zhuang asked.

"Not fire her. What would people say if we fired her so soon after hiring her? I'm thinking about finding another family for her. A few days ago, when my cousin came to see my mother, I mentioned Liu Yue to her, and she said we should marry her to her son. That got me thinking. Sure, Liu Yue is three years older than the boy, but it's an appropriate age, for as the saying goes, a wife three years older is better than gold. For a girl from the mountains in northern Shaanxi to marry into a suburban family would be like stumbling into a den of good fortune. I'll bet that's something she never dreamed of. And people would say we cared enough about her to help her find a family for the rest of her life."

Reassured by what he was hearing, Zhuang said, "Better not get involved in this. What could she do in the suburbs? With her looks and talent, she could easily find a husband in the city. Besides, I'm not so sure about an engagement to your cousin's son. He's a scrawny little monkey. I don't much like him. And don't forget that people in the countryside want a wedding soon after an engagement. When she's gone, how are we going to find a clean, hard-working helper like her? I'll lose face if you hire an ugly girl or a dimwit, and I won't have that. Then you'll have to do everything yourself."

"Is it her work or her face you're afraid to lose? She bought another pair of jeans today. Did you see how she tucked her blouse into the jeans and strutted around with her chest thrown out? She was showing off her thin waist and ample hips."

He got an erection listening to her, so he climbed on top and tried to enter her.

"Talking about Liu Yue turns you on, I see." She grew quiet but did not stop him. □□ □□ □□ [The author has deleted 60 words.]

He asked her again to change positions, but she refused. He wanted a little fire.

"I'm not a whore."

He got off her. "So I'm having sex with a corpse."

They fell silent and stopped moving. She moved over to touch him.

"All right, come on up."

But he didn't move, and she started belching again.

❋

The court date approached. The defendants read each other's rebuttals before consulting with their lawyers to go over possible questions that the other side might raise. They then made the necessary preparations for every one of them. On the day before they were due in court, Zhong Weixian asked Zhou Min to take the fourth version of his statement to Zhuang to look at. In return, Zhuang told Zhou to take a bottle of tranquilizers to Zhong, telling the old man to take two pills at bedtime and try not to think about anything. Zhou told Zhuang that the old man had more sleeping pills than he could ever take. For over a year, he had been relying on pills to combat his insomnia. He had been looking terrible in recent days, and when he climbed stairs, he was sweating profusely and had to stop several times to rest.

Niu Yueqing overhead their conversation.

"Zhou Min, pull yourself together tomorrow, and be sure to shave. That way you can intimidate the other side."

"What will Zhuang Laoshi wear?"

"He has a new suit, but no new tie. So I'll have Liu Yue buy a red one this afternoon."

"No need. It's not the Nobel Prize ceremony," Zhuang said.

"Just pretend you're accepting the Nobel, all right? Let the woman, Jing whatever, see what she missed by not marrying you years ago. I'll be there tomorrow. Liu Yue and Tang Wan'er both say they're going. I've also talked to Wang Ximian's wife and Xia Jie. We're all going, wearing our finest clothes, to cheer you on, give you moral support, and show the judge that the wives of Zhuang Zhidie and his friends are fairy-like beauties." She continued, "Every one of us is prettier than that Jing So-and-So. She'd be wise not to think too highly of herself, as if she were a flower who can ruin your reputation just because you slept with her."

Zhuang was fed up with his wife. He told Zhou Min to get some rest and sent her off to bed, while he phoned Meng Yunfang, asking him to come over and perform some divination.

When Meng arrived, they shut themselves up in Zhuang's study, where they talked and talked. Niu Yueqing and Liu waited up for them until 11:30, when they went to their rooms to sleep. Meanwhile, in the study, Meng kept his eyes on his watch, and at midnight, a time when the yin and yang intersected, he lit a stick of incense. Telling Zhuang to hold his breath and keep still, he held a pinch of milfoil in his hands for a moment before dividing it into six trigrams, to form the earth-water symbol. Mumbling an incantation, he scribbled it down for Zhuang.

丙寅，　巳酉，　丁酉，　庚子时

六神

• • 父母酉金 ——应	• • 子孙酉金 —— 世	青龙
• • 兄弟亥水 ——	• • 妻财亥水 ——	玄武
• • 官鬼丑土 ——	• • 兄弟丑土 ——	白虎
• • 妻财午火 —— 世	• • 官鬼卯木 —— 应	腾蛇
⊙ 官鬼辰土 —— 动	• • 父母巳火 ——	勾陈
• • 子孙寅木 ——	• • 兄弟未土 ——	朱雀

3rd heavenly stem, 46th heavenly stem, 34th heavenly stem, midnight

Six deities

Left column
- ∘ ∘ Parents—10th earthly branch—gold—corresponds to
- ∘ ∘ Brothers—12th earthly branch—water
- ∘ ∘ Officials and Demons—2nd of the earthly branch—earth
- ∘ ∘ Wife and Fortune—7th of the earthly branch—fire—seeker
- ∘ ∘ Officials and Demons—5th of the earthly branch—earth—change
- ∘ ∘ Descendants—3rd of the earthly branch—wood

Right column
- ∘ ∘ Descendants—10th of the earthly branch—gold—seeker green dragon
- ∘ ∘ Wife and Fortune—12th of the earthly branch—water—black turtle-snake
- ∘ ∘ Brothers—2nd of the earthly branch—earth—white tiger
- ∘ ∘ Officials and Demons—4th of the earthly branch—wood—corresponds to winged snake
- ∘ ∘ Parents—6th of the earthly branch—fire—unicorn
- ∘ ∘ Brothers—8th of the earthly branch—earth—red phoenix

"This is an intriguing sign," Meng said.

"Is it good or bad?" Zhuang asked.

"It's not bad. The earth-water symbol signifies one yang surrounded by five yin, to indicate taking command, which can mean trouble from competition. You are the second defendant, but you must take the lead. The fifth trigram, the apex, has Brothers—12th earthly branch—water; and Wife and Fortune, a sign of monetary expenditure. That's not surprising, since a lawsuit is a drain on finances and energy. The second trigram, Officials and Demons, likely means more trouble. But does this mean you will have more problems now or more problems in the future? Let me see. The lawsuit was caused by a written article, and that is fire with an overabundance of yang. It is going to require more effort. Kun is the yin sign, related to petty people and to women, in the southwest direction. You can probably expect more trouble coming from the southwest. In accordance with the Four Factor divination system—year, month, day, and time—the sign also refers to monetary losses."

"Does this mean there will be problems at tomorrow's court hearing?" Zhuang asked.

"The earth image also means unearthing, so it could be positive, like a mare that likes to run against the wind but has a gentle nature. Everything will turn out all right if you calmly keep to the righteous path. In this case, tomorrow's hearing probably will not completely eliminate your problems, but you should make it through and come out on top, so long as you remain pure and honest while adapting to changes in circumstances." As if reminded of something, Meng removed a handkerchief from his pocket and unfolded it, giving Zhuang a small scrap of bloodied paper to keep in his pocket. Zhuang asked what it was. Meng told him it was a Xijing practice to carry a virgin's menstrual blood to ward off evil spirits. He had gotten it specifically for Zhuang.

"I don't want that. Which girl did you ruin this time? How could it be a virgin's menstrual blood if you could get hold of it?"

"You're being unfair. These days, no one can guarantee that an unmarried girl is a virgin. But this blood is from a virgin. Well, I'll tell you the truth. Yesterday I went to the Clear Void Nunnery to see Huiming. When she went out to get water, I spotted a wad of bloody paper under her bed, which told me she had been changing her pad when I arrived. She couldn't discard it properly and just tossed it under the bed. Reminded of your court appearance, I secretly tore off a small piece for you. I can't guarantee the purity of others, but Huiming is certainly purer than most. I suspected that she was involved somehow with Huang Fude, but she probably would not have let him soil her Buddhist body. Besides, Huiming belongs to the order that is gentle yet strong-willed, and her menstrual napkin has a fine spirit."

"Gentle yet strong-willed? What an interesting way to put it," Zhuang said.

"There are many types of women: the svelte, light-skinned, elegant type; the fair, delicate type; the sallow, puffy type; and the dark, scrawny, coarse type. Tang Wan'er is the fair, delicate type. Had she been a virgin, her menstrual napkin would have been ideal."

Zhuang stuffed the scrap into his pocket.

"You've never been to court before," Meng said. "In movies they look scary, but in reality a local court is quite simple. There is a small room with three tables. The judges sit at the middle one, with the presiding judge in the center; the court clerks sit at side tables. Other tables, perpendicular to those in front, are for the lawyers. There are also two rows of wooden chairs, one for the plaintiffs and the other for the defendants. It's like holding a meeting, nothing to worry about. I'll stay home and use my mind to help you with qigong."

"I was going to tell you I don't want to go. I asked you over to see if you wouldn't mind going in my place."

"Have me go in your place? That won't work. You need a court's approval to send a proxy, and you'll have to fill out forms."

"Earlier I placed a call to the judge, Mr. Sima. He hemmed and hawed before finally agreeing to my request. He told me to write a power of attorney for you to take along tomorrow morning, and that will do it. To be honest, I don't want to see Jing Xueyin in a place like that. You're the only one who knows this. I don't want anyone to try to force me to go. You can bed down here tonight. That will give you time to familiarize yourself with my defense."

"You got me this time. I must have owed you something in a previous life," Meng said, before he shouted, "Ai-ya! Now I understand what the trigrams meant. The sign of a major figure was referring not to you, but to me."

"In that case, it's your fate and I don't owe you a thing."

Zhuang got up at first light and, after a few words with Meng, sneaked out the door. There were few people out at that hour—street sweepers sending dust flying and elderly joggers holding pocket radios to their ears. Zhuang, who had never been up that early, had no idea where to go, so he walked toward the small lane of banner makers. Vehicles were normally not allowed in the lane, where colorful banners hung on wires, a minor scenic sight in the city. It had been a long time since Zhuang had been there, so he decided to go in and take a look. He had another idea in mind: if he won the case, he would ask Zhou Min to have one made and send it to the court. When he got deeper into the lane, he saw no banners; instead, all the shop signs had been changed to "Advertisement Workshop," "Business Card Studio," and the like. Early risers were already putting up advertising signs of various types above their shops.

"What happened to all the banner makers?" Zhuang asked one of them.

"Haven't you heard the song 'Follow Your Feelings'? In the past, the Communist Party had so many meetings where banners were given out that everyone in this lane made banners for a living. Once the party started to focus on practical economic matters, the banner business went downhill. On the other hand, ad wars are everywhere, and no one goes out without business cards. The shift has improved our business ten times over."

Zhuang voiced his understanding and amazement before heading down another lane, where he had barely taken twenty steps before meeting up with the woman Liu and her milk cow. He stopped and drank some fresh milk right from the cow. When he was done, he walked off, taking the cow's lead.

"Don't do that. People will laugh at you or say I have no sense of propriety."

"I have nothing to do today, so let me lead the cow for you. It's my turn now, after drinking her milk for a year."

❋

The cow was moved by what she heard Zhuang say, but instead of snorting or flicking her ears and tail, she walked slowly, as if her legs were lead pipes. She listened as her mistress chatted with Zhuang.

"She's acting weird these days. She doesn't eat much and gives less milk than she used to. Every time we walk through the city gate, she digs in her hooves, refusing to move, as if I were taking her to the slaughterhouse."

"Could she be sick? You can't keep milking her without any concern for her health."

"You're right. I should take her to see a veterinarian."

The cow's eyes grew moist when she heard the exchange; she was not feeling well, was weak, with no appetite. She had no idea why she was so agitated about walking through the gate, except that she was reminded of her earlier days on Mount Zhongnan. It had been a long time since she had left her own kind, and she wondered what they were doing now. How refreshing the air was in the trees atop mountains shrouded in a blue mist and in the grass along the river. How crisply the birds sang and how clearly the water flowed. Were they grazing by the river, sticking out their long tongues to bring in mouthfuls of tender grass like scythes? Were they standing together atop a gentle rise, twisting and turning freely, comparing bones and muscles, sneezing, mooing? Were their long lowing sounds traveling far off to the cliffs before returning to fill the mountains and valleys with their echoes? Were they running over to an expansive grassy land, sending grasshoppers flying in all directions, while a tiny bird with a green beak stood firm on one cow's back? Did it refuse to fly away even when other cows butted up against it? Or were they raising their tails to relieve themselves, their droppings shapeless on the ground like puddles of watery mud, steaming up in the gentle sun and incurring curses from the land's owners? Did the men still use terrible language, so awful that they sounded more like they were scolding their wives or sons? Every time the cow thought about all this, she realized how much she longed for what she had not cherished in the past and could never return to now.

She recalled how everyone, male and female, young and old, had looked at her with envy when she was chosen to come to the city. They had circled her joyously, licking her head and tail with their soft tongues. She was smugly happy, of course. Even now, they might still be talking about her and envying her on their way back to the pen from the field under a starry sky. They probably tried to imagine the glorious city life as they worked the fields or rested between turns around the millstone. How could they know the loneliness, the isolation, and the indefinable distress she felt? It was true that she ate good food and saw new sights, and her new mistress did not make her work the field or carry any burdens. But she felt suffocated by the city air, with its mixture of odors from face powder, cigarettes, and sulfur, which congested her chest and made her nauseous. The hard cement road surface lacked the sponginess of newly tilled land, causing her hooves to blister and fester. What had worried her was finally happening: her strength was weakening and her personality changing; even her stomach was acting up. With a diminished appetite and a depressed mood, how could she be expected to give much milk? She wished she could yield vast quantities every day, even fantasizing that it was her milk, not water, coming out of the faucets for all the city's residents to drink and thus become cows, or at least be endowed with the strength of cows. But that was not possible. Not only could she not change the people and their temperament, she was actually slowly losing bovine traits because of her surroundings. Imagine this: she often thought about going back to the mountains, but her own kind might not recognize her, and she would likely have trouble adjusting to the life there if she were to return one day. The cow regretted coming to the city whenever such thoughts visited her, for that had led to a miserable fate and a cruel punishment, rather than honor and good fortune. She had thought of slipping away at night several times, but the new owner loved her so much that she kept her tethered inside the house, making escape impossible. And of course, there was no way she could leave without telling her owner why. How sad that she could not talk like humans; otherwise she could tell the mistress, "Please let me go eat grass and drink water in the wild. I would rather starve to death in the mountains or be bitten to death by gadflies than stay here. City life is not for cows." Every night she dreamed of tall mountains and flowing water, dark forests and vast expanses of grass and newly tilled soil. She even dreamed about running away; in her dream, she fought a leopard that was terrorizing the city, dying together with it in the end from exhaustion, after which her soul happily escaped from the city, once she repaid her owner and Zhuang Zhidie for their kindness.

But she woke up with tears in her eyes and sighed, "I'm afraid I'm sick. I'm truly sick."

With this thought, the cow's strength left her, so she lay down, foaming at the mouth, spittle dripping from her lolling tongue. Zhuang tugged at her but could not get her up, so he felt her here and there.

"The cow is definitely sick. Maybe you shouldn't milk her today. You should take her over by the city wall to graze instead," he said.

The woman looked at her cow and sighed.

"Go on with your errands, Mr. Zhuang. She's sick. After she rests awhile, I'll do that."

Zhuang patted the cow on the rump and walked off.

But he did not know where to go. He had left home early because he didn't want to hear Niu Yueqing and Liu Yue nag him about not going to court. His feet were soon sore from walking aimlessly. Then he recalled Niu Yueqing mentioning Wang Ximian's wife, who would also be at court that day. He wondered if her boils had disappeared. What would she say when she realized he was not at court? He lit a cigarette and spotted a crowd across the street. Their appearance and attire told him they were from the countryside. Some were holding saws, some paintbrushes; some were squatting in front of painted wooden signs, smoking, spitting, and whispering, their heads tucked down between their shoulders, their backs bent. Wondering what they were doing so early in the morning, he was about to walk over when three of them ran up to him.

"Do you have any work for us, sir? We won't charge you much."

It was, he realized, a spontaneous labor market; he waved them off to show he had nothing for them.

"I'm on my way to see Ruan Zhifei," he blurted out.

He spun around and hurried off, heading toward Ruan's dance hall. After reaching a bus stop, he wondered why he had told them he was going to see Ruan. In his current state, he couldn't possibly appreciate the song and dance and would end up ruining others' pleasure. Maybe he should see how the bookstore was doing or how work was coming along at the gallery. But then he changed his mind again and thought about the House of Imperfection Seekers, where he could take a nap. So that's where he went. When he passed the Clear Void Nunnery, he spotted a young nun sweeping the ground outside the gate.

"You're not doing a very good job there, young abbess. It's more like painting a beard on an old man's portrait."

She looked up, her face turning red.

"This surface makes the job hard," she said, and turned to sweep a second time.

He found her modesty and candor endearing, despite her homely appearance.

"I was just joking. Is Abbess Huiming in?"

"Oh, so you're here to see her. She's meditating. You're awfully early."

Zhuang walked in with a smile without asking where Huiming was meditating. He skirted a pond and looked into the Main Hall, but saw no sign of her. He then went to the Holy Mother's Hall, and she was not there, either, though he heard the faint sound of wooden fish being beaten. He stood still to listen carefully; it appeared to be coming from behind the pavilion with Ma Lingxu's grave marker. He followed the sound to the rear of the pavilion, where he saw a sparse stand of bamboo through which ran a brick path lined with red leafless stalks, each with a single flower that resembled a chrysanthemum. Morning mist hung over the area, as if gossamer had drifted above the path, occasionally hiding the flowers from view. After a few light steps, he spotted a small room off to the side; through the bamboo curtain, he saw Huiming seated lotus-style on a mat with a lotus embroidery. She was beating a wooden fish rhythmically and reciting sutras. He saw the outlines of a table, a chair, a lamp, and a sacred book in the dark room. Transfixed, he stared for a while, immersed in the serenity of the place. If one day a rush mat were placed beside her for him, Zhuang, dressed in black and shorn of hair, could sit by her and talk about the arcane Tao. How wonderful it would be to find such a spiritual world in this bustling city. He was lost in his fantasy when he recalled the bloody scrap of paper in his pocket, which led him further into a sort of daze. Wild thoughts ran through his head, conjuring up all sorts of possibilities: If he were to do that, how surprised would Xijing's writers and artists be? How about the politicians? Would they say the degenerate writer had finally turned repentant? Or would they say that sex-crazed Zhuang Zhidie wanted only to disturb the pretty Huiming? He did not want to make any noise as the gossamer mist rose up to his feet. With another look at Huiming, he walked away, secretly loathing his reputation. He had worked hard for more than a decade to gain fame, but in the end it had brought him nothing but trouble that was beyond his control. He had become a hypocrite, a contemptible person. He ended up back at the pavilion, where he rubbed the inscription on the tombstone and wept.

Instead of going to the House of Imperfection Seekers, he dragged himself back to his flat in the Literary Federation compound. Niu Yueqing and Liu were not back yet, so he had no way of knowing what had happened in court. With no news, he sat quietly by the phone and waited, until the clock on the wall struck twelve. The phone rang; it was Liu Yue.

"Is that you, Liu Yue?"

"How are you, Zhuang Laoshi?"

"I'm fine. How did it go today?"

"Everything went well. Jing Xueyin was the only one on their side who was articulate. That man talked so much nonsense that the judge had to interrupt him three times. Now I know why she was interested in you back then."

"What else?" Zhuang persisted.

"The arguments wrapped up for the morning and will start again this afternoon. Meng Laoshi went to buy some tape, saying he wanted to tape up the left side of his mouth and argue with them with only the right half."

"Tell him not to make jokes."

"That's none of my business. Why not let him humiliate the other side? Oh, you're feeling sorry for her, is that it? I assumed she was a raving beauty whose looks could topple a city wall. She's average looking. I have to question your taste. Really!"

"What do you know?"

"We're not coming home right away," she said after a pause. "We have to take the lawyer out to lunch. Are you listening? I knew you'd be waiting at home, and that's why I called. There are some noodles in the refrigerator. Can you make your own lunch?"

He put down the phone, but instead of preparing the noodles, he sat down and started drinking.

That afternoon, he went to the gallery to see Zhao Jingwu and told him to go to Bai Yuzhu's house and wait till the arguments were finished, then ask Bai to call Sima Gong to get his views on how it had gone. The judge's attitude was critical, no matter how convincing each side sounded at the hearing. As expected, Zhao agreed to go, but said there was no need to hurry. The afternoon hearing wouldn't be over for a while yet; it would likely be dark by the time court was adjourned. He could still make it if he went to Bai's house after five. Instead, he showed Zhuang the potted flowers he was growing. The gallery's interior was more than half-done by then. Zhao's combined office and lounge was located in a room at the rear, where all kinds of plants filled the steps and windowsills. It was the blooming season for many of the plants, and the flowers dazzled. As he looked at them, Zhuang recalled the unusual flower he had grown years before.

"The flowers are all very nice, but I don't see any rare ones."

"I can't match what you did. But you have your standards, and I have my ideas about flowers. I don't want rare plants, because one, they're too expensive, and two, they're hard to cultivate. And they don't instill pleasure; you feel like you're doing it for show. All I want from my flowers is for them to be pretty. What are flowers, anyway? In my understanding, they're the reproductive organs of plants. Humans' reproductive organs are located in the darkest spots, which is why people sneak around. The plants, by contrast, have theirs on top, which means sexual activity is the purpose of their existence. They use their vitality to grow in order to display their reproductive organs to attract bees. Many plants beautify their reproductive organs to lure bees in pursuit of an enchanting love."

"Where did you get such weird ideas, Jingwu?" Zhuang said. "You're still single because you're surrounded by reproductive organs, is that it?"

With a laugh, Jingwu invited Zhuang to sit in the little room, where three rows of pots stood on the desk by the window. In them were dahlias the size of rice bowls and green cacti the size of fingernails. Flowerpots took up even the head and foot of the bed and the floor in front of the four walls. A jade-colored porcelain vase with a dark narcissus rested atop a finely made square table in the middle of the room. Zhao had stored his furniture at his mother's place when his old residence was torn down, all but this small table and the vase, a Ming object.

"Flowers fill the room, and yet the most conspicuous spot is reserved for a plant with no reproductive organs," Zhuang said.

"Flowers are the plants' reproductive organs, and to me they're different types of women. The narcissus is not blooming now, and its flower isn't flashy even when it is. So you're going to make fun of me for favoring this one. In our Eastern tradition, narcissus is often the symbol for a pure, noble, chaste woman. But in the West, in Greek mythology, Narcissus was a beautiful young man, one who, with little sexual desire and emotion, loved no girls. One day, when he went to a spring to drink water, he saw his reflection and fell hopelessly in love with the image. He fell in and drowned when he leaned forward to embrace his reflection; his soul separated from his body, and he turned into a narcissus."

Zhuang had not heard that the narcissus was transformed from a man.

"So you consider yourself a narcissist?"

"Yes, I do. I know I'm not as handsome as the Pan An portrayed in ancient texts, but I think I cut quite a figure among Xijing's literary types.

When I look at these plants, I think about all the girls in the world, but this narcissus is my favorite. I feel deeply for the separation of its body and soul."

"I see," Zhuang said. "Jingwu, are you planning on getting married?"

"The narcissus is content to live with some fresh water and a few rocks. I do want to get married, but which flower-like woman will be mine? Zhuang Laoshi, you're a sensitive man. You know what I'm thinking. So I'll be frank with you. Could you give Liu Yue to me?"

Zhuang managed to hide his shock at Zhao's confession. He had sensed that Zhao had feelings for Liu, but had not expected him to think about marrying her.

"I can't *give* her to you," Zhuang said with a soft laugh. "She works for my family, but she's an independent person. I can't decide who she marries."

Zhao grabbed his hands.

"I just want you to be the matchmaker. She doesn't have a city residency or a career, but I don't care about that. I really like her. She's pretty, she's clever, and she's been living under the influence of your family. I'd be totally devoted to her and would never mistreat her. I know I haven't accomplished much and have no standing in cultural circles, but I will make her happy if she marries me."

"I'll be your matchmaker, but don't be in a hurry. Wait till I sound her out. I don't think it will be a big problem. Since coming to work at my house, she has read a lot and has met many people. She's looking more and more like a young lady from a fine family. So, Jingwu, you recommended her to come to work for us because you wanted me to educate her for you!"

An elated Zhao brought out a bottle and toasted Zhuang. "That's why I call you Laoshi, Teacher."

They talked about the gallery until Zhuang saw that it was getting late and pressed Zhao to go see Bai Yuzhu. Niu Yueqing and Liu Yue were in when he got home. They had both showered.

"Why did the afternoon argument end so early?"

"Mr. Zhong, the editor, fell ill an hour after we started, so the judge adjourned for the day, saying they had the basic picture and will now move to the discovery and investigation phase. If needed, there will be a second round of arguments, so we should be prepared to answer a summons to appear."

"Mr. Zhong is ill? What happened? How could he choose now, of all times, and at court? Others will think he got sick because he was losing the argument."

"The judge wouldn't make that kind of assumption. Mr. Zhong was standing there making his argument. He had written out thirteen pages and was reading it carefully, logically, and coherently. In the meantime, Jing Xueyin was sitting there, her face bathed in sweat, while the judge kept nodding his head. Then I heard a thud and looked up. Mr. Zhong was nowhere in sight. He had collapsed. People were in shock and rushed up to help him. His face was ashen, his eyes were shut. He was unconscious, so the judge had him sent to the hospital and adjourned the court. He was awake when we reached the hospital. Doctors had no idea of the cause and were conducting tests."

Zhuang had assumed it was something common, like a headache or a stomachache, and was now thrown into a minor panic by the news of Zhong's possibly serious illness.

"It looks like he'll be all right," Niu Yueqing said. "Zhou Min said Mr. Zhong was in a bad mood when he arrived at court this morning. He'd had a fight with the leadership at the Department of Culture, apparently over his job title. Zhou said he tried to make the old man feel better on the way over, but Mr. Zhong kept sighing, saying that nothing was going his way. He didn't get the job title he wanted, and someone had suffered a broken leg. I asked Zhou Min what the broken leg was all about, and he said he had no idea."

Zhuang knew, and he was about to explain it to Niu Yueqing, but he changed his mind. Instead, he voiced his anger at the Provincial Office about job titles and the leadership.

"You'd better stay put," his wife said. "I was angry when you didn't show up this morning, but now that Mr. Zhong is ill, it was probably a good thing for you not to be there. Seeing Jing face to face might have excited you. I was frightened by the sight of Mr. Zhong falling ill, and all I want now is for everyone on our side to stay calm. Anger is bad for your health. If more people get sick, that would please the Jing woman no end, and other people would cover their mouths and laugh out their rear ends."

Zhao Jingwu came in while they were having dinner, a huge stuffed puppy in his hands. When Liu Yue opened the door, he put the stuffed animal up to her neck, so elating her that she rolled around on the sofa, hugging and kissing the toy.

"That's quite a present for Liu Yue," Zhuang said. "It must have set you back sixty or seventy yuan."

Zhao was embarrassed. "I liked it so much I just had to buy it."

"Not so fast. You can't be happy unless I get something, too," Zhuang said.

“Let’s see if this makes you happy. Judge Sima said that after hearing today’s arguments, he thinks Jing Xueyin’s claim is on shaky ground. He said there’s just one sticking point. We argued that the image of the woman in the article was a composite, a generalization, and the epitome of many women’s experience, while they countered that this was just sophistry, since that is not how documentary works are written. They’re not knowledgeable enough to know whether or not documentary works can be as we said, so they will have to consult specialists and literary scholars.”

“That worries me,” Zhuang said. “Strictly speaking, documentary articles can’t be written in a fictional format, where characteristics are collective and generalized.”

“So what do we do?” Zhao asked. “Does that mean we’ll lose the case, like dropping a piece of meat just as it’s getting to your mouth?”

Zhuang said nothing for a long time. Niu Yueqing summoned Zhao to the kitchen with her eyes.

“Why did you have to tell him that?” she complained. “He was already worried enough, and you’ve just made him feel worse.”

“Come out here, Jingwu,” Zhuang shouted.

Zhao returned. “Let’s talk about something else,” he said. “I’m getting a headache thinking about this all day long. Some other time, all right? Besides, when the cart reaches the mountains, a road will open up. Liu Yue, why don’t you give the dog a name?”

“How about Gou-wu, taking the ‘wu’ from Jingwu’s name?”

“Stop clowning around. We have serious matters to discuss.” Zhuang turned to Zhao. “We have to get ahead of the court. Let’s ask some of Xijing’s writers, critics, and professors of literature to come up with arguments and opinions for the court to influence the judge’s view. Don’t do anything else over the next few days. You and Hong Jiang go get Li Hongwen and Gou Dahai to start looking up writers, scholars, and professors. Use whatever means necessary, and act on my behalf to ask them to formulate opinions that collective generalization is acceptable in documentary works. I will give you a list of names. Some will have no trouble writing what we want, while for others it may not be that easy. Don’t force them. Maybe they can write something that says pretty much the same thing. As for those who refuse to write, just ask them not to write anything to prove Jing Xueyin’s points.”

He wrote out a list and handed it to Zhao. Zhuang had Liu Yue see him off, while he said to his wife, “Without me, a hundred people would not be able to do shit in this lawsuit.”

"Yes, you're the best. You're a hero at home, but afraid to show up in court. Let's leave it at that and get some rest. I'm so exhausted I can barely move."

Liu Yue walked Zhao to the main gate, where he said, "We can get spicy hot pot with lamb's blood at the lane entrance. Let's go, my treat."

"You'll get all sweaty eating something like that on such a hot day," she said.

"Well, then, how about ice cream?"

"What's gotten into you today to make you so generous? I don't want anything. I'll walk you out past the gate as a way of thanking you. How's that?"

They walked out the gate, and stopped in a dark spot beyond the streetlight.

"Come over here, Liu Yue."

"What for? It's too dark there. I'm scared." She walked over nonetheless.

"Look over there," Zhao whispered and pointed. She looked to the spot, about ten meters away, and when she saw two people in a tight embrace in a dark corner, she lowered her head and giggled.

"Love fears neither darkness nor ghosts. Let's get closer to hear what they're saying."

She poked him.

"You've learned some bad tricks, I see," she chided him. "Go find yourself a girl on the street if you've got it in you. What's the point in eavesdropping on someone else? You rascal."

He surprised her by crying out and covering his face.

"Did I hurt you? Where? Your eyes?" She pried his fingers loose and looked at his face. He threw his arms around her and nibbled her tender face before taking off running. A taxi glided over from across the street and held her in its headlights for a moment, so alarming her that she pressed herself against the wall and spread her arms out. When the taxi drove off, she regained her composure and, to her amusement, saw that Zhao was gone. *Everyone says Zhao Jingwu is a playboy*, she said to herself. *He's actually a silly goose. Who else would run away after stealing a kiss?* Her cheek felt sore. She rubbed it as she headed back to the compound, where the taxi stopped to drop someone off. It was Zhou Min.

"What were you doing there, Liu Yue? I spotted you when the headlights were on you."

"You spotted me?" She tensed up. "What was I doing?"

"You looked lost there by the wall. I thought you were crying after fighting with Shimu. Are you all right?"

She laughed. "If she ever picks on me again, I'll move into your house and never return. Why would I cry? I'm not like you, a grown man getting all weepy in court. Did you just come from the hospital? How's Old Mr. Zhong?"

"Let's go in and talk. Is Zhuang Laoshi home?"

They went in, but Zhuang and his wife were already in bed. Liu Yue went to knock on their bedroom door to tell them that Zhou Min was there. Niu Yueqing came out in her pajamas; Zhou walked into the bedroom to talk to Zhuang. Before he was finished, Zhuang got out of bed and was crying bitterly before he finished getting dressed. The hospital had run tests on Zhong Weixian, and they thought the old man had late-stage liver cancer. Balling up his fists, Zhuang shouted, "It's all their fault, making him so angry he got sick. It's the anger."

He would have gone immediately to see the head of the Department of Culture if Niu Yueqing and Liu Yue hadn't stopped him, telling him it was too late, that everyone had gone home.

"Sick as he was, Mr. Zhong made it to court, where he passed out," Zhuang roared. "If he had died, we wouldn't have been able to do a thing for him. I'll go see the department head at home. How can they treat an intellectual like that? Is a job title more important than a man's life?"

Niu Yueqing let him go. Zhou Min, for his part, was worried that the cancer meant that Zhong might not live long enough to make the second court hearing. If he was gone, the magazine would lose its influence.

Niu Yueqing was enraged by the comment.

"Why are you saying that at a moment like this?" she said. "Are you still hoping that Mr. Zhong will attend the second hearing? I'd rather see that he was misdiagnosed and that it was a false alarm, even if that made us lose the case."

Knowing he had misspoken, Zhou Min quickly explained, "That's not what I meant. I was just saying that Mr. Zhong has suffered a serious health issue before the case is resolved."

Niu Yueqing quickly backtracked, for fear that Zhou might be unsettled by her tirade. "Zhao Jingwu just went to see the judge, and it looks like it's in our favor." She then updated Zhou Min on Zhuang's preemptive measures to take care of the problem. He had recovered enough that he offered to go back to the hospital to watch over Mr. Zhong. Saying she would go with him, Niu Yueqing told Liu Yue to stay home to wait for Zhuang to return and then make him a bowl of soup. She hurried down the stairs with Zhou Min.

As promised, Zhuang went to the department head's home, where he argued and pounded on the man's desk, as if ready for a fight. Never realizing that Zhuang could be so combative, the man did his best to explain while trying to duck responsibility. He did offer to visit Zhong that night and take care of his medical expenses, including extra pay for the caregiving staff.

"What's the point of visiting him if you can't solve his real problem?" Zhuang asked. "You could hasten his death by showing your face." He managed to scare the man enough that he went with Zhuang to see the four deputy heads. At four in the morning, he got the five of them to get together to work on a solution, reaching a decision that they would give Zhong Weixian the title of senior editor and report that to the provincial job certification office for final approval. It was only at this point that Zhuang shook hands and thanked them, at the same time asking their forgiveness for his brazenness. It was nearly dawn when he arrived home.

Later that day, around noon, all the mid-level officials from the Department of Culture visited Zhong in the hospital, bringing with them tonics and supplements. Niu Yueqing called Zhuang from the hospital to say that the patient was in a good mood after finishing a bowl of dumplings and walking around a bit. Putting down the phone, Zhuang called out for Liu Yue, who was pulled into his arms the moment she walked in. He laughed and kissed her. "I'm sweaty," she said. She took a basin of water into her bedroom to wash up, then lay naked on her bed, but he did not come to her. Instead, he left for the Job Assignment Office to tell them what had happened, with the request that they make an exception when they received Zhong's material and quickly conduct the review to approve the application. Then he called Niu Yueqing at the hospital and told her to help Zhong over to take the call.

"Mr. Zhong," he said, "you just rest and worry about getting better."

"Zhidie," Zhong said, "how can I ever thank you? Nothing is easy in the city except when it's time to die."

"We don't have to wait that long. You got sick, and everything's been taken care of."

"Yes, I'm lucky," Zhong said, "I'm truly lucky. Zhidie, they just handed me the decision to present my case to a higher authority. That decision is more effective than hundreds of doses of medication."

"The Job Assignment Office will give their approval soon. I'll bring your assignment certificate letter in its red plastic cover tomorrow, and you're on the road to recovery."

"Ah, an assignment letter," Zhong said. "An assignment letter. Is that all I'm worth? Zhidie, do you think that's all I want?" He broke down and sobbed. Zhuang, too, was choking on his tears.

Zhuang slept well that night. Liu Yue, dressed only in panties, walked back and forth outside his bedroom door. He was dimly aware of her before falling back to sleep. Even when she brushed his lashes with the tip of her hair, all he said was, "Let me sleep." Then he turned over and was fast asleep. At one point she pushed him, pulled back the blanket, and tapped him.

"Go away," he said angrily.

"Look outside," she said. "Do you know what time it is? The phone has been ringing off the hook. Dajie is getting mad. Are you going to answer or aren't you?"

He finally woke up. The sun was high on the window sash. He hurried over, picked up the phone, and sped to the hospital on his motor scooter, without washing his face or rinsing out his mouth.

Editor Zhong was lying in bed, visibly thinner, and nearly unrecognizable without his glasses. At five in the morning, he had coughed up so much blood it filled half a spittoon. The emergency doctor complained about Niu Yueqing, Zhou Min, and Gou Dahai, who were there to help with the care, saying that the patient had been in stable condition since coming to, and there was no reason he should be coughing up blood. That was a bad sign, for it could signal ruptured blood vessels in the stomach. The internal bleeding had to be stopped. "He was in such high spirits the day before that he ate dumplings and took a walk around," Niu Yueqing said. "Everyone was saying it was a miracle. How could it have turned around so suddenly?" The doctor asked what had gotten Zhong so worked up. When Zhou Min said it was about his job title, the doctor scolded them for telling him at a time like this. Even a healthy person can suffer all sorts of problems when excited. The bleeding stopped after a series of rescue treatments, and Zhong regained consciousness. He gave Zhou a key to his room at the magazine, asking him to bring him the case under his pillow. When it was brought over, he held it and sobbed. Though puzzled, no one tried to pry the case out of his hands.

"Mr. Zhong," Niu Yueqing said, "you prefer your old hard pillow over the soft one here, don't you?"

He shook his head.

"Maybe Mr. Zhong's savings are in there," Zhou offered. "Why don't you give it to me for safekeeping? I promise nothing will happen to it."

Zhong would not budge. By nine o'clock, he said he wanted to see Zhuang.

"Why hasn't Zhidie come to see me? Go find him and bring him over."

When Zhuang arrived, Niu Yueqing took him aside and whispered what this was about. "Don't mention the job title again. The doctor said he shouldn't get excited and that he mustn't cough up blood again. He won't let go of the case that was under his pillow. Does it contain his money or his bank deposit book? He and his wife never got along, so maybe he doesn't want her to have it. But we have to tell her now that he's in this condition. If he won't let us keep it for him, what would keep her from taking it? But then what's the point of us keeping the case for him if he's not going to make it?"

"Let me see him first," Zhuang said as he walked up and took Zhong's hand. "I'm here, Mr. Zhong."

Zhong opened his eyes and smiled. "I wasn't going to die before you got here."

Zhuang teared up. "Don't talk like that. Don't think about anything. There'll be a miracle, Mr. Zhong. There will be."

Zhong nodded. "That's what I thought, too. I should have been dead long ago, so I am a miracle."

A tear rolled down his cheek, nearly disappearing in the creases, leaving a shiny trail as if a snail had crawled over his face. "I'm not going to make it this time, Zhidie. I can sense that I'm dying. Do you think I'll die a worthy death?"

"It's been tough all these years, but you have lived a full life in spite of it. The social value you created has given your life great worth. You're truly a man who has lived a pure and noble life. You're better than any of us. That's why you're a miracle."

"You're better than me," Zhong said, showing signs of fatigue. He rested awhile before continuing, "But I'm finally going to have the certificate, along with this case. It's a shame I couldn't help produce the desired result with the lawsuit. People will laugh at me."

"No one would dare laugh at you. People are amazed and astounded by you," Zhuang said, noticing the color draining from the old man's face and his labored breathing. He knew Zhong would not last long, so he held back tears and asked: "Is there anything else I can do for you, Mr. Zhong?"

"Hold on, old Zhong," Li Hongwen said. "I sent a telegram to your family. They'll likely get it this morning. In a little while the head of the department will be here, and many writers have inquired about your condition. They all said they'll come see you."

"No, I don't want anyone to come," Zhong said, waving his hand for everyone but Zhuang to leave. Though they were puzzled, they had to abide by his wish. When they were gone, he handed the case to Zhuang and said: "No one lives forever, Zhidie, and I'm not afraid of dying. I just don't want someone to suffer from the grief. She wanted to come but has a broken leg, and I'll probably be dead by the time she arrives. So please give her this case, along with the issue of the magazine dealing with the lawsuit. And that's everything I have. Don't ask me who the person is. You'll know when she comes."

Zhuang took the case; it felt heavy in his hands. Sensing he was deceiving the old man, he wanted to tell Zhong everything before he died, but he could not bring himself to do it. He would rather be tormented for the rest of his life over the guilt of lying to the old man and squandering his emotional attachment than to have the man leave for another world with the despair of learning the truth. Nodding to Zhong, Zhuang watched as his body convulsed violently; he waved his hands in front of his chest as blood gushed out through his tightly closed lips. It spread evenly, like fireworks in the sky, some drops landing on the white wall while others rained down on his head, face, and body. Zhuang did not call out or wail; instead, he quietly watched Zhong, who had a series of strong spasms before a smile blossomed and slowly froze on his face.

When Zhuang walked out with the case in his arms, the others rushed up and asked, "How is he?"

"He's gone," Zhuang said as he walked down the hallway with the case and out of the building, where he stood still. The blistering sunlight stung his eyes so much he blinked several times, but he couldn't keep them open.

The others went into the room, followed by doctors and nurses. They watched quietly while the nurses removed the breathing tube from Zhong's nose and picked up the two ends of the bed sheet to tie into a knot. Two nurses pushed a gurney in and moved Zhong, now bundled in the white sheet, onto it. "Is his family here?" one of them asked. When no one responded, she asked again, "Are any of you family?"

Niu Yueqing, who was leaning blankly against the wall, suddenly roused herself. "What was that?"

"This is his sheet now, so you need to pay five yuan at the inpatient department."

They pushed the gurney out; with badly aligned wheels, it wobbled and creaked along the way. Zhuang turned to look as the gurney came down the brightly lit staircase, like a steel slab dragged out of a furnace, or a cartful of crystal from the crystal palace in a fairy tale. The gurney went down three flights of low steps, carrying a round object that rolled from side to side, like a watermelon enclosed in a sack.

❋

The Department of Culture took care of Zhong's funeral arrangements. Being unaffiliated with the department, Zhuang and others could only learn from Zhou Min what was done and make some suggestions. Zhong's wife, her mentally handicapped son in tow, went to the hospital morgue, where she pulled back the sheet for a quick look, then went outside to burn spirit money and have the son smash the filial son bowl, which contained noodles and paper ashes. Then she began negotiating with the department leadership, demanding five thousand yuan in assistance and a job for her son. That went on for three days, but Zhuang Zhidie and Zhou Min did not inquire about the results. Li Hongwen told her that Zhong had given a case to Zhuang. She asked for it, so he had no choice but to open it and show her a stack of letters. "You see, these are all business letters dealing with the editorial office. Your husband asked me to take care of them. There's no money in here."

"So he treasured letters about his job so much that he put them in a case and was still concerned about office business on his deathbed. He didn't give a damn about me or our son. Where did he spend all his money, anyway? He didn't leave us anything." She took the case with her, leaving the letters with Zhuang. He stayed away for a few days, until he heard that the eulogy was finished. He went to the Department of Culture for a copy, which he would read aloud; he made a few changes. People in the office told him not to be too emotional. "Well, then," he replied sarcastically, "I'll call together a hundred of our cultural figures for their opinion." He also drafted an obituary, which he gave to Zhou Min to be published in the newspaper. Zhou came back with the paper's response: as a party publication, it would only publish obituaries for party cadres above a certain rank. So Zhuang spent the night composing a short memorial essay and had it published in the supplement. More than a hundred people came to the department office with wreaths that day. The eulogy was approved, and it was decided to hold a memorial in the morning and a viewing two days later at the crematorium. Zhuang spent another evening composing the mourning couplets for the memorial site, suffering from a searing headache when he was finished. Meng Yunfang, Zhao Jingwu, Gou Dahai, and Zhou Min came to see him.

"Get word to as many people as possible, so we'll have a full house," he told them. "I really need to rest. Here's a mourning couplet I drafted. I didn't have time to worry about parallel word usage or a rhyming scheme. Why don't you take a look to see if I've said what needed to be said and make the necessary changes. Then buy a few yards of white gauze, and no matter what else you have to do, make sure to find Gong Jingyuan and ask him to write the couplet on the cloth. Hang it in the compound at the Department of Culture for a day before taking it to the memorial site."

The others took a look; it was a long couplet:

Do not sigh over the lack of fortune
water lilies look lovely in mud
The trees are capacious and the birds can keep warm
the winter plum bursts into bloom.
Do not laugh at the brevity of life
glowworms scatter in the dying night
The moon is lusterless and the stars hide in the dark
an autumn cicada is losing its voice.

As the others walked off in different directions, Niu Yueqing went to the store to buy black crepe for Zhong's closest friends to wear at the memorial. Zhuang was still up when she got home. Tang Wan'er was sitting by his bed, while Liu Yue was brewing ginger tea in the kitchen. The moment Niu Yueqing stepped in, Tang lowered her head to dry her tears. "Get some rest, Shimu, so you don't ruin your health. Without these friends, I'm sure Mr. Zhong's funeral would be dealt with hastily and casually. Did you see that wife of his? She barely shed a tear; she's more intent upon filing a grievance. What kind of wife is that?"

"They never got along."

"Only a ghost could get along with someone like that," Tang said, unconsciously tugging a corner of the blanket over Zhuang, a sight that stunned Niu Yueqing, who walked up to pull the corner of the blanket out and tuck it back down. Knowing she had overstepped her bounds, Tang awkwardly moved to a chair by the bed. "Back at Tongguan," she said, "I saw a performance of a funeral chant that went, 'What's good about living in this world, for you can die at any time and neither friend nor family knows about it.' I didn't quite get the sadness in the chant, but now, after Mr. Zhong's death, my eyes water whenever I think about it."

"Weren't all his friends around when Mr. Zhong died?" Niu Yueqing asked.

"Those were just friends, not the person on his mind."

"The person on his mind? Who could that be?"

"Wan'er is referring to a school friend from Suzhou, Anhui," Zhuang said.

"You knew about that?" Niu Yueqing asked Tang.

"I told her."

She glared at her husband. "You told me not to breathe a word, but you couldn't keep your mouth shut. Wan'er, everyone thought there was money in Mr. Zhong's case, but it was in fact filled with love letters that your Zhuang Laoshi wrote to Mr. Zhong pretending to be the schoolmate. You mustn't tell anyone. It would make Mr. Zhong look bad, not to mention your Zhuang Laoshi."

"What's wrong with letting people know now that he's dead? When the truth is out, people will be impressed by how Mr. Zhong and Zhuang Laoshi fought for true love," Tang said.

"Of course we all understand Mr. Zhong's heart, but if it were made known, how many people do you think would be as understanding as we are? He was, after all, a married man. As for love, he and his wife spent a lifetime together and produced that idiot of a son, so how can anyone say there was never any love?"

"Those are two different things. When I think about it at night, I feel sad for Mr. Zhong, but then I don't. With his gray hair and the beauty in his heart, he had an enviable life, except for the fact that his lover wasn't real."

"Would she have dared to come if she had been real?" Niu Yueqing asked.

"Why not?" Tang said. "If it were me and I'd known about his feelings, I'd have come and had a good cry over his body."

"You? No one can be a match for you," Niu Yueqing said, and then, sensing the inappropriateness of her words, she added, "I can't stand all this talk about a lover. A lover is nothing but a prostitute, a whore. Stop talking about this, Wan'er. It's all right for you talk about it with me, but who knows what kind of trouble we'd have if others knew about it? Liu Yue, isn't the ginger tea ready yet?"

Feeling disconcerted by Niu Yueqing's reproach, Tang stood up. "I'll go look." She went to the kitchen.

"What are you going to do with the letters?" Niu Yueqing asked her husband. "Should we put them in with Zhong when he's cremated?"

"There are six from the woman to him and fourteen from him to her, twenty altogether. Each has five to eight thousand words. I'm thinking about writing a long preface and having them published in a volume."

"You wrote the letters, but now you're referring to her, the woman. It was fake, but it's become real to you. If you had it published, I'm sure people would gossip. Haven't you learned your lesson from the Jing Xueyin incident? I hate to say it, but it seems you've lost your head since Zhong's death."

"You don't know what you're talking about," Zhuang retorted impatiently.

"You're right, I don't. I don't know a thing. But I'm afraid you know too much."

Tang was on her way over with the ginger tea, and when she heard their harsh voices, she coughed and waited until they fell silent before she walked in.

Zhuang's head still ached on the day of the viewing, so he took a painkiller before leaving for the memorial site. An unusually large number of people showed up. Wreaths filled the site and overflowed all the way outside. When the memorial was over, Zhuang insisted on accompanying the coffin to the crematorium. It took several people to stop him. One of them who knew massage techniques worked on Zhuang's head on the steps outside. Li Hongwen walked up.

"There's such a long line at the crematorium," he said, "he may have to wait until the day after tomorrow. They told us to put his body in the freezer for now."

"That won't do," Zhuang said. "Folks in the countryside can't be at peace until the body is in the ground, and for us in the city, it has to go in the crematorium. So many people came today that it would be terrible if the cremation wasn't carried out. Besides, you know your colleagues at the Department of Culture very well. If the cremation isn't done today, who will take care of it later?"

"That's what I thought. I kept telling them that, but all they said was, 'Go line up.' You're famous; why don't you go talk to them?"

Meng Yunfang came running over from the crematorium. "Problem solved," he said.

Zhuang asked how he had managed to talk the people around.

"I saw a red sign saying 'Special treatment for intellectuals.' You see, the government is promoting respect for knowledge and talent. This place knows to respect intellectuals."

Saying that he hadn't seen the sign, Li complimented Meng on his sharp eyes. The three of them went over and said that Zhong Weixian was a highly regarded intellectual who should be moved ahead of others.

"Intellectual?" the man in charge said, "Can you prove it?"

"He was editor-in-chief of *Xijing Magazine*," Zhuang said.

"Got any proof?"

"What proof? Do you mean you have to bring an ID for a person to be cremated? Can't we vouch for him?"

"This is Zhuang Zhidie you're talking to," Li said.

"What does he do? There are one-point-one billion people in China, and I can't remember all their names. What office do you work for?"

"You mean you don't know who Zhuang Zhidie is? He's with the Writers' Association," Li said.

"Riders' Association? There are intellectuals among riders? We only accept IDs for high-ranking positions, like professors or chief engineers."

"It doesn't matter what I ride, but the deceased did have a high-ranking position. He was a senior 'editor,' not a 'creditor,'" Zhuang said.

"You've got more of a temper than me! I need proof."

They could only stare wide-eyed. Zhuang told Li to get the head of the Department of Culture, who came to tell the man that the deceased was truly an editor, a high-ranking intellectual who died before he got his ID. He would vouch for him, leaving his name and phone number for the man to check. The man told him to write a memo. When that was done, he asked for the seal from the Assessment Office, saying that since there was only one crematorium in Xijing, people sometimes posed as leading cadres or intellectuals when there were too many bodies waiting to be cremated.

"I've sent too many like that into the fire. You can't put anything over on me, because I know what the Assessment Office seal looks like."

Left with no choice, Li Hongwen and Gou Dahai raced off in the department head's car to have the memo stamped with the Assessment Office seal. About an hour later, they came back happily, one of them waving a red plastic certificate holder. "The Assessment Office made an exception and issued the certificate as soon as they heard about the problem."

Zhuang walked up to get the certificate to show the man, who wordlessly wheeled Zhong's body to the front and pushed it into the furnace with a long hooked pole. Zhuang gritted his teeth as he watched, then abruptly tossed the little red pamphlet into the furnace before spinning around and walking out of the memorial auditorium, getting on his motor scooter, and tearing down the street without a word to anyone.

❋

Zhuang did not feel like seeing anyone for two weeks. Tang Wan'er sent several notes with her pigeon; he caught the pigeon and took off the notes, but sent the bird back without a response. But his plan to stay home was disrupted by so many visitors that he got on his motor scooter to roam the lowland redevelopment area early each morning after drinking milk from the cow. He wasn't really sure why he was there, but he watched a group of old-timers squatting on a dirt mound chatting, accompanied by the roar of a bulldozer razing crumbling walls. They talked about the lowland, where there had been several brothels, one of which was called the Duck Pit. The prostitutes at the Duck Pit were cheaper than those from Yingchun Pavilion, who could sing and dance. Visitors to the Duck Pit were usually horse grooms, colliers from Mount Zhongnan, or manual laborers from north of the Wei River transporting touch paper, porcelain ware, cotton, and tobacco on the backs of mules. The women were so cheap they could be bought with a bowl of wontons, and the men could satisfy their needs and warm their feet in the women's arms all night long. The old-timers also talked about a cotton fluffer who used to live around there somewhere and pounded used cotton with a club, his back bent all day. He was so poor he couldn't afford a hat, so he wrapped a colorful headscarf of his wife's around his head, leaving the tips of his ears to freeze, to the point that they shriveled up. But he seemed quite content. He would bang the strings on the cotton-fluffing frame while his feet tapped along with the rhythm his hand created. The man and his wife were the perfect match: a cracked wok with a dented ladle. She had been with a performing troupe from the midwestern loess, playing the clappers, which was known as banging the pigskin. Once she was married, she stopped doing that, but the moment her husband started fluffing cotton, she sang a piece from *The Butterfly Lovers* in a creaky voice: "Squatting to pee, the women write essays; standing to pee, the men wet walls like dogs." The old-timers also gossiped about the Lu Family Spicy Noodle Shop, a small place renowned for its pure Yaozhou peppers. Old Man Lu was a hunchback who had produced a beautiful daughter who was later taken by an army officer as his concubine. Her father got rich and stopped selling noodles; instead he brewed a pot of tea early every morning to sip at his lane entrance. For some reason the officer's concubine came home one day and hanged herself from the red toon tree in the backyard, a great loss of face for the father, who then sold the house and moved away. Three more families moved in, one after the other, but within two years the wives had all hanged themselves. Zhuang listened to them without going up to ask for details or inquiring whether there were other unusual events or people in the area; instead, he was curious about why these old-timers were so interested in these stories. Why did they appear so attached to the place now that the redevelopment was underway, though they might have complained about the lack of progress before? Later, when they started a game of mahjong, he saw them shuffle the tiles and swat their heads and faces; one of them grumbled, "What's going on here? Why am I itchy all over? How did my skin become so delicate in my old age? I'll have to buy a scratcher tomorrow." Zhuang was amused, but then he began to itch; there were no mosquitos around, and the itch was worse than a mosquito bite, creating such a burning pain that he decided to go home. He went out again the next day; there were noticeably fewer people on the street, and the faces of nearly all of them were covered with scarves, like people in Beijing protecting themselves against a sandstorm in March. He stood there and watched with a smile until he was itching all over. He rolled up his sleeve and saw patches of red bumps on his arms. When he took a closer look, he discovered two white specks on his arm, like dandruff, but the spots itched and ached as the dandruff turned red and three-dimensional. Some kind of insect, he saw. He took off, scratching himself all the way home. Niu Yueqing, who had come home early, blocked him at the door and told him to take off everything but his underwear before coming in. Once he was inside, she disinfected him in a tub.

"What's the hurry?" she said as he tried to get away. "Do you want those bugs to suck your blood dry?"

Zhuang asked her what was going on.

"It's horrible. Xijing is on the verge of a plague. No one knows where these strange bugs came from, but the leaves on the trees to the north of the west gate have been chewed up so badly they look like nets. It's scary the way the bugs fly around. Everyone's saying it's a bad sign. Shanghai is having an epidemic of hepatitis A, and the bodies are piling up. The bugs here in Xijing may be worse than hepatitis A and could take down half the population."

Liu Yue was bitten in five spots when she went out to do the grocery shopping, so she took off her clothes to be disinfected when she came back. Standing naked before a mirror in her room, she dabbed the spots with a medicinal ointment, then rubbed her eyes without washing her hands, which stung them badly. She got dressed.

"So that's what it is? They bit me in five spots, and I got a rash."

"Even the bugs are drawn to Liu Yue's tender skin," Zhuang said.

"You get what you deserve," Niu Yueqing said. "In order to look pretty, you walk around in a super-short miniskirt and show off your stumpy legs."

Peeved, Liu Yue turned and went back to her room.

"Look at her," Niu Yueqing said. "Not even a farewell fart before she left."

"No one would like to hear what you just said," Zhuang said before shouting in the direction of Liu's room, "Liu Yue, use soap on the rash, that'll stop the itch. What's the date today? I have to remember this phenomenon. Xijing has magic sacks and supernatural covers, so how did we get these damned bugs?"

"The more you back her up, the worse I look. Is that what you want?"

Zhuang just smiled and ducked into his study. Later in the evening, the three of them sat quietly watching TV, on which the head of the city's Sanitation Bureau showed up to talk to the residents about the bugs. It turned out that when the old houses were torn down in the lowland area, bugs that had dried up from near-starvation were released from cracks in the walls to fly around the city. They were revived once they fell on animals and humans. But the residents had no reason to panic and should ignore all rumors. The city's Sanitation Bureau had sent out cleaning teams to fumigate the area. The pestilence would stop soon.

"So those are bedbugs." Liu Yue heaved a long sigh. "Their bite gives you a heartache."

"What are you talking about, Liu Yue?" Niu Yueqing asked.

"I was just saying that bites from the bugs are unnerving."

Niu Yueqing did not respond to Liu's comment; instead she wrinkled her nose and said, "What's that foul smell?"

"Did Zhuang Laoshi forget to wash his feet again?" Liu said.

"It's not from stinky feet. The bugs only bite stinky things, and your Zhuang Laoshi has no bites on his feet."

Zhuang laughed. "Listen to you two. Where did you learn to bicker like that?"

The women laughed.

"I'm no match for Liu Yue," Niu Yueqing said.

"You're too modest," Liu said. "There's a lot I can learn from you."

"You have no manners, and you argue with me all day long."

"It's no fun if we don't argue. I wouldn't bother if it were someone else."

That pleased Niu Yueqing so much that she wrapped her arms around Liu and said: "We are karmic enemies."

The phone rang. Liu Yue got up to answer, not missing a beat in her retort: "I'm not your karmic enemy. That would be Zhuang Laoshi. You have a moon [yue] in your name and so do I, but there can only be one moon in the sky, so with two moons, we can only be rivals."

The call was from Shuangren fu. When Niu Yueqing heard that it was from her mother, she told Liu Yue, "Ask her if the bugs have gotten to her."

"Why would I have been bitten?" she said to Liu Yue. "I knew they were bedbugs days ago, after your uncle came to tell me they would bite city folks. Do you know why there are bedbugs? Your uncle said they were wiped out decades ago because the spirits in charge protected the residents. Now all those houses are being torn down. Know who built them? The spirits. When they came to raze the houses, not a single descendant from the families offered a sacrifice to their ancestors, who could not watch over their offspring on empty stomachs. So it's no wonder the bedbugs are biting people. Spirits of dead ancestors inhabit them, and they will suck the blood of anyone who forgets to offer a sacrifice. Was your dajie bitten? Zhuang Laoshi? The bites are from Uncle, for no one burned any spirit money for him on his birthday."

"Are you having another episode, Granny?" Liu Yue asked. "Has this become a people city or a ghost city? How about catching one for me?"

"I can't catch one in the daytime. Not when they're up high in the sky. Maybe if you gave me an airplane. They're everywhere when it's overcast or raining, or pitch-black. People come and go in the world. None of you has ever seen your dajie's granddad, but I saw him when I was married into the family. He looked just like your uncle, except he had a full beard. When your uncle got old and Granddad's old friends came to visit, they all thought it was Granddad. They kept calling him Desheng, Desheng. That was his nickname. Your dajie looks just like Uncle now, a smaller version. We're made that way, as if we came out of the same mold—the old are enlarged versions of the young, the young are shrunken copies of the old, but they all become ghosts after they die. That's why there are so many spirits. Tell your dajie that she needs to see Uncle. When she comes back here, I'll get him to talk to her at night."

"I don't want to hear any more," Liu Yue said. "No more. I'll call Dajie."

Niu Yueqing took the phone.

"What are you talking about now, Mother? We'll come see you tomorrow. Now, get a good night's sleep."

The old lady made a resentful noise over the phone. "So that's how you talk to me. Let me tell you, you can come over if you want, or stay away if that's how you feel. Your foster sister came. She's pregnant and has morning sickness the moment she sits down. But you don't even come to see her. She said you promised to marry Liu Yue to her son, so why has nothing been done? She came specifically for an answer."

Niu Yueqing's feelings were a mix of happiness and anxiety. She was happy about the cousin's pregnancy and anxious about Liu Yue's marriage. "We'll talk about it tomorrow when I get there." She hung up and asked Zhuang to come into the bedroom.

"Is Mother up to her old tricks?" Zhuang asked.

"Still the same old batty things." Niu Yueqing laughed.

"What's the good news? Why are you laughing like that?"

"My foster cousin came. She's expecting."

"She's here again? What's she expecting?"

"You seem to know everything under the sky when you write your novels, but in real life you're a total idiot."

"She's pregnant? I told you I don't want this."

"You don't want it? Don't you think I'd rather have one myself? Let's have one of our own if you can. Now that it's come to this, what I want counts more than what you say."

Zhuang got up angrily and started for the door, but she stopped him.

"There's one more thing for you to decide. My cousin is asking about Liu Yue. They want a definitive answer."

"When you go over tomorrow, tell Mother not to meddle and muddy the water. Liu Yue wouldn't want to marry your cousin's son. The other day, Zhao Jingwu came to me with a proposal; he wants to marry Liu Yue, and asked me to be the matchmaker. Wouldn't it be better if she married him?"

"Zhao Jingwu? Jingwu has higher standards than that. Why would he be interested in Liu Yue? Did you say anything to her?"

"Not yet. I'm waiting for the right moment to sound her out. So don't mention it yet."

"I won't. I'm not a busybody. You like her too much to let her go, and you think my cousin's son is beneath her, so go ahead and marry her off to whoever you want. What would it matter to me if someone living in a mansion fell for her and she became a palace consort? My views mean nothing in this house. Even a maid has more say than I do."

She went to Shuangren fu the next day, leaving Zhuang at home. He heard the sound of flapping wings and knew it was the pigeon. When he went to the balcony, Liu Yue had already caught the bird with a laugh. "Shameless," she said after reading the note. "So shameless!"

Zhuang took a look at the note, which turned out to be blank. Threes short hairs had been pasted on the paper beside a red circle. "What's this?" he wondered, pretending to be in the dark. "How is this shameless?"

"Do you think I'm that stupid? The red circle is lipstick. What kind of hair is this? It's curly. The shameless one didn't need to write anything.

She just sent something from the top and something from down below. She's asking you over."

"How did you recognize the hair?" he whispered.

"You thought I wouldn't know because I don't have any? They say a girl with no hair is as good as gold."

"I never heard that. A hairless girl is a white tiger who will bring a man harm."

Unhappy, she got up to leave, but he picked her up and carried her into the bedroom to take off her pants. Still upset, she grabbed hold of her pants and wouldn't let go.

"I'm a white tiger, and if I harm you, who's going to fuck Tang Wan'er?"

"Things are bad enough already, so what's to be afraid of?"

"So I have to let you do it whenever you want? I went to you the other day, when you pretended to be asleep. I'm not in the mood now, so don't try to force it on me. You took my virginity. Now you come to me whenever you feel like it. I'm still single. How am I going to find a husband?"

Seeing that she was not feigning anger, he told her about Niu Yueqing's plan to marry her off to the son of Niu Yueqing's cousin and about Zhao Jingwu's marriage proposal, as well as his own effort to convince Niu Yueqing to pair her with Zhao. When he asked her what she thought, she began to sob.

"Why are you crying? Are you upset because I didn't bring this up with you before?"

"I'm crying out of self-pity, about my terrible fate, my lack of self-awareness, and my naïveté." She went to her room and sat blankly as tears continued to stream down her face.

After puzzling over the girl's wrenching comment, he realized that she was pinning her hopes on him. Was she hoping to replace Niu Yueqing? That thought made her look calculating, which he found repugnant. He decided he would not try to talk her around; instead, he went into the living room to shine his shoes. She walked out, leaned against the wall, and said, "Zhuang Laoshi."

Zhuang kept shining his shoes.

"Zhuang Laoshi," she called out again.

"Zhuang Zhidie is no longer a worthy teacher to you. He's a horrible person, a crafty old scoundrel who took advantage of naïve Liu Yue."

She laughed. "Was I wrong to say that? Wasn't it because I was naïve? I'm just a girl. Why can't I have thoughts about being with you? I now understand that I'm just a maid from the countryside. What do I have except for my looks? Nothing. I was too naïve to let my thoughts run wild. But I don't regret being with you, so don't think badly of me. I'll be happy to be with you as long as you want me. I'll have enough to remember for the rest of my life, no matter who I marry. All I want now is for you to tell me the truth about Zhao Jingwu. Did he really say that? Did he mean it, or did he just want to take advantage of me?"

Saddened by what she said, Zhuang put down the shoes and walked over to her. "Liu Yue," he said as he picked her up, "forgive me. Please forgive me. I want you to know that Zhao is a good man. He's young, good-looking, and talented. He's better than me in many ways. He really meant it when he asked me to be your matchmaker. I'll turn him down if you're not happy with him. I'll take time to find you a better man."

She put her arms around his neck and raised her head to kiss him. They were all over each other when a button broke loose and fell to the floor. She strained to pick it up, but he held her so tightly that her upper body was bent nearly double while her lower body was still in his arms. She shook with laughter. He felt something slippery and took a look at his hands. She was so mortified she lay motionless. □□ □□ □□ [The author has deleted 200 words.] When it was over, she said, "I can't do this anymore. What would Zhao Jingwu think of me if he knew?"

"How would he know? When your dajie comes home, tell her I've gone to lead a writing workshop at the newspaper."

"You're going to see her?"

"She's asked several times and I haven't gone. I don't know what she'll do if I don't go today."

Unable to suppress her jealousy, Liu Yue said, "Go, then. In your mind I'm worth less than one of her toes. But tell her you had me first today before she can have you."

After he left, Liu Yue sat alone turning things over in her mind: So that's what Zhao was thinking. She had always thought he was nice to her, but it had never seemed to be more than that. Zhuang did love her, but he was more taken by Tang Wan'er. If one day his relationship with Niu Yueqing got so bad they divorced, he would choose Tang over her if he wanted to remarry. Besides, she would fare worse than Tang if everything stayed the way it was; Tang was married, which gave her a good cover, while she was single and might have trouble finding a good husband. Now Zhao wanted her. He was not Zhuang's equal, to be sure, but he was a much better catch than Tang's Zhou Min in terms of city residency, money, and looks. Following that line of thought, Liu Yue suddenly felt that she was a desirable commodity, and she let her thoughts begin to dwell on Zhao Jingwu. Then again, Zhuang might be toying with her, so she mustered the courage to phone Zhao. When she hinted at Zhuang's idea, Zhao could not stop saying how wonderful it was. Now that the paper-thin barrier was broken, he loosed a string of expressions about his feelings, making her hot all over. She responded with tender words of her own. He said he loved her; she responded with such intensity that she reached down between her legs and was soon moaning.

Niu Yueqing came in and heard Liu Yue's voice. "Who are you talking to?"

Startled, Liu Yue broke out in a cold sweat. She put down the phone. "Just a girl calling to ask if Zhao Jingwu was here. I asked her who she was. She said she was his cousin, and she went on and on about Cousin Jingwu. So I told her your Cousin Jingwu isn't here and hung up. What was Zhao Jingwu thinking, giving our phone number to his cousin?"

Niu Yueqing heard the explanation but didn't quite believe her.

⁂

The Mid-Autumn Festival was approaching. In the past, Xijing's four celebrities would customarily get together over holidays, with a different group of three men taking their families to the fourth man's house each day. They entertained themselves with music, chess, calligraphy, and painting, followed by drinking while they admired the moon. The festivities would last for days. On the ninth day of the eighth lunar month, Ruan Zhifei sent an invitation on red paper, asking Zhuang and his wife to his place on the fifteenth. He had gotten his hands on some Hami melons and giant grapes from Xinjiang. After they enjoyed the fruit, he would hire cars to take everyone to see the lanterns at the Giant Wild Goose Pagoda, where, according to him, a new wall had been set up for visitors to write on. They would amuse themselves by reading the lousy poems by people who longed to get published but lacked a venue, and they would add their names to the wall to show up the stupid monks at the temple. A gift was included in the invitation, an enlarged copy of a U.S. dollar bill with the image of Washington replaced by a headshot of Ruan. Zhuang laughed. "Ruan Zhifei is obsessed with money. He thinks those poems on the wall are terrible, but he could probably only write 'I was here.'"

Zhuang told his wife that he didn't want to go anywhere over this holiday and that she should decline all the invitations by phone the next day, telling everyone that he had left on a long trip. By the time the fourteenth rolled around, he regretted turning down Ruan's invitation. So he wrote out a shopping list for Liu Yue to buy some gifts for his friends.

"Dajie already told them you're away and can't make it back on time," Liu Yue said. "If you send gifts now, they'll be upset that you can't be bothered to join them when you're right here in Xijing."

"Just tell them it was Dajie's idea."

Liu read the list: for Ruan Zhifei, one cattie of Dragonwell tea and some spring liquor from Jiannan; for Gong Jingyuan, a bottle of Shaoxing liquor, three catties of slow-cooked mutton, and a carton of State Express cigarettes; for Wang Ximian, a jar of Nescafé, a can of Coffeemate, a pack of chewing gum, and a box of Winfong cosmetic products. "Except for Wang Ximian," she said, "they're all edibles. Why cosmetics for him?"

"Why can't men use cosmetics? You haven't seen enough of the world, so you think that's strange."

"You're right. I've seen so little that everything is strange to me. That pockmarked face of Wang's does need some powder to smooth it over. I just thought you seem to worry about too many things."

"Don't be petty. Haven't you gotten enough from me? Go deliver the gifts and then come right back. Oh, and buy a stack of hemp paper to burn for Zhong Weixian tonight."

A feeling of sadness rose up in Zhuang; the mention of Zhong reminded him of Ah-lan, then Ah-can. If only he had a gift . . . He sighed, lowered his head, and went to read in his study. A while later, Zhou Min, Li Hongwen, and Gou Dahai came by with five lawyers. The court had summoned Jing Xueyin and Zhou Min. Sima Gong had not let on whether or not there would be a second round of arguments, but Zhou Min was uneasy, so he brought the lawyers over to strategize about the second court session. The other side had raised some issues that had not been examined during the first session. They tossed around a number of possible responses but had not yet reached a consensus when Liu Yue returned. After greeting everyone, she brought out a teapot and added tea, then leaned up against the door and waved at Zhuang. He was reading a guide to nonfiction writing that some friends had provided. He got up, went over, and asked in a low voice, "Is everything all right? Did you deliver the gifts?"

She backed into another room. "Yes. Some even returned the favor." She took out a pastel yellow scarf and a small pipe. "This is for Dajie, and the pipe is for you. I don't understand why they gave you this since you smoke cigarettes, not a pipe."

"Really?" He put the pipe in his mouth and puffed on it until his mouth filled with saliva. "I can't smoke it like this. Tomorrow go out and buy some tobacco. I'll smoke this from now on."

"Now I see," Liu Yue said. "I was so stupid."

"What do you see?"

"When you smoke a pipe, it's kissing you the whole time."

"Ah, Liu Yue, I see I hired a little fox fairy, not a maid. Why don't you keep the scarf for yourself? It'll come in handy in the winter." He started to walk away.

"Don't you want to know who it's from?" she asked him.

He just smiled and went out to talk to the lawyers.

When Niu Yueqing came home from work, she invited them all to stay for dinner. She and Liu Yue went out to buy dumplings. They ate and talked and finally reached an agreement. As they were leaving, Niu Yueqing gave each of them a pack of moon cakes she had just bought, while Zhuang suggested that they all go burn paper money for Zhong Weixian. They went out onto the street to do so and then left.

"I'm sure you didn't buy that many moon cakes, Shimu." Zhou Min handed his back to Niu Yueqing. "And you've given them all away. We have some at home, so why don't you keep these for yourselves?"

"The others all took theirs, so you have to take yours," she said. "It's not a big deal. A few moon cakes can't cost as much as several meals, can they?"

"It's the Mid-Autumn Festival, and we should have invited people to a celebration. So go ahead and take them," Zhuang joined in.

Liu Yue handed the bag back to Zhou Min. "Take it. It's an order from Zhuang Laoshi. If you don't want them, maybe Wan'er would like them." He walked off with the bag. As they watched him recede into the distance, Niu Yueqing said, "Zhou Min just told me that since Mr. Zhong's death, Li Hongwen is fearful he'll be held responsible for things, so the magazine is rudderless. You'll definitely have to show up if there's a second court session."

"Let's worry about that later," he said and walked home.

Over the days that followed, Zhuang stayed home and read instead of writing a new rebuttal. The festival passed with no festivities, so Niu Yueqing and Liu Yue, who wanted some excitement, decided to go see the chrysanthemum show at Xingqinggong Park. After they returned, she phoned Meng Yunfang and invited him over. He spent the rest of the day there, while Niu Yueqing and Liu Yue went to Shuangren fu. Meng had a suggestion for Zhuang: Since the case was not going to be resolved any time soon, constantly living on pins and needles served no one. He would organize a literary salon at the House of Imperfection Seekers, and Zhuang would be the speaker. Zhuang replied that he didn't feel like it, that everything seemed to have lost meaning after Zhong's death.

"Others can say that, but not you," Meng said. "What a pity for someone of your status to be so passive and negative."

With his head in his hands, Zhuang said that he had indeed fared better than many other people, but in name only. Now that he was living a different life, why not keep at it? It was no small feat to find a place like the House of Imperfection Seekers in Xijing, and he wouldn't mind joining them if Meng had friends over, but he had nothing to share and would not be a good speaker. Meng encouraged him to at least show up at the gatherings.

He invited some people who were into metaphysics to talk about qigong, but not only were their friends puzzled, they thought the speakers were strange, that they must suffer from some sort of mental disorder and lived with a different mindset, which was why they could produce qi to cure illness and predict the future. Zhuang's circle of friends decided to let them keep talking, for it was amusing, if nothing else. One day, Meng invited another "guru," a man who claimed to belong to the Mount Tian School. He opened with a self-deprecating remark about his inferior powers. According to him, his master, who was 125 years old, could rise up with the wind and travel under the ground. After looking at Xijing from a distance one day, his master concluded that the one-time capital should be a site with a denser concentration of unusual talent, but there was too much yin circling the city, making it impossible to see if that could be so. So the guru was sent by his master to check out the place. After his arrival, he met all sorts of people, including Master Zhixiang at the Yunhuang Temple, but that only made him lament the fact that true masters, like his, had yet to descend to the mundane world. Someone asked him to share his views about the future world. That spurred him into a seemingly endless monologue: how the universe had started; how the sun and moon were formed; Darwin's theory of evolution; the idea of being one with nature promoted by Laozi and Zhuangzi; the mystery of the Egyptian pyramids; the riddles in the rock paintings on the Yunnan-Guizhou Plateau; the effects of the moon's phases on ocean tides; the impact of the tides on women's menstruation; how the man from Qi worried that the sky would fall, something that had already happened once; and how Mao Zedong practiced qigong, which was why he could make a million Red Guards cry with a wave of his hand at Tiananmen Square.

Though what he was saying seemed absurd and preposterous, his listeners weren't sure what to think of him, since he peppered his talk with modern technical terms. "What is a philosopher?" he demanded. "And what is a man of letters?"

No one had an answer, so he smiled. "It's simple. A philosopher knows everything before everyone else, a shepherd sent by God to watch over the others. As for you, the writers and poets, you are at best sheepherding dogs."

"The master is a font of knowledge," someone in the audience said. "You're so different from others we've met before, who could only spout nonsense and crazy ideas."

"Don't call me master. I'm just my master's disciple. There's nothing I loathe more than those who claim to be qigong practitioners but actually deceive others with their tricks. Do they know qigong? They do. But qigong is in the lowest rank of our field of practice. An elementary school student has a fountain pen in his pocket and a middle-school student has two, but can we argue that the more you know, the more fountain pens you need in your pocket? Writers like you have no pens, so what do you call those who have three or four pens in their pockets? Pen repairers! Chinese traditions are the best in the world, but sadly, the heirs to these traditions have a most annoying problem, and that is boasting. As the saying goes, He who is all talk does nothing, he who does things makes no noise. The true masters have a vapid appearance but great intelligence. Nowadays in Xijing there are many magic power sacks and magic belts. Television ads peddle products to strengthen men's kidneys and increase their sexual prowess, or to cure women's ailments they cannot talk about. In the parks and along the city wall, you see people breaking stone steles with their heads and splitting bricks with their bare hands, but can that solve humanity's problems? Those are insignificant skills that real men would not deign to practice."

The others turned to look at Meng Yunfang, who was red in the face from embarrassment. "What you're saying is all well and good," he said, "but too lofty and distant, for we are just ordinary people who would like to know what will happen to Xijing in the future."

The man was quiet, as if unable to extract himself from the scene he had just set. After a moment he finally said, "I don't possess the power to know that." That was met by sighs all around. "But," he continued, "I can receive messages from outer space. Let's give it a try." Scrunching up his shoulders and puffing out his chest, he relaxed, took off his shoes and belt, and sat in the lotus position, head down. Making the shape of a lotus flower with his fingers, he randomly rattled off a string of numbers for about a quarter of an hour before opening his eyes. "There will be a drought in Xijing. Are there any signs of that?"

"Well, we've heard that Xijing once had eight rivers, but only four are left. The factories in the western suburb often have to cease operations due to water shortages, while residents in the northwest could not get any water to the second floor all summer long. Everyone lives in multistory modern buildings, and yet they must keep storage vats for water that will run for a few minutes only in the middle of the night."

The man's face came alive. "That's it." He asked everyone to face north, avoiding the south, the direction of Mount Zhongnan, where masters in the mountain would interfere with their field of qi. Then he continued to receive transmissions from outer space before blurting out something that scared them out of their wits: "All of Xijing will sink in a few years."

Zhuang Zhidie, who had been listening attentively, fidgeted, as the man was sounding increasingly outlandish. Using a bathroom visit as an excuse, he walked out; when he heard two girls in the next room giggling softly, he went in to ask, "What are you two silly girls laughing at?"

"Xiaohong passed gas when the master was chanting his incantation. She was afraid of making a noise, so she forced it to come out real slow in tiny bits. It was so funny, we had to run out here to laugh."

The second girl blushed and put her hand over her friend's mouth. "Don't listen to Cuiling. She's full of nonsense."

"Don't overreact, Xiaohong. It's just a fart in the wind," Zhuang said, sending the girls into another laughing fit. With a straight face he looked out the window. Dusk was descending.

Their giggling finally subsiding, the girls walked up to the window. "You're so funny, Zhuang Laoshi. We recognized you but didn't dare approach you," one of them said. "We came to listen to you talk about art, but the master monopolized everything."

"Listen to me talk about art?" Zhuang said. "You two are the essence of art." He leaned against the window to gaze at the night scene outside. The distant streets and lanes were brightly lit, and people could be heard talking, but the large area to the right was shrouded in darkness and completely silent. One of the girls asked him what the area was. Zhuang told them it was the Clear Void Nunnery, where the lights were turned off when the worshippers left. The dozen or so nuns had probably gone to bed a while ago.

"What's that?" Xiaohong yelled out.

Zhuang saw a red light flicker in the dark; it went out but flickered again. He had no idea what it was, and the girls were frightened, saying it was a will-o'-the-wisp. The others came out and asked the master to take a look. He did so, then asked about the place. Meng told him it was a temple and that the red flicker seemed to be coming from the bamboo grove behind it. But the grove was usually deserted, even in broad daylight. No more red flickers came. "I said too much today without knowing there was a temple nearby," the master said. "It must be an ancient one, with buried Buddhist relics reacting to my talk." Meng said the temple, built in the Tang dynasty, indeed had a long history, but he knew of no objects there, except for Ma Lingxu's grave marker, which had been dug up during the renovations. "Could it be her spirit?" The master made a gesture in the form of a lotus flower before saying there might be more red flickers, but he could not stay long. He left.

The others went back inside, while Zhuang stayed with the girls to gaze out the window. There was another red flicker. Saying that the master was right in his prediction, Cuiling was so frightened she wanted to close the window. Just then it flickered again, and a large red light drifted forward to meet with the first red dot. "How many did you get?" a shrill voice asked. "Why did it take so long?" The larger red flicker drifted away, followed by a woman's crisp laughter. "What Buddhist relics?" Zhuang grumbled. "It's the nuns out catching fireflies." Inside, no one laughed as they stared at each other, while doubts about what the master had said crept in.

"We might gain some inspiration from him," Meng said.

"So who do you plan to invite for the next lecture, the shepherd dogs?" Zhuang asked. Everyone had a good laugh before going their separate ways. Zhuang and Meng decided to spend the night there. As they were getting ready for bed, Zhuang said, "Huiming must know a lot about these things. For a while, you were talking about inviting her, but no more. How come?"

"Every time I went to see her, the son of the chairman of the People's Consultative Conference was with her having tea. She was aloof. When I asked how she'd come to know the Number Two Knave, she told me not to use that awful term. She even said she would introduce me to Knaves One, Three, and Four. Why would I want to know them?"

"You're jealous?" Zhuang laughed. "That's better, actually. I was worried that the city might have one less real nun and gain a powerful woman if you spent too much time there."

Meng turned off the light, and they passed the night without another exchange.

❋

On the twenty-second, Hong Jiang came with an account book to go over the revenue and expenses for the previous period. After checking, they realized they hadn't lost money, but they hadn't made much, either. Hong mentioned several items that needed to be taken care of, with the expectation that things would improve the following month. Then he brought out a bolt of light yellow silk from Hangzhou sprinkled with tiny pastel green flowers, two bottles of liquor from Sichuan, a package of swallows' nests, and a carton of Japanese Seven Star cigarettes. "I spent several days in Xianyang during the Mid-Autumn Festival, Shimu," he said with a broad smile. "I couldn't make it here to wish you a happy holiday, so here I am today with these gifts. It's not much, but I don't think you need any more moon cakes, snacks, or canned goods. They're nothing special. This package of swallows' nests isn't too shabby; it's from a bookseller in Guizhou, a token of his gratitude after I helped him get a publication permit number at the beginning of the year, when he came to Xijing. A delicacy like this is too good for me, so I brought it over for Shifu, a good tonic for his health."

"Why are you doing this?" Niu Yueqing said. "I don't know anything about running a bookstore, and Zhuang Laoshi washes his hands of everything, even though he's the nominal owner. We have to rely on you. We've never expressed our thanks, while you're always giving us gifts on holidays. You're like a brother now, so please don't act like an outsider."

"That's not how it is. I do know a bit more about running a business, but without you two, I'd be out selling mutton skewers. These are not from me alone; someone else pitched in."

"Who?" she asked. "It's even worse to receive gifts from people you don't know. Your Zhuang Laoshi can't do anything but write. When friends like Meng Laoshi come, they help themselves to something to eat, which is a sign of friendship. Everyone else comes to ask Zhuang Laoshi for help. What can he do? And when he can't do something, he complains about me."

"There's nothing you need to do. The man just wants to invite you to a meal."

She took a look at the silk fabric, and saw a card embossed in gold. She opened it: "With the permission of the national marriage code, we have become husband and wife to share our happiness forever. To express our gratitude for your kindness and generosity over the years, we cordially invite you to a banquet to be held at ten in the morning of the twenty-eighth of this month." In the host column were two names: Hong Jiang and Liu Xiaoka.

Stunned, Niu Yueqing let out a cry. "What's going on, Hong Jiang? Don't you have a wife and a child? When did you get a divorce? Who's this Liu Xiaoka? When did this happen?"

"It's a surprise, I know," Hong said with a smile. "I didn't want to bother you and Laoshi with this. In fact, I wanted to mention it several times, but changed my mind. The lawsuit had everyone on edge, so I decided to keep it quiet. You know my former wife and I were always fighting. We simply couldn't get along and didn't have a day of peace together. So we said to each other, 'Let's split up,' and we did. I thought I'd be a bachelor again after the divorce, but my friends said I'd ruin my health running around taking care of the business if I didn't get married. I might even become a different person. Besides, those who didn't know might even say I had physical issues that caused my wife to divorce me. And they mentioned the girl we hired at the bookstore. I thought it over and decided it wasn't a bad idea. Since she works there, we could look after one another, so we went ahead and filed our marriage registration Luckily she's an only child with a house, so you can say I married up. We went to see her grandmother over the holiday. Her uncle, who works in Sichuan, brought these two bottles of liquor for us. Xiaoka insisted that we give them to you. I know you can't drink hard liquor, but you must try this."

"Liu Xiaoka?" Niu Yueqing said. "I can't tell the three girls at the bookstore apart."

"I know which one it is," Liu Yue, who was smiling the whole time, cut in. "The slender one with sloping shoulders, isn't it?" She stroked a finger on her face to shame Hong, who replied with a smile, "You're so wrong, Liu Yue. It's the tall, long-legged one."

"A new girl!" Liu shouted.

"Stop the nonsense, Liu Yue," Niu Yueqing said. "You don't know anything. They're all pretty, and I can't tell who's who. I must congratulate you, now that you went ahead and got married. But I'm not happy that you kept us in the dark about something so important."

"That's why you're the first to get the invitation. You have to come, no matter what. Liu Yue, too. You can be a bridesmaid."

"I'm not going," she said with a pout. "I'm not going to be the bridesmaid, either. I know you want ugly me there to highlight your beautiful bride."

Hong complimented Liu Yue on how articulate she'd gotten after only a few months in the Zhuang household. She might even be a writer one day.

They chatted for a while before he got up to leave, repeating his request for them to attend the banquet. "It won't start until Laoshi and Shimu are there."

"Where is Zhuang Laoshi?" Niu Yueqing asked after Hong left. Liu Yue said Meng had invited him for a drink. After putting the gifts away, Niu Yueqing sat down to think about what kind of wedding presents they'd take to the banquet. In the afternoon, an inebriated Zhuang returned and went to the toilet, where he stuck his finger down his throat and threw up. Niu Yueqing told him to get some rest, without mentioning Hong's marriage. Later that night, when Zhuang got up to read in the study, she went in, closed the door, and told him.

"The girl with the long legs?" Zhuang was equally dumbfounded. "I don't think I've seen her more than twice. I didn't pay much attention when he asked to hire some salesgirls. Later Zhao Jingwu told me that Hong's standards are higher than you'd find for a model. He detailed the required height, weight, and skin condition, as well as their BWH measurements."

"What's BWH?"

"Bust, waist, and hips. So he was already thinking about finding someone for himself."

"With his sallow skin and puffy face, how did he manage to get remarried so easily after the divorce? What did the girl see in him?" Niu Yueqing wondered.

"Young people these days don't think twice about getting a brand-new family. You're too old-fashioned to understand that."

"His first wife wasn't very refined, but she seemed trustworthy. The saying has it that one day as husband and wife portends a lifetime of affection. How could it end so abruptly? I can't understand it. But it's none of our business, so why worry about it? What concerns me is the bookstore. Won't the two of them run it from now on?"

"We certainly can't fire the girl. Maybe you should drop by to check things out more frequently and make sure the accounts are in order. But don't let on what you're up to. He may be sincere and aboveboard, and we don't want to offend him. No matter what we think about the marriage, you should send wedding gifts, and not something cheap."

Niu Yueqing took out a sheet of paper. "Let's draw up a list."

"Can't you handle it? Why bother me with that?" Zhuang said impatiently. She swallowed hard before walking out without a word.

She went out the next day and bought a bedspread, a coffee maker, and a set of cups. Later that night she went to her mother's place to find an iron she had left there, a gift to Zhuang from a factory where he'd given a lecture. It had never been used, so she decided to add it to the list of wedding gifts. Her mother recommended a chamber pot, saying it was the most important item, an indispensable object in a bride's dowry in the old days. But these days people didn't follow the rules, she told her, so the bride's family would not include one, and friends and relatives never gave one as a gift. Niu Yueqing thought an enamel spittoon to be used as a chamber pot would indeed be an ingenious gift. People often said that so-and-so could piss in the same pot with someone else. A chamber pot was important to the older generation because it symbolized lifelong affection between husband and wife. But she knew that no one sold spittoons in the mall these days, since someone from her office had failed to find one after going to every shopping center in town; it ultimately would have to be purchased at the ghost market outside the west gate.

She went there early the next morning, where she talked to several stall owners, who told her they were out of spittoons. But she could check out the Hong Jiang purchasing station. The Hong Jiang purchasing station? The name mystified her. She knew a man named Hong Jiang, of course, but could there also be a shop called Hong Jiang?

"That's an unusual name. Where did they get it?" she asked.

"It's nothing special. People started out calling it the place run by Hong Jiang, and after a while it just became Hong Jiang's station."

"That Hong Jiang, what does he do?"

"He runs a bookstore. We hear he struck it rich and opened a purchasing station to get even richer." The man paused, "Are you from the Household Registration Office?"

She then asked where the station was located. When it was pointed out, she saw it, located in the middle of the lane. It was being tended by an old man. "Is this the Hong Jiang purchasing station?" Niu Yueqing asked him.

"It was, but not anymore."

"What happened?"

"What happened? You'll eat anything when you're hungry and marry any woman when you're poor, but illicit thoughts begin to crop up when you're well fed and warmly clothed. Once he was well off, he laid eyes on a young, fresh girl and wanted a divorce. His wife refused, of course, so he gave her fifty thousand, plus this station, for her consent. Money as payment for a divorce is very popular these days."

With a jumble of thoughts running through her mind, Niu Yueqing returned home to tell her husband.

"He hid it from us all that time, which must mean it was a messy divorce," he said.

"That's not what I meant. Don't you think something fishy is going on here? He was dirt-poor, and we never heard of a purchasing shop. Where did he get the money to set it up? And when he got the divorce, he gave his first wife fifty thousand. Where did that come from?"

"Don't you check the accounts with him regularly?"

"Every bookstore makes money, but not ours. At best we break even. I was suspicious, but as a woman, I know little about running a business. And you, when did you bother to check the books?"

"Without any evidence, we can't confront him."

"So we'll continue to raise pigs to supply him with pork, is that it?"

"I have a gallery. Business will improve once it merges with the bookstore."

"Are you going to have Jingwu keep an eye on him?"

"Well, weren't you dead set on marrying Liu Yue off to your cousin's son?"

A happy smile broke out on Niu Yueqing's face. "Ai-ya! You're so cunning. So you knew about the problem all along!"

"You thought you were so clever," Zhuang said, embarrassing his wife.

On the twenty-eighth, Niu Yueqing went to the wedding on behalf of Zhuang, loaded down with gifts. Hong Jiang and his wife were so pleased they laid them out at the head table. They toasted her first during the banquet and announced: "Shimu is drinking for two today. Zhuang Laoshi could not be here, owing to an urgent meeting, so you must drink this one for him." Niu Yueqing had so much to drink that her face was burning, but Zhuang was not at a meeting. He had gone to see Zhao Jingwu to hurry the project along. Zhao told him that the interior was nearly finished, but they couldn't open until they had more art. Zhuang suggested they go see the man who forged famous artists' work.

"It's better that you don't. I'll be honest with you, it's Wang Ximian, but he told me not to tell anyone, including you. He's afraid someone might let it slip and ruin everything."

"I could have guessed even if you hadn't told me. I know just about every painter in Xijing, and there's no one better at making counterfeits. A while ago, I heard that Guangzhou and Hong Kong were inundated with fake Shi Lu paintings, and that the family has launched an investigation. There have been rumors implicating Wang, so why didn't he keep a low profile?"

"I knew about that, too. Those fake Shi Lu paintings were intended for us, with a forty-sixty split in his favor. But a tour guide from a travel agency managed to talk him into taking all the forgeries to Guangzhou.

These fakes can only deceive non-Chinese, so they won't do well in the domestic market. When foreigners visit China, they rely upon their tour guides to show them where to buy Chinese paintings and calligraphy. I managed to strike up a friendship with some guys at a travel agency who promised to bring foreign visitors to our gallery once we open. We'll only have to give them a commission. Wang has three students helping him forge old paintings for us, like Zheng Banqiao's bamboos in the wind, Qi Baishi's shrimps, and Huang Binhong's landscapes. He's not doing much Shi Lu, but he'll still forge a few, since they're so popular. A few days ago, when I went to take a look, Wang had just finished *Grazing Cattle*, one of Shi's earlier works, and *Plums and Rock*, done after Shi fell ill. They're incredible. I took *Plums and Rock* to show Shi's daughter, who couldn't tell it was a fake. She even asked me how I got it. I told her I bought it from someone at a roadhouse. She said, 'After my father fell ill, people like that often took him out to drink, and he'd do a painting to pay for the drinks if he didn't have money.'" Zhao finished with a hearty laugh.

"Wang didn't want me to know, but does he know that the gallery is mine?" Zhuang asked with a smile. "In fact, his wife and your shimu are like sisters, and she keeps me up to date on what he's doing." He took out his pipe, added some tobacco, and puffed away.

"Where did you get that?" Zhao asked. "It looks old, maybe an antique."

Zhuang just smiled.

"What about Mao's calligraphy in Gong Jingyuan's collection? Still no news?"

"I was going to talk to you about that. Once we get it, we'll be ready to open. We'll hold a press conference and be in business. I've found a way to deal with Gong Xiaoyi."

"How?"

"He's shrewd when he's sober but would call you grandpa if he needed a fix. I told him I could get Liu Yezi to sell him opium at a lower price. But of course I can have Liu jack up the price if I want, or refuse to sell him anything, even if he offers gold. So I told Liu to cut off his supply for ten days unless he brings out the scroll."

"Who is this Liu Yezi, anyway? Be careful with opium dealers. You know it's illegal."

"Of course I know. I don't smoke it and I don't share in the profits. We were classmates. She and her husband have been in the opium-trafficking business for years, and they're Gong Xiaoyi's only supplier."

"People in that kind of business treat money like their life. Why would she abide by your request to force Xiaoyi's hand?"

"You'll understand when I give you the whole story. Last year she sold a shipment of poppy pods to a guy named Ma on Dongyanshi Street. Ma owns a Chongqing hot pot diner, where he adds the pods to his soup to attract customers. Everyone was saying the hot pots at Ma's place were so good that people felt terrible if they missed even one day. Someone suspected that he was adding poppy pods and, after observing him in secret, reported him to the police. The police shut him down and wanted to know where he got the pods. He ratted on Liu Yezi, who told the police that a doctor in the countryside had given her a package of them to make medicinal drinks for her father, who had stomach cancer. After he died, she didn't want to throw away the pods, so she sold them to Ma. Of course the police didn't believe her. The station chief is a buddy of mine, so I spoke to him on her behalf; in the end they noted her story in their report and released her. Why would she not listen to me now? Let's go see her. Maybe Xiaoyi has already given her the scroll."

They hailed a taxi and arrived at a traditional housing compound. Zhuang did not want to go in, saying it would be better if he didn't meet Liu Yezi. Zhao told him to wait in a nearby bar while he went in to see Liu. He was pleased that she and her husband were both home. "Gong Xiaoyi is having a fix upstairs. He came with the scroll today but was afraid we wouldn't give him anything, so he demanded that first. He said he'd hand it over after we sold him some opium. Let him have his smoke. We'll take tea in the other room." For reassurance, Zhao tiptoed upstairs and looked in through a crack in the door. Gong Xiaoyi was lying on the bed, out like a light, with the scroll beside his emaciated body. Zhao smiled and went down to have tea.

❋

Gong Xiaoyi had been suffering from withdrawal symptoms for days. He went to see Liu Yezi several times a day, but she refused to sell him anything without the scroll. He went home and tried to cope, but soon returned when he could not stand it any longer. She turned him away each time, and the pattern was repeated. Again and again, five trips altogether, until his body ached so much that he rammed his head against the wall, slammed his arms against the bed boards, and pulled out handfuls of his hair. Eventually he took the scroll to Liu's house. He fell to the floor the moment he got in, kowtowing to her and foaming at the mouth. She unrolled the scroll. It was indeed Mao's calligraphy, with its elegant strokes, majestic and grand, the embodiment of a leader. *No wonder Zhao Jingwu has to have it*, she said to herself. She gave Xiaoyi some opium, which he took upstairs to satisfy his need first. As she had told Zhao, he would not part with the scroll until he was given more opium.

Once upstairs, he had begun smoking and lay down on the bed, feeling remorseful about his unseemly behavior in recent days. He had been a treasure to his father, smart, incisive, and good-looking. When the two of them had gone out together, people had praised both the father's calligraphy and his son. Legions of families had wanted to marry their daughters to him, and countless pretty girls had smiled flirtatiously when they saw him. But none of them had been good enough for him at the time. Now he had no job, was ignored by his father, and was despised by friends and relatives. Even flat-nosed Liu Yezi showed him no pity. On his earlier visit, Liu and her husband were having sex and did not stop when they saw him. He was on the floor, sniveling and begging, while she pulled up her pants, talking to him as she took a kerchief out from between her legs. In her eyes he was subhuman. He fumed over how the world treated him when he was out of opium, which was why he resorted to seeking happiness in his opium-induced state, a way for him to exact revenge on the world. The thought inevitably created a beautiful scene before his eyes; he was his former self again, young, handsome, spirited. An ingenious idea came to him: stop the movements of the hour and minute hands on the wall clock, stop time, and let him grow a pair of wings to fly around the city and see what families were doing. Sure enough, the hands stopped moving; even a buzzing fly was halted in mid-flight. He sprouted wings and flew over houses by the west gate until he reached the east gate, then headed to the north gate and finished at the south gate. He saw everything: naked men and women were copulating in just about every house in the city, displaying a myriad of positions and body movements. He walked in and collected the filthy semen from the beds, filling three large tubs. When the tubs were full, he put them on one of the trucks that sprayed the streets with water, then drove up and down the streets. A pungent, putrid smell filled his nostrils.

"I've exterminated all your children!" he shouted.

Then he gathered up all the men and cut off their genitals, which he tossed into the city moat, quickly filling it up. So he razed the city wall to bury more of the human debris. He wanted to rape all the women in front of the men, to make the women scream and the men suffer. That would make him feel better. Finally, putting on a gigantic pair of straw sandals, he ran across eight hundred li of the Qin River, over the hilltop imperial tombs that were the pride of Xijing's residents. He saw the Qian Mausoleum, which his father said had been built by Empress Wu Zetian to look like a woman lying on her back on the open plain. It was no longer a tomb, but a full-figured, beautiful, noble Wu Zetian lying there in the flesh. He raped her. Yes, he did. A wind blew, sending colorful clouds roiling in the sky. He turned to see that every one of the hilltop imperial tombs had sunk, and realized that the tombs had risen so high before because the emperors' genitals continued to grow after their deaths. Now that he owned the world and had conquered Wu Zetian, their genitals wilted and died off, out of despair. Xiaoyi was euphoric: he was the mayor of a city where the residents were either men who could no longer copulate or women whose bodies he frolicked on, where all the money and all the treasures belonged to him, where he owned all of the opium . . .

Zhao had finished off three pots of strong tea, and Xiaoyi had still not come down. Liu cracked melon seeds and chatted with him. Her husband, who was at the gate, shouted: "Hey, you crazy old man. Do you buy wastepaper? We have a pile of used toilet paper. You can have it for free."

Zhao heard a hoarse chant:

Clipped to the belt is a BP, held in the hand is a walkie-talkie, in the diner a roasted chicken to enjoy, and at a hotel a streetwalker to bed with me.

"Great! That was wonderful." Liu's husband laughed heartily.

"Would you stop sparring with that old junkman, Fatso," Liu grumbled.

Ignoring her, he called out, "Do you collect used women? If you do, I guarantee you that every man on this block would give you his and get a new one."

Liu Yezi ran out and dragged her husband inside by the ear. "You want to get a new spouse? If something like that could be done, I'd be the first to get a replacement for a scabby pig like you."

Instead of trying to mediate, Zhao sat there enjoying the junkman's distant shouts: "Junkman! Collecting junk and scraps!"

The scuffle between husband and wife went on for a while. "Is he is still up there?" she asked Zhao.

"Why don't you go take a look?"

Liu went out into the yard and shouted up, "Gong Xiaoyi, haven't you enjoyed yourself enough? Gong Xiaoyi!"

Startled out of his hallucinations, Gong came downstairs. Still immersed in his heroic fantasy, he grumbled, "What are you hollering for? Need some sex?"

"Bullshit!" Liu woke him up with a savage slap. His legs were too weak to hold him up. He fell to the steps. She reached out to snatch the scroll away.

"Good sister, we have an agreement. You can't have that unless you sell me twelve packets."

Liu laughed and handed him twelve small packets, receiving a roll of money in return.

"Zhuang Zhidie is a good friend of my father's, but I wouldn't trade the scroll to him. Now I'm pretty much giving it away."

"Go on home. Go." She shoved him out and shut the gate.

❖

With Mao's "Everlasting Sorrow" calligraphy in hand, Zhuang went to friends in the media and artistic and literary circles, inviting them to a press conference for a gallery he owned jointly with a friend. He was received with little enthusiasm; another art gallery was a hard sell, even though his name made it somewhat more interesting. There was simply too much news about galleries and bookstores. Mention of a piece of authentic calligraphy by Mao Zedong changed their minds. That was newsworthy. They were awestruck when they saw it, and some readied stories for immediate publication once the press conference was announced. Private press conferences were expensive, so Niu Yueqing got Zhao and Hong together to talk about financing the event. Hong brought out his books and managed to come up with three thousand. He complained about the difficulty of running a bookstore. Niu Yueqing said that was precisely why they were opening an art gallery. The bookstore would be part of the gallery, which would be the main source of revenue. She asked Hong to help Zhao as much as possible; he was unhappy to learn that that he would no longer be in charge, but could find no reason to object. "Sure thing. Jingwu is more resourceful than I am, so I'll do whatever I'm asked to do. Since I can't sit still, I'll run errands. I'm no rear-echelon commander, but I can be a good front-line soldier."

"Hong Jiang admires you, Jingwu, so respect his views and talk things over with him."

As they were leaving, she let Zhao walk out first before stuffing a piece of fabric into Hong's hands. "Someone brought this from Shanghai for me," she whispered. "It will be perfect for a blazer for Xiaoka. Put it away so Jingwu won't see it, or he'll be unhappy with me."

The gallery kept Zhuang too busy to visit Tang Wan'er for several days; she was as anxious as an ant in a frying pan. There were changes in her body: she had no appetite, her eyelids were puffy, and bile kept rising up.

Suspicion sent her to the hospital, where a test confirmed that she was pregnant. After arriving in Xijing, Zhou Min had insisted that there be no children as long as they lacked a permanent home. He took precautions every time, keeping her safe from pregnancy. But after beginning her affair with Zhuang, she had begun taking birth control pills. She could not carry them with her all the time, and when an opportunity arose, her desire for intimacy trumped the need for contraception. Luckily she hadn't gotten pregnant after a few of those episodes, which had so emboldened her that she stopped taking them altogether. Now she knew that the physical signs would give her away sooner or later; it was all she could do to hold off until Zhou left home before throwing up. She couldn't wait to tell Zhuang, hoping he'd come up with a solution and give her courage; she was desperate to tell him how miserable she was. But he did not show up after she sent the pigeon twice with a message. She became suspicious, wondering if he was avoiding her or had been detained by something else. Looking him up at his house was out of the question, so she could only shed private tears. The baby would not be born, she was sure of that. Even if Zhuang still loved her, she would have to have an abortion after he came to see her. But when would he come? Why not take care of the problem herself, instead of suffering all that fear and anguish? She congratulated herself for coming up with the idea. The pregnancy was proof that Zhuang was not infertile; taking care of it herself meant that she would not look pampered or cause him any trouble. He would surely feel she was better than his wife and would love her even more. So one morning after Zhou left for work, she went to a clinic for an abortion. A woman waiting her turn was so frightened by the bloody mess, she began to cry. The woman disgusted Tang.

"Where's your husband? Why isn't he here with you?" the doctor asked.

"He's waiting outside in a hired car," she replied, but was sad when she walked out of the treatment room. After sitting in the lounge for a while, she calmed down and, feeling strangely relaxed, smiled and said to herself: "I, Tang Wan'er, could swallow a brick and shit fine tiles."

She got up to go home. When she walked past Meng Yunfang's lane, she was thirsty, though she felt fine. She decided to stop in for a drink of water and to ask about Zhuang's whereabouts. Meng wasn't home; Xia Jie was inside feeling bored.

"I was going to get you to go out with me, and here you are. A see-all, know-all fox fairy."

"Yes, a fox fairy. And I smelled a stinky fox fart way over here," Wan'er said. "Look at you. Has someone made you unhappy?"

"Who else?"

"Are you upset that Meng Laoshi went with Zhuang Laoshi? You're not a child anymore, so why act like you have to tie your man to your belt?"

"Zhuang Laoshi has been too busy with the gallery to find time for him. I wouldn't be so upset if they were just sitting somewhere talking. There's this guy from Xinjiang who seems to know everything but isn't good at anything. Yunfang treats him like a god and keeps inviting him over. He even got his son to be the man's disciple. I was so mad I sent them away. I don't want to talk about him. What's wrong, Wan'er? You're so pale."

Tang felt better now that she had learned that Zhuang was tied up with gallery business. "Really? I haven't been sleeping well lately. I walked too fast on my way here and I'm thirsty. Do you have any brown sugar? Could you make me a glass of sugar water?"

Xia got up to get the water. "Not sleeping well? Maybe you and Zhou Min should give it a rest at night. Why drink water with brown sugar on a hot day like this?"

"I have cold qi in my stomach. The doctor told me to drink it." The water made her sweat and energized her. They chatted for a while. Xia suggested that they go for a walk. Tang wanted to go home for a nap, but Xia was so insistent that she couldn't say no.

They walked out through the city's south gate in high spirits, but when Tang felt a dull pain down below, she leaned against the bridgehead and said, "Let's rest here awhile." She gazed at the riverside park. A few puffy clouds and a brilliant sun hung high in the sky. The water in the city moat ran loudly past clumps of frog eggs congealed in waterweeds. Some of the eggs had hatched, releasing countless little tadpoles. The sight brought a smile to Tang's face, but she avoided the reference when Xia asked her what she was smiling about. Instead she said, "Look at the wind." A gust of wind rose from the water, climbed the riverbank, and crossed over the railings around the park, where it eddied and refused to die down. She had casually mentioned the wind, but now their attention was drawn to a tree it was attacking, a river locust whose trunk had been split in two. Interestingly, a large rock was inlaid at the split.

"The two sides of the split were quite close at first, but a gardener put in a rock to keep them apart. As the tree grew bigger and taller, the rock got stuck in there," Xia said.

"What does the tree remind you of?"

"It looks like a Y."

"Look again," Tang said.

"An upside-down character for man, 人."

"What kind of man?" Tang insisted.

"Just like a man. What else is there to see?"

"Look at the rock."

"You little slut. How in the world did you think of that?" Finally understanding what Tang was getting at, Xia pinched her; they giggled as they got tangled up in their horseplay, drawing the attention of passersby.

"No more. People are looking at us," Xia said.

"Who cares, they're just looking."

"Be honest with me, Wan'er. How many times can Zhou Min give it to you in a day? You're like a nymphomaniac. Have you seen how thin he's gotten?"

"You have it all wrong. We barely do it once a month, and we've just about forgotten it altogether."

"I don't believe you. Not counting Zhou Min, I'm sure you could stop any man in his tracks."

"Then I'd be a real fox fairy."

"That reminds of something. Last night I was reading *Strange Tales from a Scholar's Studio*, and the stories about foxes and ghosts frightened me. Yunfang said he wasn't afraid of fox fairies and was in fact wishing that one would open the window and come in late at night. I told him to dream on. With his stinky body, not even fleas or bedbugs care to bite him. When I went to bed, I marveled over Pu Songling's fantastic stories. How could a fox become a fairy? If there's a woman everyone could love, I've only seen one in my life, and that's you."

"When I read Pu Songling," Tang Wan'er said, "he strikes me as the romantic type. He must have had many lovers. He loved them but could not be with them forever, so his longing turned them into fox fairies in his stories."

"Where did you get a thought like that? Have you fallen for someone, or is someone in love with you?"

With Zhuang Zhidie's image filling her mind, Tang smiled, her eyes turning into crescent moons as she blushed. "It was just a thought. Where would I get a lover? The world is strange, Xia Jie. If there are men, there have to be women—how do you feel when you're with Meng Laoshi?"

"We regret making love because it's so lifeless, but then a few days later, the desire returns."

"Then you could both be leaders."

"Leaders?"

"Which government office these days doesn't have a leader who frequently makes mistakes? They conduct self-reflections for their superiors and then go out and make the same mistakes again. It goes on and on, and nothing happens to their official positions."

They had a good laugh over that.

"That's why we say that food and sex are the basis of human nature," Xia Jie said.

"Actually, God played a trick on us humans, and there's nothing we can do about it."

"What do you mean?"

"He wants us to live, so we need to eat. But eating is so much trouble. First we have to grow the crops; then, after we harvest the grain, we have to mill it and turn it into food. When we eat, we have to chew, swallow, digest, and get rid of the waste. So much heavy-duty work is involved. But He gave us a desire for food, so we do all this willingly. Take what men and women do, for example. Its original purpose was procreation, but who would go through all the trouble if we weren't given sexual urges? So just when you're enjoying the pleasure, you fulfill your responsibility of having children. It would be great if we could go halfway, having the fun without the duty."

"Is that what that crazy brain of yours thinks about?" Xia said as she reached out to tickle Tang under her arms. Overcome with laughter, Tang struggled out of Xia's reach and ran across the bridge, with Xia hot in pursuit. One following the other, they ran through the gate and into the park, where Tang collapsed on the lawn. Xia ran over and pounced, but Tang was motionless. So Xia picked up a leg and took off her shoe. "Let's see you run now."

"Xia Dajie." Tang turned her head to call out, her lips bloodless and her face bathed in sweat. Her eyes rolled up as she passed out.

❋

Xia Jie hailed a pedicab to take her friend to the hospital, but Wan'er woke up on the way and refused to go. She said she'd had fainting spells before and had been overtired recently, which must have brought on another attack. She'd be fine once she got home and rested. Touching Tang's forehead, Xia noted that the sweat was no longer cold and that the color was returning to her cheeks, so she gave the driver an additional five yuan to take them to Tang's place. When they got into the quiet house, Tang went to lie down.

"Are you feeling better now, Wan'er?"

"Much better. Thank you so much, Xia Dajie."

"You really scared me today. I wouldn't want to live if something terrible were to happen to you."

"Then you and I would become a pair of sexy ghosts."

"You can still joke at a moment like this! I'll make something for you. What do you feel like eating?"

"Nothing." Tang smiled weakly. "I just want to sleep. I'll be fine after I wake up. Why don't you go on home?"

"Why isn't Zhou Min home? Did he go to work? Let me call him at work."

"Call on your way home. Why not try Zhuang Laoshi's place first? He might be there."

Xia made her another cup of water with brown sugar and set it by her bed before going out to make the phone call.

When she reached Zhuang and told him that Tang had fallen ill, he hopped on his scooter and raced over. Zhou was still at the magazine. Tang wept the moment she saw Zhuang's face. As he dried her tears, he asked what had happened. After she told him, he was stunned into silence and sat on the bed for a long time. He thumped himself on the forehead. The sight brought secret joy to her, but she said, "You must hate me now. I'm so sorry that I got rid of your child."

"No, Wan'er, you've done nothing wrong. I let you down." He wrapped his arms around her head and said softly. "I should have been the one to go through the torment, but you had to endure it all alone. You're really a good woman. But why didn't you take care of yourself? Why did you have to keep Xia Jie company after you'd just had the procedure?"

"I thought I was fine. Besides, there was no way I could let her know about this. How are things at the gallery?"

"How did you know I've been busy with the gallery? I haven't been able to come see you, but why didn't you send a message with the pigeon?"

"I did. I waited day and night for you to come, but you didn't, so I made the decision on my own."

Cursing Liu Yue, he told Wan'er he knew nothing about that. He pulled back the blanket to check on her body, then pulled it back up and tucked her in before going out to buy tonics. When he returned, he sat with her until Zhou got home.

Over the following week, he went to see her every other day, taking chicken or fish each time. When he was back home, Liu Yue would make him a drink with essence of longan.

"So you know how to be nice to people?" he said to her one day.

“As a maid in your house, can I afford not to be attentive, especially when you’re hard at work with her?”

“I don’t dare go out,” he said with a smile, “since you think I go to see Tang Wan’er each time I do. I’m not going anywhere today, so I want you to run some errands. Go see Zhao Jingwu and ask him to take Dr. Song with him to the nunnery.”

“Is Huiming not feeling well? When I went to Tanshi Street to buy fish last Sunday, I saw her on my way home. She was sitting in a car with Secretary Huang, but she didn’t see me and I pretended not to notice her. Hmph! What’s a nun doing using lipstick? I have no respect for her. She shouldn’t be a nun if she wants to pretty herself up. Unlike the other nuns, she wants to know this person and be friends with that one. She’s such a show-off. There are so many pretty girls in the city, but few people have ever heard their names, and yet everyone knows about Huiming, the nun with the fair face and big tits. How did she get sick? Has the Buddha stopped looking out for her?”

“Listen to you. You’re like a hod carrier who looks down on a flour vendor. You’re upset over her good looks, aren’t you?”

“Why would I be upset?”

He was about to mention Tang’s message with the pigeon, but he changed his mind, for he hadn’t told Niu Yueqing or Liu Yue that Tang was laid up. But Liu Yue wasn’t done yet. “I don’t give a damn. That stinky-mouth Meng used to go there all the time, but he stopped after losing the sight in one eye. So now you’re the one who’s there all the time.”

“Are you finished? I ran into Secretary Huang, who told me that Huiming’s back hurt so much she couldn’t sit up straight. So I want Jingwu to have Dr. Song take a look at her. Forget it if you don’t want to go.”

“Can I say no? I won’t be home to make lunch, so you and Dajie will have to eat out.”

“How long will it take to relay a message? I’ll tell her if you get lost there.”

“All right. And I’ll tell Dajie to poison the pigeon.” She walked off smiling.

Liu Yue saw Zhao Jingwu often after they got together. Niu Yueqing noticed but decided not to say anything. She was none too happy about it and had warned the girl with veiled comments, but Liu pretended not to understand. With a foolish grin, she continued to go about everything in her own way. Distracted, she often failed to get food ready at the right time, and she let the laundry pile up. On the day after Tang fainted, Zhao came to see Zhuang at noon, but neither he nor Niu Yueqing was home, which emboldened him to steal a kiss from Liu. After putting him off for a while, she kissed him, so encouraging him that he started groping her. "You're getting too daring," she said, but then she undid her skirt and dropped her panties. Zhao had never dreamed they would go that far, but they did, since she was willing. He was too inexperienced and too fearful to last very long. With a laugh of annoyance, Liu sent him to wash the soiled underwear, which he did while making sure she wouldn't tell anyone about it.

"Do you think I'd tell people and make them feel sorry for you?"

"I can do better. It's just that I was too excited and too nervous, because this is Zhuang Laoshi's house. I'll show you what I can do once we're married. Don't talk about me too much around here. Zhuang Laoshi is the observant type. If you say too much and something slips out, he may sense we've had sex, and he'd look at me differently."

"Ai-ya! Why are you so afraid of him? He's human too, you know. Do you think he doesn't do this?"

Sensing something hidden in her reply, Zhao pressed her: "What does he do?"

Zhao was astounded when Liu Yue told him about Zhuang and Tang, but he warned her not to tell anyone else. "Zhuang Laoshi has a fine reputation and plenty of credibility, and his disciples and friends all need his help. If people knew that, it could ruin his reputation, and we'd all be done for. As his disciples, we must help promote his good standing in society and be aware of the impact of his authority."

Liu nodded in agreement but added, "I've given you everything, including my body, and something has to come out of this. I'll go to your place if it's inconvenient here."

"I didn't believe it when Meng Laoshi said that the more women do this, the more daring they get." He winked to embarrass her.

"Why should I be shy after what we did today? Besides, I'll be yours one of these days, won't I?"

"My place is even worse. Let's see. I'll get a key to the House of Imperfection Seekers from Zhuang Laoshi tomorrow, and we'll have our fun there."

"What's the House of Imperfection Seekers? I've never heard of it."

Liu oohed and aahed when Zhao told her about the place. "Sounds like a wonderful place. I always wondered why Zhou Min was never home when Zhuang Laoshi went to see Tang Wan'er after she sent the pigeon with a message. So they had a secret place for their trysts."

The next day Zhao asked Zhuang for the key, making up a story about a friend who needed a place to spend a night. Zhao then secretly made a copy and sneaked over there with Liu Yue.

One day Niu Yueqing came home for lunch at noon, but no one was home. She waited awhile until Liu Yue came up the stairs humming a tune. "Where have you been? There's not even a shadow in the house," Niu Yueqing grumbled when Liu opened the door. The girl had run into Zhao on the street, and they had talked until long past the time she was supposed to be home to make lunch, so she had bought some steamed buns. "I went out to buy buns to go with a chicken soup I'm making."

"How convenient to buy buns. What have you been doing all morning?"

"I've been home."

"Rubbish. I called and no one answered," Niu Yueqing fumed as she sat down. "Where's your Zhuang Laoshi?"

"How should I know?"

"No time for food. I need to talk to him about an urgent matter. Call Meng Laoshi's house to see if he's there." Liu called, but Zhuang wasn't there. Niu Yueqing then called the magazine office, her mother's place, Wang Ximian, Ruan Zhifei, the newspaper offices, and every other place he frequented. There was no sign of him.

"Could he be at Zhou Min's house?" Liu Yue offered when she saw how anxious Niu Yueqing was.

Niu Yueqing got on her bike and rode over to Zhou's place. Zhou, who had just returned from delivering mock-up copy to the printer, was cooking instant noodles. When he told her Zhuang hadn't been there, she asked about Tang. Zhou said he hadn't seen her when he got home, adding that she might have gone window-shopping, her favorite activity. Niu Yueqing turned and rode home, venting her frustration from hunger and anger at Liu Yue, who said, "How would I know where he is? You've been to every place he could possibly be, except for the House of Imperfection Seekers." She regretted it the moment she said it.

"Where is this place?"

"I seem to recall Zhuang Laoshi mentioning it once, but I don't know if it's an office or someone's house. I'll go check it out."

"I'll go myself. This is an urgent matter that can't be delayed even a moment. Just tell me where it is."

She had no choice but to give her the address. Niu Yueqing got back on her bike and rode out.

On this day, Zhuang happened to be spending the noon hour with Tang at the House of Imperfection Seekers. She had more or less recovered but was still spotting, and they had agreed to meet there, as he wanted to hear details of the abortion, which brought hot tears to his face when she was finished. She wanted him to swear that he loved her. He did, adding that he wanted to marry her. She asked when that would happen. Someday in the future? Three years? Five years, eight or ten years? Everyone would think that Zhuang Zhidie had married a rare beauty who turned out to be an old hag, she said. Caught in a difficult state, he sighed in agony, while she smiled and, calling him a poor man, tickled his armpit to make him laugh. Seeing the frown on his face, she said, "Don't be like that. It hurts me to see you suffer. I'll wait for you no matter how long it takes. Even if you stop loving me, at least you will have loved me once. With your disposition, you'd eventually look for someone better than me even if the heavens helped us become husband and wife. When that happened, I wouldn't hate you, nor would I stop you."

"What would that make me then? Nothing you say or do can make me lose interest in you or allow me to be with anyone else."

She laughed, saying she sometimes felt guilty about his wife, but then she was convinced that he should be hers. She told him she wasn't sure if she was a good woman or a bad one, but she knew she was a woman. If he stopped loving her, she would become a loose woman and sleep with any man, including a madman, an idiot, even bandits and thieves. Taken by surprise, Zhuang responded with a stern face, "Stop the nonsense. Don't say things like that."

She started to cry, saying she would never say those things again, and asked if he was angry with her. He spanked her, saying he was upset.

"Women's minds are confusing."

She put her arms around him and kissed him, and before long they were fused together. □□ □□ □□ [The author has deleted 38 words.] Afterward, they looked down; the red spot on the pillow under her body brought instantaneous remorse. The doctor had told her not to have sexual intercourse for a month. When Zhuang asked her how she felt, she said she was fine, but the pillow was soiled. She took out a red pen and turned the spot into a maple leaf. He laughed.

"That's great! The frosted leaf is redder than flowers in February. Later, when we go down for lunch, we'll buy a needle and thread for you to embroider the spot. No one could tell and might even comment on how a bed pillow can be turned into art."

It was past lunchtime by the time they had spent more pleasurable moments in each other's arms, so they got up to go out for something to eat. They met Niu Yueqing at the bottom of the stairs, which sent them into such a fright they turned pale.

"Wan'er, look who's here," Zhuang said to a panicky Tang.

"I've been looking all over for you, including into the rats' nests. So here you are. You don't look well, Wan'er."

"She has every right not to. She asked me to find her a temporary job, so I thought I'd go see Mr. Yang, a section head at the Sanitation Board. When I took her there, he acted all high and mighty and had no interest in talking to us. We left. How dare he treat me like that!"

"How much can you earn with a temp job? Why don't you just stay home and let Zhou Min write more essays? These days it's easier to see the King of Hell than to deal with underlings. You should go straight to the head of the board."

"That's easier said than done. I'd go hungry if we had to live on what his articles bring in. If he were as talented as Zhuang Laoshi, I'd stay home and wait on him, not go out to work like you."

"Then let's do this," Niu Yueqing said. "When Hong Jiang publishes more books, I'll ask him to get Zhou Min to help out."

"Don't make that kind of offer yet. What would you say to Zhou Min if Hong refused?" Zhuang said. "You said you were looking all over for me. What's it about?"

"An urgent matter."

"I'm sorry I've delayed you. I'll leave now," Tang said and walked off.

"Gong Xiaoyi came to see me at work this morning," Niu Yueqing said. "He started crying the moment he came in. I was stunned. What has happened to him? He looks more dead than alive. I asked him what was wrong, and he said he wanted to see you about his father. He was arrested for the same old problem and told Xiaoyi to find someone to smooth things over so he would only have to pay a fine. But Xiaoyi's mother went to Tianjin to see her parents. Xiaoyi didn't know who to see, and he had no money to pay a fine. So he came to see you."

"Could he have made up the story to get opium money from us? I saw him a few days ago, and I heard nothing about his father."

"That's what I thought, too, and I told him to tell the truth. So he showed me a note from Gong Jingyuan. I know Old Gong's handwriting. It was from him."

"Old Gong has been arrested many times because of this problem. And each time he gets out by giving away calligraphy. He'll be fine unless they chop off his hand."

"That's what I figured. But Xiaoyi said it was different this time. When someone from the Ministry of Public Security came to review job performances here, he received several letters of complaint about Old Gong's gambling habit, and the fact that he's been released after each arrest. That angered the man, who criticized the local police. Who could have guessed that the very next day, Old Gong and his friends would be gambling at the same hotel where the man was staying? So he was arrested and threatened with severe punishment."

Finally sensing the gravity of the situation, Zhuang cursed Gong Jingyuan for being so careless.

"Old Gong does have his problems," Niu Yueqing said, "but he's an old friend. And now that his son has come to us, we can't wash our hands of him. Think about who you know, and see if you can find someone to help him out. Even if it doesn't work, our consciences will be clear knowing that we've done our best. No one could accuse us of being disloyal or unkind."

Zhuang frowned and remained silent for a while before saying, "I haven't eaten yet. Let's go get some lunch first."

They went to a diner for some hand-cut noodles, after which he told his wife to go home, while he went to see Zhao Jingwu about the problem.

"I do know a few people at the Public Security Bureau, but I'm afraid they won't be much help," Zhao said, looking uncomfortable. "Ai! Maybe it's good for him to suffer a bit."

"I thought it over and decided we have to help him this time no matter what," said Zhuang. "Go see Xiaoyi and find out more about the situation. Tell him how bad it is this time, and that his father could get at least three years. Scare him a bit."

"I'm sure he's already scared witless. Why scare him more?"

"I have a plan. I'll tell you after I see Meng Laoshi."

Zhao hurried off when he heard Zhuang's explanation.

Zhuang went to see Meng Yunfang and told him what he knew.

"Who should we see?" Meng asked. "You know the mayor, why don't you go see him?"

"I can't. The repercussions would be too much for him to deal with. Did you say you've met Knave Number Two several times at Huiming's place?"

"Are you asking me to get Huiming to talk to him? I can't do that."

"But you have to. As a favor to me. We need the man's help, not to get Gong released, but to reduce the punishment to a fine. I'm pretty sure he can get it done."

Meng went with great reluctance, and returned to say that Huiming had agreed to talk to the man on their behalf. They were to wait for her call. After lunch at Meng's place, Huiming phoned that afternoon to say that the Public Security Bureau had agreed to fine Gong. But it would be a heavy fine, sixty thousand yuan. Zhuang sighed before going to Zhao Jingwu's place with Meng. Zhao had just returned from Xiaoyi's house, so they sat down to discuss the situation. Zhuang told Zhao to have the money ready within three days.

"Are you going to lend Xiaoyi the money? That would be like hitting a dog with meat buns, with no hope of getting it back. He'd buy opium instead of paying the fine."

"You're usually very smart, Jingwu, so why are you so dense all of sudden? Xiaoyi squanders everything, so I can't possibly lend him that much money. We've worked hard to get Gong off the hook by having the punishment reduced. We've done right by Gong Jingyuan. Xiaoyi is a hopeless addict who would steal all his father's calligraphy and sell it to buy opium. We might as well buy Gong's works now."

Zhao and Meng both applauded Zhuang's idea.

"That's it! We'll save Gong Jingyuan and keep his works with us. Maybe Xiaoyi will quit opium when there's nothing more for him to sell," Meng said.

"Why don't you and Jingwu work on this?"

Zhao went to see Xiaoyi and spent the whole evening talking to him. Xiaoyi, who was moved to tears by what he heard, asked to borrow money from Zhao when he was told about the fine. Zhao said he would have gotten married long ago if he had that kind of money. Then he told Xiaoyi that he knew of an art dealer who he hoped would buy Gong Jingyuan's calligraphy. The art dealer had agreed to buy only two, but Zhao told him to buy enough for them to bring in sixty thousand yuan. As a favor to save Gong, Zhao stressed.

"The art dealer reluctantly agreed, but he said he wanted a discount, since he was asked to buy so many pieces at one time," Zhao said.

"How much is he offering?" Xiaoyi asked.

Zhao signaled with his fingers.

"But that's half of what my father's works usually fetch," Xiaoyi cried out. "That's like robbery. I won't sell to him. I'll sell the pieces on my own."

"We only have four days. How many do you think you can sell off in that time, even if you manage to find buyers? Your father will have been sentenced by then."

Xiaoyi had to agree with Zhao. So he led Zhao to his father's house, where he ferreted out nearly four-fifths of the finished works. Zhao also discovered some antique scrolls in Gong Jingyuan's possession.

"You need to give those away, too, Xiaoyi. I don't want them, and neither does your Uncle Zhuang. We've run our legs off doing what's right. But when we talked to the people at the Public Security Bureau, Number Two, and Abbess Huiming, they all said they could help, but they'd want some works from the famous calligrapher. I don't see how we can refuse them. We have to make sure they don't go back on their word and hurt your father's chances, but at the same time we can't let them make exorbitant demands. Why not give one to each of them?"

Xiaoyi scratched his head and fell silent for a moment before giving Zhao seven pieces, adding one for Zhuang and one for Zhao.

"We can't take these. If this were anyone else, even ten antiques would not get me to do such a thing, let alone your Uncle Zhuang. But we are friends with you and your father, two generations of the Gong family. Tomorrow, Uncle Zhuang and I have to treat some people to a meal at the Xijing Restaurant, and you don't have to worry about how much we spend."

Xiaoyi was beside himself with gratitude, saying he would never forget their kindness and would make sure his father thanked them personally once he was released. After walking Zhao out of the house, he went back inside, took out a few antiques and his father's calligraphy, then returned home.

❋

With the addition of Gong Jingyuan's calligraphy, they held the press conference ahead of schedule, generating reports in all the media outlets. On the day the gallery opened, a huge crowd showed up to see Mao Zedong's calligraphy. When the great man was alive, they could only see copies of his work, so it was a feast for the eyes when they could view the original 148 large characters. They had come mainly for Mao's handwriting, but were pleasantly surprised to see a dazzling array of art by famous ancient and modern artists. The small gallery located outside a bustling business district gained instant fame, attracting many out-of-towners, even foreigners.

Niu Yueqing had been apprehensive about how they would get their hands on the bulk of Gong Jingyuan's treasured collection. She brought it up once, but Zhuang told her to shut up. They sold a few pieces on opening day, and when Zhao brought over the money, Zhuang tossed it at Niu Yueqing. "This accomplished two things at once. As long as Gong Jingyuan gets out and has his hands intact, money will continue to flow in for him. Besides, we may be able to wean the father and son off their evil habits, and they'd thank us for that. No one has raised any concerns, so why must you worry so much? If people got wind of this, they would be convinced that we'd done something unsavory."

Niu Yueqing kept her mouth shut from then on. Soon they heard that Gong had been released, and she prepared some gifts to take to him. They were not prepared for the news that came that afternoon—Gong Jingyuan had died. Shocked, Niu Yueqing ran over to see Zhuang at the gallery. He was busy putting up signs under some of the works, indicating that one was "sold at twenty-one thousand," another "sold at five thousand," and yet another "sold at thirty-five hundred." It was a ploy to spur potential buyers into action by marking the works as sold. Tang Wan'er was there to decorate a newly installed display case for folk artwork, such as paper-cuts, shadow-play figurines, pillow covers, and shoe pads, as well as the pillowcase with a red maple leaf that had been nicely embroidered with red and green thread. People praised the handiwork, which went to Tang's head; trying to be smart, she said that the so-called culture T-shirts that were popular on the streets had only a witty phrase or two. It would show good taste and draw buyers if a passage from an ancient text were copied onto a shirt in tiny print. They were having a good time talking and bantering, so they reeled from the shock when Niu Yueqing rushed in to inform them of Gong's death. They quickly placed a call to Wang Ximian and Ruan Zhifei to verify the news; Wang and Ruan said they had heard it, too, but weren't sure what had happened. Leaving everyone behind, Zhuang went home with Niu Yueqing. He thought about going to Gong's house after lunch. Even if it turned out not to be true, he should go to see Gong anyway.

Xiaoyi came with the news while they were eating. Niu Yueqing cried before rushing out to buy black gauze. Zhuang called Zhao and asked him to buy a wreath, a stack of hemp paper, two packs of incense, and four large candles. Zhao quickly got them and came back, followed by Niu Yueqing, who had bought three yards of wool fabric instead of black gauze.

"Why did you buy such fine fabric?" Zhao asked "Do you think the dead can wear it in the underworld?"

"With Gong Jingyuan dead, life will be tough for his wife and Xiaoyi, so what's the use of giving them black gauze? They could at least make some clothes out of the fabric here. There's nothing you can do for the dead, so we should worry about the living. It's just that they were used to a good life when he was alive, so his death means the disappearance of their wealth god. It's easy for the poor to become rich, but hard for the rich to turn poor. I'm afraid mother and son will have a tough time from now on," Niu Yueqing said tearfully.

"Your shimu is right," Zhuang said to Zhao. "I've asked around and learned that Gong lost his mind before he died and destroyed everything in the house. His wife is still in Tianjin, and, Xiaoyi being Xiaoyi, well, it will be a sad sight at their house, with nothing left. Oh, right. Go buy three packages of opium from Liu Yezi and take them with us. Xiaoyi needs to take charge now, and I don't think he has any opium left. He's useless without it."

It was dark out when the three of them rushed over to Gong's house as soon as Zhao returned with the opium.

It was a well-preserved old-style compound, with four main rooms flanked by side rooms. In the relatively small yard, a toon tree as thick as a bucket had been planted at the spots where the eaves of the main rooms met the side room walls. There were artificial hills and trellises in the middle of the yard; on the sides of the entrance were a small room, a toilet, and the furnace room to heat the house in the winter. Zhuang, Zhao, and Niu Yueqing went straight to one of the central rooms; it was brightly lit, with no one inside. The lights were on in only two of the central rooms. To the east was Gong Jingyuan's study, and to the west was the couple's bedroom, with a room to receive guests in the center. In the middle of the main room, two black lacquered square tables had been pushed together, both with inlaid tabletops made of Lantian jade, surrounded by eight low drum-shaped stools. On each side of the door was an old-fashioned lattice window with plum flower carvings linked by carved ropes. Hung on the main wall were eight mahogany images carved in relief showing the famous calligraphers Wang Xizhi, Wang Xianzhi, Yan Zhenqing, Ouyang Xun, Liu Gongquan, Zhan Xu, Mi Fei, and Yu Youren. On the walls on the eastern and western sides hung framed calligraphy by Gong himself, one reading "Enjoy Life" and the other "Harmony."

"No one died here. See, there's no bier and no one is wailing," Zhao said when a man with a mourning cloth wound around his head came out of one of the side rooms. "Ah, we have guests," the man shouted. "In here." Now they knew that the bier had been set up in a side room to the east, so they left the main room. In the middle of the room was a screen to separate a sleeping area from Gong's large writing desk. On the desk, which had been prepared to serve as the bier, lay Gong's body. It was covered in rice paper, with no blanket or sheet. Zhuang walked over to pull back the paper. Gong's hair was a mess, framing his bluish-black face; his eyes and mouth were twisted, making for a terrifying sight. Niu Yueqing put her hands over her face and cried, "Why is he covered in paper? Don't you have a blanket and sheet?"

One of the grieving relatives said that they had chosen to use rice paper because the blankets and sheets were too dirty. Niu Yueqing cried again while smoothing Gong's lapel; she wailed until she fell to the edge of the bier when she saw that Gong was wearing the same old pair of shoes he had been wearing the time she ran into him at the City God Temple. Patting Gong's face, Zhuang also teared up. "Brother Gong, how could you just die like that? How?" His chest tightened and he burst into tears. One of the relatives came over and offered them tea after they sat down.

Earlier, when Gong Jingyuan had come home and heard the story from Xiaoyi, he was enormously grateful to Zhuang, whom, to his regret, he hadn't visited often, owing to his inflated view of his own talent and his addiction to gambling. Gong was particularly pleased when he learned how well his son had done this time, so he retrieved a suitcase from under the bed that contained bundles of bills totaling a hundred thousand yuan. He took out a stack and gave it to Xiaoyi to buy four bottles of Maotai, ten cartons of Hongtashan cigarettes, and three skeins of yarn and silk. He wanted to thank Zhuang Zhidie personally. Xiaoyi was astounded to see so much money.

"You have all this money and you hid it from me? Do you know how much trouble I had to go through to get sixty thousand yuan?"

"No matter how much I have, it would never fill that opium pit of yours. If I didn't save the money, what would we do in an emergency? Your mother is away, and that's why you've had a tough time. But you did well. I thought that no one would help you out with the way you are, but you actually managed to borrow the needed amount. Tell me who the lenders were, and we'll pay them back tomorrow."

"Who would lend me so much money? The Public Security Bureau gave me four days to pay the fine, so urgently it was like trying to put out a fire. Luckily an art dealer bought your calligraphy and paid enough for me to get you out."

It was like a thunderclap to Gong, who hurried to open the closet. Ninety percent of his favorite works were gone, and a quick check told him that not much was left of the antique scrolls he had collected over the years. He overturned his desk and flew into a rage.

"You're fucking hopeless. You sold off everything, all for sixty thousand yuan! You stupid shit. And you say you've saved me? You just killed me. I didn't need you to save me. I'd rather spend five years in jail than have you destroy me like this. Why didn't you sell the house while you were at it? Why didn't you sell your mother, too?"

"Why are you so upset, Dad? You're so tightfisted, it was like slicing off a piece of your flesh whenever I asked for a few measly yuan. How was I supposed to know we had that much money in the house? I didn't have time to worry about how much I'd get for those scrolls; all I cared about was getting you out. You have talent and can produce more calligraphy, so what's the big deal?"

Gong kicked Xiaoyi out the door. "What the fuck do you know?" he screamed. "You think I can write whenever I want? Am I a printer?" He continued his tirade, calling his son all sorts of names. Having finally tired himself out, Gong lay down on the bed, wondering how someone like him could have a prodigal son like that. Xiaoyi smoked so much opium that he barely looked human, and worse yet, the idiot had squandered nearly everything over a minor incident. What would become of them if he kept at it? Then his thoughts shifted to himself. In the past, he had spent up to three days in jail after being arrested, but few people knew about that. But this time the news had gotten around, and everyone would be calling him a gambling addict. Cradling his money, he had to curse the way the ease of getting money had ruined him and his son. Overcome by extreme sadness, he decided to end his life. He looped a rope over the rafter, made a noose, and climbed onto a stool.

But then his thoughts turned to the despicable man who had brokered the deal between his son and the art dealer. Who was the man, and who was the dealer? "Damn you, you thieves; you took advantage of me when you thought I didn't have any money. You deserve to die a terrible death. I'm going to show you my wealth today before I die." Jumping off the stool, he pasted hundred-yuan bills on the wall until all the cash was used up. He chortled when it was done before regretting his action, for that might bring more derision. With so much money in the house, why would the son have to sell everything for sixty thousand yuan to get his old man out of jail? He splashed ink on the walls before using a coal rake to scratch and scrape the walls until the money, along with the wall, was turned to pulp. Throwing the rake down, he sat on the floor and cried like a lowing old cow. "It's over. It's all over. Now I'm truly penniless."

He slapped his hands on the floor, then bit off the three rings on his fingers, swallowing them one by one.

⁂

After a cup of tea, Zhuang was about to leave when Wang Ximian and Ruan Zhifei walked in, followed by several people who brought with them a large custom-made case for sacrificial implements. It was an intricate case: the bottom had a gold mountain and silver ridges made of colored slices of pigs' heads, while the top displayed flour figurines depicting the eight immortals crossing the ocean, the several sages in the bamboo grove, the twelve beauties of Nanjing, and the eighteen club-wielding monks of Shaolin Temple, all delicately created and lifelike.

After greeting Wang and Ruan, Zhuang said: "I just got here. I figured you'd come soon. Let's offer the sacrificial drinks together." They laid the case on the bier, lit some incense and candles, and knelt on one knee to burn spirit money in a clay bowl by the bier. Then, a cup of liquor in hand, they each offered three kowtows and six bows and, calling out "Brother Gong," sprinkled the liquor into the burning paper.

"It's dark out; why don't they have lights in the yard?" Ruan asked as they got to their feet. "And no one is crying. It's so quiet, it doesn't look like someone has died in this house. Where's Gong Xiaoyi? Xiaoyi, where are you? Why aren't you holding the wake and greeting the guests?"

The mourning relatives wailed a few times before stopping. Some went into the yard to fetch a lamp from one of the side rooms, while another walked to the bedroom to get Gong Xiaoyi. A while later the relative came out to say, "Cousin Xiaoyi is sick."

Zhuang and some of the others went to the bedroom; it was in total disarray, with the walls in tatters, though edges of the money were still visible. Xiaoyi was curled up in bed, foaming at the mouth, his limbs quivering with spasms, his body shaking uncontrollably. Ruan walked up and slapped him. "Why couldn't you be the one who died? The vice will be gone only when you're dead." With his eyes fixed on Zhuang, Xiaoyi did not respond.

"All right; that's enough. He just needs a fix. You can scream at him, you can hit him, he won't know," Zhuang said. "Let's go sit out there and talk about what needs to be done now, since Xiaoyi is not going to be much help."

They all went to another side room, all but Zhao Jingwu, who stayed behind and took out three small packages of opium when everyone was gone. "These are from your Uncle Zhuang. He was afraid you'd need it during the funeral preparations. And he was right."

"Uncle Zhuang is the only one who's nice to me," Xiaoyi said as he lit up. A few puffs later he was a different person, fully energized. "Go on out there, Brother Zhao. Let me lie here for a while."

"Are you looking to get revenge again?" Zhao knew what he was like.

"No, no more revenge. I've killed everyone in the city many times over. This time I'm just going to enjoy it and ask Buddha, the Holy Mother, and the immortals to sing."

"Don't enjoy it too much. Friends of your father's have come to pay their respects and are outraged that you, the filial son, did not go out to greet them. Do you need another slap? Your mother isn't home yet, and if the elders get angry and leave, what are you going to do with your father's body? Leave it out there to stink and rot away?" Zhao dragged Xiaoyi over to the side room.

Zhuang, Wang, and Ruan were assigning tasks to the relatives—contacting the crematorium, hiring a vehicle to transport the corpse, buying funeral garb, and getting an urn. Someone asked if Xiaoyi's mother had been notified and was told that a telegram had been sent. She would fly back early the next morning, and would need to be picked up at the airport. They had to make sure that nothing happened to her if she was overcome by grief. Xiaoyi, who was listening quietly off to the side, kowtowed to each of them when they were done. "Everything requires money; where am I going to get it? Why don't I sell the two jade-inlaid tables tomorrow?"

"You're still thinking about selling stuff?" Ruan Zhifei said. "Do you want your father to turn over in his grave? When your mother gets back, we will talk to her about it. You just go kneel there and burn some paper for your father."

The three of them scrounged up a writing brush and ink to decorate the mourning hall. It looked terrible for a famed calligrapher to have nothing but his picture in the hall after his death, so Zhuang took up the brush and wrote *In Mourning for Mr. Gong Jingyuan*, to be pasted above his photo. For the two sides of the picture, he wrote *In Life and Death a Son, Xiaoyi* and *Here and There, the Companionship of Four Friends*. Then he wrote two long couplets for the gate: *A big eater and drinker, he could make and spend money for the good life* and *A great calligrapher and painter, he could come and go at ease for a carefree departure.*

"This couplet is perfect," Ruan said. "It could not have been a more accurate depiction of his life. No one who sees this would dare say anything bad about him. But I think the couplet in the mourning hall was too highbrow for me to understand."

"What's so hard to understand?" Wang asked. "One is about how he gave Xiaoyi life and died at his son's hand, then vented his anger at the useless boy. The other one is about the four of us, who are well known to everyone in Xijing. Now that he's gone, he's there and we're here, and we feel that our time is also running out, so we express our grief. Is that what you meant, Zhidie?"

"You can read it however you want," Zhuang said as he got someone to place a wreath at the entrance before affixing a length of wire to hang black crepe and fabric. Finally the yard felt funereal. Ruan sent someone to find a tape of mourning music, which he played on a cassette deck. "He was, after all, a good friend of ours," he said, "and we often got together at hotels because of his connections. Whenever we went out for a drink, he'd be the one who paid. Now that he's gone, we'll have fewer chances to enjoy good food, if nothing else. He lived an active life, but ended up like this because of his worthless son. These days, people are opportunists; when he was alive, they nearly wore out his threshold coming for his calligraphy, but now that he's dead, not even their dogs will come when called. He's lucky he had us. Let's write more on the mourning scroll to express our sadness over his death and extol his fame one last time. That way it won't look too dreary when his wife returns from Tianjin."

Agreeing that it was essential, Zhuang spread out the paper to let Wang write something.

"I'm not very literary to begin with, and now that I'm here, my brain has dried up," Wang said. "When I came in the past, we wrote and painted together, but that will never happen again. So let me paint something." After licking the inky tip of his brush, he stood still for a moment before putting it to work, and with a carefree flick of his wrist, a vivid sketch of an orchid appeared before their eyes.

"Fantastic!" Ruan Zhifei said. "A lush orchid is the perfect portrayal of his personality. He was brilliantly talented and lived an unrestrained life. I know that some people were critical of him, but no one can deny that he wrote every single door sign on Xijing Street. And there's no official, no matter the rank, who doesn't have one of his scrolls hanging in his house. But I've never seen any painter add roots to an orchid. Why draw a jumble of messy roots, without putting it in soil or a pot?"

"I shudder when I think about how an outstanding figure like our friend Gong died with nothing, and that's why I didn't paint the soil or a pot," Wang said as he wrote *I cry for my brother Gong / Sadly, he has departed this world.* He finished up with *Respectfully, Wang Ximian.* Finally he imprinted his seal. It was now Ruan's turn.

"I'm a terrible calligrapher," he said, "but I won't ask Zhidie to write for me. It's just that I can't think of a single line and must ask for your help, Zhidie."

"Just write whatever is on your mind."

"I have a couplet, but the two parts don't match. Well, it's all I can do." He wrote: *You're gone, Brother Gong; the value of your calligraphy will triple in value. Here I am, Ruan Zhifei / When we play mahjong, we will now be only three, missing one.* He was overcome by grief when he put down the brush. "I'm leaving now." He walked out and sobbed all the way home.

Zhuang took up the brush, but his hand shook so much he had to stop several times. So he took out a cigarette, lit it, and picked up the brush again as sweat beaded his forehead.

"Aren't you feeling well, Zhidie?" Wang asked.

"I'm in emotional turmoil. I keep feeling that he's not dead and is in fact standing next to me watching me write."

"He did like to watch you write, complimenting your elegant prose while criticizing the composition of a particular character. We will never have a friend like him again."

The comment made Zhuang's heart ache; he closed his eyes as tears rolled down his cheeks. Dipping the brush in the ink, he wrote on the spot moistened by his tears: *I was born late, you died early / Visitors have never stayed long in Xijing / The wind wails for you and for the loss of a barrier between the living and the dead,* and *You are in the underworld, I am in the human world / Everywhere yellow dirt buries people / The rain laughs at you and me, blurring the line between there and here.*

His face was wet by the time he finished. After kneeling before the bier, he offered up a cup of water to the departed as he crumpled to the floor and passed out. Niu Yueqing yelled out and helped him up, pinching his philtrum and prying open his mouth to give him some water. Finally he came to; everyone sighed deeply over the extent of his grief.

"He's gone, don't be too sad," Wang said. "If he's watching us, he'd be happy to know how much you miss him." Wang told Zhuang to go home and rest and that he'd stay behind to make sure everything was done properly. Niu Yueqing and Zhao kept quiet, as they knew what was on Zhuang's mind, and it wasn't something they could bring up; instead they hailed a taxi and went home with him.

❋

At home, Zhuang did nothing but sleep for three days straight and ate very little. Niu Yueqing knew she could only advise him not to go back to the Gong house, so he stayed away, not even going to see Gong's wife when she returned. Niu Yueqing, on the other hand, bought items for the mourning rites and went over every day to help Gong's wife. That went on for several days, until she had dark circles under her eyes.

Zhuang slowly recovered, and after ten days it dawned on him that he hadn't had any fresh milk for quite some time. He asked Liu Yue, who told him she hadn't seen Aunty Liu, either. One day when he was bored, he went on an outing with Tang Wan'er. When they reached a village, Zhuang said, "Ai-ya! Isn't this Maowa Village? Aunty Liu lives on the south side. It's been a long time since I had fresh milk. Maybe she's ill. Why don't we visit her? I'd become a cow if we are what we eat."

"You and a bull do have one thing in common," she said.

"Do you mean the hair on my arms?" He rolled up his sleeves. "Or my stubborn nature?"

"Neither. Your horn." Zhuang was puzzled, so she explained with a folk tale:

"Once upon a time, there were a mother and daughter who opened an inn and got rich within a few years. It turned out that the inn had an unwritten rule: The mother and daughter would sleep with traveling merchants. If a man could not take them both, he would leave everything behind the following morning. If a man proved to be too much for mother and daughter, he could stay for free, even for ten days or two weeks if he wanted to. Every single merchant left empty-handed and shame-faced. One particular merchant rose to the challenge and came to stay at the inn with a load of merchandise. Confident that he was strong enough to make all the men proud, he nevertheless was apprehensive, so he carried an ox horn with him just in case. Early the next morning he was losing steam, so he used the horn to defeat the mother and daughter. Feeling sheepish about his ruse, he sneaked off before dawn. Later, when the two women made up the bed, a horn rolled out from under the pillow, but they didn't know what it was, so the mother said, 'Hmm! No wonder we lost. Just look at this. I wonder how that thing of his could shed something this big!'"

Zhuang couldn't stop laughing as he pelted her with pieces of clay. "Where did you hear that dirty joke?" he jeered. "You wouldn't be afraid even if it were a horn, I'm sure." Suddenly he squatted down and asked her to clean his ears.

"What's wrong with your ears?"

"I got so aroused by your story that I can't walk at the moment. If you clean my ears, I will focus on them and it will shrink back down."

"I don't care. You'll just have to live with the erection," she said and ran into the village ahead of him.

When they finally found Aunty Liu's house, she was weaving in the hallway. It was a sweltering day, so she only had a vest on top, with walnut leaves tucked around her waist. She cried out and stepped away from the loom when she saw them.

"My goodness. Why are you here? And why hasn't your wife come to enjoy the countryside? I haven't been to the city for days now, and I've missed you all. A while ago the soles of my feet were itching, which people say means I'll see my loved ones. I was wondering who would be coming, and it turned out to be you, not my mother or my uncle."

"So you've missed us. We're tired from the walk, but you haven't offered us a chair or some water," Zhuang said.

The woman cried out as she thumped her forehead and invited them in. She boiled water to poach some eggs, but Tang politely declined, saying she was full. She would just have some water. Unable to change Tang's mind, Liu put an egg in another bowl and took it outside, where she shouted for her son to come eat it. In the meantime, Zhuang moved two eggs from his bowl to Tang's. "Eat them. Don't they look like my you-know-whats? Why aren't you eating?"

"Behave yourself," Tang whispered. "She treats you like a saint."

When Aunty Liu returned, she said many nice things as she watched them eat and drink.

"I haven't seen you in a long time," Zhuang said. "See how thin I've gotten without your milk?"

"I talked to Wu San next door before he went into the city to sell vegetables this morning. I asked him to deliver a message to your house if he happened to walk by. The cow is sick."

"The cow is sick?"

"She hasn't eaten in days. I took her out for a walk three days ago, but she lay down yesterday and can't get back up. The poor animal has made money for us for so long, and I'm really afraid something bad might happen to her. I asked a vet to take a look, but he didn't know what's wrong. He just said she should be better in a few days. How can she get better if she doesn't eat or drink? My husband went to Qianbao to get Jiao the Cripple, a famous vet."

Zhuang went to the cow pen and was pained by the sight of the cow, which was reduced to skin and bones. The cow recognized him and, flicking her ears, tried to get up, but she couldn't quite make it. She looked at Zhuang, and Tang's eyes moistened.

"Poor thing. She's shedding sad tears, just like humans. Look at her udder; she's so skinny it looks huge."

They squatted down to shoo the mosquitoes and flies away.

The rings on the yard gate sounded while they were talking, and in walked two men. One of them, Aunty Liu's husband, whom Zhuang had met once before, was carrying a leather case on his back. The one behind limped in; he was obviously the vet. After a brief greeting, he squatted by the cow and observed the animal for some time before turning back her eyelids, prying open her lips, and raising her tail to check her back there. He followed that up by putting his ear on different parts of the cow's body and knocking on her back, making a loud thumping noise. When he was done, he broke into a big smile. "Can she be saved?" Aunty Liu asked.

"How much did you pay for her?"

"Four hundred and fifty-three yuan, from Mount Zhongnan. We're destined to be together; she started giving milk right after she came, and she has such a nice temper she's like family."

"How long have you been selling milk?" the vet asked.

"Over a year now. The poor thing, she walked up streets and down alleyways with me."

"Then I'll have to congratulate you. You've earned back what you paid for the cow by selling her milk. Moreover, she'll give you several thousand yuan with about a hundred jin of meat and the hide. She has a liver problem, you know. Cows, like humans, can have liver diseases, but when a cow's liver goes bad, it produces cow bezoar, which is valuable stuff. People have tried everything to get cows to produce it, but your family has this cow. It's like money raining down on you. What's your concern?"

"What are you talking about? I don't care about cow bezoar, whatever that is. I'm not so cold-hearted that I could watch my cow die just to get that stuff. She's a member of the family. Please write a prescription for her. I'll give her the medicine and let her rest."

"I've never met anyone like you. You have a good heart, but let me tell you, I can't cure her; no one can. Listen to me, find a butcher tomorrow and you can still get some meat off her. If you wait too long, you won't be able to save her, and her flesh will melt away."

Aunty Liu turned and went back to the house to cry, ignoring her husband when he told her to make the vet something to eat. Irritated, he cursed, "Would you cry that hard if your old man died?" Looking somewhat embarrassed, he turned to Zhuang and Tang. "That wife of mine is so muddle-headed that neither heaven nor earth can clear her mind. Let's go inside. I'll have her make something for us."

"Aunty Liu has had the cow for a long time," Zhuang said. "That's why she feels so bad. I only drank its milk, and I feel bad."

They heard the sound of water sloshing in a basin. "Are you preparing dough?" her husband asked. "Make us some noodle soup."

Aunty Liu walked out with a basin containing mung-bean paste for the cow. The vet frowned and said, "I'll be on my way. Someone in another village has asked me to check on their cow. You can pay me now. This cow isn't going to live much longer, so eight or ten yuan will do." Aunty Liu's husband tried to get the vet to stay, but he begged off, so her husband paid him and saw him to the gate. In the face of Aunty Liu's sorrow, Zhuang and Tang decided to leave, too; when they said good-bye and walked to the gate, the cow lowed from inside.

Zhuang shook his head. "I don't know what's happening these days. There have been so many disasters, it's enough to make you lose heart."

"Did you and Liu Yue get together again?" Tang asked him.

"Why bring that up when I'm talking about serious matters?"

"You slept with her, so naturally that will lead to a disaster. If you continue, either you or I will meet with a bad end."

Zhuang said that was nonsense, but deep down he was troubled, and as he looked back, fear set in. "Why would I do that? She's in love with Zhao Jingwu, and everything is fine with him."

"It's still early," she said.

When they reached Huancheng Road, he wanted to hail a taxi, but she preferred to walk so they could talk. For some reason, Zhuang thought of Ah-lan. He asked Tang if she would be willing to visit Ah-lan at the mental hospital. He had told her about the sisters, leaving out his relationship with Ah-can. She was unhappy that he wanted to go see Ah-lan at that moment.

"Have you been thinking about her? Do you regret not being her lover? I'm with you now, and still you're thinking about her. As people say, whatever you can't eat smells wonderful until you actually eat it."

"This is the road to the hospital, which reminded me of her. Why are you jealous? I don't know what you'd be thinking if she weren't ill."

"What am I supposed to do? All right, if it will make you happy, I'll go with you. I want to see what sort of rare beauty she is. But I'm afraid you might make her feel even worse, since she's alone on that side of the gate while you're holding the hand of a pretty girl on this side."

Zhuang wavered. "I won't go, then. She's in such a bad way, she might not recognize me anyway."

"Maybe you really don't want to go," she said with a smile and a wink. He pinched off a blade of grass to tickle her. She jumped to the side of the road, saying she had to pee. As she walked though waist-high wormwood, the tips of her hair floated in and out of sight atop the grass, creating a captivating air of mystery.

"Go in farther, or people in passing cars will see your rear end," Zhuang said.

"They'd only see a white rock." She hummed a tune, even sang a few lines, something she hadn't done before. It reminded Zhuang of the time Liu Yue had sung her folk song.

"So you can sing too, Wan'er."

"Of course."

"What's that you're singing?"

"A flower drum song from southern Shaanxi."

Zhuang was intrigued. "Keep singing, it's beautiful."

She sang softly as she watched her urine destroy an anthill:

The skin of my lips misses you so;
it's hard to tell anyone, oh no.
The tips of my hair miss you so;
the red ribbons are hard to get, oh no.
The irises of my eyes miss you so;
I mistake another man for you, oh no.
The tip of my tongue misses you so;
I can't taste the condiments, oh no.

As he listened to the song, Zhuang was worried that passersby might hear it and look in their direction, so he kept careful watch. First he saw a rabbit scamper from one side of the road to the other so swiftly that it was only a blurry shadow; then he noticed four or five people standing a ways off, which prompted him to whisper, "Enough. Stop singing." When the people didn't move, he realized they were waiting at a bus stop; his mind at ease, he took out a cigarette. A bus picked that moment to arrive and let out a passenger, who headed his way. Zhuang nervously asked Tang if she was finished. When he saw who the passenger was, it nearly took his breath away. It was Ah-can. Zhuang called out to her. She looked up. The sun was in her eyes, so she shielded them with her hand, then froze. She spun around and started running. The people waiting for the bus had boarded and the door had shut, but she banged on it and shouted until it was opened again. She hopped on; the door shut just as Zhuang ran up and the bus drove off, with the back of her blouse caught in the door. He waved and shouted, "Ah-can! Ah-can! Why won't you see me? Why did you run off? Where do you live?" He ran after the bus, but he was too late; he slumped to the grass when he got back to the spot where he had been standing.

Meanwhile, Tang had been flicking off the many grasshoppers that had jumped onto her as she was peeing. She amused herself by catching them and tying them together by the legs with her hair, until she had four in a row. As she was bringing the string of insects to show Zhuang, she witnessed his fruitless chase and dropped the grasshoppers. The sad look on his face stopped her from making a joke. "Was that Ah-can?" Zhuang nodded. "How bizarre! We were talking about Ah-lan and Ah-can shows up. Why did she run away when she saw you?"

"She said she never wanted to see me again. She must have been visiting her sister at the hospital, which means she lives around here. She didn't want me to know where she lives, so she jumped on the bus again."

"She must have loved you. Women are like that. When they're in love, they're like a moth flying into a flame with no regard for itself. It couldn't care less if it burned to ashes. But when they harden their hearts and choose not to see you, they'll avoid you like the plague. You were in love, weren't you?"

Ignoring her question, he said, "Be honest and tell me, Wan'er. Am I a terrible man?"

Caught off guard, she could only say, "No, you're not."

"Be truthful, don't lie to me. You must think that's all you need to say for me to believe you." He pulled up some grass around him. "I'm such a fool. Why did I think you'd tell me the truth? I should have known that you wouldn't be honest with me."

Her face reddened from the effort to comfort him. "You really aren't a bad man. You haven't seen the world's truly bad people. If you're a terrible man, then I'm an abominable woman. I betrayed my husband, abandoned my son, and ran away with Zhou Min, and now I'm with you. If you're an awful man, it's my fault." A surge of emotion brought tears to her eyes. Zhuang stared blankly; he had wanted to share his grief, but what she had said only made him feel that he truly had done great harm to the woman. He reached out for her, but she shrank back and fell to her knees, and they cried facing each other.

Zhou Min was not home when they finally made it back. The table was empty except for his xun, which had a tiny yellow daisy stuck in the blowhole. Zhuang fixed his empty gaze on it for a while, but he did not dare touch it. She heated up some water to wash their feet and complained about his long toenails when she saw his. "Doesn't she trim your nails?" She took out a pair of scissors to trim them for him despite his resistance. After putting his shoes back on, she placed her own small feet in his hands, "Rub my feet. I wore heels all day for your sake, and my feet hurt." Zhuang massaged her feet, making her giggle. "I can't stand it any longer," she said with a sideways glance at him.

"We can't," Zhuang said. "He gets off work around now."

"He's been coming home after dark lately. You're feeling low, and only I can help you relax. Do whatever you want, so long as it cheers you up," she said. She was removing her hairpin to let her hair cascade down when the sound of a bicycle came from the gate. She quickly pulled her hair back into a ponytail, set her feet down to put on her shoes, and shouted, "Who is it? Who's there?" She ran out to open the gate. Zhuang scooped up her stockings from the bed and draped them over the wire on the wall before walking out. Zhou Min was there to greet him, "So here you are, Zhuang Laoshi. I was going to go see you after we ate. Is dinner ready, Wan'er?"

"I ran into Zhuang Laoshi when I went out for some groceries, so I asked him to come in. We just got back. What would you like, Zhuang Laoshi? How about a fried-egg flat cake with purple rice porridge?"

"Go on in and make it." Zhou parked his bike. "I heard you were ill, Zhuang Laoshi. Are you feeling better?"

"It's nothing. I just felt terrible after Gong Jingyuan died and slept for a few days."

"Everyone's been talking about it. They're all saying how emotionally attached you were to him."

"Are they really?"

"Yes. You're both celebrities, but your image is so much superior to his."

"Let's not talk about that. You said you were going to my house. Have you heard anything new? After all this time, the second hearing still hasn't begun. Nothing seems to be moving. It could take years. Even a ghost would run out of patience. But Bai Yuzhu has been active, always wanting me to do something or other for him."

"I've been seeing Sima Gong about every third day. I don't take expensive gifts along, but each time it's twenty or thirty yuan. I went again this afternoon, and he said there would be no second hearing. They've gotten to the bottom of things. The arguments from the writers and literature professors we sent over were critical and timely. The view in the court is to bring the case to a conclusion."

"Did he say how?"

"He gave me a summary: Basically, there were some slip-ups in the article, but it didn't reach the level of defamation, and since the magazine office has dealt with the author, they suggest mediation for both sides to reach an understanding and repair the friendship. That means we won the case. But Sima Gong said Jing Xueyin went to see the chief judge when she heard the decision; she even went to see the party secretary for the Municipal Committee on Politics and the Law, and now the chief judge wants them to submit a new report. At least Sima Gong was true to his word. The decision angered him, so he submitted the original report. The chief judge said to deal with the six-member review committee. Three are leaning in our direction, while the chief judge and the other two are on their side. It's even, but if the chief judge shows his cards first, it's hard to say what those on our side would do. They could change their minds, and even if they don't, we'd lose if one of them abstained."

Zhou stopped when he saw Zhuang lying on the sofa with his eyes shut. "Do you understand what I'm saying, Zhuang Laoshi?"

"Keep going."

"That's all I know."

"So, what do you think?" Zhuang asked, his eyes still shut.

"This is a critical moment. The committee will meet again in ten days, because the chief judge is attending a meeting in Beijing. I think you should go see the mayor and ask him to work on the secretary of the Committee on Politics and the Law and the chief judge."

"I can't talk to the mayor about this. He's not a friend, like Meng Laoshi, to whom I can say whatever I want. I've asked for his help before, but nothing dealing with legal matters, which was why he was dropping hints. We can't ask him to help us this time. He's in a leadership position and can only help out with matters that won't undermine his status and authority."

"Then—" Zhou Min was chastened.

Zhuang was about to say more, but changed his mind. Alerted by the silence that followed, Tang came in and saw that the two men were having a disagreement, so she quickly brought out the first three fried cakes. After eating one, Zhuang said he had had enough and needed to leave. Zhou tried but failed to get him to stay longer. "Take care, then." Zhou walked him out to the lane entrance.

Before Zhuang arrived home, Zhou Min phoned Niu Yueqing from a pay phone at the lane entrance to tell her about his conversation with her husband. He asked her to talk Zhuang around, and she said she would try. The moment he walked in the door, she asked about the lawsuit, urging him to go see the mayor. He had to, she insisted, even if it meant a loss of face, for otherwise they might lose a lawsuit they expected to win. Zhuang blew up, cursing the devious Zhou Min; he had explained his reasons to Zhou, and yet Zhou had called their house before Zhuang even returned. Niu Yueqing kept trying, and Zhuang finally agreed to go see the mayor, though he couldn't help but grumble about how easy it was for people to get him to do something.

He went to see the mayor the following morning, but the man was out, and Zhuang returned looking cheerful.

"Why are you happy you didn't get to see him?" his wife asked. "You'll have to go again, you know that, don't you?"

"Don't push me."

"I know it's awkward to ask for help, but we only have eight or nine more days. What will we do if you can't find him at all?"

"I'll go again tomorrow, then. What kind of writer have I become? I've lost my dignity! I'll go to his house and wait for him, even if it means that I'll die waiting there. But there's one thing I have to make clear to you: You can't interfere with what I do when I ask for the mayor's help."

He went back the next day, but instead of asking for the mayor, he went straight to Huang Defu and inquired after the mayor's son. The son, whose name was Dazheng, had had polio as a child, which had led to atrophy in one leg; he could walk, but with a serious limp that made him look like a stumblebum. Still single at thirty, Dazheng worked for a foundation for the disabled.

"His physical condition hasn't changed," Huang Defu said, "but the mayor and his wife want to see him married. He hasn't liked any of the girls they've introduced to him; he wants a pretty girl, but what pretty girl would want to marry him? So he's gotten temperamental, causing lots of trouble at home, and the mayor can't do a thing about him."

"Nothing is perfect in this world," Zhuang said. "With an unmarried son, no one, not even the mayor of a major city, can live in peace. In the past, people who opposed the mayor laughed at him for having a disabled son. What will they do to humiliate him if he can't find his son a wife? I've been keeping an eye out for them, though, and I've finally found one who's the right age. She has a high school education, is sharp and competent, and is very attractive. I'm sure Dazheng will have no objections, but I don't know what the mayor and his wife will say."

"Have you really found such a girl? If she's OK with Dazheng, his parents will go along. In fact, the mayor's wife has talked to me several times, but I haven't been able to find a match. Tell me, where is this girl? What's her name and where does she work?"

"You'll recall meeting her if I tell you who it is. My wife said she ran into you once on the street. Do you remember the girl with her that day?"

"The one with double-fold eyes, a mole on her right brow, long legs, white heeled sandals, and a canine showing on the right when she smiles?"

Zhuang was amazed. "That's her, Liu Yue. She's a maid in my house. She has everything going for her except that she doesn't have Xijing residency."

"Ai-ya! I couldn't find such a charming girl if I searched with a lantern. A pretty face is a woman's best asset. Rural residency is no big deal. It would be easy to get her a city residency card and a job."

Huang accompanied Zhuang to see the mayor's wife at the Science Commission. When she heard Zhuang's idea, she was so happy that she took his hands in hers and said, "Thank you so much for working on this. I've worried about that boy's marriage so much, my hair is turning gray. Have you talked to the girl yet? I'm not sure she'd like Dazheng. It's happened before; a girl he likes doesn't like him, or he doesn't like a girl who likes him. When you talk to the girl, make sure to tell her everything about Dazheng. Don't keep anything from her."

Less assured now, Zhuang said, "I mentioned it to her in a roundabout way, and she just blushed without saying what she thought. But I don't think it will be a problem. Liu Yue has a pretty face and a good heart; she's smart but not beautiful. We can arrange a meeting for them whenever it's convenient for you."

"No need to worry about a convenient time. Bring her over tonight if you're free; if not, she can come on her own. They will know what it's about, so we won't have to say anything about what we're doing. They'll know. Just let them talk. It would be wonderful if it worked out, but if not, they could be friends. But no matter what, I thank you."

After a meeting that night, Zhuang went home. Niu Yueqing, who was chatting with Liu Yue, asked if he had managed to meet with the mayor. "I'll be the one to go jail if it comes to that, and you won't have to bring me my food, so what are you worried about?" he said to his wife before asking Liu Yue to see him in his study.

"I'll take food to you if Dajie won't," she said with a smile as she followed him into the study. When he closed the door, she whispered, "What nerve you have! She's home."

"I want to talk to you about something. When was the last time you saw Zhao Jingwu? Be honest with me."

"It's been several days." She blushed. "Did he say something to you?"

Instead of replying, Zhuang asked, "Have you been intimate?"

"I'm leaving if this is what you want to talk to me about."

"What I mean is," Zhuang said with a serious look, "do you really love him?"

"Have you had too much to drink? You were our matchmaker, and now you're asking me if I love him. Do you plan to match me with someone else?"

"Yes."

Liu Yue looked stunned, and Zhuang continued, "I've given it some thought. Zhao isn't bad, but he's been around. He's seen a lot, and he's clever enough to adapt. Handsome men like him usually have lots of girls chasing after them, and I'm worried that he won't be nice to you forever. I'd have done you wrong if that happened. I'm not your father, but you work here, and I'm responsible for you. I have another candidate in mind. His looks can't compare with Zhao's, but ten Jingwus wouldn't be his match in terms of social status and financial situation. And your residency could be arranged right way. I'll be straight with you: it's the mayor's son."

Her eyes lit up. "The mayor's son?" She immediately shook her head. "You're toying with me, aren't you? Why would the mayor's son want to marry me? I considered myself blessed to be working at your house and having had something with you for a while. I can't possibly have so many good things happen to me."

"Well, that's what miracles are all about. You're smart and you're pretty, and those are your best assets. I want to be frank with you. He's not good-looking, so you'll have to think about it. If you agree to the marriage, you won't have to worry about Jingwu. I'll talk to him."

"How bad does he look?"

"He has a problem with his leg, from polio as a child. But he's not a cripple and he doesn't use a cane. Mentally he's all there. Many girls want to marry him, but the mayor's wife hasn't liked any of them. She's seen you and likes you a lot."

"So that's it. He's disabled. You're selling me defective goods."

"You're a clever girl, and there's no need for me to say more. Take your time and think it over while I read. You can tell me when you've made up your mind." Zhuang picked up a book and sat down to read. She sighed and leaned back against the sofa with her eyes shut. Out of the corner of his eye, Zhuang saw two sparkling teardrops roll out of her eyes beneath her long lashes, the sight of which made his heart ache, so he shut the book and stood up. "All right, Liu Yue. Just forget what I said. Go chat with your dajie."

To his surprise, she rushed into his arms and said tearfully, "Do you think this will work?"

"You will have to decide for yourself." He dried her tears.

"I want you to tell me. Will it work?" He looked up at the bookcase before nodding. "All right." She got out of his arms and stood up straight. "I believe my luck is going to change for the better. I can feel it, really. I felt that way the moment I arrived in this city. Go tell them Liu Yue is willing."

Zhuang opened the door and walked out of the study.

"What were you talking about in there, sneaking around like that?" Niu Yueqing asked.

"What were we talking about? Something big just happened, I'll have you know."

"What?" Niu Yueqing was frightened.

"Hitler is dead," Zhuang said with a smile.

"What a windbag! This is the first time you've smiled at me in months!" she said angrily.

Wiping the smile off his face, he said, "I want to talk to you about something."

Liu Yue picked that moment to walk out. When she heard him, she spun around and went to her own room, locking the door behind her.

"I introduced Liu Yue to the mayor's son; they're getting engaged. What do you think of that?"

"Are you engaged in human trafficking? You promised her to Zhao Jingwu, and now you're handing her over to the mayor's son?" She was nearly shouting.

"You promised not to interfere when I sought the mayor's help. So now you have to stay out of this."

"So you're getting cold-hearted, marrying her to the mayor's son?" Niu Yueqing softened her tone. "We may win the case, but have you thought about what to say to Jingwu? We have to rely on him, since we can't trust Hong Jiang anymore."

"Would I have gotten into the water if I hadn't measured the depth?" He went to his study to sleep.

As she sat in the living room, Niu Yueqing turned the news over in her head, wondering how her husband could have dreamed up such a scheme. He was not normally a decisive man, but this time he had shown that he knew how to handle a serious matter. Still, she was beset by apprehension. This had come about because she had more or less forced him to see the mayor, so there was nothing she could say now. She decided to look at it more positively: on the surface, they were being unfair to the loyal Zhao in order to butter up the mayor, but it was in fact to safeguard many people's best interests by sacrificing those of one person. She asked Liu Yue to come out. "Are you really willing to marry Dazheng?"

"Sure, why not? He's disabled, but I think that's my fate anyway. If I married Zhao Jingwu, something might happen to him to make him lose a leg or an arm."

The girl's answer impressed Niu Yueqing; obviously she was facing reality, which pleased her. "It's not that bad, you know. I've met Dazheng, and he's much better than you think. On the other hand, even if he had no arms or legs, he'd still be ten times better than someone with ten arms and ten legs. When you marry him, you'll be living like royalty. Thousands of people will be green with envy. But you can't forget us."

"Of course I'll forget you. I'll get the police to arrest you or chase you out of the city, because I can't have you always telling people that I was once a maid in your house." Then she laughed, as did Niu Yueqing.

That evening, as Liu Yue made herself up in front of a mirror, Niu Yueqing helped apply blush to her cheeks, watched by Zhuang, who repeatedly told Niu Yueqing to add more. There was nothing bright in Liu's wardrobe, and Niu Yueqing's clothes were all too plain, so Zhuang rode his scooter over to see Tang Wan'er. Tang and Zhou were both happy, for their own reasons, when they heard that Liu Yue would be marrying the mayor's son. Tang gathered up a few items and climbed onto the back of the scooter. "Liu Yue was born with such good luck," she said along the way, "for now she'll rise above us all. She's going to wear my clothes today, but who knows what luxury items she'll be putting on tomorrow. She could toss her satin and silk clothes into a trashcan, and I wouldn't be lucky enough to get even one. Obviously you like her more than you do me, for you've been thinking about her future, while no one cares whether I live or die." She choked up.

"Would you accept it if I told you to marry a disabled man? Don't be envious. You want it all—love, money, fun, beauty, and—"

"And what?"

"You know what I mean. If I knew a man better than me, I'd fix you up with him and wouldn't even sigh over it."

She thumped him on the back and said, "I don't care about anyone else. You're the one I want. I just hope you'll marry me as soon as possible."

Liu Yue, wearing only a bra and panties, was doing her hair with the bathroom door open, so she shrieked and shut the door when Zhuang and Tang arrived. Tang went into the bathroom with a pile of her clothes and said, "He wouldn't dare look at you even if you asked him to. He'd be afraid the mayor would cut out his eyes." The two women giggled as Liu tried on the clothes. "Come take a look, Shimu," Tang said. "These look like they were made for her. The mayor's son will probably dance around when he sees her."

Liu Yue suddenly looked embarrassed, which prompted Niu Yueqing to glare at Tang, who turned her back on them, smiled, and said, "When she gets married, the photos will be on magazine covers. Schools have their campus beauties, so do colleges; Liu Yue would beat them all if Xijing were to hold a beauty pageant."

"As for beauty queens," Liu Yue said, "that would be Wan'er, the queen of Tongguan County."

"Me? I'm not pretty enough to go in through the front door," Tang said. Zhuang gave her the high sign and changed the subject, telling the girl how to behave and what to look for when she met the son. If she liked him, they would choose a date for the engagement party. But she and Dazheng would have to decide on a date for the wedding themselves. That done, he told Liu Yue they ought to get going. Tang went out with them, as she had to go home. Niu Yueqing walked them to the door, where she told the girl to act with modesty and grace. "Treat this place like your parents' house, and don't let Dazheng look down on us, whether it works out or not."

"That's enough, Zhuang said. "She's better at this than you."

After they emerged from the compound, Tang insisted on walking Liu Yue all the way to City Hall. Zhuang told Liu Yue he would pick her up in two hours, to which she responded with a wave before walking off.

"Liu Yue is meeting her future love," Zhuang said to Wan'er, "so why don't we have a little tryst of our own? Have you ever been to the woods outside Hanyuan Gate? When it gets dark, the area is swarming with couples. When I was younger, I didn't have an opportunity to enjoy outdoor romance, but now I can make up for it, even though I'm not young anymore."

"That sounds wonderful! What a great idea. You're younger than them all. You know who makes you young, don't you?"

The large wooded area outside the gate had already filled with young couples. They all tried to keep their distance from other couples as they happily whispered, cuddled, and fooled around. Zhuang and Tang walked on, feeling uncomfortable, as they couldn't find a secluded spot, and they looked whenever they passed a couple.

"Where are you going? We're too old, this place isn't for us anymore," she said as she guided him to a rock under a lilac tree, where she wrapped her arms around his neck. "The lilac smells wonderful," Zhuang said as he looked around. She turned his head to face her, and they were soon in each other's arms. Quickly getting into the mood, he sat her on his lap, took off her heels, hung them on a branch, and took her as if she were a cat or a dog.

"People are staring," she said.

"I don't care."

"How bold you've gotten!"

"Now I know why so many couples come here and why they're so uninhibited. A wooded area on such a beautiful night is the perfect time and place for romance. That's why everyone turns mute and deaf."

"What do you think Liu Yue and the disabled guy are doing now?"

"What do you think?"

"They might be having sex, too. But with polio, is that thing of his also disabled? That would be terrific. After she married him, she'd be eating ginseng and birds' nests during the day, but crying like a dripping candle at night."

"Don't jinx her. She's been nice to you."

"Are you feeling bad for her? Didn't I say she's a white tiger? Now you see? Zhao Jingwu suffers, while the mayor's son, who was destined to marry her, was stricken with polio."

Zhuang would not let her continue, so she lost her temper.

"You always take her side," she said. "I know what you're thinking. You're taken by her good looks, but you know you can only keep one woman. You don't want anyone else to have her, so you're giving her to a disabled man, and still you feel bad about losing her."

The reprove stirred up a myriad of emotions in Zhuang, so he tried to stop her, but the more he tried, the more she insisted on talking about Liu Yue. He spread his arms and dumped her on the grass. "All right, all right. I won't talk about her."

But she kept at it: "I treasure that dress so much, I've seldom worn it. Now that she's put it on, you will mistake me for her if I wear it after she's left."

"What you need is for me to buy you some new clothes. Let her have that one, since it fits her so well, and I'll buy you some new outfits."

"Don't even think about it. I can't part with that dress, because you bought it for me. I went to the mall on North Avenue yesterday and saw a stylish leather coat. You can buy that for me when winter comes."

"Consider it done, as long as it looks good on you. Jingwu went to Guangzhou to sell some calligraphy, and before he left, I asked him to buy you a gold necklace. I think he'll buy some clothes for Liu Yue, too. When he comes back and finds out about her, he will have no more use for the clothes, and I'll take them off his hands. Has Zhou Min sensed anything?"

"He just thinks you're good to me, and hasn't said anything. Besides, he has no proof. But I'm afraid he'll find out sooner or later. You have no idea how often I dream about you, and I'm worried that one of these days I'll call out your name in my sleep. You can't run away from me when that happens."

"I won't, but you have to understand the difficult position I'm in. You'll just have to wait for me, no matter what."

"Why did I mention that again? You're upset with me, aren't you?"

He shook his head. "Control yourself when you're at home so he won't notice."

"It might be better if he did. The sooner he knows, the sooner we'll break up."

"That's not a good idea."

"Why not?"

"My mind is a mess and my heart is in agony, Wan'er. Ever since I met you, I've wanted to marry you, but it's not that simple. I'm not young anymore, and I'm not a nobody. I don't want you to break up with Zhou Min, because I can't get a divorce any time soon. You will have to give me time so I can conquer my surroundings and conquer myself. With Zhou Min around, he can take care of you, though it pains me to see that; you and I should have been together already, but we each must continue to live with someone else."

"It's worse for me. I'm a woman, and when he wants sex, I reject him nine times out of ten. I have to do what he wants every once in a while. It's like I'm made of wood, with no desire or passion; all I want is for him to finish as quickly as possible. You can't understand my suffering. We must work hard until the day comes. If we can't be together, then neither of us will be at peace."

He put his arms around her and they fell silent, while their bodies shook so violently that the lilac tree rustled noisily, drawing the attention of a couple nearby. Finally they parted. "Let's go back." They stood up, both ruing their decision to come. "Let's talk about something cheerful," she said. "Yes," he said, but neither could come up with an uplifting topic.

Two and half hours had passed by the time they got back to City Hall, but Liu Yue was not outside waiting for them. "Could she have come out and left when she didn't see us?" Tang asked. "We'll wait awhile," Zhuang said. They waited another hour, until they were tired from walking, then went across the street to sit on the steps outside a store, where they fixed their gaze on the City Hall entrance. Another half-hour went by before they saw her emerge into the illuminated area near the entrance. Zhuang was about to call out to her when Tang stopped him. "Don't. Let me watch her body language, and we'll know if everything is all set."

Liu walked out and stopped; a car drove up. The driver got out and walked around to open the door for her. She got in, and the car took off noisily down Laishun Avenue. "It's only just started, and she's already acting like the mayor's daughter-in-law," Tang said. "You agreed to meet her here, yet she rode off in that car without even looking around."

Zhuang did not reply, so they stood there for a while. "Why don't I walk you home," he said. He did, then went back to the compound alone.

⁂

When Zhuang told his wife, she was upset but did not reproach the girl. Three days later, an engagement banquet was held at the Afanggong Hotel, where the mayor's wife, following the old traditions, gave Liu Yue an array of presents: a necklace, a box of imported cosmetic products, a set of sleepwear, a pair of red-and-white high heels, a pair of soft-soled casual shoes, a hair dryer, a leather coat, a fall dress, three blouses, and a blazer. She had never had so many nice things in her life, and she wanted to give the red heels to Niu Yueqing, who declined. So she bought Niu Yueqing a pair of stockings. From then on, Liu Yue made herself up every day, trying out new looks, and whenever she could, she went back into her room to look at herself in the mirror and practice her stockpile of smiles. With new clothes and a more glamorous face came a different way of thinking. She often bought more than the family could consume and then threw out the leftovers when they went bad. When they had visitors, regardless of their status or position, she would pour tea and then sit down in her black embroidered robe. She cut into conversations when she felt like it, sometimes interjecting comments while eating an apple. Puckering up her lips, she would cut a slice, pick it up with a knife, and slip it into her mouth. Displeased by the girl's behavior, Niu Yueqing said to her once, "Does your mouth hurt, Liu Yue?"

"I don't want to smear my lipstick," she said.

With a sigh, Niu Yueqing told her to boil some water. She then shut the kitchen door the moment the girl went in. Knowing that Niu Yueqing did not want her to talk to the guests, Liu Yue came back out of the kitchen looking surly and grumbled all the way to her room. Keeping her anger in check, Niu Yueqing waited until no one was around to ask: "Did you come back by car and leave Zhuang Laoshi waiting on the street that night?"

"The mayor has an official car, and Dazheng asked the driver to take me home, so I got in," Liu Yue said as she was styling her hair with the dryer. "They would have laughed at me if I hadn't, and that would have reflected badly on you, too."

"Then you should have let Zhuang Laoshi know when you came out. He walked you there and waited for you. What did he have while you were enjoying fruit and coffee inside? He waited till midnight, but you came out and just got in the car to be driven away."

"Did he complain to you about me? I didn't see him when I came out. Could he really have been waiting all that time? Who knows where they went and what they did."

"They? Did he invite Meng Laoshi out for a drink?"

Liu Yue's temper flared up when she saw that Niu Yueqing didn't believe her. "Who else would it be? Tang Wan'er didn't go home after we walked out the door; she came with us. When I entered City Hall, they were out there on the street, and I don't think they needed anything to eat or drink."

"You'd better watch what you're saying, Liu Yue. Zhuang Laoshi has many friends, men and women. You've gotten a boost in your status, but you would hurt his feelings if he heard what you just said. Besides, Wan'er has always been nice to you. Didn't she bring over her own clothes for you to choose from that night?"

"Dajie is the Happy Buddha, with a belly big enough to take in things that are too hard to swallow," Liu said with a laugh. "Just pretend I didn't say anything. You're unhappy with me anyway, but I'll be leaving soon."

Niu Yueqing mulled over what she had just heard. In the past, she and Zhuang had fought often, but each time whatever it was about was smoothed over; they continued to eat together and slept in the same bed, having sex at least once a week. But since he had met Tang Wan'er, the situation had slowly begun to change. They seemed to fight less and seldom quarreled, but they did not come together for three weeks or more. She wondered if Liu Yue was just being a blabbermouth. He was away a good deal of the time and was withdrawn at home, probably because of all his troubles.

"I don't like trouble, Liu Yue," she said to the girl. "You came to work for us because we had a karmic connection. I've always treated you like a sister, and I've never looked down on you. I wish you could stay here forever, but that's impossible. Soon you'll be married into the mayor's family, a wonderful outcome that both your Zhuang Laoshi and I worked hard to bring about. We don't expect any repayment, but you must behave well while you're still here, so that others won't gossip."

"Well, I'll tell you what I think now that you've said what's on your mind. If I were a typical girl from a family in the city, not a maid, would you have said those things to me? In your eyes, I'm always the country girl, the maid, and now you find it hard to take when I'm the equal of any city girl. Of course I'm grateful to you, and I'd be happy to spend the rest of my life here. I'm going to marry a disabled guy who's like the Monkey King eating a pear when he sits down; who can't bring his legs together in bed; who stands like a one-legged golden chicken; and who trips over himself when he walks, like a tethered cow. Am I really marrying so well? I want to live so that no one will ever think I'm a maid from the countryside." As she talked, Liu Yue started feeling sorry for herself, so she went to her room to dry her tears.

Niu Yueqing had wanted to teach the girl a lesson, but she ended up being the target of Liu's criticism. Feeling her face burn, she wanted to defend herself, but held back. The next day, Zhuang hastily downed two bowls of rice and got up to go to his study. Reminded of what Liu Yue had said about Zhuang and Tang Wan'er waiting together on the street, Niu Yueqing felt her appetite leave her. She stirred the contents of her bowl without putting anything in her mouth. "Can't you sit and talk awhile after you're done eating?" she asked.

"My mood is at its worst before and after mealtime, so please don't bother me."

"But that's the only time we have to talk. I wouldn't ask you to say a word if you weren't my husband."

The displeased tone in her voice stopped him. "You're right. If someone on the street tried to stop my wife and talk to her, I'd call him a rotten bastard. Well, let's talk, then. It's a clear day, the high is thirty-four degrees, and the low—" He flicked his wrist and went into his study.

Clamping her mouth shut, Niu Yueqing sighed and pushed aside her bowl and chopsticks. She stood and followed him into the study. "Tell me the truth. Are you involved with Tang Wan'er?" she blurted out, so surprising him that he froze before blowing out cigarette smoke.

"Yes," he said with his eyes on her face.

Though she had been suspicious of her husband and Wan'er, Niu Yueqing was hoping for the best with her question; he might deny it outright, swear his innocence, or fly into a rage, but there would be no more doubts. But he had calmly said, "Yes."

Troubled by his response, she felt her face darken. "Well, at least you're being honest. Now tell me how involved. When you walked Liu Yue to meet Dazheng that night, did you really spend all that time alone on the street? You came home late and told me that Liu Yue got into a car without telling you. Where did you and Tang Wan'er go? What did you do? Tell me."

Her questions told him that everything was coming to a head. He had said "Yes" in that calm tone because he wanted to test her reaction, but now he regretted his tactic. "Liu Yue," he called out, "what did you say to Dajie? Are you being a troublemaker?"

"No need to call her. I know everything; now I want to hear it from you."

"What did we do? She went home after we walked Liu Yue to City Hall. What do you think we did?"

Niu Yueqing had no answer for that, so he pressed on: "You don't know, do you? Well, I'll tell you. We had sex right there on the street in front of all the passersby, and then we went to her house and did the same in front of Zhou Min."

"Why are you yelling? Are you trying to pick a fight?"

"*You*'re the one who's picking a fight." He raised his voice. "Why don't you call Liu Yue in and have her explain it to you?"

"You're good at winning arguments, and I have to believe you for now. But let me tell you this. I can take any hardship regarding your life, your health, your career, and your future, but I won't stand for any fooling around. You were close to Jing Xueyin and I didn't say anything, did I? I could have washed my hands of the whole fiasco when she turned against you. She was an upright person who could be helpful in your career when you were friends. I'm not the jealous type. But societal mores have degenerated to such a degree that the country is filled with women who love money, status, power, and their own pleasure. I won't allow you to waste time with them." She walked out to resume eating.

The episode should have blown over when she went to work the next day, but Niu Yueqing could not stop thinking about Liu's comment as she sat in her office alone. "Dajie is the Happy Buddha, with a belly big enough to take in things that are too hard to swallow." Finally realizing that there was more to what the girl had said, she recalled how Tang Wan'er had always looked her best when she came to visit. Her eyes were emotional and expressive, ideal for seducing a man. Although Zhuang was on the timid side, writers tend to be sensitive, tenderhearted, and sentimental, so it was unlikely he was not affected. If Tang Wan'er had avoided tempting him, he might have had the desire, but not the nerve to act on it. But Tang was not the type to stay within bounds; she had run away from Tongguan with Zhou Min, so what was there to stop her from seducing Zhuang? The slightest hint from her could unleash the man's adulterous urges. Niu Yueqing searched her memory and recalled the day Tang Wan'er had tucked in Zhuang's blanket in front of her. That was not something an ordinary guest would do; if they hadn't been intimate, she would not have acted so naturally. Niu Yueqing then thought back to the day she had run into the two of them at the building by the nunnery. Tang Wan'er had looked uncomfortable. If she had indeed been looking for a part-time job, why hadn't she mentioned it before or since? Suspicion grew in Niu Yueqing's heart and prompted her to call Zhou Min at the magazine office. When he came on the phone, she asked him whether Tang Wan'er had been home on the night Liu Yue went to meet Dazheng. Zhou Min said it was nearly midnight when she returned. "I thought Shimu had asked her to spend the night."

"Nearly midnight?" Niu Yueqing repeated.

"It was. Is anything wrong? Why are you asking about this?"

"No reason. I was just worried that something might have happened to her, because I haven't seen her for quite some time."

Zhou Min was curious about the call when he put down the phone. *Was it just about that? Why did Niu Yueqing stress the time Tang Wan'er came home? Was it because she hadn't walked Liu Yue over? But when she came home, she said she had walked the girl over with Zhuang. So why was Shimu calling?* He went home full of questions. Wan'er was lying on the bed, counting something on a wall calendar. He craned his neck to look over her shoulder, and saw that some of the dates were circled in red, some had triangles around them, and others were marked with exclamation points.

"What are those marks for?"

She was in the habit of making a note on the calendar each time she returned from a tryst with Zhuang. When she was free, she could count them and savor the details. The question came out of the blue, and she was so startled that she shuddered, with goose bumps sprouting on her arms. She hung the calendar back up. "What for? I'm counting how many days a cattie of cooking oil lasts us, when I last bought pork, and how much we can afford to eat. Why did you sneak up on me like that? For a moment there I thought you were an intruder."

She was so convincing that he did not doubt her. "What would you have done if I had been an intruder?"

"What do you think? I'd screw him! What's the matter with you today? You're acting weird, like I'm keeping a lover at home while you're out."

Feeling certain he was in the wrong, Zhou Min laughed off the discussion.

But Niu Yueqing had a huge fight with Zhuang that night, saying that he and Tang Wan'er must have been on very good terms, better than good friends; otherwise, why would he have lied about her going home early? Zhuang tried to talk her around, but she would have none of it, insisting that he tell her how they got together, how intimate they had been, if they had made love, and if so, how and where. Zhuang decided to keep his mouth shut, but the more he refused to respond, the angrier she got. Irritated, he headed for his study, but she followed him, so he went into the bedroom, only to see her walk in behind him. He got into bed fully dressed, with a terrycloth blanket over his face, and she lay down next to him, not letting up on her interrogation. Then she went on about how hard she worked for the family, how she had been underappreciated by him since the day they were married, how he never went shopping with her on holidays or weekends, how he never went to a movie with her, how he never lifted a finger when it came to the household chores. She took care of his food and clothes, and she also had to take care of all the guests, ignoring her job and her own mother, all to please him. But in the end, he had eyes only for someone else.

"Are you giving me the silent treatment?" she asked. "You think everything will be fine if you don't say anything? I've let you off the hook in the past when you've clammed up, but it's not going to work this time. I want you to tell me what's going on. Go on, tell me everything."

But Zhuang slept on, even snoring softly. Niu Yueqing snatched the blanket away and jerked at his collar, "You're asleep? You've actually fallen asleep? You don't treat me like a human being. What kind of wife am I to you? If I were a dog or a cat, you wouldn't ignore me and fall asleep like that."

He sat up and shook her off, then got out of bed and headed to the study. She began to sob. When Liu Yue heard the sobbing from her room, she knew it was all because of her, yet she was waiting to see what would happen next. She got nervous when Niu Yueqing started to wail, so she went into the bedroom to talk to Niu, who realized that the girl had heard everything. Feeling a great loss of face in front of her maid, Niu Yueqing threw caution to the wind and ran over to the study, where she wrested a painting album out of Zhuang's hands and threw it to the floor.

"Look at this good wife, Liu Yue," he said. "She's started throwing things."

"Watch out for that pen on the desk, Zhuang Laoshi," Liu Yue said unexpectedly. "That's how you make a living, so make sure Dajie doesn't destroy it out of anger."

That only spurred Niu Yueqing into grabbing the pen and flinging it against the door. "I *am* a good wife, and I know how to throw things. I'll show you how good I am." She turned on Liu Yue. "Go back to your room. Why are you out here stirring things up?"

"What am I stirring up? Nothing. You're upset, so go ahead and vent your anger on me. I'm your maid, so I can't be mad at you."

Niu Yueqing was so furious that she went to her bedroom and let out a scream.

After a restless night, the three of them woke up with puffy eyes. Liu Yue made breakfast and brought it out; Zhuang slurped away while Niu Yueqing refused to eat. "Eat something," Zhuang said, "so you'll have enough energy to fight with me."

"You clam up when you should be talking, Zhuang Laoshi," Liu Yue said, "and you say all these clever things when you should be keeping your mouth shut."

"It's all your fault, Liu Yue. You told Dajie that Tang Wan'er and I have something going on." He winked her.

"Impossible. I just said you and Tang Wan'er were waiting for me at City Hall. What's wrong with that? Just tell her what you were talking about while you waited."

"We were just chatting. How can I remember any of that? Oh, now I see—I need to carry a tape recorder with me."

Niu Yueqing heard every word of the exchange, but she didn't say a thing.

"Eat something," Zhuang said to her. "After breakfast, go to the mayor's house with Liu Yue. We have important matters to attend to. Tell the mayor's wife about the lawsuit, and ask the mayor to see the secretary for the Committee on Politics and the Law and the chief judge. This has to be done as soon as possible, since it will take the mayor a couple of days. Time is running out. We mustn't delay."

"You want *me* to talk to the mayor's wife?" Niu Yueqing finally spoke up. "So you need me now?"

"It's easier when a woman is talking to another woman."

"I won't do it. You love Jing Xueyin, you love women. So why should you be afraid of lawsuits? A lawsuit over a sex scandal, it sounds so nice. Didn't you always say you would rather die at the hands of a woman, since you'd become a romantic ghost? It would surely be romantic if the court sentenced you to death. So why would I want to talk to her? If I try to cover things up when my own husband's affair is exposed, what kind of woman does that make me? Am I that worthless, that stupid?"

Zhuang silently listened as she continued to rant about the same thing. "Are you finished?" he asked as she fumed.

"You think you're in the right, so explain yourself," she said.

"You don't want to go see the mayor, and I'm not going to go. You say Tang Wan'er and I are seeing each other, so you can fantasize about how close we are. Well, I don't care. You can call Zhou Min again, even start an investigation with him." He walked out, but immediately returned to pick up his cigarettes.

Niu Yueqing did not go to work that day. She stayed home and cried her heart out until her hands and feet went cold. Liu Yue tried to talk her around but earned a scolding, so she sat in the study, where she stared blankly at the traffic outside. For over an hour, the junkman shouted, "Junkman—collecting junk—junk—I buy junk." It was annoying beyond words, and someone in the next unit threw open the window and shouted, "Hey, you, junkman." He looked up and said, "Over here. You've got junk?"

"Fuck you!"

Unperturbed, the old man pulled his cart along and sang another of his ditties:

First-rate writers enter politics
ink up with officials and become their aides.
Second-rate writers switch fields
they write ads instead of tirades.
Third-rate writers join the underworld
reprinting porn for accolades.
Fourth-rate writers sit down to write
going hungry, their good name made.
Fifth-rate writers fall on hard times
screwing themselves in a quest delayed.

❋

Niu Yueqing and Liu Yue went to the mayor's house that afternoon. He was busy with meetings, so his wife and son gave them a warm welcome before proposing that the wedding ceremony be held a month from that day. "Liu Yue will no longer be a guest here, but a host to Madam, our matchmaker." The comment brought a smile to Niu Yueqing's face. "Liu Yue's parents aren't here, so you'll be her family, since you've been so nice to her." The mayor's wife continued, "On the wedding day, the bride's family will have to follow the custom of providing a dowry, and we will send a car to pick her up at your house." The mention of a dowry concerned Niu Yueqing, who nonetheless kept smiling and said that was the way it should be done. The mayor's wife smiled happily and said, "But it shouldn't be. People would laugh at us if you spent money on her after you've made such a wonderful match. You don't have to spend a cent on the dowry. Dazheng will have everything delivered to your house in advance, to be brought over properly on the wedding day."

Niu Yueqing cried out cheerfully, "Ai-ya! We would never marry her off empty-handed, whether Dazheng sends the dowry over beforehand or not. But since you're being so considerate in order to make us look good, Zhidie and I would be happy to be her family forever." The two women continued their conversation as in-laws, chatting about things that concerned women: furniture styles and colors, which relatives and friends to invite, the location and cost of the banquet, who should be the bridesmaids, who should serve as the master of ceremonies and the witness, and so on. That went on for most of the afternoon, until Niu Yueqing took a moment to broach the main purpose of her visit. Trying to remain casual, she gave a detailed account of the origin of the lawsuit and related the suffering brought on by the case, before repeatedly stressing that they were coming to the mayor for help because they were simply at their wits' end. She talked fast without looking at the mayor's wife, but when she was done, she thought she might have sounded incoherent, so she repeated herself. *I can't care about saving face now, and I can't look at her face,* Niu Yueqing said to herself. *If she shows a hint of hesitation, I won't be able to say what I need to say. If she hems and haws when I'm done, I will get up and leave.* Her face was flushed when she finished, but she added: "Ai-ya! Listen to me. My husband told me again and again not to bring this up. Why did I tell you all this? It's so embarrassing. Everyone's gossiping about him, and he can't sit still at home. You probably will laugh at him now that you know about it."

"What's embarrassing about that?" the mayor's wife said with a smile. "Lawsuits aren't unusual. Writers like your husband care too much about saving face. That's why he didn't want to mention it to Dazheng's father."

"Ai, he knows only about writing and nothing else. He's a total incompetent away from his desk. A few days ago someone said to me, 'Writers know so much that your life with Zhuang Laoshi must be very exciting.' In fact, he knows nothing about real life, and we lead a boring existence. You can ask him what else he knows besides making up stories. He can't compare with a section chief, not to mention the mayor. Excellence in one area covers up all other deficiencies, as they say."

"But neither you nor I can make up stories, can we? And a mayor must run for office, while you can't elect a writer. He is our city's treasure."

"Ai-ya! You make him sound so special, and yet Jing Xueyin is suing with the intention of ruining him."

"Let me tell you this: No one can defeat you but you yourself. Xijing can't do without Zhuang Zhidie, so the mayor won't sit idly by if someone is trying to bring him down." She wiped off a tea stain on the table. "I'll talk to Dazheng's father."

That brightened Niu Yueqing's mood, but, afraid that the woman might forget, she reminded her of the possible serious consequences if the mayor didn't help.

"I won't forget," the mayor's wife said. "Liu Yue, why don't you go make a glass of lemonade for Dajie?"

Liu Yue brought the drink over and said, "You've insulted Zhuang Laoshi today, Dajie. He's a famous writer, and yet you make him sound worthless."

"She isn't insulting Zhuang Laoshi. Every word from her is a compliment."

"I said long ago that I would never, ever marry a writer if I were born a woman in my next life," Niu Yueqing said.

"Ah-ha! If you let that be known," the mayor's wife said, "you'd be shocked to see how many women would fight to marry him."

"Who would want him? Only a foolish woman like me agreed to marry him years ago. Now I will hand him over to anyone who wants him and count that as a blessing."

"Really? Are you sure?" Liu Yue said, which earned her a glare from Niu Yueqing.

At dinnertime Niu Yueqing insisted on going home, and she signaled Liu Yue with her eyes to help her out. So Liu Yue said that Dajie was worried about Zhuang Laoshi, and they needed to go home to cook for him. "He'll have to eat out if we don't. Restaurant utensils are dirty, and it would be terrible if he caught something."

"Don't worry. If something happens to him, I'll find you a section chief. Didn't you say you'd rather marry one of those?" Niu Yueqing laughed. "I've always heard that you are a good wife; now I see it's true, so I won't keep you. Dazheng, come see your matchmaker off."

He called for Liu Yue from his room instead. Staying put, she asked him what he wanted. Niu Yueqing nudged her to go inside while she chatted with the mayor's wife about clothes and food. It was some time before the girl came out. "What's the matter, Liu Yue? Your lips are so pale."

"Nothing," Liu Yue said, as Dazheng lurched out with a flushed face.

"Mom," is all he said.

The mayor's wife slapped her forehead and said to Niu Yueqing, "I'm afraid we're getting old."

It was dark by the time the two women were out on the street. Niu Yueqing wanted to eat at the night market, but Liu Yue said, "Aren't we going home? What about Zhuang Laoshi?"

"Don't worry about him. He doesn't care about me, so I'm not going to worry about him." They ordered two bowls of wontons and four flatbreads stuffed with meat.

"One's enough for me. How many can you eat?" Liu Yue asked her.

"We can take the leftovers home for our next meal," Niu Yueqing said.

Realizing what was going on, the girl said, "I'm so stupid. Why did I ask that question?" Niu Yueqing rapped her on the head with her chopsticks.

The living room was dark when they got home, but a light was on in the study. Niu Yueqing went to the kitchen, where the cold pots and stove told her that Zhuang had not cooked anything. Liu Yue went to the study and said to Zhuang, who was lying on the sofa under a blanket, "Guess where we went today? We took care of it."

"Really?"

"Dajie said she wouldn't go, but then what needed to be done was done," Liu Yue replied.

"Are you being a bigmouth, Liu Yue?" Niu Yueqing commented from the living room. "What did you tell him? Do you want him to laugh at me for being so hopeless? Where do you keep the enzyme pills? Bring me some. You ought to take some yourself. We ate so much meat tonight, we might get heartburn."

"You haven't eaten yet, have you?" Liu Yue said to Zhuang with a smile. "We bought two meat flatbreads for you."

"I ate already," he said.

"Are you being a flirt in there, Liu Yue?" Niu Yueqing called out. "Go to bed."

"I'm going." Liu Yue turned to Zhuang when she heard Niu Yueqing go into their bedroom. "Are you sleeping here again tonight? She cried her heart out at noon but went for your sake later. You ought to go show her some gratitude and make her feel better." She went to her room.

After some thought, he picked up the blanket and went into the bedroom. Niu Yueqing had turned off the light, so he undressed and went into the bathroom to wash, then groped his way into bed. She had rolled the blanket around her, but he forced his way in and climbed on top. She neither resisted nor displayed any reaction, so he got going quietly. □□ □□ □□ [The author has deleted 52 words.] Doing his best to seem eager, he pretended to be aroused. He tried to kiss her, but she clamped her teeth together and rolled her head back and forth. "I'll tell you a story about an impatient man eating quail eggs cooked with spinach," he said lightheartedly. "He picked at an egg with his chopsticks, but it rolled to the side, so he tried again, and this time it rolled to the other side. After five or six attempts, he lost his patience, knocked it to the floor, and squashed it."

She laughed. "You can squash me if you want."

"All right. Everything's fine. A husband and wife patch things up in bed after a fight."

"So you've thought it through and found your conscience?" He held his tongue. "I'd have lost all faith in you if you hadn't come to me tonight. Now that you're here, I'll let you off the hook and forget about what has happened. But I've learned my lesson, and I know I have to keep an eye on you. I want you to break off all communication with Tang Wan'er. I'll accompany you when you go to her house, and she is not to come here without my permission." He remained silent while continuing what he was doing under the blanket.

"You're in good shape tonight, but I'm not, so tell me another story." She pushed him off her. He lay in the dark for a while, since he had no story to tell her, and then got up to turn on the light, saying they could watch a video.

"An adult video?" she asked as he inserted a tape, immediately filling the screen with lots of action.

"You call those humans?" she asked. "They're animals."

"Many intellectuals have these in their houses, for husbands and wives to set the mood. What do you think? Does it work for you?"

"Turn it off. It looks awful."

He turned the TV off and got back into bed. □□ □□ □□ [The author has deleted 36 words.] "Did you and Tang Wan'er do it this way?" she asked. He fell silent again, but she persisted.

"No more talk of that," he said. "If you want to make love, talk like you do."

She tried to keep quiet, but blurted out, "No. This is no good. I keep thinking about what you two do together, and it makes me want to throw up."

He stopped in mid-action, climbed off, and shed silent tears.

❋

One morning Niu Yueqing was putting clothes out to dry on the balcony when the pigeon landed on the windowsill. Always fond of the little bird with its white feathers and sweet, cooing red beak, she put down her washbasin, picked up the bird, and laid it in her hand. The folded paper on its toe ring caught her attention. "I want you," it read, with a lipstick mark over the words. She froze as she realized it was a message from Tang Wan'er asking for another tryst. After tying the pigeon down with string, she waited in the living room for Liu Yue to return from buying cooking oil.

Niu Yueqing locked the door the moment Liu Yue got in. She placed a small round stool in the middle of the living room, fetched a leather duster from her bedroom, and told the girl to sit down.

"Let me put the oil in the kitchen first. There were so many people on the street today, I couldn't get through, so I yelled, 'Oil here, oil here,' and a little space finally opened for me."

"I told you to sit down."

"What's the matter with you, Dajie? I'm not going to sit down."

That earned her a whack from the leather duster. She cried out with an ugly look, "You hit me!"

"Yes, I hit you. I'm the mistress of the house and you're the maid. You colluded with a cheap woman to deceive me, so why can't I hit you? Even if the mayor were here, he wouldn't stop me. Tell me, how many times has that cunt been here? And how did you make the bed and get everything ready for them? How did you keep watch for them?"

Still thinking that the mistress was simply jealous, Liu Yue said, "How would I know what happened between them? I was just venting my anger when I mentioned it, but you took it seriously and stirred up trouble in the house. Now you've hit me for no reason. I may be a lowly maid, but I'm human, too. You really hurt me. Do you want to kill me? Even if you don't respect me or my peasant parents, I'm a member of the mayor's family. What gives you the right to beat me?"

Niu Yueqing brought over the pigeon and threw the note at Liu's feet. "This! You stay home all the time, feeding the pigeon and receiving notes, so you must have played a role in their trysts. If I didn't beat you, what would you expect me to do? Thank you? Show you respect?" Niu Yueqing hit the girl with each outburst of anger, raising welts on her arms and legs. Liu Yue groaned inwardly, aware that Niu Yueqing now knew everything. Feeling sheepish, she softened her tone as she reached out to grab at the duster. "What does what they did have to do with me?"

"How did it start? Tell me everything today or I'll keep hitting you, and I'll tell Dazheng and his mother. If they still want you, you can carry on your dirty deeds at City Hall. If they don't want you, then you can take off those clothes and go back to the hills of northern Shaanxi."

Liu Yue sobbed and told Niu Yueqing about how Zhuang and Tang Wan'er made love in the house, how he went to see her at her place, how the pigeon delivered messages that had her lipstick mark on them, sometimes even pubic hairs. In order to please Niu Yueqing and lessen her guilt, she told her everything, even things that hadn't happened. Niu Yueqing had had her suspicions, which had fueled her imagination, but Liu Yue's confession gave her such a vivid, detailed picture of what had gone on that she wished she hadn't asked. Weighed down by what she learned, she felt so helpless that her blood pressure soared and caused her to twitch; the room seemed to spin.

"God," she cried out, "I've been blind and deaf. They've been doing all of that, and I've been in the dark." Opening her eyes wide, she spread her hands and asked in a quivering voice, "What do I have left, Liu Yue? I'll tell you. I have nothing, not a thing."

Liu Yue got down off the stool and knelt before Niu Yueqing. "I wanted to tell you, Dajie, but I'm just a maid, and I didn't have the nerve to bring it up. Besides, would you have believed me if I'd told you back then? I helped by making it easy for them, I did. I'm truly sorry. Hit me, beat me to death."

Niu Yueqing threw down the duster and held Liu Yue in her arms as she wept, begging the girl to hate her. She had wanted to frighten her and hit her only because of her reluctance to tell the truth. "Please forgive your poor dajie. Can you ever forgive her?"

"Of course," Liu Yue said, and she too began to cry.

Niu Yueqing gradually calmed down. She wiped her own tears before drying those on Liu Yue's face.

"I'll go with you, Dajie, and rip that slut's face off."

"What is she, anyway?" Niu Yueqing shook her head. "A tramp who abandoned her husband and son to run away with another man, whom she then betrayed by seducing another man, a whore who loses all sense when she sees a man. I would soil my hands if I did that. Besides, people might hear about it, and everyone would know that your Zhuang Laoshi was having an affair with her. That would ruin his reputation and make her look good. He has so many admirers who can only dream of meeting him, while she slept with him. Moreover, you'll be marrying Dazheng soon, and I wouldn't be able to face their family if a scandal like this broke out. He did break my heart, but I still have to do my best to save him, even if he's intent on throwing away his future, his career, his fame, and his reputation. I put up with all the arguments at home because if they had occurred outside, he'd have flung caution to the wind and insisted upon being with the slut. That would have finished him. It was hard getting to where he is now, and all I want is for him to turn over a new leaf and stop seeing her. You mustn't let any of this reach anyone else's ears. Don't say a word when I confront him; pretend you don't know anything. But you have to think about me. Let me tell you this: you and I have to keep this predilection of his in mind and keep a close eye on him. Do you know what I'm saying?"

Liu Yue, who had never known that Niu Yueqing had that kind of analytical ability, felt sorry for her for what she had to put up with as Zhuang's wife. She nodded, and after Niu Yueqing gave her more instructions, she washed up and put on some makeup before leaving the house.

She was sent to see Tang Wan'er, who looked anxious as she invited her in. "Did you come from the apartment?" she asked. "Did you see the note? Isn't Zhuang Laoshi home?"

"He's home. Dajie went to Shuangren fu, so Zhuang Laoshi wants you to come over."

Elated, Tang Wan'er took a piece of candy out of a box for Liu Yue and, when she refused, unwrapped it and put it in the girl's mouth. "It's very sweet. Suck on it slowly, and you can feel the sweetness reach the bottom of your heart. Since he's home, he could have sent a message back with the pigeon. Why have you come all the way out here?"

"I'm going to buy some noodle sauce at the Yang Family Shop in Desheng Lane. It's not far from here, so I brought the message over," Liu said and left.

Tang carefully made herself up and got on her bike to head over to the compound.

When she had returned from seeing Zhuang that night, Zhou had been drinking with a man nicknamed Tiger, who worked for some corporation. After Zhou met him while working at the nunnery, he came to visit a few times, and Tang Wan'er got to know him a little. So she greeted Tiger before bringing a stool over to sit down to listen to them talk. An articulate man, Tiger had a fleshy face and thin lips. She quickly realized that he was trying to get Zhou to write a book for someone who had just made a lot of money. He told Zhou that the man was so rich he didn't know what to do with his money. He wanted to be known as a cultured person, which was why he was looking for someone to write a book for him. When it was done, he would take care of the printing and publication; all he asked was for his name to be on it. He would pay Zhou twenty thousand yuan. Zhou was reluctant at first; writing a book is hard, and putting someone else's name on it did not sound like a good deal. "You're not a famous writer, so what makes you think you can publish a book under your own name?" the man said. "Even if it got published, how much do you think you could make from it? Think about the life you and Wan'er are living. Why pass up an opportunity to make some real money and get out of your impoverished state? Besides, I'm not asking for a masterpiece; all you have to give me is two hundred thousand words. That's not too much work, is it? Many writers have come to me, and I've turned them all down. I'm saving this breeze of a job for you, so what's with the self-righteous attitude?"

Zhou told him he would be happy to take the job if not for the lawsuit. When Tiger asked him about that, Zhou told him everything, including the spot he was in at the moment. When Zhou mentioned Zhuang's plan to seek the mayor's help, Tang Wan'er cut in: "You've had too much to drink, Zhou Min. Stop the nonsense. Why would Zhuang Zhidie resort to that kind of backdoor ruse? You're smearing his reputation, and you could get the mayor in trouble."

"Stay out of men's conversations," Zhou said, making her so angry that she stormed into the bedroom. Lying in bed, she tried to hear what they were saying.

"I'm a lawyer myself. It's not a full-time job for me, but I won all five cases I helped on. Your case is no big deal, so there's no need to trouble the mayor. If Zhuang Zhidie doesn't want to say in court that he and the woman have slept together, there's another way to win the case."

"How?"

"Didn't Jing Xueyin claim that she was the woman in your article, while you argued that it wasn't her? If another woman were to file a lawsuit saying she was the one, that would muddy the water and create a mess; the court would declare that no one could prove it was Jing, and the case would be thrown out."

Tang Wan'er thought the solution sounded slightly crazy, but it was one way to end the suit. When Tiger left and Zhou came to bed, they talked about the suggestion.

"I could be that woman if that would help end the suit," Tang said.

"Great. I was so worried about finding someone to do it, I didn't even think about you."

"I was just testing you," she said. "Would you really want me to do it? You'd send me into his arms to serve your own interest?"

"It'd just be a ruse."

"What if it were real?"

Smiling, Zhou couldn't stop talking about what a great idea it was, but he dozed off as the effects of the alcohol took hold, and she regretted her offer. It would be for Zhuang's sake, but she wasn't sure he would agree to it. She had made the suggestion without talking it over with him first; what would he think of her if Zhou decided to carry out the ruse? After fretting about it the whole night, she waited for Zhuang's visit to talk to him. Two days had gone by, and he hadn't shown, while Zhou had her read the article to gain a better understanding of the case. He would carry out the plan if Zhuang's visit to the mayor yielded unsatisfactory results. She couldn't wait for him any longer, which was why she had sent the pigeon that morning.

❋

To her surprise, it was Niu Yueqing who opened the door when she knocked softly. The smile froze on her face. Niu Yueqing looked away for a second before she said, "Ah, it's you, Wan'er. I just got back. We made something delicious today, and I was saying to your Zhuang Laoshi that we ought to invite you over, since you haven't been here for some time. And here you are."

"What did you make? And you thought about me? You're just saying that because I'm here, aren't you? But I guess I'm lucky to have come in time for food."

"You have a nice large mouth, and as they say, a large mouth gets to eat everywhere."

"That's for men. For a woman, a large mouth only eats chaff."

"You won't eat chaff. You're more like the locust that eats crops in someone else's field."

That did not sound friendly to Tang Wan'er, who was about to ask whether Zhuang was home when he walked in with Liu Yue.

"Ah, you're here," he said.

"You haven't been home?" Tang Wan'er asked.

"Old Meng invited me over for tea, and Liu Yue went to get me, saying they'd made something good for some guests. I was wondering who it might be. It turns out to be you."

"So you haven't been home all day." She wondered why Liu Yue had said that Zhuang had sent her. Could Niu Yueqing have found the message on the pigeon? Sensing that something was wrong, she said to Niu Yueqing, who was in the kitchen, "Thank you so much, Shimu, for your kindness. You think I was born to eat good food, but in fact I'm only destined for tofu. Before Zhou Min went to work this morning, he said he was going to invite some people from the magazine for lunch, so I can't wait for you to get the delicacies ready. I need to go home."

"No deal," Niu Yueqing said as she came out of the kitchen. "Now that Zhuang Laoshi is back, you two can talk. Lunch will be ready soon. You can't leave today without eating, and I don't care about Zhou Min." She went over, locked the door, and put the key in her pocket.

"Stay for lunch," Zhuang said. "She really means it."

Knowing that it would not be a good idea to go into either the study or the bedroom, they sat on the sofa in the living room, where they carried on a conversation about nothing while exchanging puzzled looks. Eventually they smiled at each other silently, sharing the idea that they might be overreacting, for Shimu might really want her to stay. With that, they relaxed and talked more naturally. She signaled with her eyes all the worries on her mind, while he told her with his that everything was fine. They laughed silently when they thought it might have been a prank by Liu Yue. Finally at ease, she got animated, saying she'd had a dream about a snowfall. Was it good or bad to dream about snow on a hot summer day? She asked him to interpret the dream for her.

"For that you'd have to ask Meng Laoshi," Zhuang said. "Give me a character, and I'll give you a divination."

Not knowing which character to pick, she saw a string of peppers hanging on a wire outside the window and said, "String."

"String? By itself it's just that, but it can be used with something else, like high-strung, strung-up."

Her face paled, so he said, "I was just being silly. Dreaming about snow may simply mean that you're worried about the lawsuit, since the 'xue' in Jing Xueyin's name means snow. You curse her name in the daytime and dream about snow at night."

Feeling better after hearing the new interpretation, Tang asked about his visit to the mayor, but before she had a chance to bring up Tiger's suggestion, Niu Yueqing and Liu Yue were setting the table for lunch. Four small dishes filled with soy sauce were laid out on the table next to chopsticks. Niu Yueqing brought out a clay pot with steam sizzling out through the hole in its lid.

"Please take your seats," she said, and they all sat down.

"The mistress did the cooking today! But is there only one dish?" Zhuang asked. "I'll get something to drink."

"If there are too many dishes, you won't recall which one was the best. No need for liquor; that will only dilute the flavor," Niu Yueqing said.

“What rare delicacy do we have here?” Zhuang reached out to take off the lid, but Niu Yueqing said, “I’ll do it.” She removed the lid to reveal a plucked pigeon roiling in the liquid. Zhuang and Tang Wan’er were so shocked they froze.

“What do you think? A rare delicacy, wouldn’t you say?” Niu Yueqing said. “I killed it myself. It was a smart bird that will make you smart after you eat it. It has very tender meat. Come, try it and see how I did.” She tore off the wings and placed them in Wan’er’s dish.

“The wings are for you, Wan’er. Eating them will help you fly to the highest branch,” Niu Yueqing said. Next she tore off the legs and placed them in Zhuang’s dish. “The legs are for you. See how nice and plump they are. Ah, what have I done? I forgot to take off the toe ring.” She followed that by giving the body of the pigeon to Liu Yue and put the head on her own plate. “There’s no meat in the head, but I’ve heard that eating a pigeon’s eyes will prevent myopia. I’ve been nearsighted for so long, I’ll give the eyes a try.” She reached over, plucked out the eyes, and put them in her mouth, saying as she chewed, “Delicious. So tasty.”

Zhuang and Tang Wan’er did not touch their chopsticks; their faces were bathed in sweat. “Why aren’t you eating?” asked Niu Yueqing. “Something wrong with it?”

Tang Wan’er forced herself to sip the soup, but it made her gag, so she stood up and said, with tears in her eyes, “Please, Shimu, open the door so I can throw up outside.” Niu Yueqing tossed the key to the floor. Tang Wan’er picked it up, opened the door, and raced down the stairs. Zhuang stood up wordlessly but paused for a moment before going into his study and locking himself inside.

⁂

They did not have a chance to use Tiger’s ruse before the Municipal Intermediate Court issued its verdict, which was exactly as Sima Gong had predicted. The news spread quickly, and the phone at Zhuang’s house rang off the hook for days. Guests came one after another, keeping Liu Yue busy boiling water to make tea and sweeping mounds of watermelon seeds into the trashcan. One day a round of firecrackers went off downstairs, after which Wang Ximian and his wife, Ruan Zhifei, Zhou Min, Meng Yunfang, Xia Jie, Hong Jiang, and Hong Jiang and his new bride swarmed in. Niu Yueqing was so happy she shook hands with each of them.

“Well, you’re all here. I knew you’d come, but how did you manage to get everyone together? Who organized it?”

"Who organized it? Heaven did. I won't shake hands, Dajie. I'm so happy, I need a hug," Ruan said, drawing loud cheers from the others.

"Great. Let's see if she has the guts to do it," they said.

"Of course I do. Why wouldn't I?" Niu Yueqing said, prompting Ruan to walk up and put his arms around her, which made them roar with laughter. Zhuang had just fallen asleep on the sofa in the study, exhausted from days of receiving a continuous string of visitors expressing their congratulations. He had left early that morning to visit Bai Yuzhu and Sima Gong, then had lain down after he came home. Roused by the crowd, he came out with a smile, offering seats to everyone now that Liu Yue had given them all some Dragonwell green tea.

"What can we offer them today?" Zhuang asked his wife.

"Don't worry about the food. Liu Yue and I will take care of it. Why don't you go buy a bottle of Wuliangye, ten bottles of coconut juice, and a case of beer?"

Liu Yue was amazed by the intimate, genial attitude between husband and wife in front of the guests. Zhuang was about to leave when Zhou said that he would go. "Zhou Min is strong, so let him do it," Niu Yueqing said. "Where's Wan'er, Zhou Min? Why didn't she come?"

"She hasn't been feeling well lately. She feels like throwing up every time she eats, and she complains of a lack of energy. Her belly looks swollen. I'm worried she might have hepatitis. She sends her regards."

"I'm sorry to hear that. She should be here; she'd make it more festive. How terrible for a young woman to have hepatitis. You should take her to see a doctor, young man. Be careful. She's such a pretty girl, you need to pay more attention."

"You're so nice to be concerned. Actually, it's better she's not here," Zhou said softly. "Wang Ximian's wife is here today, and Wan'er doesn't like her." He walked away, and Niu Yueqing turned to see Zhuang peeling apples for the guests. "Go sit down," she said as she snatched the knife away from him. "I'll do it."

When she finished, she handed the apples to the guests. "Why isn't Zhao Jingwu here?" she asked Zhuang in a low voice.

"I was wondering that myself. I don't know."

"Could it have something to do with Liu Yue?" she asked.

"I've talked to him about it twice already. He was incensed over her choice of the rich and powerful."

"Save your intimate talk for later in bed," Meng Yunfang said. "You're ignoring a roomful of guests, whispering like that."

"You have a foul mouth, Old Meng," Niu Yueqing said with a smile. "I was just asking him why Zhao Jingwu isn't here. What's he up to? Hong Jiang, when you see him, tell him I'm unhappy with him. Does he think so highly of himself that I have to send a sedan chair for him?"

Hong Jiang, who was making a comment to Liu Xiaoka about the calligraphy on the wall, turned to say, "Sure, I'll tell him and shame him a bit. He must have something urgent to deal with; otherwise he'd be here."

As they talked, Zhou Min and Liu Yue returned with the liquor. Niu Yueqing set the table, went to the refrigerator to take out some cold dishes that had been prepared ahead of time, and opened cans of fish and some donkey and dog meat. After laying out twelve platters of food, she offered everyone something to drink before going to the kitchen with Liu Yue to cook. They all raised their glasses as Ruan said, "It's not easy for us all to be together like this. Let's have a toast for winning the case."

With a cheer, they downed their drinks. Zhou quickly refilled their glasses before raising his own. "I want to thank everyone, too. We managed to survive the battle."

"You should be happy now, Zhou Min," Xia Jie said. "It would have made everyone feel better if you could have gotten Jing Xueyin to come to Zhuang Laoshi's home."

"When I went to the toilet yesterday," he said, "I heard someone crying in the women's room. I couldn't tell who it was, so I waited in the hallway to see who came out. She had on dark glasses. I was going to hand her a handkerchief to dry her tears, but decided to let her off the hook."

"Let her off the hook? You're such a pushover," Hong Jiang said. "Everyone who knew about this has been spreading the news, and people are wondering why she even filed the suit, since her affair with Zhuang Laoshi was so long ago. Zhuang Laoshi crushed her by providing the dates and places where they'd made love, and she lost."

"That's just gossip," Zhuang said. "I didn't even go to court, so how could I do that? "I've learned an important lesson, and that is to never get involved in a lawsuit."

"If that's gossip, then don't stop it," Hong said. "In my view, this must be considered another glorious event in the life of Zhuang Laoshi. Other men couldn't get a woman to do that even if they wanted to, and there's no way they could have created such a storm."

"Zhuang Laoshi's only mistake was trying to be clever," Meng Yunfang said. "If it had been me—"

"What if it had been you?" Xia asked him.

With his eyes on his wife, Meng raised his glass, "I'd finish this coconut juice." He gulped down the contents, making everyone laugh. Someone jeered, saying he was henpecked. Someone else joked that Xia Jie was keeping her man on a short leash.

"Xia Jie is right to do that," Niu Yueqing said. "A woman must keep a close eye on her man, or something can happen when you least expect it."

"You're right," Meng said. "It's precisely because she watches me so closely that I'm still a virgin."

Forcing an awkward smile, Zhuang picked up his pipe. "So you're Tripitaka, the monk from the Tang dynasty," he said. "His trip to India for the sutras was made hard because he was a virgin, and all those demons wanted to eat his flesh."

Wang Ximian's wife smiled.

"Famed Painter," Meng said, "why are you so quiet today? Being good when your wife is around?"

"He's not much of a talker," Wang's wife said. "Don't blame me."

Meng reached out to snatch the pipe from Zhuang's mouth and smoke it himself, prompting Wang's wife to say, "That's not hygienic, Yunfang. Pipes, like toothbrushes, are for personal use only."

Meng handed the pipe back to Zhuang. "Women are always worried about hygiene. You say Wang Ximian isn't much of a talker, so how come that day at the Sheraton Dance Club the two of you were talking each other's ear off? Is he only a talker with you?"

"Sheraton? I've never been there," she said.

"Ai-ya! I shouldn't have said that. Let me slap myself."

"Stop causing trouble, Yunfang. I can tell stories about you if you insist upon telling them about me," Wang said.

"Go ahead," Xia Jie said. "I won't be jealous. Men can have lovers, and so can women."

"I guess you've already done that," said Ruan. "How come you never told us?"

"I've learned my lesson after what Zhidie has been through."

"Perfect!" Ruan clapped. "Perfect. I'll drink to that."

They cheered again, and everyone drank a toast.

"Stop talking about lovers," Niu Yueqing said. "I can't stand that word; it sounds more like a prostitute to me."

She had thrown cold water on the party, and no one knew what to say now. Wang Ximian finally said, "Fill the glasses. We're here to congratulate Zhidie on winning the case, so I suggest we each toast him."

Instead of picking up his glass, Ruan reached for some food with his chopsticks. "Don't drink too much in the morning, since you need to work; drink your fill at noon because you have to attend a standing committee meeting; drink less at night because you have to go home and face your wife."

Everyone laughed.

"Did you get that from that junkman?" Wang asked. "What standing committee meeting do you have to attend? And today isn't Saturday, so why would you be facing your wife? Fill up his glass, Liu Yue."

"I'll drink it up. I will," Ruan said. "Down the hatch. You down the glass when the feeling is deep, you lick the glass when it's not."

Ruan clinked glasses with Zhuang and then downed the contents.

"Let's not copy his uncivilized way of drinking," Wang said.

The others clinked glasses with Zhuang and drank. When Niu Yueqing came out with the food, Meng Yunfang gave her a glass so she could toast with the others. Zhou Min clinked his glass with hers twice, saying it was for Wan'er's sake.

"Let Liu Yue toast Zhuang Laoshi," Niu Yueqing said, which she did.

Zhuang thanked everyone when he saw that they had emptied their glasses. He raised his, but his hand shook so much he had trouble bringing it down to drink. When he finally did, he tossed down the contents and teared up, causing the room to fall silent. Zhou Min went over and rested his hand on him. "Did the liquor go down too fast?"

Zhuang's lips quivered. He sniffled loudly, eventually choking up.

"He's moved," Niu Yueqing added. "That's how he is. He cries when he's sad, but he also cries when he's happy. The case dragged on for so long, and so much happened during the process, that now that it's over, he's worked up to see you all here." She turned to Zhuang. "Why don't you go rest? Come back and have a drink with us after you calm down."

"I'll do that. I'm sorry, everyone. Enjoy yourselves." He went into their bedroom.

Wang's wife followed him in and asked softly, "What's bothering you, Zhidie?" He shook his head. "You can't hide it from me. You shouldn't have that look on your face now that you've won the case. I noticed it the moment I came in," she persisted.

"No more questions, please," Zhuang said. "Go on out there with the others. I'll be fine once I rest up." She was about to sit on the edge of the bed to talk to him when Niu Yueqing came in.

"Zhidie has lost weight, so I'm afraid it's up to you to make him feel better," Wang's wife said. "After Gong Jingyuan's death, we all understand how fragile life is, so it's more important than ever for us to take care of ourselves."

"That's what everyone says," Niu Yueqing said, "and I feel the pressure. He belongs to everyone now, and I'm just his keeper. I'd have trouble explaining myself if his health suffered, but does he listen to me? He knows he's in poor health, but he's so willful that no matter what he does, he doesn't know when to stop. It would be a miracle if he *didn't* lose weight."

"Men are all like that," Wang's wife said.

With his head down, Zhuang silently filled his pipe. Niu Yueqing snatched it away and put it on the bedside table. "Look at him. He's smoking again. I keep telling him not to smoke so much, but he won't listen to me. Now he's even smoking a pipe."

"What are you doing in there, Yueqing?" Meng shouted from the living room. "Both hosts have left the table before their guests. Afraid we'll drink all your liquor?"

"I'll be right there," she said. "And I'll get you good and drunk." She took Wang's wife out with her.

They all drank another round as firecrackers exploded again downstairs, followed by the sound of hurried footsteps. "Who could that be?" Niu Yueqing wondered aloud. "Go greet them, Liu Yue."

The girl went out, but returned quickly. "Dajie, it's—"

"Who is it?" Niu Yueqing asked.

"It's—you know," Liu Yue said as she went to her room.

"Anyone who comes is a guest, so why are you acting like that?" Niu Yueqing looked up to see a refrigerator being carried in, followed by more people bringing in more things: a TV set, a washing machine, a stereo system, an air-conditioner, a toaster oven, four blankets, two pillows, vacuum water bottles, washbasins, mirrors, rinsing cups, toothbrushes, toothpaste, towels, a porcelain bowl, and a pair of chopsticks. After putting down their loads, the newcomers went out into the hallway, since there was no place for them to sit. The last to enter was Dazheng, whose appearance elicited a cry from Niu Yueqing.

"Ai-ya! It's you, Dazheng. Why didn't you call first? We'd have gone down to meet you at the gate."

"My mother told me to have these dowry items delivered. There are also two large modular cabinets, sofas, and loveseats, but they're too bulky to move, so we put them in the new place. You have a lot of guests today."

"Zhidie, come out here!" Niu Yueqing shouted. "Come see who's here!"

Zhuang was pleasantly surprised when he came out of the bedroom. After inviting Dazheng to have a seat, he asked the men in the hallway to come in.

"No need for that," Dazheng said. "I'll send them home." They waved and walked off, but Zhuang caught up with them and passed out cigarettes.

When he came back inside, he said to his friends, "Do you know who this is? It's Dazheng, our mayor's son and Liu Yue's future husband."

Supporting himself on the sofa back, Dazheng stood up, smiled, and took out a pack of cigarettes. He tore it open and passed them around. He was grinning. Everyone had heard about the engagement between the mayor's son and Liu Yue, and that had made them envious of the girl's good fortune. Now, after seeing what he was like, they entertained their own thoughts about the pair; they stood up to accept the cigarettes. He was invited to sit with them amid a cacophony of "Pleased to meet you," "Congratulations on your engagement to a beauty." Someone even mentioned the mayor's accomplishments and asked Dazheng to pass on their regards. Business cards were offered.

"You're all Xijing celebrities," Dazheng said as he read the cards.

"Stop that celebrities nonsense," Meng said. "Have a drink. I've been looking for someone to play finger-guessing games with. Now I can do that with the bridegroom."

"Are you drunk on coconut juice?" Niu Yueqing said. "They're not married yet, so he's not a bridegroom. Raise your glasses, everyone, and toast the mayor. Dazheng, you are your father's surrogate. Pick up your glass. Make yourself at home. Liu Yue, where are you? Why are you acting so shy?"

Liu Yue came out of her room in a new outfit. "You go ahead and drink," she said bashfully. "I can't hold my liquor."

"At least you'll have to toast him."

"I thought she'd disappeared," Meng said. "Turns out she went in to put on makeup. Like they say, a woman makes herself up for the one she loves." They all laughed.

Dazheng raised his glass to toast Liu Yue, who clinked hers with his and ran into the kitchen.

"Why is she acting like that? After bringing over so many dowry items, Dazheng will send a festooned sedan to fetch her on the wedding day, and that will surely dazzle the people along the streets," Meng continued. "You'll have to deliver the invitation yourself, Liu Yue. Tell us what we should give you, so the gifts won't overlap. What else do you need?"

"I need a bank," she said from the kitchen.

"Ouch!" Meng exclaimed. "I won't go to the wedding, then. I was hoping for your help if we become beggars one day, but obviously we can't rely on you."

"I'd like to thank you for your kind thoughts," Dazheng said. "Of course Liu Yue will deliver the invitations, and I hope you will all come celebrate with us. Here's to you all."

"Just this one and no more," Wang said. "We've been at this for quite some time, so why don't you drink with Meng Yunfang."

"Meng Laoshi is having a soft drink. He'd surely get me drunk," Dazheng said.

"Go ahead and play the finger-guessing game, Meng Laoshi," Hong cut in. "I'll drink for you when you lose."

Meng and Dazheng began the game, creating a din as the other men watched. The women, on the other hand, sat idly around. Soon, however, Wang's wife left to chat with Liu Yue, while Xia Jie went to check out the dowry, followed by Hong Jiang's wife, who touched the items and commented appreciatively, trying to guess their prices.

"The mayor has power and status, but he's no match for you business types when it comes to spending money. This skirt of yours had to cost at least two or three hundred."

"Twelve hundred. It's a luxury brand."

"Wow, that much!" Xia Jie said. "There are celebrity writers, painters, performers, and braggarts among the guests today. Now I know there's even a fashion celebrity. You are really doing much better than the mayor."

"We may have more money than the mayor, but there's more gold in his cache," the woman said, before joining Wang's wife and Liu Yue to gossip about Liu's good fortune. She took them all into her room and closed the door. "You're mocking me, aren't you? Look at him. Who but a housemaid like me would marry him?"

"Don't talk like that," Wang's wife said. "The mayor's family has so much to offer you. Besides, he's really not that bad."

"My dear sister, you've been around, and you think Dazheng's not too bad?"

"His thick brows are nice, and he looks dependable," Wang's wife said.

"He looks fine except for that leg," Xia Jie added.

"That's right," Hong Jiang's wife said, but Liu Yue began to cry.

"I know what you're saying. He's a dependable man with thick brows. But what's so fine about him with that leg? I'm so mad at him. Why did he have to pick today to bring the dowry?" Liu Yue said tearfully. The others tried to console her.

"You can't have everything," one of them said. "Besides, no average girl could have your kind of good fortune."

"Liu Yue, your husband is failing," Meng shouted from the living room. "Come drink for him."

"He lacks common sense," Liu Yue complained. "He's a guest here, so how could he let himself go like that? Obviously Meng Laoshi is trying to make a fool of Dazheng by getting him drunk." She refused to go out, as the people in the other room clamored for Dazheng to drink more. Soon Zhou Min and Hong Jiang carried him in, so drunk he looked like a mountain of mud. As they tried to put him on Liu Yue's bed, his shoes fell off. One of his feet was straight, the other one crooked with the toes pinched together. Liu Yue sobbed as she draped a blanket over his feet.

When the men saw her crying, they thought she was upset with them for getting Dazheng drunk. Ruan Zhifei, who was fairly drunk himself, complained that Dazheng was no fun, that he got drunk too easily. He bragged that in his crazy younger days he could match Gong Jingyuan glass for glass, and once single-handedly finished off four jin of liquor as if it were water. But the mention of Gong saddened him, and he was soon sobbing. A couple of the women talked about Liu Yue in whispers; everyone's mood soured.

"What are you crying about? You're just making things worse," Wang said to Ruan. "It's getting late, we'd better leave. You can cry as hard as you want at home, but not here." He turned to Zhuang. "Zhidie, we're going now. Dazheng may have come because he has something to say to the two of you."

Niu Yueqing and Zhuang tried to get them to stay longer, but they insisted on leaving. So Zhuang walked them out to the gate, where he said to Zhou Min, "Is Wan'er ill?"

"It's nothing serious. I'll tell her to come see you another day."

"Let her rest, then. From what Yueqing told me, it could be indigestion. Here's something she can take." Zhuang handed Zhou Min a sealed medicine box.

❋

Tang Wan'er opened the box and took out a pill bottle that contained nothing but a wrinkled piece of paper: "Take care of yourself." She cried at the note. Since the day she had returned shamefaced from the compound, she had felt the sting of humiliation. The bigger the balloon, the more likely it is to burst, she knew, but once it gets started, it's hard to suppress the desire and excitement to make the balloon bigger. Unable to control her feelings for Zhuang, she felt that the nicer Niu Yueqing was to her, the more guilt and apprehension she would experience; so she resolved to avoid Niu Yueqing and refrain from going to their house to meet Zhuang. It was clear why he had asked her several times whether he was a bad man. She had even said to him, "If this is too hard on you, let's just be friends. Let's not do that again." It was a test, and he had not responded to her suggestion, so naturally, without thinking, they had sex every time they met. Niu Yueqing had cruelly killed the pigeon and cooked it to feed them, which canceled out Tang Wan'er's guilt feelings. *I hurt you, but you hurt me, too. We're even, we don't owe each other a thing, and now we're like strangers,* she thought on her way back that day; a sense of tranquility washed over her when she was back home. Suddenly feeling industrious, she cleaned the house and did the laundry. That night she said to Zhou Min, "Why aren't you in bed already?" He was writing the book that would not bear his name, after coming home from playing his xun, so he said, "I'll be there in a minute." He put away his paper and pen, heated some water to wash up, and came to bed in high spirits, only to find her asleep and snoring. She stayed in bed and did not get up for three days; she had such a terrifying dream that she was drenched in sweat when she woke up. Unable to recall the details, she remembered only that she had felt profoundly lonely and forsaken; she thought of herself as a fish roasting in a pan. Three days later, she struggled to sit on the edge of the bed before moving to a sofa, where she sat for a long while before going back and sitting up in bed. Thinking she heard the cooing of a pigeon, she tiptoed outside and leaned against the pear tree, where she looked into the high, cloudy sky—there was no pigeon. Tears slipped down her cheeks. Zhuang lived in the same city, but no street connected them, and now even their conduit in the air had been cut off. The yard was littered with fallen leaves; more were drifting down from the branches. Autumn was in the air, and the cicadas had grown quiet. Night winds had turned the lush pear tree scrawny, and she sensed that her hips were losing their shape and her face had become gaunt. Life seemed to have lost its meaning, to the point that only the sighing wind was left to disturb the bamboo curtain at the door.

When Zhou Min came home from work, she wouldn't let him go play his xun at the city wall. Instead she told him to play it under the pear tree, saying she was had no objection to his playing; in fact, she liked it. He looked at her quizzically. "I told you it had a pleasant tone, but you said you didn't like it. Well, now you finally appreciate its sound." He began to play. He winked and raised his brows to please her. Leaning against the door and listening, she had a hunch that she should go to the bridge outside the south city gate, where she would find a certain tree. She believed in her presentiment, because Meng Yunfang had once read her palm and told her that she had the hand of someone with strong premonitions. Now she was seized by a thought: with her routes to him cut off, she would have to wait for him under that tree if she wanted to see him again. So she went in, applied some makeup, changed clothes, and put on the pair of heels.

"Are you going out?" Zhou Min asked. "Where to?"

"I'm going to buy some sanitary napkins. I'm having my you-know-what." Saying it actually made it happen, and she had to put some paper in her panties before hurrying out.

"It's late. I'll go with you."

"Are there wolves and leopards in the city? Why would you need to come with me? You stay home and write that book." She walked down streets bustling with traffic and pedestrians. When she reached the stone bridge, there was no sign of Zhuang, not even after she waited until midnight. It was so late that the area was deserted, except for her, who had only menstrual blood to show for the wait. Her hands were stained with blood when she changed the napkin, which gave her the idea to smear them with blood and leave her handprints on the railing, the tree, and a rock on the tree. The last one came out clearly enough to show the handprint lines. Meng had also told her that a handprint was the map of life. *Zhuang Zhidie, if you show up here, you will be able to recognize this map of my life; I've waited for you here.*

For several days in a row she waited by the tree, but she never saw him. She thought he must be unable to leave the house and no longer had control of his actions. So when he finally sent a message through the medicine box, she had a good cry and vowed to herself: *I must see him, even if it's for the last time in my life.*

Liu Yue was set to be married on September twelfth. On the day before, she and Niu Yueqing prepared food and drinks for the people who would come get her. Saying that the expense was too much for them, Dazheng's mother wanted to send food over, but Niu Yueqing wouldn't hear of it. Liu Yue was not her own daughter, nor her sister, but she had gained a great deal of face when the mayor's family said that they considered her and Zhuang to be their in-laws and then sent the dowry to their house, giving invited guests the impression that it was from her and Zhuang.

Naturally, she would offer the best Maotai to accompany dishes with chicken, duck, fish, and pork. After everything was ready, she told Liu Yue to bathe, while she dragged her aching feet to the mayor's house. Still worried about the actual details of the ceremony, she wanted to double-check everything with Dazheng's mother. After Niu Yueqing left, Liu Yue went into the bathroom to draw a bath. When Zhuang heard the running water from the living room, a myriad of thoughts welled up inside and sent him silently into his study to chain-smoke.

Suddenly the door to his study was pushed open, and in walked Liu Yue, draped in a bright red bathrobe, her damp hair gathered in the back in a white kerchief, her freshly washed face smooth with a red glow. But she had painted her brows, applied eye shadow, and put a thick layer of crimson red lipstick on her lips, which looked as full and round as an apricot. *She's incredibly pretty,* Zhuang said to himself, *particularly after a hot bath on the night before she's to become a bride.* He smiled before lowering his head to smoke. He took a long drag on his cigarette, making the red glow of the tip move swiftly downward, though the long ash hung on.

"Are you feeling down again, Zhuang Laoshi?" she asked.

He didn't reply. It would have been pointless to say he was.

"I'm leaving tomorrow. Aren't you going to wish me happiness one more time?"

"I wish you nothing but happiness."

"Do you really think I'll be happy?"

"Yes, I do. You'll be happy." He nodded, eliciting a sarcastic laugh from the girl.

"Thank you very much, Zhuang Laoshi. You're the one who gave me happiness."

He looked up at her in surprise and saw that her eyes were fixed on him. With a sigh, he lowered his head again.

"My stay here hasn't been long, but it hasn't been short, either. I've gotten to know you, I've read many books, I've experienced many things, and I've had my fair share of the heavy cigarette smoke in this room. I'm leaving, but I really don't want to go. Can I just sit here for a while and look at the sculpture of the Tang maiden you've said resembles me?"

"You're not leaving until tomorrow, so this is still your home tonight. Sit down. I'll give you the sculpture tomorrow."

"Does that mean you'll never again want me to be here with you?"

The question stopped him. "That's not what I meant, Liu Yue. That was not what I wanted to give you, anyway. I want to give you something else."

"What is it? Can I see it now?"

He took a lovely box out of his drawer and handed it to her. She opened it to see an ancient bronze mirror with inlaid flowers, decorated with a raised ridge encircled by an inscription: *Exacting design and superb crafting, sparkling quality with fine craftsmanship, like a pearl in the morning sky or the moon at night. Use this to paint your brows, look into it to rouge your face, as you embroider at the window, all this is reflected within it.*

"What a wonderful mirror!" she cried out. "Can you really bear to part with it?"

"I'm giving it to you because I can't bear to part with it."

"Tang Wan'er has one like this. It's about the same size, with a similar design, except for the inscription. I asked her where she got it. She said she just had it. I didn't think I'd ever have one, too."

"That one was also from me."

She paused. "You gave her that one? Since they're from you, they must be a pair. So why are you giving this one to me?"

"I can never see her again. So any time I looked at this mirror, I couldn't help thinking about the one—let's not talk about her, Liu Yue."

"I know you hate me, Zhuang Laoshi." She hiked up her robe and sat down on a leather chair in front of the sofa. "You hate me because of Tang Wan'er. I admit I told Dajie everything, but it was partly because she beat me so savagely and partly because she was the one who found the message on the pigeon. She was suspicious when she read the note, and everything would have been fine if I'd kept quiet no matter how hard she hit me. But I didn't. I told her a lot of things. Now I want to explain to you why I did that. I was jealous of Wan'er. I was jealous because, like me, she had no city residency and had run away with Zhou Min, worse than anything I'd done, yet she'd managed to win your heart. I've been at your side all along, and yet—"

"Stop it, Liu Yue. She didn't win my heart. I was the one at fault. Don't you think I ruined her? Everything is over now."

"If that's what you think, then haven't you also ruined me? You're marrying me off to the mayor's son. Do you really think I can love him? I will have to close my eyes to marry him. It was you who changed Tang Wan'er and me into real women and gave us the courage and confidence to start a new life. And in the end, it was you who ruined us. But in the process, you also ruined yourself, your image, and your reputation, along with Dajie and this family."

It finally dawned on Zhuang that this had been the root cause of his depression. He had failed to notice the girl's insights all this time. Now she was leaving and would cease to be both a maid and someone he loved. Her comments were a souvenir. Could it be that she was like a candle that shines the brightest just before it goes out, or a lantern that fades away after emitting the strongest light? He looked up at the girl, who was still in the grip of her emotions.

"Liu Yue," he said softly. She rushed toward him, and they were immediately locked in an embrace. Both were in tears.

"You're right, Liu Yue. I created everything and then I destroyed it all. Nothing can be done about that now, and I am probably beyond saving. You're still young, so be sure to start a new life once you're married."

Her tears fell onto his arms. "I'm afraid I can't save myself once I'm with Dazheng," she said. "Then what will I do? I'm scared, really scared. I'll be his tomorrow, so I beg you to let me feel like Tang Wan'er on this final night." Closing her eyes, she untied the belt of her robe. She was naked, her body like the jade-white flesh of a lychee with its bright red shell opened. He quietly examined her and moved his desk lamp over so that it would shine on her. □□ □□ □□ [The author has deleted 200 words.] She cried out as the sofa inched toward the door until it bumped noisily against the jamb and jolted them both. Her head was bent at an angle, but when he tried to straighten out her body, she said, "Don't stop. Don't stop." She kicked her feet against the door, knocking a scroll off the wall and sending it falling down to cover them. "The scroll is ruined," she said, but neither made any attempt to remove it. □□ □□ □□ [The author has deleted 422 words.]

"I'm so happy, Laoshi," she said as she was leaving the smoky room. "By this time tomorrow my body will be under that cripple, but my heart will stay in this room."

"Don't talk like that, Liu Yue. You should hate me."

"You needn't worry about that." She walked out and shut the door behind her. He listened to her receding footsteps and the sound of her opening another door. Then he collapsed onto the sofa.

❋

Niu Yueqing got up at the crack of the dawn to tidy up the room and cook the congee before she went in to wake up Liu Yue. The girl got up and, embarrassed, went to get Zhuang, so they could eat together. After breakfast, she sat in the living room to brush her hair, paint her brows, place flowers in her hair, and put on her necklace and earrings, while insisting that Niu Yueqing and Zhuang sit next to her as her consultants. Two hours later, she was finally ready from head to toe, just as thunderous firecrackers went off. Niu Yueqing told her to take off her shoes and sit down on her bed, as she flung open the front door. Outside, a contingent of bridal escorts, who had come in twenty-two sedans, overflowed onto the streets outside the gate. Old Mrs. Wei, who had been given a red envelope containing money, tottered back and forth, smiling at each escort and keeping a close watch to stop any idlers from entering the compound gate. Dazheng, with a red flower in his lapel, was helped in to kowtow and bow to Zhuang Zhidie and Niu Yueqing, but Zhuang stopped him when he stretched his weak right leg back to get down on his knees. Zhuang said a bow would be enough, so Dazheng bowed deeply before going into the bedroom to put Liu Yue's shoes on her. He then carried her off the bed and pinned a flower as red as his own to her dress. She watched him quietly, and when he brought her hand up to his lips to kiss it after pinning on the flower, she twisted the corners of her mouth and said to Niu Yueqing and Zhuang, who were standing at the door to watch, "He's copying Westerners." Dazheng was so embarrassed, even his neck turned red. The escorts sat down to eat, drink, and smoke, admiring the scrolls on the wall and checking out the room full of books through the study door. When the clock struck ten, someone said, "Time to go." An escort who was sprawled atop the gate entrance lit a huge string of firecrackers and let it hang down, creating an ear-shattering roar. Taking Liu's hand in his, Dazheng started down the stairs, as three cameras clicked and a video camera rolled. He giggled and she glared at him, so he put on a serious look. Straining to keep his balance, he swayed from side to side and kept bumping into her. In the end, instead of letting him hold her hand, she clutched his hand tightly in hers, turning his arm into a lever to steady his body movements.

The firecrackers continued to explode by the gate, sending scraps of red paper flying around like butterflies. Afraid that one of the firecrackers might come loose and fall on her head, Liu Yue rushed through the gate, nearly sending Dazheng to the ground when she let go of his arm too quickly. "Liu Yue!" Niu Yueqing cried out next to her. "Liu Yue!" She turned to wait for him, and saw that the yard was filled with people. This time she looped her arm in his and stayed as close as possible to prevent him from staggering again. "That's good," Niu Yueqing said as she had four people sprinkle confetti over them, immediately bathing the couple in glittering gold and silver. The escorts began transferring the dowry into cars, forming a long procession as they walked out into the yard in an orderly fashion for the sake of onlookers, who made comments about how the bride was a head taller than the groom, how she would surely be the head of the new family, and how he would soon be cuckolded. Someone countered that the groom, being the mayor's son, must be ill tempered and would surely assert his authority and power over the bride. Another one chimed in that the groom had to wait for his pretty bride to help him onto the bed before he could beat her. Liu Yue heard every word and could not wait to get into the bridal sedan.

The wedding ceremony was held in the Xijing Hotel restaurant. When the car carrying Zhuang and Niu Yueqing stopped at the hotel entrance, they saw Dazheng and Liu Yue enter the restaurant, surrounded by a large crowd. Firecrackers went off nonstop amid loud, festive music. They were surprised to see so many people.

"The seats of honor have been reserved for you," they were told. "The mayor and his wife are waiting for you inside."

They walked into the restaurant to see dazzling lanterns everywhere and smiling people dressed in brightly colored clothes. Waitresses in qipaos shuttled from table to table to lay out flower baskets, fruit, pastries, melon seeds, cigarettes, tea, and soft drinks. The guests, mostly people they did not know, were making quite a din. After they each accepted a bouquet of flowers from a child at the door, Dazheng and Liu Yue were directed to walk down a red silk runner six feet wide and fifty feet long. At the end of the silk walkway was a slightly raised red-carpeted platform, encircled with pots of flowers. A microphone had been set up in front of four tables for the guests of honor. Huang Defu, the master of ceremonies, told the couple to turn around, then invited the guests with cameras to take pictures. The guests noisily called for the couple to stand closer, to smile, to raise their bouquets, for one of them to put a hand on the other's shoulder or place an arm around the other's waist. The couple refused to comply, but the guests would not take no for an answer; someone even went up to make them pose for the cameras, drawing laughter and loud cheers.

Zhuang paused at one end of the red walkway to read a couplet by Zheng Xie that had been copied into a book sprinkled with gold powder: *A spring wind boldly combs the willows / Evening rain secretly nourishes the flowers.* Next to the couplet was *Respectful Congratulations to Dazheng and Liu Yue on Their Wedding*, surrounded by hundreds of signatures from well-wishers. Aware that attendees at meetings and ceremonies usually sign their names on rice paper, Zhuang wondered who had come up with the idea of using a piece of silk instead, which was then turned into a walkway. As he admired the unusual and amusing setup, someone came over with a pen: "Please sign your name." When he did, the man cried out,

"Ah, you're Mr. Zhuang Zhidie!" Zhuang nodded with a smile, and the man said, "I'm a fan of literature. I'm so happy to meet you here today."

"Thank you," Zhuang said and started to walk away. "Mr. Zhuang," the man continued, "the bride was a maid at your house, so you've taught her well."

"You flatter me."

"I envy her. I have a request, a wish I hope you will grant. I'd like to be a helper at your house so I could wait on you while I'm studying creative writing."

"We're not hiring another helper, but thank you for your offer."

"You think I'm no good because I'm not a woman, is that it? I can cook and do laundry."

Seeing that Zhuang was having trouble shaking the man off, Niu Yueqing went up to talk to Huang Defu, who was introducing the guests of honor. He announced loudly, "Among the guests of honor today is the celebrated writer Mr. Zhuang Zhidie. Let's welcome him with a round of applause. Please come join us at the head table, Mr. Zhuang."

A loud cheer broke out in the hall amid thunderous applause, so the man had to let Zhuang go. He went up to one of the tables, where he greeted the city's VIPs and celebrities. He had barely sat down when two girls came up for his autograph. He was waiting for them to offer their notebooks, but they stuck out their chests and said, "Here, we've saved this spot near our hearts for you, Mr. Zhuang."

He took a closer look and saw that signatures had been scribbled all over their white cotton blouses. "What a shame to ruin such nice blouses."

"Signatures from celebrities make them valuable," they said. "It's impossible to meet so many of you at any other time. When we heard that the mayor's son was getting married, we thought you'd all be here. We can travel around the city with your autographs on our blouses, making them true culture shirts."

"Then I must see who has already signed." Seeing signatures from Wang Ximian, Ruan Zhifei, Meng Yunfang, Sun Wu, Zhou Min, Li Hongwen, and Gou Dahai, he took a pen and scribbled his name on one of the girls' chests. The other girl wanted more: "Mr. Zhuang, we know you're talented and quick-witted, so would you write a poem instead? Four lines will do."

"This is not the place for composing poetry," Zhuang said. "So what should I write?"

"You're here for a wedding, so why not something about love?"

After Zhuang wrote one on the girl's back, she asked her friend to read it for her:

Put a stick in the ground and hope for a red blossom;
Throw a stone into water and hope for a tail;
Place paper under the pillow and hope for a picture of a dream;
Paste a stamp on the heart and hope to send it to a woman far away.

"Are you thinking about someone, Mr. Zhuang?" The girl laughed.

"It's called unrequited love," he said.

"Great, that's what I like the best," she said. "I've dated a lot of men, and it never takes me long to say good-bye to any of them. There's no one left in the world I can trust or love. Yet I need love, though I have no idea whom to love. The best kind of romance is one-sided, for I can freely love anyone in my imagination; it's like having a key to every apartment."

Zhuang laughed. "With that kind of understanding, you must be in love with a real person. So how can you say you don't know whom to love?"

"It didn't work out, so I vowed to stop loving him. I warn myself against that every day."

"But you can never shake off your love for him, which shows you don't know how to have a one-sided romance. If you did, you'd think about him because you can't stop."

"Ai-ya! You're older than us, Mr. Zhuang, and yet you're just like us." She sat down in a chair next to him, looking excited and ready for a prolonged discussion. He sent her off, reminding her that the ceremony would begin soon, and it would not look good for them to still be talking. But then someone else came up and whispered to him:

"Mr. Zhuang, someone is waiting to have a few words with you outside, just to the left of the entrance."

Who could it be? He was puzzled. Everyone he knew should be attending the ceremony. He got up and walked out of the hotel; with all the onlookers inside the restaurant, the area near the entrance was deserted, except for the rows of cars. After taking a look around and seeing no one, he was about to go back inside when someone inside a taxi by the side of the road rolled down the window and shouted, "Hey." He looked over and saw a pair of oversized sunglasses. He knew who it was and ran over.

"Are you here for the wedding?"

"I came to see you," Tang Wan'er said.

He looked up and sighed.

"Can you meet me at the House of Imperfection Seekers after the wedding?" she asked.

After turning back to look at the hotel entrance, he opened the door and got into the taxi. "Take us to the street by the Great Void Nunnery."

She immediately locked her arms around him and planted urgent kisses on his forehead, face, nose, and lips, as if she were gnawing on a cooked sheep's head, leaving red lipstick marks all over his face. The driver flipped his rearview mirror.

"Are they all gone?" she asked when they reached the street by the nunnery.

"Yes."

"Then let's go to your apartment at the compound." Without waiting for his consent, she gave the driver ten yuan, and the taxi turned around to head north.

Once they were in the apartment, she asked him to hold her, saying she missed him so much she could die; she had been trying to find a way to see him, confident that God would somehow give her the opportunity. She had found it that day, and she wanted to spend this noontime meeting making up for all the days they had been apart. Telling him to hold her tighter and tighter still, she lost her composure.

"Zhuang-ge, tell me what to do, Zhuang-ge. Tell me."

Not knowing what to tell her, he could only try to make her feel better, but his words soon sounded hollow, phony, and meaningless even to himself. He could only murmur her name, "Wan'er, Wan'er." Assaulted by a splitting headache, he felt as if his head were filled with water. Waves of pain surged when his head moved and the water sloshed around.

They held each other as if holding onto silent rocks; at some point, without being aware of it, they undressed each other, until they were both naked and wondering whether they were going to make love again. They exchanged a look and a smile, sharing the knowledge that only when their bodies became one would they be able to forget their suffering for a while, and that they would have fewer and fewer chances to do that until one day they would not be able to do it ever again. When he laid her down on the sofa, she said:

"No, I want to do it on your bed. I want you to carry me into your bedroom."

They replaced the sheets and pillowcases and laid out the best blanket. She lay down with her arms and legs spread out to quietly watch him turn on all the lights in the room, start the stereo system, spray the room with perfume, and light some sacred Indian incense.

"I have to pee," she told him.

He brought a chamber pot decorated with peony flowers out from under the bed and handed it to her, but she said: "I want you to hold me up." She had such an alluring look on her face that he had to get onto the bed and hold her up like a child, listening to the sound of water falling into the pot like strings of beads. □□ □□ □□ [The author has deleted 666 words.] But no matter how hard he tried, he could not do what they wanted. He sat there dejected, his head down, listening to the tick-tock of the pendulum clock in the living room.

"I can't, Wan'er," he said. "My problem again, I think."

"How can that be? Would you like a cigarette?"

He shook his head. "I just can't. I'm sorry, Wan'er. It's getting late. Let's go where it's quiet, all right? I'll be able to do it again. I can satisfy you. When we go out and calm down, we can go to the House of Imperfection Seekers and spend the afternoon, even the whole night, there if you want."

She lay there quietly before saying, "Don't talk like that, Zhuang-ge. You're nervous and you've been depressed. We didn't do anything, and yet I'm satisfied. I'm completely contented. Being with you on this bed in your room lets me feel like the mistress of the house, and that makes me very happy." Fixing her eyes on Niu Yueqing's photo on the wall, she continued, "She hates me and is probably calling me a shameless slut. She's one of the city's happy women, but she doesn't understand me; she'll never know the pain of another woman in different circumstances." She got up and turned the photo around.

After leaving the compound, they walked aimlessly before stopping at a diner to get something to eat. When they passed a theater, they bought tickets and went in to see a movie, agreeing that they would return to the House of Imperfection Seekers after the show. They would buy enough food and drink to fully savor the feeling of being together all day and all night.

"One whole day," he said.

"Two days."

"No, three days."

"Then we'll die in our sleep."

"If we do, it will be a beautiful death."

"If that happened and we were found, would people eulogize the House of Imperfection Seekers as a place to die for love or as a den of iniquity?" They laughed at the thought, and then continued to talk and laugh while they watched another story play out on the screen. As she put her head on his shoulder, he recalled the picture they had taken together, but he quickly put it out of his mind; instead, he whispered to her that their posture reminded him of an interesting Chinese word.

"Which word?"

He wrote it on her palm, and she wrote another, even more suggestive, one on his. Lifting her legs to lay them on his lap, he took off her shoes to massage her feet and whispered in her ear, "I'm hopeless. When I wanted to use it, it was useless, but now, when I can't, it's ready for action."

She groped in the dark, and indeed it was as hard as a stick, so she unbuttoned his fly and bent down. □□ □□ □□ [The author has deleted 39 words.] Concerned that people behind them could see, he pushed her away. "I'm wet." He touched her and found she was very wet. Pinching her nose to shame her, he said, "I'll go buy some melon seeds." He got up, and as he walked up the aisle, he saw two men squatting by the wall. They looked like latecomers who were looking for seats, so he gestured to show them there were empty seats up front, which made him laugh, since they wouldn't be able to see his signal in the dark. Besides, why was he worrying about those people?

He went to the concession stand for watermelon seeds, but they were out. "I'll have some pumpkin seeds, then," he said. Pumpkin seeds were good for summer days, but they were out of those, too. All they had were sunflower seeds. He recalled seeing a grocery store not far from the theater, so he told the ticket taker where he was going, and walked out. When he went back inside, there was no sign of her, other than her handbag. She must have gone to the toilet. He even wondered whether she had gone to the toilet to pleasure herself after the earlier moment of intimacy. But ten minutes later, she was still not back. Growing suspicious, he went out and called her name from outside the toilet, there was no response. He asked a woman who was going in to look for her. She came out and told him she wasn't in there. Worry built as he wondered where she could have gone. The lounge? She wasn't there. She liked pranks, so surely she was hiding somewhere in the theater waiting to jump out and scare him when he walked by. He began checking the seats, row by row, before looking around the front and back of the theater. When the movie was over and the viewers were filing out, he stood at the exit to check everyone, until the theater was empty. There was still no sign of her, and he panicked. He phoned Meng Yunfang, who asked him why he had disappeared from the wedding. What had he been doing? Zhuang had no choice but to tell Meng everything and ask him to go to Zhou Min's house to see if she had gone back on her own. Meng told him that he had gone to Zhou's house with Zhou Min right after the wedding ceremony; he hadn't seen Wan'er there and had in fact just gotten back from their place. Zhuang put down the phone. His one remaining hope was that she had gone ahead of him to the House of Imperfection Seekers; he hailed a taxi, but she wasn't there, either. His last stop was Meng Yunfang's house. Zhuang burst out crying the moment he went inside.

❈

Niu Yueqing was immediately suspicious when Zhuang did not return after walking out of the wedding ceremony. Since all his friends were there, he might have gone to meet Tang Wan'er. But she could not leave the restaurant; when the mayor and his wife asked about Zhuang, she had to lie and say he had been called away on urgent business. The mayor insisted that she go take a look at the newlyweds' room after the banquet and stay until the guests had their customary antics with the couple. It was eleven that night when Niu Yueqing finally got home, and one look told her that someone had been in the bedroom. Suspicious, she combed through the bed and found a long strand of hair and three curly pubic hairs, along with the overturned picture of her on the wall. Outraged, she snatched everything on the bed and began throwing it out, starting with the pillow, then the sheets, and then the blanket. She screamed and kicked open the study door and knocked down the books, writing paper, stone carvings, and pottery. When she finished stomping and smashing the objects, she sat down to await his return.

She waited the whole night, but he did not come home. Another day went by, and there was still no sign of him. Her anger finally spent, she lacked the energy to smash anything else; instead she packed some clothes in a large suitcase. Then she heard someone knocking at the door. She walked over and pulled the latch but left the door shut. She went to the bathroom to wash her face, and felt terrible when she spotted a new wrinkle, which spurred her to massage her face using Princess Diana's method. "You're back," she said without turning to look. "There's longan extract in the fridge; go make a glass to replenish your energy. Make sure to clean up the hair when you finish in the future." She got a loud wail for a response.

She turned at the unusual sound and saw someone keeling over in the living room. But it wasn't Zhuang Zhidie; it was Mr. Huang, the pesticide factory owner. Niu Yueqing came out and, making no attempt to help him up, asked in a cold voice, "What's wrong with you? Did your factory go under?"

"I want to see Mr. Zhuang."

"Well, go see him, then. Why are you kneeling there and wailing like that?"

"My wife took pesticide again."

She sat down to paint her brows with a mirror. "She did it again? Then she must have been hungry or thirsty."

"I mean she ingested the pesticide."

"Hasn't she done that before?"

"But this time she died," he said as he got to his feet.

Her body twitched, and she dropped the mirror. It cracked. "Dead?"

"I always thought that 102 couldn't kill anyone, so she could drink as much as she wanted. I was out all morning. When I went back at noon, the pot was empty, so I flew into a rage. I yelled at her for getting lazy and not cooking for me. Then I went to the bed and saw her lying in there, one leg raised high in the air. I pulled at it and she rolled over, cold and stiff."

She was quiet for a while as Huang talked on about what had happened. "I don't get it. The pesticide was harmless when it needed to be lethal, but now it was actually toxic when it shouldn't have been."

"Mr. Huang, it's good she died, isn't it?" Niu Yueqing said with a smile. "With all your money, you can have anything that strikes your fancy. Now all you need is a foreign wife. She died because she was no good for you, and now she's moved aside to make room for an eighteen- or twenty-year-old, which I'm sure you'll have no trouble finding."

"That was what she said before taking the pesticide. But why not ask for a divorce? I promised her a hundred thousand yuan, and yet she chose to kill herself. I know she didn't mean it, that she just wanted to scare me. Who would have thought that the pesticide was lethal again? Now that she's dead, her brothers got someone to write up a complaint and send it to the court, the District Government Office, and, I heard, even the mayor's office. They're all accusing me of selling fake 101 and 102 pesticides."

"Ah—so you're here to see Zhidie so he can write another article to promote your products or speak to the mayor to help you get off?"

"Right. He's my only hope. He can't refuse to help me."

"Then you'll need to wait for him at the compound entrance. I'm going out, and I'll have to lock the door."

"But—but—" Huang looked troubled. Niu Yueqing picked up the mirror and smashed it on the floor.

"Get your ass out of here! What do all you stinking men have, except money? You killed your wife, and instead of taking care of her funeral, you came here with that sad face for someone to find a way out for you? And you have the nerve to tell me about it? Who did you bring with you? Is your shameless slut here also? Is she waiting for you downstairs? Bring her up here so I can take a good look. I want to see what kind of woman would hurt another woman. Did it ever occur to you that after killing your wife, someone would be waiting to kill you next? Get out. Get the hell out!" She pushed him out and slammed door.

She turned around and saw the muddy prints from his shoes; disgusted, she got a mop and ran it over the floor before sitting back on the bed breathless.

Zhuang was still out that afternoon, so she sat down and wrote him a long letter about the dozen or so harmonious years they had shared since their wedding. She recalled how he had looked like a country bumpkin and how dirt-poor he had been; it was only after she married him and sacrificed everything to encourage him and devotedly care for him that he had been able to struggle to where he was today. Now that he was successful, with fame and wealth, naturally she was no longer good enough to be his wife, for she was old. She hadn't been good-looking to begin with, but it was also because she had sacrificed herself over the years, to the point that she pretty much had never lived for herself. Their marriage had been dead for a long time, and they had different dreams even though they shared the same bed. It would be better to end it than to suffer together. Then she changed the subject: She didn't understand what she had done wrong to have everything turn out this way. For him and for their family, she had made diligent efforts, but he had repeatedly hurt her. Did that mean that nothing was real? Was that any way to live? She scratched out the passage, for it was no longer important to bring that subject up. Instead she wrote that in order to protect his reputation and to ensure his future happiness, she refused to raise a stink at the end of their marriage and turn them into enemies, like so many other women. She hoped for a peaceful dissolution without going to court; they could take care of it at the community office. She added that she was moving back to Shuangren fu and asked him not to look her up there, except when the divorce agreement was drawn up and they were ready to file. After finishing the letter, she picked up her suitcase and walked out of the compound with a curious sense of liberation.

When Niu Yueqing got home, she spotted her mother sitting on a stone at the gate with a blank look. "Mother," she called out, but there was no response. The elderly woman remained motionless except for a quick glance at Niu Yueqing, who squatted down in front of her and said, "Why are you ignoring me, Mother? What's wrong?"

The old lady came to suddenly, but her eyes still looked glazed over. "Who are you?"

"It's me, Yueqing. Don't you recognize me?"

The old woman, her mouth hanging open and her lips quivering, began to cry. At the sight of her mother weeping, Niu Yueqing could not hold back her own tears. At first mother and daughter were crying over the same thing, but soon they were engrossed in their own sad thoughts, which only made them cry harder.

It took considerable effort for Niu Yueqing to get her mother inside so she could ask the old woman why she hadn't recognized her own daughter. Her mother said she had not been able to sleep for three nights, and there had been a buzzing in her head. But when neither her daughter nor her son-in-law came to see her, she tied her daughter's clothes in a bundle to hang in the dry well in the yard to summon Niu Yueqing home.

"You lost your soul, Yueqing, and I got it back for you."

Niu Yueqing knew that her mother was losing touch with reality again, but this dazed look was something new. Mother and daughter had always been close, and she thought that her mother must have intuited something, which made Niu Yueqing start crying again.

"It's all my fault, Mother. I should have come to see you sooner so you wouldn't be like this. I will never leave you again. I'm going to live here, cook you three meals a day, sleep with you at night, and talk to you when we're awake. Mother, what do you feel like eating?"

When she said she wanted some noodle soup, Niu Yueqing went into the kitchen to prepare it. She removed the lid from the pot and saw that it had not been washed thoroughly, and that too made her sad. For over a decade, she had devoted most of her care to Zhuang, with little concern for her mother; she had let her mother down, the person closest to her in the whole world.

With her daughter around, the old lady's face regained signs of vitality, but she kept saying that the wall needed to be washed because the corners were crawling with centipedes and scorpions. When Niu Yueqing poured her some water, the woman complained about the knot of worms in her bowl; when her daughter drew water for her to wash her feet, the old lady said there was an even larger knot of worms in the basin. At bedtime, Niu Yueqing would not let her mother sleep in the coffin and made a bed large enough for both of them. Saying she couldn't sleep, the elderly woman talked about how chubby and well behaved Yueqing had been at the ages of three and four, and then she waved a fan at Niu Yueqing's feet because they were covered with flies. She must wash her feet the next day, the old lady added. Niu Yueqing turned to sleep facing the old lady and, with her mother's arms around her, sobbed.

⁂

Zhuang Zhidie, Meng Yunfang, and Zhou Min looked all over the city for Tang Wan'er, but after searching nearly every one of the main streets and small lanes, they were still unable to find her. They then went to see Zhao Jingwu, who had been drinking alone for days. He still looked dejected, so Zhuang said, "Liu Yue was dead set on marrying Dazheng. I tried many times to talk her out of it, but she wouldn't listen. I said, 'Liu Yue, if you put aside Jingwu's good looks, his talent alone would likely bring him great success, and you would want for nothing.' But she was too shortsighted. She even said, 'Zhuang Laoshi, you're like the man who draws a picture of a flatbread to stave off hunger.' You see, that's how she looked at it, and there was nothing I could do. I'm not her father, we're not even related, so I couldn't control her mind even if I could restrain her body. Since that's what she wanted, we had to let her be."

"I think it's a good outcome," Meng said. "I was unhappy when I first heard that Jingwu and Liu Yue were getting engaged, but I couldn't say so. Now that she's married to that cripple, just you wait and see—he's going to suffer."

"What do you mean, Meng Laoshi?" Zhou asked Min.

"My wife told me she once went to a bathhouse with Liu Yue and discovered that the girl was born under the star of a white tiger, someone who could kill a man without a knife. I read that in a book."

"You don't have to say any more," Jingwu said. "I'm not the type to kill myself over a woman. To each his own. If she didn't want to marry me, it wouldn't have worked. Like they say, a melon that's torn from the vine won't taste as sweet. I hate myself for being worthless. Too bad she only cared about the advantages in front of her. You've come today, and I appreciate your concern. So don't go yet; I'll go get something to drink with you."

"We feel better now that we know what's on your mind," Zhuang said. "If you feel like drinking, come to my house some other day, and we can drink ourselves silly. But we're on an urgent mission today, and we need you to join us. Did you know that Tang Wan'er has disappeared?" Zhuang followed up with details, leaving out the part about her disappearance at the movie theater.

"Elder Brother Zhao," Zhou Min said tearfully, "what's happening to us? Your woman married someone else, while mine has disappeared. We've combed every corner of the city, but there's no sign of her. I'm afraid she's run into some terrible people and was either killed or kidnapped by human traffickers."

"Stop that nonsense," Zhuang said. "She had no enemies in this city, so who would do her harm? And she's too smart to be tricked. Jingwu, you have many connections and you know people in all walks of life, so we will need your help to find her."

"Why didn't you tell me earlier? The underworld has gotten into this sort of thing lately. I do know someone, and we'll likely find out if she's fallen into their hands."

They took a taxi to Beixin Street, crossed a lane, and stopped at a shop with a wreath on the door. Telling the others to wait, Zhao walked in to speak to an old woman making papier-mâché flowers. He came right back out. "Muzi is out."

"Who is Muzi?"

"Someone who has access to the criminal world," Zhao said. "He studied martial arts as a youngster and has become very good at it. Let's get something to eat and then come back later."

They went to a restaurant, and the moment they got there, Ruan Zhifei pulled up with a woman in a car. The car stopped, and Ruan got out. "I was on my way to see you," he said to Zhuang. "Imagine running into you here. What luck."

Meng glanced at the woman in the car. "Another of your women?" he whispered.

"No, she's my assistant. I'm too lazy to get a divorce right now. So you're free to be out window-shopping, I see. Hop in. We're recruiting fashion models; it's a recent fad at dance halls. I have four already. Come tell me what you think."

"We have something important to do, so you'll have to go on without us."

Meng wanted to get Ruan to help with their search, but he kept his mouth shut when Zhuang gave him a look.

"What are you into now that's such a big secret? Well, I'll leave you to it. Give me a ring when you want to come check out the models." He ducked back inside the car and said something to the woman before driving off amid salacious laughter. The four men walked into the restaurant.

The place was packed, so Zhao Jingwu got in line to place their orders. The other three found an empty table and sat down next to a table where two young men were whispering furtively. Then a stocky fellow outside looked in through the window. Annoyed by the flattened face against the windowpane, Zhuang said to Meng, "Another sluggard," then turned to block the man's view. A moment later the man walked in; he was not tall, but he had a square, solid build. Without getting in line, he bought four oily flatbreads and carried them two in each hand to the young men's table. Without a word, they got up to leave, but he reached out, still holding the flatbreads, and said, "Give me a hand, pals, and roll up my sleeves for me." They silently did as he asked, and spotted the yellow insignias sewn onto them. "A cop!" They spun around to leave, but were stopped by oily flatbreads slapped against their cheeks.

"Don't move," he ordered, and they froze.

"Did you just steal a wallet on the number 12 bus? Don't lie."

"How did you know?" one of them asked. "But we didn't steal it, we found it."

"We'll see. Put it here in my right pocket. The person who lost it is in tears at the police station."

"We did find it, sir." One of the men put the wallet in the policeman's pocket. "We found it by the bus door."

"That sounds fishy to me. You can go now, but you won't get off if I ever catch you 'finding' another wallet. Now get out. Button up your shirts and get out of here."

They buttoned their shirts and gave him a respectful hand gesture before running off. The man laughed, picked up the flatbreads, and started eating. Zhuang and the others were amazed by what they had just witnessed.

"Do you think he'll return the wallet to its owner?" Meng whispered.

"I know the type," Zhou Min said. "He's not someone you want to mess with, so don't let him hear you."

"You know what he does?" Zhuang asked.

"He's a deadbeat who sometimes works for the police. I did that back in Tongguan."

"Muzi!" Zhao yelled out when he returned with the receipts for their orders. "I've been looking for you. Imagine running into you here."

Unable to talk because his mouth was stuffed, Muzi offered one of the flatbreads to Zhao, who declined and turned to Zhuang. "We've been looking for Muzi," he said, "and he's sitting right beside you. Muzi, let me introduce you. This is Zhuang Zhidie, the celebrated writer; this is Meng Yunfang, a researcher; and he's Zhou Min, a magazine editor."

Finally managing to swallow his food, Muzi asked, "Who? Who did you say this is?"

"Zhuang Zhidie. Haven't you heard of him?"

"I may not know the name of our governor, but I'd be laughed at as a cultural idiot if I said I hadn't heard of Zhuang Zhidie." The man rubbed his oily hand on the table before offering it to shake with everyone. "I heard your books are terrific, so I bought some, but I haven't had a chance to read them. My wife has, though, and she's a fan. What do you need to see me for? Were you really looking for me?"

"Yes," Zhao said. "Go home and ask your wife if you don't believe me."

"I'm honored that Mr. Zhuang is looking for me." Muzi reached his oily hand into his pocket and took out some money for Zhao. "Go buy a bottle and let's have a drink."

"There's no need for that," Zhuang said. "You're open and direct. I like your style. Come have a drink at my house some other time." Zhao had Muzi sit down and told him what they needed.

"I'll make a phone call." Muzi walked out and headed for a phone booth. He returned in a few moments. "I checked with some people in the east and south, but they didn't have the woman, nor had they seen her. The ones in the north said she lived outside their territory. I don't know Black Three in charge of the west side, so I told Wang Wei, who heads the north faction, to check with him and get back to me. He'll call."

That all sounded like an urban myth to Zhuang, who said, "So there are territorial boundaries."

"Well, a country has its borders, and so does a province," Muzi said. "It's easy to find a lost object, but a person, that's hard."

"The thieves you nabbed just now," Meng said with great interest, "how did you know they were thieves?"

"I was at the number 12 bus stop as people were getting off. The last one was an old man who was shouting that his wallet was gone. I took a closer look and knew immediately that it was them. Every profession gives off an aura, and I know it, even if I can't tell what it is."

"Sort of like the 'feel' for something that writers talk about," Meng said.

Muzi's pager chirped. "He's calling back," he said as he got up and walked out. The others sat wordlessly, their hearts in their throats, and stood up when Muzi appeared in the doorway. "Did you find her?"

"He said no."

Their faces fell. Sitting back down, they finished their meal distractedly before taking another taxi to Meng's place.

"What do we do now, Yunfang?" Zhuang asked.

"Should we report it to the police?" Meng asked.

"That's not necessary," Zhao said. "What can the police do if Muzi can't find her?"

"Since it's gotten to this point, Yunfang, why don't you do a divination with the eight trigrams?" Zhuang asked.

"I can do it for fun, but this is too serious for that. Let me try something else. We often use *Master Zhugu's Magic Numbers* to look for people. Give me three characters, Zhou Min," he said, but Zhou came up blank. "Anything that pops into your head."

"Rock beside door," Zhou said. "I noticed one there."

Meng began working on the number of strokes for the characters, coming up with three numbers that led him to a poem:

To the east by the water / a grove of peach trees / the birds call in the evening / the clouds obscure and dim the moon.

They puzzled over the lines.

"East?" Zhuang asked him. "Where would that be? It would be the eastern district if it's in the city, and outside the city it would be the eastern suburb. So where is it?"

"Could she have returned to Tongguan?" Zhou Min blurted out. "Tongguan is in the east."

"Very likely. Do you still have pals there?" Zhao asked.

"Lots of them."

"Then start calling," Zhao said.

"But I didn't notice any signs of her wanting to go back there," Zhou said. "She'd have told me if she wanted to return."

It took him a while to get through, but when he did, he learned that she had indeed returned to Tongguan. According to his old pals, news of her return had spread all over town. People were saying that after Zhou Min tricked this woman from a good family into running away with him, her husband had hired two men to look for her in Xijing and found her at a movie theater within a week. So he and one of the men hailed a taxi while the third man went inside. She knew the man, and when she inquired about her child, he asked her to come outside to talk. There her husband and the other man grabbed her, shoved her into the taxi, stuffed a towel in her mouth, and tied her hands and legs. They drove all the way back to Tongguan.

Zhuang was the first to sob after Zhou Min told them what he had learned. "That's how you treat criminals. How could they do that to her? Who knows how much she's suffered since returning. Zhou Min, take the train back. You have to save her."

Zhou Min squatted down and said nothing.

"What's wrong with you? Don't you want to go?" Zhuang asked.

"This is what I feared would happen one day. If they can find her in Xijing, like finding a needle in a haystack, I wouldn't be able to see her if I went back there."

"What nonsense is that? If that's what you think, then why did you bring her here in the first place? You're a grown man. Can't you even protect a woman? She must have been blind to be in love with you." Zhou Min slapped himself, and then Zhuang did the same thing.

❋

Meanwhile, Niu Yueqing had taken up residence at Shuangren fu. The lowland reconstruction project was underway, and the people in the lanes to the north had begun moving out, causing her elderly mother to panic. It would be her turn the next month or when winter came. Soon the lane with the former Water Board and the kiosk with the ancient well platform would be gone. She took out the water tokens to look at several times a day, chattering to her daughter about the former dynasty and later generations, mixing human words with ghost talk. Niu Yueqing took care of her mother's daily needs, but her mind was always on Zhuang Zhidie. She had thought that after leaving the compound and its many distractions, she would be able to think about her relationship with Zhuang with a clear head, but she had grown so used to all the activity that the absence of it now made her feel lonely. She had left the place out of anger and vowed never to see him again; she hadn't realized how much she loved him until she was alone. She tried to imagine his reaction after reading her letter. Did he fly into a rage, or was he beset by grief? If the latter, then he would have rushed over to explain things to her tearfully, showing remorse for his errors and vowing to leave Tang Wan'er right away. When that happened, she had said to herself, she would kick him out the door, humiliate him with a broom, and dump a basin of filthy water on him; she wouldn't take him back until she had vented her anger and resentment. But Zhuang never showed; he did not even call. Had she done precisely what he had been wishing for? He might have been looking for a reason to divorce but did not want to initiate the discussion, so he waited for her to say those things and start a fight. That would have been what he was waiting for, wouldn't it? Or maybe he was really upset, she thought. He was normally easygoing, but he had a stubborn streak; he might be holding out, unwilling to relent until she returned on her own. As a celebrity, he was used to being revered, and she had coddled him at home. After he hurt her feelings, might he have been waiting for her to mollify him before coming back? Several times she went to check the compound, but turned back halfway there, afraid she might further incur his displeasure by giving him the erroneous impression that she could not live without him. Besides, why had she written that letter and walked out on him if she planned to go back all along?

She phoned Meng Yunfang, who, after learning what had happened, reprimanded her for her unwise move. How could she leave home and not go back? How could she be thinking about a divorce? Her temper flared at his reproachful attitude. "Why is it all my fault? I might not have dealt with the situation properly, but was he right to do such sordid things? Should a wife treat a whoring husband with respect? He's a celebrity, so naturally you're all protecting him. Even a sore on his body is like a lovely peach blossom to you."

She slammed down the phone after her outburst. Meng had also gone to the dark side, she thought, so she was surprised to see him show up that evening. He was all smiles as he walked in, even saying that he was there to receive a tongue-lashing from her. They sat down to talk, and she told him she couldn't understand how Zhuang had become so degenerate.

"I can't figure it out, either," he said. "Other men have done worse, and they got off scot-free; poor Zhuang Zhidie, on the other hand, after meeting Tang Wan'er, sank to the point of losing his family, though he managed to stay alive."

"Do you think he's not degenerate enough?"

"What I can say is, he's better than the other people in the city's literary circles."

"But he's different from the others," Niu Yueqing said after a moment of silence. "No one would think twice about it if it had been Ruan Zhifei, but people see Zhidie as an upright man with high moral standards, and they'd be hard-pressed to accept what's happened. Who knows how many people he's destroyed, in addition to himself? He didn't walk out on the marriage, but he's been sleeping in the study; he hasn't asked for a divorce, but it's only a matter of time. Why would I want to hang on to him if that's what will happen eventually?"

"You're right about that. Other men's affairs are for temporary pleasure, but Zhidie has truly fallen in love. He's really a forthright man. I have never been thrilled about his relationship with her. It's all right to seek diversions in life, but how is she different from a wife, the way they are now?"

That did not please Niu Yueqing. "So do you mean it would be okay for him to fool around, falling for every woman he meets and then tossing them aside one by one, while sweet-talking me into accepting his behavior?"

"Marriage is one thing, love is another; they're not the same but are two halves of the same thing. He's lived in this city for decades, but instead of adopting modern ideas, he still has the mentality of country folk."

"What I want is, marriage is love and love is marriage."

"You and Zhidie have never agreed with me on this point, and see what's happened? See the suffering you're experiencing?"

"Let's not talk about that now, Yunfang, since we'll never agree. I'll bring you a glass of water if you want; if not, you can go do whatever you need to do."

"Are you trying to get rid of me?" His face reddened and he laughed awkwardly. "Well, I'm not leaving yet. I've gotten so used to your cooking, I won't leave till you feed me."

Niu Yueqing sobbed over her sad state. The more she cried, the more forlorn she looked, which prompted Meng to apologize. "Yueqing, I have a big mouth. You probably don't like what I've said, but I can tell you from the bottom of my heart that you have my total sympathy. When Zhidie talked about having you stay here, I didn't go along with him. Instead, I said, 'Zhidie, in all honesty, you have to admit that Yueqing is a good wife. She's been married to you for over a decade, and she has no serious flaws. Could you live with yourself if you left her?'"

"I don't need your sympathy. I could tell he didn't ask for a divorce because he felt sorry for me and was worried about my future. That shows he hasn't lost his conscience. But do I need sympathy? No, what I need is love. Don't think I don't love him. It's precisely because I still love him that I want to let him have what he's wishing for and marry Tang Wan'er."

"Marry Tang Wan'er? So you don't know that she's been taken back to Tongguan by her husband."

That caught her by surprise. "Well, the slut's gotten her just deserts. So she's back home after stirring up so much trouble?"

"No need to curse her, the poor thing."

"Poor thing? She's a slut."

"Now that she's gone, why don't you and Zhidie get back together? You've both gotten your feelings hurt over this, and you'll need time to recover, but it would be good for everyone if you two could patch things up. Take me, for example: I will still have a place to go for food and drink."

"I'll feed you when you come," Niu Yueqing said. "I'm just worried you'll never come here again."

"If I don't get to eat or drink, that's no big deal, but do you think the two of you will be happy for the rest of your lives once you've gotten past what you're suffering now?"

"With his status and fame, if he can't marry Tang Wan'er after the divorce, he could easily find an eighteen-year-old or a twenty-year-old. He won't be unhappy. I will never be able to find another celebrity, but I think it wouldn't be all that hard for me to marry a factory worker or an office clerk. Or I may just stay single and be with my mother."

"Why are you so stubborn? If wives had been like you in the old polygamous society, they would all have killed themselves. I'll go talk to him if you think you could let him off the hook. I've said this before: Never lose your foundation, no matter what. Don't end up like me. I loathed my first wife, so I divorced her and remarried, but now I think my first wife was better. I dream about Meng Jin's mother and have never once dreamed about Xia Jie."

"So you want him to keep two burners going at the same time, is that it? That's a lousy idea."

Meng had no response. Saying she was sleepy, she sent him out of her bedroom; he had no choice but to walk out with an awkward smile. The old lady was sitting in the living room. "What were you talking about, all that whispering and chattering? My hearing is terrible, and all I heard was that someone was lost."

"It's better to have bad hearing, Aunty, and even better not to be too clear-headed. It's Tang Wan'er. She has disappeared. Do you remember her, Zhou Min's woman? She's been gone several days now."

"I've always said you must hold your shoes in your arms when you sleep, but no one listens. See, now Tang Wan'er has gone missing. What matters most to a woman are her shoes. What kind of shoes was she wearing when she disappeared?"

"I heard she was wearing a pair of black heels."

"Mother, you're talking too much," Niu Yueqing said from her bedroom.

"Well, I'll be going." Meng laughed as he walked out.

When Meng was gone, Niu Yueqing thought about their conversation and wondered if she ought to forgive Zhuang this time, now that Tang Wan'er was gone. But on second thought, she knew he was obviously unhappy with her and would surely stay away after what she had written in the letter and what she had said to Meng. So even if Tang Wan'er was gone, there was no guarantee he would not have a Zhang Wan'er or a Li Wan'er. If that turned out to be the case, then better to suffer the short-term pain and get it over with. Gritting her teeth and steeling her heart, she still could not fathom why he was unhappy with her. Had she ever been unfaithful? Hadn't she treated him well enough? She could only conclude that he was not the same Zhuang Zhidie anymore, and she was destined to live a life of misery.

For the next few days, Meng returned every day, followed by Zhao Jingwu and Wang Ximian and his wife. They were all there to try to talk her around. It would have been fine if Zhuang had come in person to apologize and admit guilt; it would also have been fine if their friends and acquaintances had stayed out of it. But the fact was, Zhuang was nowhere in sight, while their friends were taking turns coming to pressure her. As someone who had never enjoyed being mollified, she found their visits increasingly annoying, which made her hold more firmly to her views, and eventually she refused to see anyone. After losing her appetite and sleeping badly for a few days, she was visibly thinner and her hair was falling out in clumps. Every morning when she looked at herself in the mirror, she was worried that the second half of her life would be even worse if she kept losing hair until she was bald. One day when she was feeling despondent, she recalled Huiming at the Clear Void Nunnery. She went there in the afternoon as flocks of birds and a fiery red sun hung over the city.

A sheet of red paper was pasted on the entrance: *The Yankou Incantation will be recited on the first of the month, with the following lines: Rid the living of illness and calamities extend their life span bring them happiness good fortune and peace . . . help the deceased escape suffering in hell and reach Nirvana.* Niu Yueqing had no idea what the Yankou was, but she walked in anyway. She was greeted by the sounds of Buddhist instruments in Guanyin Hall, but instead of going in for a look, she headed for a small garden to the right and pushed open the gate. Huiming was sitting in there rubbing some medicinal lotion on her head, which was very round, sparsely dotted with hair. When she saw Yueqing, she offered her a seat as she continued to rub in the lotion.

"What kind of magic is that?" Niu Yueqing asked.

"Hair-growing magic."

"Hair-growing magic?" Niu Yueqing was intrigued. "But every nun has to shave her head. Why are you doing that?"

"We've known each other for some time, so I'll honest with you. Yes, every nun has to shave her head, but I was the opposite; I became a nun because I had no hair. I had a full head of thick hair until I was eighteen, but I lost every strand that summer. A hairless woman is not a woman at all, so I avoided going out for six months before finally deciding to become a nun at Mount Zhongnan. Then I attended a Buddhist college. But now I want hair; I want hair to grow on my head so I can shave it off. This hair-growth lotion comes from Beijing and is very effective."

"I wish my hair would shed overnight and I could become a nun here."

"Even if you went completely bald, at most you'd be like me when I first became a nun. Whether as a nun or not, women are just women and can't live without men. How can women stay away from men? When a farmer harvests the wheat, he has to collect the stalks, and even an emperor can't avoid finding fleas in his dragon robe."

"That's true."

"You must find it odd to see a nun using a hair-growth product. But I find it strange that you're here. Zhuang Laoshi is not just anybody, so how could you, of all people, have worries?"

Two teardrops snaked down her face, but Niu Yueqing refused to open up, so Huiming decided not to press her. Instead, she made a pot of tea to share with Niu Yueqing before walking her out to the main entrance, where they bade one another farewell.

Niu Yueqing returned to the nunnery three days later. Huiming was sitting in bed. "I knew you'd be back," she said. "I called Meng Yunfang and asked about you. He was upset and asked me to talk you around. But I won't do that. It doesn't matter to me whether you're here to become a nun or simply to find some peace. To each her own, and it would be useless for me to say anything to try to change your mind. But I can tell you that you are the only one who can find relief for yourself. When I first became a nun, I thought I'd find peace in everything. Then I realized that not every woman can be a nun; if that were case, then a nunnery would be nothing but a refuge, and the sacred purity of the Buddha would not be able to shine through. I do understand what's on men's minds. It's their nature to prefer the new over the old and to be fickle, but this is still a man's world. Women are like children: Adults play with them when they're happy, because they want to share that happiness with them. Or they scold them when they're unhappy, treating them as a diversion, because they want them to share in their misery. They say that women hold up half the sky and can do whatever they want, like soar into the sky or bore down into the earth, but how many women can actually do that? Stores all over town sell women's clothes and cosmetics, and it appears that all of society is waiting on women. But for what? To make women beautiful for men to appreciate and enjoy. In a world dominated by men, women must accept that reality while learning to live well. The single woman must make sure she is well liked, while the married one seeks to sustain her husband's love. So women have to constantly make adjustments, enrich and reshape themselves, so they can maintain the impression that they never have to worry about their appearance. If one tries to please a man with her looks, she must know that her beauty will fade as time passes. Besides, there are many types of beauty out there, and how do you expect to satisfy a man's insatiable appetite? If your life revolves around a man, then he will become your everything, which can only lead to a terrible life until you're tossed aside. Confucius once said that it's hard to deal with women and petty people, but in fact men are the hard ones to deal with. You can't be too far from him, but he will become annoyed when you're too close. A woman must learn to keep the proper distance when dealing with a man, slipping away like an eel in his hand. If you're like a melon seed that teases the taste buds without filling him up, then he will be enamored and boldly chase after you. So a woman must live for herself, enjoying a life filled with vigor and excitement. Then she will truly know how to live in a man's world."

Niu Yueqing's heart raced after hearing Huiming's lengthy discourse, which was almost like a sutra. For a while she thought the nun was talking about Tang Wan'er, who knew how to make everyone like her. Could she have known all these things? Then she felt that Huiming must be talking about her. Had she lost Zhuang's love because she lacked the necessary understanding? What surprised her most was how much the young nun knew about men and women. "I'm amazed by what you know, Abbess Huiming."

"Is that so? Then you'll be shocked if I continue."

"What do you mean by that?"

"Well, I'll be frank with you, since you treat me like a friend and have come to see me. Has it occurred to you that I'm being very rude sitting in bed while talking to you? I had an abortion two days ago."

"An abortion?" Niu Yueqing cried out.

"Close the door so the others won't hear us. Yes, I had an abortion. You're probably going to change your opinion of me and will never come again. But it's true. When I noticed something different, I put an herbal formula together and aborted the fetus. Well, you can go now if you want."

Niu Yueqing was tongue-tied, too worked up to even look at the nun, not because she did not want to embarrass Huiming, but because she felt so awkward. Muttering something incomprehensible, she got up and went home.

For seven days in a row, she asked for sick leave and stayed home. Since her discovery of Zhuang's affair with Tang Wan'er, nothing had pained her more than the actions of her beloved husband. But now even Huiming, a nun, had had an abortion. So what else was real in this world? What was left that was credible and admirable and worthy of her belief? She turned these things over and over in her mind, to the point that she actually fell ill. Dander fell from her body, which she didn't even notice until she was putting on her socks one day and saw a pile of something that looked like chaff. The following morning when she made her bed, she spotted the same thing on the bed, which made her itch all over. Taking off her clothes, she realized that her skin was rough and scaly, like snakeskin or tree bark. That night she got undressed and, using a brush, washed her body over and over. She went back to work on the eighth day and didn't return home until very late. Her mother stopped her in the doorway and examined her closely.

"What are you doing, Mother? Can't you see it's me?"

"I don't really recognize you. What's happening to you?"

"Take another look, then, Mother," Niu Yueqing said with a smile. "Have I gotten prettier or uglier?"

"Your brows are darker, and what happened to the sun spots on your face?"

"Well, that's better." Niu Yueqing told her mother she had had some work done on her face—her brows had been tattooed, and the dark spots had been removed with a chemical peel. She would have to continue that treatment for seven days, after which the spots would be gone. Besides that, she wanted to surgically raise the bridge of her nose, eliminate the wrinkles in her forehead and her belly fat, and reduce the size of her feet.

"Then you won't be my daughter anymore."

From that day on, the old lady could not stop grumbling that Niu Yueqing was a fake, no longer her daughter. When they went to bed at night, she reached out to touch Niu Yueqing's brows, nose, and chin, and was besieged by doubts. One day she said that someone had replaced the TV with a fake; on another day she complained that the pot, too, was a fake. She even doubted the relatives and neighbors who came to visit them, which led her to wonder about her own authenticity. She demanded to know the truth from her daughter.

⁂

After admonishing Zhou Min to get him to return to Tongguan and rescue Tang Wan'er, Zhuang returned to his apartment, where he discovered that Niu Yueqing had left him. He had suddenly become a lonely man in a cheerless house, like a nest with broken eggs after the hens have flown the coop. He saw her request for a divorce. Before that time, he would have jumped at the suggestion, and he was astounded to see the letter in front him. After reading it, he let out a loud laugh and made himself a strong cup of coffee, feeling an unusual sense of relief. But after spending a day in the room alone, the emptiness got to him; he had to put on the funereal music and turn the volume all the way up before he could lie down peacefully in bed to think. In the past, whenever he'd had a dalliance with Tang Wan'er, Liu Yue, or even Ah-can, he had come home hoping that Niu Yueqing would scream hateful words at him. If she ignored him, he felt bad; if she devoted all her care to him, he felt guilty. Tormented by these reactions from his wife, he had hoped more than once to end the marriage. Now it was finally going to be over, and all he could think about were her positive traits, which, however, did not motivate him to go to Shuangren fu and ask for her forgiveness. It was obvious to him that getting back together would be virtually impossible. First of all, would she be able to live with the shadow of his relationship with Tang Wan'er? Besides, how would he deal with his feelings for the woman? It was she who had infused him with new emotions and new desires, and now that she had been plunged into an abyss of suffering, could he continue to live as if nothing had happened with a clear conscience? Even if he could bear the pain, wouldn't that mean he would carry the burden of double crimes on his back for the rest of his life? But—but on second thought, it was precisely because of his encounter with Tang Wan'er, to which he had given himself body and soul, that he had inched closer and closer to the quagmire. In order to extricate himself, he judged her by applying the moral standards and norms for women, hoping that he would come to hate her and be able to forget her. But he could not think of any sinfulness on her part, or anything that would make him loathe her. He tried many times to forget her, but each time he ended up missing her more. It was like knowing that the glass of wine in front of him was laced with poison, but, unable to resist the tempting color and heady aroma, he took a drink. Meng came to see him once, criticizing him for being cocooned so long in literary creation that he no longer knew how to live in society. He dealt with everything as if it were art, which was what had gradually put him in this state, and look where that had gotten him. Now did he plan to continue the way it was? "You worry that you can't let this one or that one go. But what about yourself? You're a celebrity, and a celebrity must live a more carefree and expansive life than others, while you, just look how you suffer."

Zhuang laughed silently, saying that Meng's ideas were alien to him. He hadn't agreed with Meng's opinions before, and he wouldn't agree with them now; all he wanted was for his friends to butt out. He said that Tang Wan'er was gone and Niu Yueqing had left home, which was a punishment from God. He and he alone would have to endure it.

After buying a case of instant noodles and doing his laundry for a few days, he was so bored that he went to Meng's place and invited Zhao and Hong over to drink. He turned into a glutton at the sight of liquor, getting so drunk that he disgusted himself. So he got on his scooter each day, Walkman headphones over his ears, and roamed the city listening to music, his hair flying. Sometimes he wondered if a woman might stop him and ask for a ride; or he might even block the way of a pretty woman on the open road. But all he did was return after a frenzied ride, his face nearly unrecognizable from dust and sweat.

On this day, when he was out on his usual roam, an idea flashed into his mind, so he rode to the southern suburb to see the cow. The late autumn sun was still powerful; the corn had been harvested, but the soil had yet to be turned over, leaving dust to roll across a brownish-yellow expanse. When he got to the grounds outside Aunty Liu's house, he was greeted by dozens of farm cattle; none was tied to a rope, and none was tethered to a stump or a millstone. Instead, they were looking into Liu's yard through the crumpled fence, so he followed their eyes. The cow was lying down, looking like a pile of hide-covered bones. Aunty Liu was squatting by the cow's head, stirring feed in a wooden basin. After parking his scooter, Zhuang walked in. Aunty Liu looked up silently, tears running down her cheeks. Knowing that the cow would not survive, he consoled himself with the fact that his timely arrival had made it possible for him to see her one last time. He pulled up a blade of pungent silver grass and put it by the cow's mouth. She twitched her ears with difficulty, as a way to greet him; there was something sticky around her eyes, which were only half-open. She smelled the grass that lay on her drooling tongue. "Didn't I tell you to go buy a bottle?" A man's thick voice could be heard from inside the house. "What are you doing out there? There's no use giving her food now." He came out with another man and stood on the steps. All Zhuang sensed at first was a white glare, which turned out to be a long, thin blade in the man's hand. Liu's husband had a stubble-covered face, bloodless and ghastly pale. "Oh, you're here," he said when he spotted Zhuang. "Come inside for tea."

"Are you killing the cow?" Zhuang asked.

"There's nothing else we can do. It's been too long, so we'd be better off to kill her to give her release than to let her continue to suffer. If she could talk, she would want it this way. You're a celebrity who came to see her when she was sick. And you returned today when she has reached the end of her life."

"The cow and I have a karmic connection."

The blade-wielding man laughed. "Old Qi, I'm afraid no one will come to see you when you die."

"I deserve that," Liu's husband said. "The cow is going to die by my hand, and that makes me guilty, too."

The man walked up to the cow with the blade between his teeth, tightening his belt. "Old Qi, you and your wife come hold down the horns." Liu's husband went up while Aunty Liu covered her face and ran inside. "Women!" her husband cursed, holding both horns. She paused at the door, unable to bear the sight, but also unable to face the fact that she would not be with the cow when she died. Facing the door, she held tightly onto the rings. With the blade still in his mouth giving off a white glint, he felt around the cow's throat before taking the instrument out of his mouth.

"Would you mind holding the cow's tail, mister?" he asked. When Zhuang did not move, the man sneered and knelt down on one leg.

"Your suffering is reaching its end today. Don't be reborn as a cow in your next life." With a swish, he plunged the blade into the cow's neck so deeply that part of the handle was invisible. Zhuang saw her eyes, the color of egg whites, roll up, as hot, gamey air gurgled around the entry point and blood ran down onto the warm earth in pink bubbles. Suddenly drained of energy, Zhuang squatted down when he saw Aunty Liu's hands slip out of the rings as she slumped to the doorsill. At that moment, the cattle outside the yard bellowed and ran in circles as if crazed, kicking up so much dirt that the area was blanketed in dust. The butcher yelled and went over to shut the gate, picking up a leather whip. One crack of the whip stopped the cattle from stampeding. One let out a bleak lowing as it raced toward a trench, followed by the others, all emitting the same sound. Zhuang watched for a while, then turned back to see a cowhide spread out on the ground. The man rummaged in the messy cow flesh before retrieving a small golden-yellow object.

"Would you look at this cow bezoar!" He was so excited, he raised it in his bloody hands to look at it in the sunlight. Steam still hovered around the object.

Aunty Liu's husband dragged Zhuang inside to sit at a table with food and drink.

When Zhuang finally woke up from his dazed state, he noticed that there was a large basket next to him filled with chunks of beef, while the bloody hide was spread over the fence to dry. He did not have anything to drink.

"I would like to buy the hide," he said.

The man tossed down a mouthful of liquor and said, "Oh, so you're a leather merchant? This is an excellent hide. What are you offering?"

"I'll give you whatever you want."

"Don't talk about price," Liu cut in. "If you want it, Mr. Zhuang, it's yours."

❋

After arriving at Dazheng's house, Liu Yue immediately realized that her husband's house, like Zhuang's, had a constant stream of visitors, with one difference: Zhuang's guests were cultural figures, while those coming to Dazheng's house were mostly high-ranking officials from government bureaus and departments, factory owners, and businessmen. They never came empty-handed, bringing gifts ranging from big-ticket items like refrigerators and color TVs to smaller presents such as cigarettes, liquor, and fruit; and they all followed the same rule, placing the gifts in a small windowless storage room next to the shoe rack while changing into slippers. They would then sit in the living room to talk to the host, the former saying nothing about the gifts, the latter offering no thanks for them. Liu Yue did not have to come out to greet visitors, except when her mother-in-law or husband called to her, "Come join us, Liu Yue." She would then come out of the bedroom, as pretty as a flower, and smile charmingly at the guests, occasionally engaging in a bit of idle chat. She knew unerringly when they had finished their tea, but instead of attending to it herself, she called out, "Come pour some more tea, Xiaoju."

Liu Yue had met the maid Xiaoju on the morning after the wedding. She was sorting chives in the kitchen. Unconsciously Liu Yue went over and picked up a handful, but she quickly dropped them to wash her hands at the sink. The maid snorted. As she scrubbed her hands with a bar of perfumed soap, Liu Yue asked, "What's your name?"

"Xiaoju."

"Let's have some dumplings today, Xiaoju," Liu Yue said. "Don't skimp on the dried shrimps. Let me know before you add them and I'll do it."

Without responding, Xiaoju continued to sort the chives for a moment. "The dumplings at the mayor's house never have dried shrimps."

Liu Yue paused and scowled. "I don't care. That's how I want them." She flicked the water off her hands and, without turning off the faucet, walked back to her room, accompanied by the sound of gushing water. "Turn off the faucet."

Bored to tears after ten days, she told Dazheng she wanted a job. He said they had someone working on her city residency, and she couldn't work until it was finalized. Saying she didn't care, she insisted on finding a job. He relayed her demand to his mother, who, after lengthy consideration, called Ruan Zhifei and asked him to find something for Liu Yue at his dance hall. She started the next day.

Liu Yue was neither a singer nor a dancer, but she had a pretty face and a good figure, so she learned to walk the runway with the models. The long-legged, narrow-waisted models were all attractive, but their faces betrayed a lack of education. Liu Yue, on the other hand, had read enough to give her a refined look, and since she knew how to highlight her graceful bearing, she soon became the top model. When the residents of the city came to a fashion show, they were there for the models, not for the clothes. In other words, no matter what the fashion designers put on the models, in the spectators' eyes the women were naked, which was why the members of the audience were often heard to say that a certain one had a pretty face but was too big in the butt, or another one was too skinny and could use larger breasts. In the end, they all thought the sexiest and most fetching woman was the model Liu Yue, who elicited whistles and lewd shouts every time she showed up. Talk of the beautiful model at Ruan Zhifei's dance hall spread, and his business boomed.

One day Meng Yunfang arranged a noontime meeting between the old man who had the sole copy of *Master Shao's Magic Numbers* and the master from Xinjiang. After the manager at the Changhong Hotel provided them with free room and board, the two masters, in order both to express their gratitude and, most importantly, to show each other up, offered to use their magic to improve the manager's health and to predict the future business at the hotel. That went on throughout the day. To repay Meng, the manager gave him an old-style copper hot pot shaped like a lotus flower, along with five jin of mutton and three types of condiments. Accepting everything with a broad smile, Meng took the gift home and called Zhuang and Zhao over to share the food. Still in low spirits, Zhuang ate little; instead he turned on the TV, where an imported fifty-episode gangster drama was playing. First came an ad for Ruan's dance hall.

"Did you know, Zhidie, that Liu Yue is working at the dance hall as a model, and a very popular one, too?"

"Great. That's a good job for her. How did you hear that? Do you go dancing often?"

"Me? No way."

"He's never been, but his son goes all the time," Xia Jie said.

"What's a youngster like Meng Jin doing there? Can he afford it?" Zhuang asked.

"That's the problem," she said. "I ran into Ruan Zhifei three days ago, and he said, 'That son of yours is quite the clever one. He comes to the dance hall every three or four days with his classmates, and when the doorman asks to see their tickets, he tells them that Ruan Zhifei is his uncle and that Liu Yue is his older sister, and then he walks right in.' When the doorman asked Ruan if he had such a nephew, Ruan saw that it was Meng Jin. He said the kid would surely grow up to be just like his old man, someone to be reckoned with. When I got home, I told Meng to have a talk with the boy, but all I got in return was a frown. Look at him. He's upset."

"I'm not upset." Meng forced a smile onto his unhappy face and said, "Let's go see Liu Yue one of these days. We don't want to make her think she's like that proverb—a married daughter is like splashed water."

"Sure," Zhuang replied. "Why don't you set it up?"

"What's there to set up? After we're done here, I have to go to the Propaganda Department. The head of the department called yesterday and asked me to come over this afternoon. It's nothing important, just to get Meng Jin's master to use qigong to help his wife pass a bladder stone. I'm going today not to help with the treatment, but to set up an appointment."

"Aren't you the busy man," Xia said. "One moment you're talking about visiting the mayor's daughter-in-law, and the next you have to set up treatments for the department head's wife. Are you going to get up and leave your writer friends here?"

"Now you're making me sound like a petty snob. It will only take half an hour to deal with the department head. Keep up the conversation. Let's meet at the dance hall at four."

"You can go, but count me out," Zhao said.

"Don't be small-minded, Jingwu," Meng Yunfang said. "Are you afraid to see Liu Yue now that she's married to someone else? She should be afraid of seeing you. You don't have to interact with her if you don't want to. Just dance. You might actually meet someone."

"You're driving me nuts with all this chatter. Go if you want," Xia Jie said. "But I'm telling you, Yunfang, since you're going for a good time, don't take Meng Jin with you and get more complaints from the door-man. I can't afford any more embarrassment."

Meng uttered a curse as he walked out. Xia Jie put the dishes away, but instead of washing them, she called a neighbor over to join them in a round of mahjong.

Meng Yunfang went to the Propaganda Department not to work on any bladder stone, but to talk about something that would impact the whole city. It turned out that the mayor had always wanted to use culture to promote the city's economic growth. When he heard that the Xijing

Zoo had just gotten three giant pandas from the Beijing Zoo, he was inspired to host an Ancient City Cultural Festival, using the pandas as the logo. He then called a meeting with officials from the Propaganda Department and the Bureau of Culture. Everyone thought it was a great idea, for not only would it raise the city's visibility to outsiders, it would also put Xijing in the vanguard of economic improvement. A preparatory committee was formed. The head of propaganda wanted to hear what Meng had to say about the program. Meng suggested that Zhuang Zhidie be included, to which the propaganda head readily agreed, adding that they wouldn't have to bother Zhuang with everyday business; his talent would be best reserved for drafting announcements and other related documents. After reading three pages of possible activities for the festival, Meng knew he could stay till dark and they still wouldn't finish their discussion. "This is big," he said. "Let me take these pages home and give it some careful thought. I'll be back tomorrow afternoon with specific comments." He left and hurried toward the dance hall.

The performances had ended, and the paying guests had just started to dance. The floor was filled with couples holding each other tightly and swaying to the music. A strobe light swirled its vivid colors, turning the dancers into indistinguishable phantoms. Meng Yunfang had heard from his son that Liu Yue danced with guests, so he sat at a table straining to locate her. But he was blind in one eye and had poor vision in the other, and it looked to him as if all the girls were strangely dressed, and that each one of them looked like Liu Yue. When the music ended, she was not among the girls leaving the dance floor. So Meng decided to look for Ruan, but the music started up and the couples went back out and merged together again. He cursed himself for poor planning; if Zhuang and Zhao were unable to find Liu Yue and Ruan Zhifei, they would give him a hard time. As he was wondering what to do, he heard someone say, "You must be Mr. Meng." He turned and saw that it was a pretty girl at the next table; she was studying him with her chin in her hands.

"Are you talking to me?" Meng asked. "My name is Meng, but who are you?"

The girl gave him her hand, so he shook it. "You look familiar," he said, "but I have such a terrible memory, I don't remember you. I'm sorry."

"No need to apologize. Actually, we've never met. I just thought you looked like Meng Yunfang, so I ventured a guess. So it is you."

"You noticed that I only have one good eye?"

"I've heard that Mr. Meng has a sense of humor, and it's true," she said with a smile. "But I'm not the witty type. I work at the Public Prosecutor's Office, and I'm sure you know who I am now. No? Well, Jing Xueyin is married to my second brother."

Meng nearly got up and ran out, but instead he smiled and said, "Ah, now I know. I'm sure you're quite witty yourself. It's a pleasure to meet you. I do know your sister-in-law. You look a bit like her; I guess that's because you're from the same family. How is she doing?"

"How do you think she's doing? Your friend's lawsuit has nearly driven her to suicide."

"You're looking at it the wrong way. I know something about the case, and in my view it didn't have to end like that. They were once close friends. Zhuang Zhidie has been in a funk lately, complaining that it was all Zhou Min's fault that a friend was turned into an enemy."

"If he really cared about their past friendship, why did he violate her privacy and say all those things? He hurt a former friend in order to save his own reputation. That is immoral!"

"It wasn't like that at all," Meng said. "Well, let's not talk about that, since the case is settled anyway."

"Mr. Meng, you don't understand the law. The judgment from the Intermediate Court doesn't mean that the case is settled. There's still the appeal to the Superior Court."

"Appeal? Is that necessary?"

"No matter what, she won't accept that judgment. She has devoted all her energy to the lawsuit and will fight to the bitter end. Do you understand what I'm saying?"

"Of course I do. With certain people behind her, she might get what she wants."

"Well, then, I'll drop the subject." The girl smiled. "Would you do me the honor of a dance?"

"I'm sorry, but I don't know how to dance. In fact, this is my first time here. Why don't you ask someone else?"

"What a shame. All right, I will." She waved to a waiter. "Bring a Coke for this gentleman, on me." She walked off.

Meng was so humiliated, he could only ask the waiter where to find Liu Yue.

"She didn't come down today, so she must be in her room. Go through that door and take the staircase to your right to the third floor. She's in room 18."

He took some money out and handed it to the waiter. "Please give this to the lady. Tell her I can't let my lover pay for drinks after I asked her out."

Meng rang the doorbell at room 18, but heard nothing, so he rang again.

"Who is it?" Liu Yue asked.

"It's me."

"Go see the business office. I'm with an important guest."

"It's me, Meng Yunfang."

The door opened. She was so heavily made up, he barely recognized her. "It's so hard to get to see you now, Liu Yue. What's that perfume? You smell awful, like a Westerner."

She signaled with her eyes. "There's a Western guy in my room," she whispered. She motioned toward a suite inside; the door was ajar. Meng went into the room. "Meng Laoshi," she said, "none of you have come to see me since you married me off." Then she lowered her voice. "Who's your dance partner today?"

"I'm half-blind and half-deaf, so who would have me? Zhuang Laoshi has been in a terrible funk, so we thought we'd come see you."

"Don't use me as an excuse if you're looking for fun. What could be bothering Zhuang Laoshi? Now that I'm gone, he should be worry-free."

"You're an ungrateful little monkey." He told her about Tang Wan'er's disappearance, Niu Yueqing's departure, and Zhuang's sad, lonely state. Her eyes reddened. "Where is he now?" she asked.

"We agreed to meet here at four, but I couldn't find you on the dance floor. Try to cheer him up. See if you can talk him into apologizing to your dajie and patching things up with her."

"I've been busy here since I got married. I've wanted to go visit them, but I can never find the time. Luckily no one looks down on me here, and I've been thinking about inviting you all to watch my performance. But after Ruan Zhifei got beaten up, I had to take over for a while. That's why I haven't had time to return to the compound. I didn't know all this had happened to him."

"What did you say? Ruan Zhifei was beaten up?"

"You didn't know? He collects the take every night after the place closes. Two nights ago, someone stopped him at the top of the stairs. 'Are you Mr. Ruan?' he asked. Ruan didn't know the guy, who said he was a secretary at the Pacific Company. They were having some sort of celebration and wanted some fashion models to help with the festivities. Ruan told him the models never perform outside the dance hall. The guy asked whether Ruan could talk to their manager, who was waiting in a car downstairs. Ruan followed him down. There were three men in the car. One of them, a fat guy, reached out to shake Ruan's hand, but the moment their hands touched, the man jerked him forward as the so-called secretary shoved him into the car, which sped off. Knowing he was in trouble,

Ruan held on to his money pouch and asked what this was all about. The fat guy punched him in the eye, smashing his glasses. A shard punctured his eye, which bled. The fat guy told him, 'That's what it's about. We know you've gotten rich, but you can't leave us hungry all the time. If we ask for a loan, you won't give it to us, so we're sorry, but this is the way it has to be.' Ruan said, 'Before you do this, you need to know that Liu Yue works at my dance hall. Do you know who she is?' The fat guy said, 'Sure. She's married to the mayor's son; so what? You've made plenty, and now you're holding on to your left eye in order to identify us.' He slugged Ruan again, this time in the left eye. They drove to Nanhuang Road, where they dumped him out and sped off. Luckily, a vegetable vendor found him and took him to the hospital, but he'd been blinded. It was big news. I'm surprised you haven't heard. Dazheng's father was outraged and ordered the police to catch the criminals. They set up roadblocks at the four city gates, but didn't turn up anyone suspicious. When they asked Ruan what the three men looked like, he was unable to say for sure, only that one of them was fat and they drove a red car."

Meng was shocked by the news. Liu Yue told him how difficult it was going be to solve the case, even though the police had been working hard on it. Uninterested in what the police were doing, Meng asked which hospital Ruan was in and how he was doing. She told him he was at the Western Medical School Hospital, but she didn't know his condition, since she had been too busy to visit him.

"Ruan was smart to have you take over, but you need to be careful. Working here is more complicated than being a maid."

"If the bad guys aren't afraid of the mayor, I'll give them whatever they want. I'm not going to be like Ruan Zhifei, who values money more than his life."

Meng laughed as he eyed the suite inside. "Where's he from?" he whispered. "Is the dance hall engaged in international trade?"

"He's a teacher at the foreign language school. He knows some Chinese and comes here to dance, which was how we met. He's an American. Want to meet him?"

"I can't stand their cologne," Meng said. "How long has he been here? Why is he hanging around?"

"He's just here to talk. Americans are like that. Don't get any ideas, OK?"

"You're not a young girl anymore. You're married to the mayor's son, and everyone is watching you."

"I'm old enough to know how to take care of myself."

Meng looked at his watch. It was four o'clock, so he said he would go down to wait for Zhuang and the others at the door and come back up with them later. Liu Yue said she would stay in her office and send the American away so she would be free to dance with Zhuang.

Meng waited downstairs for a long time without seeing his friends, even after Liu had sent the American away. Worrying about Ruan, Meng went up to tell her that he was going to the hospital, adding that she shouldn't tell Zhuang what had happened to Ruan, so as not to ruin the outing. When he returned from the hospital with a better sense of Ruan's injury, he would talk to everyone and settle on a day when they could go see him together. Moved by Meng's thoughtfulness, Liu Yue stayed at the dance hall till dark, but Zhuang never showed up, nor did Meng return to see her, which led to a night of anxiety.

Meng did not get to see Ruan at the hospital; the doctor told him that Ruan had just had a double eye transplant, and no visitors were allowed. The news of a successful operation put Meng's mind at ease, and he wondered what the transplant surgery was all about. "Can you really get a new eye?" he asked. "Of course," said the doctor. "When did you lose sight in that eye? Why don't you come in for surgery?"

"One eye is enough for me. With all the robberies occurring these days, what has the world come to? One more eye to see what's happening would simply upset me more."

"How can you talk like that, comrade?" The doctor looked annoyed.

Telling himself that this doctor had no sense of humor, Meng asked where Ruan had gotten the new eyes.

"From a dog."

"A dog!" Meng cried out. "What's that saying—to a dog, people all look small?"

The doctor snorted and walked off, ignoring Meng, who left the hospital feeling snubbed. It was getting late, so he decided not to go back to the dance hall. Instead he went home, where he found Zhuang, Xia Jie, Zhao Jingwu, and Zhou Min sitting around listlessly.

"Ha! I waited at the dance hall until I'd just about sunk roots, but you're still sitting here. Doesn't what I say mean anything? Or are you playing a trick on me?"

"I'm so mad I could kill you." Xia poked him on the forehead before dragging him into the kitchen to talk in private.

She told him they had played mahjong until 3:40 that afternoon. Just as they were ready to leave for the dance hall, Zhou Min arrived. He had returned from Tongguan, and instead of coming back with Tang Wan'er, he walked in with a bandaged head. His sorry look told everyone that he had been in a fight in Tongguan. They asked when he had come back and why he hadn't called to have them meet him at the station. He said he'd been back for two days.

"Two days?" Zhuang said. "Why did you wait that long to come see us?"

"I didn't see a need to tell people anything," Zhou said. He shifted his attention to the mahjong table, asking to play a round.

"So you came back, and that's it?" Zhuang was so mad his face looked almost black. "We were looking forward to your return so much that our eyes nearly bled, but you waited two whole days to come see us. And now here you are, looking nonchalant. Tell me, what happened to Tang Wan'er?"

"I failed to rescue her," Zhou said, obviously frightened by Zhuang's outburst.

"I can see that. But don't you have any news about how she's doing?"

Zhou told them he had been cursed, jeered at, and mocked by nearly everyone in Tongguan when he got there, so he had to stay out of the public eye. He asked a few old pals to go to her house to check things out and learned that her husband had stripped her naked and beaten her until her body was covered with welts. He wanted her to promise that she would be content to stay home with him, but she refused to say anything, neither yes nor no, so he tied her up and raped her over and over. He tortured her, burning her privates with cigarettes, cramming a flashlight up . . . Zhuang was weeping before Zhou had finished.

"It's all right," Zhou said with a laugh. "Don't shed any tears over her. None of us may ever get to see her again, so we have to learn to forget her." He went on to say that he had sent a mutual friend to see her after he talked to some lawyers and learned that she could get a divorce by sending a request to the court, whether her husband agreed or not. But the man did not get to see Tang Wan'er, since she was locked up in a shed in the back yard. Zhou said he couldn't stand it any longer, so he put on a straw hat as a disguise one afternoon and stormed into her house. Her husband had prepared for that possibility by keeping four bruisers around. The moment Zhou was inside, they tensed up, raising their fists and glaring at him. "I don't want a fight," he told them as he sat down at a table and took out a bottle, inviting everyone to drink. Seemingly reassured by his behavior, Tang's husband opened some cans of snacks, and the six of them commenced to drink.

"Let's talk now that it's reached this point," Zhou said. "When Wan'er went to Xijing with me, I knew she was married, but I loved her and she loved me, so we took off anyway. Then you went to Xijing to get her back. That's fine, but you should have let me know, so I wouldn't worry about her."

"Well, how should I put this? I'm not the cultured type, so let's not beat around the bush. You're well known in Tongguan, but she cheated on me for a long time. Now that we're sitting here, I won't beat you up or even curse you; all I ask is for you never to see her again. Do it for our child's sake, if not for mine."

"Are you begging me?" Zhou said.

"Yes, I am."

"But how can I forgive you? You tied her up and brought her back here to beat her to within an inch of her life. Then you sexually abuse and torture her. She's your wife, not some farm animal. Besides, you can't beat her into loving you."

"That's none of your business. She's my wife, and no one can tell me how to rein her in."

"I won't allow you to treat her like that. If you still want to be with her, then you have to treat her with care. Get a divorce if you plan to continue abusing her."

"I'll die before I divorce her."

"All right, then. You begged me, and now it's my turn to beg. Would you let me see her?" Zhou had filled out a divorce application, which he had planned to have Tang Wan'er sign with her fingerprint when he saw her and then take it to court on her behalf. But the husband refused, so they began to argue. When Zhou tried to force his way out back, one of the bruisers knocked him to the floor. "Beat him, beat the damned hooligan! He came here to stir up trouble, and we won't be breaking the law if we beat him to death." All four of the men went at him with their fists and feet, so he jumped up onto a table, knocking two of them down with one kick each. When Tang's husband grabbed hold of him, he bit down on his hand so savagely that the bone showed, but one of the men cracked his skull with the liquor bottle. Finally the neighbors, alerted by the scuffle, ran over. Zhou jammed on the straw hat and ran out, his head bloody. He took to bed the moment he got home, and was so ashamed he stayed there for three days. On the fourth day, he learned that Wan'er's husband and his lackeys had smashed the glass case at the small sundry shop run by Zhou's mother. He jumped out of bed, ready to fight them again, but his parents held him back, asking him to let them live in peace. They said he had already stirred up enough trouble on account of a woman, as people were talking about how he had tricked another man's wife into running away with him. Even they had been affected, which was why so many people had looked on silently while the shop was vandalized.

"You'll kill us if you stir up more trouble. With all the available women, why did you have to fall for somebody's wife? At your age, other men are already providing for their parents. We don't expect money or help from you. All we ask is for you to let us live in peace, son, and not make us worry about you all the time!"

His anger now spent, he slept for several more days before returning to Xijing.

After hearing the story of Zhou's visit, Meng Yunfang walked out of the bedroom with a heavy heart and headed straight to the refrigerator for a bottle. "Wan'er won't be returning, so be it," he said. "At least Zhou Min's back. I want to drink today, and I want to eat meat. Xia Jie, go buy four catties of dog meat."

"Liquor and dog meat?" she said. "That produces too much heat in the qi."

"Just do as I say. No more backtalk," Meng said, and she left. Everyone else was still quiet, so Zhou said, "Why doesn't someone say something? Wan'er was my woman, and I'm no longer sad, so why are you feeling bad? Life is like a dream, so we'll just wake up from this dream and go on with our lives."

Zhuang reached for the bottle, but he couldn't open it no matter how hard he tried. Zhou offered to open it for him, to which Zhuang responded by using his teeth, making a cracking noise before finally uncapping the bottle. He poured a glass for himself and drank, followed by the others, who each downed a glass. By the time Xia Jie returned with the dog meat, there was hardly any left.

"Yunfang," Xia Jie said, "people at the store were saying that Ruan Zhifei was kidnapped and blinded. Did you know that?"

Meng tried to give his wife the high sign, but she missed it. "They also said he got a new pair of eyes from a dog. Can you really do that?"

Zhao and Zhou were so stunned, the hands holding glasses stopped in midair. Meng looked at Zhuang, who belched several times before wordlessly raising his glass and tossing down the contents.

"Are you sure you can handle that, Zhidie?" Meng asked. Zhuang refilled his glass.

"Are you worried he'll drink too much of your liquor?" Xia asked him. "We have plenty of beds. If he's drunk, he can spend the night here."

"Well, drink up, then. Come on, let's drink. Yes, Ruan Zhifei did get kidnapped, and I went to the hospital to see him. He deserved it, though.

He likes to show off his wealth, sponsoring one thing after another, so it's only natural that someone would try to get something out of him. Come on, Zhidie, I'm letting myself go today. Let's get good and drunk. Bottoms up."

By now red-eyed, Zhuang stood up and said, "I'm going home." He walked out, surprising everyone, though no one dared say anything to get him to stay longer. They merely watched as he staggered out the door. Meng emptied his glass as tears rolled from his eyes.

❋

Zhuang passed out the moment he walked in the door. When he woke up the next morning, he had a terrible headache. Over the next few days, he ate nothing but instant noodles and pain pills. He didn't go to Meng's house to drink for several days, so Meng went with his son's master to help Zhuang recuperate with qigong. Meng could see that the anti-burglary door was open, but Zhuang would not open the wooden door no matter how hard he banged on it. So Meng walked down to the gatehouse and asked Mrs. Wei to make an announcement over the PA system: "You have a visitor, Zhuang Zhidie. Come down to see your visitor, Zhuang Zhidie." That got no response. Meng then went out to call him from a pay phone. Zhuang picked up the phone and answered with a complaint: "Why are you bothering me? Are you working for the grim reaper?"

"You can't stay home forever. I know you're feeling down, so I asked Meng Jin's master to help you feel better with qigong."

"Why do I need qigong therapy? I'm not sick. I'm feeling perfectly fine."

"All right, then. If you don't want qigong treatment, at least take care of yourself. Don't worry about Ruan Zhifei. I've been to see him with Jingwu and the others, on your behalf, so you don't have to go. He's doing fine, recovering well after the transplant. I do want to remind you of something, though. You're having a terrible year, with all sorts of trouble, so after giving it some thought, I did a study of the Qimen Dunjia Astrology, and it dawned on me that there's a problem with the way your furniture is arranged. The bad fengshui has ruined everything. You mustn't use a room in the northwestern corner as a bedroom. You should have been sleeping in the northeast. And the living room sofa should not face the front door. Put it by the eastern wall. Have you got all that?"

Zhuang was so annoyed he hung up. Hearing nothing but a loud slam followed by a busy signal, Meng could only smile unhappily as he invited Meng Jin's master to a dinner of steamed beef and rice before sending the man back to his hotel. He then went to the dance hall to see Liu Yue, hoping she would tell Niu Yueqing what had been happening with Zhuang. If the two women could go see Zhuang, it might make him feel better; if not, he might really fall ill and destroy himself.

Liu Yue went to Shuangren fu, but the place was deserted. A bulldozer was razing Shunzi's house, the one next door, and she knew that Niu Yueqing and her mother had moved. Standing alone under the peach tree, she was lost in thought for a long time before dejectedly heading over to the apartment at the Literary Federation compound. After opening the door to let her in, Zhuang went on about what had happened to Tang Wan'er after she had been taken home. Liu Yue decided not to say too much to him; she cooked something for him and hurried off after making sure he ate it. Over the next two weeks, she came over every day. Later, when she got too busy at the dance hall, she arranged for a woman who ran a noodle stand to deliver food to Zhuang twice a day. When the woman showed signs of reluctance, Liu Yue took out a handful of U.S. dollars and said: "I'll pay you with these. Will that work for you?"

One day, after dining with the American at a newly opened Western restaurant on Drum Tower Street, Liu Yue thought she would take him to meet Zhuang Zhidie. But as they were walking down the street, she changed her mind and told the man to go back to the school while she went to see Zhuang alone. At his door, she saw someone crouching by the wall, fast asleep. It was Zhou Min. She shook him awake. "Were you out rustling cattle last night, Zhou Min? Why are you sleeping here?"

When Zhou Min opened his eyes and saw her face, he wiped the slobber from the corners of his mouth and said, "I looked all over for Zhuang Laoshi, but couldn't find him, and I thought he might be at home. I knocked, but he won't open the door, so I decided to wait outside. Sooner or later he'll have to come out, won't he? I didn't realize I was so exhausted. What time is it?"

"Four o'clock."

"I slept for two hours?"

Liu Yue knocked on the door, then switched to banging. "Open up, Zhuang Laoshi," she shouted. "I hear you coughing inside. It's me, Liu Yue. Do you refuse to see even me?"

Finally they heard footsteps inside, and the door opened to reveal a sallow-faced Zhuang in the doorway. "So you're here, too, Zhou Min."

"I slept out here for two hours."

"What's happened to make you do that?"

"I would never disturb you if it weren't urgent. I went to see Sima Gong yesterday, and he told me the Superior Court has sent down its final judgment. They've overturned the Intermediate Court's decision and changed the verdict to slander against Jing Xueyin. I heard that one of Jing's sisters-in-law set up a honey trap and colluded with the person who reviewed the case, while we didn't take immediate action to see the chief judge at the Superior Court. I told you to go see him, and I just learned that you didn't. If we don't act now, everything will be lost."

"Is that so?" Zhuang said as he boiled some water for tea. "Let them change the verdict. I don't care. We lose if they say we lost, and we lose even if they say we won. Have some water."

Declining the water, Zhou said anxiously, "So we'll just sit around and let them do this to us? One of the rulings required the judgment to be publicized in the papers."

Zhuang sat down; the scroll on the wall behind the sofa was gone, replaced by a cowhide. "So? Let them. You can go see the chief judge of the Superior Court if you want to, but count me out. I refuse to ask anyone for help again."

"What's the use of my going to see him, Zhuang Laoshi?" Zhou was about to cry. "Please go see him, I beg you. We've fought so hard for so long only to end up like this?"

"What can I say to you, Zhou Min? Would you let me off the hook and stop talking about this? I'm writing a novel. I'm a writer, and I need peace and quiet to write."

"All right, then. I won't beg you anymore, Zhuang Laoshi. Go write your book and be the celebrity you want to be. I've been ruined by your name, but I deserve it." Zhou walked out and slammed the door behind him.

The Provincial Superior Court issued its final verdict seven days later, which was published in every newspaper in the city on the same day. For several nights, Zhou Min followed Jing Xueyin home after she left work in order to find out where she lived. Finally, on a rainy night, he hid at a street corner until Jing's husband came out on his bike. Zhou pounced like a wolf, knocking him down. "Why won't you pay back the money you owe my friend, Liu Sanguai?"

With his raincoat over his head, Jing's husband replied, "You've got the wrong man, buddy. I'm not Liu Sanguai, and I don't owe anyone any money."

Secretly pleased, Zhou went on with his demand. "Are you a man or not? Why won't you admit the debt? You're a prick is what you are. Don't blame me for getting rough. I'm just doing what I'm paid to do. Since you don't want to pay back the money you owe, you'll have to use that money to see a doctor." Zhou lifted his foot and stomped on the man's skinny calf; a loud crack told him he had broken a bone, so he got on his bike and sped off.

A drunken Zhou Min showed up at the magazine office the following morning, where everyone was talking about how Jing Xueyin's husband had been sent to the hospital with a broken leg. They were all saying that he got what he deserved, adding that the six hundred yuan the court had ordered as compensation for the defamation wouldn't be enough to pay his medical bills.

"Who did it?" Zhou Min said. "We ought to find the man and shake his hand. How did it happen?"

"They say it was a case of mistaken identity," Li Hongwen said. "Hmm, who would do that without checking his identity? He must have done something wrong to deserve that. If you can manage it, Zhou Min, why don't you take something to him at the hospital? The magazine will pay for it, of course."

"I'd go if I were still working here, but I'm no longer an employee of the magazine."

"Did they fire you?"

"They would have sooner or later, so I decided to quit first." Zhou took a carton of cigarettes out of his bag and handed everyone a pack. "I want to thank you all for watching out for me over the past few months. I'm sorry I brought the magazine so much trouble. I'm leaving now, and I ask that you forget me after you finish the cigarettes. I'm like the ash that dissipates when you blow on it."

The others could only stare blankly until Li spoke up. "But Zhou Min, we can't finish them completely, since there's always the butt. Which means we will never forget you."

"Then spit the butt into the trash can by the wall," Zhou said with a smile. He headed to the door, giving them a casual wave before he walked out.

All of Xijing was abuzz after the news appeared in the newspaper. Those who hadn't known about the lawsuit searched for the issue of *Xijing Magazine* carrying Zhou Min's article, prompting Li Hongwen to secretly sell the remaining copies at a high price to a wholesaler, who raised the price and sold them to street vendors. In the meantime, the tabloids sent reporters to interview the magazine employees and Jing Xueyin, increasing their circulation with a flurry of stories. Gossip flew with every new version. Zhuang's door was knocked on at least ten times a day, but he never opened it; his phone rang constantly, with the callers wanting to ask him about the case, to offer consolation or share their indignation, even to revile him. In the end, he unplugged the phone. When he couldn't stay holed up at home any longer, he donned a pair of dark glasses and walked outside, planning either to play mahjong at Meng's house, to go ask Zhao Jingwu or Hong Jiang for some money, or to visit Ah-lan at the mental hospital. But when he reached the intersection, he was seized by indecision. A bicycle came toward him, so he moved to the left just as the cyclist pedaled to the same side, and the same thing happened when he shifted to the right. The man cried "Aha" as they both hit the ground along with the bike. When Zhuang got to his feet, he saw that people were looking at him and laughing, so he hurried off; the cyclist rode by and cursed him, "Are you blind?"

Zhuang froze on the spot, at which point the man turned back and rode past him slowly. "Zhuang Zhidie?" he said. Zhuang didn't know the man, whose face was covered in zits. "Looks like him, but no, it's not Zhuang Zhidie." Finally he rode off. Zhuang was glad the man didn't recognize him; otherwise it would have been awkward. He continued walking aimlessly, telling himself that he wouldn't have confirmed his identity even if the man had known who he was. He laughed silently at the thought, and then spotted a tiny yellow banner flapping under a willow tree down a lane. "Liquor" was written on the banner, so he walked over and saw that it was a small tavern. He went in and ordered a drink. After downing a cup, he recalled that he had been there before—on the day he saw the funeral with filial sons and grandsons and heard the slow but beautiful funeral music. Feeling a sense of affinity with the tavern, he decided not to play mahjong with Meng or to go see Zhao and Hong. He fished another bill out of one of his shoes to buy a second cup, which he silently nursed until the sunshine glided off the table. With a casual turn of his head, he saw someone who looked like Liu Yue hurrying by. He called out to her, but she didn't respond, so he leaned against the door to look that way. It was Liu Yue. He called her name again, taking in a mouthful of wind, and took off after her. After about ten meters, he fell to the ground and threw up.

Thinking she heard someone call her name, Liu Yue slowed down, but she quickened her steps again when she didn't hear anything more. *I must have heard wrong*, she told herself, but something kept nagging at her, so she turned and saw a man fall to the ground; curious, she walked back to the spot and cried out, "Zhuang Laoshi! Are you drunk?" She tried but failed to help him up, so she ran out to the street to hail a taxi. Every taxi that drove by was taken. By the time she managed to get one and talk the driver into helping her get him into the car, a dog was already there, licking the former contents of Zhuang's stomach. It was even licking his face. He was too weak to drive the dog away and could only wave weakly. "Get the dog," he said. "The dog." Liu Yue sent it off with a kick before getting Zhuang into the taxi with the driver's help. They tore down the street and arrived at the compound, where she helped him inside to wash his face and rinse his mouth.

Liu Yue stayed with him until he sobered up and she reproached him for drinking so much and damaging his health. She then took some money from her purse.

"What are you doing?" he asked.

"I know you're short on money at the moment. Tell me when you need more. I'm not rich, but I'm not that poor maid any longer, either. Even if you think it would be demeaning to take money from me, at least it's better than getting drink money by prostituting your reputation and humiliating yourself."

Zhuang had no clue what she was talking about.

"Are you still trying to hide this from me? Hong Jiang told me everything," she said, confusing him even further.

"What did he say?"

"Look at this." She pulled a thin pamphlet out of her pocket. He took it from her. The cover was virtually devoid of design, just the words *The Ins and Outs of Zhuang Zhidie's Scandalous Lawsuit*, followed by a table of contents listing the chapters: "Lingering Feelings for Old Flame Jing Xueyin / Article about the Romance by Zhou Min," "Humiliated and Angry, the Beauty Seeks Redress from the Leadership / A Confidential Letter as a Pacifying Attempt," "Sparks Fly Inside and Outside the Court / Zhou Min Deserved the Betrayal," and so on.

"What's this all about?" He flung the pamphlet away.

"I saw someone at the dance hall reading it. I asked him where he got. He said the Dazhong Book Shop, so I went there. Hong Jiang was helping people bundle pamphlets to be sent to other counties. I asked him who wrote it and why he was participating in a moneymaking scheme that would ruin Zhuang Laoshi's reputation. He said he didn't know who wrote it, but since others were making money off of it, why should he miss out on it? Zhuang Laoshi said that after he and Dajie split up, he didn't feel right taking money from her, so he went to Hong Jiang. And the bookstore has to make money. He even said that the booklet was produced with your tacit approval and told me to mind my own business. Is that true?"

Zhuang was outraged. "Fuck that son of a bitch. How dare he do that to me?" Then he laughed softly. "I'll stop complaining about him, Liu Yue. He's a businessman, so what's the use of cursing him? I'm not going to try to find out who wrote it; it could have been Zhou Min or Hong Jiang, even Zhao Jingwu or Li Hongwen or one of the others. It doesn't matter. They can write what they want. Rumors have been swirling around the city, and you can stop one or two people from talking about it, but you can never plug up everyone's mouth. Meng Laoshi once said there's a group of people around me who profited from writing articles about me. I never expected that even our own bookstore would secretly print stuff like that to make money. I guess it's my turn to profit from myself!"

As sadness welled up inside, she tried to console him. "I'm glad you're looking at it that way. Are you still dizzy? Let me help you into bed to rest for a while."

He shook his head, saying he couldn't sleep. The expression on his face was pitiful. "How did my life turn out like this, Liu Yue? Shouldn't everything have been over when the verdict was announced? How did it get so much worse?"

"It's because you're a celebrity."

"Celebrity. You're right; I'm a celebrity, and now I'm an even bigger celebrity, a celebrated laughingstock and an object of condemnation."

"Don't mind them, Zhuang Laoshi. You're a writer, and you have to let your works speak for you. Aren't you writing a novel? Then pull yourself together and finish it. That will allow you to clear your name and even gain wider acceptance and a better reputation."

"You think so?" he asked. "Could it work?"

"Of course."

"Then I won't write it. I don't want that kind of fame."

⁂

After seeing Liu Yue off, Zhuang was even firmer in his determination not to write anymore, for that was the only way he could detach himself from fame. In the end, he penned an article, his last, to conclude his writing career. An announcement of 1,028 words, it said that due to severe insomnia, Zhuang Zhidie had lost his ability to write and was hereby formally announcing his retirement from the literary scene. When it was done, he sent it anonymously to the *Literary Field Guide* in Beijing. Within a week of its publication, the Xijing tabloids reprinted the article as a news item. One night Meng Yunfang came to see Zhuang. "Do you know what the rumor mill is spreading about you now, Zhidie? People say you've lost the ability to write and have retired from the literary scene. What a joke. The mayor even called me today to ask about it. I told him that was impossible. He was very unhappy, and said he would find out who started the rumor. How could the media work to destroy our own celebrity like that? Do you know who wrote it, Zhidie?"

By then Zhuang had shaved his head, which glistened. "I wrote it."

"You wrote it? What were you doing, playing a prank on yourself? You can't do that, no matter how terrible you feel. Tell me, what else can you do besides write? Be a cobbler, a street vendor?"

"I don't think I'd go hungry doing something else. Even if that happened, you wouldn't turn me away if I came to you for something to eat, would you?"

"Well, you never listen to me anyway. But I'm telling you, you are not just Zhuang Zhidie's Zhuang Zhidie; you're Xijing's Zhuang Zhidie. Go explain yourself to the mayor. I came with another task today, entrusted by the mayor. He would like you to write some pieces for the Ancient City Cultural Festival, including a description of the festival logo. I told him you haven't been feeling well lately, so he asked me to write a draft, but he didn't like what I wrote. He wanted you to revise and embellish it." Meng took out a manuscript, which Zhuang tossed aside without taking a look. "I've lost the ability to write, so I can't write or revise it for you."

"You can pull that on other people, but not me. If you're determined not to be known, then I will put my name on this, but you have to work on it for me."

"I can help you, but only this one time. And you must keep this from the mayor."

After Meng left, Zhuang began working on the article. He had to laugh over the logo they had picked; there were so many things they could have used for the Ancient City Cultural Festival, so why did they have to choose the giant panda? It was his least favorite animal. Though a rare animal, it was stupid, lazy, and childish, and then there was its saccharine, silly look. How could it represent the city and its culture? He threw down his pen and stopped working on the article, but on second thought he decided that it might just be the perfect image for the logo. This ruined city deserved such a symbol. He didn't want to suggest that the festival logo be changed to a hawk, a horse, a cow, or even a wolf, but he was reluctant to improve the eulogy to the giant panda. Hence he crossed out several paragraphs and replaced them with a long section of jumbled, illogical, and ungrammatical description. When he was done, he went to the post office to mail it to the mayor, without waiting for Meng to come for it.

He ran into Ruan Zhifei when he came out of the post office. Zhuang was surprised to see no dark glasses on his friend's face; in fact, Ruan's eyes were sparkling bright. "Your eyes are fine now?" Zhuang asked.

"Yes, they are. I wanted to come see you when I got out of the hospital, but the mayor sent me to Shanghai to purchase some musical instruments. I was assigned to the preparatory committee for the Cultural Festival, and see what happened? I got back three days ago and have been running around like a headless chicken, so I haven't been able to visit you." Ruan paused to stare at Zhuang's face with a puzzled look. "What happened to you? Are you ill? I want you to be well and not make me worry, like Wang Ximian."

"What wrong with him?"

"You haven't heard? Don't tell anyone what I'm going to tell you now. He got himself some more fake paintings and is now under investigation."

"Is it serious?"

"Hard to say, but let's hope not. Go get yourself checked at the hospital, Zhidie. You look like you're coming down with something."

"I'm fine."

"Then why are you suddenly a few inches shorter?"

Knowing that he couldn't have shrunk, Zhuang nevertheless checked himself out and laughed. "So a single trip to Shanghai has made you so arrogant that nothing looks good to you anymore."

"You've got a point there. The city of Shanghai—"

"Enough. Just because I say you have tiny feet, don't walk with your hands on a wall for support. In fact, it's the same with me. Every time I return from Shanghai, I feel that the streets of Xijing have become narrower and dirtier and that the people look like country bumpkins. But the feeling usually goes away within a few days. Are you free? Come have a drink at my place."

When they got there and started drinking, Zhuang asked about Ruan's treatment. Ruan said he was given a pair of dog's eyeballs. "You can't tell, can you?" Zhuang couldn't, and he chortled. "What are you laughing about?" Ruan said. "I thought the new eyes would be ugly, but then I realized that all eyes look the same. Pretty women have pretty eyes, don't they? But when you take them out and put them on a table, they're no different than pig's eyes. The face that goes with the eyes is what makes them pretty."

"You have a good-looking face, so the new eyes are pretty, but you said I'm shorter. That must be what's meant by 'to a dog, people all look small.'"

Ruan took a swing at Zhuang. "Yes, you do look shorter to me. Maybe this new pair of eyes has given me invisible powers." Seeing the cowhide on the wall, he suddenly exclaimed, "Where did you get that? Are you making a leather coat? Can you sell it to us? I had an idea for the Cultural Festival. Besides getting all the folk artists to perform and exhibit their works, I think we ought to redecorate the clock and drum towers, so that during the festival the clock would sound at seven each morning and the drum would be beaten at seven at night. Those are the sounds of heaven and earth, as indicated by ancient texts. Moreover, eighteen drums and eighteen clocks would be set up at each of the four city gates to echo the sounds from the towers. How impressive would that be! That cowhide is great. Sell it to us, and we will make a big drum to place at the north city gate, the grandest one of all. What do you say?"

Zhuang mulled it over for a while and said, "I won't sell it, but you can take it to make a drum, as long as you promise it will be hung over the north city gate even after the festival. It will be good enough for me if its sounds could remain in this city forever."

Elated, Ruan asked if he could take the hide down right away, so Zhuang went over to give him a hand; to their surprise, it crashed down from the wall and wrapped itself around Zhuang, who had to struggle out of it. Ruan then rolled it up and got ready to leave.

"Are you really going to take it?" Zhuang asked.

"I really am. Hate to part with it?"

"At least leave me the tail."

Ruan went to the kitchen for a knife. He lopped off the tail, then walked out with the hide over his shoulder to hail a taxi.

Zhuang had not anticipated giving away the hide, something that made him unhappy. When the shop owner delivered his noodles over the next few days, they didn't taste as good as they had before. "Why do the noodles seem to lack flavor? In the past I'd be drooling as I waited for you to deliver them." The woman just smiled. "Does that mean I'm unhappy with what I'm eating?" he asked.

"I'm going to be frank with you, but you can't tell anyone else. If you do, they'd shut me down. I'd suffer and you'd go hungry. In the past the noodles tasted so good because there were opium poppy pods in the soup."

"Poppy pods! No wonder it was so fragrant. But how could you do something like that for money?"

"Now I regret telling you. Of course we shouldn't do that, but it's not the same as smoking opium. It makes you just addicted enough that you'll return to our diner. It can't hurt you. Do you prefer it that way? I was worried you might find out, so I didn't use the soup the past few days."

"Well, I guess I'll have it the old way."

As he requested, she brought him the delicious noodles that afternoon.

If she hadn't told him, he would have thought only that she made delicious noodle soup. But now that he knew about the poppy pods, he had the sensation of smoking opium after finishing the soup, which gave him a buzz as he lay in bed. The sensation intensified over time, and he often had trouble distinguishing between reality and illusion. One night, after watching television for a while, he felt that he was walking into the TV as the characters on the screen came out to bring him in. He went deeper and deeper into the set until he saw tiny openings on the sides. One of the openings had a sign for "spirit writing." He opened the door and walked in; four people were using planchettes to write in sand. He laughed at their superstitious practice and began cursing all the health products that were so popular in Xijing, complaining that everyone was obsessed with their health, which was why there were products such as magic head covers, magic stomachers, even magic shoe inserts. Now a turnip was no longer just a turnip, but a health product that warmed the stomach and increased virility. And bok choy? It wasn't just cabbage; it was a nutritious health food that nourished the yin and supplemented the qi. Vegetable market vendors even put on white smocks and caps with a red cross. Hearing his fulminations, the four men told him to shut up, adding that what they were doing provided accurate predictions. So Zhuang said he would offer a word for the deity to interpret. When he wrote the character for vagina, he did not expect to see a poem appear in the sand, a sight that made him cry out in shock and that brought him out of his reverie. His eyes snapped open. The same gangster drama was playing on TV, which told him he had been dreaming. But he had never been able to remember his dreams in the past, yet now he actually recalled the poem: *Standing it's a monk with palms together / sitting it's a lotus with blooming petals / stop the horseplay / it's where you came from.*

Filled with confusion and questions, he could not get the poem out of his mind all that night. Then he began reliving his relationship with Tang Wan'er, followed by a trancelike trip to Shuangren fu to see Niu Yueqing. She wasn't there, and her mother stopped him at the gate. "Why haven't you been to see me for so long? Your uncle was mad at you, so I had to lie and tell him you were off writing somewhere. But what have you been doing? Can't you even find time to stop by? Has Zhou Min's woman come back yet? I tied a rope around her clothes and shoes and hung them down the well to make sure she'd return. Have you done the same thing?"

"Zhou Min's woman? Who's that?"

"Have you forgotten her? I just saw her yesterday. She was crying in a room; she couldn't move because her legs were bent. I asked her what happened, and she showed me. My god! Her privates were a bloody mess under a lock. I asked her why. Didn't she need to pee? She said it didn't affect her peeing, but it had gotten rusty from the urine, and she couldn't open it. I asked her to give me the key and I'd open it for her. She said Zhuang Zhidie has the key. Since you have the key, why don't you open it for her?"

"What crazy talk is this, Mother?"

"I didn't say anything crazy. I did see Tang Wan'er. Go ask your father-in-law. He was there, and I had to push him aside. I said to him, 'What are you looking at? You can't see this.'"

Zhuang woke up drenched in sweat. He didn't dare fall asleep again, so he drank some coffee and sat up till dawn. He then went to see Meng Yunfang, hoping to tell him about his dream, to see if he could make sense of it. But Meng wasn't in, while his wife was home crying her heart out. When he asked her why, she told him that Meng had left for Xinjiang with his son and his son's master. With her face wet from crying, she added that Meng Jin's master had said that the boy was highly intelligent and would grow up to be an extraordinary man. Yunfang's doubts were allayed when Meng Jin could recite the "Diamond Sutra" from memory after six months of reading, and he believed that his son might indeed become something special. So he was determined to make the boy meditate, recite sutras, practice qigong, and study Buddha's Dharma Eye, while lamenting that he had nothing to show for half a lifetime of dedication; he figured he must have been sent by heaven simply to wait on and enlighten Meng Jin, which led him to give up his own studies. He had not planned to go to Xinjiang, not until the mayor, who complained that the revised text seemed worse than the original, had called him. Had Zhuang Zhidie really lost his ability to write? Meng understood why Zhuang had sent the revised article directly to the mayor, so he echoed the mayor's speculation and said Zhuang was indeed a has-been. Then the mayor ordered him to write the articles himself. He complained about it when he got home, but he had no choice other than to copy the original and send it back to the mayor, which convinced him to go to Xinjiang. Xia Jie opposed the trip, and they ended up fighting, but Meng left anyway.

After telling Zhuang about Meng's trip, she continued to moan about what she'd gone through at home, grumbling that she couldn't live with Meng anymore; in her view, he was someone who needed an idol, and that had turned out to be his own son. How could she live with a man like that? Zhuang waited silently for her to finish, then got up to walk out. When Xia Jie, who had begun to cry again, saw that he was nearly out the door, she came after him with a note, saying it was from Meng. There was nothing on it but a line of six digits. "Is this an incantation he wanted me to recite to avert calamities and prevent troubles?" Zhuang asked. She replied that Meng had said it was a phone number, of someone who had asked about Zhuang's situation, but he did not say who it was. He said only to give it to Zhuang, who would understand. Zhuang took the note, but he did not recognize the number. If it was a friend, there was no need to ask Meng. He shrugged, tucked the note into his pocket, and walked off mournfully, his head down.

Doubt and incomprehension filled Zhuang's heart after he was unable to see Meng Yunfang. When he walked by a butcher shop under the clock tower, he decided to buy a pig's bitter gallbladder, which he would lick to help him stay awake if he was visited by strange visions when he shut his eyes at home. Before he knew it, he was standing in line at the butcher shop. The mayor happened to ride by just then on his way to inspect the progress of the site construction for the opening ceremony of the Cultural Festival. He spotted Zhuang, who now sported a shaved head and a long beard, and told his driver to stop so he could watch through the window.

"Can I help you?" the butcher asked Zhuang when it was his turn.

"I want some bitter gallbladder."

"Gallbladder?" the butcher said. "Are you nuts? We sell pork, not gallbladder."

"That's what I want. And nuts to you, too."

The butcher slammed his cleaver down on the butcher block and said, "Stand over there if you're not here to buy pork. Next."

The crowd pushed him out of the line. "The man's crazy. Totally nuts."

Standing outside the line, Zhuang just smiled stiffly, which was witnessed by the mayor. "Care to get out, sir?"

The mayor responded with a wave of his hand, and the car drove off. "Too bad about Zhuang Zhidie," he said.

Without the gallbladder, Zhuang fell into another daze that night after finishing his noodles. He imagined that he was writing a letter to Jing Xueyin; it seemed to be the fourth or even the fifth letter he had written. The contents appeared to be the same: he was telling her he loved her more and more, no matter what came of the lawsuit. Since she and her husband had never gotten along and he had become a cripple, Zhuang hoped they would both leave their spouses and live together to fulfill the wishes of years ago. He had the impression that he had posted the letter and had been waiting for her reply at home, when there was a knock at the door. He thought it must be the noodle shop owner, but it was Jing Xueyin. They stood there looking at each other, but neither spoke, like two people who barely knew each other. But a moment later they were talking with their eyes, and they knew why they were meeting; each finally understanding what was being said, they rushed into each other's arms. And then they planned their wedding. In that room, he saw her in a variety of hairstyles, a bun, a single braid draped loosely around her shoulders. He spotted the tips of a pair of white shoes on feet peeking out from under the door curtain, then a pair of crossed feet under the sofa, followed by a pair in high heels at the side of a table. Urging her to buy some fine furniture and bedding, he published a wedding announcement in every newspaper. The ceremony was held at a luxury hotel. When the usual wedding night pranks were over, he would not let the guests leave, but shut the door to their bedroom. Imitating both ancient Chinese and modern Westerners, he invited her to bed, where he read her passages from the pornographic novel *Golden Lotus* and showed her adult videos to arouse her. When they lay naked in bed, he touched her all over, using his hands, a feather, and his tongue to so excite her that she lost control, while he continued to caress her and arouse her; he was laughing as he touched her most sensitive spot, until finally, amid her moans, he saw fluid bubbling out from her splendid hair. After rubbing his fingers on her belly to clean them, he picked up a broken tile he had hidden under the bed earlier to gently cover her, put on his clothes, and walked out. The guests were still in the living room. He announced in a loud voice, "This marks the formal dissolution of the marriage between Jing Xueyin and me." His declaration was immediately broadcast on TV, stunning the guests. "Didn't you just marry her?" they wondered aloud. "Why divorce her so quickly?" He laughed. "Mission accomplished!"

When that miserable night was finally over and the day was breaking, he still could not tell if the marriage and divorce had been a sweet fantasy or a real experience, but he was in a good mood. After downing half bottle of rice wine that morning, he said to himself: "I have finally accomplished what I needed to do in this city."

Dusk had descended as Zhuang Zhidie, suitcase in hand, arrived at the train station alone. As he lined up to purchase a ticket, he was aware that he was about to leave a city where a woman was carrying within her a tiny him. He was about to leave, but felt he ought to say good-bye to that self. He turned and walked toward a phone booth. The train station was located outside the north gate; the phone booth was beneath an old pagoda tree. It was dark outside, but the distant city was ablaze with light. The wind turned gusty as he stepped inside the booth, only to see that it had been vandalized. The dial, now filled with sand, was useless, while the handset hung down like an enormous black spider or a worn shoe. Among the several improvements the mayor's office proclaimed to have accomplished for the people, sidewalk phone booths were at the top of the list. Yet three or four out of every ten had been damaged, like this one, in short order. He opened his mouth to curse but stopped before a sound emerged; instead, he gave the handset a vicious kick, which produced a gratifying noise. When he came out into the dim light, he noticed that the tree trunk was plastered with all sorts of ads, one to teach self-defense, one to share a family secret formula for lasting erections, another to report on the accomplishments of the master of a certain school. There was even a scandal rag with two items called "Strange News from Xijing." After giving it a cursory look, he felt compelled to walk up and read more carefully. One of the pieces went like this: A woman in X Lane of X Street in the city had not come out of her house for several days, and her neighbors thought that something must have happened. They broke down her door and found her dead in bed. An examination of her body showed no sign of injury, so she hadn't been murdered, but there was a corncob stuck in her vagina. A pile of corncobs was found near her bed, all smeared with blood. Obviously she had masturbated herself to death. The other item was about a hospital in the city where on such and such date a woman had given birth to a limbless baby with a belly so transparent its internal organs were all visible from the outside. The terrified doctor threw the newborn into a trashcan, but the mother bundled the baby in her clothes and left.

For no reason at all, he reached out and tore off the sheet before walking away, his heart racing. He took out a cigarette, but each of the three matches he struck went out in the wind. The wind grew stronger, and he heard an eerie sound, like the cries of a ghost or the howl of a wolf. He looked up and saw, over the north gate, a horizontal banner proclaiming "An Exuberant Celebration of the Arrival of the Ancient City Cultural Festival." Above the banner hung a leather drum. Zhuang could tell that it was the old cow's hide. The drum was humming in the wind.

He walked into the station waiting room, where he ran into Zhou Min. They stopped.

"Zhou Min, how are you doing?" Zhuang called out.

"Zhuang—" Zhou stopped and greeted him without calling him "Laoshi."

"Leaving town?" Zhuang asked. "Where to?"

"I'm leaving for the south. How about you?"

"We'll be fellow travelers again," Zhuang said, and they laughed. Zhou picked up Zhuang's suitcase and helped him over to a bench. Telling Zhuang he would go buy them some soft drinks, he went to the station shopping mall. When he returned, Zhuang was asleep, his face covered with a newspaper.

"Here," Zhou offered, but Zhuang remained motionless, so he removed the paper. Zhuang was holding Zhou's backpack, which contained his xun, but his eyes had rolled up and his mouth was twisted to the side.

Outside the waiting room, the old junkman was standing with his cart under a giant panda created from thousands of potted plants and flowers.

"Junkman! Collecting junk and scraps! Give me your junk!"

Zhou banged repeatedly on the window until the glass pane broke. His hand bled, sending blood streaming down the cracked window like red earthworms. Through his blood, he could see that the old man did not hear him calling out to him. Instead, he saw a woman's bony face pressed against the other side of the pane, her thin lips moving. It was the wife of Wang Ximian.